PRAISE FOR THE NOVELS
OF STEPHEN

For Liars &

"This book is vintage Coonts . . . pl
the added benefit of a new lead cha.

—Dallas Morning News

"Former Grafton sidekick Tommy Carmellini, ex-burglar and CIA
operative, has been promoted to star in what's sure to be another
excellent, long-lived series. . . . Tommy is smart, brave, skilled, and
possessed of enough self-deprecating, wisecracking wit to endear
him to readers . . . readers of the Jake Grafton series will easily
make the leap to Tommy Carmellini, and new readers can be
expected to sign up for this hipper hero."
—Publishers Weekly (starred review)

"Tommy is a self-deprecating and wisecracking narrator who
brings a welcome energy to the genre. And fans will be pleased to
see a now retired Jake Grafton and his wife, Callie, make an
appearance."
—Library Journal

"Readers who have not previously treated themselves to a Coonts
thriller should definitely pick up this one."
—Bookreporter.com

For Liberty

"Frighteningly realistic."   —Maxim

"Gripping . . . Coonts's naval background and his legal education
bring considerable authority to the story, and the narrative is loaded
with detailed information about terrorist networks, modern
weaponry, and international intrigue . . . the action is slam-bang."
—Publishers Weekly

For America

"This master of the techno-thriller spins a bone-chilling, worst-case
scenario involving international spies, military heroics, conniving
politicians, devious agencies, a hijacked nuclear sub, lethal computer hackers, currency speculators, maniac moguls, and greedy mer-
cenaries that rivals Clancy for fiction-as-realism and Cussler for

spirited action. . . . [Coonts] never lets up with heartracing jet/missile combat, suspenseful submarine maneuvers, and doomsday scenarios that feel only too real, providing real food for thought in his dramatization of the missile-shield debate."

—Publishers Weekly (starred review)

"Give a hearty welcome back to Admiral Jake Grafton . . . thrilling roller-coaster action." —The Philadelphia Inquirer

For Hong Kong

"High-octane . . . [Coonts] skillfully captures the postmodern flavor of Hong Kong, where a cell phone is as apt as an AK-47 to be a revolutionary weapon." —USA Today

"The author gives us superior suspense with a great cast of made-up characters. . . . But the best thing about this book is Coonts's scenario for turning China into a democracy."

—Liz Smith, The New York Post

For Cuba

"Enough Tomahawk missiles, stealth bombers, and staccato action to satisfy [Coonts's] most demanding fans."

—USA Today

"[A] gripping and intelligent thriller."

—Publishers Weekly (starred review)

"Dramatic, diverting action . . . Coonts delivers!"

—Booklist

For Flight of the Intruder

"Coonts knows how to write and build suspense . . . this is the mark of a natural storyteller." —The New York Times Book Review

"Flight of the Intruder kept me strapped in the cockpit of the author's imagination for a down-and-dirty novel."

—St. Louis Post-Dispatch

CUBA
HONG KONG

CUBA

HONG KONG

Stephen Coonts

ST. MARTIN'S GRIFFIN ❧ NEW YORK

www.stmartins.com

ISBN 0-312-35561-0
EAN 978-0-312-35561-6

Cuba was originally published by St. Martin's Press in August 1999

Hong Kong was originally published by St. Martin's Press in September 2000

First St. Martin's Griffin Edition: October 2005

10 9 8 7 6 5 4 3 2 1

CUBA

To Tyler

ACKNOWLEDGMENTS

In theory a speculative work of adventure fiction has the same requirement for technical accuracy as a story about space aliens set in the thirtieth century, yet as a practical matter many readers demand that this author at least stay in reality's neighborhood while spinning his tales. For their aid in contributing to technical accuracy the author wishes to thank Michael R. Gaul, Captain Sam Sayers USN Ret., Mary Sayers, Captain Andrew Salkeld USMC, and Colonel Emmett Willard USA Ret., as well as V-22 experts Colonel Nolan Schmidt USMC, Lieutenant Colonel Doug Isleib USMC, and Donald L. Byrne Jr. As usual, the author has taken liberties in some technical areas in the interest of readability and pacing.

Ernestina Archilla Pabon de Pascal devoted many hours to helping the author capture the flavor of Cuba and earned the author's heartfelt thanks.

A very special thank-you goes to the author's wife, Deborah Buell Coonts, whose wise counsel, plot suggestions, and endless hours of editing added immeasurably to the quality of this tale.

Cultivo una rosa blanca,
  En julio como en enero,
  Para el amigo sincero
  Que me da su mano franca.
Y para el cruel que me arranca
  El corazón con que vivo,
  Cardo ni oruga cultivo;
  Cultivo la rosa blanca.

José Martí

I grow a white rose
  In July the same as January,
  For the sincere friend
  Who gives me his open hand.
And for the cruel one who pulls me
  away
  from the dreams for which I live,
  I grow neither weeds nor thistles,
  I grow the white rose.

PROLOGUE

His hair was white, close-cropped, and his skin deeply tanned. He wore only sandals, shorts, and a paper-thin rag of a shirt with three missing buttons that flapped loosely on his spare, bony frame. A piece of twine around his waist held up his shorts, which were also several sizes too large. His dark eyes were restless and bright behind his steel-framed glasses, which rested on a large, fleshy nose.

The walk between the house and barn winded him, so he sat on a large stone in a bit of shade cast by a cluster of palm trees and contemplated the gauzy blue mountains on the horizon and the puffy clouds floating along on the trade wind.

A man couldn't have found a better place to live out his life, he thought. He loved this view, this serenity, this peace. When he had come here as a young man in his twenties he had known then that he had found paradise. Nothing in the first twenty-six years of his life had prepared him for the pastel colors, the warmth and brilliance of the sun, the kiss of the eternal breeze, the aroma of tropical flowers that filled his head and caressed his soul.

Cuba was everything that Russia wasn't. After a lifetime in Siberia, he had wanted to get down and kiss the earth when he first saw this land. He had actually done that, several times in fact, when he had had too much to drink. He drank a lot in those days, years and years ago, when he was very young.

When the chance to stay came he had leaped at it, begged for it.

"After a time you will regret your choice," the colonel said. "You will miss Mother Russia, the sound of Russian voices, the young wife you left behind. . . ."

"She is young, intelligent, ambitious. . . ." he had replied, thinking of Olga's cold anger when informed she could not accompany him to Cuba. She was angry at *him* for having the good fortune to go, not angry at the state for sending him. She had never in her life been angry at the state for anything whatsoever, no matter how bleak her life or prospects—she didn't have it in her. Olga was a good communist woman, communist to the core.

"She will be told that you have died in an accident. You will be proclaimed a socialist hero. Of course, you may never write to her, to your parents, to your brother, to anyone in the Soviet Union. All will believe you dead. For them, you will be dead."

"I will have another life here."

"These are not your people," the colonel observed pointedly a bit later in the discussion, but he didn't listen.

"Olga is a patriot," he remembered telling the colonel. "She loves the state with all her soul. She will enjoy being a widow of a socialist hero. She will find another man and life will go on."

So he stayed, and they told her that he was dead. Whether she remarried or stayed single, got that transfer to Moscow that she dreamed about, had the children she didn't want, he didn't know.

Looking at the blue mountains, smelling the wind, he tried to conjure up the picture of her in his mind that he had carried all these years. Olga had been young then so he always remembered her that way. She wouldn't be young now, of course, if she still lived; she would be hefty, with iron gray hair which she would wear pulled back in a bun.

His mind was blank. Try as he might, he couldn't remember what Olga looked like.

Perhaps that was just as well.

He had found a woman here, a chocolate brown woman who cooked and washed for him, lived with him, slept with him and bore him two children. Their son died years ago before he reached manhood, and their daughter was married and had children of her own. His daughter cooked for him now, checked to make sure he was all right.

Her face he could remember. Her smile, her touch, the warmth of her skin, her whisper in the night . . .

She had been dead two years next month.

He would join her soon. He knew that. He had lost seventy pounds in the last twelve months and knew that something was wrong with him, but he didn't know just what.

The village doctor examined him and shook her head. "Your body is wearing out, my friend," the doctor said. "There is nothing I can do."

He had had a wonderful life here, in this place in the sun in paradise.

He coughed, spat in the dirt, waited for the spasms to pass.

After a while he slowly levered himself erect and resumed his journey toward the barn.

He opened the board door and stepped into the cool darkness within. Little puffs of dust arose from every footfall. The dirt on the floor had long ago turned to powder.

The only light came from sunbeams shining through the cracks in the barn's siding. The siding was merely boards placed on the wooden frame of the building to keep out the wind and rain . . . and prying eyes.

In truth the building wasn't really a barn at all, though the corners were routinely used to store farm machinery and fodder for the animals and occasionally to get a sensitive animal in out of the sun. Primarily the building existed to hide the large, round concrete slab in the center of the floor. The building was constructed in such a way that there were no beams or wooden supports of any kind above the slab. The roof above the slab was merely boards cantilevered upward until they touched at the apex of the building.

The white-haired old man paused now to look upward at the pencil-thin shafts of sunlight which illuminated the dusty air like so many laser beams. The old man, however, knew nothing about lasers, had never even seen one: lasers came after he had completed his schooling and training.

One corner of the building contained an enclosed room. The door to the room was locked. Now the old man fished in his pocket for a key, unlocked the door, and stepped inside. On the other side of the door he used the key to engage the lock, then thoughtfully placed the key in his pocket.

He was the only living person with a key to that lock. If he collapsed in here, no one could get in to him. The door and the walls of this room were made of very hard steel, steel sheathed in rough, unfinished gray wood.

Well, that was a risk he had agreed to run all those years ago.

Thirty-five . . . no, thirty-eight years ago.

A long time. ,

There was a light switch by the door, and the old man reached for it automatically. He snapped it on. Before him were stairs leading down.

With one hand on the rail, he went down the stairs, now worn from the tread of his feet.

This door, these stairs . . . his whole life. Every day . . . checking, greasing, testing, repairing . . .

Once rats got in down here. He had never found a hole that would grant them entrance, though he had looked carefully. Still, they had gotten in and eaten insulation off wiring, chewed holes in boards, gnawed at pipes and fittings. He managed to kill three with poison and carried the bodies out. Several others died in places he couldn't get to and stank up the place while their carcasses decomposed.

God, when had that been? Years and years ago . . .

He checked the poison trays, made sure they were full.

He checked consoles, visually inspected the conduits, turned on the electrical power and checked the warning lights, the circuits.

Every week he ran a complete set of electrical checks on the circuitry, checking every wire in the place, all the connections and tubes, resistors and capacitors. Occasionally a tube would be burned out, and he would have to replace it. The irony of burning up difficult-to-obtain electrical parts testing them had ceased to amuse him years ago. Now he only worried that the parts would not be available, somewhere, when he needed them.

He wondered what they were going to do when he became unable to do this work. When he died. Someone was going to have to take care of this installation or it would go to rack and ruin. He had told the Cuban major that the last time he came around, which was last month, when the technicians came to install the new warhead.

Lord, what a job that had been. He was the only one who knew how to remove the old nuclear warhead, and he had had to figure out how to install the new one. No one would tell him anything about it, but he had to figure out how it had to be installed.

"You must let me train somebody," he said to the major, "show someone how to take care of this thing. If you leave it sit without maintenance for just a few months in this climate, it will be junk."

Yes, yes. The major knew that. So did the people in Havana.

"And I am a sick man. Cancer, the doctor says."

The major understood. He had been told about the disease. He was sorry to hear it.

"This thing should be in a museum now," he told the major, who as usual acted very military, looked at this, tapped on that, told him to change a lightbulb that had just burned out—he always changed dead bulbs immediately if he had good bulbs to put in—then went away looking thoughtful.

The major always looked thoughtful. He hadn't an idea about how the thing worked, about the labor and cunning required to keep it operational, and he never asked questions. Just nosed around pretending he knew what he was looking at, occasionally delivered spare parts, listened to what the old man had to say, then went away, not to reappear for another three months.

Before the major there had been a colonel. Before the colonel another major . . . In truth, he didn't get to know these occasional visitors very well and soon forgot about them.

Every now and then he would get a visitor that he could not forget. Fidel Castro had come three times. His first visit occurred while the Russians were still here, during construction. He looked at everything, asked many questions, didn't pretend to know anything.

Castro returned when the site was operational. Several generals had accompanied him. The old man could still remember Castro's green uniform, the beard, the ever-present cigar.

The last time he came was eight or ten years ago, after the Soviet Union collapsed, when spare parts were so difficult to obtain. That time he had asked questions, listened carefully to the answers, and the necessary parts and supplies had somehow been delivered.

But official visits were rare events, even by the thoughtful major. Most of the time the old man was left in peace and solitude to do his job as he saw fit. Truly, the work was pleasant—he had had a good life, much better than anything he could have aspired to as a technician in the Soviet Rocket Forces, doomed to some lonely, godforsaken, windswept frozen patch of Central Asia.

The old man left the power on to the console—he would begin the tests in just a bit, but first he opened the fireproof steel door to reveal a set of stairs leading downward. Thirty-two steps down to the bottom of the silo.

The sight of the missile resting erect on its launcher always took his breath for a moment. There it sat, ready to be fired.

He climbed the ladder to the platform adjacent to the guidance compartment. Took out the six screws that sealed the access plate, pried it off, and used a flashlight to inspect the wiring inside. Well, the internal wiring inside the guidance unit was getting old, no question about it. It would have to be replaced soon.

Should he replace the guidance wiring—which would take two weeks of intense, concentrated effort—or should he leave it for his successor?

He would think about the work involved for a few more weeks. If he didn't feel up to it then, it would have to wait. His health was deteriorating at a more or less steady pace, and he could only do so much.

If they didn't send a replacement for him soon, he wouldn't have enough time to teach the new man what he needed to know. To expect them to find someone who already knew the nuts and bolts of a Scud I missile was ridiculous. These missiles hadn't been manufactured in thirty years, were inaccurate, obsolete artifacts of a bygone age.

It was equally ridiculous to expect someone to remove this missile from the silo and install a new, modern one. Cuba was poor, even poorer than Russia had been when he was growing up. Cuba could not afford modern missiles and the new, postcommunist Russia certainly could not afford to give them away.

Not even to aim at Atlanta.

Those were the targeting coordinates.

He wasn't supposed to know the target, of course, but that rule was another example of military stupidity. He took care of the missile, maintained it, tested it, and if necessary would someday fire it at the enemy. Yet the powers that be didn't want him to know where the missile was aimed.

So when he was working on the guidance module he had checked the coordinates that were programmed in, compared them to a map in the village school.

Atlanta!

The gyros in the guidance module were 1950s technology, and Soviet to boot, with the usual large, forgiving military tolerances. No one ever claimed the guidance system in a Scud I was a precision instrument, but it was adequate. The guidance system would get the missile into the proper neighborhood, more or less, then the warhead would do the rest.

The old warhead had an explosive force equal to one hundred thousand tons equivalent of TNT. It wouldn't flatten all of Atlanta—Atlanta was a mighty big place and getting bigger—but it would make a hell of a dent in Georgia. Somewhere in Georgia. With luck, the chances were pretty good that the missile would hit Georgia.

The new warhead ... well, he knew nothing about it. It was a completely different design than the old one, although it weighed exactly the same and also seemed to be rigged for an airburst, but of course there was no way for him to determine the altitude.

Not that it mattered. The missile had never been fired and probably never would be. Its capabilities were mere speculation.

The old man took a last look at the interior of the control module, replaced the inspection plate and inserted the screws, then carefully tightened each one. Then he inspected the cables that led to the missile and their connectors. From the platform he could also see the hydraulic pistons and arms that would lift the cap on the silo, if and when. No leaks today.

Carefully, holding on with both hands, he climbed down the ladder to the floor of the silo, which was just a grate over a large hole, the fire tube, designed so the fiery rocket exhaust would not cook the missile before it rose from the silo.

The rats may have got into the silo when he had the cap open, he thought. Yes, that was probably it. They got inside, found nothing to eat, began chewing on wire insulation to stay alive.

But the rats were dead.

His woman was dead, and he soon would be.

The missile ...

He patted the side of the missile, then began climbing the stairs to the control room to do his electrical checks.

Nobody gave a damn about the missile, except him and maybe the major. The major didn't really care all that much—the missile was just a job for him.

The missile had been the old man's life. He had traded life in Russia as a slave in the Strategic Rocket Forces for a life in paradise as a slave to a missile that would never be fired.

He thought about Russia as he climbed the stairs.

You make your choices going through life, he told himself, *or the state makes the choices for you. Or God does. Whichever, a man must accept life as it comes.*

He sat down at the console in the control room, ran his fingers over the buttons and switches.

At least he had never had to fire the missile. After all these years taking care of it, that would be somewhat like committing suicide.

Could he do it? Could he fire the missile if ordered to do so?

When he first came to Cuba he had thought deeply about that question. Of course he had taken an oath to obey and all that, but he never knew if he really could.

Still didn't.

And was going to die not knowing.

The old man laughed aloud. He liked the sound so much he laughed again, louder.

After all, the joke was really on the communists, who sent him here. Amazingly, after all the pain and suffering they caused tens of millions of people all over the planet, they had given him a good life.

He laughed again because the joke was a good one.

CHAPTER ONE

Guantánamo Bay, on the southeast coast of the island of Cuba, is the prettiest spot on the planet, thought Rear Admiral Jake Grafton, USN.

He was leaning on the railing on top of the carrier *United States*'s superstructure, her island, a place the sailors called Steel Beach. Here off-duty crew members gathered to soak up some rays and do a few calisthenics. Jake Grafton was not normally a sun worshiper; at sea he rarely visited Steel Beach, preferring to arrange his day so that he could spend at least a half hour running on the flight deck. Today he was dressed in gym shorts, T-shirt, and tennis shoes, but he had yet to make it to the flight deck.

Grafton was a trim, fit fifty-three years old, a trifle over six feet tall, with short hair turning gray, gray eyes, and a nose slightly too large for his face. On one temple was a scar, an old, faded white slash where a bullet had gouged him years ago.

People who knew him regarded him as the epitome of a competent naval officer. Grafton always put his brain in gear before he opened his mouth, never lost his cool, and he never lost sight of the goals he wanted to accomplish. In short, he was one fine naval officer and his superiors knew it, which was why he was in charge of this carrier group lying in Guantánamo Bay.

The carrier and her escorts had been running exercises in the Caribbean for the last week. Today the carrier was anchored in the mouth of the bay, with two of her larger consorts anchored nearby. To seaward three destroyers steamed back and forth, their radars probing the skies.

A set of top-secret orders had brought the carrier group here.

Jake Grafton thought about those orders as he studied the two cargo ships lying against the pier through a set of navy binoculars. The ships were small, less than eight thousand tons each; larger ships drew too much water to get against the pier in this harbor. They were *Nuestra Señora de Colón* and *Astarte*.

The order bringing those ships here had not come from some windowless Pentagon cubbyhole; it was no memo drafted by an anonymous civil servant or faceless staff weenie. Oh, no. The order that had brought those ships to this pier on the southern coast of Cuba had come from the White House, the top of the food chain.

Jake Grafton looked past the cargo ships at the warehouses and barracks and administration buildings baking in the warm Cuban sun.

A paradise, that was the word that described Cuba. A paradise inhabited by communists. And Guantánamo Bay was a lonely little American outpost adhering to the underside of this communist island, the asshole of Cuba some called it.

Rear Admiral Grafton could see the cranes moving, the white containers being swung down to the pier from *Astarte*, which had arrived several hours ago. Forklifts took the steel boxes to a hurricane-proof warehouse, where no doubt the harbormaster was stacking them three or four deep in neat, tidy military rows.

The containers were packages designed to hold chemical and biological weapons, artillery shells and bombs. A trained crew was here to load the weapons stored inside the hurricane-proof warehouse into the containers, which would then be loaded aboard the ship at the pier and transported to the United States, where the warheads would be destroyed.

Loading the weapons into the containers and getting the containers stowed aboard the second ship was going to take at least a week, probably longer. The first ship, *Nuestra Señora de Colón*, Our Lady of Colón, had been a week loading, and would be ready to sail this evening. Jake Grafton's job was to provide military cover for the loading operation with this carrier battle group.

His orders raised more questions than they answered. The weapons had been stored in that warehouse for years—why remove them now?

Why did the removal operation require military cover? What was the threat?

Admiral Grafton put down his binoculars and did fifty push-ups on the steel deck while he thought about chemical and biological weapons. Cheaper and even more lethal than atomic weapons, they were the weapons of choice for Third World nations seeking to acquire a credible military presence. Chemical weapons were easier to control than biological weapons, yet more expensive to deliver. Hands down, the cheapest and deadliest weapon known to man was the biological one.

Almost any nation, indeed, almost anyone with a credit card and two thousand square feet of laboratory space, could construct a biological weapon in a matter of weeks from inexpensive, off-the-shelf technology. Years ago Saddam Hussein got into the biological warfare business with anthrax cultures purchased from an American mail-order supply house and delivered via overnight mail. Ten grams of anthrax properly dispersed can kill as many people as a ton of the nerve gas Sarin. What was that estimate Jake saw recently?—one hundred kilograms of anthrax delivered by an efficient aerosol generator on a large urban target would kill from two to six times as many people as a one-megaton nuclear device.

Of course, Jake Grafton reflected, anthrax was merely one of over one hundred and sixty known biological warfare agents. There were others far deadlier but equally cheap to manufacture and disperse. Still, obtaining a culture was merely a first step; the journey from culture dishes to a reliable weapon that could be safely stored and accurately employed— anything other than a spray tank—was long, expensive, and fraught with engineering challenges.

Jake Grafton had had a few classified briefings about CBW—which stood for chemical and biological warfare—but he knew little more than was available in the public press. These weren't the kinds of secrets that rank-and-file naval officers had a need to know. Since the Kennedy administration insisted on developing other military response capabilities besides nuclear warfare, the United States had researched, developed, and manufactured large stores of nerve gas, mustard gas, incapacitants, and defoliants. Research on biological agents went forward in tandem at Fort Detrick, Maryland, and ultimately led to the manufacture of weapons at Pine Bluff Arsenal in Arkansas. These highly classified programs were undertaken with little debate and almost no publicity. Of course the Soviets had their own classified programs. Only when accidents occurred—like the accidental slaughter of 6,000 sheep thirty miles from the Dugway Proving Ground in Utah during the late 1960s, or the deaths of sixty-six people at Sverdlovsk in 1979—did the public get a glimpse into this secret world.

Nerve gases were loaded into missile and rocket warheads, bombs, land mines, and artillery shells. Biological agents were loaded into missile warheads, cluster bombs, and spray tanks and dispensers mounted on aircraft.

Historically nations used chemical or biological weapons against an enemy only when the enemy lacked the means to retaliate in kind. The threat of massive American retaliation had deterred Saddam Hussein from the use of chemical and biological weapons in the 1991 Gulf War, yet these days deterrence was politically incorrect.

In 1993 the United States signed the Chemical Weapons Convention, thereby agreeing to remove chemical and biological weapons from its stockpiles.

The U.S. military had been in no hurry to comply with the treaty, of course, because without the threat of retaliation there was no way to prevent these weapons being used against American troops and civilians. The waiting was over, apparently. The politicians in Washington were getting their way: the United States would not retaliate against an enemy with chemical or biological weapons even if similar weapons were used to slaughter Americans.

When Jake Grafton finished his push-ups and stood, the staff operations officer, Commander Toad Tarkington, was there with a towel. Toad was slightly above medium height, deeply tanned, and had a mouthful of perfect white teeth that were visible when he smiled or laughed, which he often did. The admiral wiped his face on the towel, then picked up the binoculars and once again focused them on the cargo ships.

"Glad the decision to destroy those things wasn't one I had to make," Toad Tarkington said.

"There are a lot of things in this world that I'm glad I'm not responsible for," Jake replied.

"Why now, Admiral? And why does the ordnance crowd need a battle group to guard them?"

"What I'd like to know," Jake Grafton mused, "is why those damned things were stored here in the first place. If we knew that, then maybe we would know why the brass sent us here to stand guard."

"Think Castro has chemical or biological weapons, sir?"

"I suspect he does, or someone with a lot of stars once thought he might. If so, our weapons were probably put here to discourage friend Castro from waving his about. But what is the threat to removing them?"

"Got to be terrorists, sir," Toad said. "Castro would be delighted to see them go. An attack from the Cuban Army is the last thing on earth I would expect. But terrorists—maybe they plan to do a raid into here, steal some of the darn things."

"Maybe," Jake said, sighing.

"I guess I don't understand why we are taking them home for destruction," Toad added. "The administration got the political credit for signing the Chemical Weapons Treaty. If we keep our weapons, we can still credibly threaten massive retaliation if someone threatens us."

"Pretty hard to agree to destroy the things, not do it, and then fulminate against other countries who don't destroy theirs."

"Hypocrisy never slowed down a politician," Toad said sourly. "I guess I just never liked the idea of getting naked when everyone else at the party is fully dressed."

"Who in Washington would ever authorize the use of CBW weapons?" Jake muttered. "Can you see a buttoned-down, blow-dried, politically correct American politician ever signing such an order?"

Both men stood with their elbows on the railing looking at the cargo ships. After a bit the admiral passed Toad the binoculars.

"Wonder if the National Security Agency is keeping this area under surveillance with satellites?" Toad mused.

"No one in Washington is going to tell *us*," the admiral said matter-of-factly. He pointed to one of the two Aegis cruisers anchored nearby. "Leave that cruiser anchored here for the next few days. She can cover the base perimeter with her guns if push comes to shove. Have the cruiser keep her gun crews on five-minute alert, ammo on the trays, no liberty. After three days she can pull the hook and join us, and another cruiser can come anchor here."

"Yes, sir."

"There's a marine battalion landing team aboard *Kearsarge*, which is supposed to rendezvous with us tomorrow. I want *Kearsarge* to stay with

United States. We'll put both ships in a race-track pattern about fifty miles south of here, outside Cuban territorial waters, and get on with our exercises. But we'll keep a weather eye peeled on this base."

"What about the base commander, sir? He may know more about this than we do."

"Get on the ship-to-shore net and invite him to have dinner with me tonight. Send a helo in to pick him up."

"Sir, your instructions specifically directed that you maintain a business-as-usual security posture."

"I remember," Jake said dryly.

"Of course, 'business as usual' is an ambiguous phrase," Toad mused. "If anything goes wrong you can be blamed for not doing enough or doing too much, whichever way the wind blows."

Jake Grafton snorted. "If a bunch of wild-eyed terrorists lay hands on those warheads, Tarkington, you and I will be fried, screwed, and tattooed regardless of what we did or didn't do. We'll have to will our bodies to science."

"What about the CO of the cruiser, Admiral? What do we tell him?"

"Draft a top-secret message directing him to keep his people ready to shoot."

"Aye, aye, sir."

"*Nuestra Señora de Colón* is sailing this evening for Norfolk. Have a destroyer accompany her until she is well out of Cuban waters."

"Yo." Toad was making notes on a small memo pad he kept in his hip pocket.

"And have the weather people give me a cloud-cover prediction for the next five days, or as far out as they can. I want to try to figure out what, if anything, the satellites might be seeing."

"You mean, are they keeping an eye on the Cuban military?"

"Or terrorists. Whoever."

"I'll take care of it, sir."

"I'm going to run a couple laps around the deck," Jake Grafton added.

"May I suggest putting a company of marines ashore to do a security survey of the base perimeter? Strictly routine."

"That sounds feasible," Jake Grafton said. "Tonight let's ask the base commander what he thinks."

"Yessir."

"Terrorists or the Cuban Army—wanna bet ten bucks? Take your pick."

"I only bet on sure things, sir, like prizefights and Super Bowls, occasionally a cockroach race."

"You're wise beyond your years, Toad," the admiral tossed over his shoulder as he headed for the hatch.

"That's what I tell Rita," Toad shot back. Rita Moravia was his wife.

Jake Grafton didn't hear the rest of Toad's comment. "And wisdom is a heavy burden, let me tell you. Real heavy. Sorta like biological warheads." He put the binoculars to his eyes and carefully studied the naval base.

CHAPTER TWO

The night was hot and sultry, with lightning playing on the horizon. From his seat on the top row of the stadium bleachers Hector Juan de Dios Sedano kept an eye on the lightning, but the storms seemed to be moving north.

Everyone else in the stadium was watching the game. Hector's younger brother, Juan Manuel "Ocho" Sedano, was the local team's star pitcher. The eighth child of his parents, the Cuban fans had long ago dubbed him El Ocho. The family reduced the name to "Ocho."

Tonight his fastball seemed on fire and his curve exceptional. The crowd cheered with every pitch. Twice the umpire called for the ball to examine it. Each time he handed it back to the catcher, who tossed it back to the mound as the fans hooted delightedly.

At the middle of the seventh inning Ocho had faced just twenty-two batters. Only one man had gotten to first base, and that on a bloop single just beyond the fingertips of the second baseman. The local team had scored four runs.

Hector Sedano leaned against the board fence behind him and applauded his brother as he walked from the mound. Ocho looked happy, relaxed—the confident, honest gaze of a star athlete who knows what he can do.

As Hector clapped, he spotted a woman coming through the crowd toward him. She smiled as she met his eyes, then took a seat beside him.

Here on the back bench Hector was about ten feet from the nearest fans. The board fence behind him was the wall of the stadium, fifteen feet above the ground.

"Did your friends come with you?" he asked, scanning the crowd.

"Oh, yes, the usual two," she said, but didn't bother to point to them.

Sedano found one of the men settling into a seat five rows down and over about thirty feet. A few seconds later he saw the other standing near the entrance where the woman had entered the stadium. These two were her bodyguards.

Her name was Mercedes. She was the widow of one of Hector's brothers and the current mistress of Fidel Castro.

"How is *Mima*?"

Tomorrow was Hector's mother's birthday, and the clan was gathering.

"Fine. Looking forward to seeing everyone."

"I used the birthday as an excuse. They don't want me to leave the residence these days."

"How bad is he?"

"*Está to jodío*. He's done in. One doctor said two weeks, one three. The cancer is spreading rapidly."

"What do you think?"

"I think he will live a while longer, but every night is more difficult. I sit with him. When he is sleeping he stops breathing for as much as half a minute before he resumes. I watch the clock, counting the seconds, wondering if he will breathe again."

The home team's center fielder stepped up to the plate. Ocho was the second batter. Standing in the warm-up circle with a bat in his hands, he scanned the faces in the crowd. Finally he made eye contact with Hector, nodded his head just enough to be seen, then concentrated on his warm-up swings.

"Who knows about this?" Hector asked Mercedes.

"Only a few people. Alejo is holding the lid on. The doctors are with him around the clock." Alejo Vargas was the minister of the interior. His ministry's Department of State Security—the secret police—investigated and suppressed opposition and dissent.

"We have waited a long time," Hector mused.

"*Ese cabrón*, we should have killed Vargas years ago," Mercedes said, and smiled at a woman who turned around to look at her.

"We cannot win with his blood on our hands."

"Alejo suspects you, I think."

"I am just a Jesuit priest, a teacher."

Mercedes snorted.

"He suspects everyone," Hector added.

"Don't be a fool."

El Ocho stepped into the batter's box to the roar of the crowd. He waggled the bat, cocked it, waited expectantly. His stance was perfect, his weight balanced, he was tense and ready—when he batted Hector could see Ocho's magnificent talent. He looked so . . . perfect.

Ocho let the first ball go by . . . outside.

The second pitch was low.

The opposing pitcher walked around the mound, examined the ball, toed the rubber.

The fact was Ocho was a better batter than he was a pitcher. Oh, he was a great pitcher, but when he had a bat in his hands all his gifts were on display; the reflexes, the eyesight, the physique, the ability to wait for his pitch. . . .

The third pitch was a strike, belt-high, and Ocho got around on it and connected solidly. The ball rose into the warm, humid air and flew as if it had wings until it cleared the center field fence by a good margin.

"He caught it perfectly," Mercedes said, admiration in her voice.

Ocho trotted the bases while everyone in the bleachers applauded. The opposing pitcher stood on the mound shaking his head in disgust.

Ocho's manager was the first to greet him as he trotted toward the dugout. He pounded his star on the back, pumped his hand, beamed proudly, almost like a father.

"What else is happening?" Hector asked.

"The government has signed the casino agreement. Miramar, Havana, Varadero and Santiago. The consortium will provide fifty percent of the cost of an airport in Santiago."

"They have been negotiating for what—three years?"

"Almost that."

"Any sense of urgency on the part of the Cubans?"

"I sense none. The Americans were happy with the deal, so they signed."

"Who are these Americans?"

"I thought they were Nevada casino people, but there were people in the background pulling strings, criminals, I think. They wanted assurances on prostitution and narcotics."

The Cuban government had been negotiating agreements for foreign investment and development for years, mainly with Canadian and European companies. Tourism was now the largest industry in Cuba, bringing 1.5 million tourists a year to the island and keeping the economy afloat with hard currency. Now the Cuban government was openly negotiating with American companies, with all deals contingent upon the ending of the American economic embargo. Fidel Castro believed that he could put political pressure upon the American government to end the embargo by dangling development rights in front of American capitalists. Hector Sedano thought Fidel understood the Americans.

"The tobacco negotiator, Chance—how is he progressing?"

"He is talking to your brother Maximo. Then he is supposed to see Vargas. Tobacco will replace sugarcane as Cuba's big crop, he says. The cigarettes will be manufactured here and marketed worldwide under American brands. The Americans will finance everything; Cuba will get a fifty-percent share of the business, across the board."

"Is this Chance serious?"

"Apparently. The tobacco companies think their days are numbered in the United States. They want to move offshore, escape the regulation that will eventually put them out of business."

Hector sat silently, taking it all in as the uniformed players on the field played a game with rules. What a contrast with politics!

Mercedes was a treasure, a person with access to the highest levels of the Cuban government. She brought Hector Sedano information that even Castro probably didn't have. The big question, of course, was how she learned it. Hector told himself repeatedly that he didn't want to know, but of course he did.

He glanced at the woman sitting beside him. She was wearing a simple dress that did nothing to call attention to her figure, nor did it do anything to hide it.

She was a beautiful woman who needed no makeup and never wore any. Every man she met was attracted to her, an unremarkable fact, like the summer heat, which she didn't seem to notice. Extraordinarily smart, with a near-photographic memory, she had almost no opportunities to use her talent in Cuban society.

Except as a spy.

"Will Maximo be at *Mima*'s party tomorrow?"

"He said he would."

"Should I be shocked if he acts possessive?"

Mercedes glanced at him, raised an eyebrow. "He would not be so foolish."

Well, just who was she sleeping with? Hector glanced at her repeatedly, wondering. She appeared to be concentrating on the ball game.

The only thing he knew for sure was that she wasn't sleeping with him, and God knows he had thought about *that* far more than any priest ever should. Of course, priests were human and had to fight their urges, but still . . .

Castro . . . Of course she slept with him—she was his mistress—that was how she got access. But did she love him?

Or was she a cool, calculating tramp ready to change horses now that Castro was dying?

No. He shook his head, refusing to believe that of her.

Where did Maximo fit in? As he sat there contemplating that angle, he wondered how Maximo saw her?

Mercedes left after watching Ocho pitch an inning. He faced three batters and struck them all out.

When the game was over, Hector Sedano stayed in his seat and watched the crowd file out. He was still sitting there when someone shouted at him, "Hey, I turn out the lights now."

The darkness that followed certainly wasn't total. Small lights were illuminated over the exits, the lights of Havana lit up the sky, and lightning continued to flash on the horizon.

Sedano lit another cigar and smoked it slowly.

After a few minutes he saw the shape of a man making his way along the aisle toward him. The man sagged down on the bench several feet away.

"Good game tonight." The man was the stadium keeper, Alfredo Garcia.

"Yes."

"Your brother, El Ocho, was magnificent. Such talent, such presence."

"We are very proud of him."

"Why do you call him El Ocho?"

"He was the eighth child. He has the usual half dozen names, but his brothers and I just call him Ocho."

"I saw that she was here, with her security guards circling. . . . What did she say?"

"What makes you think she tells me anything?"

"Come, my friend. Someone whispers in your ear."

"And someone is whispering to Alejo Vargas."

"You suspect me?"

"I think you are just stupid enough to take money from the Americans and money from Alejo Vargas and think neither of them will find out about the other."

"My God, man! Think of what you are saying!" Alfredo moved closer. Sedano could see his face, which was almost as white as his shirt.

"I am thinking."

"You have my life in your hands. I had to trust you with my life when I first approached you. Nothing has changed."

Sedano puffed on the cigar in silence, studying Garcia's features. Born in America of Cuban parents, Garcia had been a priest. He couldn't leave the women alone, however, and ultimately got mixed up with some topless dancers running an "escort" service in East St. Louis. After a few months the feds busted him for violation of the Mann Act, moving women across state lines for immoral purposes, i.e., prostitution. After the church canned him, he jumped bail and fled to Cuba. Garcia had been in Cuba several years when he was recruited by the CIA, which asked him to approach Sedano.

Hector Sedano had no doubt that Garcia had the ear of the American government—in the past four years he had supplied Sedano with almost a million dollars in cash and enough weapons to supply a small army. The money and weapons always arrived when and where Garcia said they would. Still, the question remained, who else did the man talk to?

Who did his control talk to?

Hector had stockpiled the weapons, hidden them praying they would never be needed. He used the money for travel expenses and bribes. Without money to bribe the little fish he would have landed in prison years ago.

Hector Sedano shook his head to clear his thoughts. He was living on the naked edge, had been there for years. And life wasn't getting any easier.

"Castro is dying," he said. "It is a matter of weeks, or so the doctors say."

Alfredo Garcia took a deep breath and exhaled audibly.

"I tell you now man-to-man, Alfredo. The records of Alejo Vargas will soon be placed in my hands. If you have betrayed me or the people of Cuba, you had better find a way to get off this planet, because there is no place on it you can hide, not from me, not from the CIA, not from the men and women you betrayed."

"I have betrayed no one," Alfredo Garcia said. "God? Yes. But no man."

He went away then, leaving Sedano to smoke in solitude.

Fidel Castro dying! Hector Sedano could hear his heart beat as he tried to comprehend the reality of that fact.

Millions of people were waiting for his death, some patiently, most impatiently, many with a feeling of impending doom. Castro had ruled Cuba as an absolute dictator since 1959: the revolution that he led did nothing more than topple the old dictator and put a new one in his place. Castro jettisoned fledgling democracy, embraced communism and used raw demagoguery to consolidate his total, absolute power. He prosecuted and executed his enemies and confiscated the property of anyone who might be against him. Hundreds of thousands of Cubans fled, many to America.

Castro's embrace of communism and seizure of the assets of the foreign corporations that had invested in Cuba, assets worth several billions of dollars, were almost preordained, inevitable. Predictably, most of those corporations were American. Also predictably, the United States government retaliated with a diplomatic and economic blockade that continued to this day.

After seizing the assets of the American corporations who owned most of Cuba, Castro had little choice: he had to have the assistance of a major power, so he substituted the Soviet Union for the United States as Cuba's patron. The only good thing about the substitution was that the Soviet Union was a lot farther away than Florida. Theirs was never a partnership of equals: the Soviets humiliated Fidel at almost every turn in the road. When communism collapsed in the Soviet Union in the early 1990s, Cuba was cut adrift as an expensive luxury that the newly democratic Russia could ill afford. That twist of fate was a cruel blow to Cuba, which despite Castro's best efforts still was a slave to sugarcane.

Through it all, Castro survived. Never as popular as his supporters believed, he was never as unpopular as the exiles claimed. The truth of the matter was that Castro was Cuban to the core and fiercely independent, and he had kept Cuba that way. His demagoguery played well to poor peasants who had nothing but their pride. The trickle of refugees across the Florida Straits acted as a safety valve to rid the regime of its worst enemies, the vociferous critics with the will and tenacity to cause serious problems. In the Latin tradition, the Cubans who remained submitted to Castro, even respected him for thumbing his nose at the world. A dictator he might be, but he was "our" dictator.

A new day was about to dawn in Cuba, a day without Castro and the baggage of communism, ballistic missiles, and invasion, a new day without bitter enmity with the United States. Just what that day would bring remained to be seen, but it was coming.

The exiles wanted justice, and revenge; the peons who lived in the exiles' houses, now many families to a building, feared being dispossessed. The foreign corporations that Castro so cavalierly robbed wanted compensation. Everyone wanted food, and jobs, and a future. It seemed as if the bills for all the past mistakes were about to come due and payable at once.

Hector Sedano would have a voice in that future, if he survived. He sat smoking, contemplating the coming storm.

Mercedes was of course correct about the danger posed by Alejo Vargas. Mix Latin machismo and a willingness to do violence to gain one's own ends, add generous dollops of vainglory, egotism, and paranoia, stir well, and you have the makings of a truly fine Latin American dictator, self-righteous, suspicious, trigger-happy, and absolutely ruthless. Fidel Alejandro Castro Ruz came out of that mold: Alejo Vargas, Hector knew, was merely another. He could not make this observation to Mercedes, whom Hector suspected of loving Fidel—he needed her cooperation.

Alfredo Garcia found a seat near the ticket-taker's booth from where he could see the shadowy figure on the top row of the bleachers. He was so nervous he twitched.

Like Hector Sedano, he too was in awe of the news he had just learned: Fidel Castro was dying.

Alfredo Garcia trembled as he thought about it. That priest in the top row of the bleachers was one of the contenders for power in post-Castro Cuba. There were others of course, Alejo Vargas, the Minister of Interior and head of the secret police, prominently among them.

Yes, Garcia talked to the secret police of Alejo Vargas—he had to. No one could refuse the Department of State Security, least of all a fugitive from American justice seeking sanctuary.

And of course he cooperated on an ongoing basis. Vargas's spies were everywhere, witnessed every conversation, every meal, every waking moment . . . or so it seemed. One could never be certain what the secret police knew from other sources, what they were just guessing at, what he was their only source for. Garcia had handled this reality the only way he could: he answered direct questions with a bit of the truth—if he knew it—and volunteered nothing.

If the secret police knew Alfredo had a CIA contact they had never let on. They did know Hector Sedano was a power in the underground although they seemed to think he was a small fish.

Garcia thought otherwise. He thought Hector Sedano was the most powerful man in Cuba after Fidel Castro, even more powerful than Alejo Vargas.

Why didn't Hector understand the excruciating predicament that Alfredo Garcia found himself in? Certainly Hector knew what it was like to have few options, or none at all.

Alfredo was a weak man. He had never been able to resist the temptations of the flesh. God had forgiven him, of that he was sure, but would Hector Sedano?

As he sat in the darkness watching Hector, Alfredo Garcia smiled grimly. One of the contenders for power in post-Castro Cuba would be Hector's own brother, Maximo Luís Sedano, the finance minister. Maximo was Fidel's most trusted lieutenant, one of his inner circle. Three years older than Hector, he had lived and breathed Castro's revolution all his life, willingly standing in the great man's shadow. Those days were about over, and Maximo's friends whispered that he was ready— he wanted *more*. That was the general street gossip that Garcia heard, and like most gossip, he thought it probably had a kernel of truth inside.

For his part, Maximo probably thought his only serious rival was Alejo Vargas. He was going to get a bad shock in the near future.

And then there were the exiles. God only knew what those fools would do when Fidel breathed his last.

Yes, indeed, when Fidel died the fireworks would begin.

Hector Sedano was taking the last few puffs on his cigar when his youngest brother, El Ocho, climbed the bleachers. Ocho settled onto a bench in front of Hector and leaned back so that he could rest his feet on the bench in front of him.

"You played well tonight. The home run was a thing of beauty."

"It's just a game."

"And you play it well."

Ocho snorted. "Just a game," he repeated.

"All of life is a game," his older brother told him, and ground out his cigar.

"Was that Mercedes I saw talking to you earlier?"

"She is here for *Mima*'s birthday."

Ocho nodded. He seemed to gather himself before he spoke again.

"My manager, Diego Coca, wants me to go to the United States."

Hector let that statement lie there. Sometimes Ocho said outrageous things to get a reaction. Hector had quit playing that game years ago.

"Diego says I could play in the major leagues."

"Do you believe him?"

Ocho turned toward his older brother and closest friend. "Diego is a dreamer. I look good playing this game because the other players are not so good. The pitch I hit out tonight was a belt-high fastball right down the middle. American major league pitchers don't throw stuff like that because all those guys can hit it."

"Could you pitch there?"

"In Cuba my fastball is a little faster than everyone else's. My curve breaks a little more. In America all the pitchers have a good fastball and breaking ball. Everyone is better."

Hector laughed. "So you aren't interested in going to America and getting rich, like your uncle Tomas?" Tomas had defected ten years ago while a team of baseball stars was on a trip to Mexico City. He now owned five dry-cleaning plants in metropolitan Miami. Oh, yes, Tomas was getting rich!

"I'm not good enough to play in the big leagues. Diego tells me I am. I think he believes it. He wants me to go, take him with me, sign a big contract. I'm his chance."

"He wants to go with you?"

"That's right."

"On a boat?"

"He says he knows a man who has a boat. He can take us to Florida, where people will be waiting."

"You believe that?"

"Diego does. That is what is important."

"You owe Diego a few hours of sweat on the baseball field, nothing else."

Ocho didn't reply. He lay back on his elbows and wiggled his feet.

"Why don't you tell me all of it," Hector suggested gently.

Ocho didn't look at him. After a bit he said, "I got Diego's daughter pregnant. Dora, the second one."

"He knows this?"

Ocho nodded affirmatively.

"So marry the girl. This is an embarrassment, not dishonor. My God, *Mima* was pregnant when Papa married her! Welcome to the world, Ocho. And congratulations."

"Diego is the girl's *father*."

"I will talk to him," Hector said. "You are both young, with hot blood in your veins. Surely he will understand. I will promise him that you will do the right thing by this girl. You will stand up with her in church, love her, cherish her. . . ."

"Diego wants the best for her, for the baby, for me."

"For himself."

"And for himself, yes. He wants us to go on his friend's boat to America. I will play baseball and earn much money and we will live the good life in America. That is his dream."

"I see," said Hector Sedano, and leaned back against the fence. "Is it yours?"

"I haven't told anyone else," Ocho said, meaning the family.

"Are you going to tell *Mima*?"

"Not on her birthday. I thought maybe you could tell her, after we get to America."

"*Está loco,* Ocho. This boat . . . you could all drown. Hundreds— thousands of people have drowned out there. The sea swallows them. They leave here and are never heard from again."

Ocho studied his toes.

"If they catch you, the Americans will send you back. They don't want boat people."

"Diego Coca says that—"

"Damn Diego Coca! The Cuban Navy will probably catch you before you get out of sight of *Mima*'s house. Pray that they do, that you don't die out there in the Gulf Stream. And if you are lucky enough to survive the trip to Florida, the Americans will arrest you, put you in a camp at Guantánamo Bay. Even if you get back to Cuba, the government won't let you play baseball again. You'll spend your life in the fields chopping cane. Think about *that*!"

Ocho sat silently, listening to the insects.

"Did you give Diego Coca money?" Hector asked.

"Yes."

"Want to tell me how much?"

"No."

"You're financing his dream, Ocho."

"At least he's got one."

"What's that mean?"

"It means what I said. At least Diego Coca has a dream. He doesn't want to sit rotting on this goddamned island while life passes him by. He doesn't want that for his daughter or her kid."

"He doesn't want that for himself."

Ocho threw up his hands.

Hector pressed on, relentlessly. "Diego Coca should get on that boat and follow his dream, if that is his dream. You and Dora should get married. Announce the wedding tomorrow at *Mima*'s party—these people are your flesh and blood. Cuba is your country, your heritage. You owe these people and this country all that you are, all that you will ever be."

"Cuba is *your* dream, Hector."

"And what is yours? I ask you a second time."

Ocho shook his head like a mighty bull. "I do not wish to spend my life plotting against the government, making speeches, waiting to be arrested, dreaming of a utopia that will never be. That is life wasted."

Hector thought before he answered. "What you say is true. Yet until things change in Cuba it is impossible to dream other dreams."

Ocho Sedano got to his feet. He was a tall, lanky young man with long, ropy muscles.

"Just wanted you to know," he said.

"A man must have a dream that is larger than he is or life has little meaning."

"Didn't figure you would think it was a good idea."

"I don't."

"Or else you would have gone yourself."

"Ocho, I ask you a personal favor. Wait two weeks. Don't go for two weeks. See how the world looks in two weeks before you get on that boat."

Hector could see the pain etched on Ocho's face. The younger man looked him straight in the eye.

"The boat won't wait."

"I ask this as your brother, who has never asked you for anything. I ask you for *Mima*, who cherishes you, and for Papa, who watches you from heaven. Have the grace to say yes to my request. Two weeks."

"The boat won't wait, Hector. Diego wants this. Dora wants this. I have no choice."

With that Ocho turned and leaped lightly from bench to bench until he got to the field. He walked across the dark, deserted diamond and disappeared into the home team's dugout.

Although he was born in Cuba, El Gato's parents took him to Miami when he was a toddler, before the Cuban revolution. He had absolutely no memory of Cuba. In fact, he thought of himself as an American. English was the language he knew best, the language he thought in. He had learned Spanish at home as a youngster, understood it well, and spoke it with a flavored accent. Still, hearing nothing but Cuban Spanish spoken around him for days gave him a bit of cultural shock.

He and two of his bodyguards had flown to Mexico City, then to Havana. He had always kept his contacts with the Cuban government a deep, dark, jealously guarded secret, but rumors had reached him, rumors that Castro was sick, that important changes in Cuba were in the wind. The rumors had the feel of truth; his instincts told him.

El Gato, the Cat, didn't get rich by ignoring his instincts. He decided to go to Cuba and take the risk of explaining it away later. If the exiles in Florida ever got the idea that he had double-crossed them, money or no money, they would take their revenge.

Courage was one of El Gato's long suits. He didn't accumulate a fortune worth almost a half billion dollars by being timid. So he and his bodyguards boarded the plane. That was almost a week ago. He had been steadily losing money in the casinos every day since while waiting. Now the waiting was over.

Tonight he was to see the man he came to meet, Alejo Vargas. In five minutes.

He checked his watch, then pocketed his chips and walked for the door of the club, the Tropicana, the jewel of Havana. His bodyguards joined him, like shadows.

El Gato left the casino via the back entrance. The three men walked a block to a large black limousine sitting by the curb and climbed into the rear seats.

Two men were sitting on the front-facing seats.

"El Gato, welcome to Havana. I confess, I didn't think we would ever meet on Cuban soil."

"Miracles never cease, Señor Vargas. The world turns, the sun rises and sets and we all get older day by day. Wise men change with the times."

"Quite so. This is Colonel Santana, head of the Department of State Security."

El Gato nodded politely at Santana, then introduced his bodyguards, men Santana didn't even bother to look at.

"I was hoping, Señor Vargas, that you and I might have a private conversation, perhaps while these gentlemen watched from a small distance?"

Vargas nodded his assent, pushed a button, and spoke into an intercom to the driver. After about fifteen minutes of travel, during which nothing was said, the limo pulled up to a curb and all the men got out. The car was sitting on a breakwater near Morro Castle, with the dark battlements looming above them in the glare of Havana reflecting off the clouds.

Vargas and El Gato began strolling.

"The cargo is aboard," El Gato said, "and the ship has sailed. I presume you kept me waiting to see if that event would occur."

"When you proposed this operation, I had my doubts. I still do."

"I cannot guarantee success," El Gato said. "I do everything within my power to make success possible, but sometimes the world does not turn my way. I understand that, and I keep trying anyway."

"The waiting will soon be over," Vargas said.

"Indeed. In many ways. I hear rumors that Fidel will not be with us much longer."

Vargas didn't reply to that remark.

"Change is rapidly coming to Cuba," El Gato began, "and the thought occurred to me that a man with friends in Cuba under the new order would be in an enviable position."

"You have such friends?"

"I am here to test the water, so to speak, to learn if I do."

"After your years of opposition to Castro, any friends you have will not be very vocal about it."

"Noisy friends I have aplenty in Florida. No, the kind of friends I need are the kind who keep their friendship to themselves and help when help is needed, who give approvals when asked, who nod yes at the appropriate time."

"How much money have you given the exiles' political movements over the years?"

"You wish to know the figure?"

"Yes. I wish to learn if you will be honest with me. Obviously I have sources and some idea of the amount. Come now, impress me with your frankness and your honesty."

"Over five million American," El Gato said.

This was twice the figure Vargas expected, and he looked at the American sharply. If El Gato was lying, exaggerating the number to impress Vargas, it didn't show in his face.

"Some of that money, a small amount it is true, came directly from the Cuban government," El Gato said. "I believe you authorized those payments."

"You have a sense of the sardonic, I see," Vargas said without humor. One got the impression he had not smiled in his lifetime, nor would he.

El Gato nodded.

"You had a commodity to sell, we wished to buy. We paid a fair price."

"Come, come, Señor Vargas. Let's not pretend with each other. I arranged for you to acquire the equipment and chemicals necessary to create a biological warfare program. What you have done with those chemicals and equipment I don't know, nor do I want to know. But you know as well as I that if the American government found out about the sale I would be ruined. And you know that I made no profit in the transaction."

Vargas nodded, a dip of the head.

"Nor have I asked for money for arranging to steal *Nuestra Señora*."

"That is true, but if the operation succeeds, we would have paid a fair amount."

"I do not want your money."

"You want something. What?"

El Gato walked a few paces with his hands in his pockets before he spoke. "After Castro I envision a Cuba much more friendly to American interests, more open to a free flow of capital in and out. A great many people in the United States have a great deal of money accumulated that they want to invest in Cuba, which they will do as soon as the United States government allows them to do so, and as soon as the Cuban government guarantees these investors that their investment will not be confiscated or stolen with hidden taxes or demands for graft. A man who could guarantee that his friends would be fairly treated in Cuba could make a lot of money. He would be a patron, if you will. And if he carefully screened his friends, Cuba would get a vetted flow of capable investors who would perform as promised."

"Something for everyone," Vargas said.

"Precisely."

"Just so that I understand—are you suggesting that you want to be that man, *el jefecito*?"

"I could do it, I believe."

"The exiles expect to come to Cuba at Castro's death and take over the country. They want billions in repatriations. I tell you now, you have helped fuel their expectations with your five million dollars."

What he failed to mention was the fact that the Cuban government had played to the fears of the peons who stayed, telling them they would be thrown from their homes if the exiles ever returned.

El Gato smiled. "Like the exiles, you fail to clearly see the situation. They are Americans. They make more money in America than they ever could in Cuba. They will never return in significant numbers. In fact, if the borders are thrown open, the net human flow will be toward the United States, not back to Cuba. If the American government would allow it, a million Cubans a year would leave this island. You would be wise to let people go where they wish to go."

"You are saying the exile problem will just disappear?"

"Except for a few bitter old men, yes, I believe it will. The young ones have gotten on with their lives. They have no old scores to settle."

"So you betray these old ones for your own profit?"

"Señor Vargas, if they wish to nurse old grudges and dream of a time which is long past and will never come again, who am I to tell them no? Most of these people are quite harmless. Those who aren't can be dealt with when they 'cause problems. A public apology to dispossessed old people, a plea for healing, a few pesos, and the exiles could be appeased."

"Assassination plots against Castro and the like?"

"Plots that never get off the ground are harmless. Let them have their meetings and their thunderous denunciations. These people will pass from the scene soon enough."

Vargas made a gesture of irritation. He had his own opinions and didn't really wish to hear other people's. "Colonel Santana will take you and your men to your hotel."

"Thank you."

"I can promise you very little, El Gato. I understand that you cannot guarantee the future, but the North Koreans must fulfill their part of our bargain. If they do, there is a chance, just a chance, that I may rule after Castro."

El Gato waited.

Vargas continued: "I will not forget what you did for me, for Cuba. If the day ever comes when I am in a position to help you, feel free to ask. What I can do then will have to be decided upon that day."

"That is more than I hoped for," El Gato said, genuine warmth obvious in his voice. "I thank you for that promise."

CHAPTER THREE

The F-14 Tomcat hung suspended in an infinite blue sky, over an infinite blue sea. Or so it seemed to Jake Grafton, who sat in the front cockpit taking it all in. Behind him Toad Tarkington was working the radar, searching the sky ahead. The air was dead calm today, so without a visual reference there was no sensation of motion. The puffy clouds on the surface of the sea seemed to be marching uniformly toward the rear of the aircraft, almost as if the sky were spinning under the airplane.

The fighter was cruising at 31,000 feet, heading northwestward parallel with the southern coast of Cuba, about a hundred and fifty miles offshore.

"I sure am glad you got us off the ship, sir," Tarkington said cheerfully. "A little flying helps clean out the pipes, keeps everything in perspective."

"That it does," Jake agreed, and stretched.

He had the best job in the navy, he thought. As a battle group commander he could still fly—indeed, an occasional flight was part of the job description. Yet his flying days would soon be over: in just two months he was scheduled to turn over the command to another admiral and be on his way somewhere.

He searched the empty sky automatically as he thought again about where the next set of orders might send him. If the people in the flag detailing office in the Pentagon had a clue, they certainly weren't talking.

Ah, it would all work out. The powers that be would send him another set of orders or retire him, and it really didn't matter much which way it went. Everyone has to move on sooner or later, so why not now?

Maybe he should just submit his retirement papers, get on with the rest of his life.

With his right hand he hit the emergency disconnect for the autopilot, which worked as it should.

Without touching the throttles, Jake Grafton smoothly lifted the nose and began feeding in left stick. Nose climbing, wing dropping . . . rolling smoothly through the inverted position, though with only seventy degrees of heading change. The nose continued down—keep the roll in!—and the G increased as the fighter came out of the dive and back to the original heading, only 1,400 below the entry altitude. Ta-ta! There you have it—a sloppy barrel roll!

Jake kept the stick back and started a barrel roll to the right.

"Are you okay up there, sir?" Toad Tarkington asked anxiously.

"You ask that of me? The world's finest aerobatic pilot? Have you no respect?"

"These whifferdills are not quite up to your usual world-class standards, so one wonders. Could it be illness, decrepitude, senility?"

They were passing the inverted positon when Jake said, "Just for that, Tarkington, you can put us on the flight schedule every day so we can practice. An hour and a half of high-G maneuvers seven times a week will teach you to respect your elders."

"You got that right," Toad replied, and moaned as if he were in pain as Jake lifted the Tomcat into a loop.

"War Ace One Oh Four, this is Sea Hawk. You have traffic to the northwest, one hundred miles, heading south at about 30,000."

"Roger, Sea Hawk."

Coming down the back side of the loop, Jake turned to the northwest.

"Admiral, I know you think I was loafing back here," Toad said obsequiously, "but I had that guy on the scope. Honest! I was just gonna say something when that E-2 guy beat me to the switch."

"Sure, Toad. These things happen. If you're going to nap, next time bring a pillow."

"This guy is coming south, like he's out of some base in central Cuba, about our altitude. Heck of a coincidence, huh?"

The F-14 had an optical camera mounted in the nose that was slaved to the radar cross-hairs.

"Tell me when you see him," Jake murmured.

"Be a couple miles yet. Let's come right ten degrees just for grins and see what happens."

Jake again had the fighter on autopilot. He pushed the stick right, then leveled on the new course.

At fifty miles Toad had the other airplane on the screen of his monitor. A silver airplane, fighter size, with the sun glinting off its skin. The electronic countermeasures (ECM) panel lit up as the F-14's sensors picked up the emissions of the other plane's radar.

"A MiG-29," Jake said.

"What's he doing out here?" Toad wondered.

"Same thing as we are. Out flying around seeing what is what."

"I thought the Cubans had retired their MiG-29s. Couldn't keep paying the bills on 'em."

"Well, at least one is still operational."

Even as they watched, the MiG altered course to the left so that he would have a chance to turn in behind the F-14 when their flight paths converged.

Jake Grafton was suddenly sure he didn't want the MiG behind him. The Soviets specifically designed the MiG-29 to be able to defeat the F-14, F-15, F-16 and F/A-18 in close combat; it was, probably, the second-best fighter in the world (the best being the Sukhoi Su-27 Flanker). Jake altered course so the two planes would converge head-on.

What would the MiG pilot do?

If the Cuban pilot opened fire over the ocean, over a hundred miles from land, who would ever know?

"Sea Hawk, One Oh Four, are you getting this on tape?"

"Yes, sir. We're recording."

"This bogey is a MiG-29."

"Roger that. We've been tracking him for twenty-five minutes now."

The range was closing rapidly, but still Jake didn't see the MiG. He looked at the target dot in the heads-up display, but the sky was huge and the Cuban fighter too far away, although it was almost as large as the F-14.

The MiG was about four miles away when Jake finally saw it, a winged silver glint that shot by just under his right wing. Jake Grafton disconnected the autopilot and slammed the stick over.

He pulled carefully, cleanly, craned his head and braced himself with his left hand as he kept the turning MiG in sight.

The Cuban fighter rolled out of his turn heading north. Jake leveled out on a parallel course. Careful not to point his nose at the Cuban, Jake let the Tomcat drift closer on a converging course.

When the planes were less than a hundred yards apart, he slowed the closure rate but kept moving in.

Finally the two planes were in formation with their wingtips about twenty yards apart.

"Look at that thing, would you?" Toad enthused. "Have you ever seen a more gorgeous airplane?"

"I hear it's a real dream machine," Jake agreed.

"Oh, baby, the lines, the curves... The Russians sure know how to design flying machines."

"If this guy has to jump out of that thing," Jake asked Toad, "do you think Cuban Air-Sea Rescue is going to come pick him up?"

"I doubt it," Toad replied. "And I suspect he knows that."

"He's got a set of cojones on him," Jake said. "Bet he can fly the hell out of that thing, too."

In the Cuban fighter, Major Carlos Corrado took his time looking over the American plane. This was the first time he had ever seen an F-14. Amazing how big they were, with the two men and the missiles under the wings.

Carlos was lucky he had this hunk of hot Russian iron to fly, technical generations ahead of the MiG-19s and 21s that equipped the bulk of Cuba's tactical squadrons, and he damn well knew it. Cuba owned three dozen MiG-29s and had precisely one operational—this one—which Corrado kept flying by the simple expedient of cannibalizing parts from the others.

He checked his fuel. He had enough, just enough, to get home. Sure, he had no business being out here over the ocean, but he wanted to fly today and the Cuban ground control intercept (GCI) controller said the American was here. One thing led to another and here he was.

Now Carlos Corrado was on course to return to his base near the city of Cienfuegos, on Cuba's southern coast. He checked the compass, the engine instruments, then turned back to studying the American plane, which hung there on the end of his wing as if it were painted on the sky.

A minute went by, then the man in the front seat of the American plane raised his hand and waved. Carlos returned the gesture as the big American fighter turned away to the right and immediately began falling behind. Carlos twisted his body in his seat to keep the F-14 in sight for as long as possible. Big as it was, the F-14 disappeared into the eastern sky with startling rapidity.

Carlos Corrado turned in his seat and eased the position of his butt.

The Americans were two or three technical generations beyond the Cubans, so far ahead that most Cuban military men regarded American capabilities as almost superhuman. They had read of the Gulf War, of the satellites and computers and smart weapons. Unlike his colleagues, Corrado was not frightened by the Americans. Impressed by their military capability, but not frightened.

If I were smarter, he thought now, *I would be frightened.*

But the Americans and Cubans would never fight. They had not fought since the Bay of Pigs and doubtless never would. Castro would soon be gone and a new government would take over and Cuba would become a new American suburb, another little beach island baking in the sun south of Miami, Key Cuba. When that happy day came, Carlos Corrado told himself, he was going to America and get a decent flying job that paid real money.

Doña Maria Vieuda de Sedano's daughters arrived first, in the early afternoon, to tidy up and do the cooking for the guests. They had married local men who worked the sugarcane and saw her every day. In truth, they looked after her, helped her dress, prepared her meals, cleaned and washed the clothes.

It was infuriating to be disabled, to be unable to *do!* The arthritis that crippled her hands and feet made even simple tasks difficult and complex tasks out of the question.

Doña Maria managed to shuffle to her favorite chair on the tiny porch without help. Her small house sat on the western edge of the village. From the porch she could see several of her neighbors' houses and a wide sweep of the road. Across the road was a huge field of cane. A cane-cooking factory stood about a half mile farther west. When the harvest began, the stacks belched smoke and the fumes of cooking sugar drifted for miles on the wind.

Beyond all this, almost lost in the distance, was the blue of the ocean, a thin line just below the horizon, bluer than the distant sky. The wind coming in off the sea kept the temperature down and prevented insects from becoming a major nuisance.

The porch was the only thing Doña Maria really liked about the house, though after fifty-two years in residence God knows she had some memories. Small, just four rooms, with a palm-leaf roof, this house had been the center of her adult life. Here she moved as a young bride with her husband, bore her children, raised them, cried and laughed with them, buried two of the ten, watched the others grow up and marry and move away. And here she watched her husband die of cancer.

He had died . . . sixteen years ago, sixteen years in November.

You never think about outliving your spouse when you are young. Never think about what comes afterward, after happiness, after love. Then, too soon, the never-thought-about future arrives.

She sat on the porch and looked at the clouds floating above the distant ocean, almost like ships, sailing someplace. . . .

She had lived her whole life upon this island, every day of it, had never been farther from this house than Havana, and that on just two occasions: once when she was a teenage girl, on a marvelous expedition with her older sister, and once when her son Maximo was sworn in as the minister of finance.

She had met Fidel Castro on that visit to the capital, felt the power of his personality, like a fire that warmed everyone within range. Oh, what a man he was, tall, virile, full of life.

No wonder Maximo orbited Fidel's star. His brother Jorge, her eldest, had been one of Castro's most dedicated disciples, espousing Marxism and Cuban nationalism, refusing to listen to the slightest criticism of his hero. Jorge, dead of heart failure at the age of forty-two, another dreamer.

All the Sedanos were dreamers, she thought, poverty-stricken dreamers trapped on this sun-washed island in a sun-washed sea, isolated from the rest of humankind, the rest of the species. . . .

She thought of Jorge when she saw Mercedes, his widow, climb from the car. The men in the car glanced at her seated on the porch, didn't wave, merely drove on, leaving Mercedes standing in the road.

"*Hola, Mima.*"

Jorge, cheated of life with this woman, whom he loved more than anything, more than Castro, more than his parents, more than *anything*, for the Sedanos were also great lovers.

"*Hola*, my pretty one. Come sit beside me."

As she stepped on the porch, Doña Maria said, "Thank you for coming."

"It is nothing. We both loved Jorge. . . ."

"Jorge . . ."

Mercedes looked at Maria's hands, took them in her own, as if they weren't twisted and crippled. She kissed the older woman, then sat on a bench beside her and looked at the sea.

"It is still there. It never changes."

"Not like we do."

The emotions twisted Mercedes's insides, made her eyes tear. Here in this place she had had so much, then with no warning it was gone, as if a mighty tide had swept away all that she valued, leaving only sand and rock.

Jorge—oh, what a man he was, a dreamer and lover and believer in social justice. A true believer, without a selfish bone in his body . . . and of course he had died young, before he realized how much reality differed from his dreams.

He lived and died a crusader for justice and Cuba and all of that . . . and left her to grow old alone . . . lonely in the night, looking for someone who cared about something besides himself.

She bit her lip and looked down at Doña Maria's hands, twisted and misshapen. On impulse leaned across and kissed the older woman on the cheek.

"God bless you, dear child," Doña Maria said.

Ocho came walking along the road, trailed by four of the neighborhood children who were skipping and laughing and trying to make him smile. When he turned in at his mother's gate, the children scampered away.

Everyone on the porch turned and looked at him, called a greeting as he quickly covered the three or four paces of the path. Ocho was the Greek god, with the dark hair atop a perfect head, a perfect face, a perfect body . . . tall, with broad shoulders and impossibly narrow hips, he moved like a cat. He dominated a room, radiating masculinity like a beacon, drawing the eyes of every woman there. Even his mother couldn't take her eyes from him, Mercedes noted, and grinned wryly. This last child—she bore Ocho when she was forty-four—even Doña Maria must wonder about the combination of genes that produced him.

Normally an affable soul, Ocho had little to say this evening. He grunted monosyllables to everyone, kissed his mother and Mercedes and his sisters perfunctorily, then found a corner of the porch in which to sit.

Women threw themselves at Ocho, and he never seemed to notice. It was almost as if he didn't want the women who wanted him. He was sufficiently different from most of the men Mercedes knew that she found him intriguing. And perhaps, she reflected, that was the essence of his charm.

Maximo Luís Sedano's sedan braked to a stop in a swirl of dust. He bounded from the car, strode toward the porch, shouting names, a wide grin on his face. He gently gathered his mother in his arms, kissed her on both her cheeks and forehead, kissed each hand, knelt to look into her face.

Mercedes didn't hear what he said; he spoke only for his mother's ears. When she looked away from Maximo and his mother she was surprised to see Maximo's wife climbing the steps to the porch. Maximo's wife—just what *was* her name?—condemned forever to be invisible in the glare of the great man's spotlight.

Another dominant personality—the Sedanos certainly produced their share of those—Maximo was a prisoner of his birth. Cuba was far too small for him. Amazingly, because life rarely works out just right, he had found one of the few occupations in Castro's Cuba that allowed him to travel, to play on a wider field. As finance minister he routinely visited the major capitals of Europe, Central and South America.

Just now he gave his mother a gift, which he opened for her as his sisters leaned forward expectantly, trying to see.

French chocolates! He opened the box and let his mother select one, then passed the rare delicacy around to all.

The sisters stared at the box, rubbed their fingers across the metallic paper, sniffed the delicious scent, then finally, reluctantly, selected one candy and passed the box on.

One of the sister's husbands whispered to the other, just loud enough for Mercedes to overhear: "Would you look at that? We ate potatoes and plantains last month, all month, and were lucky to get them."

The other brother-in-law whispered back, "For three days last week we had absolutely nothing. My brother brought us a fish."

"Well, the dons in government are doing all right. That's the main thing."

Mercedes sat listening to the babble of voices, idly comparing Maximo's clean, white hands to those of the sisters' husbands, rough, callused, work hardened. If the men were different, the women weren't. Maximo's wife wore a chic, fashionable French dress as she sat now with Doña Maria's daughters, whispering with them, but inside the clothes she was still one of them in a way that Maximo would never be again. He had traveled too far, grown too big. . . .

Mercedes was thinking these thoughts when Hector arrived, walking along the road. Even Maximo stopped talking to one of his brothers, the doctor, when he saw Hector coming up the path to the porch.

"Happy birthday, *Mima*."

Hector, Jesuit priest, politician, revolutionary . . . he spoke softly to his mother, kissed her cheek, shook Maximo's hand, looked him in the eye as he ate a chocolate, kissed each of his sisters and touched the arms and hands of their husbands and his brothers, the doctor and the automobile mechanic.

Ocho was watching Hector, waiting for him to reach for his hand, his lips quivering.

Mercedes couldn't quite believe what she was seeing, Hector hugging Ocho, holding him and rocking back and forth, the young man near tears.

Then the moment passed.

Hector refused to release his grip on his bother, led him to Doña Maria, gently made him sit at her feet and placed her hands in his.

Ah, yes, Hector Sedano. If anyone could, it would be you.

"They do not appreciate you," Maximo's wife told him as they rode back to Havana in his car.

"They are so ignorant," she added, slightly embarrassed that she and her husband should have to spend an evening with peasants in such squalid surroundings.

Of course, they were his family and one had duties, but still . . . He had worked so hard to earn his standing and position, it was appalling that he should have to make a pilgrimage back to such squalor.

And his relatives! The old woman, the sisters . . . crippled, ignorant, dirty, uncouth . . . it was all a bit much.

And Hector, the priest who was a secret politician! A man who used the Church for counterrevolutionary treason.

"Surely he must know that you are aware of his political activities," she remarked now to her husband, who frowned at the shacks and sugarcane fields they were driving past.

"He knows," Maximo murmured.

"Europe was so nice," his wife said softly. "I don't mean to be uncharitable, but truly it is a shame that we must return to *this*!"

Maximo wasn't paying much attention.

"I keep hoping that someday we shall go to Europe and never return," she whispered. "I do love Madrid so."

Maximo didn't hear that comment. He was wondering about Hector and Alejo Vargas. He couldn't imagine the two of them talking, but what if they had been? What if those two combined to plot against him? What could he do to guard against that possibility, to protect himself?

Later that evening Hector and his sister-in-law, Mercedes, rode a bus into Havana. "It was good of you to stay for *Mima*'s party," Hector said.

"I wanted to see her. She makes me think of Jorge."

"Do you still miss him?"

"I will miss him every day of my life."

"Me too," Hector murmured.

"Vargas knows about you," she said, after glancing around to make sure no one else could hear her words.

"What does he know?"

"That you organize and attend political meetings, that you write to friends, that you speak to students, that most of the priests in Cuba are loyal to you, that many people all over this island look to you for leadership. . . . He knows that much and probably more."

"It would be a miracle if none of that had reached the ears of the secret police."

"He may arrest you."

"He will do nothing without Fidel's approval. He is Fidel's dog."

"And you think Fidel approves of your activities?"

"I think he tolerates them. The man isn't immortal. Even he must wonder what will come after him."

"You are playing with fire. Castro's hold on Vargas is weakening. Castro's death will give him a free hand. Do not underestimate him."

"I do not. Believe me. But Cuba is more important than me, than Vargas, than Castro. If this country is ever going to be anything other than the barnyard of a tyrant, someone must plant seeds that have a chance of growing. Every person I talk to is a seed, an investment in the future."

" 'Barnyard of a tyrant.' What a pretty phrase!" Mercedes said acidly. The last few years, living with Fidel, she had developed a thick skin: people said the most vicious things about him and she had learned to ignore most of it. Still, she deeply admired Hector, so his words wounded her.

"I'm sorry if I—"

She made sure her voice was under control, then said, "Dear Hector, Cuba is also the graveyard of a great many martyrs. There is room here for Vargas to bury us both."

He was remembering the good days, the days when he had been young, under a bright sun, surrounded by happy, laughing comrades.

All things had been possible back then. Bullets couldn't touch them, no one would betray them to Batista's men, they would save Cuba, save her people, make them prosperous and healthy and strong and happy. Oh, yes, *when we were young* . . .

As he tossed and turned, fighting the pain, snatches of scenes ran through his mind; student politics at the University of Havana, the assault on the Moncada Barracks in Santiago, guns banging and bullets spanging off steel, off masonry, singing as they whirled away. . . . He remembered the firefights on the roads, riding the trucks through the countryside, evenings making plans with Che and the others, how they would set things right, kick out the capitalists who had enslaved Cuba for centuries.

Che, he had been a true believer.

And there were plenty more. True believers all. Ignorant as virgins, penniless and hungry, they thought they could fix the world.

In his semiconscious state he could hear his own voice making speeches, explaining, promising to fix things, to heal the people, put them to work, give them jobs and houses and medical care and a future for their children.

Words. All words.

Wind.

He coughed, and the coughing brought him fully awake. The nurse was there in the chair watching him.

"Leave me, woman."

She left the room.

He pulled himself higher in the bed, used a corner of the sheet to wipe the sweat from his face.

The sheets were thin, worn out. Even *el presidente*'s sheets were worn out!

A sick joke, that.

Everything in the whole damned country was broken or worn out, including Castro's sheets. You didn't have to be a high government official to be aware of that hard fact.

On the dresser just out of reach was a box of cigars. He hitched himself around in bed, reached for one, then leaned far over and got his hand on the lighter.

The pain made him gasp.

Madre mia!

When the pain subsided somewhat he lay back in the bed, wiped his face again on the sheet.

He fumbled with the cigar, bit off the end and spat it on the floor. Got the lighter going, sucked on the cigar . . . the raw smoke was like a knife in his throat. He hacked and hacked.

The doctors made him give up cigars ten years ago. He demanded this box two days ago, when they told him he was dying. "If I am dying, I can smoke. The cancer will kill me before the cigars, so why not?"

When the coughing subsided, he took a tiny puff on the cigar, careful not to inhale.

God, the smoke was delicious.

Another puff.

He lay back on the pillow, sniffed the aroma of the smoke wafting through the air, inhaled the tobacco essence and let it out slowly as the cigar smoldered in his hand.

The truth was that he had made a hash of it. Cuba's problems had defeated him. Oh, he had done the best he could, but by any measure, his best hadn't been good enough. The average Cuban was worse off today than he had been those last few years under Batista. Food was in short supply, the economy was in tatters, the bureaucrats were openly corrupt, the social welfare system was falling apart, and the nation reeled under massive short-term foreign debt, for it had defaulted on its long-term international debt in the late 1980s. The short-term debt could not be repudiated, not if the nation ever expected to borrow another peso abroad.

He puffed on the cigar, savoring the smoke. Then he shifted, trying to make the ache in his bowels ease up.

Of course he knew what had gone wrong. When he took over the nation he had played the cards he had . . . evicted the hated Yanqui *imperialistas* and seized their property, and accepted the cheers and adulation of the people for delivering them from the oppressor. Unfortunately Cuba was a tiny, poor country, so he had had to replace the evicted *patrón* with another, and the only one in sight had been the Soviet Union. He embraced communism, got down on his knees and swore fealty to the Soviet state. With that act he earned the undying hatred of the politicians who ruled the United States—after several assassination attempts and the ill-fated Bay of Pigs invasion debacle, they declared economic warfare on Cuba. Then the cruelest twist of the knife—the Soviet Union collapsed in 1990–91 and Cuba was cut adrift.

Ah, he should have been wiser, should have realized that the United States would be the winning horse. The Spanish grandees had bled Cuba for centuries, worked the people as slaves, then as peons. After the Americans ran the Spanish off, American corporations put their men in the manor houses and life continued as before. The people were still slaves to the cane crop, living in abject poverty, unable to escape the company towns and the company stores.

A few things did change under the Americans. The island became America's red light district, the home of the vice that was illegal on the American mainland: gambling, prostitution, drugs, and, during Prohibition, alcohol. Poor Catholic families sent their daughters to the cities to whore for the Yanquis.

The capitalists bled Cuba until there was no blood left—they would keep exploiting people the world over until there were no more people. Or no more capitalists. Until then, the capitalists would have all the money. He should have realized that fundamental truth.

He had grown up hating the United States, hating Yanquis who drank and gambled and whored the nights away in Havana. He hated their diplomats, their base at Guantánamo Bay, their smugness, their money . . . he despised them and all their works, which was unfortunate, because America was a fact of life, like shit. A man could not escape it because it smelled bad.

God had never given him the opportunity to destroy the Yanquis, because if He had . . .

Fidel Castro was intensely, totally Cuban. He personified the resentment the Cuban people felt because they had spent their lives begging for the scraps that fell from the rich men's table. Resentment was a vile emotion, like hatred and envy.

Well, he was dying. Weeks, they said. A few weeks, more or less. The cancer was eating him alive.

The painkillers were doing their job—at least he could sit up, think rationally, smoke the forbidden cigars, plan for Cuba's future.

Cuba had a future, even if he didn't.

Of course, the United States would play a prominent role in that future. With the great devil Fidel dead, all things were possible. The economic embargo would probably perish with him, a new *presidente* could bring . . . what?

He thought about that question as he puffed gingerly on the cigar, letting the smoke trickle out between his lips.

For years Americans had paraded through the government offices in Havana talking about what might be after the economic embargo was lifted by their government. Always they had an angle, wanted a special dispensation from the Cuban government . . . and were willing to pay for it, of course. Pay handsomely. Now. Paper promises . . . He had enjoyed taking their money.

He had made no plans for a successor, had anointed no one. Some people thought his brother, Raúl, might take over after him, but Raúl was *impotente*, a lightweight.

He would have to have his say now, while he was very much alive.

But what should the future of Cuba be?

The pain in his bowels doubled him up. He curled up in the bed, groaning, holding tightly to the cigar.

After a minute or so the pain eased somewhat and he puffed at the cigar, which was still smoldering.

Whoever came after him was going to have to make his peace with the United States. They were going to have to be selective about America's gifts, rejecting the bad while learning to profit from the good things, the gifts America had to give to the world.

That had been his worse failing—he himself had never learned how to safely handle the American elephant, make the beast do his bidding. His successors would have to for the sake of the Cuban people. Cuba would never be anything if it remained a long, narrow sugarcane field and way point for cocaine smugglers. If that was all there was, everyone on the island might as well set sail for Miami.

Maybe he should have left, said good-bye, thrown up his hands and retired to the Costa del Sol.

Next time. Next time he would retire young, let the Cubans make it on their own.

Like every man who ever walked the earth, Castro had been trapped by his own mistakes. The choices he made early in the game were irreversible. He and the Cuban people had been forced to live with the consequences. Life is like that, he reflected. Everyone must make his choices, wise or foolish, good or bad, and live with them; there is no going back.

There is always the possibility of redemption, of course, but one cannot unmake the past. We have only the present. Only this moment.

When the pain came this time, the cigar dropped from his fingers.

He lay in the bed groaning, trying not to scream for the nurse. If he did, she would give him an injection, which would put him to sleep. The needle was going to give him peace during his final days, but he wasn't ready for it yet.

The pain had eased somewhat when he felt a hand on his forehead. He opened his eyes. Mercedes.

"You dropped your cigar on the floor," she whispered.

"I know."

"Shall I call the nurse?"

"Not for a while."

She used a damp cloth to wipe the perspiration from his face. The cloth felt good.

"Light the cigar."

She did so, put it in his hand. He managed one tiny puff.

"You talked to Hector?"

"Yes."

"What did he say?"

"He was surprised. He didn't know it would be so soon."

"That was your impression?"

"Yes."

"And the tobacco deal with the Americans? What did Hector say when you told him about it?"

"Just listened."

"The birthday party, Maximo came?"

"Yes. Brought a box of French chocolates and his wife, who wore a Paris frock."

Fidel's lips twisted. He could imagine what the other people at the party thought of that. Maximo could charm foreign bankers and squeeze a peso until it squealed, but he was no politician.

"Did you warn Hector about Alejo?"

"Yes."

"What did he say?"

"He made light of it."

Fidel thought about that. Remembered the cigar and took another puff.

"He thinks the threat will be the generals," he said finally, "but it won't. The generals don't know it, but the troops will follow Hector. Alejo Vargas is his most dangerous opponent, and if Hector Sedano doesn't understand that, they will bury him a few days after they bury me."

"Admiral, next weekend when we're in the Virgin Islands, what say we put the barge in the water and go water-skiing?"

The person asking the question was the admiral's aide, a young lieutenant who flew an F/A-18 on her last cruise. Her boyfriend was still in one of the Hornet squadrons; the last time Jake Grafton approved the barge adventure, the boyfriend was invited to go along.

Now Jake sighed. "I'm not sure where we're going to be next weekend, Beth." He had no intention of getting very far from Guantánamo Bay while those warheads were still in that warehouse, but of course he couldn't say that. "Check with ops, Commander Tarkington."

"Yes, sir," Beth said, trying to hide her disappointment.

The new Chief of Staff, Captain Gil Pascal, Toad Tarkington, and the admiral had put their heads together, carefully listed the forces available should an emergency arise, and drafted a contingency plan. "Nothing's happened in all these years," Jake told them, "but Washington must have had a reason for telling us to keep an eye on the place. They must know something we don't."

Gil Pascal met the admiral's gaze. He had reported to the staff just a week ago. "Sir, as I recall, the orders said to 'monitor' the loading of the weapons onto the containership."

" 'Monitor'?" muttered Jake Grafton. "What the hell does that mean? Is that some kind of New Age bureaucrat word? It doesn't mean anything."

"I guess my question really is, how much force are you willing to use without authorization from Washington?"

A faint smile crossed the lips of Toad Tarkington. Only a man who didn't know the admiral would ask that question. Anyone who started shooting in Jake Grafton's bailiwick had better be ready for a war, Toad thought. He had managed to wipe off the smile by the time the admiral answered:

"Whatever it takes to keep those warheads in American hands."

Pascal took his time ordering his thoughts. "Shouldn't we be talking contingencies with Washington, Admiral?"

Jake Grafton opened a top-secret message folder that lay on his desk in front of him. "I already sent a query to CNO. This is the answer."

He passed the message to Pascal. "Monitor weapons on-load diligently, using your best judgment," the message read, "but do not deviate from normal routine. Revealing presence of chemical and biological weapons in Cuba not in the national interest. Risks of transfer have been carefully considered at the highest level. Should risk assessment change you will be informed." The final sentence referred to the original message.

"Five sentences?" Toad Tarkington asked when he had had his chance to read the message. "Only five sentences?"

Reading naval messages was an art, of course. One had to consider the identity and personality of the sender, the receiver, the situation, any correspondence that had passed before. . . . The situation in Washington was the unknown here, Jake concluded. If the CNO had been at liberty to say more, he would have: Jake knew the CNO. The lack of guidance or illumination told Jake that the chief of naval operations wanted him to be ready for anything.

"We'll have to do the best we can with what we have," the admiral said now to Pascal and Tarkington. "I want a plan: we need someone watching at all times, a quick reaction force that can meet any initial incursion with force, a reserve force to throw into the fray to absolutely deny access, and flash messages ready to go informing Washington of what we have done."

Toad and Gil Pascal nodded. A plan like this with the forces that the admiral had at his disposal would be simple to construct. No surprises there.

"There is always the possibility that we may not be able to prevent hostiles from getting to the warheads, if they choose to try. We also need a plan addressing that contingency."

"Surely this nightmare won't come to pass," Gil Pascal said. "Your assessment of the risk differs remarkably from that of the National Security Council."

"I'm sure the powers that be think it quite unlikely anybody will try to prevent us from removing the weapons from Cuba, and I agree. On the other hand, they must know something they can't share with us. If the risk were zero, they wouldn't have sent us here with orders to monitor, whatever the hell that is. Gentlemen, I just want to be ready if indeed we win the lottery and our number comes up."

Toad thoughtfully put the message from Washington back into its red folder. He pursed his lips, then said thoughtfully, "One thing is for sure—something is up."

CHAPTER FOUR

Alejo Vargas thought he had the finest office in Havana, indeed, in all of Cuba, and perhaps he did. He had the whole corner of the top floor, with lots of glass. Through the large windows one got a fine view across the rooftops of Morro Castle and the channel leading into Havana Harbor from the sea. The desk was mahogany, the chairs leather, the carpet Persian.

William Henry Chance paused to take in the view, then nodded appreciatively. He turned, saw the old United Fruit Company safe in the corner, now standing open, and the display of gold and silver coins from the Spanish Main under glass. He paused again, ran his eye over the coins just long enough to compliment his host.

"Very nice," Chance said, and took the chair indicated by Alejo Vargas. At a nearby desk sat Vargas's Chief of Staff, Colonel Pablo Santana, who nodded at Chance when he looked his way, but said nothing.

Colonel Santana was dark, with coal black eyes and black hair combed straight back; he had some slave and Indian somewhere in his bloodline. He slit the throats and pulled the trigger for Alejo Vargas whenever those chores needed to be done.

Chance forced himself to ignore Santana and look at his host. "I appreciate you taking the time from your busy day to see me, General," the American said, and gave Vargas a frank, winning smile.

Chance was tall and angular, with craggy good looks, and dressed in a light gray suit of a quality one could not obtain in Cuba for love or money. He appeared perfectly at ease, as if he owned the building and were calling on a tenant.

No wonder the Russians lost the race to the Americans, Vargas thought ruefully. A true Latin male, he was acutely aware of his own physical and social shortcomings, his lack of grace and self-assurance, so he was quick to appreciate the desired qualities in others.

"I understand you have been discussing a business arrangement for the future with officials of several departments," Vargas began.

"That is correct, General. As you probably know, I represent a consortium of stockholders in several of the major American tobacco companies. My errand is discreet, not for public discussion."

Vargas certainly did know. He had a complete dossier on William Henry Chance in the upper right-hand drawer of his desk, a dossier decorated with a half dozen photos, photocopies of all the pages of Chance's passport, and one of his entry in *Who's Who.* A senior partner in a major New York law firm, Chance had represented tobacco companies for twenty-five years. That Chance was the man in Havana talking to the Cuban government was a sure signal that major money was behind him.

Indeed, Chance was in Vargas's office today because Fidel Castro had asked Vargas to see him.

"Alejo," Fidel had said, "our future depends on Cuba getting a piece of the world economy. The Americans have kept us isolated too long. If we can make it profitable for the Americans to lift the embargo, sooner or later they will. The Yankees can smell money for miles."

If William Henry Chance knew that Castro had personally asked Vargas to see him, he gave no sign.

The less he understands about our government, the better, Vargas thought. He cleared his throat, and said, "I am sure you understand our concern, Señor Chance. Cuba is a poor nation, dependent on sugarcane as the mainstay of the economy, a crop that is, as usual, a glut on the world market. Your client's proposal, as I understand it, is to cultivate tobacco in Cuba instead of sugarcane."

Chance gave the tiniest nod. A trace of a grin showed on his lips. He glanced at Santana, who was scrutinizing him with professional interest, the way a cat examines a mouse.

"Your comprehension is perfect, General."

"Through the years, señor, the price of tobacco on the world market has been even lower than that of sugar."

"This meeting shall be a great help to my clients," Chance declared. "Here today I will show you the many benefits that will accrue in the future to the nation that keeps an open mind about tobacco. I am not talking about cigar leaf, you understand, which is a tiny percentage of the world market. I am talking about cigarette tobacco."

"The price of which will collapse in America when the American government ends its subsidy to American tobacco farmers."

"Indeed," said William Henry Chance. "The United States government *will* soon cease supporting the price. But of greater interest to our clients, the government will increasingly regulate and tax the cigarette business. Plainly stated, the government is hostile to our industry. The current administration has stated that their eventual goal is to put the industry out of business."

Chance moved his shoulders up and down a millimeter, settled deeper into his chair. "The American public is gradually giving up the cigarette habit. In a few years the only Americans smoking will be rebellious youth and addicted geriatrics."

Chance leaned forward slightly in his chair and looked Alejo Vargas straight in the eye. "The future of the cigarette industry is to sell American brands to non-Americans. All over the world people in developing countries want the image American cigarettes present: prosperity, sex appeal, luxury, a rising status in the world. These images are no accident. They have been carefully created and nurtured at great expense by the American cigarette companies."

Chance paused here to see if his host had anything to say. He didn't. Alejo Vargas sat silently with a blank, expressionless face. Not a single muscle revealed a clue about its owner's thoughts. Through the years Alejo had had a lot of experience listening to Castro's long-winded expositions.

William Henry Chance summed up: "Minister, under the benevolent eye of a government that wants the industry to succeed, the prospects for profit are enormous. In the future the cigarette companies will grow the tobacco, process it, advertise, and sell the cigarettes. Cubans could own part of the companies, which would pay taxes and employ Cubans at a living wage. Here is a product that could be produced locally and sold worldwide. Cigarettes could be gold for Cuba in the twenty-first century."

Now Alejo Vargas smiled. "I like you, Señor Chance. I like your style."

"You can't fool me," Chance shot back. "You like my message."

"Cuba needs industries in addition to sugar."

"The key, General, is a stable government that will protect the industry. Let me be frank: my clients have a great deal of money to invest, but they will not do so without the clear, unequivocal prospect of a stable government that will guarantee their right to do business and earn a fair profit."

"Any promises or guarantees must come from the proper ministries of our government, with the consent of our president, Señor Castro," Alejo Vargas said from the depths of his padded leather chair.

"It is the future of Cuba I wish to discuss with you, General. I state unequivocally that my clients will not invest a dime in Cuba until such time as the American government lifts the economic embargo. Candidly, the embargo will not be lifted as long as Castro remains in office."

"Your candor deserves equal honesty on my part," General Vargas said. "Castro will remain in office until he chooses to leave of his own free will or until he dies. Do not be mistaken—regardless of what drivel you hear from the exiles, Fidel Castro is universally admired, loved, revered as a great patriot by virtually everyone in Cuba. There is no opposition, no movement to remove him . . . none of that."

"It is the distant future I wish to discuss with you."

"Very distant," the general said.

"After Castro."

"I do not have a crystal ball, Señor Chance. I may not live so long."

"Nor I, sir. But very likely the cigarette industry will still be in business and looking for new opportunities to grow."

"Perhaps," Alejo Vargas admitted, and cocked his head slightly. He had seen transcripts of Chance's telephone calls to the United States and a transcript of the conversations that had taken place in his room. The man hadn't said one word about Castro's health nor had anyone mentioned it to him.

Still, it was a remarkable coincidence that he was here in Havana talking about post-Castro Cuba, and Castro was dying.

Alejo Vargas didn't believe in coincidences. His instincts told him that William Henry Chance was not who he appeared to be. As he listened to Chance talk about cigarette marketing and demographics in the Third World, he removed the file on Chance from his desk drawer. Holding the file in his lap where Chance could not see it, he carefully reviewed the information it contained. The photographs he could not scrutinize closely but he was willing to accept them as genuine. Mr. William Henry Chance of New York City was probably a senior partner in a large law firm—after looking once more at the file Vargas would have been shocked if he weren't. All the right things were in the file. At least the file collectors were thorough, if nothing else, Vargas thought. Still, Chance's position and profession might be an elaborate cover.

When he finished with the file Vargas returned it to the desk drawer just as Chance was summing up. The lawyer had charts and graphs. Vargas didn't even glance at them. He studied Chance's eyes, the way they focused, how they moved, how the muscles tensed and relaxed as he talked.

It was possible, Vargas decided. William Henry Chance might be CIA.

Thirty minutes later when Chance was packing his charts and graphs to leave he pulled a small package from his briefcase and offered it to Vargas. "Here's something you might enjoy, General. Sort of an executive pacifier. These things are hot right now in the States so I picked up a few at the airport."

Vargas unwrapped the tissue paper. He was looking at a small plastic frame from which three odd-shaped crystals dangled, suspended by strings.

"These crystals are man-made and react to differential heating," Chance explained. "You put this on the windowsill and the crystals dance around, refracting the sunlight. Very colorful."

"Thank you," Vargas said mechanically, and sat the toy on his desk.

When Chance was gone Colonel Santana called an aide, who examined the device visually, then took it away to be examined electronically.

An hour later the aide returned with the toy in hand. "It is what it appears to be, sir, merely three lumps of oddly shaped crystal on strings. The crystals and frame are entirely solid; they contain nothing."

"Americans! Executive pacifier!" Vargas said contemptuously.

Colonel Santana put the toy on a south-facing windowsill, watched the crystals dance in the sun for a moment, then forgot about it.

William Henry Chance took his time walking to his hotel, the Nacional, a classic 1930s masterpiece near Havana harbor. He left his locked briefcase in his room, then went downstairs to the hotel restaurant, which charged truly stupendous amounts of American dollars for very modest food. In fact, the only currency the hotel staff would accept was American dollars. Colorful wooden panels and ceramic accents, and peacocks wandering around like refugees from an aviary, gave the place an over-the-top Caribbean look, Chance thought, sort of South Miami Beach racheted one notch too tight.

Chance ordered a sea bass, blackened and grilled, black beans and rice, avocados, and a *mojito*, a delicious concoction of lime juice, sugar, mint leaves, and rum—just what the doctor ordered to prevent scurvy. He savored the fish, sipped a second *mojito,* contemplated the state of the universe and his fellow diners.

The hotel staff, he knew, were employees of the Cuban secret police. When they weren't rushing here and there with daiquiris and fruit drinks they worked for Vargas, spied on the guests, listened to their conversations, searched their luggage, filled out written reports.

Chance knew the routine. He also knew that the Cubans would learn nothing by watching him because there was nothing to learn.

As he drank his second *mojito* he carefully reviewed everything Vargas had said during his interview. He thought about the general's face, the total lack of expression when the demise of Fidel Castro was discussed.

Of course Alejo Vargas knew that Castro was dying. He must know. What Vargas didn't know was that the CIA was equally aware of Castro's medical condition.

When Chance finished dinner he went out on the street for a walk. First he had to work his way through the crowd of Cubans loafing around the entrance to the hotel. Knots of poor, bored Cubans with nothing to do and nowhere to go thronged the sidewalks in front of every nightclub and casino listening to the music that floated out through open doors and windows. Occasionally people danced or sang, but mostly they just passed the time chatting and watching the tourists, and beggars and prostitutes trying to extract dollars from them.

Several blocks away Chance stopped to buy bread. The man who sold him the bread gave him a peso in change.

One peso meant yes, two meant no.

Chance smiled, nodded his thanks, and walked on.

The crystal device was working. The vibrations of human voices in the room changed the motion of the crystals in predictable, minute amounts. When a powerful optical device was focused on the crystals, the refracted light was processed through a computer into human speech. The crystals were a totally passive listening device.

So far so good, Chance reflected, and walked on aimlessly, for the exercise, drinking in the sights, sounds, and smells of Havana. She was like a painted old whore, he thought, trying to keep up appearances. The tourist attractions were gay and lively, temples of hedonism set in a gray communist wasteland.

Outside the tourist area the city reeked of destitution and decay. The crumbling, rotting buildings were choked to the rafters with people, often four families to every apartment. The people fought daily battles to get enough food and basics to sustain life. Away from the clubs and hotels, the faces of the people were gloomy, drawn, without hope.

The poison of communism had done its work here, as it had in every nation that had ever embraced it. After the revolution the government expropriated almost all private property, from the vast estates of the rich to the corner grocery. Hopeless, grinding poverty became nearly universal. Forty years after the revolution the average wage was ten dollars a month, girls from all over Cuba flocked to Havana to prostitute themselves on the streets, everything necessary for a decent life was outrageously expensive or unavailable at any price. The social justice that the communists had promised was as far away as ever: the pain and misery that blighted and made wretched millions of lives had not brought that goal one step closer.

The tourist attractions were the supreme irony, of course. These monuments to greed and sins of the flesh were owned and operated by the socialist state to attract hard currency. The dollars were brought in and spent here by decadent capitalists who earned the money exploiting the workers of the world somewhere else.

If Karl Marx only knew. With the banners of social justice flying in the blue tropic sky, the Cubans had joined the Pied Piper of the Sierra Maestra as he marched bravely down the road to hell. The crumbling buildings, decrepit old cars, hookers on every corner, universal hopelessness—it looked as if the whole parade had almost arrived.

Very curious, William Henry Chance thought. Curious as hell.

From this vantage point he could see all of it, his whole life, as if it were a play being performed before him. The memories came back vivid and clear, the scenes scrolling before his eyes. The mistakes and lost opportunities and petty vendettas played endlessly, inevitably, and he lived it all again, powerless to change a word or gesture.

He was in pain these days, a lot of it, and the doctor this morning had given him a strong narcotic. Now he floated, half-asleep, the pain that had doubled him into the fetal position now a tolerable dull ache. Even as his mind raced, his body relaxed.

Mercedes Sedano sat in a chair in the darkened room beside the bed, looking into the gloomy darkness and lost in her own thoughts.

She reached for Fidel when he moaned and put her hand on his forehead. He had always liked the sensual coolness of her fingers. Her touch now seemed to quiet him. He relaxed again, then tossed restlessly as the ghosts of the past paraded through the recesses of his mind.

An hour later, his eyes opened, though they didn't focus. Finally the head moved and the eyes sought her out.

Fidel Castro said nothing, merely looked.

He could feel the narcotic wearing off. The pain was coming back. He opened his mouth to ask for the doctor, then thought better of it.

He licked his lips. "I want to make a videotape," he whispered, barely audible.

"Are you strong enough?"

"For a little while, I could be, I think. It must be done."

"What will you say?"

"I don't know exactly. I need to think about it."

"When do you wish to do this tape?"

"Soon, I think, or never."

"Tomorrow?"

"Yes, tomorrow. Tell the doctor. I must be alert tomorrow, if only for a little while."

"Why?"

"I want to dictate my political will."

She leaned forward and put her face next to his. "Can you visit a moment with me?"

"*Te quiero, mujer.*"

"*Y yo te adoro, me viejo.*"

"We will talk for a little bit, then the doctor and the needle." He was perspiring now, his body becoming tense.

"I am being selfish. I will call the doctor now."

"In a moment. I want to tell you . . . I love you. You have been the rock I have held on to the last few years."

She wiped away her tears and kissed him.

Then he said, "I have made many mistakes in my life, but I have always tried to do what I thought best for Cuba. Always. Without fail."

"Why do you think I love you so?"

"I want the Cuban people to remember me well. They are my children."

"They will never forget."

"I must help them march into the future."

He drew his knees to his chest. His eyes were bright, perspiration coursed from his forehead and soaked into the pillow.

"Tomorrow," he whispered. "I will think. Get the doctor now."

She squeezed his hand, then left the room.

Maximo Sedano spent the evening on his yacht cruising in sight of Morro Castle. The breeze blew the tops off occasional waves under a deep blue sky. Maximo's two guests looked decidedly pale as they huddled with him around the small table near the galley.

"If Castro dies, will the drug smugglers continue to do business with us?" asked Admiral Delgado, head of the Cuban Navy. For the last fifteen years he had limited his nautical activities to visiting patrol boats tied to piers.

"If we can guarantee the continued safety of their products and their people, of course," Maximo said.

"We can't guarantee anything," General Alba, Chief of Staff of the Cuban Army, said bitterly. "The whole thing is going to fall apart; we are going to lose something very sweet."

It was typical of Delgado and Alba, Maximo thought, that their very first thought of the future was of their pocketbooks. Money. These small, petty men lived for the bribes. Truly, they were unable to see what lay outside of the tiny circle where they lived their miserable, corrupt lives.

Alas, the best military man in Cuba under the age of eighty, the air force chief, died last month. Castro had yet to name a replacement, and probably would not.

Maximo sighed. "Nothing lasts forever," he said. "But change always presents opportunity, if one knows where to look for it. Gentlemen, it all boils down to this: Who will rule Cuba when the dust settles after the funeral?"

"It won't be you," General Alba said curtly. "Five of my regional commanders are in Hector Sedano's pocket, and there is little I can do about it unless I relieve them and put someone else in their place." He gave a tiny shrug. "Castro must endorse the order. If I make a major move like that without his consent, he will sack me."

"He is sick."

"His aides will sack me, using his authority. I cannot disobey Fidel while he draws breath. You know that as well as I."

"Perhaps you should shoot these disloyal subordinates," the admiral said slowly, eyeing his colleague.

"If you have some loyal men who will wait until the right moment," Maximo added.

"When Castro dies?"

"No. When I give the word. Not until then."

"I have some loyal men, certainly," the general said. "I have spread the money around, made sure it got all the way down the chain. Only a fool plays the pig or hands great wads of money to someone else to distribute. My men get their share. The devil of it is that the disloyal ones think Alejo Vargas puts it in their pockets. They think he is the good fairy."

"Will they obey you without question?"

"The loyal men will obey *me*, yes."

"And will *you* obey *me*?" Maximo Sedano demanded.

General Alba stared at Maximo impudently. "I will not lift a finger to put you on the throne as the new Fidel unless..." he said roughly, still looking Maximo straight in the eye, "unless you represent my interests, which are also the interests of my men, and you have a chance to win. I don't think that you have such a chance."

"I hear you, Alba. We have worked together for years; there is enough sugar here for all of us." Maximo glanced at the admiral. "Do you agree?"

"Oh, there's enough. But money isn't everything. The fact is that Alejo Vargas is a blackmailer and has been gathering his filth for twenty years. His spies are everywhere; he sees and hears everything."

The admiral picked up the thought. "Vargas has corrupted people you would not suspect, and those he can't corrupt, he blackmails. I give you my honest opinion: You have no chance against this man."

"Without friends, I do not, that is true."

"I tell you now, Maximo, you have no friends who wish to die with you. Few men do."

"What I cannot understand," the soldier said, "is why Fidel tolerated your brother's antics. He has been told repeatedly of Hector's activities, of the meetings, the speeches, the subtle criticism of Fidel and the choices he made. Why does Fidel tolerate this?"

"I asked him that question once," Maximo said, "a year or so ago. Believe me, he has been carefully briefed on Hector Sedano."

"What did he say?"

"He said Hector was a barometer. The people's reactions to his message told Fidel how unhappy they were with him, with the government. People routinely lie to government clerks, but if they go out of their way to listen to Hector Sedano make a speech, that means something. For my part, I think Fidel wisely considers what the Church might think. Like it or not, Hector is a priest. Fidel has carefully reached out to the Vatican the last few years—he cannot afford to antagonize the pope."

"Are you saying he doesn't care what Hector says?"

"Three or four years ago when Hector first came to his attention, I think Fidel found him extremely irritating. Believe me, I warned Hector repeatedly, tried to get him to use reason, to control his tongue. He ignored me. Flouted me.

"I think Fidel intended to imprison Hector when he had said enough to convict himself with his own mouth. I told Hector he was playing with fire. But as Fidel got sicker, I think he lost interest. He just listens to the reports now, asks a few questions about the size of the crowds, who was there, and goes on to another subject."

"Surely Fidel doesn't intend that Hector Sedano rule after him?" Admiral Delgado asked, his disapproval of Castro's attitude quite plain.

"If we are to have a chance at the prize, we must strike when Fidel breathes his last," Maximo said. "And quickly. Alejo Vargas must be assassinated within hours of Castro's death. Within minutes."

"We would have to kill Santana too," the general said. "I have trouble sleeping nights knowing he is out there listening to everything, planning, scheming at Alejo's side."

"Who is going to do this killing?" the admiral asked.

No one spoke.

"Our problem is going to be staying alive," the general said, "because Alejo Vargas and Santana will eliminate us at the slightest hint that we might be a threat."

"What about Hector?"

"Hector will have to dodge his own bullets."

"You are sheep," Maximo muttered, loud enough for them to hear, "without the courage to take your fate in your own hands. The wolves will rip out your throats."

Toad Tarkington and his wife, Lieutenant Commander Rita Moravia, were seated in the back corner of the main wardroom aboard *United States*, drinking after-dinner coffee and conversing in low tones. A naval test pilot, Rita was on an exchange tour with the Marine squadron aboard *Kearsarge* so that she could gain operational experience on the tiltrotor Osprey prior to its introduction into navy squadrons.

As usual when he was around Rita, Toad Tarkington had a smile on his face. He felt good. *Life is good*, he thought as he watched her tell him what their son, Tyler, now four years old, had said in his most recent letter. She had received the missive earlier today. Of course Tyler wrote it with the help of Rita's parents, who looked after him when Rita and Toad were both at sea.

Yes, *life is good!* It flows along, and if you surround yourself with interesting people and interesting problems, it's worth living. Toad grinned broadly, vastly content.

"May I join you?" Toad and Rita looked up, and saw the new chief of staff standing there with a cup of coffee in his hands.

"Please do, Captain. Have you met my wife, Rita Moravia?"

Gil Pascal hadn't. He and Rita shook hands, said all the usual getting-acquainted things.

After they discussed the command that the captain had just left, Pascal said, "I understand that you two have known Admiral Grafton for some years."

"Oh, yes," Toad agreed. "I was just a lieutenant in an F-14 outfit when I first met him. He was the air wing commander, aboard this very ship in fact. We went to the Med that time, had a run-in with El Hakim."

"I remember the incident," Pascal said. "The ship went to the yard for a year and a half when she got back to the States. And Admiral Grafton was awarded the Medal of Honor."

Toad just nodded. "Rita met the admiral a few months later in Washington," Toad said, trying to move the conversation along. Conversations about El Hakim made him uncomfortable. That was long ago and far away, when he was single. Now, he realized with a jolt, things were much different—he had Rita and Tyler.

He was thinking about how being a family man changed his outlook when he heard Rita say, "Toad has served with Admiral Grafton ever since then. Somehow he's always found a billet that allowed him to do that."

"You know Admiral Grafton pretty well then," Pascal said to Toad.

"He's the second best friend I have in this life," Toad replied lightly. He was smiling, and deadly serious. "Rita is *numero uno*, Jake Grafton is number two."

From there the conversation turned to Rita's current assignment, evaluation of the new V-22 Osprey. After a few minutes Toad asked Rita, "May I get you more coffee?"

At her nod, Toad excused himself, took both cups and went toward the coffee urn on a side table. Normally a steward served the coffee, but just now they were cleaning up after the evening meal.

Captain Pascal asked, "Have your husband's assignments hurt his career?"

Rita knew what he meant. Toad had not followed the classic career path that was supposed to lead to major command, then flag rank. "Perhaps." She gave a minute shrug. "He made his choice. Jake Grafton appeals to a different side of Toad's personality than I do."

"Oh, of course," said the captain, feeling his way. "Spouses and friends, very different, quite understandable . . ."

"Jake Grafton can trade nuances with the best bureaucrats in the business, and he can attack a problem in a brutally direct manner." Rita searched for words, then added, "He always tries to do the right thing, regardless of the personal consequences. I think that is the quality Toad admires the most."

"I see," said the chief of staff, but it was obvious that he didn't.

As Toad walked toward the table with a coffee cup in each hand, Rita Moravia took a last stab at explanation: "Jake Grafton and Toad Tarkington are not uniformed technocrats or clerks or button pushers. They are warriors: I think they sense that in one another."

The shadows were dissipating to dusky twilight as Ocho Sedano walked the streets toward the dock area. Over each shoulder he carried a bag which he had stitched together from bedsheets. One contained a few changes of clothes, a baseball glove, several photos of his family—all that he wished to take with him into his new life in America. Truly, when you inventory the stuff that fills your life, you can do without most of it. Diego Coca said to travel light and Ocho took him literally.

The other bag contained bottles of water. He had searched the trash for bottles, had washed them carefully, filled them with water, and corked them. Diego hadn't mentioned water or food, but Ocho remembered his conversation with his brother, Hector, and thought bringing water would be a wise precaution.

He also had two baked potatoes in the bag.

Diego would laugh at him—they were not going to be at sea long enough to get really hungry, or so he said.

Please, God, let Diego be right. Let us be in America when the sun rises tomorrow.

There would be a man waiting in the Keys, waiting on a certain beach. Diego showed Ocho a map with the beach clearly marked in ink. "He was a close friend of my wife's brother," Diego said. "A man who can be trusted."

The boat was fast enough, Diego said, to be in American waters at dawn. They would make their approach to the beach as the sun rose, when obstructions to navigation were visible, when they could check landmarks and buoys.

Diego was confident. Dora believed her father, looked at him with shining eyes when he talked of America, of how it would be to live in an American house, go to the huge stadiums and watch Ocho play baseball while everyone cheered . . . to have a television, plenty to eat, nice clothes, a *car*!

Dios mio, America did sound like a paradise! To hear Diego tell it America was heaven, lacking only the angel choir . . . and it was just a boat ride away across the Florida Straits.

Of course, Diego said they would probably get seasick, would probably vomit. That was inevitable, to be expected, a price to be paid.

And they could get caught by the Cubans or Americans, get sent back here. "We'll be no worse off than we are now if that happens," Diego argued. "We can always try again to get to America. God knows, we can't get any poorer."

Dora with the shining eyes . . . she looked so expectant.

She was the first, the very first woman he had ever made love to. And she got pregnant after that one time!

When she first told him, he had doubted her. Didn't want to believe. She became angry, threw a tantrum. Then he had believed.

He thought about her now as he walked the dark streets, past people sitting in doorways, couples holding hands, past bars with music coming through the doorways. He had spent his whole life here and now he was leaving, an event of the first order of magnitude. Surely they could see the transformation in his face, in the way he walked.

Several people called to him, "El Ocho!" Several fans wanted to shake his hand, but no more than usual. This was the way they always acted as he walked by—this was the way people had treated him since he was fifteen.

He left the people behind and walked past the closed fish markets and warehouses. His footsteps echoed off the buildings.

The boat was in a slip, Diego said, behind a certain boatyard.

He rounded the corner, saw people. Men, women, and children standing in little knots. Hmm, they were right near the slip.

They were standing around the slip.

He saw Diego standing on the dock, and Dora.

People stepped out of the way to let him by.

"All these people," he said to Diego, "Did you announce our departure at the ballpark? I thought we were going to sneak out of here."

Diego had a sick look on his face. "They're going with us," he said. "*What?*"

"The captain brought his relatives, my brother heard we were leaving, talked to some of his friends. . . ."

Ocho stared at the boat. The boat's name on the stern was written in black paint, which was chipping and peeling off. *Angel del Mar*, Angel of the Sea. The boat was maybe forty feet long, with a little pilothouse. Fishing nets still hung from the aft mast. The crowd—he estimated there were close to fifty people standing here.

"How many people, Diego? How many?"

"Over eighty."

"On that boat? In the Gulf Stream? *Está loco?*"

Diego was beside himself. "This is our chance, Ocho. We can make it. God is with us."

"God? If the boat swamps, will He keep us from drowning?"

"Ocho, listen to me. My friends are waiting in Florida. This is our chance to make it to America, to be something, to live decent.... This is *our* chance."

People were staring at him, listening to Diego.

Ocho looked into the faces looking at him. He tore his eyes away, finally, looked back at Diego, who had his hand on Ocho's arm.

"No. I am *not* going." He pulled his arm from Diego's grasp. "Go with one less, you will all have a little better chance."

"You *have* to go," Diego pleaded, and grabbed his arm.

"Ocho," Dora wailed.

"You have to go," Diego snarled. "You got her pregnant! Be a man!"

CHAPTER FIVE

Eighty-four people were packed aboard *Angel del Mar* as she headed for the mouth of the small bay under a velvet black sky strewn with stars. A sliver of moon cast just enough light to see the sand on the bars at the entrance of the bay.

The boat rode low in the water and seemed to react sluggishly to the small swells that swept down the channel.

"This is insane," Ocho said to Diego Coca, who was leaning against the wall of the small wheelhouse.

"We'll make it. We'll reach the rendezvous in the Florida Keys an hour or two before dawn. *Vamos con Dios.*"

"God had better be with us," Ocho muttered, and reached for Dora. The baby didn't show yet. She was of medium height, with a trim, athletic frame. How well he knew her body.

As far as he knew, he was the only one on the boat who had brought water or food. Oh, the other passengers had things, all right, sacks and boxes of things too precious to leave behind: clothes, pictures, silver, Bibles, rosaries, crucifixes that had decorated the walls of their homes and their parents' and grandparents' homes.

Boxes and sacks were stacked around each person, who sat on the deck or on his pile. Men, women, children, some merely babies in arms . . . It appeared to Ocho as if the Saturday night crowd from an entire section of ballpark bleachers had been miraculously transported to the deck of this small boat.

The breeze smelled of the sea, clean, tangy, crisp. He took a deep breath, wondered if this were his last night of life.

He pulled Dora closer to him, felt the warmth and promise of her body.

Well, this boatload of people would make it to Florida or they wouldn't, as God willed it. He had never thought much about religion, merely accepted it as part of life, but through the years he had learned about God's will. He was not one of those athletes who crossed himself every time he went to the plate or prepared to make a crucial pitch, vainly asking God for assistance in trivial matters, but he knew to a certainty that most of the major events of life—be you ballplayer, manager, father, husband, cane worker, whatever—are beyond your control. Events take their own course and humans are swept along with them. Call it God's will or chance or fate or what have you, all a man could do was throw the ball as well as he could, with all the guile and skill he could muster. What happened after the ball left your fingers was beyond your control. In God's hands, or so they said. If God cared.

For the first time in his life Ocho wondered if God cared.

He was still thinking along these lines when the boat buried its bow in the first big swell at the harbor entrance. Spray came flying back clear to the wheelhouse. People shrieked, some laughed, all tried to find some bit of shelter.

People were moving, holding up clothing or pieces of cardboard when the next cloud of spray came flying back.

The boat rose somewhat as she met each swell, but she was too heavily loaded.

"We're not even out of the harbor," muttered the man beside Ocho. His voice sounded infinitely weary.

Dora hugged Ocho, clung to him as she stared into the night.

She barely came to his armpit. He braced himself against the wall of the wheelhouse, held her close.

The boat labored into the swells, flinging heavy sheets of spray back over the people huddled on the deck.

The door to the wheelhouse opened. A bare head came out, shouted at Diego Coca: "The boat is overloaded, man! It is too dangerous to go on. We must turn back."

Diego pulled a pistol from his pocket and placed the muzzle against the man's forehead. He pushed the man back through the door, followed him into the tiny shack and pulled the door shut behind him.

The man next to Ocho said, "We may make it . . . if the sea gets no rougher. I was a fisherman once, I know of these things."

The man was in his late sixties perhaps, with a deeply lined face and hair bleached by the sun. Ocho had studied his face in the twilight, before the light completely disappeared. Now the fisherman was merely a shape in the darkness, a remembered face.

"Your father is crazy," Ocho told Dora, speaking in her ear over the noise of the wind and sea. She said nothing, merely held him tighter.

It was then he realized she was as frightened as he.

Angel del Mar smashed its way northward under a clear, starry sky. The wind seemed steady from the west at twelve or fifteen knots. Already drenched by spray, with no place to shelter themselves, the people on deck huddled where they were. From his position near the wheelhouse Ocho could just see the people between the showers of spray, dark shapes crowding the deck in the faint moonlight, for there were no other lights so that the boat might go unnoticed by Cuban naval patrols.

"When we get to the Gulf Stream," the fisherman beside Ocho shouted in his ear above the noise of the wind and laboring diesel engine, ". . . swells . . . open the seams . . . founder in this sea."

In addition to heaving and pitching, the boat was also rolling heavily since there was so much weight on deck. The roll to starboard seemed most pronounced when the boat crested a swell, when it was naked to the wind.

Ocho Sedano buried his face in Dora's hair and held her tightly as the boat plunged and reared, turned his body to shield her somewhat from the clouds of spray that swept over them.

He could hear people retching; the vomit smell was swept away on the wind and he caught none of it.

On the boat went into the darkness, bucking and writhing as it fought the sea.

Late in the evening William Henry Chance met his associate at the mahogany bar in El Floridita, one of the flashiest old nightclubs in Old Havana. This monstrosity was the dazzling heart of prerevolutionary Havana in the bad old days; black-and-white photos of Ernest Hemingway, Cary Grant, and Ava Gardner still adorned the walls. The place was full of Americans who had traveled here in defiance of their government's ban on travel to Cuba. As bands belted out salsa and rhumba, the Americans drank, ate, and scrutinized voluptuous prostitutes clad in tight dresses and high heels.

Chance's associate was Tommy Carmellini, a Stanford law school graduate in his late twenties. The baggy sportscoat and pleated trousers did nothing to show off Carmellini's wide shoulders and washboard stomach. Still, a thoughtful observer would conclude he was remarkably fit for a man who spent twelve hours a day at a desk.

"Looks like the Cubans have come full circle," Chance said when Carmellini joined him at the bar. He had to speak up to be heard above the music coming through the open windows.

"Goes around and comes around," Tommy Carmellini agreed. "I wonder just how many different social diseases are circulating in this building tonight."

When they were outside on the sidewalk strolling along, William Henry Chance pulled a cigar from the pocket of his sports jacket, which was folded over his left arm. He bit off the end of the thing, then cupped his hands against the breeze and lit it with a paper match. The wind blew out the first two matches, but he got the cigar going with the third one. After a couple puffs, he sighed.

"Smells delicious," Carmellini said.

"Cuban cigars are the real deal. Gonna be the new in thing. You should try one."

"Naw. I just might like cigars. I've made it this far without smoking, I'm going to try to go all the way."

They paused outside a nightclub and listened to the music pouring out. "That's a good band."

"If you close your eyes, this sorta feels like Miami Beach."

"Miami del Sud."

They walked on. "So what do you hear?"

"The pacifiers are working. All three of them. This afternoon Vargas talked to his subordinates about this and that, the minister of finance had phone sex with a girlfriend, and Castro's top aide talked to the doctors for an hour."

"How is the old goat doing?"

"Not good, the man said. The doctors talked about how much narcotics to administer to ensure he didn't suffer."

"Any guesses when?"

"No."

"The Cuban exile, El Gato, where does he fit in?"

"Don't know yet."

"He's in the casino now with three Russian gangsters, people he knows apparently, playing for high stakes."

"El Gato is supposed to be an influential and powerful enemy of the Castro regime," Chance muttered. "Sure does make you wonder."

"Yeah," said Carmellini. He and Chance both knew that the FBI had an agent and three informers in El Gato's chemical supply business looking for evidence that it was the source of supply for some of the makings of Fidel Castro's biological warfare program. So far, nothing. Then El Gato unexpectedly swanned off to Havana. Chance and Carmellini were coming anyway, but now they had a new item added to their agenda.

And Castro was dying.

"I'd like to know what the Cat is going to tell all his exile friends when he gets back to Florida," Tommy Carmellini said. "Maybe if he winds up in the right offices we'll find out, eh?"

That reference to the executive pacifiers made Chance grin. He puffed the cigar a few times while holding it carefully between thumb and forefinger.

"You don't really know much about smoking cigars, do you?"

"Is it that obvious?"

"Yes, sir."

Chance put the cigar between his teeth at a jaunty angle and puffed fearlessly three or four times. Then he took the thing from his mouth and held it so he could see it. "Wish I could get the hang of it," he said. "Cuba seemed like a good place to learn about cigars."

He tossed the stogie into a gutter on the street.

"Makes me a little light-headed." Chance grinned sheepishly and wiped a sheen of perspiration from his brow.

He stood listening to the sounds of the crowd and the snatches of music floating from the bars and casinos, thinking about biological weapons.

Angel del Mar was only a half hour past the mouth of the harbor when the fisherman beside Ocho Sedano pulled at his arm to attract his attention. Then he shouted, "We will reach the Gulf Stream soon. The swells will be larger. We are too deeply loaded. We must get rid of what weight we can."

The boat was corkscrewing viciously. Ocho nodded, passed Dora to the fisherman, pulled open the wheelhouse door and carefully stepped inside.

The captain worked the wheel with an eye on the compass. The faint glow from the binnacle and the engine RPM indicator were the only lights—they cast a faint glow on the captain's face and that of Diego Coca, who was wedged in beside him, the gun still in his hand. Both men were facing forward, looking through the window at the sheets of spray being flung up when the bow smacked into a swell with an audible thud. The shock of those collisions could be felt through the deck and walls of the wheelhouse.

"You are suicidal," the captain shouted at Diego. "The sea will get worse when we reach the Gulf Stream. We are only a mile or two from it!"

Diego backed up, braced himself against the aft wall of the tiny compartment, pointed the pistol in the center of the captain's back. He held up his hand to hold off Ocho.

"You took the money," Diego said accusingly to the captain.

"Don't be a fool, man."

"*America!* Or I shoot you, as God is my witness."

"You want to drown out here, in this watery hell?"

"You took the money!" Diego shouted.

Ocho stepped forward and Diego pointed the pistol at him. "Back," he said. "Get back. I don't want to shoot you, but I will."

Ocho Sedano leaned forward. "I think they are right, what they say. You *are* crazy. You will kill every man and woman on this boat. Even the babies."

"The boat is overloaded," the captain said without looking at Ocho. "We have to get some weight off. Throw the fishing gear over, the baggage, everything."

Ocho pulled the door open and stepped out onto the pitching deck. He took Dora from the fisherman, pushed her into the wheelhouse, and pulled the door until it latched.

"We must get rid of some weight. Everything goes overboard but the people."

The fisherman nodded, took the bags near his feet and threw them into the white foam being thrown out by the bow. Then he grabbed Ocho's bag and tossed it before the young man could stop him.

Madre mia!

Walking on that bucking deck was difficult. Ocho made his way forward, picking up every sack and box in reach and throwing it into the sea. Some people protested, grabbed their belongings and tried to prevent their loss, but he was too strong. He tore the bags from the women's grasp and heaved heavy boxes as if they were empty.

Up the deck he went toward the bow, drenched every time the bow went in, throwing everything he could get his hands on into the foam created by the bow's passage.

Other people were throwing things too. Soon the deck contained only the people, who huddled in small groups, their backs to the spray. The nets hanging on the mast were lowered to the deck, then put into the sea and cut loose.

Near the bow the motion was vicious. The salt sea spray slamming back almost took him off his feet. He caught himself on a line that stabilized the mast, then worked his way aft holding on to the rail.

He thought the boat was riding easier, but maybe it was only his imagination.

Then they got into the Gulf Stream. The swells grew progressively larger, the motion of the boat even more vicious.

How much of this could the boat take?

People cried out, praying aloud, lifted their hands to heaven. He could hear the women wailing over the rumbling of the engine, the pounding of the sea.

He tried the door to the wheelhouse.

Locked!

He rattled the knob, twisted it fiercely, pulled with all his strength.

"Open up, Diego."

He pounded futilely on the door.

Six people were huddled in the lee of the tiny wheelhouse, blocking the door. One of them was Dora. He leaned over her, pounded futilely on the door with his fist.

He looked down at Dora, who had her head down.

Frustrated, drained, sick of himself and Diego and Dora, he found a spot against the aft wall of the wheelhouse and buried his head in his arms to keep the spray from his face.

He was drifting, thinking of his mother, reviewing scenes from his child-hood when Mercedes shook him awake. Still under the influence of the painkilling drugs, Fidel Castro opened his eyes to slits and blinked mightily against the dim light.

"Maximo is here, Fidel, as you asked."

He tried to chase away the past, to come back to the present. His mouth was dry, his tongue like cotton. "Time?"

"Almost midnight."

He nodded, looked around the room at the walls, the ceiling, the dark shapes of people and furniture. He couldn't see faces.

"A light."

She reached for the switch.

When his eyes adjusted, he saw Maximo standing in the shadows. He motioned with a finger. Yes, it was Maximo: now he could see his features.

"*Mi amigo.*"

"*Señor Presidente,*" Maximo said.

"Closer, in the light."

Maximo Sedano knelt near the bed.

"I don't have much time left to me," Castro explained. His mouth was so numb that he was having trouble enunciating his words.

"I want the money brought back."

"To Cuba?"

"Yes. All of it."

"You will have to sign and put your thumbprints on the transfer cards."

"The money was never mine, you understand."

"I had faith in you, *Señor Presidente*. We all had faith."

"Faith . . ."

"I will go to my office now, then return."

"Mercedes will admit you."

Ocho Sedano was soaked to the skin, covered with vomit from the woman beside him, when he heard the cry. Holding onto the wheelhouse wall with one hand and the net boom mast with the other, he levered himself erect, braced himself against the motion of the boat.

Waves were washing over the bow, which seemed to be lower in the water. The bow wasn't rising to the sea the way it did when he sat down an hour ago, or maybe the waves were just higher.

Someone was against the rail, pointing aft.

"Man overboard!"

"*Madre mia*, have mercy!"

Another swell came aboard and two people braced against the lee rail were swept into the sea as the boat rolled.

Ocho turned to the wheelhouse, pulled people from against the door and savagely twisted the latch handle. He pounded on the door with his left fist.

"Let me in, Diego! So help me, I will kill you if you don't turn the boat around."

The bow began turning to put the wind and swells more astern.

A muffled report came from inside the wheelhouse.

Ocho braced himself, then rammed his left fist against the upper panel of the door. The wood splintered, his fist went through almost to his elbow. He reached down, unlatched the door, jerked it open.

The captain lay on the floor. Diego Coca stood braced against the back wall, his hands covering his face. The pistol was nowhere in sight. The wheel snapped back and forth as the seas slammed at the rudder.

Ocho bent down to check the captain.

He had a wet place in the middle of his back, right between his shoulder blades. No pulse.

At least the boat seemed more stable with the swells behind it.

For how long? How long would the engine keep running?

The fisherman opened the door, saw Ocho at the wheel, the dark shape lying on the floor.

"Is he dead?" the man shouted.

"Yes."

"We must put out a sea anchor in case the engine stops. If the boat turns broadside to the sea, it will be swamped."

"Can you do it?"

"I will get men to help," the fisherman said, and closed what was left of the door.

A great lassitude swept over Ocho Sedano. His sin with the girl had brought all of these people here to die, had brought them to this foundering boat in a rough, windswept night sea with a million cold stars looking down without pity.

Then he realized that the forward deck was empty.

Empty!

The people were gone. Into the sea . . . that must be it! They were swept overboard.

"Ocho."

Diego put his hand on the young man's shoulder, gripped hard.

"I didn't mean to shoot him. As God is my witness, I did not mean for this to happen. It was an accident."

Ocho swept the hand away.

He pointed through the glass at the forward deck. "They are gone! Look. *The people are gone!"*

"I did not mean for this to happen," Diego repeated mechanically.

"What?" Ocho demanded. "What did you not intend? For the captain to die? For your daughter to drown at sea? For all of those people on that deck to die? What did you not intend, Diego?"

Oh, my God, that this should happen!

"*Answer me!"* he roared at Diego Coca, who refused to look forward through the wheelhouse windshield.

"Look, you bastard," Ocho ordered through clenched teeth, and grabbed the smaller man by the neck. He rammed his head forward against the glass.

"See what your greed and stupidity have cost."

Then he threw Diego Coca to the floor.

The impact of the disaster bowed Ocho's head, bent his back, emptied his heart. Diego's guilt did not lessen his, and oh, he knew that well. He, Ocho Sedano, was *guilty.* His lust had set this chain of events in motion. He felt as if he were trying to support the weight of the earth.

Maximo Sedano's office in the finance ministry reflected his personal taste. The furniture was simple, deceptively so. The woods were hardwoods from the Amazon rain forest, crafted in Brazil by masters. Little souvenirs from his travels across Europe and Latin America sat on the desk and credenza and hung on the walls, small things of little value because expensive trinkets would be impolitic.

He turned on the light, then walked to the huge floor safe, which he unlocked and opened. He found the drawer he wanted, removed a stiff document envelope, took it to his desk and adjusted the light.

With the contents of the envelope spread out on the highly polished mahogany, Maximo Sedano paused and looked around the room with unseeing eyes. He blinked several times, then leaned back in his chair and stretched.

There were four bank accounts in Switzerland, all controlled by Fidel Castro. The last time Maximo computed the interest, the amount in the accounts totaled $53 million. Castro had been very specific when the accounts were opened years ago; the accounts were to be denominated in United States dollars. This choice had worked out extraordinarily well through the years as the currencies of every other major trading nation underwent major inflation or devaluation. The United States dollar was the modern-day equivalent of gold, although it would certainly be poor politics for any member of the Castro regime to say so publicly.

Fifty-three million dollars.

Quite a sum.

Enough to live extraordinarily well for a millennium or two.

Fidel kept that little nest egg in Switzerland just in case things went wrong here in this communist paradise and he had to skedaddle. No sense living on government charity in some other squalid communist paradise, like Poland or Russia or the Ukraine, when a little prior planning could solve the whole problem. So Fidel rat-holed a fortune where only he could get at it and slept soundly at night.

Now he wanted the money back in Cuba.

Not that the money ever really belonged to the Cuban government. The money came from drug dealers, fees for using Cuban harbors for sanctuary, fees for being able to send shipments directly to Cuba, stockpile the drugs, then ship them on when the time was right.

The money was really just Castro's personal share of the drug fees. An even larger chunk of the profits had gone to army, navy and law enforcement personnel, all of them, every man in the country who wore a uniform had been paid; another chunk went to Castro's lieutenants and political allies. Maximo had received almost a half million dollars himself. All in all, the deals with the drug syndicates had been good public policy—the drug business was highly profitable, giving Castro money to buy loyalty and so remain in power, and the business corrupted America, which he hated. Ah, yes, the money came from the United States despite the best efforts of the American government to prevent it. Fidel had savored that irony too.

Fifty-three million.

Maximo pursed his lips as he thought about the life of luxury and privilege that a fortune that size would buy. The money could be invested, some hotels, bank stock, invested to earn a nice income without touching the principal.

He could stay in the George V in Paris, ski in St. Moritz, shop in London and Rome and yacht all over the Mediterranean.

God, it was tempting!

Fifty-three million.

All he had to do was get Castro's thumbprint on the transfer order. Without that thumbprint, the banks would not move a solitary dollar.

Really, those Swiss banks . . . Maximo had urged Castro to transfer the money to Spanish and Cuban banks for months, ever since the dictator was diagnosed with cancer. If he died with the money still in Switzerland, prying money out of those banks was going to be like peeling fresh paint from a wall with fingernails. And the drug dealers thought their racket was profitable!

But why be a piker? Why settle for $53 million when there was a lot more, somewhere?

From his pocket he removed a coin, a gold five-peso coin dated 1915. There was a portrait of José Martí on one side and the crest of Cuba on the other.

Gold circulated in Cuba until the revolution, until Fidel and the communists declared it was no longer legal tender and called it in, allowing the peso to float on the world market.

Maximo rubbed the gold coin with his fingers. By his calculations, based upon Ministry of Finance records, almost 1.2 million ounces of gold were surrendered to the government in return for paper money.

One million, two hundred thousand ounces . . . about thirty-seven *tons* of gold. On the world market, that thirty-seven tons of gold should be worth about $360 million.

A man who could get his hands on that horde would be on easy street for the rest of his life. Yes, indeed.

The only problem was finding it. It wasn't in the Finance Ministry vaults, it wasn't in the vaults of the Bank of Cuba, on account at banks in Switzerland or London or New York or Mexico City . . . it was gone!

Thirty-seven tons of gold, vanished into thin air.

If a man could lay hands on that gold . . . well, Alejo Vargas and Hector Sedano could fight over the presidency of Cuba, and may the better man win. Maximo would take the gold. If he could find it.

He had a few ideas about where it might be. In fact, he had been quietly researching the problem since he took over the Finance Ministry. Eight years of ransacking files, talking to old employees, looking at clues, thinking about the problem—the gold had to be in Cuba, in Havana. Thirty-seven tons of gold.

A life of ease and luxury in the spas of Europe, mingling with the rich and famous, surrounded by beautiful women and the best of everything . . .

But first the $53 million.

He would type the account numbers on the transfer orders and the accounts the money was to be transferred to. He would use the secretary's typewriter. He had the account numbers written in the notebook he removed from the safe. He flipped through the notebook now, found the page, stared at the numbers.

How closely would Fidel check the order?

The man is sick, drugged, dying. He is barely conscious. Unless he has the numbers of the accounts in the Bank of Cuba by his bedside, he'll be none the wiser.

But what if he does? What if he has the numbers written down in a book or diary and hands the transfer order to Mercedes to check? What then?

Fifty-three million. More money than God has.

He remembered the old days when he was young, when Castro walked the earth like Jesus Christ with a Cuban accent. Ah, the fire of the revolution, how the true believers were going to change the world!

Instead, time changed them, America bled them, and life defeated them.

Maximo had been loyal to Fidel and the revolution. No one could ever say he was not. He had been with Fidel since he was twenty-four years old, just back from the university in Spain. He had endured the good times and the bad, never uttered a single word of criticism. He had faith in Fidel, proclaimed it publicly and demanded it of others.

Now Castro was dying. In just a few days he would be beyond regrets.

Fifty-three million.

The pounding the overloaded boat had taken bucking the heavy Gulf Stream swells opened the seams somewhat, and now the fisherman was pumping out the water with the bilge pump, which received its power from the engine-driven generator.

"As long as we can keep the engine running, as long as the seams don't open any more than they are, we'll be all right."

"How much fuel do we have on board?"

The fisherman went to check.

Ocho was at the helm, steering almost due east. With the wind and sea behind her, the *Angel del Mar* rode better. Now the motion was a rocking as the swells swept under the stern. Very little roll from side to side.

Of the eighty-four people who had been aboard when the boat left the harbor in Cuba, twenty-six remained alive. The captain's body lay against the wheelhouse wall.

Ocho found Diego's pistol and put it in his belt. He physically carried Diego from the wheelhouse and tossed him on the deck.

Fifty-seven living human beings, men, women, and babies, had gone into the sea. There was no way in the world to go back to try to rescue them. Even if he and the fisherman could find those people in the water, in the darkness, in this sea, the pounding of heading back into the swells would probably cause the boat to take on more water, endangering the lives of those who remained aboard.

No, the people swept overboard were lost to their fate, whatever that might be.

The living twenty-six would soon join them, Ocho told himself. The boat was heading east, away from Florida.

Perhaps if the sea calmed somewhat, they should bring the boat to a more southerly heading and return to Cuba.

That, he decided, was their only chance.

Cuba. They would have to return.

Why wait? Every sea mile increased the likelihood of the engine quitting or the boat sinking.

He turned the helm a bit, worked the boat's bow to a more southerly heading. The roll became more pronounced. The wind came more over the right stern quarter.

How long until dawn? An hour or two?

The door to the wheelhouse opened. Diego was standing there, the whites of his eyes glistening in the dim light. "Turn back toward Florida! No one wants to go back to Cuba."

"It's the only way. We'll all die trying to make it to Florida in this sea."

"I was dead in Cuba all those years," Diego Coca shouted. "I refuse to go go back! I refuse."

Ocho hit him in the mouth. One mighty jab with his left hand as he twisted his body, so all his weight was behind the punch. Diego went down backward, hit his head on the deck coaming, and lay still.

Dora wailed, crawled toward her unconscious father.

Ocho closed the door to the wheelhouse, brought the boat back to its southeast heading.

Soon the door opened again and the fisherman stepped inside. "We have fuel for another ten or twelve hours. No more than that."

"We'll be back in Cuba then."

"That's our only chance."

The stars in the east were fading when the engine quit. After trying for a minute to start the engine, the fisherman dashed below.

Ocho abandoned the helm. The boat rolled sickeningly in the swells.

At least the swells were smaller than they were earlier in the night, in the middle of the Gulf Stream.

The fisherman came up on deck after fifteen minutes, his clothes soaked in diesel fuel. "It's no use," he said. "The engine has had it."

"What about the water in the bilges? Is it still coming in?"

"We'll have to take turns on the hand pump."

"What are we going to do about the engine?" Ocho asked.

The fisherman didn't reply, merely stood looking at the swells as the sky grew light in the east.

CHAPTER SIX

The van drove up to the massive, 250-feet-tall extra-high-voltage tower beside the drainage canal on the southern outskirts of Havana and backed up toward it. The base of the tower was surrounded by a ten-foot-high-chain link fence with barbed wire on top. The access door in the fence was, of course, padlocked.

The driver of the van and his passenger were both wearing one-piece overalls. They stretched, looked at the wires far above, and scratched their heads while they surveyed the ramshackle four-story apartment buildings that backed up to the canal. One of the men extracted a pack of cigarettes from his overalls and lit one. The nearest apartments were at least sixty meters away, although for safety reasons the distance should have been much more. Each of the extra-high-voltage (EHV) lines overhead carried 500,000 volts.

The driver of the van was Enrique Poveda. His passenger was Arquimidez Cabrera. Both men were citizens of the United States, sons of Cuban exiles, and bitter enemies of the Castro regime.

Poveda had parked the van so that the rear doors, when open, almost touched the gate in the chain-link fence. Now he reached into the van, seized a set of bolt cutters, and applied the jaws to the padlock on the gate. One tremendous squeeze and the bar of the padlock snapped.

Cabrera threw the remnants of the padlock into the back of the van.

He opened the gate in the fence, set a new, open padlock on the hasp, and stood looking up at the tower.

The best way to cut the power lines the tower carried would be to climb the tower and set shaped charges around the insulators. Unfortunately, the lines carried so much juice that the hot zones around the wires were eleven feet in diameter, more in humid weather. No, the only practical way to cut the lines was to drop the towers, which would not be difficult. A shaped charge on each leg should do the job nicely. Cabrera looked at the angle of the wires leading into the tower, and the angle away. Yes, once the legs were severed, the weight and tension of the line should pull the tower down to the side away from the canal, into this open area, where the lines would either short out on the ground or break from the strain of carrying their own weight.

Timing the explosions would be a problem. This close to all that energy, a radio-controlled electrical detonator was out of the question. Chemical timers would be best, ones that ignited the detonators after a preset time, although chemical timers were not as precise as mechanical ones.

All that was for a later day, however. The decision on when the tower must come down had yet to be made, so today Cabrera and Poveda would merely set the charges. They would return later to set the timers and detonators.

Poveda finished his cigarette and strapped on his tool belt. This was the fourth tower today. Only this one and one more to go.

"You ready?" he asked Cabrera.

"Let's do it."

Ocho Sedano lived with his older brother Julio, Julio's wife, and their two children in a tiny apartment atop a garage just a few hundred yards from Doña Maria's house. Julio worked in the garage repairing American cars. The cars were antiques from the 1950s and there were no spare parts, so Julio made parts or cannibalized them from the carcasses behind the garage, cars too far gone for any mechanic to save. When he wasn't playing baseball, Ocho helped.

Hector found his brother Julio working in the shop by the light of several naked bulbs. "Where is Ocho?"

"Gone."

"Gone where?"

Julio was replacing the valves of an ancient straight eight under the hood of an Oldsmobile. The light was terrible, but he was working by feel so it didn't really matter. He straightened now, scowled at his older brother.

"He has gone to try his luck in America."

"You didn't try to stop him?"

Julio looked about at the dimly lit shop, the dirt floor, the shabby old cars. He wiped his hands on a dirty rag that hung from his belt. "No, I didn't."

"What if he drowns out there in the Gulf Stream?"

"I have prayed for him."

"That's it? Your little brother? A prayer?"

"What do you think I should have done, Hector? Tell the boy that he was living smack in the middle of a communist paradise, that he should be happy here, happy with his labor and his crust? Bah! He wants something more from life, something for himself, for his children."

"If he dies—"

"Look around you, Hector. Look at this squalid, filthy hovel. Look at the way we live! Most of Cuba lives this way, except for a precious few like dear Maximo, who eats the bread that other men earn. You saw him yesterday at *Mima*'s—nothing's too good for our dedicated revolutionary, Maximo Sedano, Fidel's right-hand ass-wipe man."

Julio snorted scornfully, then leaned back under the hood of the Olds. "I told Ocho to go with God. I prayed for him."

"What if he dies out there?"

"Everybody has to die—you, me, Fidel, Ocho, all of us—that's just the way it is. They ought to teach you that in church. At least if Ocho dies he won't have to listen to any more of Fidel's bullshit. He won't have to listen to yours, either. God knows, bullshit is the only thing on this island we have a lot of."

"Have you told *Mima* that he left?"

"I was going to keep my mouth shut until I had something to tell her." Julio turned his head to look at Hector around the edge of the car's hood. "Ocho is a grown man. He has taken his life in his own two hands, which is his right. He'll live or die. He'll get to America or he won't."

"He should have waited. I asked him to wait."

"For what?" Julio demanded.

Hector turned to leave the garage.

"What are we waiting for, Hector? The second coming?"

Julio came to the door and called after Hector as he walked away down the street: "How long do I have to wait to feed my sons? Tell me! I have waited all my life. I am sick and tired of waiting. I want to know now—*how much longer?*"

Hector turned in the road and walked back toward Julio. "Enough! *Enough!*" he roared, his voice carrying. "You squat here in this hovel waiting for life to get better, waiting for someone else to make it better! You have no courage—you are not a man! If the future depends on rabbits like you Cuba will always be a sewer!"

Then Hector turned and stalked away, his head down, his shoulders bent forward, as if he were walking into a great wind.

The Officers' Club at Guantánamo Bay Naval Station was sited on a small hill overlooking the harbor. From the patio Toad Tarkington and Rita Moravia could see the carrier swinging on her anchor near the mouth of the bay.

These days the O Club was usually sparsely populated. The base was now a military backwater, no longer a vital part of the U.S. military establishment. For the last few years the primary function of the base was to house Cuban refugees picked up at sea.

Still, the deep blue Caribbean water and low yellow hills under a periwinkle sky packed picture-postcard charm. With cactus and palm trees and magnificent sunny days, the place reminded Toad of southern California. If the Cubans ever got their act together politically, he thought, this place would boom like southern California, with condos and high-tech industries sprouting like weeds. Hordes of people waving money would come here from Philly and New Jersey to retire. This place had Florida beat all to hell.

He voiced this opinion to Rita, the only other person on the patio. It was early in the afternoon; the two of them had ridden the first liberty boat in after the ship anchored. Jake Grafton sent them packing because today was their anniversary.

They had a room reserved at the BOQ for tonight. They intended to eat a relaxed dinner at the club, just the two of them, then retire for a private celebration.

"The Cubans may not want hordes from Philly and Hoboken and Ashtabula moving in," Rita objected.

"I wouldn't mind having a little place in one of these villages around here my own self," Toad said, gesturing vaguely to the west or north. "Do some fishing, lay around getting old and fat and tan, let life flow by. Maybe build a golf course, spend my old age selling balls and watering greens. This looks like world-class golf country to me. Aaah, someday."

"Someday, buster," Rita said, grinning. Toad liked to entertain her with talk about retirement, about loafing away the days reading novels and newspapers and playing golf, yet by ten o'clock on a lazy Sunday morning in the States he was bored stiff. He played golf once every other year, if it didn't rain.

Now he sipped his beer and inhaled a few mighty lungfuls of this clean, clear, perfect air. "Feel that sun! Ain't life delicious, woman?"

They had a nice dinner of Cuban cuisine, a fresh fish, beans and rice. By that time the club was filling up with junior officers from the squadrons aboard ship, in for liberty. The noise from the bars was becoming raucous when Toad and Rita finished their dinner and headed back to the patio with cups of coffee.

"Maybe I better check on my chicks," Rita said, and detoured for the bar.

Toad paused in the doorway, staring into the dark room, which was made darker by the brilliant sunlight shining outside the windows.

"Commander Tarkington!" Two of the young pilots came over to where Toad stood with his coffee cup. "Join us for a few minutes, won't you? We're drinking shooters. Have one with us."

Rita was already standing by the table. Toad allowed himself to be persuaded.

A trayful of brimming shot glasses sat on the small round table. As Toad watched, one of these fools set the liquor in the glasses on fire with a butane cigarette lighter.

"Okay, Commander, show us how it's done!"

Toad looked at Rita, who was studying him with a noncommittal raised eyebrow.

He sat down, one of the youngsters placed a glass in front of him. The blue flame was burning nicely.

It had been years since he did this. Was it Rota, that time he got so blind drunk he passed out while waiting for the taxi? Ah, but the navy was politically correct now. Nobody got drunk anymore.

Toad steadied himself, took a deep breath, exhaled, and poured the burning brandy down his throat. It seemed to burn all the way down. Some of the liquid trickled from his lips, still on fire, but he licked it up with his tongue. Was he burning? He didn't think so. He wiped his mouth with the back of his hand just to make sure.

The members of his audience were gazing at him with openmouthed astonishment. "Jesus, sir! We always blow the fire out before we drink it."

Toad didn't know whether to laugh or cry. "You goddamn pussies," he said, and tossed off another one.

"Our anniversary, and you're drunk!"

Toad Tarkington felt like he had been hit by a large truck, an eighteen wheeler, at least. He turned in the bathroom door and looked carefully at his spouse. He squinted to make his eyes focus better.

"I am *not* drunk! A bit tipsy, I will grant you that. But not drunk." He swelled his chest and tried to look sober. "Those puppies, thinking they could drink an old dog like me under the table." He snorted his derision. " 'We blow the fire out before we drink.' Ha, ha, and ha!"

Rita was sooo mad! "Oh, you—"

"Excuse me." Toad held up a finger. "Just a minute or two, and we will continue this discussion until you have said everything that needs to be said. There is undoubtedly a lot of it and I am sure it will take a while. Just one little minute." He closed the bathroom door and retched into the commode. Then he swabbed his forehead with a wet washcloth.

He felt better. He stared at himself in the mirror.

You look like hell, you damned fool.

He took a long drink of water, swabbed his face with a towel, then opened the door, and said, "Okay, you were saying?"

She wasn't there. The room was empty.

Even her bag was gone.

He lay down in the bed. Oh, that felt gooood. Maybe he should just lie here for a few minutes until she cooled off and he sobered up completely, then he would find her and apologize.

The room was whirling around, but when he rolled on his side it steadied out somewhat and he drifted right off.

Jake Grafton was alone at a table in the corner of the O Club dining room when Rita Moravia saw him and came over. He stood while she seated herself.

"You're by yourself? Where's Toad?"

"Sleeping it off. He was in the bar with your young studs and had four drinks. Four! He's whacked."

Jake Grafton chuckled. "I don't think I've seen him drink more than an occasional beer or glass of wine with dinner in years."

"He doesn't," she said. "Poor guy can't handle it anymore."

"Heck of an anniversary celebration," Jake said, eyeing her.

"I've been lucky," Rita said simply. "Toad Tarkington and I were made for each other. I don't know how the powers that rule the universe figure out who marries whom, but I sure got lucky."

"I know what you mean," Jake said. Then he smiled, and Rita knew he was thinking of his wife, Callie. Jake Grafton always smiled when he thought of her.

"So, maybe you should join me for dinner," Jake said, "since Toad is temporarily indisposed and Callie is temporarily not here."

"I've already eaten, and tongues might wag, Admiral," she said with mock seriousness.

"And probably will. Won't do me or thee any good."

"I'm not going to live my life to please pinheads," Rita replied. "I'll join you for a drink."

After they gave their orders to the waiter, Jake said, "Tell me about the V-22. I've been wondering about that plane but haven't had the chance to talk to you."

Away Rita went, talking about airplanes and flying, two subjects they both enjoyed immensely. The breeze coming through the open doors of the dining room stirred the curtains and made the candles on the tables flicker in the evening twilight.

They were drinking after-dinner coffee when Rita remarked, "Toad says that you still haven't heard from Washington about your next set of orders."

"That's right."

"I don't want to talk about something you would rather not discuss, but he says they may ask you to retire."

"They might. I've thrown my weight around a few times in the past and made some enemies, in uniform and out." He shrugged. "Every flag officer gets passed over for a promotion at some point and asked to retire. My turn will come sooner or later. Maybe sooner."

"Are you looking forward to retirement?"

"Haven't thought about it that much," he said. "To be honest, the prospect of spending more time with Callie has great appeal." He rubbed his forehead, then grinned ruefully. "It'll hurt if they don't find me another job, give me another star next year. Yet even a CNO gets told it's time to go. When it happens to me, Callie and I will get on with the rest of our lives. The truth is, when I decided to stay in the navy after Vietnam I never expected to get this far: thought it'd be terrific if I made commander or captain. Here I am with two stars in charge of a carrier battle group." He snorted derisively. "Guess it all goes to prove I'm an ungrateful bastard, huh?"

"It goes to prove you're human."

"You are very kind, Rita."

"You've really enjoyed the navy, haven't you?"

"Every tour has been a challenge, an adventure. Every set of orders I've had, I've thought, Oh, wow, this will be fun. I can't say I've enjoyed every day of it, because I haven't, but it's been a good career. Like most people who have worn the uniform, I did the best I could wherever they needed me. I've worked with great people all along the way. I have no regrets."

One of Jake's aides came over to the table, smiled at Rita, then whispered in the admiral's ear. "The ship that left here four days ago carrying biological warheads to Norfolk never arrived. It is overdue."

"Civilization begins when the strong finally realize they have a duty to protect the weak. That duty is the foundation of civilization, the bedrock on which everything else rests."

Hector Sedano stood in the pulpit and looked at the sea of sweating, glistening faces that packed the church to overflowing. He could feel the heat from their bodies. There must be close to two hundred people jammed in here.

Hector continued: "For centuries we, the people, have abdicated our duty to a few strong men. Rule us, we said, and do not steal too much. Do not be too corrupt, do not betray us too much, do not shame us beyond endurance. Protect the weak, the elderly, the helpless, the sick, the very young, protect them from those who would prey upon them. And protect us. If you grant us protection you may steal a little, enough to become filthy rich, as long as you do not rub our faces in it.

"We give unto you the strong one a great trust because the faith to face the evil in the world is not in us.

"O strong one, protect us because we lack the courage to protect ourselves."

The crowd was rapt, wanting more.

Hector Sedano had given this very same speech more than a hundred times. Only the faces in the audience were different. He leaned forward, reached out as if to grab the people. They had to understand, to feel his passion, or Cuba would never change. Perspiration ran down his face, soaked his shirt.

"I say to you here tonight that our duty can be ignored no longer. The hands that made the universe are delivering our destiny into our very own human hands. We must seize the day when it comes. We must acknowledge before God and before each other that the future of this nation is *ours* to write, *ours* to invent, *ours* to live, and *ours* to answer for before the throne of heaven on Judgment Day."

A thunderous applause shook the tiny church.

When it died, Hector continued, "I say to you that the future of *our* families is on *our* heads, that the fate of this people is *our* responsibility and *our* destiny.

"We shall drink every drop that God pours for us, be it sweet or bitter, be it thin or full, be it a tiny trickle or a great river. We shall not turn aside from that righteous cup."

The applause swelled and swelled and filled the room to overflowing; it spilled through the open doors and windows and rushed bravely away to do battle with the silence and darkness of the night.

"We pulled it off," Admiral Delgado told Alejo Vargas. "*Nuestra Señora de Colón* is stranded on a rocky reef near the entrance to Bahia de Nipe. Santana is ready and waiting."

"What took so long?"

"When she left Guantánamo the Americans sent a destroyer to accompany her. The captain was beside himself—he thought the destroyer would accompany them all the way to Norfolk. He faked an engineering casualty in the Windward Passage, crawled along at three knots. Of course, then the destroyer refused to leave. He finally had to announce that he had fixed the problem and steam off at twelve knots before the destroyer turned back."

Vargas smiled. "If this works, I will be very grateful to you, Delgado."

"There are real problems, which we have discussed. I give this operation no more than a fifty percent chance of success."

"Fifty percent is optimistic," Alejo Vargas replied. "I suspect the odds are a lot worse than that. Yet they are good enough to take a chance, and if we don't do that, we have only ourselves to blame, eh?"

"Doing business with the North Koreans is an invitation to be double-crossed. How do you know they will perform?"

"We need long-range ballistic missiles, the North Koreans want well-designed, well-made biological warheads. The exchange is fair."

"I still do not trust them," Delgado countered. "This is a once-in-a-lifetime deal."

Vargas changed the subject: Delgado was not a partner, he was the hired help. "Tell me about your evening cruise with Maximo Sedano."

"He wants political backing when Castro dies."

"What did you promise him?"

"I told him you buy people or blackmail them, that he has no chance."

"And Alba?"

"He agreed with my assessment."

Vargas smiled. "Let us hope Maximo stifles his ambitions. For his sake. You told the man the honest truth; if he chooses to disregard it the consequences are on his head."

Delgado said nothing. He suspected Vargas had already talked to Alba: the admiral hoped the general didn't try to dress up the tale. Telling Vargas the truth was the only way to stay alive.

Toad Tarkington was sitting by the window in the BOQ room thinking about biological weapons and marines dug in around a warehouse when Rita unlocked the door and came in. She was still in uniform. His head was thumping like a toothache and he felt like hell.

"Some anniversary," he said. "I feel like an ass."

She came over to the chair, knelt and put her arms around him.

"This wasn't the way the evening was supposed to go. I'm sorry, Rita."

"Our life together has been terrific, Toad-man. You're still the guy I want."

He hugged her back.

"Let's go to bed," she said.

CHAPTER SEVEN

The emotional impact of what he had done didn't hit Maximo Sedano until the jet to Madrid leveled off after the climbout from Havana airport.

He took the transfer cards bearing Castro's thumbprint from his inside left breast pocket, and holding them so no one else in first class could read them, studied them carefully.

He was holding $53 million in his hands and he could feel the heat. Hoo, man! He had done it!

He took a chance, a long chance. When he walked into Castro's bedroom he had had the real transfer cards in his left jacket pocket and the ones bearing his bank account numbers in his right. Mercedes wasn't there that second time he was admitted, which was a blessing. His former sister-in-law was too sharp, saw too much. She might have decided something was wrong merely from looking at his face.

So it was just Fidel and a male nurse, a nobody who handled bedpans and urinals. There wasn't a notebook or ledger anywhere in sight, and Fidel certainly was in no condition to closely scrutinize the cards. He signed the cards, transferring the money to Maximo, then let Maximo put his thumb in an ink pad and press it on each of them.

Fidel said little. He had obviously been given an injection for pain and was paying minimal attention to what went on around him. He merely grunted when Maximo said good-bye.

The Maximo Sedano who walked into that bedroom was the soon-to-be unemployed Cuban finance minister with a cloudy future. The Maximo Sedano who walked out was the richest Cuban south of Miami.

Just like *that*!

The icing on the cake was that the Swiss accounts should have perhaps a million more of those beautiful Yankee dollars as unpaid interest. Every penny was going to be transferred to Maximo's accounts at another bank in Zurich. It wouldn't be there long, however. Tomorrow morning after he turned in these transfer cards to Fidel's banks, he would walk across the street and send the money from his accounts to those he had opened in Spain, Mexico, Germany, and Argentina. These were commercial accounts held by various shell corporations that Maximo had established years ago to launder money for Fidel and the drug syndicates, accounts over which he had sole signature authority. The shell corporations would quickly write a variety of very large checks to a half dozen other companies Maximo owned. After a long, tortuous trail around the globe and back again, the money would eventually wind up in Maximo's personal accounts all over Europe.

The scheme hinged on the bank secrecy laws in various nations, not the least of which was Switzerland, and the fact that anyone trying to trace the money would see only disorganized pieces of the puzzle, not the big picture.

Maximo smiled to himself and sighed in contentment.

"Would you care for a drink, sir?" the flight attendant asked. She was a beautiful slender woman, with dark eyes and clear white skin.

"A glass of white wine, please, something from Cataluña."

"I'll see what we have aboard, sir." She smiled gently and left him.

Maximo told himself that he would find a woman like that one of these days, a beautiful woman who appreciated the finer things in life and appreciated him for providing them.

His wife was expecting him to return to Cuba in three days: "I must go to Europe in the morning," he had told her. "An urgent matter has arisen."

She wanted to go with him on this trip of course—anything to get off the island, even for a little while.

"Darling, I wish you could, but there wasn't time to make reservations. I got the only empty seat on the airliner."

She was not happy. Still, what could she say? He promised to bring her something expensive from a jeweler, and that promise pacified her.

The flight attendant brought the glass of wine and he sipped it, then put his head back in the seat and closed his eyes. Ah, yes.

He had a new identity in his wallet: an Argentine passport, driver's license and identity papers, a birth certificate, several valid credit cards, a bank account and a real address in Buenos Aires, all in the name of Eduardo José Lopéz, a nice common surname. This identity had been constructed years before and serviced regularly so that he might move money around the globe when drug smugglers sought to pay Fidel Castro. Becoming the good Señor López would be as easy as presenting the passport when checking into a hotel.

He had the papers for two other identities in a safe deposit box in Lausanne, across the lake from Geneva.

Maximo Sedano fingered the bank transfer cards one more time, then reclined his seat.

How does it feel to be rich? Damned good, thank you very much.

Lord, it was tempting. Just walk away with the money as Señor López, and poof! disappear into thin air.

And yet, the gold was there for the taking. His plans were made, his allies ready . . . all he had to do was find the gold and get it out of the country.

He reclined his seat, closed his eyes, and savored the feeling of being rich.

Doña Sedano was sitting on her porch, inhaling the gentle aroma of the tropical flowers that grew around her porch in profusion and watching the breeze stir the petals, when she saw Hector walking down the road. He turned in at her gate and came up to the porch.

After he kissed her he sat on the top step, leaned back so he could see her face.

"Why aren't you in school, teaching?" she asked.

He made a gesture, looked away to the north, toward the sea.

There was nothing out that way but a few treetops waving in the wind, with puffy clouds floating overhead.

He turned back to look into her face, reached for her hand. "Ocho went on a boat two nights ago. They were trying to reach the Florida Keys."

"Did they make it?"

"I don't know. If they make it we won't hear for days. Weeks perhaps. If they don't reach Florida we may never hear."

Doña Maria leaned forward and touched her son's hair. Then she put her twisted hands back in her lap.

"Thank you for telling me."

"Ocho should have told you."

"Good-byes can be difficult."

"I suppose."

"You are the brightest of my sons, the one with the most promise. Why didn't you go to America, Hector? You had plenty of chances. Why did you stay in this hopeless place?"

"Cuba is my home." He gestured helplessly. "This is the work God has given me to do."

Doña Maria gently massaged her hands. Rubbing them seemed to ease the pain sometimes.

"I might as well tell you the rest of it," Hector said. "Ocho got a girl pregnant. He went on the boat with the girl and her father. The father wants Ocho to play baseball in America."

"Pregnant?"

"Ocho told me, made me promise not to tell. He did not confess to me as a priest but as a brother, so I am exercising an older brother's prerogative—I am breaking that promise."

She sighed, closed her eyes for a moment.

"If God is with them, they may make it across the Straits," Hector said. "There is always that hope."

Tears ran down her cheeks.

It was at that moment that Doña Maria saw the human condition more clearly than she ever had before. She and Hector were two very mortal people trapped by circumstance, by fate, between two vast eternities. The past was gone, lost to them. The people they loved who were dead were gone like smoke, and they had only memories of them. The future was . . . well, the future was unknowable, hidden in the haze. Here there was only the present, this moment, these two mortal people with their memories of all that had been.

Hector stroked his mother's hair, kissed her tears, then went down the walk to the road. When he looked back his mother was still sitting where he had left her, looking north toward the sea.

Ocho was probably dead, Hector realized, another victim of the Cuban condition.

When, O Lord, when will it stop? How many more people must drown in the sea? How many more lives must be blighted and ruined by the lack of opportunity here? How many more lives must be sacrificed on the altar of political ambition?

As he walked toward the village bus stop, he lifted his hands and roared his rage, an angry shout that was lost in the cathedral of the sky.

The pain was there, definitely there, but it wasn't cutting at him, doubling him over. Fidel Castro made them get him up, had them put him in a chair behind his desk. He wanted the flag to his right.

Mercedes and the nurse helped him into his green fatigue shirt.

He was perspiring then, gritting his teeth to get through this.

"Do you know what you want to say?" Mercedes asked.

"I think so."

The camera crew was fiddling with the lights, arranging power cords.

"I want to say something to you, right now," she whispered, "while you are sharp and not heavily sedated."

His eyes went to her.

"I love you, Fidel. With all my heart."

"And I you, woman. Would that we had more time."

"Ah, time, what a whore she is. We had each other, and that was enough."

He bit his lip, reached for her hand. "If only we had met years ago, before—"

He winced again. "Better start the tape," he said. "I haven't much time." He straightened, gripped the arms of the chair so hard his knuckles turned white.

With the lights on, Fidel Castro looked straight into the camera, and spoke: "Citizens of Cuba, I speak to you today for the last time. I am fatally ill and my days on this earth will soon be over. Before I leave you, however, I wish to spend a few minutes telling you of my dream for Cuba, my dream of what our nation can become in the years ahead. . . ."

The door opened and Alejo Vargas walked in. Behind him was Colonel Pablo Santana.

"Well, well, *Señor Presidente*. I heard you were making a speech to the video cameras this afternoon. Do not mind us; please continue. We will remain silent spectators, out of the sight of the camera, two loyal Cubans representing millions of others."

"I did not invite you here, Vargas."

"True, you did not, *Señor Presidente*. But things seem to be slipping away from you these days—important things. The world will not stop turning on its axis while you lie in bed taking drugs."

"Get out! This is my office."

Alejo Vargas settled into a chair. He turned to the camera crew. "Turn that thing off. The lights too. Then you may take a short break. We will call you when we want you to return."

The extinguishment of the television lights made the room seem very dark.

Colonel Santana escorted the technicians from the room and closed the door behind them. He stood with his back against the door, his arms crossed.

"If you are pushing the button near your knee to summon the security staff, you are wasting your time," Vargas said. "Members of my staff have replaced them."

"Say what you want, then get out," Castro said.

Vargas got out a cigarette, lit it, taking his time. "I am wondering about Maximo Sedano. The night before last he was here, you signed something for him, he left this morning on a plane to Madrid, with a continuation on to Zurich. What was that all about?"

Fidel said nothing. Mercedes noticed that he was perspiring again.

"I am in no rush," Vargas said. "I have all the time in the world."

Fidel ground his teeth. "He went to move funds. On a matter of interest to the Finance Ministry."

"The question is, where will the funds end up when their electronic journey is over? Tell me that, please."

"In the government's accounts in the Bank of Cuba, in Havana."

"I ask this question because the man who was here last night did not see you check the account numbers in any book or ledger. You have the account numbers memorized?"

"No."

"So in reality you don't know where Maximo Sedano will wire the money?"

"He is a trustworthy man. Loyal. I cannot be everywhere, see everything, and must trust people. I have trusted people all my life."

"How much money are we talking about, *Señor Presidente?*"

"I don't know."

"Millions?"

"Yes."

"Tens of millions?"

"Yes."

"*Dios mio,* our Maximo must be a saint! I wouldn't trust my own mother with that kind of money."

"I wouldn't trust your mother with a drunken sailor," Mercedes said. "Not if he had two centavos in his pocket." She handed some pills to Castro, who glanced down at them.

"Water, please," he whispered. He put the pills on the desk in front of him.

Vargas continued: "If we ever see the face of Maximo Sedano again, *Señor Presidente,* you have me to thank. I am having one of my men meet the finance minister in Zurich. We will try to convince Maximo to do his duty to his country."

Mercedes handed Fidel a glass of water. He picked up several of the pills, put them in his mouth, then swallowed some water. Then he put the last pill in his mouth and took another swig.

Vargas was a moral nihilist, Castro thought, a man who believed in nothing. There were certainly plenty of those. He had known what Vargas was for many years and had used him anyway because he was good at his job, which was a miserable one. *We entrusted it to a swine so that we need not dirty our hands.*

Another mistake.

"I need rest," he said, and tried to rise.

"No," Vargas said fiercely. He leaned on the desk with both hands, lowered his face near Fidel. "You still have a statement to make before the cameras."

"Nothing for you."

"You think you have nothing to lose, do you not? You think, Alejo could kill me, but what is that? He merely speeds up the inevitable."

Fidel looked Vargas square in the eye. "I should have killed you years and years ago," he said. He took his hands from the arms of his chair and wrapped them around his stomach.

"There is no regret as bitter as the murder you didn't commit. How true that is! But you didn't kill me because you needed me, Fidel, needed me to ferret out your enemies, find who was whispering against you and bring you their names. Help you shut their mouths, cut out the rot without killing the tree.

"Kill me? Without me how would you have kept your wretched subjects loyal? Who would have kept these miserable *guajiros* starving on this sandy rock in the sea's middle from cutting the flesh from your bones? Who would have provided the muscle to keep you in office when the Russians abandoned you and nothing went right? When everything you touched backfired?

"Kill me? *Ha!* That would have been like killing yourself.

"Now I have come for mine. Not centavos, like in the past. I want what is mine for keeping you in power all these years, for keeping the peasants from slicing your throat when in truth that was precisely what you deserved. You are a miserable failure, Fidel, as a man and as a servant of Cuba. And you are going to die a revered old man—God, what a joke! Hailed as the Cuban Washington for the next ten centuries. . . ."

Vargas sneered.

"Now *I* have the power of life or death, Fidel. I think you will make your statement in front of the camera. You will name me, Alejo Vargas, your loyal, trusted minister of interior as your successor; you will plead with all loyal Cubans everywhere to recognize the wisdom of your choice."

Sweat ran in rivulets from Fidel's face, dripped from his beard. His voice came out a hoarse whisper. "Forty years service to my country, and you expect me to hand Cuba over to you? To rape for your profit? Not on your life."

"Don't be a fool. You have nothing to bargain with."

"Kill me. See what you gain," Fidel said, his voice barely audible.

"You'll die soon enough, never fear. But before you do Colonel Santana will butcher Mercedes on this table while you watch."

"Have you no honor?"

"Don't talk to me of honor. You have told so many lies you can't remember ever telling the truth. You have profaned the Church, denied God, sent loyal Cuban soldiers to die in Angola, demanded that generation after generation give their blood to fulfill your destiny as Cuba's savior. You have impoverished a nation, reduced them to beggary to salve your ego. I spit on you and all that you would have us become."

And he did.

Fidel brought a hand up to wipe away the spittle. "Fuck you!" he whispered.

"And you too, *Líder Maximo*!" Vargas shot back. "I do not pretend to be God's other son, strutting in green fatigues and spouting platitudes while the people worship me. But enough of this. Before we get to the camera, tell me where the gold is."

"The gold?"

"The gold, Fidel. The gold from the peso coins that the Ministry of Finance melted down into ingots, the gold ingots that you and Che and Edis López and José Otero carried away. How much gold was there? Forty or fifty tons? You certainly didn't spend it on the people of Cuba. Where is it?"

A grimace twisted Castro's lips. "You'll never find it, that's for certain. Edis and José died within weeks of Che. I am the only living person who knows where that gold is; I am taking the secret to my grave."

"The gold isn't yours."

"Nor is it yours, you son of a pig."

"We will let you watch us cut up Mercedes. We will make a tiny incision on her abdomen, pull out a loop of small intestine. I will ask you questions, and every time you refuse to answer Colonel Santana will pull out more intestine. You will tell us everything we want to know or we will see what her insides look like. Colonel?"

Santana grabbed Mercedes by the arms. With one hand he grabbed the front of her dress and ripped it from her body.

Fidel Castro's jaw moved. Then he went limp, slumping in his chair.

"*Fidel!*" Mercedes screamed.

Vargas leaped for Castro, pried open his jaw and raked a piece of celluloid from his mouth with his finger.

"Poison," he said disgustedly. He felt Castro's wrist for a pulse.

"Stone cold dead." He tossed down the wrist and turned toward Mercedes.

"*You* gave him the poison! He had the capsule in his mouth."

Alejo Vargas slapped her as hard as he could.

"And this is for insulting my mother, *puta*!" He slapped her again so hard she went to her knees, the side of her face numb. "If you do it again I will cut your tongue out," he added, his voice almost a hiss.

Then Vargas took a deep breath and steadied himself. The sight of

Fidel Castro's corpse drained the rage from him and filled him with adrenaline, ready for the race to his destiny. He had waited all his life for this moment and now it was here.

"Listen to this," the technician said, and handed the earphones to William Henry Chance. They were crammed into a tiny van with the logo of the Communications Ministry on the side. The van was parked on a side street near Chance's hotel, but with an excellent view of the Interior Ministry.

Chance put on the headphones.

"We recorded this stuff early this morning," the technician told Chance's associate, Tommy Carmellini. "Getting to you without stirring up the Cubans was the trick. Wait until you hear this stuff."

"What is it?" Carmellini asked.

"Vargas and his thug, Santana, in the minister's office. They're talking about a speech they want Castro to make in front of cameras. A political will, Vargas called it. They are writing it, debating the wording."

"What do they want it to say?"

"They want Castro to name Vargas as his successor, his heir."

"Will he do that?"

"They seem to think he will."

"Have we heard anything back from Washington about that ship reference—the *Colón?* . . . *Nuestra Señora de Colón?*"

"No. Something like that will take days to percolate through the bureaucracy."

"I was hoping the reference to North Koreans and biological warheads would light a fire under somebody."

"It always takes a while before we smell the smoke of burning trousers."

Carmellini watched Chance's face as he listened to the tape. William Henry Chance, attorney and CIA agent, certainly didn't look like a man who would be at home in the shadow world of spies and espionage. But then appearances were often deceiving.

Carmellini had been a burglar—more or less semi-retired—attending the Stanford University Law School when he was visited one day by a CIA recruiter, a woman who took him to lunch in the student union cafeteria and asked him about his plans for the future. He still remembered the conversation. He was going into business, he said. Maybe politics. He thought that someday he might run for public office.

"A prosecution for stealing the Peabody diamond from the Museum of Natural History in Washington would probably crimp your plans, wouldn't it?" she said sweetly.

He gaped. Sat there like a fool with his mouth hanging open, the brain completely stalled.

He had seen her credentials, which certainly looked official enough. Central Intelligence Agency. The Government with a capital G. But there had never been the slightest hint that anyone was on his trail. Not even a sniff.

"It would do that," he managed.

After a bit, the question of how she knew formed in his mind, and he began trying to figure out how to ask it in a nonincriminating way.

"You're wondering, I suppose," she said matter-of-factly between sips of her coffee, "how we learned of your involvement."

Unable to help himself, he nodded yes.

"Your pal talked. The Miami PD got him on another burglary, so he threw you to the wolves to get a lighter sentence."

Well, there it was. His very best friend in the whole world and the only guy who knew everything had sold him out.

"You need some better friends," she said. "Your friend is a pretty small-caliber guy. A real loser. He got eight years on the state charge. Moving stolen property across state lines is a federal crime of course, and Justice hasn't decided if they will prosecute."

It quickly became plain that at that moment in his life, the CIA was his best career choice.

After finishing law school, Carmellini spent a year in the covert operations section of the agency. Now he was an associate of William Henry Chance, who had been with the CIA ever since he left the army after the Vietnam War. The cover was impeccable—both men were really practicing attorneys and CIA operatives on the side.

Carmellini remembered the first time he met William Henry Chance. He was running a ten-kilometer race in Virginia one weekend when Chance came galloping up beside him, barely sweating, and suggested they have lunch afterward.

Chance mentioned a name, Carmellini's boss at the agency. "He said you were a pretty good runner," Chance said, then began lengthening his stride.

Tommy Carmellini managed to stay with Chance all the way to the tape but it was a hell of a workout. Chance didn't work at running; he loped along, all lean meat, bone, and sinew, a natural long-distance runner. Carmellini, on the other hand, was built more like a running back or middle linebacker.

About half of Carmellini's time was spent on agency matters, half on the firm's business. He was a better covert warrior than he was a lawyer, so he had to work hard to keep up with the bright young associates who had not the slightest idea that Carmellini or Chance were also employed by the CIA.

Sitting in a telephone company van in the middle of Havana listening to intercepted conversations, Tommy Carmellini wondered if he should have told the CIA to stick it. He would probably be getting out of prison about now, free and clear.

And broke, of course. His friend had fenced the diamond and spent all the money, never intending to give Carmellini his share.

On the table were a set of photos the technicians had taken of the University of Havana science building. They had had the place under surveillance for the last two days.

Carmellini looked at the photos critically, as if he were going to burgle the joint. There were guards at every entrance, some electronic alarms: getting in would take some doing.

After a while Chance handed the headphones to a technician. He sat looking at Carmellini with a frown on his face.

"I think Vargas plans to kill Fidel," Chance said finally.

"When?"

"Soon. Very soon. Today or tomorrow, I would imagine."

"And then?"

"Your guess is as good as mine."

The men left alive aboard *Angel del Mar* were unable to get the engine restarted, so it drifted helplessly with the wind and swell. Ocho took his turn in the tiny, cramped engine compartment. Something down inside the engine was broken, perhaps the crankshaft. Rotating the propeller shaft by hand made a clunky noise; at a certain point in the shaft's rotation it became extremely difficult to turn. Admitting finally that repairing the motor was hopeless, Ocho backed out of the small compartment. His place was taken by someone else who wanted to satisfy himself personally that the engine was indeed beyond repair.

After a while they all gave up and shut the door.

Without the engine they had to work the bilge pump manually. Fifteen minutes of intense effort cleared the bilges of water. With daylight coming through the hatch one could just see the water seeping in between the planks where the sea had pounded the caulking loose. It took about fifteen minutes for the bilges to fill, then they had to be pumped again. A quarter hour of work, a quarter hour of rest.

"If we can just keep pumping," the old fisherman said, "we stay afloat."

"If the water doesn't come in any faster," Ocho added. He was young and strong, so he spent hours sitting here in the bilge working the pump, watching the water come in.

Twenty-six people remained alive. The captain's body was still in the wheelhouse, where he had fallen. No one wanted to take responsibility for moving him.

After a morning working the bilge pump, Ocho Sedano stood braced against the wheelhouse and, shading his eyes, looked carefully in all directions. The view was the same as it was yesterday, swells that ran off to the horizon, and above it all a sky crowded with puffy little clouds.

At least the sea had subsided somewhat. The wind no longer tore whitecaps off the waves. The breeze seemed steady, maybe eight or ten knots out of the southwest.

One suspected the boat was drifting northeast, riding the Gulf Stream. The nearest land in that direction was the Bahamas.

The United States was north, or perhaps northwest now. A whole continent was just over the horizon, with people, cities, restaurants, farms, mountains, rivers . . . if only they could get there.

Well, someone would see this boat drifting before too long. Someone in a plane or fishing boat, perhaps an American coast guard cutter or navy ship looking for drug smugglers. They would see the *Angel del Mar* drifting helplessly, give the people stranded on her water and food, then take them to Guantánamo Bay and make them walk through the gate back to Cuba. Or maybe they would be taken to hospitals in America.

Already some of these people needed hospitals. They had vomited too much, been without water for too long. They had become dehydrated, their electrolytes dangerously out of balance, and if left unattended would die. Just like the people swept over the side last night.

Of course, knowing all this, there was absolutely nothing Ocho Sedano could do. He too felt the ravages of thirst, felt the aching of the empty knot in his stomach. Fortunately he had not been seasick, had not retched his guts out until he had only the dry heaves like so many of these others lying helpless in the sun.

The wheelhouse cast a little shade, so he dragged several people in out of the sun. Maybe that would help a little.

The sea seemed to keep the boat broadside to it, so the shade didn't move around too much, which was a blessing.

There wasn't room in the shade for everyone.

"The sail," said the fisherman. "There is an old piece of canvas around the boom. Let's see if we can get it up."

They worked with the canvas in the afternoon sun for over an hour, trying to rig it as a sail. It wasn't really a sail, but an awning. Finally the fisherman said maybe it was best used to catch rain and protect people from the sun, so they rigged it across the boom and tied it there.

Ocho dragged as many people under it as he could, then lay exhausted on the board deck in the shade, his tongue a swollen, heavy, rough thing in his dry mouth.

Sweating. He was going to have to stop sweating like this, stop wasting his bodily fluids. Stop this exertion.

Nearby a child cried. She would stop soon, he thought, too thirsty to waste energy crying.

He sat up, looked for Dora. She was sitting in the shade with her back against the wheelhouse. Her father, Diego Coca, lay on the deck beside her, his head in her lap. She looked at Ocho, then averted her gaze.

"What should I have done?" he asked.

She couldn't have heard him.

He got up, went over to where she was. "What should I have done?"

She said nothing, merely lowered her head. She was stroking her father's hair. His eyes were closed, he seemed oblivious to his surroundings and the corkscrewing motion of the drifting boat. His body moved slackly as the boat rose and fell.

Ocho Sedano went into the wheelhouse. Above the captain's swollen corpse the helm wheel kicked back and forth in rhythm to the pounding of the sea.

Ocho held his breath, turned the body over, went through the pockets. A few pesos, a letter, a home-made pocketknife, a worn, rusty bolt, a stub of a pencil, a button . . . not much to show for a lifetime of work.

Already the body was swelling in the heat. The face was dark and mottled.

He dragged the captain's stiff body from the wheelhouse, got it to the rail and hooked one of the arms across the railing. Then he lifted the feet.

The dead man was very heavy.

Grunting, working alone since none of his audience lifted a hand to help, Ocho heaved the weight up onto the rail and balanced it there as the boat rolled. Timing the roll, he released the body and it fell into the sea.

The corpse floated beside the boat face up. The lifeless eyes seemed to follow Ocho.

He tore himself away, finally, and watched the top of the mast make circles against the gray-white clouds and patchy blue.

When he looked again at the water the captain's corpse was still there, still face up. The sea water made a fan of his long hair, swirled it back and forth as if it were waving in a breeze. Water flowed into and out of his open mouth as the corpse bobbed up and down.

The long nights, the sun, heat, and exhaustion caught up with Ocho Sedano and he could no longer remain upright. He lowered himself to the deck, wedged his body against the railing, and slept.

"That freighter that left Gitmo last week, the one carrying the warheads?"

"I remember," Toad Tarkington said. "The *Colón*, or something like that."

"*Nuestra Señora de Colón.* She never made it to Norfolk."

"What?" Toad stared at the admiral, who was holding the classified message.

"She never arrived. Atlantic Fleet HQ is looking for her right now."

Toad took the message, scanned it, then handed it back.

"We sent a destroyer with that ship," the admiral said. "Call the captain, find out everything you can. I want to know when he last saw that ship and where she was."

In minutes Toad had the CO on the secure voice circuit. "We went up through the Windward and Mayaguanan passages," Toad was told. "They were creeping along at three knots, but they got their engineering plant rolling again and worked up to twelve knots, so we left her a hundred miles north of San Salvador, heading north." The captain gave the date and time.

"The *Colón* never arrived in Norfolk," Toad said.

"I'll be damned! Lost with all hands?"

"I doubt that very much," Toad replied.

Toad got on the encrypted voice circuit, telling the computer technicians in Maryland what he wanted. Soon the computers began chattering. Rivers of digital, encrypted data from the National Security Agency's mainframe computers at Fort Meade, Maryland, were bounced off a satellite and routed into the computers aboard *United States*.

On the screens before him he began seeing pictures, radar images from satellites in space looking down onto the earth. The blips that were the *Colón* and her escorting destroyer were easily picked out as they left Guantánamo Bay and made their way through the Windward Passage.

The screens advanced hour by hour. The three-knot speed of advance made the blips look almost stationary, so Toad flipped quickly through the screens, then had to wait while the data feed caught up.

Jake Grafton joined him, and they looked at the screens together.

The two blips crawled north, past Mayaguana, past San Salvador, then they sped up. The destroyer turning back was obvious.

As Jake and Toad watched, the blip that was the *Colón* turned southeast, back toward the Bahamas archipelago. Then the blip merged into a sea of white return.

"Now what?"

"It's rain," Jake said. "There was a storm. The blip is buried somewhere in that rain return. Call NSA. See if they can screen out the rain effect."

He was right; the rain did obscure the blip. But NSA could not separate the ship's return from that caused by rain.

"See if they can do a probability study, show us the most probable location of the *Colón* in the middle of that mess."

The computing the admiral requested took hours, and the results were inconclusive. As the intensity of the showers increased and decreased, the probable location of the ship expanded and contracted like a living circle. Jake and Toad drank coffee and ate sandwiches as they waited and watched the computer presentations.

Jake wandered around the compartment looking at maps between glances at the computer screen and conversations over another encrypted circuit with the brass in the Pentagon. The White House was in the loop now—the president wanted to know how in hell a shipload of chemical and biological warheads could disappear.

"What do you think happened, Admiral?" Toad asked.

"Too many possibilities."

"Do the people in Washington blame you for not having the *Colón* escorted all the way to Norfolk?"

"Of course. The national security adviser wants to know why the destroyer left the *Colón*."

Toad bristled. "You weren't told to escort that ship, you were told to guard the base. Escorting that ship out of the area wasn't your responsibility."

"Somebody is going to second-guess every decision I make," Jake Grafton said, "all of them. They're doing that right now. That comes with the stars and the job."

"Hindsight is a wonderful thing."

"I'll be out on the golf course soon enough, and the only person who will second-guess me then will be my wife."

Despite the best efforts of the wizards in Maryland and aboard ship, the location of the *Colón* under the rain of the cold front could not be established. Jake gave up, finally.

"Tell them to move forward in time. Let's see where the ship was after the storm."

But when the rain ceased, the computer could not identify the *Colón* from the other ship returns. There were thirty-two medium-to-large sized vessels in the vicinity of the Bahamas alone.

Toad stayed on the encrypted circuit to the NSA wizards. Finally he hung up the handset and turned to the admiral.

"They can assign track numbers to each blip, watch where they go, and by process of elimination come up with the most likely blips. There is a lot of computing involved. The process will take hours, maybe a day or two."

Jake Grafton picked up the flight schedule, took a look, then handed it to Toad. "Put the air wing up in a surface search pattern. Let's see what we can find out there now."

Toad turned to the chart on the bulkhead. "Where do you want them to look?"

"From the north coast of Cuba north into the Bahamas. Look along the coast of Hispaniola, all the way to Puerto Rico. Do the Turks and Caicos. Have the crews photograph every ship they see. Have NSA establish current ship tracks, then match up what the air crews see with what the satellite sees. Then let's run the current plot backward."

"Someone got a lucky break with the rain storm," Toad commented. "Maybe they were playing for the break, maybe it just happened."

"Send a top secret message to the Gitmo base commander. Find out everything they know about the crew of that ship."

Jake Grafton tapped the chart. "The president gave everyone in uniform their marching orders. Find that ship."

CHAPTER EIGHT

Maximo Sedano flashed his diplomatic passport at the immigration officer in the Madrid airport and was waved through after a perfunctory
glance. His suitcase was checked through to Zurich, and of course customs passed his attaché case without inspection. Traveling as a diplomat
certainly had its advantages—airport security did not even x-ray a diplomat's carry-on bags.

The Cuban minister of finance wandered the airport terminal luxu-
riating in the ambiance of Europe. The shops were full of delicacies,
books, tobacco, clothes, liquor, the women were well turned out, the
sights and smells were of civilization and prosperity and good living.

In spite of himself, Maximo Sedano sighed deeply. Ah, yes . . .

Spain or one of the Spanish islands would be his choice for retirement.
With Europe at his feet, what more could a man want? And retirement
seemed to Maximo to be almost within reach.

What was the phrase? "Fire in the belly?" Some Yanqui politician
said to win office one must have fire in the belly.

After a morning of thinking about it, Maximo concluded he didn't
have the fire. After Fidel died, Fidel's brother, Raúl or Maximo's brother
Hector, or Alejo Vargas, or anyone else who could kill his rivals could
rule Cuba—Maximo had given up trying for that prize. He'd take the
money.

And all the things money can buy: villas, beautiful women, yachts, gourmet food, fine wine, beautiful women . . . Someone else could stand in the Plaza de la Revolucion in Havana and revel in the cheers of the crowd.

He filed aboard the plane to Zurich and settled cheerfully into his seat. He smiled at the flight attendant and beamed at the man across the aisle.

Life is good, Maximo told himself, and unconsciously fingered his breast pocket, where the cards were that contained Fidel's signature and thumbprints.

Why go back?

Fifty-three or -four million American dollars was more than enough. To hell with the gold!

As the jet accelerated down the runway, Maximo told himself that the only smart thing was to take the money and retire. Now was the hour. Reel in the fish on the line—don't let it off the hook to cast for another.

He could transfer the money, spend three or four days shuffling it around, then leave Zurich on the Argentine passport as Eduardo José López. Maximo Sedano would cease to exist.

Off to Ibiza, buy a small cottage overlooking the sea, find a willing woman, not too young, not too old . . .

Yes.

He would do it.

The sudden death of Fidel Castro caught Alejo Vargas off guard. The dictator's death was supposed to be days, even weeks, away. Unfortunately Vargas's political position was precarious, to say the least. He really could have used Fidel's endorsement, however obtained. At least now no one would get it.

Although he had lived his whole life in his brother's shadow, Raúl Castro nominally held the reins of government. Alejo Vargas thought that without Fidel, Raúl was completely out on a limb, without a political constituency of his own.

While he tried to analyze the moves on the board, Vargas had Colonel Santana lock Mercedes in a bedroom, seal the presidential palace, and put a security man on the telephone switchboard. He didn't want the news of Fidel's death to get out before he was ready.

Vargas left Santana in charge of the palace and took his limo back to

the ministry. Of course he refrained from using the telephone i̶
to issue orders. The Americans listened to every radio transmiss̶
telephone frequencies and would soon know as much about his busi̶
as he did. He sat silently as the limo carried him through the afternoo̶
traffic to the ministry.

There he called his most trusted lieutenants to his office and issued
orders. Bring Admiral Delgado and General Alba to this office immediately. Find and arrest Hector Sedano.

Alejo Vargas stood at the window looking at Morro Castle and the
sea beyond. Far out from shore he could just make out the deep blue of
the Gulf Stream, which appeared as a thin blue line just under the
horizon. An overcast layer was moving in from the southeast and a
breeze was picking up.

A historic day . . . Fidel Castro, the towering giant of Cuban history
was dead. The end of an era, Vargas thought, and the beginning of a
new one, one he would dominate.

Despite the timing surprise, Vargas really had no choice: he was going
to have to go forward with his plan. He had concluded a month or so
ago that the only course open to him upon the death of Castro was to
create a situation that would induce the Cuban people to rally around
him. He would need boldness and a fierce resolve if he were to have a
chance of success, but he was just the man to risk everything on one roll
of the dice. After he personally loaded them.

Colonel Santana brought an American artillery shell to Havana yesterday, one removed from *Nuestra Señora de Colón*. The thing was in
the basement of the ministry now, under armed guard. The Cuban leadership had known for years that the Americans had CBW weapons
stored at Guantánamo. Now the Americans were removing the things,
but too late! Thanks to El Gato, Vargas had one he could show the
world. Soon he hoped to have a great many more.

Alejo Vargas took a deep breath, stretched mightily, helped himself
to a cigar. He lit it, inhaled the smoke, and blew it out through his nose.
Then he laughed.

"I want a little house with a garden. Every day food to eat. Children.
A doctor to make them well when they get sick. A man who loves me.
Is that so much?"

Dora's mouth was so dry she didn't enunciate her words clearly, but meant. They lay head to head under the awning *l del Mar* pitched and rolled endlessly in the long

erse of water they couldn't drink, the twenty-
oat were tortured by thirst and baked by the
rns now, raw places where the skin had blis-
off, leaving oozing sores. The old fisherman dipped
kets of water from the sea and poured salt water over the burns. He gently poured sea water on the small children, who had long ago ceased crying. Perhaps the water would be absorbed by their dehydrated tissues. If not, it would at least help keep them cool, ease their suffering somewhat.

Near Dora a woman was repeating the Rosary, over and over, mumbling it. Now and then another woman joined in for a few minutes, then fell silent until the spirit moved her again.

It seemed as if everyone left alive had lost someone to the sea that first night. The cries and grief were almost more than people could bear when they realized who had been lost, and that they were gone forever. Mothers cried, daughters were so distraught they shook, the hopelessness hit everyone like a hammer. The mother of the captain, who saw him dead, shot in the back, could neither move nor speak. As Dora talked, Ocho watched the woman, who sat now at the foot of the mainmast, holding on to it with one hand and a daughter or daughter-in-law with the other.

Every now and then Ocho sat or stood and searched the horizon. Nothing. Not a boat, not land, not a ship. Nothing.

Oh, three airplanes had gone over, two jets way up high making contrails and a twin-engine plane perhaps two miles up that had crossed the sky straight as a string, without the slightest waver as it passed within a half mile of *Angel del Mar,* rolling her guts out in the swells.

To see the airplanes, with their people riding inside, safe, full of food and drink, on their way from someplace to somewhere else, while we poor creatures are trapped here on this miserable boat, condemned to die slowly of thirst and exposure . . .

Surely the boat would be found soon . . . by somebody! Anybody! How can the Americans not see us? How?

Do they see us and not care?

Ocho was standing, watching for other ships and listening to Dora talk of the house she wanted, with the flowers by the door, when he realized that the dark place he could see to the west was a rain squall.

"Rain," he whispered.

"*Rain*." He shouted the word, pointed.

The squall was upon them before anyone could muster the energy to do anything. The people stood with their mouths open as raindrops pounded them and soaked their clothes and ran off the awning and along the deck, to disappear into the scuppers.

"The awning! Quickly. Make a container from the awning to trap the water!"

Ocho untied one corner with fingers that were all thumbs, the old fisherman did another corner, and they held the corners up, trapping water.

They had a few gallons when the rain ceased falling.

Several of the men tried to lean over, drink from the awning.

"No. Children first."

Ocho managed to catch one man by the back of the neck and throw him to the deck.

"Children first."

One by one the children were allowed to drink all they could hold. Then the women.

Several of the men got a swallow or two each, then the water was gone.

Ocho sat down, wiped the sweat and water from his hair and sucked it from his fingers. The only water he had gotten had been from holding his mouth open.

Dora had drunk her fill. Now she lay on the deck with her eyes closed.

Diego Coca had even gotten a swallow. He looked about with venomous eyes, then lay down beside his daughter.

"We must rig the awning so that it will catch water if the rain comes again," Ocho said to the old fisherman.

They worked at it, cut a hole in the low place in the canvas and put a five-gallon bucket under the hole.

If it will just rain again, Ocho thought, studying the clouds. *Please God, hear our prayer.*

"Why are you here, on this boat?" the old fisherman asked Ocho, who stared at him in surprise.

"Why are you here?" the fisherman repeated. "You aren't like us."

Ocho looked around at his fellow sufferers, unable to fathom the old man's meaning.

"These people are all losers," the old man said, "including me. We came looking for something we will never find. Why are you with us?"

"It's time for someone to relieve López on the pump. I will do it for a while, then you relieve me, old man."

"We are going to die soon, I think," the old man said.

Ocho hissed, "There are children listening. Watch your mouth."

"When we can pump no more we will swim. Then we will die. One by one people will drown, or sharks will come."

"Look for a ship," Ocho said harshly, and went below.

Sharks! The old windbag, scaring the children like that.

Of course sharks were a possibility. Blood or people thrashing about in the water would attract them, or so he had always heard. Sharks would rip people apart, pull them under.

He pumped for a bit over twenty minutes, then took a break. The water came in fast. After five minutes he began pumping again. Another twenty-one minutes of vigorous effort was required to empty the bilge.

The water was coming in faster than it did yesterday. Pumping the handle manually seemed to require more effort too, though he knew he just had less energy. Pump, pump, pump, take a brief rest in the stinky bilge, then pump again. . . .

The more tired he grew the more hopeless he felt. All of them were doomed. Dora, the baby growing within her, the baby that he had put in her womb . . .

It was his fault. If he had been man enough to say no, to not surrender to lust, all these people would still be in Cuba, they would have a future to look forward to, not watery death. All the people who had been swept to their death would still be alive.

Alive! He had no idea of the horrible things he was setting in motion when he opened her dress, felt the ripeness of her body, felt the heat of her.

The guilt weighed on him, made it hard to breathe. He must do what he could to save them all. That was the only honorable choice open to him. Save as many as possible and maybe God would forgive him.

Maybe then he could forgive himself. . . .

And he shouldn't give up hope yet. As he worked the pump handle he scolded himself for being so negative, for not having faith in God, in His plan for the twenty-six human beings still alive on *Angel del Mar*.

Soon a ship would come. The sailors would see the boat and rescue them. Give them cool, clean water, all they could drink; and food. Let each of them eat their fill. Soon it would come. Any minute now.

He pumped and pumped, sweat burned his eyes and dripped from his nose, though not so much as he sweated yesterday. He was very dehydrated. The salt had built up in his armpits, his groin, and it cut him. With his free hand he scratched, which only made the burning worse.

Any minute now a ship will come over the horizon. Soon . . .

Maximo Sedano took a taxi from the Zurich airport to an excellent hotel in the heart of the financial district where he had stayed on six or eight previous visits. The hotel was old, solid, substantial, almost banklike, yet it was not the primo hotel. This was the last time he stayed here, he told himself. Eduardo José López would stay at the best hotel in town because by God he could afford it. And because the staff over there had never seen him as Maximo Sedano.

He would have to make many adjustments, avoid photographs, avoid places where prominent Cubans might see him, like the heart of Madrid or London or Paris. Of course, if Vargas was assassinated in the turmoil following Fidel's death, he could relax his vigilance somewhat. Vargas was a bloodhound, a humorless man with a profound capacity for revenge. Still, if Vargas came out on top after the succession struggle in Havana, he would have many things on his mind, and a missing ex-finance minister would of necessity be far down on the list.

Maximo would take his chances. He was in Europe, the money was in the banks just down the street, the loud and clear call of destiny was ringing in his ears.

He was sipping a drink and thinking about where he might go for dinner when he heard a knock on the door.

"Yes?"

"Delivery."

"I ordered nothing. There has been a mistake."

"For the Honorable Maximo Sedano."

Curious, he opened the door.

The man standing in the hallway was European, with thinning hair and bulging muscles and a chiseled chin. And he was holding a pistol in his right hand, one pointed precisely at Maximo's solar plexus.

The man backed Maximo into the room and closed the door.

"Your passport, please?" A German accent.

"I have little money. Take it and go."

"Sit." He gestured toward a chair by the bed with his pistol. Maximo obeyed, thankfully. His knees were turning to jelly and he had a powerful urge to urinate.

"Now the passport."

Maximo took the diplomatic passport from his inside pocket and passed it across. Taking care to keep the pistol well away from Maximo and still pointed at his middle, the man reached for the passport with his left hand.

He glanced at the photo and name, grinned, and tossed the passport on the bed. The man took a seat.

"You look white as a sheet, man. Are you going to pass out?"

He felt dizzy, light-headed. He put his hand to his forehead, which felt clammy.

"Loosen your tie," the German ordered, "unbutton your collar button, then put your head between your knees."

Maximo obeyed.

"Don't breathe so fast. Get a grip on yourself. If you aren't careful you'll hyperventilate and pass out."

Maximo concentrated on breathing slowly. After a few seconds he felt better. Finally he straightened up. The pistol was nowhere in sight.

"Vargas said you were a jellyfish." The German shook his head sadly.

"Do you work for him?" He was shocked at the sound of his own voice, the pitch of which was surprisingly high.

"I do errands from time to time," the German replied. "He pays well and the work is congenial."

"What do you want?"

"Vargas wanted me to remind you that you were sent to do an errand. You are to transfer the money to the proper accounts tomorrow and return to Cuba. If you do not, I am to kill you."

The German smiled warmly. "I will do it too. There is a side of my personality that I am not proud of, that I do not like to admit, but it is only fair that I should tell you the truth: I like to kill people. I enjoy it. I don't just shoot them, bang, bang, bang. I see how long I can keep them alive, how much I can make them suffer. I own a quiet little place, out of the way, isolated. It is perfect for my needs."

The German's eyes narrowed speculatively. "You seem a miserable specimen, but I like a challenge. I think with a little prior planning I could probably make you scream for at least forty-eight hours before you died."

Maximo's heart was hammering in his ears, thudding along like a race horse's hooves.

The German picked up the telephone, told the operator he wished to place a call to Havana. He gave her the number.

One minute passed, then another.

"Rall here. For Vargas."

After a few seconds, Rall spoke again. "*Buenos días, señor.* I have given him your message."

The German listened for a few more seconds, then passed the telephone to Maximo.

The Cuban minister of finance managed to make a noise, and heard the voice of Alejo Vargas:

"The money must arrive tomorrow, Maximo. You understand?"

"Your thug has threatened me."

"I hope Señor Rall has made the situation clear. It would be a tragedy for you to die because you did not understand your duty."

The line went dead before Maximo could answer. He sat with the instrument in his hand, trying to keep control of his stomach. Rall gestured, so he handed the phone to him.

The German listened to make sure the connection had been severed, then placed the instrument back in its cradle. He stood.

"I don't know what else to say. You understand the situation. Your destiny is in your hands."

With that the German went to the door, opened it and passed through, then pulled the door shut behind him until it latched.

Maximo ran to the bathroom and vomited in the commode.

William Henry Chance was lying on the bed in his hotel room reading a magazine when he heard the knock on the door. He opened it to find Tommy Carmellini standing there.

"Hey, boss," Carmellini said. "Let's take a walk."

"Give me a moment to put on my shoes."

Chance did so, pulled on a light sportscoat, and locked the door behind him on the way out.

Neither man spoke as they rode the elevator downstairs. Out on the

sidewalk they automatically checked for a tail. No one obviously following, but that meant little. If the Cubans had burned them as CIA, they
could have watchers in every building, be filming every move, every
gesture, every movement of the lips.

So neither man said anything.

Carmellini directed their steps toward one of the larger casinos on the
Malecon. Latin music engulfed them as they walked into the building.
The place reminded Chance of Atlantic City, complete with crowds of
gray-haired retirees buying a good time, mostly Americans, Germans,
English, and Spaniards. No Cubans were gambling, of course, just for-
eigners who had hard currency to wager.

The only Cubans not behind the tables were prostitutes, young, gorgeous, and dressed in the latest European fashions. At this hour of the
evening the cigar smoke was thick, the liquor flowing, and the laughter
and music loud.

The two men drifted around the casino, taking their time, checking
to see who was watching them, then finally sifted out of the building
through a side door. At the basement loading dock a man was inven-
torying supplies in a telephone repair van. Chance and Carmellini
climbed in, the man closed the door, and the van rolled.

"Vargas is having a powwow in his office," Carmellini reported. "It
sounds as if Castro is dead."

"Nobody lives forever," Chance said lightly. "Not even dictators."

"That isn't the half of it. They're talking about biological weapons
again."

"Bingo," Chance said, a touch of satisfaction creeping into his voice.

"Yeah. Vargas says there is a warehouse full of biological warheads
at Gitmo."

It took a whole lot to surprise William Henry Chance. He gaped.

"Not only that," Carmellini continued, "he has one of the things. He's
going to show it to the Cuban people, prove to the world what perfidious
bastards the Americans are."

"He's got an American CBW warhead?"

"You'll have to listen to the tape. Sounded to the technician like the
thing was stolen from a ship."

"Biological warheads at Guantánamo Bay? That's gotta be wrong!
Have these guys been smoking something?"

"I think Vargas and his pals have gone off the deep end. Either that or they plan to plant some biological agents in Guantánamo after they crash through the fence."

"Maybe they know we're listening to them," Chance said. "Maybe this whole thing is a hoax."

"Could be," Tommy Carmellini agreed, but to judge by his tone of voice, he didn't think so.

Maximo Sedano was committed. He couldn't transfer the money to Cuban government accounts in Havana because the transfer cards contained the wrong account numbers. Changing the numbers was out of the question: any alteration to the cards would be instantly spotted and cause the Swiss bankers to suspect forgery.

Maximo carefully arranged the combination locks on his attaché case and opened it. At the bottom was a pistol, a very nice little Walther in 7.35 mm. The magazine was full, but there was no round in the chamber. Maximo chambered a round and engaged the safety.

He put the pistol in his right-hand trouser pocket and looked at himself in the mirror.

He put his hand in his pocket and wrapped his fingers around the butt of the weapon.

He had to go to the banks tomorrow, act like a bureaucrat shuffling money for his government while they shoveled $53 million plus interest into his personal accounts. Well, if he could kill the German and get away with it, he sure as hell could keep his cool while the Swiss bankers made him rich.

Could he kill Rall?

How badly did he want to be rich?

He stood at the window looking at the Limmat River a block from the hotel, and beyond it, the vast expanse of Lake Zurich. Beyond the lake half-hidden in the haze were the peaks of the Alps, still white with last winter's snow.

He certainly didn't want to go back to Cuba.

A drink of scotch whiskey from the minibar helped settle his nerves.

An hour later he left the hotel. He turned left, crossed the Limmat River on the nearest bridge, and headed for the main thoroughfare. Perhaps an hour of daylight left, but not more. He didn't look around him, sure that Rall was somewhere near. He took his time strolling along, pretending to enjoy the early summer day and the ebb and flow of the crowd, many of whom were young people on school holiday.

Finally he turned into an old cobblestoned street too narrow for vehicles and walked up it toward the hill which loomed above the downtown area. Medieval buildings rose up on either side and seemed to lean in, making the street seem even narrower and more confining than it really was as the daylight faded from the sky.

He found the restaurant he remembered and went inside. Yes, it was as he recalled, with the tables and chairs just so, the kitchen beyond, and past the kitchen, the rest room. One with an old tank mounted high in the wall with a pull chain.

How long had it been?

Two years, at least.

The waiter was new, didn't seem to recognize him. Not that he should, but it might be inconvenient if he should later recall seeing Sedano here this evening.

Maximo sat with his back against the wall, so that he could see both the front doorway and the door to the kitchen.

He ordered an Italian red wine, something robust, while he studied the menu.

The truth was Maximo was so nervous that he didn't think he could eat anything. The automatic felt heavy on his thigh, its weight an ominous presence that he couldn't ignore.

He tried to slow his breathing, make his pulse stop racing.

He used his handkerchief to wipe his hands, his face. He was used to the heat of Cuba; he should not be perspiring like this! *Get a grip, Maximo—if you cannot control yourself you will soon be dead. Or a subject for that pervert's experiments.*

He wondered if Rall had told the truth about torturing people.

Just thinking about that subject and the way the bastard told him about it—with obvious relish—make his forehead break out in a sweat. He swabbed with the handkerchief again.

There were two couples and another single man in the restaurant. Only one waiter shuttled back and forth through the kitchen door.

Maximo moved to a different seat at the same table so that he could see through the kitchen door. Yes, now when the waiter came through the door he could see most of the length of the narrow kitchen. The chef was moving back and forth, working on something in a pot, checking the oven, taking things from a refrigerator. . . .

"More wine?"

The waiter was there, holding the bottle.

"If you please."

As the waiter poured, Maximo murmured, "Have you a rest room?"

"Yes, of course. Through the kitchen, on the left in back."

"I do not wish to disturb the chef."

"Do not stand on ceremony, sir."

He waited, sipping the wine, trying not to stare through the kitchen door. When the waiter returned he ordered, something, the first thing he saw on the menu.

One of the two couples left, the second finished their dinner and ordered coffee, the other man's meal came at about the same time as Maximo's.

He was just starting on the main course when the chef came to the door, wiped his hands on a towel, and said something to the waiter. Then he stepped outside into the narrow street and lit a cigarette. Night had fallen.

Maximo got up and headed for the rest room.

As the kitchen door closed behind him, he looked for the drawer or shelf that held the tools.

Quickly now...

He opened one drawer... the wrong one.

Next drawer, forks, knives and spoons.

Next drawer... *yes!*

He saw what he wanted, and quick as a thought reached, palmed it, and strode for the rest room.

Ten minutes passed before he was ready for the dining room again. The chef was back at his pots and pans. He nodded as Maximo walked by.

Maximo resumed his seat, took his time, stirred the food around on his plate but could eat nothing more. He took a few more sips of wine, then ordered coffee.

He was just reaching for the bill at the end of the meal when Rall dropped into a seat at his table.

"I should have come in earlier, let you buy me a meal."

"Get out."

"Oh, don't be impolite. I wish to talk to you awhile, to learn what you do for the Cuban government."

"If you wish to know can I pay more than Vargas, the answer is probably no. I am just a civil servant. I suggest you take up the question with Vargas."

Maximo took enough money from his wallet to pay for the meal and a tip and dropped it into the tray on top of the tab.

"I have a diplomatic passport. If you do not leave I will have the waiter call the police."

"And have me arrested?"

"Something like that."

Rall stared into Maximo's eyes. "I don't think you appreciate your position."

"Perhaps. Have you properly evaluated yours?"

"A roaring mouse." Rall pushed himself away from the table, rose, and walked out the front door.

Maximo lingered, considering.

He left the restaurant a half hour later, his right hand in his pocket around the butt of the pistol. He looked neither right nor left, walked purposely along the thoroughfares. He crossed the Limmat River and walked toward the main train station, which was well lit and still crowded with vacationing students laden with backpacks. The students sat around in circles, sharing cigarettes and talking animatedly as they waited for their trains.

Maximo Sedano had no doubt that Rall was a killer. He didn't know anything about the man except what he had said, but he knew Alejo Vargas. Vargas was just the man to order a killing, or to do it himself. The list of Castro's enemies who had disappeared through the years was long enough to convince anyone that Vargas's enmity was not good for one's health.

Maximo could hear footsteps behind him as he walked through the train station.

A few students looked up at him, glanced behind him at whoever was following. . . .

That had to be Rall.

What if it were someone else? What if Rall were not alone?

If there were two men, he was doomed. He was betting everything that there was only one man, one man who thought him an incompetent coward.

Well, he was a coward. He had never had to live by his wits, face physical danger. He was frightened and no doubt it showed. He was perspiring freely, his temples pounding, his breath coming in short, quick gasps.

He entered a long, dingy hallway, following the signs toward the men's room. The hall was empty.

He could hear the footsteps coming behind, a steady pace, not rushed. The man behind was making no attempt to walk softly. He was confident, in complete control, the exact opposite of the way Maximo Sedano felt.

He fought the urge to run, to look over his shoulder to see precisely who was back there following him.

Time seemed to move ever so slowly. He was aware of everything, the noise, the people, the dirty floor and faded paint, and the smell of stale urine and feces wafting through the door of the men's room as he entered.

No one in the room. The stalls, empty.

Maximo walked to the back wall, turned, and faced the door. He kept his hand in his pocket. He grasped the butt of the pistol tightly, his finger wrapped around the trigger.

Rall walked into the room, stopped facing him.

"Well, well. We meet again."

Maximo said nothing. He swallowed three or four times.

"Are you going somewhere on the train? Am I delaying your departure?"

Maximo bit his tongue.

"What do you have in your pocket, little man?"

He tilted the barrel of the pistol up, so that it made a bulge in his trousers.

Rall grinned. The naked bulb on the ceiling put the lower half of his face in shadow and made his grin look like a death's-head grimace.

The German reached into his jacket and pulled out his pistol. He leveled it at Maximo.

"If you are going to shoot me, little man, go ahead and do it."

Sweat stung Maximo's eyes. He shook his head to clear the sweat.

Rall advanced several paces, moving slowly.

"Take your hand out of your pocket."

Now the German leveled his pistol. Pointed it right at Maximo's face. "I will shoot you with great pleasure unless you do as I say."

"Everyone will hear," Maximo squeaked, and withdrew his hand from his pocket. Automatically he raised both hands to shoulder height.

Rall kept advancing. When he passed under the lightbulb his eye sockets became dark shadows and Maximo couldn't see where he was looking.

Rall came up to him, slapped him with his left hand, then felt Maximo's right trouser pocket. At this distance Maximo could see Rall's eyes. His hands were together above his head.

"A gun!" the German said with a hint of surprise in his voice.

He reached for it, put his left hand into Maximo's pocket to draw it out.

As he did so he glanced downward.

With his right hand Maximo pulled the handle of the ice pick loose from the strap of his wristwatch and drew it out of his sleeve. With one smooth, quick, savage swinging motion he jabbed the pick into the side of Rall's head clear up to the handle.

Rall collapsed on the floor. Maximo kept his grip on the handle of the ice pick, so the shiny round blade slipped out of the tiny wound, which was about an inch above Rall's left ear.

Maximo bent down, retrieved his pistol. Rall's pistol was still in his hand, held loosely by his flaccid fingers.

There was almost no blood on the side of Rall's head.

Rall tried to focus his eyes. His body straightened somewhat; one hand tightened on the pistol in an uncontrolled reflex, then relaxed.

The German groaned. Muscle spasms racked his body.

Maximo took a deep breath and exhaled explosively. He wiped at the perspiration dripping from his face. His shirt was a sodden mess. Squaring his shoulders, he walked out of the men's room without another glance at the man sprawled on the floor. As he walked down the hallway toward the main waiting room he passed two male students carrying backpacks, but he purposefully avoided eye contact and they didn't seem to pay him any attention.

He walked at a steady, sedate pace through the terminal and out into the night.

CHAPTER NINE

William Henry Chance sat in the back of the van listening to the tape of Vargas's conversation with his generals. Normally the fidelity of this system was acceptable. Every now and then a word or phrase was garbled or inaudible, the same drawback that affected every listening technology. People mumbled or talked at the same time or turned their heads the wrong way or talked while smoking. Still, this evening he was only catching occasional words.

Chance strained his ears. Phrases, occasionally a plain word, lots of garbled noise . . .

"Is this the best we can do?"

"The sky was overcast, the window was in shadow with the evening coming on."

"What about the laser?"

If the crystals were illuminated with a laser beam in the nonvisible portion of the spectrum, the vibrations could be read with the large magnification spotting scope at the usual distance. The problem was getting the laser close enough to the crystals. Maximum range for the laser was less than one hundred meters, so the van with the laser had to be parked literally in front of the building.

"We didn't want to take the risk without your permission."

Ah, yes, risk. This equipment had been brought into Cuba by boat.

The four technicians—of Mexican or Cuban descent—had arrived the same way.

Miguelito was from south Texas, the son of migrant laborers. He didn't learn English until he was in his late teens. He had recorded the conversations, listened to the audio as the computer processed it. "What did you think, Miguelito?" Chance asked. Chance's Spanish was excellent, the result of months of intense training, but he would never have a native speaker's ear for the language.

Miguelito took his time answering. "It is difficult to say. I hear phrases, pieces of sentences, stray words . . . and my mind puts it all together into something that may not have been there when they said it. You understand?"

Chance nodded.

"What I hear is a conversation about biological weapons in Guantánamo Bay."

"You mean using biological weapons against Guantánamo Bay?"

"That is possible. But my impression was that the weapons were already there."

"Castro. Did they talk about Castro?"

"His name was mentioned. It is distinctive. I think I heard it."

"Is he still alive?"

"I do not know." Miguelito looked apologetic.

"Biological weapons inside the U.S. facility is impossible. They must be intending to use them against the people there."

Miguelito said nothing.

"I'd better listen," Chance said.

"I will play for you the best part," Miguelito said. "Give me a few moments." He played with the equipment. After about a minute he announced he was ready with a nod of his head. Chance and Carmellini donned headsets.

Noise. They heard noise, occasionally garbled voices, but mostly computer-generated noise as the machine tried without success to make sense of the flickering light coming through the high-magnification spotting scope. Every now and then a word or two in Spanish. "Guantánamo . . . attack . . ." Once Chance was sure he heard the word "biological," but even then, he wasn't certain.

Finally he removed his headset.

Miguelito did likewise.

"Perhaps they are talking about possible targets when and if," Carmellini suggested. "After all, they can spray this stuff into the air from a truck upwind and kill everyone on the base."

Chance grimaced. What he had here was absolutely nothing. He was going to need something more definite before he started talking to Washington via the satellite.

"They did a lot of talking about political matters, people and districts, whom they supported and so on," Miguelito said. "It is not much better than what you have just heard—they talked of this before the sun went down—but I got the impression that Vargas wanted Delgado and Alba to abandon any commitments they had to Raúl Castro or the Sedanos and throw in with him."

"Hmmm," said William Henry Chance. He tried to focus on Miguelito's comments and couldn't. Biological weapons were on his mind.

He recalled Vargas's face, remembered how he had looked as Chance had sat there discussing a Cuban-American cigarette company. The strong, fleshy face had been a mask, revealing nothing of its owner's thoughts. That poker face . . . that was his dominate impression of Vargas.

The man certainly had a reputation: he was ruthless efficiency incarnate, a thug who smashed heads and sliced throats and got answers from people who didn't want to talk. Every dictatorship needed a few sociopaths in high places. He was also subtle and smooth when that was required. Nor had he yet surrendered to his appetites, surrendered to the absolute corruption that absolute power inevitably causes. Not yet, anyway.

Yes, Alejo Vargas was a damned dangerous man, one who apparently possessed the brains and managerial skills necessary to produce biological weapons and the brutality to use them.

El Gato may have shipped the Cubans material that they could use to culture bacteria or viruses, but as yet there was no hard evidence that the Cubans had done so.

That tantalizing word, "biological." Why would the interior minister and the head of the Cuban Army and Navy use that word if they weren't talking about weapons? Sure as hell they weren't talking about barracks sanitation or the condition of the mess halls.

If there was a biological weapons program, Chance told himself, the evidence would be inside the ministry, the headquarters of the secret police. There must be paper, records, orders, letters—something! No one could run a serious project like that without paper, not even Vargas.

The evidence is *inside that building,* he told himself.

After Fidel died of poison she had handed him, Mercedes was locked in her bedroom by Vargas and Santana. Which was just as well.

She pulled a blanket over herself and curled up on the bed in the fetal position. The silence and afternoon gloom were comforting.

Amazingly, no tears came. Fidel had been dying for months, she was relieved that he had finally come to the end of the journey, the end of the pain.

In the stillness she listened to the sound of her breathing, the sound of her heart pumping blood through her ears, listened to an insect buzzing somewhere, listened to the distant muted thump of footfalls and doors closing, people engaged in the endless business of living.

She saw a gecko, high on the wall, quite motionless except for his sides, which moved in and out, just enough to be seen in the dim light coming in through the window drapes. He seemed to be watching her. More likely he was waiting for a fly, as he did somewhere every day, as his ancestors had done since the dawn of time, as his progeny would do until the sun flamed up and burned the earth to a cinder. Then, they say, the sun would burn out altogether and the earth, if it still existed, would wander the universe forever, a cold, lifeless rock, spinning aimlessly. Until then geckos clung to walls and God provided flies. Amazing how that worked.

She wondered about Hector, wondered if he would be found and arrested, or murdered and shoveled into an anonymous grave. God knows she had done everything possible to warn him. Perhaps the man didn't want to be warned: perhaps he knew the task before him was impossible. Perhaps he really believed all that Jesuit bullshit and in truth didn't care if he lived or died. Most likely that was it.

The truth was that the more you knew of life, of the compromises one must make to get from day to day, the more you realized the futility of it all. None of it meant anything.

Man lived, man died, governments rose and fell, justice was done or denied, venality was crushed or triumphant; in the long run none of it mattered a damn. The world spun on around the sun, life continued to be lived. . . .

When we perish from human memories we are no more. We are well and truly gone, as if we had never been.

She threw aside the cover and sat up in bed, hugging her knees. She thought again of Fidel, and finally let him go. She then had only the twilight, the room falling into darkness.

Toad Tarkington was waiting for Jake Grafton beside the V-22 Osprey on the flight deck of *United States*.

The Osprey was a unique airplane, with a turbo-prop engine mounted on the end of each wing. Just now the pilot had the engines tilted straight up so that the 38-foot props on each engine would function as helicopter rotor blades. The machine could lift off vertically like a helicopter or make a short, running takeoff. Once airborne the pilot would gradually transition to forward flight by tilting the engines down into a horizontal position. Then the giant props would function as conventional propellers, though very large ones. The machine could also land vertically or run on to a short landing area. A cross between a large twin-rotor helicopter and a turbo-prop transport, the extraordinarily versatile Osprey had enormous lifting ability and 250-knot cruise speed, capabilities exceeding those of any conventional helicopter.

Jake Grafton stood looking at the plane for a few seconds as it sat on the flight deck. With its engines mounted on the very ends of its wings—a position dictated by the size of the rotor blades—the machine could not stay airborne if one of the rotor transmissions failed. It could fly on one engine, however, if the drive shaft linking the good engine to the transmission of the distant rotor blade remained intact.

The Osprey's extremely complicated systems were made even more so by the requirement that the wings and rotors fold into a tight package so that the plane could be stored aboard ship. The transitions between hovering and wing-borne flight were only possible because computers assisted the pilots in flying the plane. Complex controls, complex systems—Jake thought the machine a flying tribute to the ingenuity of the human species.

The evening looked gorgeous. The sky was clearing, visibility decent. The late afternoon sun shone on a breezy, tumbling sea. Jake took a deep breath and climbed into the plane.

He put on a regular headset so that he could talk to the flight crew. " 'Lo, Admiral."

"Hello, Rita. How are you?"

"Ready to rock and roll, sir. Let me know when you're strapped in."

"I'm ready." Jake settled back and watched Toad and the crewman strap in.

Lightly loaded, the Osprey almost leaped from the flight deck into the stiff sea wind, which was coming straight down the deck. Rita wasted no time rotating the engines forward to a horizontal position; the craft accelerated quickly as the giant rotors became propellers and the wings took the craft's weight.

An hour later Rita Moravia landed the Osprey vertically on a pier at Guantánamo between two light poles. The sun was down by then and the area was lit by flood lights.

A marine lieutenant colonel stood waiting. He had the usual close-cropped hair, a deep tan, the requisite square jaw, and he looked as if he spent several hours a day lifting weights.

As they walked toward him Toad muttered, just loud enough for Jake to hear, "Another refugee from the Mr. Universe contest. If you can't make it in bodybuilding, there's always the marines."

"Can it, Toad."

The lieutenant colonel saluted smartly. "I am deploying a company around the warehouse, Admiral. We're taking up positions now."

"Excellent," Jake Grafton said. "I brought an aerial photo that was taken this afternoon"—Toad took it from a folder and passed it over—"if you would show me where you are placing your people?"

"Yes, sir." Lieutenant Colonel Eckhardt, the landing team commander, used the photo and a finger to show where he would put his company. He finished with the comment, "My plan is to channel any intruders into these two open areas formed by these streets, then kill them there."

"What are your alternatives?"

They discussed them, and the fact that Eckhardt planned to divide one platoon between several empty warehouses and use them as reserves. "I think this will be a very realistic exercise, sir," the colonel finished. "I have even had ammunition issued to the men, although of course they have been instructed to keep their weapons empty."

"Colonel Eckhardt, this is not an exercise."

"Sir?"

"That warehouse, warehouse nine, contains CBW warheads. They are being loaded aboard this freighter and the one that left the other day for transport back to the states, where they are supposed to be destroyed. The first ship that left carrying the damned things has disappeared. We're hunting for it now. I don't know just what in hell is going on, so I'm putting your outfit here just in case."

"What is the threat, sir?"

"I don't know."

Jake could see Eckhardt was working hard to keep his face under control.

"If the Cubans or anybody else comes over, under, around, or through the perimeter fence, start shooting."

"Yes, sir," Eckhardt said.

"Have your people load their weapons, Colonel. They will defend themselves and this building. No warning shots—shoot to kill."

"If we are assaulted, sir, how much warning would you expect us to have?"

"I don't know. Maybe days, maybe hours, maybe no warning at all."

"The more warning I have, sir, the fewer lives I am likely to lose."

"I will pass that on to Washington, Colonel. When I know something is up, you'll hear about it seconds later. That's the best I can do."

"Yes, sir."

"Just so we're on the same sheet of music, Colonel, I want that warehouse defended until you are relieved or the very last marine is dead."

Eckhardt said nothing this time. Toad Tarkington's grim expression softened. Eckhardt could have said something like, "Marines don't surrender," or some other bullshit, but he didn't. Toad was taking a liking to the lieutenant colonel.

"Anything you need from me," Jake Grafton continued, "just ask. The battle group and the base commander will supply you to the extent of our resources. The cruiser will provide artillery support—I want you to interface with the cruiser people in the next hour or two, make sure you're ready to communicate and shoot."

"Yes, sir."

"Which brings up a point: I see that your people are building bunkers from sandbags."

"Yes, sir. We're trying to fortify some positions, create some strongpoints."

"Get a couple of backhoes from the base people, get someone to locate the utilities, and dig fortifications. Jackhammer the concrete. By dawn I want your people dug in to the eyes." This order might be stretching the phrase "business as usual," but Jake wasn't worried. Freighters carrying weapons don't normally turn up missing.

"Yessir."

"What are you going to do if the Cubans send tanks through the fence?"

"Their tanks are old Soviet T-54s, I believe," Lieutenant Colonel Eckhardt said. "We'll channel them into these two avenues," he pointed at the aerial photo, "then kill them—cremate the crews inside the tanks."

"Okay. When your people are dug in, dig any tank traps that you want. You have carte blanche, Colonel."

"Nobody is going into that warehouse, sir."

"Fine. We'll keep the Cuban Navy off your back and give you air support. The cruisers will provide artillery. Call us if you see or hear anything suspicious."

Toad passed the colonel a list of radio frequencies and they discussed communications for several minutes.

Jake took that opportunity to wander off, to look at the warehouse from all angles.

He was standing beside six large forklifts that were parked near the main loading dock when Toad and Eckhardt walked over to him. "Don't isolate these forklifts from the pier when you're digging up concrete," Jake advised.

"Of course not."

"One other thing," Jake said. "You'd better break out the MOPP suits and have them beside every man." MOPP stood for mission-oriented protective posture, a term designed by career bureaucrats to obfuscate the true nature of chemical and biological warfare protection suits.

The colonel was going to say something about the suits, then he decided to pass on it.

They talked for several minutes about the battalion's problems, how the colonel was deploying it. The colonel told Jake he was putting people on the roofs of all the warehouses.

As Jake and Toad walked back to the Osprey, Lieutenant Colonel Eckhardt turned toward warehouse nine and scratched his head. He didn't for a minute believe that building contained chemical and biological weapons.

He frowned. A hijacked freighter? He had been in the Corps long enough to know how the navy operated: this was just another readiness exercise but the admiral didn't have the courtesy or decency to say so.

"Let's keep the grunts' assholes twanging tight." MOPP suits, in the heat of the Cuban summer!

Yeah.

"Cuba must learn to live with the elephant," Hector Sedano told the crowd of schoolteachers and administrators. "Our relations with the United States have been the determining factor in our history and will be the key to our future. Any Cuban government that hopes to make life better for the people of Cuba must come to grips with the reality of the colossus ninety miles north."

That was the nub of his message, pure and simple. He was careful never to criticize Fidel Castro or the government, knowing full well that to do so would be the height of folly, an invitation to a prison cell. Most of the people in this room were teachers, a few were agents for the secret police. Cuba was a dictatorship, a fact as unremarkable as the island status of the nation.

Still, he was talking about the future, about a day still to come when all things might change, a day that Cuba would have to face someday, sometime. Everyone in the room understood that too, including the secret police, so no one objected to his remarks. Hector Sedano talked on, talking about education, jobs, investment, opportunities, the building blocks of the life sagas of human beings.

When he finished he sat down as the thunder of applause rolled over him. He thought that his audience's reaction was not to his message, which in truth was not that new or fresh or interesting, but to the fact that he was a private citizen speaking aloud on sensitive political subjects. This his audience found most remarkable. They stood on their feet, applauded, pressed forward to touch him, to give him a greeting or blessing, reached between people to touch his clothes, his hands, his hair.

Afterward he sat and spoke privately to a knot of people who wanted to be with him when that someday came. He was more open, spoke about specifics but still spoke guardedly, careful not to speak openly against the government or to criticize Fidel.

In his heart of hearts Hector Sedano knew that Fidel Castro must know what he had to say, must know his message almost as well as he himself did. Everything that the government knew, Fidel knew, for he was the government.

And still Fidel let him speak. That was the remarkable thing, and Hector had a theory about why this might be so. When he was a young revolutionary in jail, Fidel had written a political tract in defense of the Cuban revolution that became its manifesto. He entitled it, "History Will Absolve Me." In it he defined "the people" as "the vast unredeemed masses, those to whom everyone makes promises and who are deceived by all."

Maybe, Hector thought, Fidel Castro was still looking for absolution from those who would come after. Maybe he was thinking about "the people" even now, thinking of the promises he had made and the reality that had come to pass.

When he was leaving the school, on the way to the borrowed car with two friends who accompanied him, Hector found himself surrounded by well-dressed men, obviously not local laborers.

"Hector Sedano," said one, "you are under arrest. You must come with us."

He was stunned. "What am I charged with?" he demanded.

"That is not for us to discuss," the man said, and took his elbow. He pushed him toward a government van.

"They are arresting Sedano," someone shouted. The shout was taken up by others. As a crowd gathered, shoved closer, shouting threats and obscenities, the men around the van pushed Hector into it and jumped in themselves. In seconds it was in motion.

Hector protested. He had done nothing wrong, he was not wanted for any crime.

The man showed him a badge. "You are under arrest," he said. "We have our orders. Now be silent."

The van raced through the streets of the city, then took the highway toward Havana.

Maximo Sedano was too excited to sleep. The adrenaline aftershock of stabbing an ice pick into Vargas's thug should have floored him, but the thought of $53 million, plus interest, kept him wide awake. That and the possibility of sirens.

He lay in the darkness listening. Every now and then he heard a siren moaning, faint and faraway. He waited in dread suspense for that moan to join others and become a wailing convoy of police vehicles converging on his hotel, followed by the stamping of a horde of policemen charging upstairs to arrest him. He twitched with every howl in the night, though they were few and faint and never seemed to grow louder. In the silence between moans he amused himself by trying to calculate the amount of interest that might be due on Castro's horde.

He hadn't seen a statement in about six months . . . call it six months exactly, half a year. Interest at 2.45 percent, on $53 million . . . almost 650,000 American dollars.

Ha! The interest alone would buy a nice small villa on Ibiza. Of course he should not rule out Majorca, nor Minorca for that matter, until he had traveled over each of the islands and seen local conditions for himself, and checked the real estate market. No, indeed. He would visit all the Balearic Islands in turn, including Formentera and Cabrera, stay at local inns, drink local wine, eat lamb and beef and fish prepared as the islanders preferred . . .

Ahh, his dream was within his grasp. Tomorrow. In just a few short hours. When the banks opened he would go immediately to the one with the largest account, submit the transfer card, then to the next one, and finally, the one with the smallest amount on deposit, a mere $11 million.

Maximo paced the room, stared out the window at the lights of the city that housed his fortune, paced some more.

He was full almost to bursting, too excited too sleep.

He had almost run back to the hotel from the railroad station. He had taken his time though, walked slowly and unhurriedly, paused to feed the ducks under one of the Limmat bridges, slipped the ice pick into the river when no one was watching, then walked on to the hotel so full of joy and happiness he could barely contain himself.

At about four in the morning he began to wind down somewhat, so he lay down on the bed. In minutes he was asleep.

When Maximo awoke the sun was up, he could hear a maid running a vacuum sweeper in the next room.

He checked his watch. Almost eight-thirty.

He showered, shaved, put on clean clothes from the skin out, then packed his bags. He would come back to the hotel this afternoon when he had finished his banking and check out. He wanted to be long gone if Santana showed up looking for Rall and the money.

There was a continental breakfast laid out in the hotel dining room, so Maximo paused there for coffee and a French roll.

Suitably fortified, with his attaché case in his left hand and the transfer cards signed by Fidel in his inside breast pocket, Maximo Sedano set off afoot for the bank that was to be his first stop. It was a mere two blocks away, a huge old building of thick stone walls and small windows, a building hundreds of years old with the treasure of the ages in its vaults.

He spoke to a clerk, was ushered into a small windowless office to see a middle-aged man who wore a green eyeshade and spoke tolerably good Spanish. Maximo surrendered the appropriate transfer card and settled down to wait after the clerk left the room.

The bank was quiet. Footsteps were lost on the vast wood and stone floors. Humans seemed to be the intruders here, temporary visitors who came and went while the bank endured the storms of the centuries, a monument to the power of capital.

Five pleasant minutes passed, then five more.

Maximo was in no hurry. He was prepared to wait quite a while for $53 million, even if it took all day. Or several days. After all, he had waited a lifetime so far. But he wouldn't have to wait long. The clerk would be back momentarily.

And he was.

He came in, looked at Maximo with an odd expression, handed him back the transfer card with just the slightest hint of a bow.

"I am sorry, señor, but the balance of this account is so low that the transfer is impossible to honor."

Maximo gaped uncomprehendingly. He swallowed, then said, "What did you say?"

"I am sorry, señor, but there has been some mistake."

"Not on my part," Maximo replied heatedly.

The clerk gave a tight little professional smile. "The bank's records are perfectly clear." He held out the transfer card. "This account contains just a few dollars over one thousand."

Maximo couldn't believe his ears. "Where did the money go?"

"Obviously, due to the bank secrecy laws I have limited discretion about what I can say."

Maximo Sedano leaped across the table at the man, grabbed him by his lapels.

"Where did the money go, fool?" he roared.

"*Someone with the proper authorization ordered the money transfered, señor. That much is obvious. I can say no more.*" And the clerk wriggled from his grasp.

The story was the same at the next two banks Maximo Sedano visited.

Each account contained just a few dollars above the minimum amount necessary to maintain the account.

The horror of his position hit Maximo like a hammer. Not only was there no money here for him, Alejo Vargas would kill him when he got back to Cuba.

He told the bank officer at the last bank he visited that he wanted to make a telephone call, and he wanted the bank officer there to talk to the person at the other end.

He called Vargas at home, caught him before he went to his office.

After he had explained about the accounts, he asked the bank officer to verify what he had said. The officer refused to touch the telephone. "The bank secrecy laws are very strict," he said self-righteously. Maximo wanted to strangle him.

Vargas had of course listened to this little exchange. "There is no money," Maximo told the secret-police chief. "Someone has stolen it."

"You ass," Vargas hissed. "*You* have stolen the money. *You* are the finance minister."

"Call the other banks, Alejo," he urged. "They are here in Zurich. I will give you their names and the account numbers. Listen to what the bank officers have to say."

"You are a capital ass, Sedano. The Swiss bankers will not talk to me. The money was deposited in Switzerland precisely *because* those bastards will talk to no one."

"I will call you from their office and have them speak to you."

"Have you lost your mind? What are you playing at?"

This was a scene from a nightmare.

"If I had the money I would not set foot in Cuba again, Vargas. We both know that. Use your head! I don't have the money: I'm coming home."

He tried to slam the instrument into its cradle and missed, sent it skittering off the table. Fumbling, he picked it up by the cord, hung the thing properly on the cradle.

The account officer looked at him with professional solicitude, much like an undertaker smiling at the next of kin.

Perhaps the banks have stolen Fidel's money, Maximo thought. *These Swiss bastards pocketed the Jews' money; maybe they are keeping Fidel's.*

He opened his mouth to say that very thing to the account officer sitting across the table, then thought better of it. He picked up his attaché case with the pistol in it and walked slowly out of the bank.

The van took Hector Sedano to La Cabana fortress in Havana. It stopped in a dark courtyard where other men were waiting. They took him into the prison, down long corridors, through iron doors that opened before him and closed after him, until finally they stood before an empty cell in the isolation area of the prison. Here they demanded his clothes, his shoes, his watch, the things in his pockets. When he stood naked someone gave him a one-piece jumpsuit. Wearing only that, he was thrust into the cell and the door was locked behind him.

The journey from the everyday world of people and voices and cares and concerns to the stark, vile reality of a prison cell is one of the most violent transitions in this life. The present and the future had been ripped from Hector Sedano, leaving only his memories of the past.

Hector was well aware of the fact that he could be physically abused, beaten, even executed, at the whim of whoever had ordered him jailed. People disappeared in Cuban prisons, never to be heard from again.

The parallels between his situation and that of Christ while awaiting his crucifixion immediately leaped to Hector's Jesuit mind. Not far behind was the realization that Fidel Castro had also been imprisoned before the revolution.

Perhaps prison is a natural stage in the life of a revolutionary. Imprisonment by the old regime for one's beliefs was de facto recognition that the beliefs were dangerous and the person who held them a worthy enemy. The person imprisoned was automatically elevated in stature and respect.

These thoughts swirled through Hector's mind as he sat on a hard wooden bunk without blankets and gave in to his emotions. He found himself shaking with anger. He paced, he pounded on the walls with his fists until they were raw.

Finally he threw himself on the bunk and lay staring into the gloom.

Angel del Mar pitched and rolled viciously as she wallowed helplessly in the swells. In every direction nothing could be seen but sea and cloudy sky. The sky was completely covered now with cloud, the wind was picking up, and the swells were getting bigger, with a shorter period between them. Aboard the boat, many people lay on their stomach and hugged the heaving deck.

Everyone on board suffered from the lack of water, some to a greater degree than others. Ocho Sedano, who had had only a few mouthfuls since the boat left Cuba and had pushed himself relentlessly, without mercy, was desperate. His eyes felt like burning coals, his skin seemed on fire, his tongue a thick, lifeless lump of dead flesh in a cracked, dry mouth.

He wasn't perspiring much now. Of all his symptoms, that one worried him the most. As an athlete he knew the importance of regulating body temperature.

Dora lay in the shade cast by the wheelhouse and said nothing. She had been sick a time or two, vomit stained her dress. She seemed to be resting easier now.

Beside her lay her father, Diego Coca. He was conscious, his eyes fierce and bright, his jaw swollen and misshapen. He hadn't moved in hours, unwilling to let anyone else have his spot in the shade.

Ocho sat heavily near Dora, scanned the sea slowly and carefully.

My God, there must be a ship! A ship or boat—something to give us food and water . . .

In all this sea there must be hundreds of fishing boats and yachts, dozens of freighters, smugglers, American Coast Guard cutters hunting smugglers, warships . . . Where the hell are they? Where are all these goddamn boats and ships?

From time to time he heard jets flying over, occasionally saw one below the clouds, but they stayed high, disappeared into the sea haze.

Under the mast an old woman sat weeping. She was the one who grieved for the captain, for some of the people who were washed overboard that first night. She wept silently, her shoulders shaking, her breath coming in gasps.

He wanted to hug her, to comfort her, but there was nothing he could say. His brother Hector would have known what to say, but Ocho did not.

He looked longingly at Dora, Dora who was once beautiful, and he could think of nothing to say to her. Nothing.

All the promise that life held, and they had thrown it away on a wild, stupid, doomed chance. Diego had led them, prodded them, demanded they go, and still he could think of nothing to say to Diego.

He was so tired, so lethargic. He had pumped for hours, just keeping up with the water. If the water came in any faster . . . well, he didn't

want to think about it. They would all die then. They would have little
chance swimming in the open sea.

Ocho slumped over onto the moving deck. He was so tired, if he
could just sleep, sleep. . . .

The old fisherman shook him awake. The sun was setting, the boat
still rolling her guts out in the swell.

"A fish . . ." He held it up, about eighteen or twenty inches long. "No
way to cook it, have to eat it raw. Keep up your strength."

With two quick swipes of his knife, the fisherman produced two
bleeding fillets. He offered one to Ocho, who closed his eyes and bit into
the raw fish. He chewed.

Someone was clawing at him, tearing at the fish.

He opened his eyes. Diego Coca was stuffing a piece of the fish in his
swollen mouth.

The old man kicked Diego in the stomach, doubled him over, then
pried his jaws apart and extracted the unchewed fish.

"He's manning the pump that keeps you afloat, you son of a bitch.
He has to eat or every one of us will die."

Diego got a grip on the fisherman's knife and lunged for him.

He grabbed for the slippery flesh, swung wildly with the knife.

This time the old man kicked him in the arm. The knife bounced
once on the deck, then landed at an angle with the blade sticking into
the wood, quivering.

The fisherman waited for the boat to roll, then kicked Diego in the
head. He went over backward and his head made a hollow thunk as it
hit the wooden deck. He went limp and lay unmoving.

Retrieving his knife, the fisherman ate his chunk of raw fish in silence.
Ocho chewed ravenously, letting the moisture bathe his mouth and
throat. He held each piece in his mouth for several seconds, sucking at
the juices, then reluctantly swallowing it down.

Dora watched him with feverish eyes. He passed her a chunk of the
fish and she rammed it into her mouth, all of it at once, chewed greedily
while eyeing the old man, almost as if she were afraid he would take it
from her.

After she swallowed it, she tried to grin.

Ocho averted his eyes.

"Your turn on the pump," the old man said.

Diego lay right where he had fallen.

Ocho got up, went into the wheelhouse and down into the engine room. The water in the bilge was sloshing around over his shoes as he began working the pump handle, up and down, up and down, endlessly.

Hours later someone came to relieve him, one of the men in the captain's family. Ocho staggered up the stairs, so exhausted he had trouble making his hands do what he wanted.

The people on deck had more fish. Ocho sat heavily by the wheelhouse. In the dim light from the stars and moon, he could see people ripping fish apart with their bare hands, stuffing flesh into their mouths, wrestling to get to fish that jumped over the rail when the boat rolled.

He collapsed into a dreamless sleep.

CHAPTER TEN

One of the butlers unlocked the bedroom door and took Mercedes to see Colonel Santana, who was standing behind Fidel's desk sorting papers. He didn't look up when she first came in. She found a chair and sat.

"The government has not yet decided when or how to announce the death of *el presidente*. No doubt it will happen in a few days, but until it does you are to remain here, in the residence, and talk to no one. Security Department people are on the switchboards and will monitor all telephone calls. The telephone lines that do not go through the switchboard have been disconnected."

He eyed her askance, then went back to sorting papers. "After the official version of Fidel's death is written and announced, you will be free to go. I remind you now that disputing the official version of events is a crime."

"Everyone swears to your history before you write it?" she snapped.

Santana looked at her and smiled. "I was searching for the proper words to explain the nub of it and they just came to you"—he snapped his fingers—"like that. It is a gift, I think. When you say it so precisely, I know you understand. Ignorance will not be a defense if there is ever a problem."

Mercedes got up from the chair and left the room.

She wandered the hallways and reception rooms, the private areas, the offices, all now deserted. Every square foot was full of memories. She could see him talking to people, bending down slightly to hear, for he had been a tall man. She could not remember when he had not been the president of Cuba. When she was a girl, he was there. As a young woman, he was there. When she married, was widowed, when he took her to be his woman . . . always, all her life there was Fidel.

Such a man he had been! She was a Latin woman, and Fidel had been the epitome of the Latin man, a brilliant, athletic man, a commanding speaker, a perfect patriot, a man who defined machismo. The facets of Fidel's personality that the non-Latin world found most irritating were those Cubans accepted as hallmarks of a man. He was self-righteous, proud, sure of his own importance and place in history, never admitted error, and refused to yield when humiliated by the outside world. He had struggled, endured, won much and lost even more, and in a way that non-Latins would never understand, had become the personification of Cuba.

And she had loved him.

In the room where he died the television cameras and lights were still in place, the wires still strung. Only Fidel's body was missing.

She stood looking at the scene, remembering it, seeing him again as he was when she had known him best.

Still magnificent.

Now the tears came, a clouding of the eyes that she was powerless to stop. She found a chair and wept silently.

Her mind wandered off on a journey of its own, recalling scenes of her life, moments with her mother, her first husband, Fidel. . . .

The tears had been dry for quite a while when she realized with a start that she was still sitting in this room. The cameras were there in front of her, mounted on heavy, wheeled tripods.

These cameras must have some kind of film in them, videotape. She went to the nearest camera and examined it. Tentatively she pushed and tugged at buttons, levers, knobs. Finally a plate popped open and there was the videocassette. She removed it from the camera and closed the plate. There was also a cassette in the second camera.

With both cassettes concealed in the folds of her dress, Mercedes strode from the room.

A wave breaking over the deck doused Ocho Sedano with lukewarm water and woke him from a troubled, exhausted sleep. *Angel del Mar* was riding very low in the water. Even as he realized that the bilges must be full, another wave washed over the deck.

Ocho dashed below. The old fisherman slumped over the pump, water sloshed nearly waist-deep in the bilge. Ocho eased him aside, began pumping. He could feel the resistance, feel the water moving through the pump. He laid into it with a will.

"Sorry," the old man said weakly. "Worn out. Just worn out."

"Go up on deck. Dry out some, drink some water."

The old man nodded, crawled slowly up the steep ladder. He slipped once, almost smashed his face on one of the steps. Finally his feet disappeared into the wheelhouse.

Three rain showers during the night had allowed everyone on board to drink their fill, to replenish dehydrated tissue, and when Ocho last looked, there were several gallons of water in the bucket under the tarp that no one could drink.

Ocho was no longer thirsty, but he was hungry as hell. There had been no more fish. Without line, hooks, bait, or nets they were unable to catch fish from the sea. Unless the creatures leaped onto the deck of the boat they were out of reach. So far, there had been no more of those.

The tarp they caught the water in gave the liquid a brackish taste, which everyone ignored. Still, water on an empty stomach made one aware of just how hungry he was.

Ocho pumped, felt his muscles loosen up, enjoyed the resistance that meant the pump was moving water. After fifteen minutes of maximum effort he could see that the water level was down about six inches. He settled in to work at a steady, sustainable pace.

The horizon remained empty. Empty! Not a boat or sail. Endless swells and sky in every direction.

It was almost as if the Lord had abandoned them, left them to die on this leaky little boat in the midst of this great vast ocean, while planes went overhead and boats and ships passed by on every side, just over the horizon.

We won't have to wait long, Ocho thought. *Our fate is very near. If the chain on this pump breaks, if we run out of energy to pump, if the swells get larger and waves start coming aboard, the boat will break up and the people will go into the sea. That would be our fate, to drown like all those people who went overboard that first night.*

They are dead now, surely. Past all caring.

Amazing how that works. Everyone has to die, but you only have to do it once. You fight like hell to get there, though, and when you arrive the world continues as if you had never been.

As he pumped he wondered about his mother, how she was doing, wondered if he should have told her he was going to America.

An hour later Ocho was still pumping, the water was down several feet and the boat was riding better in the sea. And he was wearing out. He heard someone coming down the ladder, then saw feet. It was Dora.

She clung to the ladder, watched him standing in water to his knees working the pump handle up and down, up and down, up and down.

"It's Papa," she said.

He said nothing, waited for her to go on.

"I think he has given up."

Ocho kept pumping.

"Speak to me, Ocho. Don't insult me with your silence."

Ocho switched arms without missing a stroke. "What is there to say? If he has given up, he has given up."

"Will we be rescued?"

"Am I God? How would I know?"

"I am *sick* of this boat, this ocean!" she snarled. "Sick of it, you understand?"

"I understand."

She sobbed, sniffed loudly.

Ocho kept pumping.

"I don't think you love me," she said, finally.

"I don't know that I do."

She watched him pump, up and down, rhythmically, endlessly.

"Doesn't that make you tired?"

"Yes."

"We're going to die, aren't we?"

He wiped the sweat from his face with his free hand. "All of us, sooner or later, yes."

"I mean now. This boat is going to sink. We're going to drown."

He looked at her for the first time. Her skin was stretched tightly over her face, her teeth were bared, her eyes were narrowed with an intensity he had never seen before.

"I don't know," he said gently.

"I don't want to die now."

He lowered his face so that he wouldn't have to look at her, kept the handle going up and down.

She went back up the ladder, disappeared from view.

Ocho paused, straightened as best he could under the low overhead and looked critically at the water remaining in the boat. He was gaining. He stretched, crossed himself on the off chance God might be watching, then went back to pumping.

The CIA's man in Cuba was an American, Dr. Henri Bouchard, a former college professor who lived and worked inside the American Interest Section of the Swiss embassy, a complex of buildings that in former days housed the American embassy and presumably someday would again. The Cubans watched the American diplomats very closely, so this officer had no contact with the agency's covert intelligence apparatus on the island. He kept himself busy watching television, listening to radio, collecting Cuban newspapers and publications and writing reports based on what he saw, heard, and read. His diplomatic colleagues were congenial and the life was semi-monastic, which he found agreeable.

The man who ran the covert side of the business was a Cuban who had never set foot inside the U.S. Interest Section and probably never would. He owned a wholesale seafood operation on the waterfront in Havana Harbor. Every day the fishing boats brought their catch to his pier and every day he purchased what he thought he could sell. Both the price he paid and the price he charged were set by the government: had there not been a black market for fish he would have starved.

The cover was decent. A Cuban fishing boat could meet an American boat or submarine at sea, passing messages or material in either direction. The spymaster's delivery trucks visited every restaurant, casino, and embassy in the capital. With people and things coming and going, the old man could keep his pulse on Cuba. He was called el Tiburón, the Shark.

William Henry Chance had no intention of ever meeting el Tiburón unless disaster was staring him in the face. The CIA man in the American Interest Section was another matter.

"Ah, yes, Mr. Chance. Delighted to meet you, of course."

Dr. Bouchard shook hands with Chance and Carmellini as he peered at them over the top of his glasses. He led them down several narrow hallways to a tiny, windowless cubicle in the bowels of the building.

"Sorry to say, this is the office. Security, you know. They used to store food in here. Damp but quiet." He took a stack of newspapers off the only guest chair and moved them to his desk, extracted a folding metal chair from behind his desk and unfolded it for Carmellini, then settled into his chair.

The knees of all three men almost touched. "So how are you enjoying Cuba?"

"Fascinating," Chance muttered.

"Yes, isn't it?" Professor Bouchard beamed complacently. "Six years I've been here, and I don't ever want to leave. I don't miss the snow, I'll tell you, or the faculty politics, feuds, dog-eat-dog jealousy over department budgets—thank God I'm out of all that."

Chance nodded, unwilling to get to the point.

"We met once or twice before, I think," Chance reminded Bouchard.

"Oh, yes, I do seem to recall. . . ."

They discussed it.

"My associate, Mr. Carmellini. I don't think you've met him."

The pleasantries over at last, Chance edged around to business. "You have a few items in your storeroom that we need to borrow, I believe."

"Certainly. The inventory is in the safe. If you gentlemen will step into the hall for a moment . . ."

They did so and he fiddled with the dial of the safe. When he had the file he wanted and the safe was closed and locked, he seated himself again at his desk. Chance sat back down. Carmellini remained standing.

"This is the inventory, I'm sure. Yes. What is it you want?"

"Two Rugers with silencers, ammunition, two garroting wires, two fighting knives, a dozen disposable latex gloves, two self-contained gas masks—"

"Let's see . . ." The professor ran his finger down the list. "Guns, check. Ammo, okay. Knives . . . knives . . . oh, here they are. Wires, garroting, check . . . gloves . . . masks. Yes, I think we have what you need. Do you want to take this stuff with you?"

"I think so. In a suitcase of some kind, if you can manage that."

"I'll have to give you one of mine. You can return it or pay me for it, as you prefer."

"We'll try to return it."

"That's best, I think. The accounting department is so difficult about expense accounts. You gentlemen wait here; I'll see what I can do. While you're waiting would you like a cup of coffee, a soft drink?"

"I'm fine," Chance said.

"Don't worry about me," Carmellini said.

"This will take a few minutes," the professor advised. "Would you like to wait in the courtyard? The flora there is my hobby, and the eagle from the Maine Memorial is a rare work of art."

"That's the big eagle over the doorway?"

"Yes. After the revolution Castro demanded it be removed from the Maine Memorial. That was about the time he announced he was a communist, before the Bay of Pigs. Difficult era for everyone."

"Ah, yes. We'll find our way."

"I'll look for you in the courtyard when I have your items," the professor said, and scurried off.

The eagle was huge. "Quite a work of art," Carmellini muttered.

"Too big for you," Chance said.

"I don't know about that," Carmellini replied, and glanced around to see if there was any way to get the thing out of the mission ground with a crane. "Run a mobile construction crane up to the wall, send a man down on the hook, haul it out. I could snatch it and be gone in six or seven minutes."

Chance didn't even bother to frown. Carmellini had a habit of chaffing him in an unoffensive way; protest would be futile.

"The professor is the most incurious man I've ever met," Tommy Carmellini said conversationally a few minutes later.

"He doesn't want to know too much."

"He doesn't want to know anything," Carmellini protested. "People who don't ask obvious questions worry me."

"Hmmm," said William Henry Chance, who didn't seem at all worried.

The professor came looking for them a half hour later. After he had scrawled an illegible signature on a detailed custody card, Chance offered the professor a photo of a man that his surveillance team had taken outside the University of Havana science building. The man was in his sixties, slightly overweight, balding, and looking at the camera almost full face. He didn't see the camera that took the picture, of course, since it was in the van.

"If you could, Professor, I would like you to send this to Washington. I want to know who this man is."

"American?" Dr. Bouchard asked, accepting the photo and glancing at it.

"I have no idea, sir. We've seen him around here and there and wondered who he might be. Would you have the folks in Langley try to find out?"

"Of course," the professor said, and put the photo in his pocket.

Toad Tarkington was in a rare foul mood. He snapped at the yeomen, snarled at the flag lieutenant, fumed over the message board, and generally glowered at anyone who looked his way.

This state of affairs could not go on, of course, so he went to his stateroom, put on his running togs, and went on deck for a jog. The tropical sea air, the long foaming rollers, the puffy clouds running on the breeze, the deep blue of the Caribbean—all of it made his mood more foul.

None of the leads to find the *Colón* had borne fruit. The ship was still missing, the captain and crew had stayed aboard her all the time she was tied to the pier in Guantánamo, the gloom seemed impenetrable. The air wing was still searching, but as yet, nothing! And of course the temperature of the rhetoric coming from the White House and Pentagon was rising by the hour.

Toad was jogging aft from the bow when a petty officer from the admiral's staff flagged him down. "The AIs have a photo of the *Colón*!"

"Where is she?"

"Aground on a reef off the north shore of Cuba."

Toad bolted for the hatchway that led down into the ship, the petty officer right behind.

The photo was of the *Colón*, all right. The ship looked as if it were wedged on some rocks, almost as if it grounded during a high tide. Now the tide was out and the *Colón* was marooned.

"When was this picture taken?" Toad demanded of the air intelligence officers.

"Yesterday."

"And no one recognized it?"

"Not until today."

Toad growled. "Have you passed this to the admiral?"

"Yes, sir."

"Show me the location."

The AI pinpointed the location on a sectional chart.

Toad called Jake Grafton. "I want to see that ship," Jake said. "As soon as possible. We'll take an F-14 with a TARPS package." TARPS stood for tactical air reconnaissance pods. Each pod contained two cameras and an infrared line scanner.

Cuba is an island surrounded by islands, over sixteen hundred of them. Most of the islands on Cuba's north shore are small, uninhabited, rocky bits of tropical paradise, or so they looked to Jake Grafton, who saw them through binoculars from the front seat of an F-14.

The ship was about three miles offshore, stranded on rocks that just pierced the surface of the sea. The breaking surf looked white through the binoculars.

The freighter was plainly visible, listing slightly. Some of the weapons containers were visible on the main deck. Jake checked the photo in his lap, which was taken yesterday by an F/A-18 Hornet pilot with a hand-held 35-mm camera. Yep, the containers visible in the photo were still in place aboard the ship.

Although the Cubans claimed a twelve-mile territorial limit, the United States recognized but three. *Nuestra Señora de Colón* was stranded on a reef in international waters, the AIs assured Jake. They had checked with the State Department, they said.

South of the ship was the entrance to Bahia de Nipe, a decent-sized shallow-water bay.

Was the ship on her way into the bay when she went on the rocks?

Jake was making his initial photo passes a mile to seaward of the *Colón*. In the event the Cubans chose to send interceptors to chase him away, he had a flight of F-14s ten miles farther north providing cover. Above them was an EA-6B Prowler electronic warfare airplane, listening for and ready to jam any Cuban fire-control radar that came on the air. According to the electronic warfare detection gear in Jake's cockpit, he was being painted only by search radars. That, as he well knew, could change any second.

He had just completed a photo pass from west to east and was turning to seaward when the E-2 came on the air. "Battlestar One, we have company. Bogey twenty miles west of your posit, heading your way. Looks like a Fulcrum." A Fulcrum was a MiG-29.

Jake keyed his radio mike. "Roger that. I'll make one more photo pass before he gets here, then exit the area to the north."

He tucked the nose down and let the Tomcat accelerate. The plane was alive in his hand—the descending jet bumped and bounced in the swirling, roiling tropical air under the puffy cumulus clouds drifting along on the trade wind.

"Cameras are on and running," Toad Tarkington said from the back seat.

Staying just outside the three-mile limit, Jake flew past the stern of the stranded freighter one more time, which meant he was probably getting fine views of her stern and oblique views of her flanks.

"Since we're here . . ." he muttered, and dropped a wing as he eased the stick and throttles forward.

In the back seat, Toad Tarkington was monitoring the recon package. "I sure am glad we're staying out of Cuban airspace," he told Jake. "I'd feel a lot more comfortable outside the twelve-mile limit, but that's asking too much of this technology. A ship sitting on the rocks like this, looks like a setup to me. They're looking to mousetrap some dude flying by snapping pictures and perforate his heinie."

"Yeah," said Jake Grafton, and leveled off at a hundred feet above the water. He had the F-14 flying parallel with the axis of the ship, offset with the ship to his right since the recon package was mounted under his right engine.

"Got the cameras and IR scanner going?"

"Oh, yeah, looking real good," Toad said, just as he picked up the seascape passing by the canopy with his peripheral vision. He looked right just in time to see the freighter flash by, then Jake Grafton pulled back on the stick and lit the afterburners. The Tomcat's nose rose to sixty degrees above the horizon and it went up like a rocket, corkscrewing back toward the ocean, as the E-2 Hawkeye radar operator called the bogey for the Showtime F-14 crews who were Jake's armed guard. Both RIOs said they had the bogey on radar.

"Like I said," Toad told Jake, "sure is great we're staying outside Cuban airspace."

"Great," his pilot agreed.

"Don't want to piss anybody off."

"Oh, no."

"Wonder why that ship ended up where it did?"

"Maybe the photos will tell us."

"Bogey is six miles aft, Battlestar One," the E-2 Hawkeye radar operator said, "four hundred knots, closing from your eight o'clock."

"You wanna turn toward him, Admiral, let me pick him up on the radar?" Toad asked this question.

"No, let's clear to seaward."

"I got him visual," Toad said as the Tomcat climbed past fifteen thousand feet. "He's a little above us, pulling lead."

"Pulling lead?" Jake looked over his left shoulder, found the MiG-29.

"He could take a gunshot anytime," Toad said.

"He's rendezvousing," Jake said, "Gonna join on our left wing, looks like."

And that is what the MiG did. He closed gently, his nose well out in front, his axis almost parallel, a classic rendezvous. The MiG stabilized in a parade position, about four feet between wingtips, stepped down perhaps three feet. Despite the bumpy air the MiG held position effortlessly.

Jake Grafton and Toad Tarkington sat staring at the helmeted figure of Carlos Corrado in the other cockpit. Toad lifted his 35-mm camera, snapped off a dozen photos of the Cuban fighter and the two air-to-air missiles hanging on the racks.

"Think he knows we were inside the three-mile limit?" Toad asked Jake.

"His GCI controller told him, probably."

Corrado stayed glued to the F-14. He paid no attention to the other Tomcats that came swooping in to join the formation, didn't even bother to glance at them.

Jake Grafton slowly advanced his throttles to 95 percent RPM. The MiG was right with him. Leaving the power set, he got the nose coming up, began to roll away from the MiG, up and over to the inverted and right on through, coming on with the G to keep the nose from scooping out . . . a medium-sloppy barrel roll.

Now a barrel roll to the left. The two F-14s behind Carlos Corrado moved into trail position, behind and stepped down slightly, to more easily stay with the maneuvering airplanes, but Corrado held his position in left parade as if he were welded there.

Now a loop. Up, up, up and over the top, G increasing down the backside, the sea and sky changing position very nicely, the sun dancing across the cockpit.

"This guy's pretty good," Toad remarked grudgingly.

"Pretty good?"

"Okay, he's a solid stick."

Now a half loop and half roll at the top, fly along straight and level for a count of five, roll again and half turn into a lopsided split S, one offset from the vertical by forty-five degrees. Coming out of the dive Jake let the nose climb until it was pointed straight up; he slowly rolled around his axis, then pulled the plane on over onto its back and waited until the nose was forty-five degrees below the horizon before rolling wings level and beginning his pullout. Through it all Carlos Corrado stayed glued in position on Jake's wing.

Coming out of the last maneuver, Jake Grafton turned eastward. The MiG-29 stayed with the American fighters for fifteen more minutes, until the flight was near the eastern tip of Cuba, Cape Maisi, and turning south. Only then did Carlos Corrado wave at Jake and Toad and lower his nose to cross under the F-14.

Out of the corner of his eye Jake saw Toad salute the MiG pilot as he turned away to the west.

"Wonder why that ship ended up on those rocks?" Toad Tarkington mused aloud. Jake Grafton, Gil Pascal, Lieutenant Colonel Eckhardt, Toad, and several of the photo interpretation specialists were bent over a table in the Air Intelligence spaces studying the photographs from the F-14's reconnaissance pod.

"Maybe the person at the con was lost," the senior AI speculated.

"Or didn't know the waters," the marine suggested.

"Maybe the Cubans wanted it there," Gil said.

Jake Grafton used a magnifying glass to study photos of the island closest to the stranded freighter.

"Here's a crew setting up an artillery piece," he said, and straightened so everyone could see. "If they planned to strand the ship on those rocks, one would think they would have set up guns and a few SAM batteries in advance."

"Maybe that's what they want us to think."

"How far is the ship from the nearest dry land?"

"Three point two nautical miles, sir." That was one of the photo interpretation specialists, a first class petty officer. "If you look at this satellite photo of the main island, Admiral, you will see that there are two SAM batteries near this small port ten miles south of where the Colón went on the rocks."

"That's probably where the ship was going when it hit the rocks," Jake said. "Or where it had been. So how many artillery and missile sites are in the area?"

"Four."

"We'll have EA-6B Prowlers and F/A-18 Hornets overhead, HARM missiles on the rails, F-14s as cover. The instant one of those fire-control radars comes on the air, I want it taken out."

"When do you want to land aboard the ship?" Eckhardt asked.

Jake Grafton looked at his watch. "One in the morning."

"Five hours from now?"

"Can we do it?"

"If we push."

"Let's push. I talked to General Totten in the Pentagon. He agrees—we should inspect that ship as soon as possible. For me, that's five hours from now. We will go in three Ospreys. The lead Osprey will put Commander Tarkington and me on the ship; Lieutenant Colonel Eckhardt will be in the second bird leading a rescue team to pull us out if anything goes wrong. The third Osprey will contain another ten-man team, led by your executive officer."

Captain Pascal zeroed in immediately. "Do the people in Washington know that you intend to board that ship, Admiral?"

"No, and I'm not going to ask."

"Sir, if you get caught—a two-star admiral on a ship stranded in Cuban waters?"

"The ship is in international waters. We must find out what happened aboard the *Colón* after it left Guantánamo. The stakes are very high. I am going to take a personal look. While I'm gone, Gil, you have the con."

"Admiral, with all due respect, sir, I think you should take more than just one person with you. Why not a half dozen well-armed marines?"

"I don't know what's on that ship," Jake explained. "There may be people aboard, there may be a biological hazard, it may be booby-trapped. It just makes sense to have a point man explore the unknown before we risk very many lives. I am going to be the point man because I want to personally see what is there, and I make the rules. Understand?"

The news about the loss of a ship loaded with biological weapons arrived in Washington with the impact of a high-explosive warhead on a cruise missile.

When the National Security Council met to be briefed about the ship the president was there, and he was in an ugly mood.

"Let me get this straight," he said, interrupting the national security adviser, who was briefing the group. "We decided to remove our stockpile of biological and chemical warheads from Guantánamo Bay when we heard Castro might be developing biological weapons of his own. Is that correct?"

"The timing was incidental, sir. They were scheduled to be moved."

"Scheduled to be moved next year," the president said acidly. "We hurried things along when the CIA got wind that El Gato might be shipping lab equipment to Cuba. Will you grant me that?"

"Yes, sir."

"Just for the record, why in hell were those damned things in Gitmo in the first place?"

"A computer error, sir, back when the Pentagon was prepositioning war supplies at Guantánamo. Somehow the CBW material got on the list, and by the time the error was discovered, the stuff was on its way."

The president's lip curled in a sneer. "Did this circle jerk happen under my administration?"

"No, sir. The previous one."

The president glanced at the ceiling. "Thank you, God."

He took a deep breath, exhaled, then said, "So we decided to clean up old mistakes. We didn't want to take the chance Castro knew of our CBW stockpiles at Gitmo when we started fulminating about his." The president was addressing the national security adviser. "But to cover our asses, you wanted a carrier battle group that just happened to be in the Caribbean to keep an eye on things while you got the weapons out. Just having the navy hanging around would keep the Cubans honest, you said."

"Yes, sir."

"And now a ship full of weapons from the Gitmo warehouse is on the rocks off the Cuban coast."

"The ship is on the rocks, but we don't know if any weapons are still aboard."

"Are you going to court-martial the admiral in charge of the battle group?" the president asked the chairman of the joint chiefs, General Howard D. "Tater" Totten, a small, gray-haired man who looked like he was hiding inside the green, badged, bemedaled uniform of a four-star army general.

"No, sir. He was told to quote monitor unquote the situation in Guantánamo, not escort cargo ships. He actually had the cargo ship that was hijacked escorted out of Cuban waters, but he didn't direct that it be escorted all the way to Norfolk. No one did, because apparently no one thought an escort necessary."

"Was the ship hijacked?"

"We don't know, sir. We've been unable to contact it by radio."

"How are we going to find out if the weapons are still aboard?"

"Send marines aboard tonight to look."

"I don't think that ship is stranded in international waters," the secretary of state said.

"Your department told us it was," Totten shot back.

"That was a first impression by junior staffers. Our senior people demanded a closer look. We are just not sure. The determination depends on where one draws the line that defines the mouth of the bay. Reasonable people can disagree."

Totten took a deep breath. "Mr. President, we don't know what happened aboard that ship. We don't know if the weapons are aboard. If they have been removed, we need to learn where they went. Now is not the time to split hairs over the nuances of international law. Let's board the ship and get some answers, then the lawyers can argue to their hearts' content."

"That's the problem with you uniformed testosterone types," the secretary of state snarled. "You think you can violate the law anytime it suits your purposes."

The president of the United States was a cautious man by nature, a blow-dried politician who had maneuvered with the wind at his back all his life. His national security adviser knew him well, General Totten thought, when he said, "Preliminary indications are that the stranded ship is in international waters, Mr. President. The naval commander on the scene has the authority to examine a wreck in international waters if he feels it prudent to do so. Let him make the decision and report back what he finds."

"That's right," the president said. "I think that is the proper way for us to approach this."

"Will you pass that on to the battle group commander?" the national security adviser asked General Totten.

The general reached for an encrypted telephone.

Jake Grafton and Toad Tarkington went aboard the V-22 parked at the head of the line on the flight deck of USS *United States*. Marines filed aboard the second and third airplane. Tonight the carrier was thirty miles northeast of Cape Maisi—the distance to the stranded freighter was a bit over a hundred miles.

Jake was more nervous than he had been in a long, long time. Before he left the mission planning spaces this evening, he looked again at the chart that depicted the threat envelope of the two surface-to-air missile sites on the Cuban mainland just a few miles from the stranded freighter, *Nuestra Señora de Colón*. The freighter was well inside those envelopes, and the Ospreys would be also.

Jake had had a long talk with the EA-6B electronic warfare crews and the four F/A-18 Hornets that would be over the Ospreys carrying HARMs. HARM stood for high-speed antiradiation missile. Enemy radars were the targets of HARMs, which rode the beams right into the dishes. HARMs even had memories, so if an enemy operator turned off his radar after a HARM was launched, the missile would still fly to the memorized location.

"If the Cubans turn on the SAM radars, open fire," Jake told his guardian angels. "Don't wait until their missiles are in the air."

"Yes, sir."

Jake had heard nothing from Washington waffling on the assertion that the *Colón* was in international waters, so as far as he was concerned, that fact was a given. The Cubans had no right to fire on ships or planes in international waters. If they did, Jake Grafton would shoot back. Of course, if the Cubans shot first, they would probably kill a planeload or two of Americans, Jake Grafton included. The crews of the EA-6B Prowlers and Hornets were well aware of that reality.

As he sat in the Osprey Jake Grafton wondered if the enlisted marines in the other two planes understood the risks involved in this mission. He suspected they didn't know, and in truth probably didn't want to. Their job was to obey their officers; if the officers led them into action, fretting about the odds wasn't going to do any good at all.

That thought led straight to another: Did he understand the risks?

"You okay, Admiral?"

That was Toad.

Jake Grafton nodded, smiled. A friend like Tarkington was a rare thing indeed. He hadn't asked Toad if he wanted to risk his life on this mission; the commander would have been insulted if he had.

The warm noisy darkness inside the plane seemed comforting, somehow, as if the plane were a loud, safe womb. After takeoff Jake sat for five minutes with his eyes closed, savoring the flying sensations, recharging his batteries. Then he made his way toward the cockpit and squatted behind the pilots, both of whom were wearing night-vision goggles. From this vantage point Jake could see the computer displays on the instrument panel. The flight engineer handed him a helmet, already plugged in, so that he could talk to the pilots and listen to the radio.

He heard the Prowler and Hornets checking in, the F-14s, the S-3 tankers.

He heard Rita call twenty miles to go to the mission coordinator in the E-2 Hawkeye. She had the Osprey flying at a thousand feet above the water, inbound at 250 knots.

"Visibility is five or six miles," she told Jake over the intercom. "Some rain showers around. Wind out of the west northwest."

"Okay."

"We'll do it like we planned," she continued, making sure Jake, the copilot, and her crew chief all understood what was to happen. "I'll hover into the wind, then back down toward the ship, put the ramp over the fantail."

"Ten miles," the copilot sang out.

Jake took off the aircraft helmet and donned a marine tactical helmet, which contained a small radio that broadcast on one of four tactical frequencies. Repeaters in the Ospreys picked up the low-powered helmet transmissions and rebroadcast them so that everyone on the tactical net could hear, including the mission coordinator in the E-2, the people aboard the carrier, and the pilots of the airborne planes.

Jake pulled on a set of night-vision goggles and looked forward, through the Osprey windscreen. The night was gone, banished. He could see the stranded freighter, still several miles away, see the surf breaking on the rocks, the containers stacked on deck, the empty sea in all directions. He looked toward the nearest land, an island just over three miles away; he could just make out the line of breaking surf.

The Osprey was slowing: Rita rotated the engine nacelles toward the vertical position as she transitioned from wing-borne cruising flight to pure helicopter operation. Computers monitored her control inputs and gradually increased the effectiveness of the rotor swashplates as flaperons, elevators and rudders lost their effectiveness due to the decreasing airspeed. The transition from wing-borne to rotor-borne flight was smooth, seamless, a technological miracle, and Jake Grafton appreciated it as such.

Jake Grafton kept his eyes on the ship. No people in sight. The bow of the ship was on the rocks. The ship had a small forecastle superstructure, with the main superstructure and bridge on the stern of the ship. The ship's cargo was in holds amidships, with extra containers stacked between the bridge and forecastle. The ship had two large cranes, one forward, one aft. She had a single stack, and probably—given her size—only one screw.

Jake could see that the containers on the deck were jumbled about, several obviously open and empty. Others, a whole bunch, seemed to be missing.

Now Rita swung into the wind, away from the *Colón.*

The ramp at the back of the aircraft was open, with Toad and the crew chief waiting there. Jake Grafton walked aft to join them.

The crew chief gave Rita directions on the ICS, back fifty feet, down ten, as she watched her progress on a small television screen that had been rigged in the cockpit for this mission.

Lower, closer to the ship . . . and the ramp touched the deck.

"Go, go, go," the crew chief shouted.

Jake spoke into his voice-activated boom mike: "Let's go!"

The fixed deck of the stranded freighter felt strange after a half hour in the moving Osprey. The wash from the mighty, 38-foot rotors was a mini-hurricane here on the fantail, a mixture of charged air and sea spray, dirt, and trash from the deck and containers.

Jake and Toad crouched on the deck as the Osprey moved away. The ramp had been against the deck for no more than fifteen seconds.

Jake spoke into his lip mike, made sure the mission coordinator could hear him. Gripping an M-16 in the ready position, Toad led them forward along the main deck. Jake Grafton carried a video camera, which was running, and two 35-mm cameras. The video and one of the still cameras were loaded with infrared film, the other 35-mm contained regular film and was equipped with a flash attachment.

First stop was the main deck, where he inspected the containers there.

Many had doors hanging open, some still had the doors closed, but all the containers were empty. Although he wasn't sure how many containers were supposed to be there, the area around the main hatches was remarkably clear. The hatches themselves were not properly installed. One hatch was ajar.

No people about. None. The ship seemed totally deserted and firmly aground. Jake could feel no motion.

He used a flashlight to look into the hold. This section of the hold didn't seem to be full. Many of the containers were open.

Filming with the video camera, pausing now and then to shoot still photos, the two men searched until they found a ladder that led down into the hold. Toad waited by the hatchway, his M-16 at the ready.

Jake went down the ladder into the dark bay.

He had his night-vision goggles off now; in total darkness they were useless. He snapped on the flashlight, looked around, fingered the pistol in the holster on his hip.

This hold was half-empty, with the packing material that had been wrapped around the warheads strewn everywhere. The place was knee-deep in trash. The containers that were there were obviously empty.

Jake didn't stay but a minute or so, then he climbed back up the ladder.

"Let's check the bridge," he said to Toad over the tactical radio.

They went aft along the main deck and climbed an outside ladder to the bridge, which stretched from one side of the ship to the other.

"They've cleaned her out," Toad remarked over the tac net.

"Yeah," Jake replied, and kept climbing.

On the bridge Jake again removed the night-vision goggles and used a flashlight. He wanted to see whatever was there in natural light.

What he found were bloodstains. A lot of blood had been spilled here on the bridge; pools of congealed, sticky black blood lay on the deck. People had walked in it, tracking the stuff all over.

"Not everyone was on the payroll," Jake muttered, and quickly completed his search. He aimed the video camera at the stains, then snapped a couple photos with the regular camera using the flash.

Toad used a flashlight to search for the log book and ship's documents. "The safe is open and empty," he told Jake Grafton. He came over to watch the admiral work the cameras.

"Where in hell are the warheads?" Toad asked aloud.

"The Americans are aboard the *Colón*, Colonel."

The man shook Santana awake. He held a candle, which flickered in the tropical breeze coming through the screen.

Santana sat up and tossed the sheet aside. He consulted his watch.

He got out of bed, walked out onto the porch of the small house and searched the night sea with binoculars. Nothing.

He lowered the binoculars, stood listening.

Yes, he could hear engine sounds, very faint . . . jet engines, the whopping of rotors. . . .

"How long have they been aboard?"

"I don't know, sir. With this wind it is hard to hear helicopter noises. When I heard the voices on the radio, I came to wake you."

"Admiral, look at this." Toad came over to where Jake was standing, showed him the screen of a small battery-operated computer. "I'm picking up radio transmissions, even when we are not using the tactical net. Something on the ship is broadcasting."

Jake Grafton pulled his mike down to his lips. "Hawkeye, this is Cool Hand. Has anyone been picking up radio transmissions from the target?"

"Cool Hand, Hawkeye. They started about a minute ago, sir, when you went up on the bridge. We have them now."

"What kind of transmissions?"

"Amazingly, sir, I'm receiving clear channel radio. I'm actually hearing you talk on this other frequency."

"What the hell? . . ."

Oh, sweet Jesus!

"This damned ship is wired to blow. The bastards are listening to us right now. We gotta get off!" With that he gave Toad a push toward the door of the bridge. Toad ran. Jake Grafton was right behind him.

Colonel Santana couldn't see anything through the binoculars, but he heard those American voices coming through the radio speaker. The microphones were on the bridge.

"Anytime, Tomas," he said.

Tomas keyed the radio transmit button three times. A flower of red and yellow fire blossomed in the darkness.

Santana aimed the binoculars and focused them as the last of the explosions faded. He could see the flicker of flames as they spread aboard *Nuestra Señora de Colón*. These Americans! So predictable! Santana chuckled as he watched.

"Into the ocean," Jake shouted.

Toad vaulted over the rail into the blackness. As he fell he wondered if there were rocks or salt water below.

Toad Tarkington and Jake Grafton were in midair when the bridge exploded behind them. Jake felt the thermal pulse and the first concussion.

Then the dark, cool water closed over his head and he went completely under.

As he began to rise toward the surface, he felt more explosions from inside the ship. The concussions reached him through the water like spent punches from a prizefighter.

When he got his head above water, flames illuminated the night.

Above the noise of the explosions and flames, he could hear Tarkington cursing.

CHAPTER ELEVEN

After Rita pulled them out of the ocean and flew them back to the carrier, Toad Tarkington and Jake Grafton were checked in sick bay, then they showered and tried to snatch a few hours sleep.

Toad gave up on sleep—too much adrenaline. He lay in his bunk thinking about leaping over the bridge rail without knowing whether rocks or water lay beneath, and he shivered. The shock of the impact with the water had been almost a deliverance.

He turned on the light and looked at the photos of Rita and Tyler he had taped to the bulkhead. *Really stupid, Toad-man, really stupid. Grafton must have checked the location of the rocks, knew where he could jump and where he couldn't, and you never once thought to look.*

He got up, dressed, and headed for the computers, where he typed out a classified E-mail for the people at the National Security Agency. After breakfast he was ready to brief Jake Grafton and Gil Pascal.

"Before she was stranded, *Nuestra Señora de Colón* went into this little Cuban port at the west end of Bahia de Nipe. She was there for six hours, then she steamed out and went on the rocks where we found her. If you look at this satellite photo you can see a boat nearby, probably taking the crew off after she piled up. The folks at NSA in Fort Meade say they can see ropes from the ship to this boat that the crewmen could slide down."

Toad Tarkington stood back so Jake Grafton and Gil Pascal could study the satellite photos that he had pinned to a bulletin board in the mission planning spaces.

"Where are the weapons now?" Gil Pascal asked.

"In this fish warehouse." Toad pointed at the photo with the tip of a pencil. "Right here."

"It's an easy SEAL target," the Chief of Staff commented.

"Too easy," Jake Grafton said, then regretted it.

"When did the freighter reach this port?"

"Noon, three days ago."

"And they spent the afternoon off-loading it?"

"Yes. It went onto the rocks that night."

"Too easy." Now he was sure.

"What do you mean?"

"These people aren't stupid. They know about satellite reconnaissance; they knew we would see them off-loading the ship in this port; they wanted us to see that. The question is, Why did they go to all the trouble of putting on a show for us? What are they hiding?"

Toad flipped through the satellite photos, looking at date-time groups. "Here is the ship coming into the bay, there it is against the pier at Antilla, here it is being off-loaded, here is an IR photo of it going out to the rocks after dark, here is an IR shot of the freighter and the boat that probably took the crew off."

"Radar images?"

Toad had a handful of those too.

"I want to know where this ship was between the time the destroyer left it and the time it showed up in this Cuban port."

"NSA is still working on that stuff. Perhaps in a few hours, sir," Toad said.

"Call me."

"The weapons weren't on the ship," the national security adviser told the president in the Oval Office. "The ship was empty when it went on the rocks. Apparently the Cubans booby-trapped it—the thing exploded a few minutes after the admiral went aboard to inspect it."

"Casualties?"

"None, sir. We were lucky. If the admiral had taken more people with him, I can't say the results would have been the same."

"So where are the weapons?"

"NSA thinks they are in a warehouse on the waterfront in the center of the town of Antilla. They are studying the satellite sensor data now."

"Shit!" said the president.

William Henry Chance and Tommy Carmellini ate dinner in the main restaurant of the largest casino on the Malecon. The fact that 99 percent of the Cubans on the island didn't eat this well was on Chance's mind as he watched the waiters come and go amid the tables filled with European diners. Plenty amid poverty, an old Cuban story so common as to be unremarkable.

Carmellini merely played with his food; he was too tense to enjoy eating, had too much on his mind. Chance tried to concentrate on a superb string quartet playing classical music in the corner of the room.

To the best of his knowledge, he and Carmellini had not been followed on their expeditions around the capital, although he knew very well that a really first-class surveillance would be impossible to detect. With enough men, enough radios and automobiles, the subjects could be kept in sight at all times yet no one would be directly behind them, following where they could be seen or noticed. The subjects would seem to be alone, moving of their own will through the urban environment, yet their isolation would be an illusion.

He knew all that, yet he could detect no tails or signs of people that might be watching, taking an interest in him or Carmellini. Chance was no neophyte—he had a great deal of experience in this line of work, he knew what was possible and he knew what was likely.

He thought about all these things as the flawlessly decked-out Cuban waiter served coffee. The music formed a backdrop to the babble of conversation from his fellow diners, who were gabbing in at least five languages, perhaps six.

Chance sipped the coffee, let his eyes wander the room. No one was paying the slightest attention. Not a single furtive glance, no hastily broken eye contact, no one studiously ignoring him.

Well, if he and Carmellini were going to do it, tonight was the night. The longer they stayed in Havana, the more likely it was that they would attract the interest of the Department of State Security, the secret police. The interest of Santana and Alejo Vargas.

The truth was that Vargas might have burned them, might have devoted the resources necessary to learn everything about them. Vargas or his minions might be waiting tonight in the science hall, waiting to catch them red-handed, to embarrass the United States, perhaps even to execute Chance and Carmellini as spies.

In this line of work the imponderables were always huge, risks impossible to quantify. Still, he and Carmellini were going to have to look inside that building, see what was there.

If there was a biological weapons program in Cuba, it had to be in that building, which housed the largest, best-equipped laboratory known to be on the island. And the most knowledgeable people were nearby, the microbiologists and chemists and skilled lab technicians that would be needed to produce large quantities of microorganisms.

Chance was well aware that the most serious technical problem a researcher faced when constructing a biological weapon was how to keep the microorganisms alive inside a warhead or aerosol bomb for long periods of time. Some biological agents were easier to store than others, which was why they were most often selected for weapons research. For example, the spores of anthrax were very stable, as were the spores of the fungal disease coccidioidomycosis, which incapacitated but rarely killed its victims. Of course, the naturally occurring strains of an infectious disease could have been altered to make the microorganisms more stable, more virulent, or to overcome widespread immunity: years ago researchers produced a highly infective strain of poliomyelitis virus for just these reasons.

Idly he wondered about the microbiologist who ran the program. Who was he? What were his motivations? Perhaps that question answered itself in a totalitarian society, but it was worth researching, when he had some time. If he ever had some time.

"Ready?" Chance muttered to Carmellini, who drained the last of his coffee.

The two men paid their bill in cash and left the casino. They got into a car parked at the curb, one driven by one of their associates, and sped off into the night.

In a dark, deserted lane on the outskirts of the city the car in which Chance and Carmellini rode met the former telephone van they had used before, but now it bore the logo of a wholesale food supplier.

Inside the van Carmellini and Chance changed into black trousers, a black pullover shirt with a high collar, black socks, and black rubber-soled shoes. When they were dressed, they sat listening to the insects, drinking water, monitoring a radio frequency. One of their colleagues was observing the science building at the university. He checked in every fifteen minutes. So far he had seen nothing out of the ordinary.

"Why did you get into this line of work?" Chance asked Carmellini as they sat listening to the chirp of crickets.

"The challenge of it, I guess. I had an uncle who cracked a few safes . . . he was a legendary figure. The only time he ever went to the pen was for tax evasion: he did a couple years that time. I was always asking him questions. He told me if I wanted to be a safecracker, go to work for a firm that manufactured and installed the things. That was good advice. I installed safes for several summers while I was in college, got too cocky for my own good. Thought I had this stuff figured out, you know? One thing led to another, and before you know it I was cracking the things."

Chance nodded.

"Here I am still at it. Only this time I won't go to the pen if they catch me."

"Yeah. The Cubans will probably execute us as soon as Vargas gets through with us, if there's anything left to execute."

"The way I figure it, I finally made the big leagues."

"You optimists, always looking on the bright side."

"Which brings up a point. You got us garroting wires and knives and pistols. I never carry weapons. I'm a safecracker, not a killer."

"You'll probably become a dead safecracker if they catch you in there."

"I've never carried weapons. Ever."

"A wise precaution if you are burgling gentlemen's safes. You're in the major leagues now."

"Listen, Chance—"

"This isn't a game, Tommy. Speaking for myself, I want to keep breathing. You'll do as I say."

The driver parked the van in an alley near the science building. He sat hunched over the wheel watching people on the sidewalks as Chance and Carmellini examined the building through binoculars. They were behind him, in the body of the van, looking forward through the windshield.

The way in, they decided, was through the roof. To get there, they would need to go into the building beside the science building, a lecture hall, ascend to the top floor, then get access to the roof. From here they would need to cross to the roof of the science hall, then find a way in.

The lecture hall was locked at night, though it was not guarded.

It was one in the morning when the van stopped in the empty alley behind the lecture hall. The two men in back pulled on latex gloves, swung on backpacks, then went out the van's side door.

The door was not wired with an alarm. Carmellini picked the lock in thirty seconds, and they were in.

The van drove away as the door closed behind them.

They stood in the darkness letting their eyes adjust to the gloom.

Carmellini led off. Behind him Chance took out his pistol and thumbed off the safety, keeping the pistol pointed downward at the floor.

The weak light filtering through windows in classrooms and thence through open doors to the hallway did little to aleviate the darkness. The floors were uncarpeted concrete, the walls massive masonry, the ceilings at least twelve feet high. The building was devoid of decoration or even a trace of architectural imagination.

Carmellini moved like a shadow, making no detectable noise. Chance seemed to be making enough noise for both of them. He could hear himself breathing and his heart pounding, could hear the echoes of his footfalls in the cavernous hallways.

Keeping near the wall, they climbed the stairs to the second floor. Carmellini moved slowly, steadily, listened carefully before turning every corner, then lowered his head, keeping it well below the place one would naturally look for it, and peeped around the corner. Then he slithered around the corner out of sight; Chance followed as silently as he could.

The top of the staircase put them out on the fourth floor of the building. There had to be another staircase, probably very narrow, leading to the roof. Where might it be?

Carmellini was ready to go explore when he suddenly held up his hand. He held a finger to his lips.

Chance listened with all the concentration he could muster.

He *could* hear something! Voices?

Carmellini slowly inched along the hallway toward an open door, then froze there.

He came back down the hallway to Chance, put his lips against Chance's ear. "A couple of kids making love."

The silenced Ruger felt heavy in Chance's hand.

"Gonna kill 'em?"

Not shooting them was a risk, sure.

Chance listened carefully. The lovers were whispering. No other sounds.

"Find the stairs up."

The stairs were at the end of a hall, behind a locked door. Carmellini worked on the lock in the darkness for almost a minute before he pulled the door open.

They closed the door behind them and climbed the totally dark staircase, feeling their way. They ended up in a stuffy, black attic. Chance used the flashlight. Furniture, desks, chairs, stacked everywhere. In the middle of the attic was another stairway up.

The door to the roof was also locked, this time with a padlock, which was on the interior side of the door.

"What if there is a padlock on the other side?" Chance asked.

"Then we're screwed. Unless you want to kick this thing down."

"No."

"Let's try to get this lock open, then the door."

"Okay."

The lock was rusty, corroded. After several minutes effort Carmellini admitted his defeat and used a wire saw to cut through the metal loop of the lock. That took two minutes of intense effort but didn't make much noise, considering.

With the lock off and hasp pulled back, they pushed at the door. It refused to open. With both men heaving, the door slowly opened with great resistance, and groaned terribly.

"That'll wake the dead," Chance muttered, and wiped the sweat from his face as Carmellini slipped out onto the roof.

Chance followed along.

The metal roof sloped away steeply in several different planes. Moving on hands and knees they worked themselves over toward the edge that faced the science building.

"Let me do this," Carmellini whispered, and extracted the rope from his backpack. "Get out of the way, up by the door."

Chance went.

The glare of the city and the streetlights below illuminated the roof quite well, too well in fact. While it was easy to see where to walk, anyone below who bothered to look could probably see the black shapes silhouetted against the glare of the sky.

Chance huddled against the dormer that formed the staircase up from the attic. He watched Carmellini on the edge of the roof, shaking out the rope, checking the grappling hook. Now he began to twirl the hook above his head, letting out more and more line to make the hook swing an ever-larger circle. Just as it seemed the circle was impossibly wide, he cast the line and hook across the chasm separating the buildings at a metal vent sticking up out of the roof.

The hook made an audible metallic sound as it hit the far roof, then it began sliding off.

Carmellini quickly pulled in line in huge coils, but too late to stop the grappling hook from sliding off the roof.

He kept pulling on the line. In seconds he had the hook in his hand and bent down against the roof.

Someone was down below. Even back here Chance could hear voices. He scanned the surrounding roofs, the streets that he could see, the blank windows looking at him from other buildings.

Minutes ticked by, the voices below faded.

Now Carmellini was standing, swinging the rope and hook, now casting it ... and it caught! He tugged at it, worked his way back up the roof to where Chance was kneeling.

Carmellini put the end of the rope around the dormer, pulled it as taut as possible, then tied it off.

"Well, there is our way across," the younger man said. "You want to go first, or should I?"

"Anchored solid, is it?"

"You bet."

"Age before beauty," Chance said, and tugged on leather gloves, wrapped his hands around the rope. He worked out hand over hand, then draped his lower legs over the rope. His backpack dangled from his shoulders.

Hanging from the rope like this took a surprising amount of physical strength. The rope sagged dangerously with his weight, becoming a vee with him at the bottom, which made it more difficult to move along it.

Gritting his teeth, trying to keep his breathing even, William Henry Chance worked his way along the rope, taking care not to look down.

At one point he knew he was over the chasm but it didn't matter: if he slipped off the rope the fall would kill him, whether he hit the roof and slid off or missed it clean.

He kept going, doggedly, straining every muscle, until he felt the bag dragging along the roof of the science building. Only then did he unhook his legs from the rope and let them down to the roof. Still pulling on the rope, he heaved himself up by the vent and grabbed it.

The grappling hook was holding by one tong. He wrapped the rope around the vent and set the hook, then tugged several times to make sure it would hold.

Wiping his forehead, he breathed heavily three or four times. He had one hand on the rope, so he felt the tension increase with Carmellini's weight. He peered at the other building. Carmellini came scurrying along the rope like a goddamn chimpanzee.

The younger man was over the gap between the buildings when the rope broke, apparently where it was anchored atop the lecture hall. Carmellini's body fell downward in an arc and disappeared from view. An audible thud reached Chance as Carmellini's body smacked against the side of the science building.

"*Our Lady of Colón* was under this storm system, out of sight of the satellites passing over, for six hours," Toad Tarkington explained to Jake Grafton. They were bent over a table in Mission Planning, studying satellite radar images. "When next it reappeared, it was steaming for Bahia de Nipe at twelve knots, yet its average speed of advance while it was out of sight was two knots."

"Two?"

"Two." Toad showed him the positions and measurements.

"So it was stopped somewhere."

"Or made a detour."

"What if the ship rendezvoused with another ship and the warheads were transferred?"

"Possible, but if you look at these other ship tracks, it doesn't seem very likely. All these other tracks were going somewhere, with speed-of-advance averages that seem plausible."

"Okay. What if the ship stopped and the crew dumped some of the weapons in the water? Maybe all of them. Dumped them in shallow water for someone to pick up later. How deep is the water in that area?"

"That area is the Bahamas, Admiral. Pretty shallow in a lot of places in there."

"Have NSA put that area under intense surveillance. Have them study every satellite image since that storm passed. If those warheads were dumped overboard from the *Colón*, someone is going to come along to pick them up. We have to get there before that somebody gets them aboard."

"Yes, sir."

"Ask Atlantic Fleet to get a P-3 out to that area as soon as possible, have the crew search for anchored or stationary ships. Any ships not actually under way. Understand?"

"Yes, sir."

Jake Grafton rubbed his forehead, trying to decide if there was anything else he should be doing.

"Uh, Admiral . . ." Toad began, his voice low. "I want to thank you for saving my assets last night. I about had a heart attack after we jumped over that rail, everything behind us blowing up, wondering if we were going to go into the water or splatter ourselves on a rock pile. That was truly a religious experience."

A wry grin crossed Jake Grafton's face. "Wish I had paid more attention to where those rocks were before crunch time arrived. Talk about jumping out of the frying pan into the fire! For a few seconds there I thought we had had the stroke."

"You didn't know?" Toad was aghast.

"What say we don't mention this to Rita or Callie," Jake said, and walked away. He had another meeting to attend.

William Henry Chance grabbed the rope, which extended over the side on the science building roof into the darkness. The rope was still taut. Tommy Carmellini must be hanging on the end of it!

Chance braced himself and began pulling, hand over hand, and almost ruptured himself.

He got no more than six feet of rope up when he realized he wasn't in the right position. Moving carefully, he braced himself against the vent pipe and got the rope over his shoulders. Now he used his whole body to help raise it.

Two more feet.

Four.

A dark spot, a head, coming above the eave, struggling to climb.

Chance held the rope steady as Carmellini heaved himself over the edge of the roof and began crawling up the slope, still holding onto the rope.

"Man, I thought I had bit the big one," Carmellini said between gasps. Leaning against the chimney, Chance blew equally hard.

"I'm getting too old for this shit," Carmellini muttered.

"Next time get a desk job."

"Why in hell do you think I went to law school?"

Chance coiled the rope and inspected it. It had frayed through where it was wrapped around the dormer on the other building. He showed the place to Carmellini, then put the rope in his knapsack.

"Let's go."

Carmellini used a glass cutter on a pane of a dormer window, then they went in.

Chance took a chance and used the flashlight. This attic was stacked with laboratory equipment: dishes, warmers, mixing units, microscopes, a spectrometer, a bunch of equipment large and small that he couldn't identify.

"Let's put on our masks," Chance said, "just in case."

They donned the gas masks, made sure the filter elements were on tight. The mask could provide only filtered air: it had an inhalation and exhalation valve and a black faceplate with two large clear lens to see through. The mask was attached to a hood that went over the head and shoulders of the user. Pull strings sealed the hood so air could not get in around the user's neck. When they had the mask on, both men removed the leather gloves they had been wearing and donned a pair of latex gloves. They stuffed their trousers inside their socks.

With Carmellini in the lead, the two men stealthily descended the stairs.

The laboratory was in the basement, so Chance and Carmellini had to pass through the main floor to get there.

The elevator would be the best way from the top of the building to the bottom, but it might be monitored from the guards' station at the main entrance. Certainly it should be: nothing could be simpler than to have a warning light come on when the electric motor that ran the elevator engaged. Chance and Carmellini took the stairs.

Carmellini was leading the way now. Using the flashlight, he examined the door to the staircase for alarms, then opened the door a crack and examined the stairwell. Fortunately the stairwell was lit. If this building were in the States it would be festooned with infrared sensors, motion detectors, microphones, and remote cameras controlled from a central station. However, this was Cuba.

At each landing, Carmellini extended a small periscope and looked around the corner.

On the second floor his inspection of the stairs leading down revealed a camera mounted on a wall above the landing, focused on the door in from the main floor. There was probably a camera mounted above the door to the main floor, a camera that looked back toward this camera.

Carmellini studied the camera through the periscope, twisted the magnification to the maximum and refocused. He kept the instrument steady by bracing himself against the wall.

The security camera was fifteen or twenty years old if it was a day. No doubt there were ten or twelve cameras on a sequential switch, so the video from each one was shown in turn on a monitor at the guard's station. The guard was probably reading something, eating, talking to another guard, if he was paying any attention at all.

From his backpack Carmellini removed a strobe unit and battery. He plugged the thing together, switched on the battery, and waited for the capacitor to charge. The bulb had a set of silver metal feathers around it so that the light could be focused. Carmellini tightened the feathers around the bulb as much as they would go. When the capacitor's green light came on, he eased the light around the corner, exposing his head for the first time. One quick squint to line up the light, then holding the thing tightly against the wall to steady it, he retracted his head, closed his eyes and buried his head in the crook of his arm. William Henry Chance did likewise. The short, intense burst of light should burn out the camera's light-level sensor, rendering it inoperative.

The flash was so bright Carmellini saw it through his closed eyelids.

The two men slipped down the stairs. Standing just under the camera that had just been disabled, Carmellini used the periscope again. Yes. Another camera, just over the door to the main floor.

He waited ten more seconds for the capacitor to fully charge, then stuck it around the corner and flashed the light.

"Let's *go!*"

With Chance behind him, Tommy Carmellini went down the stairs to the main floor and used his periscope to examine the landing on the stairs leading down. Nothing.

On down to the landing, peeking around the corner.

"Motion detector," he whispered to Chance.

Chance was breathing heavily inside the mask. It wasn't the exertion, he decided, but the tension. He must be audible at fifty paces. He tried to ignore the sound of his own rasping and listen.

Were the guards coming? Two cameras were down—had they noticed? Would they come to inspect the things?

Or were the guards congregating right now, calling in troops?

"Microwave or infrared?" Chance asked, referring to the motion detector.

"One of each."

"Beautiful."

"Probably two independent systems."

"Oh, Christ!"

"That's a poor way to install them, actually. This is old technology, *Mission Impossible* stuff. We'll just walk by the infrared detectors—all this clothing will help shield our body heat. If we move right along we should be okay."

"And the microwave system?"

Carmellini had already removed a device the size of a portable CD player from his backpack. "Jammer," he said, and examined the controls.

He turned it on and, holding it in front of him, walked down to the motion detectors. The one on the left was the microwave one, with a coaxial cable leading away from it. Carmellini pulled the cable an inch or so away from the wall and wedged the jammer into that space.

"Come on," he whispered, and opened the door into the basement.

The two men found themselves in a hallway. Directly over their head was a camera that pointed the length of the hall, covering the door halfway down that must lead into the lab.

Carmellini took a small battery-powered camcorder from Chance's backpack. He held it under the security camera for about a minute, filming the view down the hallway, then pushed the play button. The device now replayed the same scene on a continuous loop, and would do so until the batteries were exhausted. He slid a collar around the coaxial cable leading from the camera, tightened it, then used a pair of wire cutters to slice the coax away from the security camera.

The door into the lab had an alarm on it, one mounted high.

"The alarm rings if the circuit is broken," Carmellini whispered. "It's designed to prevent unauthorized exit from the lab, not entry. Won't take a minute."

He worked swiftly with a penknife and length of wire. By wiring around the contact on the door and jam, he made the contact impossible to break.

Sixty seconds later he gingerly tried the door. Reached for the handle and—

Locked!

Now to work with the picks.

"They locked an emergency exit?" Chance demanded.

"Yeah. Real bastards, huh?"

Tommy Carmellini knew his business. When the lock clicked, he put his picks back in his knapsack, pulled the knapsack into position, and palmed his pistol.

"You ready?"

"Yeah."

Carmellini eased the door open, looked quickly each way with just one eye around the jam.

The door opened into a well-lit foyer. The entire opposite wall of the room was made of thick glass, which formed a wall of a large, well-equipped laboratory. No people in sight. And no security cameras or motion detectors.

Both men came in, pistols in their hands and pointed at the floor. Chance pulled the door shut behind them.

They knelt by the long window and with just their heads sticking up, surveyed the scene.

Row after row of culture trays, units for mixing chemicals, deep sinks, storage cabinets, big sterilizing units, stainless steel containers by the dozen, analysis equipment, retorts, microscopes . . .

"Holy damn," Carmellini said softly. "They are sure as hell growing something in there."

"Something," Chance agreed.

On the end of the room to their left was a large air lock.

"That's the way in."

"Do we have to go in?"

"We need samples from those culture trays."

Chance led the way. He walked, holding the pistol down by his right thigh.

Around the corner slowly, looking first.

There were actually two air locks. After they went through the first one, they found themselves in a dressing room with a variety of white one-piece coveralls hanging on nails. Each man donned one, pulling it on over his clothes, then zipping it tightly, fastening the cuffs with Velcro strips. Gas masks were there too, but they were already wearing masks.

The second lock was equipped with a large vacuum machine which suctioned dust and microorganisms from the white coveralls.

They opened the door to the lab and stepped inside.

"The culture trays," Chance said, and led the way. From his backpack he took syringes, quickly screwed on needles.

The glass trays sat on mobile racks, three dozen to a rack. They were readily transparent, so he could look inside, see the bacteria growing on the food mix at the bottom of the tray.

He selected a rack of trays, pulled one tray from the rack and laid it on the marble-topped counter nearby. He opened it. Used a syringe. With the syringe about half-full, he unscrewed the needle, deposited the syringe in a plastic freezer bag and sealed it.

Meanwhile Carmellini had been exploring. As Chance sealed up his second sample from this rack of trays, Carmellini came back, motioning with his hand. "Better come look. Looks like they are growing several kinds of cultures."

The second kind looked similar to the first, but the organisms were of a slightly different color. Chance selected a tray, took a sample, then replaced the tray on the rack, as he had the first one.

He was finishing his second sample from this batch when, out of the corner of his eye, he saw Carmellini motion for him to get down.

He dropped to a sitting position, finished sealing the syringe bag.

He put the samples into his knapsack, reached up on the countertop for his pistol.

Carmellini was creeping along below the counter with his pistol in his hand.

Someone was in the air lock. By looking down the aisle between the counters Chance could just see the top of his head as he pulled on the gas mask in the dressing room.

Whoever it was was coming in.

Carmellini looked at Chance, lifted his hands in a query: Now what?

Chance made a downward motion. Maybe this person would just come in, get something, then leave.

It would be impossible, he decided, to sneak out while the person was in the lab. Although the lab was large, at least a hundred feet long, anyone in the air locks could be seen from anywhere in the lab unless the viewer was behind a piece of large equipment.

Shit!

Well, the Cubans were about to discover that their lab was no longer a secret. That was not a disaster; unfortunate, perhaps. Perhaps not.

The person coming in wore a complete protection suit and mask. Not a square inch of skin was exposed.

Large for a woman. A man, probably. Almost six feet. Hard to tell body weight under a bag suit like that, but at least 180 pounds.

He checked the safety on the pistol. On. With his thumb he moved it to the off position, checked it visually.

Now the person was coming out of the air lock, walking purposefully down the aisle between the counters and trays of cultures.

William Henry Chance stood up, pointed the pistol straight in the face of the masked person walking toward him.

The man froze. If it was a man. Stopped dead and slowly raised his hands.

Out of the corner of his eye Chance saw Tommy Carmellini moving toward the Cuban.

"Find something to tie him with," he said loudly, hoping Carmellini would understand his muffled voice.

Carmellini seemed to. He held up a roll of duct tape. He moved toward the man, who turned his head so that he could get a good look at Carmellini.

Carmellini had his pistol in his hand. His holster was under the white coverall, as was Chance's, so both men had carried their pistols with them in their hands.

Now Carmellini placed the pistol on a counter, well out of the man's reach. He walked behind him.

The man pushed backward, slamming Carmellini against a counter.

Damnation! Chance couldn't shoot for fear of hitting Carmellini. As if the .22-caliber bullets in the Ruger would drop a big man at this distance.

Chance walked around the counter, up the aisle, intending to shoot the Cuban in the head from as close as he could get.

Carmellini kicked violently and the Cuban went flying back into a rack of culture trays. Three or four of the trays fell from the rack and shattered on the floor.

The man launched himself at Carmellini, who ducked under a right cross. The man kept right on going, heading for the pistol lying on the counter.

Carmellini caught him by the back of his coverall and swung him bodily around. With a mighty punch he sent the man reeling backward, straight into the rack of culture trays he had already hit. The man slipped, fell amid the broken glass.

Without sights, wearing the silencer, the Ruger was hard to aim. Chance squeezed off a round anyway. Where the bullet went he never knew.

Before he could fire again the man screamed in agony. All his muscles went rigid. He bent over backward, screaming in a high-pitched wail.

"Let's go!" Carmellini yelled.

The man got control of an arm. He tore at his mask, trying to get it off, all the while screaming and thrashing around on the floor amid the broken glass.

"Holy shit."

The stricken man finally just ran out of air. All motion stopped. He was bent over backward, almost double, his head within a few inches of his heels.

Careful not to step on the broken glass, Chance bent over the man. He carefully took off the gas mask.

Eyes rolled back in his head, every muscle taut in a fierce rigor, the man seemed almost frozen.

"He must have torn his suit," Chance muttered to himself. *The Cubans must have vaccinated everyone with access. Why didn't the vaccination protect him?*

"Let's get our asses through the air lock and get the fuck outta here," Carmellini said loudly.

They stood in the vacuum room for the longest time, neither man willing to be the first to leave.

"We must go," Carmellini said at last, after almost ten minutes of suction, after using a high-pressure jet of air from a hose to blast every nook and fold of the coverall.

They hung the coveralls on the nails. Stood in the next air lock, were vacuumed again, then they were out, still wearing their gas masks.

"We might kill everyone in Havana," Chance said.

"We'll never know it," Carmellini shot back. "We'll be in hell before they are."

"Can't figure out why the vaccination didn't protect him."

"Later. How the hell are we going to get out of here?"

"The easiest way is to just walk out the front door, shoot both the guards, and walk around the corner to the van."

"They'll see us going up the stairs."

"The elevator. We'll use the elevator. Keep the pistols where they can't see them."

"You are fucking A crazy, man. One crazy motherfucker."

The elevator was right there with the door open. Chance walked in. When Carmellini was aboard, he pushed the button to take it up.

With their pistols down by their legs, they walked out of the elevator, straight for the guard shack at the front door.

Only one man was there, reading something. He looked up as they approached. Now he stood.

"*Qué pasa*—?" he began, and Chance shot him in the forehead from six feet away.

The guard toppled over backward.

Chance and Carmellini kept going, out the door at a walking pace, down the sidewalk under the streetlights looking like two refugees from a flying saucer, and around the corner. They jerked open the rear door of the van and jumped in.

Chance ripped off the mask.

"Let's get the hell outta here," he roared at the driver, who was as surprised at their sudden appearance as the guard had been. "Drive, damn it, drive!"

As the van jostled and swayed through the city streets, they sat in the back staring at each other, waiting for the disease to hammer them.

Waited, and waited, and waited...

CHAPTER TWELVE

Six hours after William Henry Chance and Tommy Carmellini walked out of the University of Havana science building, Dr. Bouchard was on his way to Washington via Mexico City with two of the culture samples in his diplomatic pouch. Three hours later one of lowest-ranking mission employees with diplomatic status left on a plane to Freeport, there to transfer to a flight to Miami, and then on to Washington. This employee carried the other two samples in her diplomatic pouch.

Chance and Carmellini were dropped at their hotel after changing clothes in the van. "Burn those clothes immediately, and don't touch them with your bare hands," Chance told the driver.

At the hotel both men went straight to their rooms, stripped, and stood in the shower for as long as they could stand it.

Standing under the shower head Chance waited for the first symptom to announce its arrival. Every now and then he shuddered, despite the hot water, as cold chills ran up and down his spine. He had a raging headache. When he got out of the shower he toweled himself dry, got in bed and arranged a wet, cool washcloth across his forehead.

The lab worker writhing on the floor, the startled face of the guard the instant before he died—these scenes played over and over in his mind. The death throes of the lab worker were bad enough, but the face of the guard, when he saw the pistol rising, saw the silencer, knew Chance was going to shoot: *that* face Chance would carry to his grave.

He shouldn't have had to kill the guard. The truth of the matter was that he panicked when the lab worker died horribly; he stood in the air locks thinking he or Carmellini would be next, any second. He had wanted out of that building so badly he had thrown caution to the wind and bolted blindly for the front door. It was a miracle that there weren't two or three guards standing by the main entrance, that they didn't have guns out as the two figures from biological hell stepped out of the elevator.

Ah, the stink of Lady Luck.

Lying there in the darkness he thought about microorganisms, wondered what was in the sample vials, wondered why the lab worker, who must have been immunized, died such a painful, horrible death.

One thing was certain: The Cubans were well on their way to having biological weapons. And the only conceivable target was the United States.

With his head pounding, unable to sleep, he turned on his small computer and typed an E-mail reporting the intrusion and his findings. After he encrypted the message, he used the telephone on the desk to get on the Web and fire the message into cyberspace.

Then he went back to bed, and finally to sleep.

The American stood amid the shards of glass looking at the body of the lab worker. He wore a protective garment that covered him head to toe and a mask that filtered the air he breathed. He looked at everything, taking his time, then exited the laboratory through the air lock.

Alejo Vargas was waiting for him. He said nothing, merely waited for the American to talk.

"The virus has apparently mutated," the American said finally. "I thought the strain was stable, but . . ." He gave the tiniest shrug.

"Mutated?"

"Possibly."

"Come now, Professor. I have not asked for scientific proof. Tell me what you think."

"A mutation. A few days with the electron microscope would give us some clues. We need to do more cultures to be sure. It would help if I could dissect the dead man, see how the disease affected him."

"Like you did the others?"

"You told me they were killers, condemned men. We had to *know*!"

"What if the disease gets away from you at the morgue? What if it spreads to the general population?"

"With the proper precautions the danger is minuscule. Man, the advancement of human knowledge requires—"

"No," Vargas said. He gestured to the lab. "If that gets away from us, for whatever reason, there won't be a human left alive on this island."

"Then don't ask me for opinions," the professor snapped. "You can guess as well as I."

Alejo Vargas's eyes narrowed to slits. His voice was cold with fury. "I wanted to use an anthrax agent, but no, you insisted on poliomyelitis. Now you tell me it mutated, as I feared it might."

The damned fool, the American thought. Of course he had insisted on a virus—for Christ's sake, his life work was studying viruses, not bacteria.

Vargas continued, pronouncing the sentence: "We spent all this money, built the warheads, installed them, and we took huge risks to do it. Don't talk to me of acceptable *risks*."

The professor was not the type to calmly submit to lectures from his intellectual inferiors. "Don't get wrathy with me, Vargas. You're a stupid, ignorant thug. I didn't design the universe and I can't take responsibility for it. I merely try to understand, to learn, to increase the store of man's knowledge."

The American lost his temper at that point and spluttered, "Biology isn't engineering, goddammit! Sometimes two plus two equals five."

Vargas turned his back on the professor. He stared into the lab, which appeared cold and stark under the lights yet was full of poisonous life.

"I don't understand what happened in there," the American said. "He didn't just fall. It looks like there was a struggle."

"Someone broke in," Vargas said.

The professor was horrified. "Broke in? Past the guards? Who would be so foolish?"

"Someone who wanted to see what was in there," Vargas said, and turned to look at the other man's face. A note of satisfaction crept into his voice as he added, "Probably Americans. Perhaps CIA."

The professor looked startled, as if the possibility had not crossed his mind.

"Come, come, Professor, don't tell me you thought your work here in Cuba would remain a secret forever."

"I am a scientist," the American said. "Science is my life."

Vargas snorted derisively. "Your life!" he said softly, contemptuously.

The professor lost it. "Fool!" he shouted. "Idiot! You sit in this Third World cesspool and think this crap matters—*fool!*"

"Perhaps," Vargas said coldly. He was used to Professor Svenson, an unrepentant intellectual snob, the very worst kind, and American to boot. "I would like to stay and trade curses with you today but there is no time. The workers are waiting outside. You are going to show them how to clean up the lab, then you will determine exactly what happened to the viruses. You will write down all that must be done to check the warheads. You will have the report hand-delivered to me. If you fail to do exactly what I say, you will go into the crematorium with the lab worker. Do you understand me, Professor?"

"You can't threaten me. I'm—"

Alejo Vargas flicked his fingers across the professor's cheek, merely a sting. He stared into his eyes. "You suffer from a regrettable delusion that you are irreplaceable—*I* can cure that. If you wish, you can go to the crematorium right now. Two body bags are not much more trouble than one."

When Vargas left, Olaf Svenson sat and hid his face in his hands.

He had never thought past the scientific problems to the ones he now faced. Oh, he should have, of course: he knew that Vargas intended to put the virus into warheads. He shut his mind to the horror—he wanted to see if the mutation could be controlled. No, he wanted to see if *he* could control the mutation of the viruses. The scientific challenges consumed him. Vargas had the money and the facilities—Olaf Svenson wanted to do the research.

He was going to have to get out of Cuba, and as soon as possible. The university thought he was in Europe—that was where he would go. The CIA probably had no evidence, or not enough to prosecute him in an American court. If he went to the airport and took a plane now they probably would never get enough—Vargas certainly wasn't going to be a willing witness.

He waited a few minutes, long enough for Vargas to clear off upstairs, then stood and took a last fleeting look at the lab. With a sigh he turned his back on what might have been and walked to the elevator. In the lobby he took the time to give detailed instructions to the workers who would clean up the lab, answered the foreman's questions, then watched as they boarded the elevator. When the elevator door closed behind the workers, Professor Svenson nodded to the guards at the entrance of the building, set off down the street and never looked back.

The P-3 Orion antisubmarine patrol plane flew over a sparkling sea. The morning cumulus clouds would form in the trade winds in a few hours, but right now the sky was empty except for wisps of high stratus.

The glory of the morning held no interest for the P-3's crew, which was examining an old freighter anchored in the lee of an L-shaped cay. A few palm trees and some thick brush covered the backbone of the little island, which had wide, white, empty beaches on all sides.

"Whaddya think?" the pilot asked his copilot and the TACCO, the tactical coordinator, who was standing behind the center console.

"Go lower and we'll get pictures," the TACCO suggested. He passed a video camera to the copilot.

The pilot retarded the throttles and brought the plane around in a wide, sweeping turn to pass down the side of the freighter at an altitude of about two hundred feet. The copilot kept the video camera on the freighter, which was fairly small, about ten thousand tons, with peeling paint and a rusty waterline. A few sailors could be seen on deck, but no flags were visible.

"I'll get on the horn," the TACCO told the pilot, "see if the folks in Norfolk can identify that ship. But first let's fly over the ship, get the planform from directly overhead."

The TACCO knew that the computer sorted ship images by silhouettes and planforms, so having both views would speed up the identification process.

Professor Olaf Svenson was standing in line at Havana airport to buy a ticket to Mexico City when he saw Colonel Santana arrive out front in a chauffeur-driven limousine. Through the giant windows he could clearly see Santana get out of the car, see the uniformed security guards salute, see the plainclothes security men with Santana move tourists out of the way.

Svenson turned and rushed away in the other direction. He dove into the first men's room he saw and took refuge in an empty stall.

Was Santana after him?

The acrid smell of a public rest room filled his nostrils, permeated his clothing, made him feel unclean. He sat listening to the sounds: the door opening and closing as men came and went, feet scraping, water running, piss tinkling into urinals, muttered comments. Sweat trickled down his neck, soaking his shirt.

Slam! Someone aggressively pushed the rest room door open until it smashed against the wall.

The minutes crawled.

Santana was an animal, Svenson thought, a sadist, a foul, filthy creature who loved to see fellow human beings in pain. Svenson had seen it in his eyes. Even the smallest of bad tidings was delivered with a malicious gleam. Svenson suspected that as a boy Santana had enjoyed torturing pets.

What would Santana do to an overweight, middle-aged scientist from Colorado who tried to escape the country?

The door slammed into the wall again, and Svenson jumped.

Torture? Of course. Santana would want to inflict pain. Svenson felt his bowels get watery as he thought about the pain that Santana could dish out.

Every sound caused him to move, to jump.

He consulted his watch again. Just a few minutes had passed.

O God, if you really exist, have mercy on me! Don't let Santana find me. Please!

Home. He wanted to go home so badly. To his apartment and cats and flowers in planters. To his neat, safe little haven, where he could shut out the evil of the world.

Someone slapped the side of the stall, said something unintelligible in Spanish. Probably wanted him to hurry up, to get out and let the next man in.

Svenson made a retching sound. And almost lost his breakfast.

He tried retching audibly again, less forcefully.

The person standing beside the stall walked away, the door to the rest room opened and closed.

Where was Santana?

Maybe he wasn't coming. Surely by now if he were searching the terminal he would have looked into this restroom.

Could it be?

Or perhaps Santana was standing outside, waiting for him to come out, for the sheer joy of dashing his hopes when he thought the coast was clear. Santana would do a thing like that, Svenson told himself now.

He felt so dirty, so wretched. He wiped at the sheen of sweat on his face, wiped his hands on his trousers.

He watched the minute hand of his watch, watched it slowly circle the dial, counted the seconds as it moved along so effortlessly.

With every passing minute that Santana didn't come he felt better. Yes. Perhaps he wasn't looking. He must not be. If he were looking he would have been in this restroom, would have opened the door, would have jerked him from the stall and arrested him and put the cuffs on him and dragged him across the terminal and thrown him into a police car.

But Santana didn't come.

After an hour of waiting, Olaf Svenson began thinking about how he was going to get out of the country. He needed another passport. If he used his own, the security people might not let him through the immigration checkpoint.

He pulled up his pants, washed his hands thoroughly, and went out into the main hall of the terminal. Keeping an eye out for Santana, he went to the ticket desk for Mexicana Airlines and stood where he could watch the agent. When handed a passport, the man glanced up, comparing the face to the photo. Just a glance, but a glance would be enough. Using a stolen passport with a photo that didn't match his face was too much of a risk. Svenson knew he would have to use his own, dangerous though it would be.

Screwing up his courage, Olaf Svenson got in line. *"Ciudad Mejico, por favor."* He handed the passport to the agent, who glanced into his face, then handed the passport back.

An hour later Svenson went through the immigration line. The uniformed official didn't look up, merely compared the passport to a typed list that lay on his desk, then passed it back. He did not stamp the document.

Olaf Svenson took a seat in the waiting area and used a filthy handkerchief to wipe perspiration from his forehead.

A reprieve. The powers that rule the universe had granted him a reprieve.

He would have liked to have had the opportunity to study the latest viral mutation, but the risk was just too great. A lost opportunity, he concluded. Oh, too bad, too bad.

When the plane from Madrid touched down at Havana airport with Maximo Sedano aboard, Colonel Santana and two plainclothes secret police officers were there to meet him. They stood beside Maximo while he waited for his luggage, then the two junior men carried it to the car while Maximo walked beside Santana.

Colonel Santana said nothing to the finance minister, other than to say Alejo Vargas wanted to see him, then he let the bastard stew. He had learned years ago that silence was a very effective weapon, one that cost nothing and caused grievous wounds in a guilty soul. All men are guilty, Santana believed, of secret sins if nothing else, and if left to suffer in silence will usually convince themselves that the authorities know everything. After a long enough silence, often all that remains to do is take down the confession and obtain a signature.

One of his troops drove while Santana rode in the back of the car with his charge. Not a word was uttered the whole trip.

Maximo seemed to be holding up fairly well, Santana thought, not sweating too much, retaining most of his color, breathing under control. The colonel smiled broadly, a smile that grew even wider when he saw from the corner of his eye that Maximo Sedano had noticed it.

Ah, yes. Silence. And terror.

The car drove straight into the basement of the Ministry of Interior, where Maximo Sedano was hustled to a subterranean interrogation room.

"I demand to see Vargas," Maximo said hotly when they shoved him into a chair and slammed the door shut.

"You demand?" asked Santana softly, leaning forward until his face was only inches from Maximo. "You are in no position to demand. You may ask humbly, request, you may even pray, but you don't demand. You have no right to demand anything."

Santana seated himself behind the desk, across from Maximo. He took out the interrogation form, filled out the blanks on the top of the sheet, then laid it on the scarred wood in front of him.

"Where," Santana asked, "is the money?"

Maximo Sedano inhaled through his nose. He smelled dampness, urine, something rotting, meat or vegetable perhaps . . . and something cold and slimy and evil. It was here, all around him, in this room—the very stones reeked of it. Before Castro the secret police belonged to Fulgencio Batista, and before him Geraldo Machado, and so on, back for hundreds of years. This was a secret room that never saw the light, where justice did not exist, where force and venality and self-interest ruled. Here shadow men without conscience or scruple wrestled with the enemies of the dictator. The room reeked of fear and blood, torture and maiming, pain and death.

Maximo pushed the images aside. With a tenuous composure, carefully, completely, honestly, he explained about the accounts and the German and the people at the bank. He related what they said to the best of his memory. He told about the ice pick and the men's room, everything, withholding only his intention of transferring the money to his own accounts.

Santana had questions, of course, made him repeat most of it two or three times. When the colonel had it all written down, Maximo signed the statement.

"Where are the transfer cards?" Santana asked.

"In Switzerland. I left them at the bank."

"Why?"

"If there has been some mistake, if the money was stolen by someone at the bank, then the banks have valid, legal transfer orders they must honor. They must send the money to the Bank of Cuba."

"So where is the money?"

"It is not in those accounts, obviously. I think the money has been stolen."

For the first time, Santana was openly skeptical. "By whom?"

"By someone who had access to the account numbers. *El Presidente* insisted on keeping a record of them in his office. I would look there first."

"Why not your office? Is it not possible one of your aides learned the numbers, passed them to someone who—?"

"All the numbers of the government's foreign accounts, including the accounts controlled exclusively by *el Presidente,* are kept in a safe in my office under my exclusive control. None of my staff has access—only me."

Again Santana smiled. "You realize, of course, that you are convicting yourself with your own mouth?"

Maximo threw up his hands. "I tell you this, Santana. I do not have the money. If I had fifty-four million dollars I would not have taken the plane back to Cuba. I would not be sitting in this shithole talking to a shithead like you."

Santana ignored the insult and jotted a few more lines on his report. Personally he believed Maximo—if the man had the money he would have run like a rabbit—but to say so would give Maximo too much leverage. And Maximo said that he killed a man with an ice pick, which certainly seemed out of character. Santana raised an eyebrow as he thought about Rall. Maximo Sedano killing Rall—well, the world is full of unexpected things.

He left Maximo Sedano sitting in the chair in the interrogation room while he went to find Vargas. The minister was in his office listening to a report of the laboratory burglary from one of the senior colonels, who had just returned from the university.

Santana knew nothing of the burglary, had not been informed before he went to the airport. He stood listening, asked no questions, waited for Alejo Vargas.

An hour passed before Vargas was ready to talk about Maximo. "He is downstairs in an interrogation room," Santana said. "Here is his statement." He passed it across. Vargas read it in silence.

"The money is not in the accounts," Vargas said finally.

"So he says."

"And you think he is telling the truth?"

"Sir, I don't think Maximo Sedano has what it takes to steal that kind of money and come back here to face you. He knew he would be met at the airport. He was expecting it."

Vargas said nothing, merely blinked.

"Actually, his suggestion about the account numbers at the president's residence is a good one. If there was a leak, it was probably there. Fidel probably left the book lying around—he had no organizational sense."

"And?"

"I know of no one in Cuba with the computer expertise to get into the Swiss banks electronically and steal that money, but there are plenty of people in America who could. A lot of them work for the American government."

"People were stealing money from banks long before computers were invented," Vargas objected. "Anybody could have bribed a bank officer and stolen that money. The Yanquis are the most likely suspects, however."

Vargas well knew that everything that went wrong south of Key West was not the fault of the United States government, but he was too old a dog to think that the people who ran the CIA were incompetent dullards too busy to give Cuba a thought.

"The Americans say that shit happens."

"They often make it happen," Vargas agreed, and stood up. "Let us talk to Maximo. Perhaps we can save a soul from hell."

Going down the stairs Vargas said to Santana, "Maximo has been plotting to get himself elected president when Castro passes. Today would be a good time to let him know that such a course is futile."

"Yes, sir."

"Some pain, I think. Nothing permanent, nothing life threatening. We will need his expertise in finance later on."

"Yes, sir."

A petty officer came to find Jake Grafton. The sailor led the admiral to the Air Intelligence spaces, where he found Toad and the AIs gathered around a television monitor.

"A P-3 took this sequence a few hours ago," Toad told the admiral, "in the Bahamas. It's an anchored North Korean freighter. The P-3 is going to fly directly overhead here in a minute and get a shot looking straight down. We'll freeze the video there."

The perspective changed as the plane came across the top of the ship. The clear blue water seemed to disappear, leaving the ship suspended above the yellow sandy bottom. Just before the P-3 crossed above the ship, Toad froze the picture.

He stepped forward, pointing to dark shapes resting on the sand under the freighter. "I think we've found the rest of the stolen warheads," he said. "The people on the *Colón* dumped them here in the ocean for the North Koreans to pick up later."

Jake stepped forward, studied the picture on the television screen. "Can this picture be computer enhanced?"

"They are working on that in Norfolk right now."

"How certain are they about the identification of the ship?"

"Very sure. Undoubtedly North Korean."

When the National Security Council met to be briefed about developments in Cuba, the president's mood was even uglier than it had been a few days before. He listened with a frozen frown as the briefer described the biological warfare research laboratory in the science building at the University of Havana. He covered his face with a hand as the briefer explained that some of the warheads from *Nuestra Señora de Colón* appeared to be resting on a sandy ocean floor in the Bahamas, with a North Korean freighter anchored nearby.

"The good news," the briefer said brightly, "is that the freighter seems to be in British territorial waters."

"Do you have a plan?" the president asked General Totten.

"Yes, sir. At our request, the British have formally requested that a United States ship board and search the North Korean freighter, which has violated their territorial waters. The nearest U.S. ship will be there in three hours."

"And if the North Koreans raise the anchor and sail away?"

"We'll stop the ship anyway, remove any United States government property that we find."

"Another international incident!" the president grumped. "The North Koreans will shout bloody murder, then the Cubans will join the chorus."

The national security adviser jumped right in. "Sir, the Cubans can't prove we had CBW warheads in Gitmo."

"Can't prove? If Fidel Castro doesn't have a stolen artillery shell on his desk right now I'll kiss your ass at high noon on the Capitol steps while CNN—"

"Sir, we think—"

"*Let me finish!* Don't interrupt! I'm the guy the congressmen are going to fry when they hear about this fiasco. Let me finish."

Silence.

The president swallowed once, adjusted his tie. "And now," he said, trying to keep the acid out of his voice, "we learn the Cubans have a biological weapons lab in a building in the heart of Havana, at the university there. Is that correct?"

"Yes, sir."

"What I would like to know is this: Have the Cubans got any way of using biological weapons on the United States right now? Today? Have they got a delivery system?"

"Sir, we don't know."

"Well, by God, in my nonmilitary opinion we ought to find out just as fast as we can. Does anybody in this room agree with that proposition?"

"Yes, sir."

"Another thing I want to know: Somebody explain again how the goddamned Chemical Weapons Treaty will make countries like Cuba decide not to build biological and chemical weapons."

The silence that followed that question was broken by the chairman of the joint chiefs, General Tater Totten:

"The Chemical Weapons Convention Agreement won't dissuade anyone who wants these weapons from building them. All it will do is force us to rid ourselves of the weapons that deter others from using these things. Chemical and biological weapons are only employed when a user believes his enemy cannot or will not retaliate in kind. Your staff knew that and wanted the treaty anyway so that you could brag about it on the stump and win votes from soccer moms who don't know shit from peanut butter."

The president eyed General Totten sourly, then surveyed the rest of them. "At least somebody around here has the guts to tell it like it is," he muttered.

The chairman continued: "Doing the right thing isn't the same as getting the right result. We could use more of the latter and less of the former, if you ask me."

"Don't push it, General," the president snarled.

The gray-haired general motored on as if the president hadn't said a word. "To get back to your question, of course the Cubans have a delivery system, or several. Biological weapons are the easiest of all weapons to employ. The delivery system could be as simple as planes rigged to spray microorganisms into the atmosphere: after all, Cuba is just ninety miles south of Key West; jets could be over Florida in minutes. Or a few teams of Cuban saboteurs could induce the toxins into the water supply systems of major cities—tens of millions of people could be infected before anyone figured out there was even a problem."

Here was the classic dilemma: The U.S. was prepared to fight a nuclear war to the finish and lick anyone on the planet in a conventional war. Hundreds of billions of dollars had been spent on networks and communications, on precision weapons and missile systems, on an army, navy and air force that were the best equipped, trained, and led armed forces on earth. So if there were an armed conflict, no sane enemy would confront the United States on a conventional or nuclear battlefield: guerrilla warfare and terror weapons were the alternatives.

"What the Cubans probably don't have," General Totten continued, "is the engineering and industrial capacity to turn tankfuls of toxins into true weapons, weapons that are safe to handle, can be stored indefinitely, and aimed precisely. That's why they want to get their hands on that shipload of biological warheads."

"So how do we prevent the use of CBW weapons?" the president asked.

"You have to deter the bad guys," Tater Totten explained. "You have to be willing to do it to them worse than they can do it to you. And they have to know that you will."

"You're saying that if the Cubans murder ten million Americans, we have to kill every human in Cuba?"

"That's right. Mutually assured destruction."

"M-A-D."

"Insane. But there is no other way. If these people think you lack the resolve to retaliate in kind, you just lost the war."

"If anyone kills Americans we will retaliate," the president said. "That's been U.S. policy since George Washington took the oath of office."

The general concentrated on straightening a paper clip, then bending it into a new shape.

Finally, when the president had had his say, when the national security adviser had summed up the situation, the chairman spoke again: "The agent in Havana who found the lab had a request. It was in the last paragraph of his message this morning. Mr. Adviser, do you wish to discuss it?"

The adviser obviously didn't wish to discuss it; he could have raised the point at any time during the meeting and hadn't. A flash of irritation crossed his face, then he said, "I've gone over that request with the staff, and with State, ah, and both staff and State feel it is completely out of bounds."

"What request?" the president asked curtly.

"Sir, staff and State feel the request is absolutely out of the question; I struck it from the agenda."

"What request?" the president repeated with some heat.

"The agent wants Operation Flashlight to happen at one-thirty A.M. tomorrow," Tater Totten said.

"And that is?" the president said, frowning.

"He wants the power grid in central Havana knocked out."

"Oh. Now I remember. You want to blow some high-voltage towers."

"That's correct, sir. This operation was discussed and approved three weeks ago."

"Oh, no. Three weeks ago I gave a tentative approval, tentative only. Sabotage of a power network of a foreign nation is a damn serious matter. Back when I was in school we called that an act of war."

"It still is," the national security adviser said. He was something of a suck-up, General Totten thought.

"I think this matter deserves more discussion," the president said.

"Yes, sir."

"What happens if the people setting these charges are arrested?"

The director of the CIA reluctantly stepped in. "Sir, that is one of the inherent risks of clandestine operations. The men who set the charges know the risks. We know the risks. The fact is that the possible gains here make the risks worth running. That's the same cost-benefit analysis we make before we authorize any clandestine operation."

"What if one of these people is arrested? Can the Cubans prove they work for the CIA?"

"No, sir. They will appear to be Cuban exiles, in Cuba creating mischief on their own hook."

"This operation gives me a bad feeling in the pit of my stomach," the president said. "There are too many things going wrong all at once."

General Totten could hold his tongue no longer. "There is no time to be lost," he said. "Four vials of microorganisms taken from a biological warfare laboratory located just ninety miles south of Key West in the capital of a communist country hostile to the United States are this very minute being examined in laboratories in the Washington area. Cuba could become another Iraq, armed to the teeth with chemical and biological weapons. This nation cannot afford to let that happen. Cuba is only *ninety* miles away. The risk is simply too great."

The president glared around the room. Looking for someone to blame, General Totten thought.

"Mr. President, Flashlight will take hours to pull off," the CIA director said. "I've already given the order for it to proceed."

"You've already given the order?" The president repeated the words incredulously.

"There was no time to be lost," the director shot back. "These things take hours to set in motion. The execution time is one-thirty A.M., less than six hours away."

The chairman of the joint chiefs leaned forward in his chair, rested both elbows on the mahogany table. "Mr. President, we have no choice in this matter. None at all. If this administration fails to move aggressively to learn exactly what the Cuban threat is and take steps to meet it, you will almost certainly be impeached and removed from office by Congress for dereliction of duty."

The president looked as if he were going to explode. This was a side of him the voters never saw. A control freak, like most politicians, he hated just being along for the ride. Watching the president seethe, Tater Totten knew his days on active duty were numbered. The CIA director had better start thinking about retirement, too.

"Who is our agent in Cuba?" the president demanded.

The director looked startled. Names of agents were closely held, never discussed in meetings like this. Yet he couldn't refuse to answer a direct question from the president of the United States. "Sir, if you need that information, I could write it on a sheet of paper." The director grabbed a notepad and did so. He tore off the sheet, folded it once, and passed it down the table. The president put the folded paper in front of him but didn't open it.

"I want to know who authorized this man"—the president tapped on the folded paper with a finger—"to go to Cuba to see what cesspools he could uncover."

"Sir, this mission was authorized by this council two months ago."

"Then why in hell didn't someone mention it when we were discussing getting our warheads home from Guantánamo Bay? Why wasn't that cargo ship escorted from pier to pier? Why in hell didn't we get those warheads out of there two months ago, two years ago? *Why in hell can't you people get a goddamn grip?*"

Silence followed that outburst. It was broken when the chairman said, "Instead of fretting over the timing, let's pat ourselves on the back for being smart enough to have an agent in Havana. It's the Cubans' weapons lab, not ours."

When Tater Totten walked out of the room, he still had his letter of resignation from the joint chiefs in his pocket. He had prepared it when the national security adviser struck Operation Lightbulb from the agenda. Maybe he should have laid the letter on the president and retired to the golf course before these fools drove this truck off the cliff. He had no doubt the mess in Cuba was about to blow up in their faces, and soon.

The American warship nearest the unnamed cay where the North Korean freighter was anchored was a destroyer out of Charleston, South Carolina, manned by naval reservists on their annual two-week tour of active duty. The destroyer had been on its way to Nassau for a weekend port call when the flash message rolled off the printer.

The destroyer's flank speed was 34 knots, and she was making every knot of it now as she thundered down the Exuma Channel with a bone in her teeth.

From five thousand feet Jake Grafton could see the destroyer plainly even though it was twenty miles away. And he could see the wake lengthening behind the North Korean freighter, *Wonsan*.

"Damn scow is getting under way," Rita said disgustedly. She was flying the V-22. "It'll be in international waters long before the destroyer gets there."

"Wonder how many warheads they pulled out of the water?"

"We're going to find out pretty soon," Jake muttered. "If this guy stops and lets us board him, he won't have a warhead aboard. If he refuses to heave to, he's got a bunch."

"What are you going to do, Admiral, if he refuses to stop?"

Jake Grafton didn't have an answer to that contingency, nor did he want to make the decision. If that eventuality came to pass he would ask for guidance from Washington, pass the buck along to people who would probably refer it to the politicians.

"The *Wonsan* is turning northeast," Rita observed. "She'll probably go between Cat Island and San Salvador."

"Let's go down," Jake Grafton said, "hover in front of this guy, see if he'll stop." He was sitting on the flight engineer's seat just aft of the pilots.

Five minutes later the Osprey was in helicopter flight with the rotors tilted up, descending gently in front of the *Wonsan*, which was up to five or six knots now. Jake Grafton could see four people on the bridge, standing close together and gesturing at the Osprey. The copilot was watching the clearance, telling Rita how much maneuvering room she had.

"Closer," Jake said.

Rita Moravia kept the Osprey moving in. Luckily the wind was from the west, so she could keep the twin-rotor machine on the starboard side of the freighter, yet pointed right at the bridge. This kept the wind on her starboard quarter.

She stopped when the distance between her cockpit and the bridge glass was about fifty yards. The right rotor was still well above the top of the freighter's crane, which was mounted amidships.

"Closer," Jake said again, "but watch your clearance."

The copilot glanced nervously at Jake. "Give me clearance," Rita snapped at him, which brought him back to the job at hand.

She maneuvered the Osprey until it was completely on the starboard side of the *Wonsan*, then she dropped it until she could see the length of the bridge.

The captain—he might have been the captain, wearing a dirty, white bridge cap—stepped through the door of the bridge onto the wing and stood looking into the cockpit, fifteen feet away. He had his hands pressed against his ears, trying to deaden the mighty roar of the two big engines. The downwash from the rotors raised a storm of sea spray, which was soaking him, and now it carried away his hat.

"Closer," Jake said one more time.

"The air is sorta bumpy coming around this superstructure."

"Yeah," the admiral said.

Ten feet separated the nose of the V-22 from the rail of the bridge wing. Rita eased the Osprey forward a foot at a time, until the refueling probe and three barrels of the turreted fifty-caliber machine gun that protruded from the nose were no more than eighteen inches from the rail.

"Aim the gun at the captain," Jake said.

The copilot flipped a switch, then looked at the captain's head, and the machine gun faithfully tracked, following the aiming commands sent to it from the gunsight mounted on the copilot's helmet.

The captain's face was now less than ten feet from Jake Grafton's. He was balding, a bit overweight, in his late fifties. The rotor wash lashed at him and tore at his sodden clothes, making it difficult for him to keep his footing. Groping for a rail to steady himself against the fierce wind, he looked at the three-barreled machine gun, which tracked him like a living thing, then at Jake Grafton on the seat behind the Osprey pilots.

The captain turned and shouted something over his left shoulder; he held on with both hands as he went through the door onto the enclosed bridge.

"Watch it," Jake muttered into his lip mike. "This guy may be fool enough to turn into you."

Rita was the first to realize what was happening. She felt the need to turn left to hold position. "The ship is slowing," she said. "I think he's stopped his engines."

In a few seconds it became obvious that she was correct. Rita backed away until the distance between the cockpit and ship was about fifty feet.

"I think he lost his nerve, Admiral."

"Look at the stuff on his deck," the copilot said, pointing. "Looks like he pulled up a bunch of warheads."

The freighter was drifting when the destroyer arrived a half hour later and coasted to a stop several hundred yards away. In minutes the destroyer had a boat in the water.

When armed Americans were standing on the *Wonsan*'s deck, Jake tapped Rita on the shoulder.

"Let's go home."

"I listened to the tape from Alejo Vargas's office this afternoon," Carmellini said to Chance. They were walking the Prado looking for a place to eat dinner. To have a decent selection and palatable food, the restaurant would have to be a hard-currency place. Although the best restaurants were in ramshackle houses in Old Havana, tonight Chance wanted music, laughter, people.

"Someone told Vargas all about the break-in at the university lab, the contamination, the dead lab worker. They spent most of the day running the fans at the lab, trying to lower the count of the stuff in the air before they went in."

"What did they say about the dead man, why he died?"

"That had them stumped. He was vaccinated. They called in a Professor Svenson."

"Olaf Svenson?"

"No one used a first name."

"It must be him. I've heard of him. Damned potty old fool. He was at Cal Tech for years. Thought he was at Colorado now. A genius, almost won a Nobel Prize." He snapped his fingers. "That photo we gave Bouchard—that must have been Svenson."

"Well, he is their main man down at the lab, to hear the conversation at Vargas's office."

"So why did the lab worker die? Wasn't he vaccinated?"

"The stuff mutated, according to the professor. Mutated again, he said."

"Well, what the hell is it? Did they say that?"

"Some kind of polio."

"Polio doesn't kill that quickly," Chance objected.

"This kind does. The lab worker wasn't the first, apparently. The professor wanted to dissect him like the others but Vargas ordered the body burned immediately."

They paused on a corner, watched the people who filled the sidewalks under the crumbling buildings. Just down the walk to the left a Cuban was trying to sell trinkets to a pair of Germans and having no luck. To the right a tall young white guy, American or Canadian probably, was locked in a passionate embrace with a local girl.

"Sun, sex, and socialism," Carmellini muttered. "Makes you wonder why there aren't more Cubans."

Chance closed his eyes, enjoyed the caress of the breeze on his face and hair. He could hear snatches of music amid the honk of car horns and traffic sounds. Havana was very much alive this evening, as it was every evening.

Finally he opened his eyes, looked again at the Cubans and tourists swirling about him. And Carmellini standing there, quite nonchalant, looking bored.

"Do they have any ideas about who broke in?"

"Americans. CIA scum. No evidence, but they're sure."

Chance nodded.

"There was talk," Carmellini continued, "of rounding up likely suspects, doing some thorough interrogations, just to see what might turn up. That was Colonel Santana's suggestion: apparently he is a rare piece of work. Vargas overruled him. Said they couldn't torture tourists every time the CIA did something they didn't like or soon they wouldn't have any tourists."

"Sensible."

"Anything else?"

Carmellini shrugged, scratched his chin. "I listened to almost three hours' worth of that stuff, and you know, they didn't mention Fidel Castro even once."

"Didn't say his name?"

"Nope. And the technician said he hadn't heard them mention Castro all day."

"Curious."

"It's odd. I would have thought—"

After a bit Chance said, "The lab is just the tip of the iceberg. There must be machinery for drying out the cultures, for packing the microorganisms into warheads or mixing them into some sort of chemical stew to be sprayed from planes. There must be trucks that transport this stuff from place to place. And then there are the weapons: where the hell are they?"

They went into one of the nightclubs and found an empty table. Six whores were sitting around the table beside them. The girls were drinking daiquiris and having a fine, loud time. One of the girls looked the two men over while the band tuned up just a few feet away.

"Washington wants more information," Carmellini said, ignoring the whores.

"They would." Chance chewed on his lip for a bit, then picked up the wine list. "Tonight's the night we go into Vargas's safe. Are you comfortable with that?"

Carmellini took his time answering. Chance was about to repeat the question when he said, "If the alarms are off."

"They'll be off."

"Sure."

"Trust me."

When the waiter came they ordered dinner.

"So tell me again about the Ministry of Interior," Carmellini said. "Everything you can recall. Everything."

Chance leaned back, closed his eyes, tried to visualize how the building looked when he had stepped from the taxi out front on his way to his meeting with Alejo Vargas.

"There is a guard kiosk out front on the sidewalk. You then walk through the front entrance to the guard station inside. They check your credentials again, call whoever you say you want to see. This person comes to get you, leads you through the halls to the office you are to visit."

"Cameras?"

"Security cameras mounted high in corners, monitored by the main guard station. There are two separate systems, at least, with pictures playing on separate monitors."

"Infrared sensors?"

"I think so...." The fact is he should have paid more attention. Looked more carefully, consciously noted what he was seeing. "Yes, I remember seeing one."

"Motion detectors?"

"No."

"Laser alarms?"

"Yes, mounted at ankle height." Presumably these were only on when the building was not occupied.

"Alarms on the windows?"

"Yes."

"Vibrators on the glass?"

"No." If there had been vibrators, the computer would have had a much more difficult job sorting out the voices from the electronic noise of the vibrators when it tried to read the light refracted by the crystals.

"Were there internal security doors, doors that might be closed when the building is not occupied?"

"Yes. Every hall had them, but I doubt they were ever used."

"And internal security stations?"

"I saw none."

Carmellini thought about it. Closed security doors made a burglar's access more difficult, but they provided a peaceful, quiet place for a burglar to work once he had gained entry.

"Do they have backup power when the power goes off?" Carmellini mused.

"They must," Chance replied thoughtfully. "A backup generator of some type. I'm going to walk in assuming that they do, but I'll be improvising as I go."

"We'll sure as hell find out soon enough, won't we," Carmellini said, and grinned. That was the first grin he had managed all afternoon. The death of the lab worker had hit him hard, but the cool execution of the guard at the front door by William Henry Chance had hit him like a punch to the solar plexus. Chance just gunned the man down and kept on trucking, as if killing another human being were something he did every morning before lunch.

All evening Carmellini had studied the older man, watched him for a sign that the murder of the guard was anything more than absolutely routine. And he had seen nothing. Nothing at all. Chance looked as if he might be having dinner in a restaurant in the Bronx with a Yankees game from a kitchen radio as background noise.

Carmellini stared at the food on the plate that the waiter put in front of him. He didn't want a mouthful. But what he wouldn't give for a stiff drink! He sipped at a glass of water, felt his stomach knot up.

"Order a drink," Chance said as he used his knife and fork. "One. Something on the rocks. You need it. We have a long night ahead."

Carmellini looked around for the waiter, and found himself staring at one of the whores at the next table, who gave him a big grin. He grinned back. A man just has to keep things in perspective.

CHAPTER THIRTEEN

The sun had been down for several hours when Enrique Poveda and Arquimidez Cabrera drove up to the fourth EHV tower they hoped to blow. After a quick look around, they unlocked the padlock on the gate and put on their tool belts. Each of the men picked a tower leg and started up. About ten feet above the ground they found the shaped charges of C-4 plastique still firmly taped to the steel legs. Working in the darkness by feel, each man took a chemical timer from his belt, a device about the size and shape of a fountain pen, and inserted it into the plastique. The timer was already set to explode as near to 1:30 A.M. as possible.

After setting the timers, they climbed down to the ground, then ascended the other two legs. In minutes they were back on the ground.

They locked the padlock, closed up the back of the van, and drove away.

"One more," Poveda said. He wished he had a map or diagram, but all that had been left behind in Florida. There he and Cabrera and the U.S. Army power grid expert had labored for days over satellite reconnaissance photos, photographs taken from the ground by not-so-innocent tourists, and computer-generated diagrams. They selected the target towers and committed their locations to memory. Not a single sheet of paper left the room with them.

So now Cabrera pointed down one street and Poveda motioned

toward another. The men chuckled. "I am very sure," Poveda said. "Two blocks down, right turn, then on for a half mile."

"Okay."

"I am glad it was tonight," Cabrera said. "The charges had been in place too long, the new padlocks were there too long, I was getting nervous—you know what I mean, my friend?"

Poveda grunted. He knew. His stomach felt as if it were tied in a knot. He hadn't felt this uptight about an operation since his first one, fifteen years ago, when he was very young. He had been to Cuba many times since, eight as he recalled, and none of them were as tense as that first time, until now.

The Cubans had almost caught him and his partner that time. The partner was eventually caught six years later and died under interrogation, or so they heard months after that. Poveda had promised himself then and there that he would never be taken alive, that he would not die in a Cuban prison.

Communists! He made a spitting motion out the open window. The communists took everything from the people in Cuba who had worked and saved and built for the future, and gave it to the people who had not. Now look at the place! Everyone poor, everyone on the edge of starvation, the cities and towns and factories rotting from lack of investment. The communists ran off the people who could make Cuba grow, the people the nation needed to feed everyone else. Ah, these bastards deserved their misery, and by God they had had some. Universal destitution was Castro's legacy, his gift to generations yet unborn.

Poveda was a pessimist. He knew that soon Castro would be dead and things would change in Cuba. "They'll forget Fidel's faults, remember just the good," he told Cabrera, for the hundredth time. "You wait and see. In a hundred years the church will make him a saint."

"Saint Fidel." Cabrera laughed.

"I shit you not. That is the way of the world. The people he pissed on the most will call him blessed."

"Saint or devil, we'll fuck the son of a bitch a little tonight," Cabrera said as the van pulled up to the last tower.

Poveda killed the van's engine and lights and the two men got out. Silence.

"Awful quiet, don't you think?" Poveda asked.

Cabrera stood by the van's rear doors, listening, looking around. Poveda dug in his pocket for the key to the padlock, inserted it.

It wouldn't fit. He tried another.

"What's wrong?"

"Key doesn't seem to want to go in this lock."

"Let's get the fuck outta here, man," Cabrera said, and started for the van's passenger door.

A spotlight hit them.

"Put up your hands," boomed a voice on a loudspeaker.

Poveda dropped to his knees, pulled a 9-mm pistol from his pocket. He didn't hesitate—he aimed at the spotlight and started shooting.

Something hit him in the back. He was down beside the rear tire trying to rise when he realized he had been shot. People shooting from two directions, muzzle flashes, thuds of bullets smacking into the van like hailstones. A groan from Cabrera.

"I'm hit, Enrique."

"Bad?"

"I think . . . I think so." He grunted as another bullet audibly smacked into his body.

The bullet that hit Poveda had come out his stomach. He could feel the wetness, the spreading warmth as blood poured from the exit wound. Not a lot of pain yet, but a huge gaping hole in his belly.

He lifted the pistol, pointed it at Arquimidez Cabrera, his best friend. There, he could see the back of his head. He fired once; Cabrera's head slammed forward into the dirt. Then he put the barrel flush against the side of his own head and pulled the trigger.

Sitting in the back of a van just down the street from the Ministry of Interior, William Henry Chance watched the second hand of his watch sweep toward the twelve. It passed 1:30 A.M. and swept on.

The lights stayed on. Carmellini was looking at his own watch.

"What the hell is wrong now?" Carmellini asked.

"I don't know."

"Oh, Lord."

They sat there in the van looking at the lights of the city.

"It went bad," Tommy Carmellini said. "Time for us to boogie."

"We'll give them a few minutes."

"Jesus, when it doesn't go down as planned, something is wrong. What are you waiting for, a phone call from Fidel? Let's bail out while our asses are still firmly attached."

"If I had any brains I wouldn't be in this business," Chance replied tartly.

His watch read exactly ten seconds after 1:32 A.M. when the lights of downtown Havana flickered. "All right," Carmellini said, and whacked his leg with his hand.

The lights flickered, dimmed, came back on, then went completely out. All the lights. Only automobile headlights broke the total darkness.

"That's it. Let's go," Chance said to Tommy Carmellini. They opened the back of the van and climbed out while the driver of the van started the engine. Chance walked the few steps back to an old Russian Lada parked at the curb behind the van and got into the passenger seat. Carmellini started the car and turned on the headlights while the van pulled away from the curb.

The two agents drove down the street toward the Ministry of Interior, a hulking immensity even darker than the night.

The three guards at the main entrance of the Ministry were illuminated by the headlights when Tommy Carmellini drove up. He killed the engine and pocketed the key as William Henry Chance got out on the passenger side.

Of course the guards had seen Chance's uniform from the car's interior light while the door was open—now they flashed the beam of a flashlight upon him. Then they saluted.

Chance was dressed in the uniform of a Security Department colonel. He had been to the building several days ago in the daytime wearing civilian clothes: he thought it highly unlikely that anyone who had seen him then would recognize him now. It was a risk he was willing to take. Still, his stomach felt as if he had swallowed a rock as he returned the guards' salute, and spoke:

"We were just a block away when the power failed all over this district."

"Yes, Colonel. Just a minute or two ago."

"And you are?"

"Lieutenant Gómez, sir, the duty officer."

"Have you taken steps to start the emergency generator, Gómez?"

"Ahh . . . I was about to do so, Colonel. It is in the basement. I was waiting to see if the power would come back on immediately. Often these outages last but moments and—"

"The darkness seems widespread, Gómez. Let us start the generator."

"Of course, Colonel." The lieutenant began giving directions to his two enlisted men, who obviously knew nothing about the emergency generator. The lieutenant began by telling them which room the generator was in.

Chance interrupted again. "Perhaps you would like to take them there, supervise the start-up, Lieutenant. My driver and I will guard the front entrance until you return."

"Of course, Colonel." With his flashlight beam leading the way, the lieutenant and the two enlisted men made for the stairs.

Carmellini opened the trunk of the car, extracted a duffle bag, which he swung over one shoulder. Without a word to Chance he disappeared into the dark interior of the building.

Carmellini took the main staircase to the top floor of the building, then strode quickly down the hall to Alejo Vargas's private office. The door was locked, of course.

Working in total darkness, Carmellini ran his hands over the door. One lock, near the handle. From the bag he extracted a small light driven by a battery unit that hooked on his belt. He donned a headband, then stuck the light to the headband with a piece of Velcro.

He checked his watch. It was 1:36 A.M.

He examined the lock, felt in the bag for his picks.

Hmmm. This one, perhaps. He inserted it into the lock.

No.

This one? Yes.

The latex gloves didn't seem to affect his feel for the lock.

Carmellini had always enjoyed pick work. The exquisite feel necessary, the patience required, the pressure of time usually, the treasure waiting to be discovered on the other side of the door . . . the CIA had been a damned lucky break. Without that break he would have certainly wound up in prison sooner or later when his luck ran out, because no one's luck lasts forever.

He inserted a smaller pick, felt for the contacts . . .

And twisted, using the strength of his fingers.

The bolt opened.

He stowed the picks, picked up the duffle bag, and opened the door.

Dark office, with the only light coming through the windows, the glow of headlights on the street below, somewhere the flicker of a fire.

The safe sat in the corner away from the windows. It was old, and huge, at least six feet tall, three feet wide and three feet deep. Painted on the door of the safe was a pastoral scene; above the landscape arranged in a semicircle were the words "United Fruit Company."

After a quick glance at the safe, Carmellini turned his attention to the rest of the room. He searched quickly and methodically. First the drawers of the desk. One of them held a pistol, one a bottle of expensive scotch whiskey and several glasses, one pens and pencils and a blank pad of paper. Several lists of names, phone numbers, addresses . . .

The lower right drawer of the desk was locked. A small, cheap furniture lock. He opened it with a knife, began examining files. The files seemed to be on senior people in the government, girlfriends, vices, lies told, bribes offered and accepted, that kind of thing.

He flipped through the files quickly, stacked them on the desk, and moved on.

The crystals were on the windowsill. A rack of books was below the window. A cursory check revealed no files peeking out between the books.

The displays of old coins didn't even rate a glance. Back before he worked for the government the coins would have made his juices flow, but not now.

On to the credenza. Many files in there. Carmellini sampled them, looking for anything on biology, weapons, strange code names. When he saw something he didn't understand he opened the file and glanced at the papers inside. People—most of these files were on people. Unfortunately Tommy didn't recognize the names. He added the files to the stack on the desk.

Now he came to the safe. They must have lifted it to this floor with a crane before the windows were installed, he thought. He checked every square inch of the exterior to see if the safe was wired. No wires.

Tommy Carmellini tried the handle.

No.

Turned the circular combination dial ever so carefully to the right, maintaining pressure on the handle. If the safe had been closed hastily, all the tumblers might not have gone home. He took his time.

No. The safe was locked.

He checked his watch. Now 1:47.

The lights would come on soon, powered by the emergency generator.

He opened the duffle bag and began extracting items. The first item he removed was a telescoping rod which he extended and positioned over the safe's combination dial; he secured it there with clamps placed on each side of the safe. Working quickly, with no lost motion, he clamped a small electric motor to the rod, then adjusted the jaws protruding from the motor so that they grasped the dial of the safe.

Other sensors were placed on the top, bottom, left, and right sides of the safe door. These sensors were held in place by magnets.

Wires led from the sensors and electric motor to a small computer, which he now took from the bag and turned on. There was one lead remaining, which he connected to a twelve-volt battery which was also in the bag.

As he waited for the computer to boot up he checked all the leads one more time. Everything okay.

Tommy Carmellini pursed his lips, as if he were whistling.

This contraption was of his own design, and with it he could open any of the older-style mechanical safes, if he were given enough time. An electrical current introduced into the door of the safe created a measurable magnetic field. The rotation of the tumblers inside the lock caused fluctuations in the field, fluctuations that were displayed on the computer screen. Finally, the computer measured the amount of electric current necessary to turn the dial of the lock; an exquisitely sensitive measurement. Using both these factors, the computer could determine the combination that would open the safe.

Sitting cross-legged in front of the safe with the computer on his lap, Carmellini tugged the latex gloves he was wearing tighter onto his hands, then manually zeroed the dial of the lock. Now he started the computer program.

The dial rotated slowly, silently, driven by the electric motor clamped to the rod. After a complete turn the dial stopped at 32. The number appeared in the upper right-hand corner of the screen. After a short pause, the dial turned to the left, counterclockwise, as Carmellini grinned happily.

In his mind's eye he could visualize the lock plates rotating, the tumblers moving. . . .

The line on the screen that tracked the magnetic field twitched unexpectedly. Carmellini frowned. He hadn't moved, the building was quiet.

Another squiggle, so insignificant he almost missed it. And another.

Someone was coming. Someone was walking softly down the hall; the sensors were picking up the shock waves of their footfalls as the waves spread out through the structure of the building.

Careful to make no noise at all, Tommy Carmellini sat the computer on the duffle bag, stood up and moved over behind the door. As he did he drew the Ruger from its holster under his shirt and thumbed off the safety, then turned off the light attached to his headband. Now he transferred the pistol to his left hand. With his right he reached into a hip pocket and extracted a sap, a flexible length of rubber with the business end weighted with lead.

The darkness appeared total as his eyes adjusted. Gradually a bit of glare from headlights faintly illuminated the room.

Carmellini had good ears, and he couldn't hear the footfalls. He could hear the tiniest whine, however, that the electric motor made as it turned the dial of the lock, the distant honking of some vehicle blocks away, and faintly, ever so faintly, the wail of a fire or police siren.

Tommy Carmellini stopped breathing, stopped thinking, stood absolutely frozen as the knob on the door slowly turned, then the door began to open.

William Henry Chance walked slowly back and forth in front of the glass doors that marked the main entrance to the Ministry. The duty officer and his two men were in the basement, doing God knows what to the emergency generator. Chance wondered how long it had been since the generator had been fueled, oiled, checked carefully, and started.

The second hand on his watch seemed frozen. He checked his watch, walked, watched cars and trucks pass by, adjusted his duty belt and pistol, reset the cap on his head, strolled some more, promised himself he wouldn't look at the luminous hands on his watch, finally peeked anyway. A minute. One lousy minute had passed.

Someone was coming along the sidewalk . . . a uniformed guard carrying an AK-47 at high port. He must be stationed at one of the side or rear entrances. The man stopped, slightly startled, when he saw Chance's figure standing in the door. Now he peered closer. And saluted.

"Sir, I am looking for the duty officer."

"He is in the basement, starting the emergency generator. Is there someone else at your post?"

"Uh, yessir. I was coming around to check if—"

"I think you should stay at your post. The emergency power for the building will come on in a few minutes, then you can make your request of the duty officer."

"Yes, sir. But the last time we started that thing, all the alarms went off, every one of them. The duty officer always wanted the alarms off before he turned the power back on."

"I am sure he will take care of that. He knows the system."

"Yessir."

"And when was the emergency generator last used, anyway?"

"The big storm last year, sir. Eight or nine months ago, I think."

"Go back to your post."

"Yes, sir." The man saluted, turned, and marched down the sidewalk. Chance could hear his footsteps for several seconds after he disappeared into the gloom.

The guy accepted him as Cuban, as had Lieutenant Gómez and his men. If they only knew the hundreds of hours of language classes that Chance had endured to learn the accent, to get it exactly right!

All in anticipation of a moment that might never come. Yet the orders did arrive, and here he was, walking around in the foyer of secret police headquarters in Havana spouting Cuban Spanish like José Martí.

He went to the guard's station, used his flashlight to examine the equipment there. The video monitors were of course blank, everything off, but where was the tape? If the power came on while he was there he didn't want to give Alejo Vargas a souvenir videotape of the men who cracked his safe.

Ah, here was the videotape machine, in this cabinet. He pushed the eject button, futilely. Without power the machine would not eject the tape that it contained. He used the Ruger—four shots into the heads of the machine.

The brass kicked out on the floor. He picked them up, pocketed them.

More pacing. Each minute was an agony of waiting.

When the power was restored to the building, he had expected the alarms to go off in Vargas's office, and to have to cover Carmellini as he made his exit. By whatever means necessary, he intended to be the only man at the main entrance when Carmellini emerged. Yet if alarms were a normal occurrence, perhaps violence would not be necessary.

The silenced Ruger rode inside his shirt under his left armpit. The pistol was an assassin's weapon, shot a .22 Long Rifle hollow-point bullet that would do minimal damage unless fired into someone's brain at point-blank range. Wounds in the limbs or body would be painful but not immediately incapacitating. The Ruger's only virtue was the silencer that dramatically muffled the report, reduced it from an ear-splitting crack to a soft, wet pop that was inaudible beyond a few feet.

He wondered how Carmellini was coming on getting the safe open. *Come on, Tommy!*

Footsteps from within the building.

Here came a flashlight.

"Ah, Colonel, the lieutenant sent me to tell you that it will not be much longer, that the generator will start very soon."

"Yes."

"He is having difficulty, the mechanical condition is not as it should be."

"I understand. I have faith in your lieutenant."

The man went back down the hallway in the direction from whence he came.

More pacing.

At least three more minutes had passed when the lieutenant came down the hallway. The occasional flicker of passing headlights revealed him to be a large, rotund man.

"I am sorry, Colonel, but we cannot make the cursed thing run."

"No harm done, if your guards stay alert. And I can always come back tomorrow for my errand, I suppose."

"We will stay alert, sir. Our duty is our trust."

"You and your men have done what you can, have you not?"

"We could awaken Colonel Santana, I suppose. Perhaps he knows more about the generator than any of us."

Chance tried to keep his voice under control. "Colonel Santana is in the building, then?"

"Yes, sir. He came in about an hour ago. He went to his apartment on the top floor. I think he was investigating the incident of the two saboteurs that were killed near a high-voltage tower south of town."

"A high-voltage tower? That sounds like attempted sabotage."

"Oh, yes, sir."

"I hadn't heard of that incident."

"Enemies of the regime, sir. Apparently some of them were successful."

"Santana is the very man I came to see," Chance declared. "Still, I did not expect to find him asleep. I suggest you give the generator one last mighty heroic effort, and if you are unsuccessful, I shall awaken Colonel Santana."

When the doorknob had turned as far as it would go, the door to Alejo Vargas's office slowly opened. Tommy Carmellini was behind the door, still as a statute in the park, with a sap in his right hand and the silenced Ruger in his left.

Now a flashlight beam shot out, swung quickly around the room, hit the safe and swung away for an instant, then returned to the door of the safe. The apparatus Carmellini had attached to the door was quite plain in the small beam, as was the tangle of wires that ran to the computer.

Faster than he would have ever believed possible, the door smashed Tommy Carmellini in the face. The impact stunned him, threw him backward against the wall.

The man sprang into the room, swung something that smacked Carmellini in the skull and made him see stars.

He was falling, off-balance, the other man coming for him in a brutal, ferocious way, when he got the Ruger more or less pointed and began pulling the trigger as fast as he could. He could barely hear the pops.

He fell to the floor and his assailant leaped on him, began smashing him in the face with his fist, repeatedly.

Swinging his right hand with all his might, Carmellini hit the other man in the side of the head with the sap. And again.

The man was slumping, falling to the left.

Carmellini gathered his strength and smashed the man again, one more time, square in the head.

The man rolled onto the floor, slumped on his back.

Carmellini sat up, his breath coming in ragged gasps. Part of his face was numb, he was drooling from a mighty punch to the mouth.

He forced himself to his knees. He pocketed the sap, reached for the flashlight, which was lying on the floor still lit. He played the light on the face of his assailant.

Santana.

Oooh, damn!

He checked the pistol. He had fired at least five shots. A couple of the spent brass were lying near Santana, who had a bloody place on his chest, one on his neck. Hit twice, at least.

Maybe one of the little .22 bullets would kill him.

Maybe not.

Tommy Carmellini found to his surprise that he didn't care one way or the other.

He put the pistol back in its holster, wiped his face with his shirt, and went back to the computer.

The combination was right there on the screen, all three numbers. The dial wasn't moving.

He tried the handle, put some weight on it. It moved.

The safe was open!

He wiped his face on his sleeve, willed himself back to his task. First he stowed the computer and sensors and telescoping rod in his duffel bag. Then he opened the safe, examined its contents with Santana's flashlight, then turned on his headband light.

Lots of papers, files, two shelves of them. The top shelf consisted of files on people, each file had a person's name. These were the files he had come to find. He raked these into his duffel bag.

Ah, on the second shelf . . . files labeled with numbers. He looked inside one. Engineering drawings, possibly of a warhead . . .

He dumped everything that looked interesting into his duffel bag, including the stack of files on Vargas's desk.

Oh, here was a file about supplies from a Miami laboratory supply house . . . one about susceptibility studies, lethality, vaccines . . . he stuffed all these in the bag, began checking another handful.

The hell with it! He would take everything. The files on the bottom shelf might prove as interesting as those on the top. The bag would be heavy, but he could lift it. He transferred the files to the bag as quickly as he could.

When he had all the files, he hoisted the bag experimentally. Eighty pounds, at least. Room for a few more things . . .

What else did Vargas keep in his safe? A small laptop computer. Well, he certainly didn't need that anymore. Into the bag with it.

He was pawing through one of the side drawers when he sensed movement behind him.

As he turned Santana's fist grazed his jaw—his turn had been just enough to save his life. The headband and light flew away, somewhere, the little beam flashing around crazily.

He groped for his sap, swung it in a roundhouse right and connected with bone.

Santana went sideways to the floor.

No time for this! The man is too dangerous!

He pulled out the Ruger, thumbed off the safety and was ready when Santana came off the floor again. The pistol coughed.

Santana's momentum drove his body forward and he collapsed against Carmellini's feet.

The American stepped around the body. He put the pistol away, stowed the headband light, zipped the duffel bag closed.

After a quick last look around, Tommy Carmellini went to the door, made sure it would lock behind him. He came back for the duffel bag, hoisted it to his left shoulder.

Out in the dark hall, he pulled the door shut, made sure it was locked, then walked quickly down the dark hallway for the stairs.

Tommy Carmellini held the Ruger down by his leg as he descended the stair and walked across the lobby toward the shadowy figure standing in the doorway.

As he walked the lights came on. Instantly an alarm sounded, loud enough to wake the dead.

He squinted against the light. That was Chance standing in the doorway.

"Into the car, quickly now," Chance said. The alarms were wailing and every light in the building was on, with not a soul in sight. If they could be gone before the lieutenant and his men got back up here, he wouldn't have to kill them—they couldn't have seen his face very well in the darkness.

His watch read 2:04 A.M.

Chance stood in the doorway with euphoria flooding over him while Carmellini stowed the bag in the backseat of the car, got into the driver's seat, and started the engine. Three long strides, he jerked open the passenger's door and jumped inside, and Carmellini fed gas.

The lights in the rest of the city were still off, however, so when the car pulled away from the building the night swallowed it.

"What did you get?"

"I got the safe open—took two drawers full of files, everything made of paper that was in there, some files from a desk. Got a laptop, too."

"Well done."

"Someone came in while I was there. Santana, I think. Left him for dead."

"Was he dead?"

"I didn't take the time to check, and to be honest, I really don't care one way or the other. I put six bullets into the son of a bitch and whaled on him a while with the sap. If he isn't dead he ought to be."

Chance flipped on the interior light of the car, just long enough to check Carmellini's face. "Looks like he got a piece or two of you."

"Oh, yeah. He was damned quick."

"Did he get a look at your face?"

"I don't think so. Pretty dark. And he's probably dead. Don't sweat it."

Chance grunted and stared out the window at the dark, decaying city.

The voyagers on the *Angel del Mar* saw a ship during the night. It came out of one dark corner of the universe and passed within a half mile of the derelict as the people aboard shouted and waved the single working flashlight.

The ship was a freighter of some type, huge, with lights strung all over the topside and superstructure. It raced through their world and disappeared into the void as quickly as it came, leaving the people gasping on deck, exhausted, starved, devoid of hope.

A child had died earlier in the evening, just at sunset, and some of the people aboard had wanted to eat it. "She is beyond caring, and her body can give us life," one man said, a sentiment several agreed with.

The old fisherman went below to tell Ocho, who was taking his turn on the pump, which meant he had to pump out the water that had accumulated because the man before him could not keep abreast of it, as well as the water that came in on his watch. He was on the ragged edge of total exhaustion, but he listened to the old fisherman as he struggled with the pump handle.

"Maybe . . ." Ocho began, but the old man would not listen.

"To eat her would be sacrilege, the moral death of every one who tastes her flesh or watches others eat it. All flesh must die, but to face God with that on our souls would be unforgivable. Come with me! *Come!*"

He half dragged Ocho up the ladder. Together they swung hard fists left and right, reached the corpse, and tossed it into the sea.

In the fading light the old fisherman stood with his back to the wheelhouse and shouted at the others, some too weak to move. He damned them, dared them, kicked at those who came too close, punched one man so hard he nearly went overboard.

The child's body floated, supported by the great vast moving ocean, just out of reach, moving with the rise and fall of the swells. Some of the people looked at it, others refused to. When the last of the light faded the body disappeared into the total darkness.

Ocho went back down the ladder to the hold, which reeked of vomit and filth. He worked the pump handle like an automaton.

Finally the fisherman relieved him, helped him up the ladder.

He was lying by a scupper when the ship went by. He roused himself, stood with a hand on the rail, tried to shout and found he had no voice left.

Then someone tried to push him overboard.

There was no mistake. The hard shove in the back, the continuing pressure.

Only his raw strength saved him. Ocho turned and swung blindly, felt his fist connect with cartilage and bone, swung several more times before the man went down.

Ocho collapsed from the exertion. He crawled forward, intent on beating the man as long as he had strength to swing his fists, but Dora was there, sobbing, and stopped him.

"No, no, no, my God!" she howled. "You are killing him!"

"He tried to shove me over."

"Oh, damn you, Ocho. If it weren't for you, we would be safe in Cuba."

"Me?"

"You were his ticket out. You! This is your fault."

"And you are blameless. With the baby in your body you risked your life."

"I am not pregnant! I have never been pregnant! He made me tell you I was so you would come." And she dissolved in sobbing.

Ocho lay in the darkness trying to think, trying to see the boat and the people as God must see then, looking down from above.

Fortunately rain fell occasionally, enough to fill the bucket and let people drink. Maybe God was sending the showers.

He was starving, though, and oh so tired.

His whole life had dissolved into nothing and was soon to end, and he didn't care. He tried to tell Dora that it didn't matter but he couldn't and she was sobbing hysterically, and in truth he really didn't care.

After another turn at the pump, Ocho came back on deck and looked for Diego and Dora, to say something—he didn't know what—but something that would make their burdens easier to carry.

But Diego wasn't there. He wasn't in the hold and he wasn't in the wheelhouse and he wasn't on deck. Ocho scanned the sea, checking in all directions, looking for a head bobbing amid the heaving swells.

Dora was curled in a ball near the bow. He shook her.

"Where's Diego?"

She had a dazed look on her face, as if she didn't understand the words. He repeated the question several times.

She looked around, trying to understand.

"I do not see him," Ocho said, trying to explain. "Did he fall overboard?"

She stared at him with eyes that refused to focus. Her face was vacant, blank. Finally her eyes focused.

"He climbed the rail last night. Jumped in the ocean."

Ocho looked again on both sides of the boat, staggered to the port side so he could look aft past the wheelhouse. Then he returned.

She was lying down again, curled up, her chin against a knee.

He left her there, laid down and tried to rest.

CHAPTER FOURTEEN

"Who did this to you?"

Alejo Vargas asked the question of Colonel Santana while he lay on a gurney in the hospital emergency room being prepped for surgery. He had four bullets in him and a wicked wound on his forehead where a bullet had ricochetted off his skull. His jaw and one cheekbone were severely swollen, his nose smashed, he had lost two teeth, and he obviously had a concussion. The pupil in his right eye was dilated and refused to focus.

"I don't know," Santana managed. He tried to swallow, almost choked on his tongue. After gagging several times, he seemed to relax.

"American?"

"I do not know. Nothing was said, it was dark. He was waiting behind the door when I went in."

"One of the bullets penetrated the wall of his chest, Minister," the doctor said. "We must get it out and stop the hemorrhaging. He needs a transfusion and rest."

Vargas left the emergency room. The car drove him back to the ministry and he took the elevator to his office.

The workers had the worst of the damage cleaned up. Still, the door to the safe was standing open and the drawers within were empty.

The priceless files on the generals and top government people that had taken twenty years to compile, gone—like a storm in the night.

Every sin known to man was somewhere in one of those files: marital infidelity, theft, rape, incest, sodomy, even murder. Those files were the key to his power, to his ability to make things happen anywhere in Cuba. And now they were gone.

Hector Sedano was his first suspect. Of course Hector himself was in La Cabana, but someone could have robbed the safe on his behalf.

And it could be one of the generals, or Admiral Delgado. Any one of those ambitious fools.

Raúl Castro? A possibility, but he discounted it. Then the fact that he thought Raúl Castro an unlikely suspect made him suspicious. He would have Raúl checked, followed day and night, everyone he spoke to would be scrutinized.

Truly there was much to do. Much to do.

The electrical outage made the burglary possible. Four towers down, two dead saboteurs.

There was a trail out there, and some diligent investigating would eventually lead him to the man or men who did this crime.

Not that it would do any good. Whoever had those files would undoubtedly destroy them immediately.

All his plans, all that work . . . up in smoke.

Alejo Vargas didn't believe in coincidences. Whoever robbed that safe made extensive preparations. This was no spur-of-the-moment thing—the robbery was carefully, meticulously planned.

He looked again at the safe. Not a mark on it. Someone had dialed the combination. He had heard that such things were possible, but he had never seen it done. Nor heard of it being done in Cuba. Yesterday he would have said there was not a man in Cuba with that kind of talent.

And the files on the biological program were gone.

The day after the break-in at the lab.

The lab break-in wasn't Hector's style—he would have no reason to burgle the place, nor would anyone else—there was nothing there to steal.

Except poliomyelitis viruses. Would Hector gain political advantage by publicizing the biological weapons program, proving its existence?

The Americans . . .

Alejo Vargas stood looking at his empty safe, thinking about Americans.

The Americans were a possibility, he reluctantly concluded.

He got a magnifying glass from the top drawer of his desk, examined the door of the safe as carefully as he could.

There were marks, scratches, several together. He could see them. But how long had they been there? What were they made by?

There was no one to tell him, and he decided finally that perhaps it didn't matter. The people who opened this safe and stole the keys to Cuba had brought down the power grid in central Havana. That was where the trail began.

He spent a few seconds in contemplation of his revenge when he caught these men.

"Minister, here is Lieutenant Gómez, who had the duty last night."

"You saw these men, Gómez?"

"Two men arrived just seconds after the lights went out, sir. I saw the colonel for a few seconds in a flashlight beam. The driver, no."

"What did this man look like?"

"He was tall, not fat."

"His accent?"

"None that I noticed, sir."

"Come, come, Lieutenant. Was he from Cuba, from Havana or Oriente, or did he speak Castilian Spanish?"

"From Havana, I thought, sir. He sounded like you and me."

"What did he say?"

"That we should start the emergency generator."

"So you did?"

"Yes, sir. Without power the alarms were disabled, we could not talk to each other on the telephone, the security of the building was compromised. My men and I went to the basement and worked on the generator. I came back upstairs once and reported to the colonel, told him we were having difficulties; he said he had faith. When we got the generator going and went back upstairs, the colonel and his driver and vehicle were gone."

"You had never seen this colonel before?"

"Not to my knowledge, sir."

"Would you recognize him if you saw him again?"

"Oh, yes, sir."

No, he wouldn't, Vargas decided. If this colonel thought there was a glimmer of a chance Lieutenant Gómez would recognize him then or later, he would have killed him. Gómez was alive because he posed no threat.

Vargas dismissed Gómez and called in his department heads to give them orders.

With no ceremony and no conversation, Mercedes Sedano was released from the presidential palace. A butler came to the door, suggested she pack.

The electrical power was still off. It had been off when she awoke this morning, and she was given stale bread and water for breakfast.

She put the clothes she wished to keep in two shopping bags that were on the floor of the closet, sandwiched the cassettes in between them, and took a last look around the apartment. The butler returned five minutes later and led her out. Without electricity the palace looked dark and grim. She wanted desperately to be gone, to bring an end to this phase of her life. She bit her lip to keep herself under control.

The butler paused in an empty hallway, looked around to ensure that there were no maids about, then whispered, "They've arrested your brother-in-law Hector Sedano. He is in La Cabana."

Then he took her to the door of the palace, said a barely audible good-bye, and closed the door behind her.

She walked past the guards and continued down the street to the bus stop. The electrical power seemed off everywhere, yet the streets of Havana hustled and bustled as usual. Didn't they know Fidel was dead?

She dared not ask.

On the bus she saw a newspaper lying on a nearby seat and scanned the front page. The usual stuff, nothing about Fidel.

So they had not announced his death.

She transferred to another bus, left her clothes with a friend in a shop on the Malecon. The shop was closed because of the lack of electricity, but Mercedes tapped on the window until her friend came to open the door.

Her friend was very agitated. She drew Mercedes into the tiny dark storeroom. "I have heard they arrested Hector. What does it mean?"

"I do not know," Mercedes told her, shaking her head.

"Hector's friends are on fire," said the shopkeeper, "and he has many, many friends. I heard there was a riot in Mariel after he was arrested. The newspapers have nothing on it, yet the story is on everyone's lips. People are coming in, asking me about it, because they know I know you."

Mercedes assured the woman she knew nothing, that she was as mystified as everyone on the street.

She rode buses through the city to La Cabana.

The guard at the gate recognized her name and sent a man to fetch the duty officer, a Captain Franqui. He treated her with respect, took her to his office, a dark cubicle near the gate, and sent a note to the commandante. While the note was being delivered he apologized for the lack of electricity. "It has not been off this long in years."

In five minutes she and Franqui were in the commandante's office. He was a heavy-set, balding officer who looked as if he were frightened of his own shadow.

"I have my orders," he said. "I cannot admit you. He is to see no one."

"Fidel sent me," she said simply, without inflection. "Hector is my brother-in-law."

The commandante looked as if wild horses were trying to tear him in half. Obviously he knew of the relationship between Mercedes and Fidel. The blood drained from his florid face as he weighed his fear of Fidel against his fear of Vargas.

Captain Franqui understood the commandante's dilemma. "Perhaps, if I may be so bold, sir, it might be best if you were indisposed, at lunch perhaps, and I acted on my own initiative in light of the lady's impeccable credentials."

The commandante grasped at this straw. "I cannot be everywhere or make every decision, can I?"

"No, sir. If you will excuse us?" Captain Franqui took Mercedes's elbow and steered her expertly from the office into the hallway.

"I myself am an admirer of Hector Sedano," Captain Franqui confided as they walked. "He is a great patriot and a man of God. Surely he will serve Cuba well in the years ahead."

After several minutes of platitudes, she found herself standing in front of Hector's cell in the isolation wing. None of the other cells contained people. Captain Franqui disappeared, leaving the two of them alone.

"Are they listening?" she whispered.

"Probably not," he said. "The electricity is off, and they would need it to listen."

"How long have you been here?"

"Two days. For two days I've been sitting alone in this hole. No one comes to see me."

"They will admit no one. I told them Fidel had sent me, and the commandante was afraid to refuse."

"Ah, yes, Fidel."

"He is dead."

"I am sorry, Mercedes," he said softly, so softly she almost missed his words.

"It had to happen. He and I both knew it, accepted it."

Hector sighed. "That explains my arrest, then."

"Two days ago."

"The cancer finally, eh?"

"Poison! He poisoned himself rather than make a tape naming Vargas as his successor."

Hector crossed himself.

"It was not a sin," she said, desperate to explain. "He merely speeded things up a few days."

Hector leaned forward, let his forehead touch the cool steel bars.

"I heard there was a riot in Mariel after you were arrested." Her voice was very soft, a whisper in church.

"I did not know that."

"A friend told me."

"Have you heard from Ocho?"

"Nothing. Is he not at home?"

"He went on a boat with some others. They were going to America."

"I have heard nothing."

Hector sagged, fought to stay erect. He looked so . . . so different than Fidel, Mercedes thought. He was not tall, vigorous, oozing machismo. And yet Fidel thought Hector could lead Cuba!

She got as close to the bars as she could, and whispered, "I need to talk to the Americans as soon as possible. Should I see the little man you gave the Swiss bank account numbers to? The stadium keeper?"

"He might betray you. He talks to Vargas too. I tried to frighten him, and may have succeeded too well."

"Who, then?"

"Go to the American mission. Ask for the cultural aide, I think his name is Bouchard. He is CIA, I believe."

"Fidel signed bank transfer orders for Maximo, who went flying off to Switzerland, just as we thought he would. I have not heard if he got the money."

"He will not come back if he gets it," Hector said.

"Maximo would steal it," she agreed. "But do you think the Americans will ever give the money back?"

"I have heard their courts are fair. I would rather try to get the money back from them than from Maximo."

She nodded at that.

"Why do you want to talk to the Americans now?" Hector asked.

She told him.

The secret police had the bodies of the two saboteurs laid out in the basement of police headquarters when Vargas saw them. Two Latin-looking males who had spent many years in the United States, from the look of their dental work. Exiles, probably.

Vargas examined their clothes, which were in a pile, and stirred through the contents of the van. He examined the chemical timers and C-4 shaped charges, the guns and electrical tape, and tossed everything back on the table.

CIA.

No doubt in his mind.

Four extra-high-voltage towers had collapsed, killing power to the two substations that fed central Havana and the government office buildings located there.

A neat and tidy operation.

And as soon as the power went off, a team of burglars entered the Interior Ministry and robbed the safe in his office, carrying away files that he had spent twenty years collecting.

The Americans.

And he had not an iota of proof, nor would he ever get any.

The burglars also stole his laptop computer, and the thought of its loss gave him pause. Certainly not as valuable as the files, the laptop had many things on it he wished the Americans did not have.

He had used the computer to derive the trajectories for the missiles' guidance systems, which had to be reprogrammed when the warheads were changed, the new biological warheads being significantly lighter than the old nuclear ones. Still, if the Americans didn't know about the missiles, perhaps they wouldn't pay much attention to that file.

What the burglary showed, Alejo Vargas concluded, was that time was short. The Americans could move fast and decisively—to win the game he was going to have to move faster.

I'm ready, he told himself. *Now is the hour.*

"I am Bouchard, the cultural attaché."

Mercedes Sedano smiled, shook the offered hand.

"Please sit down." Bouchard looked embarrassed, as if he rarely entertained visitors in this small office, which was packed with Cuban magazines and newspapers. Four candles sat atop the piles. "The power is still out," he said by way of explanation. "And the emergency generator ran out of fuel an hour ago."

"I don't know how to begin, Doctor," she said.

"I am not a real doctor," he said apologetically. "I am a scholar."

"My brother-in-law is Hector Sedano," she explained. "He said I should come to you."

"My work is strictly cultural, señora. I work for the American state department studying the culture of Cuba. I cannot imagine how I could be of service to you, or anybody else. I write studies of Cuban music, literature, drama. . . ."

"I know nothing about the branches of the American government," she said.

Bouchard smiled. "I know very little myself," he confided.

"You still haven't asked why I am here."

"I ask now, señora. What may I do for you?"

"My brother-in-law, Hector Sedano, says you work for the CIA. He—"

Bouchard was horrified. His hands came up, palms out. "Señora, you have been severely misinformed. As I have just explained, I am a scholar who—"

"Yes, yes. I understand. But I have a problem that—"

He clapped his hands over his ears. "No, no, no. You have made a great mistake," he said.

She sat calmly, waiting for him to lower his hands. When he saw that she was not going to speak, he did so. "I must show you my work," Bouchard said, and dug into a drawer. He came up with a handful of paper, which he thrust at her. "I recently completed a major study of—"

She refused to touch the paper. "Fidel Castro is dead," she said.

Bouchard froze. After a few seconds he remembered the paper in his hand and laid it on top of the nearest pile.

"I was there when he died. We were filming a statement to the Cuban people, a political will, if you please." She produced two videotapes from her large purse and laid them on the nearest pile.

"He died before he finished his speech," she explained. "Which is inconvenient and, in a larger sense, tragic."

"I *assure* you, Señora Sedano, that I am a poor scholar, mediocre in every sense, employed here in Cuba because I tired of the publish-or-perish imperative of the academic world. My work is of little import to the United States government or anyone else. *I do not work for the CIA.* There has been some mistake."

Mercedes maintained a polite silence until he ran out of words, then she said, "Fidel and I watched an American movie a few months ago, about dinosaurs in a park—an extraordinary story and an extraordinary film. We marveled at the magic that could make dinosaurs so lifelike upon the screen. It was almost as if the moviemakers had some dinosaurs to film. Perhaps the magic had something to do with computers. However they did it, they made something that had been dead a very long time come back to life."

Bouchard didn't know what to say. Agency regulations did not permit him to tell anyone outside the agency who his employer was. He twisted his hands as he tried to decide how he should handle this woman who refused to listen to his denials.

"Did you say something?" she asked.

"I don't like movies," Bouchard muttered. "There are no good actors these days."

"Perhaps not living," said Mercedes Sedano. "But you must admit the magicians have given new life to some dead ones. You and your friends could perform a great service for Cuba if you would take these videotapes to the moviemakers and let them bring Fidel back to life. For just a little while."

Bouchard picked up the cassettes, held them in his hands as he examined them.

"I suppose the cultural attaché might be able to pass these things along," Bouchard admitted. "What is it you wish Fidel had lived to say?"

Mercedes nodded. She looked Bouchard straight in the eyes and told him.

Maximo Sedano huddled in his great padded leather chair at the Finance Ministry staring out at the Havana skyline. He took another sip of rum, eased the position of his injured hand. He was holding it pointed straight up. The doctor who set the broken bones in his fingers assured him elevating the hand would help keep the swelling down.

That pig Santana! He whipped out his pistol and smashed it down on the fingers of Maximo's left hand so quickly Maximo didn't even think of jerking it away. Three broken fingers.

Then the son of a bitch laughed! And Vargas laughed.

Vargas had whispered in his ear: "You aren't going to be the next president of Cuba, Maximo. You have no allies. Delgado and Alba will obey me to their dying day, as you will. You have a wife and daughter and your health. Be content with that."

He said nothing.

"Your brother Hector is in prison charged with sedition. I suggest you meditate upon that fact."

Maximo sipped some more rum.

His fingers hurt like hell. The doctor gave him a local anesthetic and a half dozen pills when he set the fingers, but now the anesthetic was wearing off and the pills weren't doing much good.

He probably shouldn't be drinking rum while taking these pills, but what the hell. A man has to die only once.

Where was the $53 million?

Somewhere on the other side of the black hole that was the Swiss banking system.

Face facts, Maximo. You can kiss those bucks good-bye. Those dollars might as well be on the backside of the moon.

He spent some time dwelling on what might have been—he was only human—but after a while those dreams faded. The reality was the pain in his hand, and the fact that he was stuck in this Third World hellhole and would soon be out of a job. Whatever government followed Fidel would appoint a new finance minister.

He had no chance of succeeding Castro, and he let go of that fantasy too. He didn't have the allies in high places, he wasn't well enough known, and if he had been he would be in a cell beside Hector this very minute.

Hector's plight didn't cause him much concern. He and Hector had never been close, had never had much in common. Well, to be frank, they loathed each other.

A pigeon landed on the ledge outside his window. He watched it idly. It searched the ledge for food, found none, then took off.

Maximo watched it. The pigeon circled the square in front of the ministry and landed on a statue that stood near the front door. Maximo had never liked the statue, some Greek goddess with a sword. Still, it gave the building a certain tone, so he had never ordered it moved.

Statues. At least he got the goddess instead of that larger-than-life bust of Fidel that the Ministry of Agriculture—

He stared at the goddess. She was made of bronze. Some kind of metal that had turned green as the rain and sun and salt from the sea worked on it.

The bust of Fidel in front of the Ministry of Agriculture was of course manufactured and erected after the revolution.

So were the statues in the Plaza de Revolucion. And some of the statues in Old Havana, at the Museo de Arte Colonial, at the Catedral de San Cristobal de la Havana, on some of the minor squares.

After the revolution! After the government collected all the gold pesos, or before?

The Museum of the Revolution! The old presidential palace was converted to a propaganda temple that would prove to all generations the venality of Batista, the dictator Fidel had overthrown. Maximo recalled reading somewhere that Fidel had personally supervised the renovation and conversion of the old building.

Thirty-seven tons of gold. Fidel had squirreled it away somewhere.

What he needed to do was go to the Museum of the Revolution, lock himself in a room with the collection of Havana newspapers. After the revolution, after the gold was collected, what was Fidel doing?

Thirty-seven tons of gold.

"One sample vial from the Cuban lab contained a new, super-infectious strain of poliomyelitis. The viruses are so hot they kill in seconds."

The members of the National Security Council didn't say anything.

"The scientists said they never saw anything like it," the national security adviser continued. "The four sample vials contained three different strains of the polio virus. Two of the vials contained the same type of virus."

"Is the vaccination we were all given as children effective against these strains?" The chairman of the joint chiefs asked this question.

"Apparently not. The scientists will need more time to verify that, but apparently . . . no."

The president looked glum. "Talk about a choice. We can wait until the Cubans use that stuff on us or we can bomb the lab right now."

"No, sir," the chairman said. "There is no guarantee a bomb would kill that virus. Bombing the lab would probably just release the viruses to the atmosphere and kill everyone in Cuba who happened to be downwind."

The silence that followed that remark was broken by the secretary of state, who asked, "Do the scientists have an estimate on how long those viruses can live outside the lab?"

"Not yet," the national security adviser replied. He took a deep breath and referred back to his notes. "Here is the situation in Cuba as we believe it to be: We received a report two hours ago from our man in Havana who says he was told earlier today that Fidel Castro is dead. He is sending some videotapes in the diplomatic pouch."

"Dead, huh?" said the president. "I'll believe it when they put his corpse on display in a tomb on the Plaza de Revolucion."

Someone tittered.

The national security adviser continued to read from his notes. "Review of the documents from the safe of the secret police chief, Alejo Vargas, indicates that the Cubans have installed biological warheads on intermediate-range ballistic missiles."

"*What?*" the president demanded. He pounded on the table with the flat of his hand to silence everyone else. In the silence that followed, he roared, "Where in hell did those people get ballistic missiles?"

The national security adviser looked like he was in severe pain. "From the Russians, sir. In 1962. Apparently the Russians left some behind after the Cuban missile crisis. You may recall that Castro refused to let the UN inspection team into the country to verify that all the missiles had been removed."

"How good is this information?"

"The man who sent it is absolutely reliable."

The president mouthed a profane oath, which the chairman of the joint chiefs thought a succinct summation of the whole situation.

CHAPTER FIFTEEN

In a country as poor as Cuba safe houses were hard to come by. The one that William Henry Chance and Tommy Carmellini found themselves in was an abandoned monastery on a promontory of land on the south coast of the island. Surrounded by tidal flats and dense vegetation, the sprawling one-story building was an occasional refuge for drug smugglers and young lovers, who had left their trash strewn about. The rotten thatched roof remained intact over just one room, the kitchen. A roaring fire burned in the fireplace, which apparently the monks had used primarily for cooking.

From the window three fishing boats were visible, wooden boats with a single mast, manned by one or two men. The crew of two of the boats were rigging trot lines, the other was hauling in a net. Chance examined each through binoculars. They looked harmless enough—he doubted if any of the boats had an engine or radio.

"What do you think?" Carmellini asked.

"We have a little time, but I don't know how much."

"Guess it depends on how efficient the secret police and the military are."

"Umm," Chance grunted, and after one more sweep of everything in sight, put down the binoculars.

Tommy Carmellini sat feeding sheets of paper from the secret police files into the fire as fast as they would burn. He merely scanned the pages as he ripped them from the files and tossed them into the flames.

"Vargas and his guys were certainly thorough," Carmellini commented. "They looked under every rock."

"And found every slimy thing that walks or crawls," Chance agreed. Vargas's laptop was on, so Chance resumed his examination of the files.

"Sort of like J. Edgar Hoover."

"Secret police are pretty much alike the world over," Chance muttered. He moved the cursor to the next file on the list and called it up.

"How many missiles are there on this island?" Carmellini asked as he tore paper.

"I have found six missile files, so far. There may be more—I see some references to material that doesn't seem to be on this computer."

"Six? With locations?"

"Names only. Every missile has a name: Miami, Atlanta, Jacksonville, Charleston, New Orleans, and Tampa."

"What about Mobile?"

"Don't see it on here."

"Birmingham, Orlando, the army bases in Alabama?"

"Nothing."

"I find it hard to believe that in the decades since 1962, the Cubans have managed to keep the secret of their ballistic missiles."

Chance didn't reply. He had never agreed with the agency's spending priorities, which were heavily slanted toward reconnaissance satellites. The people in Washington were sold on high-tech computer and sensor networks for the collection of intelligence. Hardware and software didn't turn traitor and were easy to justify to the bean counters. The spymasters seemed to have lost sight of a basic truth: networks could only collect the information their sensors were designed to obtain. And they could be fooled. If garbage goes in, garbage comes out.

Ah, well. The world keeps turning.

"How long is that going to take?" Chance asked, referring to the files and the fire.

"Couple hours at this rate."

Chance glanced at his watch. A few minutes after one o'clock in the afternoon. The rendezvous with the submarine was set for ten o'clock tonight, almost nine hours away. "If we have to run for it, we'll take everything we haven't burned."

He and Carmellini and the four U.S. Navy SEALS on guard in the grasses and bushes out front would try to escape if the Cubans attacked the place. Two speedboats were fueled and ready inside the old boathouse, and a submarine would meet them fifty miles south.

Unfortunately he had no way of knowing if the submarine was already lying submerged at the rendezvous position or if the skipper planned to arrive punctually. If he was already there, Chance, Carmellini, and the SEALs could leave now. If the sub wasn't at the rendezvous, the two boats would have to spend the afternoon and evening rolling in the swell, hoping and praying the Cuban Navy didn't come over the horizon.

We'll wait, Chance decided, glancing at his watch again, though Lord knows the waiting was difficult.

It would be a serious mistake to underestimate Alejo Vargas. The Cuban secret police had over forty years of practice finding and arresting people who sneaked onto the island—one had to assume they were reasonably good at it.

Chance didn't want to get into a firefight with the Cuban military or secret police. Leaving a body behind would be bad, and leaving a live person to be captured and tortured would be absolute disaster.

If the Cubans came riding over the hill, Chance and his entourage were leaving as quickly as possible. They could take their chances on the open sea. That decision made, Chance turned his attention back to the computer screen in front of him.

Two months ago when he and Carmellini were handed this mission, William Henry Chance would not have bet a plugged nickel they could pull it off. Polish the Spanish in over a hundred hours of classes, be in the right place at the right time when the power went off, break into Alejo Vargas's safe in secret-police headquarters, carry out the files that Vargas had spent twenty years accumulating, the files he could trade for political support after Castro's death.

Amazingly, they had pulled it off. Every file that went into the flames was one Vargas would never use.

Chance glanced at Carmellini, who was using a stick to stir the fire, keep the paper burning.

Yep, they had pulled it off. And stumbled upon a biological weapons program and Fidel's collection of old Soviet ballistic missiles.

Six missiles. No locations.

The locations must be well camouflaged or the satellite reconnaissance people would have seen them long ago. On the other hand, if they knew what they were looking for . . .

Chance went to the door, called softly to the SEAL lieutenant. "Mr. Fitzgerald, would you set up the satellite telephone again?"

"Of course. Take about five minutes."

"Thank you."

While the lieutenant was getting the set turned on and acquiring the com satellite, Chance continued to check the computer. When he hit a file labeled "Trajectories" he sensed he was onto something important.

The file was a series of mathematical calculations, complex formulas. Hmmm . . . *Let's see, if one could figure out where the warheads were aimed, then one could use the known trajectory to work back to the launch site. That's right, isn't it?*

"Mr. Chance, they're on." The lieutenant handed him the satellite phone.

In Washington, D.C., the director of the CIA and the national security adviser listened without comment as the voice of the agent in Cuba came over the speaker phone. He gave them the news as quickly and succinctly as he could. They had the secret-police files, were burning them now though the task would take several more hours, they had a computer containing a file of what appeared to be missile-trajectory calculations, and there were at least six ballistic missiles in Cuba, maybe more. Chance gave the men in Washington the names of the missiles.

"Well done," the director said, high praise from that taciturn public servant.

When the connection was broken, the national security adviser and the CIA director sat silently, lost in thought. The spymaster was thinking about Alejo Vargas and the possibility he might seize control of the government in Cuba upon the death of Castro. The other man was thinking about ballistic missiles and microscopic viruses of poliomyelitis.

"Another Cuban missile crisis," muttered the adviser disgustedly.

The CIA director grinned. "Why don't you look at the silver lining of this cloud for a change? Fate has just presented us with a rare opportunity to clean out a local cesspool. We ought to be down on our knees giving thanks."

The adviser didn't see it that way. He knew the president regarded the upcoming death of Castro as a political opportunity, a chance to change the relationship between Cuba and the United States and escape the bitter past. Perhaps the president would decide to just ignore the weapons, pretend they didn't exist. Then he could hold out the olive branch to the Cubans, get what he wanted from them, get credit for progressive leadership from the American electorate, and negotiate about the weapons later.

Tommy Carmellini was burning the last of the files when William Henry Chance noticed that two of the fishing boats were no longer in sight. "When did they leave?" he asked the naval officer, Lieutenant Fitzgerald.

"Several hours ago, sir. I noticed one of them going west under sail then, but I confess I haven't been paying much attention to the others."

Carmellini checked his watch—5:30 P.M. Still three or four hours of daylight left.

"Anything stirring out here?" Chance asked.

"No, sir. Pretty quiet. An old man and a girl walked along the road toward the monastery about three P.M., then turned and went back the way they had come."

"Did they see your men?"

"No, sir."

"Well . . ." In truth, Chance was nervous. He felt trapped, completely at the mercy of forces beyond his control. He took a deep breath, tried to relax as Carmellini stirred the ashes of the fire to ensure that all the paper he had thrown in was totally consumed.

"Would you like some MREs, sir?" the navy officer asked. "My men and I are getting hungry."

Surprised at himself for not noticing his hunger sooner, Chance said, "Why not?" He hadn't had a bite since last night.

They were munching at the rations when a helicopter came roaring down the coast from the west. The craft was doing about eighty knots, Chance guessed, when it went over the old monastery. It continued west for a half mile or so, then laid into a turn.

"Shit," said Tommy Carmellini.

"Lieutenant, I think he's onto us," Chance told the SEAL officer.

"If he is, his friends can't be far away," the SEAL said. Standing in the center of the room so he was hidden in shadow, he used the binoculars to look at the chopper.

"Two men, one looking at us with binoculars."

"Maybe it's time we set sail," Chance said as he folded the laptop and zipped it into its soft carrying bag. Then he put the whole thing in a waterproof plastic bag, which he carefully sealed.

"Stay down, stay clear of the windows," the lieutenant said, and darted out the door away from the chopper.

Chance and Carmellini sat on the floor with their backs to the window. The chopper noise came closer and closer, then seemed to stop. It sounded as if the craft were hovering about a hundred feet to the east of the crumbling building. The rotor wash was stirring the remnants of the roof thatch that Chance could see.

Then he heard the sharp crack of a rifle. Two more reports in quick succession. The tone of the chopper's engine changed, then he heard the sound of the crash.

He risked a peek out the window. The wreckage of the helicopter lay on the rocks by the water's edge. Amazingly, one of the rotor blades was still attached to the head and turning slowly. A wisp of smoke rose from the twisted metal and Plexiglas. Chance could see the bodies of the two men slumped motionless in what remained of the cockpit. As he watched the wreckage broke into flames.

"Sorry about that," the lieutenant said as he burst into the room, "but the copilot was holding a radio mike in his hand. I think it's time we bid Cuba a fond farewell."

"Let's go," Chance agreed.

The boats were fast, at least thirty knots. In the swell of the open sea beyond the peninsula they bucked viciously. Salt spray came back over the men huddled behind the tiny windscreen every time the boat buried its bow.

Chance settled back, wedged himself into place with the computer on his lap.

They were well out to sea, heading due south, when a Cuban gunboat rounded the eastern promontory and gave chase. A puff of smoke came from the forward deck gun and was swept away by the wind.

The splash was several hundred yards short.

The lieutenant at the helm altered course to put the gunboat dead astern. The Cuban captain fired twice more; both rounds fell short. Then he apparently decided to save his ammunition.

The boats ran on to the southwest.

Tommy Carmellini caught Chance's eye and gave him a huge grin. Yeah, baby!

The distance between the speedboats and the gunboat slowly widened over the next hour. After a while the gunboat was only visible as a black spot on the horizon when the boat topped a swell. As the rim of the sun touched the sea, the Americans realized the crew of the gunboat had given up and turned back toward the north.

Then they heard the jets. Two swept-wing fighters dropping down astern, spreading out as they came racing in, one after each boat.

"MiG-19s," the lieutenant shouted. "Hang on tight."

The shells hit the sea behind the boat and marched toward it as quick as thought. Lieutenant Fitzgerald spun the helm, the boat tilted crazily, and the impact splashes from the strafing run missed to starboard.

The jet that strafed Chance's boat pulled out right over the boat, no more than fifty feet up. The thunder of the engines was deafening.

The jet made a climbing turn to the left, a long, lazy loop that took it back for another strafing run. His wingman stayed in trail behind him.

"Turn west, into the sun," Chance shouted to Fitzgerald, who complied. The other boat did the same. The boats came out of their turns with the sun's orb dead ahead, a ball of fire touching the ocean.

The jets behind overshot the run-in line, so they made a turn away from the boats, letting the distance lengthen, as they worked back to the dead astern position.

Fitzgerald handed Chance his M-16. "As he pulls out overhead, give him the whole magazine full automatic."

Chance nodded and lay down in the boat.

As the jets thundered down, Fitzgerald turned the boat ninety degrees left, then straightened. The MiG's left wing dropped as he swung the nose out to lead the crossing boat. He steepened his dive. As the muzzle flashes appeared on his wing root, Fitzgerald spun the helm like a man possessed to bring the boat back hard east, into the attacker.

The shell splashes missed left this time: Chance let go with the M-16 pointing straight up, in the hope the MiG would fly through the barrage.

Whether any of his bullets hit the jet as it slashed overhead, he couldn't tell. The plane pulled out with its left wing down about thirty degrees, but its nose never came above the horizon. Perhaps the sun dead ahead on the horizon disoriented the pilot. The left roll continued as the plane descended toward the sea, then it hit with a surprisingly small splash. Just like that, it was gone.

The other jet was climbing nicely. The pilot had found his target: the other speedboat was upside down in the sea.

Fitzgerald turned toward the upset boat, kept his speed up.

The wingman took his time—he must realize this would be the last strafing run because the light was failing, and perhaps he was running low on fuel.

He came off the juice, kept the power back, so on this pass he was doing no more than 250 knots, a pleasant maneuvering speed.

Fitzgerald turned his boat so that he was heading straight for the jet. He had the throttle wide open. The jet steepened his dive.

The pilot held his fire and fed in forward stick.

Fitzgerald spun the helm as far as it would go and the boat laid over on its beam in a turn.

The jet didn't shoot, but began pulling out. William Henry Chance let go with a whole magazine.

Closer and closer the plane dropped toward the sea, the nose still coming up, contrails swirling off the wingtips from the G-loads. The belly of the MiG almost kissed the water, came within a hair's breath, and then the jet was climbing into the sky trailing a wisp of smoke.

"Maybe you hit him," Fitzgerald shouted.

"He sure came close enough."

Now the jet was turning toward the north, still climbing and trailing smoke. Soon it was out of sight amid the alto-cumulus clouds.

The overturned boat had been hit by cannon fire, which punched at least six holes in the bottom. One man in the water had a broken arm, the other two were dead. A cannon shell had hit one of the men in the torso.

Chance and Carmellini managed to get the injured man aboard.

"The bodies too," Fitzgerald demanded. "They're my men."

"What about the Cuban pilot?" Carmellini asked Fitzgerald.

"He's probably dead," the SEAL lieutenant said. "If he isn't, I hope he's a good swimmer."

The naval officer used a handheld GPS to set his course to the submarine rendezvous.

Jake Grafton walked down the hill from the Officers' Club and along the pier between the warehouses. He walked past foxholes and strong-points made from piles of torn-up concrete, each of which contained a handful of marines, wide-eyed young men in camouflage clothing and helmets, armed to the teeth. Someone in every strongpoint watched every step he took. He walked by the muzzles of a dozen machine guns and a few light artillery pieces.

The whole area was well lit by floodlights mounted on the eaves of every warehouse. Some marines were gathered around a mobile kitchen, eating hot MREs, and some were gathered around a headquarters tent near the hurricane-proof warehouse. They all carried gas masks on their belts.

Jake stopped at the tent and said hello to the landing force commander, Lieutenant Colonel Eckhardt, who was still awake and keeping an eye on things at this hour. The colonel poured Jake a cup of coffee.

"Your chief of staff, Captain Pascal, was here about an hour ago, Admiral," the colonel said. "He tells me that cleaning out that warehouse will take three more days. The ordnance crew from Nevada is working around the clock."

Jake nodded. Gil Pascal was briefing him four times a day.

"The men have been told that this whole operation is classified, not to be discussed with unauthorized personnel," Eckhardt replied.

"Fine. Is there anything I can do for you, anything you need?"

They discussed logistics for a few minutes, then the colonel said, "I assume you're keeping up with the news out of Havana, Admiral."

"I was briefed before I came ashore," Jake replied.

"I got a message from Central Command advising me that there are large riots going on in three or four major Cuban cities."

"I have heard that too."

"Does that have any bearing on our posture here, sir?" the marine officer asked.

"If I knew what the hell was going on, Colonel, you're the first man I'd tell. Washington isn't telling me diddly-squat. I don't think they know diddly-squat to tell. Yes, the intel summary says people are rioting in the streets in several Cuban towns, everyone in Washington is waiting for Castro to tell his people to shut up, for the troops to wade in. So far it hasn't happened."

"Maybe Castro is dead," Lieutenant Colonel Eckhardt speculated.

"God only knows. Just keep your people alert and ready. Three more days. Just three more."

CHAPTER SIXTEEN

Try as they might, Ocho Sedano and the old fisherman could not get the water out of *Angel del Mar*. With both of them pushing and pulling on the pump handle they could just keep up with the water coming into the boat. If either of them stopped, and the other lacked the strength to work the pump quickly enough, the water level rose.

They struggled all night against the rising water. At dawn they knew they were beaten. No one else on the boat was willing to come below and pump. Some said they were afraid of being trapped below deck if the boat should go under, and others plainly lacked the strength. The passengers of the *Angel del Mar* lay about the deck horribly sunburned, semiconscious, severely dehydrated and starving.

On the evening of the previous day one woman drank sea water. The old fisherman didn't see her do it, but he knew she had when she began retching and couldn't stop. She retched herself into unconsciousness and died sometime during the night. When he went up on deck in the middle of the night, she was dead, lying in a pool of her own vomit.

The other children were also dead. Three little corpses, now still forever.

No one protested when he threw their bodies overboard.

Then he went below to help Ocho.

The losing battle was fought in total darkness against an inanimate pump handle and their own failing strength in a tossing, heaving boat as water swirled around their legs. Ocho prayed aloud, sobbed, babbled of his mother, of his deceased father, of the days he remembered from his youth.

The old fisherman remained silent, not really listening to Ocho—who never stopped pumping—but thinking of his own life, of the women he had loved, of the hard things life had taught him. He would die soon, he knew, and somehow that was all right, a fitting thing, the proper end to the great voyage he had had through life. Life pounds you, he thought, knocks out the pride and piss of youth. Live long enough and you begin to see the big picture, see yourself as God must see you, as a flawed mortal speck of protoplasm whose fate is of little concern to anyone but you. You work, eat, sleep, defecate, reproduce, and die, precisely like all the others, no different really, and the planet turns and the star burns on, both quite indifferent to your fate.

He understood the grand scheme now, and thought the knowledge worth very little. Certainly not worth the effort of telling what he knew to the boy, who would also die soon and lacked the fisherman's years and experience. No, the boy would not appreciate the wisdom that age had acquired.

When the gray light from the coming day managed to find its way down the hatch and showed him the level of the water sloshing about, the old fisherman said "Enough. Out. Up the ladder before she goes under." He pulled Ocho away from the handle, shoved him up the ladder.

"Up, up, damn you. I want out of here too." The words made Ocho scramble out of the way.

The sea was empty in every direction. The old fisherman looked carefully, then shook his head sadly. Where were the ships and boats that were usually here? Why had no one seen the drifting wreck of the *Angel del Mar?*

"Into the ocean with you. The boat is sinking. You must get into the water, swim away, so the mast and lines will not trap you and pull you under when she sinks."

They stared at him uncomprehendingly.

"Into the water, or not," he said softly, "as you chose. May God be with you."

And he walked aft and stepped off the stern of the ship into the sea. The salt water felt refreshing, welcomed him.

Ocho Sedano stood on the rail a moment, then stumbled and fell in. He paddled toward the old man.

"Ocho!" Dora stood there on deck, calling to him.

"You must swim," Ocho said. "The boat is sinking." There was little freeboard remaining, the deck was almost awash. Indeed, even as he spoke a wave broke over the deck.

Dora looked wildly about, unwilling to abandon the dubious safety of the boat. Other people joined her, some on hands and knees, unable to stand. They looked at the two men in the water, at the horizon, at the swells, at the sky.

One woman rocked back and forth on her heels, moaning softly, her eyes open.

"Swim," the old man told Ocho. "Get away before it goes."

He turned his back on the boat and began swimming. Ocho followed.

After a minute or so Ocho ceased paddling and looked back. The boat was going under, people were trying to swim away. He heard a woman screaming—Dora, perhaps.

The mast toppled slowly as the swells capsized *Angel del Mar*. Then, with an audible sigh as the last of the air escaped, the boat went under.

Heads bobbed in the swells—just how many Ocho couldn't tell.

He ceased swimming. There was no place to go, no reason to expend the energy.

He was so tired, so exhausted. He closed his eyes, felt the sun burning on his eyelids.

He opened them when salt water choked him. He couldn't sleep in the sea.

So that was how it would be. He would struggle to stay afloat until exhaustion and dehydration overcame him and he went to sleep, then he would drown.

The screaming woman would not be quiet. She paused only to fill her lungs, then screamed on.

A line in the sky caught his attention. A contrail. A jet conning against the blue. Oh, to be there, and not here.

He was listening to the screaming woman, trying not to go to sleep, when he felt something bump against his foot. Something solid.

He lowered his face into the water, opened his eyes.

Sharks!

The president of the United States sat listening to the national security adviser with a scowl on his face. The president usually scowled when he didn't like what he was hearing, the chairman of the joint chiefs, General Tater Totten, thought sourly.

The adviser was laying it out, card by card: The Cubans had at least six intermediate-range ballistic missiles, which the staff thought were probably sited in hidden silos, away from the cameras of reconnaissance planes and satellites. According to the documents obtained from the safe of Alejo Vargas, the missiles now carried biological warheads, apparently a super-virulent strain of polio. Some of the warheads stolen from *Nuestra Señora de Colón* were now stacked in a warehouse on the waterfront in a Cuban provincial town, Antilla.

Complicating everything were the riots and demonstrations going on in the large cities of Cuba. No one was moving aggressively to quell the unrest; the army was not patrolling the cities; in fact, people in Cuba were openly speculating that Fidel Castro was dead.

CIA believed that Castro was indeed dead; the director said so at the start of the meeting.

"If Castro has bit the big one, who is running the show down there? Who is the successor?" The secretary of state asked that question.

"Hector Sedano, we hope," the adviser said, glancing at the president, who was examining his fingernails. "Operation Flashlight was designed to whittle Alejo Vargas down to size."

"Stealing a safeful of blackmail files will hurt Vargas, but it won't do much to help Hector Sedano," General Totten muttered. "I seem to recall a CIA summary that says Hector might be in prison just now."

"That's right," the director agreed, nodding. "We think the rioting is directly due to the fact Sedano is in prison. The lid is coming off down there."

"We've had our finger in a lot of Cuban pies," the president said disgustedly, folding his hands on the table in front of him. "Probably too many. I seem to recall that the CIA did some fast work with a computer, emptied Fidel's Swiss bank accounts."

"The money is still in those banks," the director said quickly. "We just created a few new accounts and moved the money to them. Don't want anyone to think we are into bank robbery these days."

"Why not? This administration has been accused of everything else," the president said lightly. Poking fun at himself was his talent, the reason he had made it to the very top of the heap in American politics. He laced his fingers together, leaned back in his chair. "If we had any sense we would let the Cubans sort out their own problems. Lord knows we have enough of our own."

A murmur of assent went around the table.

Tater Totten sighed, took his letter of resignation from an inside jacket pocket and unfolded it, placed it on the table in front of him. Then he took out another letter, a request for immediate retirement, and placed it beside the first. He smoothed out both documents, put on his glasses, looked them over.

The secretary of state was sitting beside him. She looked over to see what Totten was reading. When she realized she was looking at a letter of resignation, she leaned closer.

"What is today?" Tater whispered. "The date?"

"The seventh."

General Totten got out his ink pen, wrote the date in ink on the top of the letter of resignation and the letter requesting retirement. Then he signed both letters and put his pen back in his pocket.

". . . our willingness to work with the new government. In fact, I think this would be an excellent time to end the American embargo of Cuba. . . ." The national security adviser was talking, apparently reciting a speech he had rehearsed with the president earlier today. As the adviser talked, the president had been looking around the room, watching faces for reactions. Just now he was looking at Tater Totten with narrowed eyes.

He knows, the general thought.

When the adviser wound down, the president spoke before anyone else could. "General Totten, you look like a man with something to say."

"We can't ignore six ICBMs armed with biological warheads. We can't ignore a lab for manufacturing toxins. We can't ignore a warehouse full of stolen CBW warheads." He leaned forward in his chair, looked straight at the president, whose brow was furrowing into a scowl. "Fifty million Americans are within range of those missiles. We must move *right now* to disarm those missiles, put the Cubans out of the biological warfare business, and recover those stolen warheads. We have absolutely no choice. When they find out what the threat is, the American people are not going to be in the mood to listen to excuses."

Tater Totten looked around the table at the pale, drawn faces. Every eye in the room was on him. "If one of those missiles gets launched at America, everyone in this room will be responsible. That is the hard, cold reality. All this happy talk about lifting embargoes and a new era of peace in the Caribbean is beside the point. We can't ignore weapons of mass destruction aimed at innocent Americans."

The silence that followed lasted for several seconds, until the president broke it. "General, no one is suggesting we ignore those missiles. The question is how we can best deal with the reality of their presence. My initial reaction is to wait until a new government takes over in Cuba, then to talk with them about disarmament and return of the stolen warheads in return for lifting the embargo. Reasonable people will see the advantages for each side."

"Your mistake," General Totten replied, "is thinking that reasonable people will be involved in the negotiations. Reasonable people don't build CBW weapons of mass destruction—unreasonable people do. Unreasonable people use them to commit murder for ends they could achieve in no other way, ends they think are worth other peoples' blood to attain. Now, *that,* by God, is reality."

The secretary of state had snaked the chairman's letter of resignation over in front of her while he was speaking. Now she showed it to the director of the CIA, who was on her left.

"What is that document?" the president asked.

"My letter of resignation," Tater Totten said blandly. "I haven't decided whether to submit it now or later."

As the president's upper lip curled in a sneer, the secretary of state put the letter back on the table in front of the general.

"Totten, you son of a bitch! *I'm* the man responsible."

"I have to sleep nights," Tater shot back.

"You reveal classified information to the press, I'll have you prosecuted." The president knew damn well that Totten would hold a press conference and tell all. "You'll spend your goddamn retirement in a federal pen," the president snarled.

"Bullshit! When the public finds out about polio warheads on ICBMs aimed at Florida, the tidal wave is going to wash you away." General Totten pointed a finger at the president. "Don't fuck this up, cowboy: there are too many American lives at stake. Now isn't the time for a friendly game of Russian roulette."

"Okay," the president said, lifting his hands and showing the palms. "Okay! What's the date on that letter?"

"Today."

"Make it a week from today. We'll do this your way, and a week from today you're permanently off to the golf course with your mouth welded shut."

Totten got out his pen, changed the date on both the letters, and passed them across the table to the president, who didn't even glance at them.

"Better get cracking, General," the president snarled.

"Yes, sir," said Tater Totten. He rose from his chair and walked out of the room.

At the same time the president and National Security Council were meeting in Washington, the Council of State of the communist government of Cuba was meeting in Havana.

"Where is Fidel?" someone roared at Alejo Vargas as he walked into the room, flanked by Colonel Santana on one side and a plainclothes secret policeman on the other. Santana limped as he walked. He was heavily bandaged about the head and left arm, and moved like a man who was very sore.

Vice President Raúl Castro watched Alejo Vargas take his seat at the table beside the other ministers. His face was mottled, his anger palpable. He motioned for silence, smacked a wooden gavel against the table until he got it, then looked Vargas straight in the face.

"Where is my brother?"

"Dead."

"And you have hidden the body."

"The body is being prepared for a state funeral. I didn't think anyone would object."

"Liar!" Raúl Castro spit out the word. He stood, leaned on the table, and shouted at Vargas. "*Liar!* I think you murdered Fidel. I think you murdered him so that you could take over the country." He waved at the window. "The people out there think so too. You have murdered my brother and arrested the man that he hoped would eventually succeed him, Hector Sedano. Jesus, man, the whole country is coming apart at the seams; they are rioting in the streets!"

Alejo Vargas examined the faces around the table while Raúl shouted. Maximo Sedano was there, his face impassive. Many of the faces could not be read. Most of them merely wanted food to eat and a place to live, something better than the people in the cane fields had. They went to their offices every day, obeyed Fidel's orders, took the blame when things went wrong—as they usually did—watched Fidel take the credit if things went right, and soldiered on. That had been a way of life for these people for two generations—forty years—and now it was over.

"... the people loved Fidel," Raúl was saying, "honored and respected him as the greatest patriot in the history of Cuba, and I think you, Alejo Vargas, had a hand in his death. I accuse you of his murder."

"Watch your mouth," Santana told him, but Raúl turned on him like an enraged bear.

"I am vice president of the republic, first in line of succession upon the death of the president," Raúl thundered at the colonel. "Maintain your silence or be evicted."

Alejo Vargas had already removed his pistol from his pocket while he sat at the table listening to Raúl. Now he raised it, extended it to arm's length, and squeezed the trigger. Before anyone could move he pumped three bullets into Raúl Castro, who fell sideways, knocking over his chair. The reports were like thunderclaps in the room, leaving the audience stunned and slightly deafened.

Alejo Vargas got to his feet, holding the pistol casually in front of him in his right hand.

"Does anyone else wish to accuse me of murder?"

Total, complete silence. Vargas looked from face to face, trying to make eye contact with everyone willing. Most averted their eyes when he looked into their face.

"Colonel Santana, please remove Señor Castro from the room. He is ill."

As a bandaged Santana and the plainclothesman were carrying out the body, Alejo Vargas again seated himself. He placed the pistol on the table in front of him.

"I will chair this meeting," he said. "We are here today to decide what must be done in light of the recent death of our beloved president, Fidel Castro. He fought a long, valiant fight against the disease of cancer, which claimed him four days ago. Of course the news could not be publicly announced until the Council of State had been informed and decisions reached on the question of succession.

"I do hereby officially inform you of the tragedy of Fidel Castro's passing, and declare this meeting open to discuss the question of naming a successor to the office of president."

With that Vargas reached across the table and seized the gavel that Raúl Castro had used. He tapped it several times on the table, sharp little raps that made several people flinch.

"This meeting is officially open," he declared. "Who would like to speak first?"

No one said a word.

"The news of our beloved president's death has hit everyone hard," Vargas said. "I understand. Yet the business of our nation cannot wait. I hereby nominated myself for the office of president. Do I hear a second?"

"I second the nomination," said General Alba, his voice carrying in the silence.

"Let the record show that I move to make the nomination unanimous," Admiral Delgado said, his voice quavering a little.

"I second that motion," General Alba replied, "and move that the nominations be closed."

One would almost think they rehearsed that, Alejo Vargas thought, and gave the two general officers a nod of gratitude.

Sharks!

The silent predators came gliding in even as Ocho Sedano watched with his face in the water, gray, streamlined torpedoes swimming effortlessly through the half-light under the surface. They seemed to be swimming toward the place where the *Angel del Mar* had just gone under. No doubt the turbulence and noise from the sinking boat attracted them.

The people thrashing about on the surface were also making noise. Nature had equipped the sharks to sense the death struggles of other creatures, and to come to feed.

He raised his head from the water, shouted, "Sharks. Sharks." His voice was very hoarse, his throat terribly dry. He sucked up a mouthful of salty seawater, then spit it out.

"*Sharks!* Do not struggle. Swim away from the wreck, from each other."

He didn't know if anyone heard him or not.

A scream split the air, then was cut off abruptly, probably as the person screaming was pulled under.

Another scream. Shouts of "Sharks!" and calls to God.

He felt something rub against his leg, and kicked back viciously. With his face in the water he could see the shark, a big one, maybe eight feet, swimming toward the concentration of people in the water.

He turned the other way, began swimming slowly away.

The old fisherman was nearby, doing the same.

"Do not panic," the old man said. "Swim slowly, steadily."

"The others . . ."

"There is nothing we can do. God is with them."

He heard several more screams, a curse or two, then nothing. He didn't want to hear. And he was swimming into the wind, so the sound would not carry so well.

Dora was back there. If she got off the boat. He couldn't remember if she leaped from the boat before it sank. Perhaps she drowned when the boat went down. If so, that was God's mercy. Better that than being eaten by a shark, having a leg ripped half off, or an arm, then bleeding in agony until the sharks tore you to pieces or pulled you under to drown.

That there were still things on this earth that ate people was an evil more foul than anything he had ever imagined.

He tired of swimming and stopped once, but the old fisherman encouraged him.

"Don't die here, son. Swim farther, get away from the sharks."

"They're everywhere," Ocho replied, with impeccable logic.

"Swim farther," the old man said, and so he did.

Finally they stopped. How far they had come they had no way of knowing. The sea rose and fell in a timeless, eternal rhythm, the wind occasionally ripped spume from a crest and sent it flying, puffy clouds scudded along, the sun beat down.

"We will die out here," he told the old man, who was only about ten feet away.

The fisherman didn't reply. What was there to say?

Even the tragedy of Dora couldn't keep him awake. He kept dozing off, then awakening when water went into his nose and mouth.

In the afternoon he thought he saw a ship, a sailing ship with three masts and square sails set to catch the trade winds. Maybe he only imagined it. He also thought he saw more contrails high in the sky, but he might have imagined those too.

He would swim until he died, he decided. That was all a man could do. He would do that and God would know he tried and forgive him his sins and take him into heaven.

Somehow that thought gave him peace.

"Gentlemen, your backing this morning touched me deeply."

Alejo Vargas was sitting with General Alba and Admiral Delgado in his office at the Ministry of Interior. Colonel Santana was parked in a chair near the window with his leg on a stool and a bandage around his head.

"What happened to you, Colonel?" General Alba asked.

"I was in an accident."

"Traffic gets worse and worse."

"Yes."

"Gentlemen, let's get right down to it," Alejo Vargas began. "Right now I don't have the support of the people. The mobs are out of control. We must restore order and confidence in the government; that is absolutely critical."

Delgado and Alba nodded. Even a dictator needs some level of popular support. Or at least acceptance by a significant percentage of the population.

"I propose to move on two fronts. I will send a delegate to Hector Sedano, see if he can be enlisted to endorse me. Getting out of prison will be an inducement, of course, but one can't rely on anything that flimsy. I thought of naming him as ambassador to the Vatican."

"That would be a popular move," Alba thought, and Delgado agreed.

"All my adult life I have been a student of Fidel Castro's political wiles," Vargas continued. "I learned many things from watching the master. This may seem to you gentlemen to be heresy, but without the United States, Castro would have lasted only a few years in power—had the world turned in the usual way he would have been overthrown by a coup or mass uprising when it became obvious that he could not deliver on his promises. Fidel Castro survived because he had a scapegoat: he had the United States to blame for all our difficulties."

"One should not say things like that publicly, but there is much truth in that observation."

"The Yanquis never failed to play their part in Fidel's little dramas," Delgado agreed, and everyone in the room laughed, even Santana.

When his audience was again attentive, Alejo Vargas continued: "I propose to unite the Cuban people against the United States one more time, and this time I shall be out in front leading them."

Jake Grafton had dinner that evening with the commanding officers of the units in the battle group. In addition to the skippers of the ships, the marine landing force commander, Lieutenant Colonel Eckhardt, and the air wing commander aboard *United States* were also there. Held in the carrier's flag wardroom, the dinner was one of those rare official functions when everyone relaxed enough to enjoy themselves. Surrounded by fellow career officers, Admiral Grafton once again felt that sense of belonging to something bigger than the people who comprised it that had charmed him about the service thirty years ago. The tradition, the camaraderie, the sense of engaging in an activity whose worth could not be measured in dollars or years of service made the brutally long hours, the family separations, and the demands of service life somehow easier to endure.

He was basking in that glow when one of his aides slipped in a side door and handed him a top-secret flash message from Washington. Jake put on his glasses before he took the message from the folder.

He scanned the message, then read it again slowly. Ballistic missiles in Cuba, biological warheads, Castro dead—he thanked the aide, who left the room.

Jake read the message again very carefully as the after-dinner conversation buzzed around him. The message ordered him to stage commando raids on the suspected ballistic missile sites, "as soon as humanly possible, before the missiles can be launched at the United States."

"Gentlemen, let us adjourn to the flag spaces," Jake Grafton said, and led the commanders from the wardroom.

When the group was together in the flag spaces, with the door closed behind them, Jake said, "The course of human events has catapulted us straight into another mess. I just received this message from Washington." He read it to them. When he finished, no one said anything. Jake folded the message and returned it to the red folder.

He turned to the captains of the two Aegis-class guided-missile cruisers that were assigned to his battle group:

"I want you to get underway as soon as you get back to your ships. Take your ships through the Windward Passage, then proceed at flank speed to a position between the island of Cuba and the Florida Keys that allows you to engage and destroy any missiles fired from Cuba toward the United States. Make every knot you can squeeze out of your ships. Every minute counts. When you come up with an estimated time of arrival, send it to me. We won't lift a finger against the Cubans until both your ships are in position."

He shook hands with the captains, and they strode out of the room.

"The rest of us might as well get comfortable. Looks like we are in for a long evening."

Ocho Sedano looked at it for fifteen minutes before the thought occurred to him that he should find out what it was. Something white, floating perhaps fifteen feet away, slightly off to his right.

Now that the existence of the white thing had registered on his consciousness, he made the effort to turn, to stroke toward it.

He had been in the water all day. The sun would soon be down and he would be alone on the sea. After the sharks this morning there had been only Ocho and the old man; now the fisherman no longer answered his calls. Hadn't for several hours, in fact. Maybe he just drifted out of hailing range, Ocho thought. That must be it.

The sharks killed all the others, sparing only the two men who had gone off the sinking boat first and swam away from the group. At least he thought the others were dead—he had no way of knowing the truth of it.

He had thought about the decision to swim away from the sinking *Angel del Mar* all day, off and on, trying to decide just what instinct had told him and the old man to get away from the others. Drowning people often drag under anyone they can reach—no doubt that knowledge was a factor in the old man's thinking, in his thinking, for he did not want to put the responsibility for his life on anyone but himself.

Perhaps those who were attacked by the sharks were the lucky ones. Their ordeal was over.

Dora—had she been one of them?

Diego Coca was already dead, of course. He died . . . a day or two ago . . . didn't he? Jumped into the sea and swam away from the *Angel del Mar*.

Ah, Diego, you ass. I hope you are burning in hell.

He reached for the white thing, which of course skittered out of reach. He paddled some more, reached up under it.

A milk jug. A one-gallon plastic milk jug without a cap, floating upside down. Apparently intact. He lifted the milky white plastic jug from the sea, let the water drain out, then lowered it into the water. The thing made a powerful float.

He pulled it toward him.

Hard to hold on to, but very buoyant.

How could he hold it, use the power of its buoyancy to keep himself afloat through the night?

Inside his shirt? He worked the jug down, tried to get it under his shirt. The thing escaped once, shot out of the water. He snagged it, tried it again.

The second time he got it under his shirt. The thing tried to push him over backward, but if he leaned into it, he could keep his weight pretty much balanced over it. Then he could just float, ride without effort.

As long as he could keep the open neck facing downward, the jug would keep him up.

Ocho was celebrating his good fortune when a swell tipped him over. He fought back upright, adjusted the jug in the evening light.

Maybe he should just forget the jug—he seemed to be working as hard staying over it as he did treading water.

With the last rays of the sun in his face, he decided to keep the jug, learn to ride it.

"I'm going to be rescued," he said silently to himself, "going to be rescued. I must just have patience."

After a bit he added, "And faith in the Lord."

Ocho was a Catholic, of course, but he had never been one to pray much. He wondered if he should pray now. Surely God knew about the mess he was in—what could he conceivably tell Him that He didn't already know?

In the twilight the water became dark. Still restless, still rising and falling, but dark and black as the grave.

He would probably die this night. Sometime during the night he would go to sleep and drown or a shark would rip at him or he would just run out of will. He was oh so very tired, a lethargy that weighed on every muscle.

Tonight, he thought.

But I don't want to die. I want to live!

Please, God, let me live one more day. If I am not rescued tomorrow, then let me die tomorrow night.

That was a reasonable request. His strength would give out by tomorrow night anyway.

The last of the light faded from the sky, and he was alone on the face of the sea.

La Cabana Prison was an old pile of masonry. In the hot, humid climate of Cuba the interior was cool, a welcome respite from the heat. Yet in the dark corridors filled with stagnant air the odor of mold and decay seemed almost overpowering. The iron bars and grates and cell doors were wet with condensation and covered with layers of rust.

During the day small windows with nearly opaque, dirty glass admitted what light there was. At night naked bulbs hanging where two corridors met or an iron gate barred the way lit the interior; and for whole stretches of corridors and cells there was no light at all.

Hector Sedano saw the flashlight even before he heard people coming along the corridor. One flashlight and two or three, maybe even four people—it was difficult to tell.

The flashlight led the visitors to this cell, and it turned to pin him on the cot.

"There he is."

"I will talk to him alone."

"Yes, *Señor Presidente*."

One man remained standing in the semidarkness outside the cell after the others left. After the flashlight Hector's eyes adjusted slowly. Now he could see him—Alejo Vargas.

Vargas lit a short cigarillo. As he struck the match Hector closed his eyes, and kept them closed until he smelled tobacco smoke and heard Vargas's voice.

"Father Sedano, we meet again."

Hector thought that remark didn't deserve a reply.

"I seem to recall a conversation we had, what—two or three years ago?" Vargas said thoughtfully. "I told you that religion and politics don't mix."

"You even had a biblical quote ready to fire at me, Mark twelve-seventeen. Most unexpected."

"You didn't take my advice."

"No."

"You don't often follow advice, do you?"

"No."

"I came here tonight to see if you wish to make your peace with Caesar and join my cabinet, perhaps as our ambassador to the church."

"You're the president now?"

"Temporarily. Until the election."

"Then the title will become permanent."

"I don't think anyone will want to run against me."

"Perhaps not."

"But let's take it a day at a time. Temporary acting president Vargas asks you to serve your country in this capacity."

"And if I say no?"

"I want to sleep with a clean conscience, which is why I came here tonight to make the offer."

"Your conscience is easily cleansed if that is all it takes."

"It does not trouble me too much."

"A man who lives as you do, a lively conscience would hurt worse than a bad tooth."

"So your answer is no."

"That it is."

"But at least you considered my offer, so I can sleep knowing you chose your own fate."

"My fate is in God's hands."

"Ah, if only I had the time to discuss religion with you, an intelligent, learned man. Time does not allow me that luxury. Still, I have one other little thing to discuss with you, and I caution you, this is not the time for a yes or no answer. This thing you must think about very carefully and give me your answer later."

Sedano scratched his head. Vargas probably couldn't see past the glow of his cigarillo tip, so it didn't matter much what he did.

"I want to know what Fidel did with the gold from the pesos. I want you to tell me."

"Me? I was six years old when he melted the gold, if he did."

"I think you know. I think Fidel told Mercedes, and Mercedes told you. So I have come to ask you where it is. Will you tell me?"

"She didn't tell me about gold."

"I should not have asked so quickly. I told myself I would not do that, then I did. I apologize. I will ask you later, when you have had time to think about the question and all the implications."

"I can't tell you what I don't know."

"Well, think about it; that is all I ask. Of course I will talk to Mercedes. I think she also told you or the CIA about Fidel's Swiss bank accounts. When Maximo went to get the money it was not there. I would like to have been there to see the look on Maximo's face—ah, yes, *that* was a moment, my friend!"

He chuckled, then drew on the cigarillo, made the tip glow.

"Maximo thinks the Swiss stole it; he is very gullible. I smell the CIA. The CIA could reach into Swiss banks as easily as you and I breathe."

"The world is quite complex."

"Isn't it?" Vargas sighed. "All the strings lead to Mercedes. She knew too much for her own good. I think she will do the right thing. She is a loyal patriot. With Colonel Santana asking the questions, I have faith that she will do what is best for Cuba."

Hector could feel the sweat beading up on his forehead. He made sure his voice was under his complete control before he spoke. "For Cuba?"

"For Cuba, yes. Cuba and me, our interests are identical. I want the gold, Father, and I intend to get it. As you sit here rotting, you think about that."

Alejo Vargas turned and walked away, still puffing on the cigarillo.

The smell of the tobacco smoke lingered in the cell for hours. Hector fancied that he could still smell it when daylight began shining through the window high in the wall at the end of the corridor.

CHAPTER SEVENTEEN

The submariners put the computer in a plastic garbage bag to keep it dry, then put bag and computer into a backpack that one of the sailors had for his liberty gear. William Henry Chance put on the backpack and the sailors adjusted the straps.

"You should be okay, sir," they said. At a nod from the sound-powered telephone talker, Chance started up the ladder with Tommy Carmellini right behind him. They came out of the hatch on the submarine's deck forward of the island. The deck wasn't much, merely wet steel that curved away right and left into the black ocean.

Hovering in the darkness overhead was a helicopter—the downwash from the rotor blades made it hard to breathe. Amid the flashing lights and spotlights, his eyes had a hard time adjusting—Chance felt almost blind. One of the sailors on the deck put a horse collar over his head and he went up into the chopper first. Then Carmellini.

A strong set of hands pulled him into the chopper. After a wave at the officers in the sail cockpit, Carmellini used hands and feet to get over to the canvas bench opposite the open door where Chance had found a seat.

Forty-five minutes later the helicopter landed on the flight deck of USS *United States*. As the rotors wound down, an officer in khakis came to the chopper's door, and shouted, "Mr. Chance? Mr. Carmellini?"

"Right here."

"My name is Toad Tarkington. Will you gentlemen come with me, please. The admiral is waiting."

Tommy Carmellini felt completely out of place, completely lost. After the submarine and the helicopter, the strange sounds, smells, and sensations of the huge ship underway in a night sea seemed to max out his ability to adjust.

The compartment where Toad took the two agents was packed with people, all talking among themselves. Still, compared to the flight deck and the sensations of the helicopter, it was a oasis of calm. Toad led them to a corner of the room and introduced them to Rear Admiral Jake Grafton.

Grafton was a trim officer about six feet tall. The admiral's gray eyes captured Tommy's attention. The eyes seemed to measure you from head to toe, see all there was to see, then move on. Only when the eyes looked elsewhere did you see that Grafton's nose was a trifle too large, and one side of his forehead bore an old scar that was slightly less tan than the skin surrounding it.

Toad Tarkington was several inches shorter than the admiral and heavier through the shoulders. He was a tireless whirlwind who dazzled a person meeting him for the first time with quick wit and boundless energy, which seemed to radiate from him like the aura of the sun. He smiled easily and often, revealing a set of perfect white teeth that would have made any dentist proud.

Jake Grafton and William Henry Chance stood behind Toad watching him work Alejo Vargas's computer. Toad stared at the screen intently while his fingers flew over the keys.

Soon they were plotting positions on a chart. "Those missiles have to be at these locations, Admiral," Toad said, pointing at the places he had marked on the chart, "or the data in the computer is worthless." He looked over his shoulder at Chance. "Could this computer be a plant?"

Chance glanced at Carmellini, who was sitting in a chair against the wall studying the layout and furnishings of the planning space and the knots of people engaged in a variety of tasks. The roar of conversation made the place seem greatly disorganized, which Tommy realized was an illusion. Charts on the wall decorated with classified information, planning tables, file cabinets sporting serious padlocks, battle lanterns on the overhead, copy machines, burn bags—the place reminded him of the inner sanctums of the CIA's headquarters at Langley.

"Very doubtful," Chance answered, and bent over to study the chart Toad was marking.

"I make it six sites," Toad said.

"Could there be more missiles?" Jake Grafton asked. He too glanced at Carmellini, then turned to Chance. "You see the pitfalls if there are missiles we don't know about?"

"Yes, sir. I can only say we have seen evidence for at least six."

"Six silos," Toad mused, studying the locations.

"There is a warhead manufacturing facility someplace on that island," Chance said. "The viruses would have to be dried out, put in whatever medium the Cubans believe will keep them alive and virulent and dormant until the warhead explodes, then the medium sealed inside the warheads. The facility will not be large, but it will have clean rooms, air scrubbers, remote handling equipment, and I would think a fairly well equipped lab on site."

"Any ideas?" Jake Grafton.

"I was hoping that the satellite reconnaissance people might be able to find the site if we tell them what to look for."

"We'll have them look, certainly, but you have no independent information about where this facility might be?"

"No."

Jake motioned to Carmellini, who leaned in so that he could hear better. "Here is the situation," the admiral said. "The White House has ordered us to go get those missile silos as soon as possible. Bombing the silos is out—we are to remove the warheads and destroy the missiles. What my staff and these other folks here tonight are trying to decide is how best to go about doing what the president wants us to do. Obviously, if we had enough time we could bring in forces from the States and assault the silo locations with forces tailored for the job. If we had enough time we could even do a dress rehearsal, make sure everyone is on the same sheet of music. Unfortunately, the White House wants the silos taken out as soon as possible."

"How soon is possible?" Chance asked.

Jake Grafton took a deep breath, then let it out slowly. "That's the sixty-four dollar question. We must find out what's there before we go charging in."

He stood, walked over to a chart of Cuba that was posted on the bulkhead. He was looking at a penciled line on the chart that went through the Windward Passage and along the northern coast of Cuba, all the way to the narrowest portion of the Florida Straits. The cruisers should be in position by six o'clock this evening.

Jake turned from the chart and gestured at the people at the planning tables. "These folks are just looking at possibilities. We must assemble sufficient forces to do the job, yet we run huge risks if we take the time to assemble overwhelming force. There is a balance there. When we see the latest satellite stuff we'll have a better idea."

"I would be amazed if there are any troops around these silos," William Henry Chance said. "Their existence has been overlooked by two generations of photo interpretation specialists. The Cubans know that the whole island is painstakingly photographed on a regular basis—we've been looking at those damned silos for forty years and didn't know what they were. They must be underground and well camouflaged."

"I'm not sending anybody after those things until I know what the opposition is," Jake said bluntly. "I don't launch suicide missions."

"Are the silos your only target?" Chance asked.

Jake Grafton examined the tall agent with narrowed eyes. "What do you mean?"

"The Cubans grew the viruses for their warheads in a lab in the science building of the University of Havana. If we walk off with the warheads in the missiles, there is nothing to prevent the Cubans from cooking up another batch and putting it in planes to spray all over Florida and Georgia and wherever."

"You are suggesting that we target their lab?"

"I highly recommended it. Chances to step on cockroaches are few and far between: we better put Alejo Vargas out of business while we have the chance."

"All I can do is make a recommendation to Washington," the admiral said.

"And the processing facility. If we are going to take Cuba out of the biological warfare business, we should do it right."

"Can we bomb any of these places?" Toad Tarkington asked.

"Oh, no," Chance said. "A bomb exploding in a lab full of poliomyelitis virus would be the equivalent of a biological warhead detonating. The virus would be explosively liberated. Everyone downwind for a couple hundred miles, maybe even farther, would probably die. No, the only way to destroy the virus is with fire."

Jake Grafton scratched his head.

"The temperature would have to come up really quickly to kill the viruses before the place started venting to the atmosphere," Chance added. "A regular old house fire wouldn't do it. We need something a lot hotter."

"The fires of hell," Toad said, and his listeners nodded.

The first batches of satellite imagery began coming off the printers within an hour after the suspected silo locations were encrypted and transmitted. The air intelligence specialists were soon bent over the images, studying them with magnifying glasses. Before long Jake Grafton was shoulder to shoulder with the experts.

"This first location looks like it's smack in the middle of a sugarcane field," the senior Air Intelligence officer groused.

Jake Grafton didn't have to think that over very long. "Let's assume that our global positioning is more accurate than the Cubans'."

"You mean they don't know the silos' exact lat/long locations?"

"Precisely."

"Well, the nearest building to this sugarcane field is this large barn, which is about three-quarters of a kilometer away." The specialist pointed. Jake used the magnifying glass.

"That could be it," he muttered. "Let's see what we can dig out of the archives. How long has this barn been here, have there ever been any large trucks around—let's look in all seasons of the year—and are Cuban Army units nearby? I'm really interested in army units."

"Power lines," the senior AI officer mused. "Strikes me that there ought to be a large power feed nearby."

"It sort of fits," Toad Tarkington said to Jake. "If they built the barn first, then they could dig the silo inside the barn and truck the dirt out at night, pour concrete, do all the work at night."

"Install the missile at night when the thing is finished," the AI officer said, continuing the thought, "and if they had no unusual activity near the barn, no one would ever be the wiser."

"Prove to me that that is what they did," Jake said. "And prove that we won't be sending troops into an ambush."

The admiral stood amid the banks of computers and watched the operators trade data via satellite with the computers at the National Security Agency in Maryland.

The CIA agents were fed and given bunks to sleep in. They went without protest. Someone brought Jake Grafton a cup of coffee, which he sipped as he walked around the intel and planning spaces thinking about intermediate-range ballistic missiles with biological warheads.

Dawn found Ocho Sedano still afloat, still hanging grimly on to the milk jug and treading water. He had stopped thinking hours ago. Hunger and exhaustion had sapped his strength and thirst had thickened his blood. He was not asleep, nor was he awake, but in some semiconscious state in between.

He found himself looking into the glare of the rising sun as it rose from the sea. The realization that he had made it through the night crossed his mind, as did the certainty that today was the last day.

Today, someone must find me today . . . .

The television lights were on and the cameras running when Alejo Vargas walked to the podium in the main reception room of the presidential palace in Havana. For forty years Fidel Castro had used this forum to speak to the Cuban people and the world—now it was Alejo's turn.

"We are here," he began, "at a desperate hour in our nation's life. The greatest Cuban patriot of them all, Fidel Castro, died here five days ago. Everyone listening to my voice knows the details of his career and the greatness of the leadership he provided for Cuba. I was with him when he died"—here Vargas wiped tears from his eyes—"and I can tell you, it was the most profound moment of my life.

"Yesterday the Council of State elected me interim president, to hold office until the next meeting of the National Assembly, which as you know elects members of the Council of State and selects its president. I swore to the ministers and the Council of State that I would uphold the Constitution and defend Cuba with all my strength. Now I swear it to you."

He paused again and gathered himself. "Today there are people on the streets who accuse me of murdering Fidel. May God strike me dead if I am guilty of that crime."

He paused, took several deep breaths, and since God didn't terminate him then and there, continued:

"Fidel Castro died of cancer. His body shall lie in state for the next three days. If you love Cuba, I invite you to pay your respects to this great man, and to look at his corpse. See if there is a single mark of violence on the body. My enemies have accused me of many things, but the murder of Cuba's greatest patriot is the most vicious cut of all. I too worshiped Fidel. Look at the body carefully—let the evidence of your own eyes prove the falsity of these accusations against me."

Here again he had to pause to wipe his eyes, to steady himself before the podium.

"I have been accused of other crimes, so I take this opportunity to bare my soul before you, to tell you the truth as God Almighty knows it, so you will know the lies of my enemies when you hear them. My enemies are also whispering that I killed Raúl Castro at a meeting of the Council of State yesterday, when the facts of his brother's death were first announced. The truth is Raúl was murdered as he stood at the table discussing the hopes and dreams of his dead brother, by Hector Sedano. Raúl Castro was shot down before a dozen eyewitnesses, myself included. I swear to you this day that Hector Sedano will pay the price the law requires for his crime."

He paused again here, referred to his notes. Someone had to take the fall for shooting Raúl, so why not Hector?

"The story of our country is a story of struggle, a struggle between the socialist people of Cuba and the evil forces of capitalism, forces controlled and dominated by the United States, the colossus to the north. The struggle was not won by Fidel, although he fought the great fight—it continues even today. For example, while they are representing to the world that they are destroying their inventory of chemical and biological weapons, the United States has introduced these weapons to Cuban soil."

The camera panned to the artillery shell resting on its base on a table beside the podium.

"Here is an American artillery shell loaded with the bacteria that causes anthrax, one of the deadliest diseases known to man. This shell was stored in a warehouse at the American naval base at Guantánamo Bay, which is sacred Cuban soil. The Americans were unwilling to keep their poisonous filth in their own country, so they exported it to ours.

"I have this day asked the ambassadors of five of the nations who keep embassies in Havana to send their military attachés to inspect this warhead. Here is a sworn document these officers executed that states the shell is as I have represented, a biological warhead." He fluttered the paper, then held it up so the camera could zoom in.

"The revelation here today of the United States's perfidy will undoubtedly provoke a reaction from the bandits to our north. Fidel always knew that the day might come when we would have to defend ourselves again from American aggression, so he installed a battery of intercontinental ballistic missiles in Cuba for defensive purposes. These missiles are operational and ready now to defend our sacred soil. Rest assured, my fellow Cubans, that we shall resist American aggression, that we shall fight to defend Cuba from those who would destroy her, and we shall make her great for the generations to come.

"Thank you."

As a speech to a Cuban audience accustomed to Fidel's six-hour harangues full of baroque phrases and soaring rhetoric, Alejo's little effort seemed underdone. He had actually made a conscious effort not to sound like Fidel. Watching the tape of the speech, he thought it went well.

"Air it immediately," he said to the television producer, and walked back toward Fidel's old office.

Alba and Delgado were there to meet him. They had known that Vargas intended to blame Raúl's murder on Hector Sedano when he made this speech: indeed, they had already signed eyewitness affidavits swearing that they saw Hector shoot the man. That Alejo Vargas had the cojones to make the big lie stick meant a lot to these men who had spent their lives in an absolute dictatorship and knew that the man at the top had to be completely ruthless, without scruple of any kind, to survive. Fidel had been willing to crush his enemies any way he could; Vargas seemed to have the same talent, so perhaps he had a chance.

The two military men shook Vargas's hand. "Tell us, *Señor Presidente,* what the Americans will do."

"I have thrown the ballistic missiles in their face," Vargas said. "I expect the Americans to go to the United Nations Security Council and ask for sanctions, perhaps a world trade embargo sanctioned by the UN. Now that the missiles have been discussed in public, the American government cannot ignore them, even if they want to."

"Do you anticipate an attack?"

"I do not, but we must take precautions. The missiles sit in hardened silos impervious to air attack, or nearly so. It is possible that the Americans might attempt commando raids. I suggest you move troops to the sites, have them dig in around the silos."

"And if the Americans attack and we cannot repulse them?"

"This dog will bite. Fire the missiles."

Alba grinned. His hatred of the Yanquis was common knowledge. "If the Americans do attack, when would you expect it?"

"They will try diplomacy first. Only if that fails will they try military action."

"Still, I would like to move the troops immediately."

"By all means," said Alejo Vargas. "We will have television cameras film your men digging in to defend Cuba."

"And the missiles? Are you going to film them?"

"Of course. Cuba is a sovereign nation. The world has changed since the 1962 missile crisis. We have an absolute right to defend ourselves, and if necessary we shall. Any noise the Americans make will rally the Cuban people to us."

Even as Vargas talked to his military men, the president of the United States's advisers were arguing for diplomatic initiatives before military options were weighed. "We must go to the United Nations first," the secretary of state stated forcefully.

"What if the UN turns us down?" the president asked in reply.

"We need political cover," the secretary shot back. "A significant percentage of Americans think Castro was a hero, a champion of the downtrodden, and we unfairly bullied him. The fact that he was an absolute dictator with zero regard for human rights means very little to the political left. Then there is the casualty problem—the American people won't tolerate seeing their soldiers killed while fighting for oil or corporate profits in foreign wars."

"What bullshit!" snapped Tater Totten. "I'm really sick of listening to Vietnam draft evaders tell us that Americans don't have the guts to fight for civilization."

"I am *not* a draft evader," shouted the secretary of state, her face red, her cheeks quivering. "I demand an immediate apology!"

"Shut up, both of you," the president growled.

"I apologize," Tater Totten muttered, almost as if he meant it.

The president had done some hard thinking since Tater Totten demanded that the presence of the Cuban missiles be addressed before any other matter with Cuba was put on the table. Six missiles with biological warheads aimed at the southeastern United States—Cuban missiles today were every bit as serious as when John F. Kennedy had to deal with them, he decided. If the administration asked for the blessing of the UN Security Council and didn't get it, he would be worse off than if he ordered military action immediately.

The lab and processing facility worried him too. If Cuba could manufacture polio virus and put it in an aerosol solution, any plane that could fly across the Straits of Florida could attack the United States.

By the time Alejo Vargas's broadcast was translated and replayed for the National Security Council, the president strongly believed that the American people would react angrily to the presence of missiles in Cuba. The outrage of the congressmen and senators who heard the speech convinced him.

He called on Tater Totten again. "I'm getting the cold sweats just thinking about this crap. Tell me what we are going to do to make sure the Cubans don't shoot those missiles."

"Sir, the best insurance is to go after the missiles, the lab, and the processing facility as soon as humanly possible, before the Cubans get troops in there to defend them."

"When is humanly possible?"

"Tomorrow night would be the earliest possible date. Every day we wait allows us to assemble more forces. Conversely, every day we wait the risk increases: Tomorrow Vargas can move more troops to guard those silos; he could get wind of what's coming and threaten to release polio virus by airplane, by missile, or have somebody with a aerosol bomb in a suitcase turn it loose God knows where."

"So why not go tomorrow night?"

"We must put enough people and firepower in there to get the job done. It's a nice calculation."

"Do you want me to make that decision?"

"I recommend that you leave the decision to the military professional who is there, Rear Admiral Grafton. He's spent thirty years in uniform training for this moment, for this decision."

The president grunted.

The Chairman continued, "By tonight we will have two Aegis cruisers in the Florida Straits between Cuba and Florida. Jake Grafton ordered them there on his own initiative. He's a good man. The cruisers have the capability of shooting down ballistic missiles coming out of Cuba."

"Do the Cubans know that?"

"Someone in Cuba might—the information is in the public domain—

but I doubt that Alejo Vargas knows much about U.S. naval capability."

"You hope he doesn't, because if he does, they might launch before the cruisers get in range."

Tater Totten nodded affirmatively.

"This Grafton, I've heard that he goes off half-cocked, doesn't obey orders, isn't a team player."

"I don't know who said that, but Jake Grafton is the best we have. War is his profession. Alejo Vargas is an amateur playing at war—there is a vast difference."

"Grafton has enemies."

"Who doesn't?"

"What if the Cubans launch their missiles and the cruisers miss?"

"Then the shit will really be in the fan, Mr. President. Americans will die, a lot of them. You'll have to decide how much of Cuba you want to wipe off the face of the earth."

"We're going to hold a news conference to reply to Vargas this afternoon."

"I wouldn't mention biological weapons, if I were you," Tater Totten advised. "Let your audience assume the Cuban missiles still have nuclear warheads. Germs scare people more than bombs, perhaps because they are invisible. And we've lived with the bomb for fifty years."

The president pursed his lips thoughtfully.

Autrey James, Petty Officer Third Class, USN, always watched the ocean from his station in the door of the helicopter. It was a point of pride with him. He once spotted two fishermen whose boat had sunk off Long Island and was given a medal and had his name and photograph in the newspapers, but the part of that adventure that he remembered best was his grandmother's reaction when she read of his exploits. "You *save* people, Autrey, what a marvelous profession!" Grandmom's comment somehow said it all for Autrey James; whenever his helo was airborne, he watched the ocean. Maybe someday he would save another life.

So that was the reason Autrey James spotted the tiny object on the surface of the immense ocean and called it out to the pilots on the ICS.

"Yo, Mr. P., looks like a man in the water at ten o'clock, two miles," Autrey James said.

"Are you kidding me, James? You got eyes that good?"

"Looks like a man to me, sir, but I could be wrong."

"Well, we'll motor over that way just to find out if you are."

The helicopter was an SH-60B Seahawk from USS *Hue City*, one of the two Aegis-class cruisers that Jake Grafton had sent charging northwest. The cruisers were doing just that right now, running abreast of each other a mile apart, making 32 knots, twenty-five miles east of the helicopter's position.

Hue City's commanding officer had launched his helo so the crew could get some flight time and he could find out what was over the horizon, beyond the range of his surface-search radar.

"Dog my dingies, James, danged if that ain't a survivor. Is he alive, do you think?"

"His head's still up, sir. Give me a hover and I'll put the basket in the water."

The basket was just that, a basket on the end of a winch cable. All the survivor had to do was crawl in, then James could winch the basket up to the chopper and help the survivor out.

Unfortunately, with the basket in the water just in front of him, the survivor made no attempt to get in.

"He ain't gettin' in, Mr. P." Autrey James told the pilot. He was leaning out the door of the helicopter so that he could see the survivor and the basket.

"Maybe he's dead."

"I don't think so. Looks like his head is out of the water. Dead men don't float like that."

"You wanna jump in and help?"

"On my way," said Autrey James. The pilot lowered the chopper to just a few feet above the water and James jumped into the sea.

One look at the survivor's face told him the man was near death, too weak to help himself. With some pushing and pulling, James got the survivor into the basket. The other enlisted man in the chopper winched him up, then dropped the basket for James.

When James had his helmet on again, he informed the pilot, "We'd better head back quick, Mr. P. This guy is in real bad shape. His eyes don't focus."

"Try to give him some water."

"I'll try, but we need to get him to a doc."

Autrey James leaned over the survivor, who was deathly cold, and shouted to make himself heard above the loud background noise, "Hey, man, you're one lucky dude. You're gonna be okay. Just hang on for a few more minutes."

"Blankets," James said to the other crewman. Both of them wrapped the survivor in wool blankets.

"*Gracias,*" said Ocho Sedano, and tried to smile. Then exhaustion overcame him and he passed out.

The carrier and her battle group got under way at dawn. *Kearsarge* stayed in Guantánamo Bay and began loading the marines that had been guarding warehouse number nine. The last of the warheads were going aboard the cargo ship this afternoon, then it would sail. When it left, *Kearsarge* would also get underway with the marines, all nineteen hundred of them.

The battle group steamed south from Guantánamo bay. For about an hour the southern hills of Cuba were visible from the decks of the ships, but they soon dropped over the horizon and all that could be seen in any direction was the eternal ocean, always changing, always the same. It was then that the carrier launched an E-2 Hawkeye, which carried its radar up to 20,000 feet. Everything the Hawkeye's early warning radar saw was datalinked to the carrier's computers, where specialists kept track of the tactical picture.

Toad Tarkington took Jake aside and showed him the latest message from the National Security Council. He was directed to destroy the viruses in the laboratory in the University of Havana's science building, find and destroy the warhead-manufacturing facility, and to remove the warheads from the six missiles and destroy them in their silos.

As Jake read the message, Toad said, "They don't want much, do they?"

"Where in hell is the warhead-manufacturing facility?" Jake groused. He went to find William Henry Chance to ask him that question. He found Chance in the wardroom drinking coffee with Tommy Carmellini. They were the only two people there at ten in the morning.

"Do you have any idea where we might find this factory for making biological warheads?"

"Sit down, Admiral. Let me buy you a cup of navy coffee."

Jake sat. Carmellini went for the coffee while Jake repeated the question.

"It has to be someplace between the science building and the missile silos," Chance said. "No one in their right mind would want to haul that stuff very far. A traffic accident of some type . . ."

Jake Grafton's brows knitted. He tapped on the table. "If you were going to haul polio viruses around, what kind of truck would you use?"

Chance shrugged. "I don't know," he said.

"I've been thinking about it for five hours now, and I've got an idea. We'll run it though the recon computers and see what pops out." He got up from his chair.

"Mind sharing your epiphany?"

"I'd haul the stuff in milk trucks. Clean, sterile, and sealed. A dairy should have a sterile environment and the equipment to mix the viruses with some sort of a base, then load them into warheads."

Jake turned and marched from the room just as Carmellini approached with the extra coffee cup and saucer.

"He didn't stay long, did he?"

"No," Chance grunted, and sipped at the coffee Carmellini had brought from the urn in the corner of the room.

"Think Grafton's big enough for this job?" Carmellini asked.

"Yeah. I think he is."

Three dairies met Jake's specifications—they were located between Havana and the first of the missile silos, which were arranged in a line beginning forty miles east of Havana and going east from there. The silos were about fifteen miles apart.

"Cows. See if they have cows around them."

"When?"

"The latest satellite photography. Whenever that was."

Two of the dairies no longer had cattle in the adjacent fields. The one that did was scratched off the list. The other two were examined minutely by the carrier's intelligence center experts and the National Security Agency photo interpreters in Maryland, who conferred back and forth via encrypted satellite telephones. The experts decided that neither dairy could be eliminated as a possible site for the warhead factory.

"We'll do 'em both," Jake Grafton said.

By three that afternoon the staff and air wing planners had come up with a draft plan. Actually the task, destruction of eight targets, was a relatively simple military one. Tomahawk missiles could take out the lab and the dairies without muss or fuss. They could probably also destroy the missiles in their silos, as the silos were hardened in a simpler age, when the threat was unguided air-dropped bombs. With their ability to power-dive straight down on a hardened target and penetrate ten or twelve feet of reinforced concrete, Tomahawks were the weapon of choice.

And they were out of the question. The president absolutely refused to take the chance that polio viruses might escape from a bombed lab or silo and kill tens of thousands of Cubans in their beds. An event like that would be political dynamite, with repercussions beyond calculation. No, the politicians said, American troops were going to have to lay their lives on the line to prevent just such an occurrence. And, Jake Grafton well knew, some of them would die.

He had already put the wheels in motion. Preliminary messages had been sent to other commands, asking them for the assistance Jake thought he would require. A thousand details remained to be worked out by the various staffs involved, but the machine was in motion. The primary task Jake still had to address was setting the day and hour for the attack.

As he stood looking at the charts of Cuba that covered the wall in the planning space, Jake and his staff wrestled with the timing question. Captain Gil Pascal, the chief of staff, argued that the operation should be delayed until such time as U-2s could fly a photo recon mission and get the very latest enemy troop positions.

"Vargas made a speech today," Jake replied. The speech and a translation had played several times on television. Jake had even stopped once to watch it.

"*Hue City* and *Guilford Courthouse* are racing for the Florida Straits," Toad Tarkington argued. "This battle group is underway. The Cubans may find out about these ship movements and put two and two together and get their wind up. They may be able to put twenty-four hours of delay to better use than we can."

"That's the nub of it, isn't it?" Jake mused, and stood looking at the charts, trying to imagine how it would be.

Sure, things would go wrong. People were going to have the wrong frequencies, go to the wrong places, everything that could go wrong would. Still, the missions were simple.

The real issue, Jake concluded, was the follow-up. What were you going to do if the troops ran into more trouble than they could handle? How would you extract them? How would you destroy the target?

Jake called the Pentagon on the satellite telephone. He was patched through via land line to General Totten at the White House.

After the usual greetings, Jake said, "Sir, two points. First, I would like to address the proposal to delay the operation until Patriot SAM batteries can be moved into southern Florida. If we pop a Cuban missile over southern Florida the cloud of viruses may drift over to Miami or Tampa. I don't think we gain anything by waiting for Patriot batteries."

"We've about reached the same conclusion here, but there has been vigorous debate. What is your second point?"

"In my view, the key to getting this done is our willingness to do whatever is required to accomplish the mission."

"The president is listening, Admiral. Explain yourself."

"As I see it, General, our choice is to either wait until we are convinced we can pull it off, or go now before the Cubans have a chance to garrison these sites with troops. The lab in Havana presents problems that the other sites do not. We will have to tackle the lab after the missiles are destroyed."

"Okay."

"If the troops assaulting the silos run into more Cubans than they can handle, we must either add more forces or extract our men. If we elect to extract our people, we still have the problem of the missile in the silo and we will have handed the Cubans a victory in a fight we cannot afford to lose."

"What do you propose?"

"We won't be able to go back later with more people. We get one bite of the apple, sir. I propose that you authorize me to use whatever force is required to accomplish the mission, short of nuclear weapons."

Jake Grafton heard the president loudly say, "I'm not giving him or anybody else the authority to risk a catastrophic release of toxins. No."

"We'll call you back," General Totten said, and hung up.

Mercedes went to stay with Doña Maria Vieuda de Sedano, to cook for her and clean and do whatever needed to be done. She had stayed with her mother-in-law in the past, after her husband, Jorge, died—fortunately the two women genuinely liked each other.

She and Doña Maria ate lunch on the little porch of the bungalow so they could enjoy the breeze blowing in from the sea. It was strong today, whipping the palm fronds and rippling the sugarcane. Little puffy clouds threw severe shadows that raced over the ground.

Doña Maria had gone back inside for a nap and Mercedes was sewing a blouse together when a limo drove up and Maximo got out. He came up the short walk, paused at the steps, and looked at her. "I thought I would find you here," he said.

"*Mima*'s sleeping."

"I came to see you."

She nodded, continued working on the blouse. He stayed on the dirt and scraggly grass, walked around so the porch railing was between them.

"Vargas made a speech this morning. It was on television."

"Hmm," she said. Doña Maria did not have a television, and Maximo knew that.

"He is the president now."

"I have heard."

"Did he really kill Fidel?"

"No."

Her thread broke. She got out the spool of thread and rethreaded the needle.

"Would you tell me if he had?"

"What did you come for, Maximo?"

"I need your help."

She knotted the thread and began a new seam.

"You don't think much of me, do you?"

"I don't think of you at all."

He leaned on the porch railing, crossing his arms. "Where did Fidel hide the gold?"

"I didn't know he had any," she said, not looking up from her work. "He didn't even have gold in his teeth."

"The gold pesos the government called in after the revolution—that gold."

"I have no idea," she said.

"I think you do. I think Fidel told you."

"Think what you like."

"He wouldn't let the secret die with him."

"Maximo, look at me. If I had a pocketful of gold, would I be sitting here on the porch of a tiny, ninety-five-year-old bungalow with a thatched roof beside the road to Varadero, sewing myself a shirt?"

"I don't think you have it—I think you know where it is."

She snorted and went back to the needle and the seam.

"You don't want the gold for yourself, I know. But I need it. Not all of it, just a little. I must get out of Cuba."

A strand of hair fell across her face. She brushed it back.

"We could leave together, Mercedes, if we had some of that gold. You could go anywhere on earth you wanted, live the rest of your life without worry, without fear, without need. Think of it! A new life, a new beginning. How much of this heat and dirt and hopeless poverty do you want, anyway?"

"Forget the gold, Maximo. If there is any, it is not for you."

He backed away from the railing, stood in the sun with the sea wind playing at his hair. "Think about it," he said. "Vargas is no fool; he wants the gold too. One of these days he will send Santana around to see you. Think about what you are going to say to him when he comes."

He walked to the waiting limo. The driver turned the car in the road and headed back toward Havana.

Toad Tarkington was the only person in the room with Jake as they waited for the chairman of the joint chiefs to call from the White House.

"What do you want from them, Admiral?"

"I want the authority to do whatever I have to do to destroy those viruses," Jake Grafton explained. "Once the shooting starts, *we have to win*."

"What if the president won't give you that authority?"

"He has a right to say that. We'll go do our best, and if we can't cut it without using Tomahawks or laser-guided weapons, then we'll call him up and say so."

"What is the problem here?" Toad demanded. "If there is a toxin release he won't be the guy responsible. Fidel Castro and Alejo Vargas are the guilty parties. This is *their* country."

Jake shook his head. "If there is a toxin release in America, the president must be able to prove that he did everything humanly possible to prevent it. If there is a release in Cuba . . . well, he will need to show people around the world that he did what he could to prevent it while still eliminating the threat to the U.S. Elimination of the threat is the key here, and I hope they understand that in Washington." He smacked the wall with his hand. "Dammit, we only get one shot at those viruses."

"I wonder if anyone in Washington is thinking about the Bay of Pigs," Toad mused. "That turned into a debacle because Kennedy wasn't willing to commit enough resources."

"*I've* been thinking about it," Jake Grafton said.

When the telephone rang, General Totten was on the line. "Admiral, we shall word it like this: 'Your mission is to eliminate the threat to the United States. In completing your mission you are instructed to do everything within your power to minimize the possibility of a toxin release in Cuba. You may use any forces and weapons in your command except nuclear or CBW weapons, and you may request assistance from any command in the U.S. armed forces.' "

"Yes, sir."

"I'll have that on the wire as soon as possible."

"Yes, sir. I want to thank you and the president. We'll do our best."

"I know you will, sailor. When are you going?"

"Tomorrow night, sir. In view of all the factors involved, that is my choice."

CHAPTER EIGHTEEN

Over Cuba the next morning the cloud cover was typical for that time of year: as the sun rose the prevailing westerly winds spawned cumulus clouds over the warming land. The longer the clouds remained over land, the higher they grew. In the area east of Havana where the Americans believed the missile silos and processing lab were located the cloud cover averaged forty or fifty percent by ten in the morning, enough to inhibit satellite and U-2 photography of the area. Infrared photography was not affected by the clouds, nor were the synthetic-aperture radar studies done by air force E-3 Sentry AWACS aircraft.

Oblivious to the intense scrutiny that the island was now getting from the Americans, General Alba conferred that morning with Alejo Vargas, then ordered troops and tanks moved into position around the silos. There were actually eight silos, but only six held operational missiles. The other two missiles had been used as sources of spare parts through the years. Had Alba and Vargas realized what was coming, they might have elected to dissipate the American military effort by garrisoning all eight silos: as it was, they didn't think of it.

The sun had been up just two hours when two C-130 Hercules landed at the naval air station at Key West, Florida. On the civilian side of the field people stood and watched as the Hercs parked on the other side of the runway. Soon navy personnel began unloading the transports. The civilian kibitzers did not know what the pallets and canisters contained, and after a while they went on about their business. Four armed marines in combat gear took up locations where they could guard the transports.

Among other things, the transports had delivered belted 20-mm ammunition for miniguns, Hellfire missiles, flares, and 2.75-inch rockets. They also delivered tools and spare parts to work on Marine Corps AH-1W SuperCobras.

Two hours after the Hercs landed, the first two SuperCobras settled onto the military mat. By noon sixteen of the mottled green helicopters were parked in the sun.

The two-man crews didn't leave the base, but went into an old, decrepit navy hangar nearby for briefings.

Two more C-130s wearing marine markings landed an hour or so later. They parked near the first two. As navy trucks began refueling the planes, marines disembarked and spread their gear on the ramp. They lounged around, a few walked a safe distance away and lit cigarettes, and after awhile a navy truck brought hot food.

Troops, tanks, and trucks were moving in Cuba by noon, blocking roads and creating traffic jams. By midafternoon the E-3 Sentry crews had alerted the National Security Agency, which passed the information on to USS *United States.* Jake Grafton went to the ship's intelligence center to see what the computers could tell him.

After listening to the briefer, Jake Grafton muttered, "Damn."

He went over the data, then asked, "How much combat power are they moving, and when will it be in place?"

In New York City the U.S. ambassador to the United Nations paid a call on the Cuban ambassador. After exchanging civilities, the American said bluntly, "My government has asked me to inform you that if the Cuban government releases biological toxins of any kind in the United States, for any reason, the American government will massively retaliate."

" 'Massively retaliate'?" The Cuban's eyes widened. "What does that mean?"

"Sir, I was instructed to deliver the message, not to interpret it. Here is the statement in writing." The American handed over a sheet of paper and took her leave.

Aboard USS *Hue City*, now underway precisely halfway between Cuba and Key West at ten knots, Ocho Sedano awoke in midafternoon from a deep sleep. He found that he was in a hospital bed on a small ward, with two intravenous solutions dripping into his veins. His vision was blurred, he could not focus his eyes.

The doctor on the ward noticed that he was awake and came over to check him. In a few minutes an American sailor who spoke Spanish came to interpret.

"Your eyes are sore from the salt of the water. They will get better. Can you tell us your name, señor?"

"Juan Sedano," he whispered, because he could not talk above a whisper. "They call me El Ocho."

"And where are you from?"

"Cuba."

"How long were you in the sea?"

"Two days and nights, I think. I am not sure. Maybe more than that."

The doctor put a solution into Ocho's eyes while the questions and answers were flying back and forth. After blinking mightily Ocho thought he could see a little better. The doctor was examining Ocho's fingertips and the calluses on his hands. Now he held up Ocho's hand and peeled off a callus. Then he smiled. "You were very lucky."

The translator interpreted.

"Where am I?" Ocho asked.

"Aboard *Hue City*, a United States Navy ship. You were rescued by a helicopter. The man who saw you in the water wants to shake your hand when you awaken. He saved your life. May I call him?"

"I would like to meet him."

It felt very comfortable lying there, looking at the fuzzy beds and blurred people bustling about, checking him over, so different from *Angel del Mar*. Or floating on the sea.

Maybe he was dead. He examined that possibility but concluded it was not so. This was not a bit like the heaven he envisioned, and he was hungry. He told the interpreter of his hunger, and the man went to talk to the doctor, who had wandered off.

They brought food about the same time that Autrey James came breezing in with one of his pals, who had a camera. James was a happy fellow with a wide smile—the white teeth in a dark face were the only details that Ocho could see. James got down beside the bed and posed while the man with the camera took many pictures. Another man with a camera came, some kind of television camera, and he and James shook hands again. Several men in khaki stood behind the camera watching.

The interpreter relayed the questions from Autrey James and the television cameraman. When did you leave Cuba, What was the name of the boat, How many people were there?

"Eighty-four people."

"Eighty four?" asked the interpreter in disbelief.

"Eighty-four," whispered Ocho Sedano.

"What happened to the boat?"

"It sank."

"And the people?"

"They went into the water . . . sharks."

"Sharks?"

"Some people were swept over the side during a storm our first night at sea. Diego Coca shot the captain, some people died of thirst . . . Diego jumped into the sea. The children died of exhaustion and hunger, I think—it is really impossible to say. There was no food or water, only rain to drink. When the boat sank those who were left were eaten by sharks. If they didn't drown. I hope Dora drowned.

"The old fisherman and I were spared. . . . Did you find him? The old fisherman? Did you see him in the ocean?" He clawed at Autrey James, who drew back out of reach.

"No," the interpreter said. "You were the only one."

They went away then, all of them, left him to eat the food and stare at the ceiling and think about the fact that he was alive and all the others were dead.

The others were dead. He was alive. What did that mean?

Was God crazy?

Why me?

He was thinking about that when someone came to put solution in his eyes again. This time the solution made him cry.

He sobbed for a minute or two, then his body gave out and he slept.

"Why did you not put the gold in a bank vault?"

Mercedes had asked this question of Fidel several years ago, when he first told her of the gold pesos. As she sat on her mother-in-law's small porch completing her blouse, she remembered the question, and Fidel's answer:

"If we kept the gold in a bank, the international bankers would have learned of it eventually, would have demanded that we post it as security for a loan. Then a hurricane would come or the bottom would drop out of the sugar market one year, and the gold would be gone."

"But the gold does not help Cuba. Why own it?"

"The gold is ours," he said obstinately. "When it is gone it is gone for all Cubans forever."

"But you hid it, so it is gone now."

"Oh, no. You and I know where it is. As long as it is hidden, it belongs to Cuba."

She couldn't shake him—he had the peasant's love of the secret hoard, the instinctual drive to bury a can of money or hide it in a mattress, just in case. No matter how bad things got in the house, the money was always there, hidden, an asset that could be tapped to stave off starvation or disaster.

He said as much when he admitted, "In the middle of the night, when I am alone and the world is heavy on my shoulders, I remember we still have the gold."

Fidel and Che Guevara hid it together, for Cuba. Guevara was killed in Bolivia and apparently took the secret to his grave. Fidel didn't want to—he told the one person on this earth he trusted.

She wished she didn't know this thing. As she worked on the last seam of the blouse, she thought about this great secret, about what she should do.

Mercedes Sedano had confided in no one, had written nothing down. With Fidel dead the gold was only one heartbeat away from being lost forever. She must do something, but what?

Fidel had been a knot of contradictions. She had argued with him— challenged the macho man himself—and he had admitted some of his failures, which was a rare moment for him. Not all of his errors, but some.

"I am the only communist in Cuba," he said, laughing. "Becoming a communist was a mistake—of course I can never say that in public. We had to declare our independence from the American financiers and corporations. In the fullness of time it turned out that the Russian horse couldn't run the race, which was unfortunate, but that didn't mean we were wrong in the first place." He shrugged.

He had the Latin's ability to accept life's vicissitudes as they came with courage and grace.

"The best thing about communism was the dictatorship. The economic twaddle meant nothing. Someone had to show the Cuban people they could stand on their own feet, that they didn't need to sell their souls to the Americans or the Catholic Church." He smiled again, made a gesture toward heaven. "The truth is we were too poor to afford the Church or the Americans."

If Santana or Vargas tortured her, she would tell them about the gold. To suffer horribly and die for a secret that you thought illogical was worse than stupid—it would be a sin.

Did he ever wonder what she would do if she found herself in this situation?

She finished the last seam, shook out the blouse, and held it up so she could view it.

Had Fidel really trusted her to make the decision that was best for Cuba, or did he just think that she would keep her mouth shut?

For Maximo Sedano the question was simple and stark: Where was the gold?

Rumors had circulated for forty years, and not a flake had ever surfaced. Several men swore they had helped melt the coins into ingots in a smelter in the basement of the Ministry of Finance, but they never knew what happened to the ingots. Alejo Vargas had been running the secret police for twenty years and the Ministry of Interior for the last ten and probably hunting for the gold for at least nineteen, and he hadn't found it. At least Maximo didn't believe he had. In forty years no loose ends had unraveled ... so there must have been no loose ends.

The conclusion Maximo drew from these facts was that only a very few people—Fidel, perhaps his brother Raúl, maybe Che—had known the secret in the first place. Today the secret might be known by a few people who had been close to them. In any event, there were no elderly workmen about who liked to run their mouth when they drank their rum—Vargas would have found anyone like that years ago.

So the gold wasn't made into statues, poured like concrete into a floor or foundation, made into bricks and used to construct a state building, or transported to some flyspecked hovel and buried under the floor. No. If the gold had been hidden this way, someone involved in the labor would have talked during the last forty years.

If there were secret records waiting to be discovered or letters in bank vaults, Maximo would never discover them. All he had were his wits.

With Fidel dead and Alejo Vargas ascendant, Maximo was using his wits now, applying them as never before.

In search of inspiration, he walked the streets of Havana to the Museum of the Revolution.

Like so many revolutionaries who swashbuckled through the pages of human history, after his victory Fidel found it expedient to enshrine himself as the savior of the nation so that he might remain at the helm permanently. Of course, to properly do the job it was also necessary to build a monument to the venality and depravity of his enemies, because great heroes need worthy opponents. Amazingly, all this good, evil, and greatness fit neatly under one roof: the presidential palace that had been the residence of Fulgencio Batista.

Maximo walked quickly through the exhibits that detailed Batista's corruption—what he sought would not be there.

He quickly found what he was looking for. Fidel the savior, *"El Líder Maximo,"* portraits, busts, memorabilia, candid and posed photographs, heroic paintings—all of this was enough to turn the stomach of anyone who had actually known the man, Maximo thought. Alas, Fidel had been very flawed clay: megalomaniacal, filled with a sense of his own magnificent destiny, boorish, opinionated, pigheaded, insufferable, prejudiced, loquacious to a fault, and, all too often, just plain wrong. What a tragedy that this self-annointed messiah was stranded in this third world backwater and never had the opportunity to save the species, which he could have done if only God had sent him to Moscow or Washington.

Maximo tried to stifle his disgust and concentrate upon the displays before him.

Fidel and Che Guevara, Camilo Cienfuegos, the other immortals . . . The university, the Moncada Barracks, the trial, prison, handwritten letters, exile, guerrilla days . . .

He carefully looked at everything, then wandered on. He came to a room devoted to the fall of Havana; Fidel riding into the city on a tank, ecstatic children. Then Fidel the ruler; Fidel the baseball player; Fidel and Che fishing in the Gulf Stream; Fidel with Hemingway, Richard

Nixon, Khrushchev, Kosygin, the famous and the infamous, always togged out in those abysmal green fatigues; dozens of shots of Fidel with his mouth open in front of crowds . . . God, how the man could talk to a captive audience!

Maximo was in the next room looking at photos of Fidel eating rice and beans with schoolchildren when the incongruity of the photo of Fidel and Che fishing struck him. Odd, that.

He went back to it. The two were on some kind of fishing boat, with fighting chairs and big rods, fishing for marlin probably.

Wait a minute . . . The marina where Maximo kept his boat . . . When he first moved it there the harbormaster had once told him that Fidel used to leave from that marina to fish.

Now he remembered. Yes. The old man said Fidel and Che fished often, every few days, went out by themselves, often spent the night at anchor in the harbor. After a year or so they tired of it, the old man said wistfully, never came back. The boat belonged to the Cuban Navy— seized from an American—and was eventually converted to a gunboat.

He could remember the old man talking, could see the wind playing with his white hair as he stood on the dock in the sun talking about his hero, Fidel, about that moment one day long ago when their lives came close together.

The harbormaster had been dead for years. The new man was far too young to remember anything.

What if the gold were on the floor of Havana Harbor?

Each night Fidel and Che could have lowered hundreds of pounds of it over the side of the boat free from observation. Given enough nights . . .

Over time the gold could have gradually disappeared from the Finance Ministry. If no one but Fidel and Che handled the gold, there was no one to talk.

Maximo could see logistical problems with this possibility, of course, but not insurmountable ones.

He left the museum deep in thought.

"The air force's AWACS reports that the Cuban military is moving toward the silo sites, Admiral."

The briefer was a commander, the senior Air Intelligence officer on the carrier battle group's staff.

"The troops are being moved from barracks in the Havana area. We can see tanks and trucks, which presumably contain supplies and troops. The columns are moving slowly, eight to ten miles per hour. Cuban troops have already arrived at missile site number one. Just arriving on sites two and three. We estimate that there will be no Cuban military presence on sites four though six until tomorrow morning after dawn."

"Why so slow?" Jake Grafton asked.

"These are old tanks, Soviet T-54s! We think they see no reason to risk breakdowns by driving faster. The consensus seems to be that the Cubans aren't on full alert."

"Okay," Jake Grafton said, because there was nothing else to say. The god of battles was dealing the cards.

The briefer continued, pointing out bridges and crossroad choke points, and Jake tried to concentrate, which was difficult. When the briefer finished, Jake dismissed his staff and sat staring at the map on the bulkhead.

The plan was good: the weather would be typical, the forces he had should be adequate, they knew their jobs . . . but if the Cubans fired those missiles at the United States, two Aegis cruisers were all he had to prevent the missiles from reaching their targets.

Should this whole operation be delayed until antimissile batteries could be moved to south Florida?

Every hour of delay meant more American troops would die taking those missile sites. Yet if the missiles successfully delivered their warheads, the results would be catastrophic.

He looked again at the plan—at the timing, at the units assigned.

Biological weapons. Poliomyelitis.

He could always use more people, of course. One of the primary goals of warfighting—some people argued, the *only* goal—was to direct overwhelming force at the point where the enemy was most vulnerable. Or as Bedford Forrest put it, "Get there firstest with the mostest."

Already the Cubans were digging in around silos one and two. What if the forces he had committed couldn't crack those nuts?

The urge to wait for a bigger hammer had Jake Grafton in its grip now. He felt like David with his slingshot. Maybe he needed more Aegis cruisers, some Patriot missile batteries, more cruise missiles, troops, Ospreys, airplanes.

If one of those missiles got through . . .

He found a handkerchief in his hip pocket and mopped his face.

His stomach tried to turn over.

He hadn't felt like this since Vietnam. Way back in those happy days he had been responsible only for his bombardier's life and his own miserable existence. All things considered, that load had been relatively light.

This load . . .

Well, Jake Grafton, Uncle Sugar's been paying you good money all these years while you've been getting fat and sassy on the long grass. It's payback time.

In midafternoon Toad Tarkington went to the communication spaces to call his wife, Rita Moravia, on one of the ship-to-ship voice circuits. He had done this a time or two before and the chief petty officer was accommodating when the circuits were not in use for official business. This afternoon he asked the chief for an encrypted circuit but they were all busy—the chief handed him a clear-voice handset. Toad called *Kearsarge* and left a message for his wife. Ten minutes later she called him back.

"Hey, Toad-man."

"Hey, Hot Woman."

Tonight, he knew, she would be flying a V-22 Osprey, hauling troops to missile silo two.

"Just wanted to hear your voice," Toad said, as matter-of-factly as he could. He could envision this conversation coming over radios in ships throughout the battle group and in Cuban monitoring stations. He had no intention of giving away secrets nor of entertaining kibitzers.

Rita was equally circumspect. "Got a letter from Tyler. He wrote it with Na-Na's help, of course."

"How's Ty-Guy doing?"

"He has a girlfriend, the Goldman girl across the street."

"That's my boy," Toad said. "A lover already. A chip off the old brick."

Aboard *Kearsarge* Rita was holding the handset in a death grip. She loved life: her son, her husband, her job, the people she worked with—every jot and comma of her life. Oh, of course there were days when the stress and problems threatened to overwhelm her ability to cope, but somehow she managed. In the wee hours of the night when she paused to evaluate, she knew that she wouldn't change a thing. Not one single thing.

Now she realized that Toad hadn't spoken in several seconds.

"I wouldn't change a thing," Rita said.

"I was thinking the same thing," he said.

"From day one."

"I remember the first day I saw you. Wow."

"When we were at Whidbey, I thought you hated me."

"And I thought you didn't like me."

"Thank God you finally screwed up the courage to kiss me."

"Wish I could now," he shot back.

Tears ran down her cheeks. She wanted to tell him how much he had meant all these years, how grateful she was that they shared life, and nothing came out. She put her hand over the mouthpiece so he wouldn't hear her cry.

"Next time we're together, better not wear lipstick," he said.

"I never wear lipstick," she managed, her voice barely under control.

"It's a good thing, too," he said, his voice cracking.

The silence grew and grew.

"Well, I gotta go," Toad finally said. "They wanna use this circuit to trade movies or something."

"Yeah."

"*Vaya con Dios*, baby."

"You too, Toad-man."

Toad found Jake Grafton in Combat huddled with Gil Pascal, the chief of staff. He listened to the conversation for a moment, then realized that the admiral was trying to assure himself that he had adequate forces to win. Tonight!

After a bit Jake turned toward Toad. "Let's have your two cents," he said.

"If we need anything, sir, it's a bigger reserve. We have three V-22s with twenty-four marines each to go wherever they are needed. A while ago the CO of the carrier's marine det asked if he and some of his people could get in on the fun. He called *Kearsarge* and found there is one extra Osprey. It's being used as a backup to the first wave, but if it isn't needed, then it'll be an extra."

Gil Pascal frowned. "The carrier's marines haven't been briefed," he pointed out.

Jake glanced at Toad and raised one eyebrow.

"Sir, I was hoping you would let me go with them," Tarkington replied cheerfully. "I'm as briefed as it's possible to get." Actually, as Ops, Tarkington wrote the plan.

"You've been planning to spring this on me all day, haven't you?"

"I could take a satellite phone, give you a worm's-eye view of the action, let you know if there is really a problem."

"Did the marine det CO approach you with this marvelous idea, or did you approach him?"

Toad turned his eyes to the ceiling. "An officer I know well used to say, 'You know me.'"

"I think I know that guy too," Jake said, and chuckled. "Oh, all right, damn it—you can go. Gil and I will try to hold the fort without you. If the backup Osprey isn't needed, you'll be part of the cavalry. Tell the grunts to saddle up."

The Spanish-speaking sailor who acted as an interpreter shook Ocho Sedano awake. "Ocho," he said. "Ocho, a question has arisen. We wish to know if you are related to Hector Sedano."

Ocho opened his eyes and focused on the interpreter, who appeared reasonably clear. His eyes were better, much better. He rolled over, then sat up in bed. He was still in sick bay aboard *Hue City*.

"Welcome back to the land of the living," said the American sailor.

"It is good to be alive," Ocho whispered.

"Did you ever give up hope?"

"I suppose. I thought I would die, and was waiting for it. But I always wanted to live."

The sailor grinned. This was the first American he had ever gotten to know, and he had a good grin, Ocho thought.

"The officers want to know," the sailor said, "if you are related to Hector Sedano."

"He is my brother."

"I will tell them."

Ocho nodded, then rubbed his head and stretched. He was hungry and thirsty. A glass of water was sitting on a rolling table beside the bed, so he drained it.

"May I have some food?"

"I will bring some."

Ocho looked the sailor in the eyes. "I want to go back to Cuba. I should never have left."

"I will tell them," the sailor said, and left him there.

William Henry Chance and Tommy Carmellini argued with Toad about how many marines wearing CBW suits should go into the warhead factory with them. "Just Tommy and I," Chance said. "The more people that are in there the greater the chance of an accident."

"How are you going to get your gear in there?"

"An armload at a time. It will take a little longer, but with only two guys going in and out, this whole evolution will be safer."

"What if the Cuban Army shows up while you're working?"

"The marines can defend us until the place goes up."

They were in a ready room under the flight deck dressing in a corner under the television set, which was showing a continuous briefing by the Air Intelligence types. Radio frequencies, threat envelopes, timing, call signs, weather, everything was on the tube.

Carmellini was paying close attention to the briefers, Chance was arguing with Toad. "And I'm not taking a rifle or hand grenades or rations or any of that combat crap."

"A pistol, then."

"Got my own. Don't want two."

"Why are you being so obstinate, Mr. Chance?"

Chance sat down heavily in one of the ready-room chairs.

"I guess I've got a bad feeling about this commando stuff," he said. "Charging in decked out like Captain America with rifle in hand scares me silly. Everybody and his brother will start shooting, and with cultures above-ground in vulnerable containers . . ." He shivered. "If we sneak in in civilian clothes . . . well, that's what I'm used to. This military stuff frightens me."

"You're going to look funny walking into a dairy in civilian clothes with flares on your shoulders if there are Cuban troops sitting around the place guarding the cows."

"You're right, I know." Chance shrugged.

"Gonna be an adventure," Tommy Carmellini tossed in.

"You guys are big boys," Toad Tarkington said. "I'm not going to nursemaid you. But this isn't a game—a lot of lives are at stake. If you screw this up and we gotta go back in there later and fix it, you guys better be dead. Don't bother coming back."

Toad said it matter-of-factly, as if he were discussing a payroll deduction. Chance suddenly felt small.

"Okay," he said. "Two other guys in CBW suits. But I'm in charge. If I go down, Tommy is."

"Fine," said Toad Tarkington, and went to find an encrypted telephone.

Terror wasn't going to be enough to keep Alejo Vargas in office. He knew that. He could put the fear of God in the little sons of bitches and keep it there, but to sleep nights in Fidel's house he was going to have to govern the country, to give a little here, a little there, and so on. He was prepared to do that—he had watched Fidel manipulate these people all of his adult life.

Today he sat in his office at the Ministry of the Interior—he had had no time to move to the presidential palace—receiving the members of the Council of State, of which he was the president.

"Señor Ferrara, it is a pleasure to see you again."

Ferrara was short, fat, and wheezed when he moved. He was a member of the Council of State and the minister of electric power. He dropped into a chair across the desk from Vargas and wiped his forehead with a handkerchief.

"Good day, Señor President."

Colonel Santana handed Vargas Ferrara's affidavit. Vargas merely glanced at the signature, then laid it in his top right-hand drawer with the others. He didn't read it because he knew exactly what the affidavit contained—an emotional eyewitness account of the murder of Raúl Castro by Hector Sedano. Vargas and Santana had drafted the document this morning.

Before each member of the Council of State met with Vargas, Santana presented them with an affidavit for signature. Most intuitively understood that signatures were mandatory, and those that didn't had the facts of life explained to them. So far, all had signed.

"I appreciate your support in this matter, Ferrara."

"I will be frank with you, Vargas. That document means nothing."

He gestured toward the desk drawer. "You may be able to crack the whip in Havana, but the people do not support you. They want Hector Sedano in the presidential palace."

"They will find a place in their heart for me."

"Fidel Castro lasted for over forty years because he had the support of the people. The members of the National Assembly, the Council of State, the ministers, could not oppose him because they had no base of support. The Department of State Security didn't control the population—Fidel did."

"He did not tolerate opposition, nor will I."

Ferrara said nothing.

What was it about Ferrara? Something was in the files, but he hadn't looked at that file in years, and now it was gone. "Was it your daughter?"

Ferrara's face became a mask.

"Your daughter ... something about your daughter ..."

He stared into Ferrara's eyes.

"Help me a little."

Even Ferrara's wheezing had stopped.

"Maybe it will come to me." Alejo Vargas leaned back in his chair. "Or maybe I will forget completely."

Santana came in just then, handed him a sheet of paper, and said, "The ambassador to the United Nations received this note from the American UN ambassador."

"Thank you for stopping by, Señor Ferrara. I appreciate you executing this affidavit. I look forward to working with you in the future. Good Day." Ferrara went.

Vargas read the note. "Any other American reaction to my speech or their president's?"

"Yes, sir. As we expected, the American pundits generally support their president, but there are many who feel the United States has goaded Cuba into military adventurism with their political shunning of Castro. This feeling is widespread in Europe. Around the world there are many who feel that Cuba has endured much oppression at America's hands."

Vargas nodded. All the world roots for the underdog.

"The American carrier battle group that was in Guantánamo is now south of the Isle of Pines. They have only a few planes aloft."

"And General Alba? Is he getting troops into position around the silos?"

"Yes, sir."

"Make sure the air force is on full alert, the army, the navy, the antiaircraft missile batteries, everyone. If the Americans come we will bloody their nose, perhaps even launch a missile. One missile will teach them a bitter lesson. They have never seen anything like that virus: they will have no stomach for it. The error of their ways is about to become quite apparent."

"You do not believe this 'massive retaliation' threat?"

"It is laughable," he scoffed. "No American president will ever order the use of weapons of mass destruction, even in retaliation. The Americans stopped making war years ago—they use force to send messages to 'bad' governments, never to kill the civilians who support that government. Guilt is the new American ethic: they would be horrified at the murder of the hungry." He waved his hand dismissively, then became deadly serious:

"The Yanquis may, however, screw up the courage to use force against our armed forces. If so, the Cuban people will rally to the flag and we shall heroically defend our national honor. And use the missiles to show them the error of their ways."

"Cubans are patriots," Santana agreed. "After the Bay of Pigs, Castro was president for life."

"A man with the right enemies can do anything," Vargas declared, and smiled.

CHAPTER NINETEEN

While Alejo Vargas and Colonel Santana were conferring in Havana, the Americans opened fire. Three Spruance-class destroyers that had sailed from Mayport soon after sunrise were now fifty miles off the Florida coast headed south, well away from the coastal shipping lanes. They began launching Tomahawk cruise missiles from the vertical launchers buried in the deck in front of their bridges. Although each ship carried forty-eight Tomahawks in their vertical launch tubes, they only launched twenty missiles each.

On the bridge of USS *Comte de Grasse* the captain watched with binoculars as his missiles leveled out from their launch climb and disappeared into the sea haze. One of the missiles dove into the ocean, making a tiny splash.

"There went three million bucks," he muttered.

After the launch was complete, he called down to Combat on the squawk box. "How many successfully launched?"

"Nineteen, sir."

"And the other ships?"

"Twenty and eighteen, Captain."

"What is the time of flight?"

"An hour and twenty minutes, sir."

"Very well. Report the launch."

Not bad, the captain thought, and gave orders to secure from General Quarters.

God help the Cubans, he thought, then turned to the navigator to discuss the voyage to the Florida Straits, where *Comte de Grasse* and her sister ships would join the Aegis cruisers already there.

Aboard USS *United States*, Jake Grafton seated himself in the admiral's raised chair in Combat and surveyed the computer displays. Gil Pascal, the chief of staff, was also there along with the ship's air wing commander, the Combat Control Center officer and the members of his staff.

Jake leaned over and whispered to Pascal. "See if you can find me some aspirin, please."

"Yes, sir."

He was looking over the plan and watching the display of commercial traffic going in and out of José Martí International Airport in Havana when a chief petty officer handed him the encrypted satellite phone.

"Admiral Grafton, sir."

"This is the president, Admiral. How goes the war?"

"We already have Tomahawks in the air, sir, but the Cubans won't know what's coming for an hour or so."

"We're sweating the program here in Washington," the president continued. "Our feet are getting frosty. If we chicken out, could the airborne Tomahawks be intentionally crashed?"

Jake Grafton took a deep breath and exhaled before he answered. "Yes, sir. That is possible."

"Let's hold on to that option. I'm sitting here with General Totten and the senior leadership of the Congress. I want your opinion on this question: Should we postpone this show for a day or two? Or indefinitely? What are your thoughts?"

Jake Grafton licked his lips. In his mind's eye he could see ballistic missiles rising from their silos on pillars of fire, and sailors, just like the ones manning the computers here in Combat aboard *United States,* sitting in front of radar scopes and computer keyboards aboard the Aegis cruisers.

"Mr. President, I have also been thinking about the risks. The only thing I can promise is that we will do our best. No one can guarantee results. Still, in my opinion, considering just the military risks, we should go now, without delay."

"Thank you, Admiral," the president said.

"Jake, this is Tater Totten."

"Good evening, sir."

"Just wanted to say good luck," the general said, then the connection broke.

Jake Grafton handed the handset to the chief.

"Here is your aspirin, Admiral," Gil Pascal said, holding out water and three white pills.

Four EA-6B Prowlers sat on the ramp at NAS Key West. Their crews stood lounging around the aircraft. They had flown in just an hour ago, and now the fuel trucks were pulling away. The crews had huddled with the crew of the two C-130 Hercs parked on the ramp, studying charts and checking frequencies. Now it was time to man up.

As the marines in full combat gear filed aboard the Hercs, the crews of the Prowlers strapped in and started engines. Two of the Prowlers carried three electronic jamming pods on external stations and two HARM missiles. HARM stood for high-speed anti-radiation missile. The other two Prowlers carried four HARMS and one jamming pod on the center-line station.

With the engines running, the pilots closed the Prowlers' canopies and taxied behind the Hercs toward the duty runway. No one said anything on the radio.

The flight deck of USS *United States* came alive. A small army of people in brightly colored shirts swarmed around the airplanes that packed the deck as the flight crews manned up and started engines.

Light from the setting sun came in at a low angle like a bright spotlight, illuminating the towering cumulus which dotted the surface of the sea, and made everyone facing west squint or shade their eyes.

Soon the plane guard rescue helicopter engaged its rotors and lifted off the deck as the first airplanes began taxiing toward the bow and waist catapults.

Aboard USS *Hue City* and USS *Guilford Courthouse*, the two Aegis cruisers on station in the Florida Straits, the afternoon had been a busy one.

Twenty-five miles of ocean separated the two ships, but they were linked together electronically as tightly as if they were wired together at a pier.

As the Hercs and EA-6Bs taxied at Key West, and *United States* prepared to launch her air wing, the weapons officers aboard the cruisers checked the ships' inertial systems one more time, compared the GPS locations yet again, then gave the fire order.

The first of the Tomahawk missiles rose vertically from their launchers on fountains of fire. The wings of the missiles popped out, then the missiles began tilting to the south as they accelerated away into the evening sky.

The first missiles from each ship were still in sight when the second ones came roaring from the launchers. Each ship launched sixteen missiles, then turned to stay in the race-track pattern they had been using to hold station.

Sitting in the Combat Control Center aboard *United States,* Jake Grafton felt the thump as the first bow catapult fired. A second later he felt the number-three cat on the waist slam a plane into the air. His eyes went to the monitor, which was showing a video feed from a camera mounted high in the ship's island superstructure. Each catapult stroke was felt throughout the ship as the planes were thrown into the sky, one by one.

A half dozen planes were still on deck awaiting their turn on the catapults when the destroyers in the carrier's screen began launching Tomahawk cruise missiles.

The television cameraman in the ship's island swung his camera to catch the fireworks. The picture captured the attention of the people in Combat, who paused to watch the missiles roar from their launchers on fountains of reddish yellow fire, almost too brilliant to look at.

When the last of the missiles was gone, the camera returned to the launching planes.

Gil Pascal said to Jake, "It'll go well, Admiral."

Jake nodded and took another sip of water.

The sun seemed to be taking its good ol' time going down, Lieutenant Commander Marcus Gillispie thought.

He was at the controls of an EA-6B Prowler that had just launched from *United States*. He had worked his way around towering buildups reaching up to 10,000 feet and was now above them, looking at the evening sky. The last of the red sunlight played on the tops of the clouds, but the canyons between them were purple and gray shading to black. As Gillispie climbed he delayed the sun's apparent setting for a few more minutes. Soon the last of the red and gold faded from the cloud tops below.

A very high cirrus layer stayed yellow and red for the longest time as Marcus circled the carrier at 30,000 feet. Two F/A-18 Hornets came swimming up from the deepening gloom to join on him.

"You guys all set?" Marcus asked his three crewmen.

His crewmen counted off in order.

The Prowler was the electronic-warfare version of the old A-6 Intruder airframe. While the Prowler bore a superficial resemblance to its older brother, the electronic suite in the aircraft could not have been more different: the Prowler was designed to fight the electronic battle in today's skies, not drop bombs.

The airframe was also longer than the old A-6, lengthened to accommodate four people and a massive array of computerized cockpit displays. The people sat in ejection seats, two in the front, two in the back. Only one of the crewmen was a pilot, who sat in the left front seat: the other three were electronic-warfare specialists. And they were not all men. One of the guys in back tonight was a woman, a lieutenant (junior grade) on her first cruise.

Marcus looked at his watch, then keyed his mike. He waited while his encryption gear timed in with the ship's gear, then said, "Strike, this is Nighthawk One. I have my chicks and am ready to leave orbit. Request permission to strangle the parrot."

"Roger, Nighthawk One. Call feet dry."

"Wilco."

Marcus Gillispie rolled the Prowler wings level heading northwest for the city of Havana. Then he engaged the autopilot. When he was satisfied that the autopilot was going to keep the plane straight and level, he flashed his exterior lights, then turned them off, leaving only a set of tiny formation lights illuminated on the sides of the aircraft above the wing root. Finally he reached down and turned his radar transponder, his parrot, off. The Prowler and the two Hornets on her wing were no longer radiating on any electromagnetic frequency.

The pilot looked back past his wingtips at the Hornets. One was on each wing now. Like the Prowler, their missile racks were loaded with HARMs. The Hornets also carried two Sidewinders, heat-seeking air-to-air missiles, one on each wingtip, just in case.

Already the displays in the Prowler were alive with information. The electronic countermeasures officer, ECMO, in the seat beside the pilot, was really the tactical commander of the plane. His gear, and that of the two electronic-warfare officers in the back cockpit, provided a complete display of the tactical electronic picture. The information the computers used was derived from sensors embedded all over the aircraft in its skin, and from the sensors of one of the HARM missiles, which was already on line.

The ECMO with Marcus Gillispie was Commander Schuyler Cole-ridge, the squadron commanding officer, who wound up in the right seat of Prowlers because his eyes were not quite 20/20 uncorrected when he graduated from the Naval Academy. The truth of it was, he thought he had the better job. Pilots, he liked to say, just drove the bus—ECMOs fought the war.

He had one to fight tonight. The Cubans were going to get really riled when those Tomahawks started popping, he thought, and then the fireworks would start.

Just now Coleridge was busy running his equipment through its built-in tests. Everything was working, as usual. That routine fact was the greatest advance of the technological age, in Coleridge's opinion. In his younger days he had had a bellyful of fancy equipment that couldn't be maintained.

He was sweating just now, even though the cockpit temperature was positively balmy. And he knew his fellow crewmen were sweating—this was the first time in combat for all of them.

It will go all right, he thought. After the tension he had suffered through this afternoon and evening, Schuyler Coleridge actually wel-comed the catapult shot. *Let's do it and get it over with.*

All four of the squadron's EA-6Bs were aloft just now, and the other three also had pairs of Hornets attached.

As Coleridge looked at the search radars sweeping the Cuban skies, he wondered if there were going to be MiGs.

"Okay, people," Coleridge told his crew, "let's go to work."

A search radar on the southern coast of Cuba drew his attention. The signal was being received by the HARM sensors, which routed the electronic signal through the plane's computer and displayed it on the tactical screen.

Coleridge checked his watch. "Any second now," he muttered to his crewmen.

The Cubans had their search radars wired into sector facilities, which performed the functions of air traffic control (ATC) for civilian aircraft and early warning and ground control interception (GCI) for military aircraft. ATC radars in developed countries rarely searched for non-transponder–equipped targets, but due to the dual usage of these radars, such sweeps were routine. Consequently one of the controllers in the Havana sector was the first to notice a cloud of skin-paint targets closing on the Cuban coast from the south.

His call to the supervisor was echoed by a call from a controller looking at targets headed south toward the north coast of the island.

The shift supervisor stood frozen, staring over the operator's shoulder at the radar screen. He had wondered if something like this might not happen after Alejo Vargas's television speech, but when he asked the site manager about the possibility of Cuba being attacked by the United States, the man had laughed. "The world has changed since the Bay of Pigs, Pedro. You are safe—have courage." The response humiliated the shift supervisor.

Now the supervisor picked up his telephone, called the manager in his office. "You'd better come see this," he said with an edge on his voice. "Come quickly."

The manager was looking over the supervisor's shoulder when the first Tomahawk crashed into the antenna of the main search radar on the southern coast. In seconds three more radars went off the air.

The stunned men turned their attention to the radars on the north coast, and were just in time to watch the blip of a Tomahawk from *Hue City* fly right down the throat of the radar and knock it out.

The supervisor turned to the manager and calmly said, "Apparently the war you didn't believe would happen is happening now."

The stunned manager watched in horror as screen after screen went blank.

"The Americans rarely leave things half-done, or so I've heard," the supervisor continued. "I would bet fifty pesos that this building is also a target of a cruise missile. If you gentlemen will excuse me, I think I will go home for the evening."

With that, he turned and walked briskly from the room.

"Everyone out," the facilities manager shouted. "Outside, everyone outside."

The men at the consoles needed no urging. They bolted for the doors.

The shift supervisor was outside, walking quickly for the bus stop, when he heard a Tomahawk. He fell to the ground and covered his head with his hands as the missile dove into the roof of the sector control building and its 750-pound warhead exploded with a thundering boom. Within the next fifteen seconds, two more missiles crashed into the building.

After waiting another minute just to be sure, the supervisor stood and surveyed the damage. Clouds of tiny dust particles formed an artificial fog, one illuminated by flame licking at the gutted building. The stench of explosives residue and smoke lay heavy in the night air.

One hundred fifty missiles swept across central Cuba, some coming from the north, some from the south. The targeting had been done quickly, but the information that made it possible had been mined from databases painstakingly constructed from satellite and aircraft photo and electronic reconnaissance over a period of years.

Four dozen Tomahawks were targeted against every known radar dish within a hundred miles of the missile silos—search, air traffic, anti-aircraft missile, and artillery radars—all of them, two missiles for each antenna.

Another fifty Tomahawks attacked every Cuban Air Force base along the five-hundred-mile length of the island. Some of the Tomahawks carried bomblets instead of high-explosive warheads: these swept across aircraft ramps, scattering bomblets over the parked MiGs, damaging them and setting some on fire. Other cruise missiles dove headfirst into the Cuban Air Force's hangars, weapons storage facilities, and fuel farms. Fixed antiaircraft surface-to-air missile (SAM) sites received two or three missiles each.

Alejo Vargas learned of the American attack when the telephone he was using went dead in his hand. He frowned, jiggled the hook, then replaced the handset on its base. Only then did the dull boom of the explosion in the central Havana telephone exchange reach him. A Tomahawk had dived through the roof.

More explosions followed in quick succession as two more cruise missiles hurled themselves into the telephone exchange. One of the problems the Americans faced with the employment of cruise missiles was assessing damage after the attack. The solution was to fire multiple missiles at the same target to ensure an acceptable level of damage.

The thought that the presidential palace might be a target never occurred to Alejo Vargas. He went to the nearest window and stood listening to the roar of Tomahawks overflying the city on their way to radar and antiaircraft gun and missile installations sited around José Martí International Airport. The five-hundred-knot missiles were invisible in the darkness, but they weren't quiet.

The missiles had passed when someone near the harbor opened up with an antiaircraft gun firing tracers. The bursts of tracers went up like fireworks and randomly probed the darkness as the hammering reports echoed over the city.

Colonel Santana came into the room and joined Vargas at the window. "The telephone system in the city is out."

"It's probably out all over Cuba," Vargas replied.

"They are attacking much sooner than you thought they would."

"No matter. The results will be the same. Get a car to take us to Radio Havana. I will make an address to the nation."

"The Americans may use missiles on the radio stations or power plants."

"It is possible, but I doubt it. Get the car."

Santana went after a car as Vargas thought about what he would say to fan the fires of patriotism in every Cuban heart.

The two C-130s Hercs and four EA-6B Prowlers that had left Key West were level at ten thousand feet when they crossed the northern shoreline of Cuba. The C-130s actually were flying with their wingtip lights on so that the Prowlers could easily stay in formation with them. Inside the Hercs the pilots were using global positioning system (GPS) units to navigate to the missile silo sites.

The Prowler crews watched their computer displays and listened to their emission-detection gear, waiting for the Cubans to turn on a radar, any radar. The night was deathly quiet. The Tomahawks had done their work well.

As the Hercs crossed over the first of the dairy farms, two men leaped from each plane. Forty seconds later two more went as they crossed over the second possible lab site. Then the Hercs made a gentle, lazy 270-degree turn to get lined up for the run-in to the missile silos.

José Martí Airport and the surface-to-air missile sites that surrounded it were only thirty miles west. Not a peep from them. If the Tomahawks missed any of the mobile radars, the operators had not yet screwed up the courage to turn them on, for which the Hercules crews were thankful. The Prowler crews, however, with HARM missiles ready on the rails, were feeling a bit disappointed. After all the sweating, there should be more *action.*

Aboard USS *United States,* the datalink from the E-3 Sentry AWACS over Key West revealed the aerial fire drill going on over Havana as commercial flights tried to find their way into José Martí Airport without the aid of air traffic controllers with radar. Some of the flights announced they were diverting, and headed for the United States or Jamaica or the Cayman Islands. The others queued up and landed VFR as Jake Grafton watched the computer displays with his fingers crossed. While he didn't want to be responsible for the crash of a civilian airliner, he couldn't delay this operation until there was a temporary lull in civilian air activity.

As the first Herc approached silo one, two men leaped from the open rear door. Seconds later, two more leaped from the second transport.

The jumpers fell away from the airplanes like stones.

Over silo two, marines leaped in pairs from each of the Hercs, and so on, until the transports had overflown and dropped recon teams at all six silo sites. Then they turned northward, toward the sea.

The Prowlers followed faithfully.

At that moment a SAM control radar near silo two came on the air, probing for a target.

The Prowlers with the Hercs picked up the signal, of course, and two of them dropped their wings to turn back toward the threat.

Forty miles south of silo two, Schuyler Coleridge also picked up the SAM radar, an old Soviet Fansong. As he slaved the HARM to the signal, his pilot, Marcus Gillispie, turned the plane ten degrees to point at the offending radar. Although the new missiles could be fired at very large angles, a quick turn by the launching aircraft shortened the missile's flight time by a few seconds.

"Fire," Coleridge ordered, and Gillispie punched off the HARM, which shot forward off the rail in a blaze of fire.

Coleridge keyed the radio. "Fox Three," he said, letting everyone on the freq know that a beam rider was in the air.

The HARM zeroed in on the side lobes of the radiating Fansong, whose operator was trying to lock up a Herc for an SA-2 launch. The operator never realized the beam rider was in the air.

The missile actually flew into the back of the antenna dish at almost Mach 3 and went several feet through it before the warhead exploded.

The warhead contained thousands of 3/16th-inch tungsten-alloy cubes, which were three times denser than steel. The warhead blasted these cubes in all directions, obliterating the radar antenna and wave guides, shredding the trailer on which the antenna was mounted, and knocking out the equipment in the trailer. The flying cubes also killed the radar operator and severely wounded the three other occupants of the trailer.

Another HARM launched by one of the F/A-18 Hornets on the Prowler's wing arrived six seconds later and impacted a tree just a few feet from the smoking, gutted trailer. Although the target radar had been off the air for six seconds, the missile's strap-down inertial allowed it to fly to the place where the computer memory believed the radar to be. The shrapnel from the warhead severed the tree and sprayed the shell of the trailer yet again, killing one of the already-wounded men.

Major Carlos Corrado was sleeping off a hangover when the roar of a Tomahawk going over woke him. His eyes came open. He heard the staccato popping of bomblets from the Tomahawk, but had no idea what caused the sound. He thought the Tomahawk was a low-flying airplane.

Groggy, aching, sick to his stomach, he was hugging a commode when another Tomahawk went over. In ten seconds the sound of the bomblets detonating on the planes parked on the flight line reached him though his alcoholic haze. Then one of the planes exploded with a rolling crash that shook the barracks.

Corrado staggered outside and looked toward the flight line, where at least three planes were burning brightly.

"Holy Mother!"

Suddenly sober, Corrado went back inside and hastily donned his flight suit and boots.

He was jogging toward the flight line when another Tomahawk went over scattering bomblets. The missile flew on, out of sight.

As Corrado rounded the corner and the flight line came into view, the first cruise missile that had scattered bomblets dove into one of the hangers. There wasn't much of an explosion, but in seconds a hot fire was burning in the wooden structure.

Corrado's personal fighter was parked between the burning hangar and another, which would probably be struck within seconds. The maintenance men had been working on the plane today, which was why it was not on its usual parking place at the head of the flight line.

Running men helped Corrado push the plane away from the burning hangar, the wall of which was perilously close to collapse.

"There is no fuel in the plane," someone shouted.

"Get a truck," Corrado roared in reply. "And ammunition for the guns."

The words were no more out of his mouth when the second missile crashed into the untouched hangar.

Corrado seethed as linemen fueled his plane and serviced the guns. He was still on the phone in the dispersal shack talking to someone at the base armory when the truck carrying missiles braked to a squealing halt near the fighter, a silver MiG-29 Fulcrum. Now he called the sector GCI site. The telephone rang and rang, but no one answered.

Corrado stuck an unlit cigar in his mouth and stomped out to the plane. "Careful there, fools. Do it right. Do not embarrass me."

He was watching the last of the 30-mm cannon shells going into the feed trays when one of the Havana colonels showed up.

"You aren't going up in this thing, are you, Corrado?"

"We are servicing it as a joke, dear Colonel. Every Saturday night when the Americans attack we put the cannon shells in, then take them out on Sunday morning."

"Don't trifle with me, Major. I won't stand for it."

"You pompous limp-dick! Go find a whore and let the real men fight."

"Do not insult me, you sot. You stink of rum and vomit! Show some respect!"

"Why should I? Your putrid face insults you every day."

The colonel was so angry he spluttered. "I absolutely forbid you to fly this airplane without written orders from Havana."

"Court-martial me tomorrow."

"The Americans will destroy this airplane if you take it off the ground. To fly it is sabotage, a crime against the state. If you attempt to fly it, I will shoot you." The colonel pulled out his pistol and showed Corrado the business end.

Corrado ignored the gun. "You are a traitor," he roared, "who wants the Americans to win. Defeatist! Coward!"

"I will shoot anyone who helps you defect in this airplane," the colonel screamed. He pointed the pistol at the troops closing the servicing doors on the MiG-29. "Counterrevolutionaries! Saboteurs!"

Corrado used his fist on the colonel. The second punch, in the ear, did the trick. The man went to his knees, then onto his face. He didn't get up. One of the linemen picked up the pistol while the major massaged his knuckles. His hand hurt like hell but didn't seem to be broken.

In truth Corrado wasn't much of a man. He abandoned a wife and child years ago and hadn't heard from them since—didn't want to hear from them, because they would probably want money. What money he got his hands on he drank up; he even sold military equipment on the black market to pay for alcohol. His ability to fly a fighter plane was his sole skill, his only worthwhile accomplishment in thirty-six years of life. Now, unexpectedly, miraculously, he had a chance to use that skill to defend something larger than himself, to make his miserable life mean something—and no strutting Havana rooster was going to cheat him out of it.

Carlos Corrado gestured at the men. "Get the missiles loaded, you lazy bastards," he shouted. "There's a war on."

Richard Merriweather rode his parachute into a cornfield. At least, he thought it was corn—long, stiff stalks, head-high. He checked himself over; he was sore, but nothing broken. He stood and wrestled the chute toward him, then began scooping out a hole to bury it. He was finishing the job when he heard someone coming toward him.

"Sergeant?"

"Yo. You okay?"

"Yeah," said Kirb Handy.

"Set up the GPS. Figure out where we are."

With the parachute disposed of, Merriweather put on his night-vision goggles and took a careful look around. He was well out in the center of this field, near as he could tell.

Merriweather sat down in the dirt beside Handy, who was also wearing night-vision goggles. Handy punched buttons on the GPS.

"This thing says we are a mile and a half southwest."

"I'll buy that."

"Missed the landing zone by a half mile."

"Not bad at all." Merriweather unslung his weapon and checked it over. Then he got to his feet.

"The other two guys should be around," Handy muttered.

"They'd better be. We don't have much time."

After a careful check of the GPS unit, the two men started walking northeast toward missile silo number six. They had gone only about a hundred meters when they came to the bank of a stream, a fairly wide stream.

"What the hell is this?" Merriweather demanded, and got out his map. He and Handy huddled behind a tree studying the thing.

"Holy shit," Handy said. "We're in the wrong place. We're at least four miles from the damned silo. Look here." He pointed to the stream. "That has gotta be this thing in front of us."

"So where's the other half of our team?"

"Gotta be over there, near the silo."

"Let's get on the phone, give 'em the bad news."

"Oh, man," Handy moaned softly. "This ain't good."

The four-man recon team for silo number two approached the barn via a large seasonal drainage ditch that ran more or less in the right direction. Fortunately the sides were relatively dry, though the ditch contained a few inches of water and the bottom felt soft.

They stopped moving when they were about fifty meters from the barn where they believed the silo to be. They were completely surrounded by Cuban Army troops. Two tanks stood outside the barn, trucks were parked in a nearby grove of trees, and troops were setting up a cooking tent near the farmhouse's well. Other soldiers were down in the woods to the left, presumably digging latrines.

"Must be a couple hundred of 'em," Asel Tyvek whispered to Jamail Ali, who was lying in the ditch beside him.

"Sure as hell we can't stay here," Ali whispered. "It's just a matter of time before somebody inspects this damn ditch with a flashlight."

"The silo must be in that barn. Gotta be. If we crawl down this ditch, we should get within thirty yards of the thing. When the shit hits the fan, maybe we can get in there."

"Let's spread out, man, fifty yards apart," Jamail Ali suggested. "If they find one of us, the others will have a chance." Tyvek nodded and Ali whispered to the other two men, and pointed. They disappeared into the darkness.

Tyvek keyed the mike on his helmet-mounted radio. In seconds he was talking to a controller aboard USS *United States*, telling her what he saw around the missile silo.

"Twelve minutes," the female voice from *United States* said in his ear. "Twelve minutes."

"Roger that, Battlestar. Twelve minutes."

Norman Tillman and the three men of his recon team were up to their knees in cow shit. They waded through the barnyard and shoved the mooing dairy cattle out of the way so that they could get to the door of the barn, a possible biological weapons manufacturing site.

"I thought there weren't any damn cows around here," Tillman's number two muttered unpleasantly.

Tillman took off his night-vision goggles, got his flashlight in hand, and took a firm grip on his rifle. He nodded at his number two, who carefully opened the barn door, which creaked on its rusty hinges anyway. Tillman launched himself through the door opening. He slipped on something, fell, and slid for several feet on his chest. Much to his disgust, he could identify the substance he was lying in by its smell.

Tillman stood, used the flashlight. He was standing in a conventional wooden barn that had not been mucked out in several weeks. Two cows turned and stared at the light. They looked nervous, as if they wanted to run, then began bawling. Cursing under his breath, Norman Tillman went on through the building, checking it out.

Five minutes later he stepped outside and keyed his helmet radio. "Battlestar, this is Team One. Negative results. Nothing here but cows."

"Roger, Team One. Stand by for a pickup."

"Team One standing by. Out."

"I thought there weren't any cows at these sites," one of the men said.

"Yeah, but the cows didn't know they were supposed to be on vacation."

"Maybe we landed at the wrong dairy farm."

Tillman thought that over. Naw. That would be quite a screwup. More likely, the cows were being held in a nearby field when the recon photos were taken.

"Sarge, somebody coming."

The men dove facedown into the dirt-and-manure mix at their feet. The person coming turned out to be a farmhand in civilian clothes. The marines made him sit with his back against the barn wall where they could watch him, but they didn't tie his hands.

At first the man was frightened. He got over it when one of the troops offered him a cigarette and lit it for him.

Tillman crawled over a fence out of the muck and sat down under a tree to wait for the helicopter. One man watched the farmer while the other two posted themselves as sentinels.

CHAPTER TWENTY

"There are several hundred troops and three or four tanks around silos one and two, Admiral, and at least two tanks and a squad of soldiers around three. Four and five appear to be unguarded. The recon team checking out silo six seems to have been dropped in the wrong place—only two of the four have reported in; they estimate they are three miles from the silo. We haven't been able to contact the other two men."

The briefer was an Air Intelligence officer who zapped the map with a laser flashlight pointer whenever he mentioned a silo.

Jake Grafton wasn't paying much attention to the map, which he had memorized. He glanced at his watch, compared it with a clock on the bulkhead.

"Lab site Alpha is a dairy farm. The recon team checking out Bravo reports jackpot, but not many troops—no more than a dozen. The Osprey will be there in less than ten minutes."

The admiral got up from his chair, stretched, rubbed the back of his neck. So far it was going better than he expected it would. So far. Nobody shot down yet, only one recon team lost . . .

"Is someone monitoring Cuban radio and television?"

"Yes, sir. The National Security Agency. They will keep us advised."

"Ummm."

"What are we going to do about silo six, Admiral?" Gil Pascal asked.

"Nothing we can do. The assault team will have to go into the landing zone blind."

"The Cuban Army may be waiting."

"They might," Jake Grafton agreed.

He put on his headset and switched between radio channels. By simply flipping switches he could monitor the aircraft tactical channels. In addition, with the new tactical com units, he and his staff could hear everything that was said on the helmet radios worn by marine officers and NCOs.

Since the signals were rebroadcast and ultimately picked up by the satellite, they were also being monitored in the war room of the White House. One of Jake's concerns was that the politicians or senior officers would be tempted to step into the middle of the operation. Although the Washington kibitzers could not communicate on the nets, they could quickly get in touch with someone who could, and an order was an order, even if ill-considered.

He would worry about the politicians when the meddling started, he decided, not before.

Doll Hanna was the recon team leader at dairy Bravo. He was sitting on a biological warhead assembly plant and he knew it. There wasn't a cow in sight, two clean, modern dairy trucks sat near the entrance to the barn, and Hanna could hear air conditioners running. And the Cuban Army was guarding the place.

From where he lay he could see two soldiers in cloth hats with rifles in their arms standing in front of the main entrance. He knew that there were men on the door in the rear of the building and in the old thatch-roofed farmhouse nearby.

Doll Hanna touched the transmit button on his radio. "Willie, you take the two guys on the north side. Fred, you got the farmhouse. Goose, these two on the main entrance."

All three men acknowledged.

Doll was wearing his night-vision goggles so he could see Goose crawling behind the milk trucks, then under them, working his way toward the entrance. It was eerie watching Goose sneak along, knowing the guards couldn't see him.

Taking out two men was a challenge. Either one could raise the alarm.

Goose moved like he had all night.

He didn't, Doll Hanna well knew. The Osprey was out there now circling, but it wouldn't come in until he called the area clear. Still, the plane only had so much fuel and the Cubans wouldn't stay quiet forever.

In fact, a truckload of soldiers could come rolling in here any minute. The troops in the Osprey, when they arrived, would set up a perimeter to keep the Cuban military away.

"Doll, this is Fred. I'm going to make some noise over here."

"Okay."

No doubt Goose and Willie heard that transmission. Noise would cause the guards to do something. If necessary, Goose and Willie could just shoot them down.

Hanna heard the faint sound of a slamming door come from the direction of the farmhouse.

The guards near the main door to the dairy got to their feet, looked at each other, then started toward the house. One stopped, told the other to stay, then went on with his weapon at the ready. As he went around the truck out of sight of the guard at the door, Goose got him with a knife.

Then Goose waited.

The man at the door called out to his friend.

Nothing.

The guard looked worried. He called again, got no answer, then walked forward twenty feet or so. He stopped, cocked his head, stood looking into the darkness and trying to hear over the hum of the big air conditioners.

He was standing like that when Goose stepped out from behind the truck and threw a knife. The guard dropped his rifle and pitched forward on his face.

Hanna got up, trotted for the door of the barn. He passed Goose, who was bending over the second guard checking to make sure he was dead. Carefully Doll eased the door open and looked inside.

There were people inside, all right, behind transparent plastic curtains that formed biological seals. They were wearing full body-and-head CBW suits, so they looked like spacemen walking around in there between trays of cultures and rows of worktables.

They had apparently heard nothing above the noise of the air-ventilation system, which was a loud, steady hum.

Doll eased his head back. The people in there would have to wait until the experts arrived.

Major Carlos Corrado walked onto the runway of the Cienfuegos Air Base. The runway lights were off and the night was fairly dark considering that two hangars and at least five aircraft were ablaze. He could hear people shouting, about fire, about water, about missiles, about staying under cover. Straining hard he could hear several cruise missiles—and airplanes—up there in the darkness—American airplanes, because in order to save money, the Cuban Air Force, the *Fuerza Aerea Revolucionaria*, did not fly at night.

What was happening? Where was the war?

Carlos Corrado had no illusions about the difficulties involved in engaging the American military. His MiG-29, a stripped Soviet export version, had only the most rudimentary of electronic detection equipment and lacked any active countermeasures. And his GCI site was probably in the same condition as the burning hangars behind him.

If he left his radar off he would not beacon on the Americans' detection equipment. And he would be electronically blind.

Perhaps if he stayed low...

Another cruise missile roared overhead and dove into the last undamaged hangar. The 750-pound warhead rocked the base, then the hangar collapsed outward, its walls silhouetted black against the yellowish white fireball caused by the warhead.

Well, if the Americans were pounding Cienfuegos, they must be pulverizing José Martí International in Havana.

Havana. The war would be in Havana, so that was where he would go.

The V-22 Osprey twin-engine tiltrotor assault transport was the ultimate flying machine, or so Rita Moravia liked to tell her husband, Toad Tarkington. It hovered like a helicopter and flew like an airplane, operated from the deck of an airborne assault ship, and was at its best after the sun went down.

So here she was, in the pilot's seat of a V-22 on her way to a ballistic-missile silo in the Matanzas Province of central Cuba with 24 combat-ready marines, loaded for bear. She had made a vertical takeoff from *Kearsarge* and was now thundering along at two thousand feet over the Cuban countryside at 250 knots, navigating by GPS and monitoring the forward-looking infrared display (FLIR), which revealed the countryside ahead as if the sun were shining down from a cloudless sky.

Rita's copilot was Captain Crash Wade, USMC, who earned his nickname in an unfortunate series of ski adventures, not flying accidents. Wade paid careful attention to the multi-function displays (MFDs), computer presentations of everything the pilots needed to know, on the instrument panel in front of him.

Rita was paying careful attention to the voice on the radio, which was that of Asel Tyvek, NCO in charge of the marine recon team at silo number two. Rita didn't know his real name, just his call sign, Blue One.

"Old Rover, this is Blue One. I want you to hold four minutes out while we get some ordnance on this LZ. It's sizzling hot."

"Old Rover, Roger." Rita keyed the intercom. "Okay, Crash, do a holding pattern."

"How come we got the hot LZ?" Crash wanted to know.

"Just lucky, I guess," Rita replied, and selected an intercom button that would allow her to talk to the lieutenant in the cargo bay with his troops.

Asel Tyvek and Jamail Ali were side by side in the ditch, just thirty yards or so from the barn. The other two members of the team were also in the ditch, but well left and right.

"We ought to get in the barn," Ali whispered, "in case the Cubans want to get in there too."

"Man, those little boards ain't gonna protect anybody from anything. You just be ready in case the Cubans start diving into this damned ditch with us."

"Listen, I can hear our guys coming."

Tyvek strained his ears. Yep, he could just detect the distinctive beat of chopper rotors. "Snake One, Blue One," he whispered into his radio. "Cuban troops all around the barn. At least two tanks, eight or nine trucks, a couple hundred men. We're in a ditch near the barn."

"Got your head down?"

"Yeah."

Tyvek could hear the choppers distinctly now. He eased his weapon up, put his finger on the safety. The Cubans were going to be looking for cover very shortly, and he didn't want to share the ditch.

The SuperCobras eased up over the tree line, barely moving. Tyvek knew what was going to happen next, and it did. He heard the roar as Hellfire antiarmor missiles screamed toward the tanks, and he heard the explosions as they hit.

He lifted his head above the ditch line for a quick peek. The tanks were smoking hulks. Even as he watched, more missiles tore into the trucks.

Not a standing figure could be seen. Everyone was on the ground, crawling or lying still.

The two SuperCobras came closer. The noise of their engines was quite plain now. The flex three-barreled 20-mm cannons opened up and rockets shot forward from the pylons under the stubby wings.

The men in the yard realized they couldn't stay where they were—the area was a killing zone. Some jumped up and ran for the ditch. Fortunately few of them seemed to have weapons in their hands—the attack had caught them by surprise.

"Here they come," Tyvek shouted, and opened up on the men closest to the ditch. He couldn't shoot them fast enough. Men dashed for the cover of the ditch as he and Ali and the other two poured fire into them and the SuperCobras lashed the area with ordnance.

Tyvek spoke into the voice-activated mike on his helmet-mounted radio. "We're gonna need some help, Old Rover. Whenever you can get here."

Something heavy fell across Tyvek's legs. He spun and fired at the same time, but the man was already dead: Ali had shot him.

"They're going into the barn!" Ali shouted. He fired a whole magazine at three men trying to get through the front door. One of the men disappeared inside.

Jamail Ali scrambled over the edge of the ditch and ran for the barn while Tyvek screamed at the SuperCobra gunners not to shoot him.

"Snake One Four, this is Orange One." Richard Merriweather let go of the mike and waited for an answer from the SuperCobra inbound to silo six.

"Orange One, Snake One Four."

"Man, we're on the wrong side of this river or creek five or six clicks south of the LZ. How about seeing if you can find us."

"Are you standing up?"

"In plain sight."

Merriweather and his partner, Kirb Handy, stepped away from the trees. With their night-vision goggles, the SuperCobra crewmen should have no trouble seeing two men standing in an open field, and they didn't.

Both the helicopters settled to earth and the marines on the ground ran to them.

The pilot of the lead chopper opened his canopy as Merriweather ran over. "Where are the other guys?"

"Haven't seen them or talked to them. Don't know."

"Seen any bad guys?"

"Nope. How about a ride over toward the barn?"

"Sit on the wheel and grab hold. We run into trouble, you gotta get off if we drop down low."

Merriweather gave the pilot a thumbs-up and arranged himself on the wheel. Handy was clinging to the wheel on the other side.

The chopper came slowly into a hover, then dipped its nose and began moving forward. Merriweather held on for dear life as the rotor downwash and slipstream tore at his clothing, helmet, and gear, and threatened to rip the night vision goggles from his head.

What a stupid idea this was! How in hell had they ended up four miles south of the goddamned landing zone? If he ever again laid eyes on that son of a bitch who flew the Herc, he was going to stomp his ass.

Bryne and McCormick—those two were missing. If they were okay surely they would have checked in on the radio. Maybe their parachutes didn't open. Maybe they fell into that river. Maybe the Cubans captured them as soon as they hit the ground. Maybe, maybe, maybe . . .

He could see the barn now. The chopper was just a few feet above the trees, making an approach to the area right in front of the damn thing. The other chopper was flying over the trees, three or four hundred yards away—close, but not too close.

Nobody in sight around the barn. Not a soul.

Merriweather jumped when the chopper was three feet off the ground, and fell on his face. He got up, staggered out from under the rotor blast.

Handy appeared at his elbow.

The glow of a cigarette tip showed in the door. Someone sitting there! Merriweather froze, his M-16 at the ready.

A marine sat in the open door smoking a cigarette. His face and neck were coated with green and brown camo grease. His helmet and night-vision goggles lay in the dirt beside him.

Merriweather walked over to the man, who said, "No one around."

"Where's Bryne?"

McCormick nodded toward the east. "Over there about a hundred yards. Parachute streamed, backup didn't open."

"Your radio?"

"Broke. Bryne's got smashed." McCormick stood, took a last drag on the cigarette, and tossed it away. "Been sitting here waiting for you. The place is deserted, quiet as a graveyard."

"Too bad about Bryne."

"Left two little kids. Too fucking bad."

The interior of the barn was large, empty, and dark. Merriweather used a flashlight, looked in every corner, inspected the ceiling, the floor, the nooks and crannys.

Then he spoke into his boom microphone. "Let's get the Osprey into the LZ, set up a perimeter."

Through her night-vision goggles, Rita Moravia could see the silo two landing zone and the hovering SuperCobras plain as day as she made her approach in the Osprey. She saw bodies lying everywhere, still-warm bodies radiating heat, and she saw living men. She transitioned to hovering flight and lowered the Osprey toward the ground between the choppers. A cloud of dirt and dust rose up, obscuring everything. She went on instruments.

On the intercom she told the lieutenant to get ready.

As soon as the wheels hit, the marines in back charged out the door of the Osprey and kept right on going for fifty yards, when they went down on their stomachs with their rifles at the ready.

Rita didn't wait to see what was going to happen next. As soon as her crew chief said the last marine was out, she lifted the Osprey into the air, climbed straight up out of the dust cloud and only then began the transition to winged flight.

The lieutenant was named Charlie Herron, and he had his orders.

His primary responsibility was to ensure that the missile in that silo never left the ground. As his feet hit the ground, he flopped on his belly and waited while the roaring Osprey climbed away. When the dust began to clear, he spotted the barn and went for it on a run.

Bodies and body parts lay scattered everywhere. The living men he passed sat in the dirt with empty hands reaching for the sky. Herron shouted over the radio, "Cease-fire, cease-fire. They are surrendering."

Inside the barn he found Asel Tyvek standing over a dead Cuban.

"Over here, Lieutenant. I think this wooden thing is a door."

Tyvek and Herron opened the wooden door, which revealed a steel door with built-in combination lock. "Think there's anybody in there?" Herron asked. After all, Tyvek had been here longer than he had.

"I don't know, sir."

"Well, we gotta get in there. Let's blow the door."

A charge of C-4 took less than a minute to rig. The two men took cover behind a wooden stall.

The explosion was sharp, a metallic wham that rang their ears.

The demolition charge cut the lock clean out of the door and warped it. The two men pried the door open. A stairway lit by naked light bulbs led away downward. Herron and Tyvek took off their night-vision goggles and let them dangle around their necks. With Herron in the lead with his pistol in his hand, the two of them descended the stairway.

Aboard *United States* Jake Grafton was getting the blow-by-blow update. Air Intelligence officers annotated the maps and briefers told him of every report from the silos.

"Heavy firefight around silos one and two."

"No opposition at sites four, five and six."

"Ospreys on the ground at sites two, three, and four."

"SeaCobra hit and in trouble at site one."

"Team leader into silo two."

"Recon leader into silo six."

Each report was entered on a checklist: there were eight of them, one for each silo and dairy site.

First Lieutenant Charlie Herron and Asel Tyvek found the control room of silo two empty. A series of stairs and more steel doors led downward to the bottom of the concrete structure. The doors weren't locked. When he opened the last door, there was the missile towering upward. The shiny, painted fuselage reflected pinpoints of light from the naked bulbs arranged around the top and sides of the concrete silo.

Under the missile was a steel grate over a black hole. That was the flame pit, to exhaust the flame and gases when the missile was launched.

A circular steel stairway led up to a catwalk. From the catwalk it appeared a person could reach over and gain access to the missile's warhead and control panel.

Herron holstered his pistol and turned to Sergeant Tyvek. "See if you can figure out a way to safety this bottle rocket so they can't fire it from Havana while I'm working on it."

"Lieutenant, I've got bad news for you. I don't know shit about guided missiles."

"Well, you sure as hell don't want to be standing here with your thumb up your butt if they light this thing off. Now go look for a switch or something."

"Yes, *sir*," Tyvek said, and disappeared back up the stairway.

Herron took the steps two at a time. He hoped he would find what he expected when he got to the catwalk, although he thought a lot of the old Russian engineer's explanation had been pure bullshit. Somebody had found an engineer in Russia who said he helped design these missiles—the guy was in his eighties. They had him on television for an hour explaining how the business end of the missile was put together. The engineer spoke not a word of English so a translator did the talking. The man had a hell of a memory or was lying through his teeth. Herron was about to find out which was the case.

"If it's typical Russian stuff," the American briefer said, "you'll be able to work on it with pliers and screwdrivers. American designers could learn a lot from Russian engineers, who design for ease of maintenance." They gave each officer and NCO who might get near a missile a small tool pouch.

Herron examined the access panel, which was only about six inches long by six inches high, and curved, a part of the missile's skin. The screws holding it in place looked like Dzus fasteners. They weren't, though: they were plain old screws. Careful not to drop them, he unscrewed them one by one and put the screws in a shirt pocket. There were a dozen screws, just like the Russian engineer said. Okay! So far so good.

Sweat dripped down his nose, ran into his eyes. He wiped the palms of his hands on his camo pants and used his sleeve to swab his face, then went back to twisting the screwdriver. He worked as quickly as he could. Finally he took out the last screw.

Carefully, ever so carefully, Herron pulled off the access panel and laid it on the catwalk by his feet. He dug a small flashlight from his pocket. Looking through the access panel, he could see lots of wires. And a stainless-steel sphere about the size of a basketball. That, he concluded, must be the biological warhead. The missile had been designed for a nuclear warhead, which would have been round, so the biological warhead had to go into the same space. Yet the warhead was too large to come out this little six-inch access hole.

Charlie Herron reached through the hole to his elbow, felt upward with his ear against the skin of the missile. Yes, he could feel the latch. He opened it. Now down . . . one there too. Right, then left.

With the last latch open, he pulled at the panel he had his arm in. It came out in his hand, making a hole at least twenty inches across. So the engineer had been telling the truth.

Herron turned to put the panel on the catwalk . . . and dropped it.

It fell, striking the side of the missile, finally landing on the grate at the bottom with a tinny sound, much like the lid of a garbage can.

Charlie Herron grabbed the rails of the catwalk and held on to keep from falling.

He wiped his face on his sleeves, the palms of his hands on his trousers.

Using a pair of wire snips, the lieutenant began clipping wires, then pulling the ends out of the way so he could see how the warhead was held in place.

William Henry Chance and Tommy Carmellini stepped from their Osprey transport wearing their CBW suits. Two marines similarly clad followed them. Each marine carried a cylinder about six feet long and five inches in diameter balanced on his shoulder.

Doll Hanna was waiting for them as they approached the main entrance. "I count five people in the clean area," he said. "They don't know we're here yet. The air-circulation system is pretty loud."

Chance went to the partially open door and eased his head around for a peek. He counted the people inside. Five.

He had been thinking about this moment ever since Jake Grafton asked him to take out this facility. If the integrity of the sealed area was broken before the fire got hot enough to destroy the virus, some of the virus might escape. If there were any free viruses in the air inside there, or if one of the culture trays was broken, intentionally or unintentionally . . .

How much was some? Who could say?

He pulled his head back, looked at Doll Hanna, looked at the marines carrying the cylinders on their shoulders.

Well, it was a hell of a risk. A *hell* of a risk.

Just then William Henry Chance wished he were back in New York City, eating dinner at a nice restaurant or preparing a case for trial or sitting at home with the woman who had shared his life for the past ten years. Anywhere but here.

"Give me your rifle," he said to Hanna, who handed him his M-16. "Is it loaded?"

"Full. Selector is on single shot. This is the safety." Hanna touched it.

"Okay," said William Henry Chance.

He turned to Carmellini. "If worse comes to worst, you know what to do."

Carmellini didn't say anything. *The dumb shit is probably wishing he was safe and snug in a federal pen,* Chance thought.

He pointed the rifle at the ground and held it close to his leg, then eased the door open and stepped inside. No Cuban saw him. They were looking intently at something in a sealed unit with remote-control arms. A radio was playing somewhere, playing loudly.

Chance stepped into the air lock, stood there looking at the people while he waited for the interior door to unlock automatically.

He recognized the voice on the radio: Alejo Vargas. The gravelly flat delivery was unmistakable.

"My fellow Cubans, now is the hour to rally to the defense of our holy mother country. Tonight even as I speak the nation is under attack from American military forces, who have leveled the awesome might of their armed forces against the eleven million peaceful people of Cuba."

Ten seconds passed, fifteen, twenty. After a half minute, the interior door clicked. Chance pushed it open and stepped into the lab.

Racks holding eight or ten culture trays each stood beside the benches. He lifted the rifle, thumbed off the safety, walked forward toward the working figures, who still had their backs to him. The tables on both sides of the aisles contained tools, parts, glassware, specialized instruments.

"Join with me in fighting the forces of the devil, the forces of capitalism and exploitation that seek to enslave the Cuban people so that the Yanquis can manufacture more dollars for themselves. . . ."

One of the workers spotted Chance when he was ten feet away, and turned in his direction.

Chance gestured with the rifle, motioned for them to raise their hands. They did so.

I should just shoot them, he thought, acutely aware of the culture trays just beside his elbow, and theirs.

Maybe I won't have to.

Backing up between two tables, he jerked his head back the way he had come, toward the air lock, gestured with the barrel of the rifle.

"Our hour of glory is now," Alejo Vargas thundered, "an hour that will live in all of Cuban history as the supreme triumphant moment of our people, that moment in the history of the world when we humble people struck back against the enslaver and oppressor and became forever free. . . ."

Slowly, watching Chance, the closest man began moving, passed him, kept walking with his hands up.

The second man passed.

The third . . .

He was turning to look at the fourth man when the man grabbed the barrel of the rifle with one hand and stabbed Chance in the solar plexus with the other.

William Henry Chance looked down at the handle sticking out of his abdomen. A screwdriver! The man had stabbed him with a screwdriver.

The man was fighting him for the rifle!

A shot. He heard a shot over the noise of the air-circulation fans. The man who stabbed him collapsed.

More shots.

Chance fell. His legs didn't work anymore and he was having trouble breathing.

"Kill the American enslavers wherever you find them, wherever they choose to shovel their odious filth onto a committed socialist people," Vargas shouted over the radio. "Beloved Cuba, the mother of us all, needs our strong right arms."

On the floor, his vision narrowing to tiny points of light, fighting for air he couldn't get, William Henry Chance felt someone roll him over. Through the face plate on the mask of the man who held him, he could just make out Carmellini's features.

"You should have shot 'em," Carmellini shouted. "You stupid bastard, you should have shot 'em."

Chance was trying to suck in enough air to reply when his heart stopped.

Carmellini and the two marines in CBW suits carried the aluminum cylinders they had brought from the Osprey into the lab and set them down. There was not a moment to be lost. Bullets had gone through several of the men lying dead on the floor and punctured the transparent plastic walls of the facility.

The two marines went back after more cylinders while Carmellini brought plastic cans of gasoline through the air lock. He didn't have time to wait for the lock to work, so he jammed the door so it would not close.

Please God, don't let the viruses out.

With six cylinders on the floor near the cultures and ten gallons of gasoline sitting nearby, Carmellini was ready. The five Cubans who were working in the lab lay where they had fallen. Chance's body lay where he died. Carmellini ignored the bodies as he worked.

He gestured to the marines to leave, then turned to the nearest cylinder, which was a five-inch-diameter magnesium flare designed to be dropped from an airplane. A small steel ring was taped to the side of the thing—he tore that off and pulled it out as far as it would go, which was about a foot. Then he gave it a mighty tug, which tore it loose in his hand.

He laid the cylinder on the wooden floor and walked for the air lock. As he went through he released the door, allowing it to close.

He still had a few seconds, so he stood in the lock as the suction tore as his CBW suit, trying to cleanse it of dust and stray viruses.

But he was running out of time.

He pushed the emergency button and let himself out of the lock through the exterior door. Walking swiftly, he exited the barn and strode for the waiting Osprey.

Doll Hanna was standing there with a rifle in his arms.

"Let's get the men—" Carmellini began, but the ignition of the flare stopped him. The glare of a hundred-million-candlepower magnesium fire leaked out of the barn through the door and cracks in the siding.

"Let's get the hell out of here before it goes up like a rocket," Carmellini shouted, and trotted for the Osprey.

Three minutes later, with all the people aboard and the plane airborne, he went to the cockpit and looked back. The fire was as bright as a welder's torch, so brilliant it hurt his eyes to look. The heat of the first flare had set off the second, and so on. The heat from the first few flares probably caused the gasoline cans to explode, raising the temperature dramatically and helping ignite the other flares.

"Think the fire will kill all the viruses?" the pilot asked.

"I don't know," Carmellini said grimly, and went back to his seat. He didn't have any juice to waste on the merely worried.

CHAPTER TWENTY-ONE

There were just too many Cuban troops at silo one. The two Super-Cobras assigned there expended their Hellfire missiles on the tanks and trucks, then scourged the area with 20-mm cannon shells. Between them the assault choppers fired fifteen hundred rounds of 20-mm. As the first two assault choppers left the arena to refuel and rearm, Battlestar Control aboard *United States* routed other SuperCobras to the site. They began flaying the area with a vengeance.

The problem was that the troops were fairly well dug in. Almost a thousand men had arrived in the area early that morning under an energetic young commander who had ordered trenches dug and machine guns emplaced in earth and log fortifications. Two small bulldozers helped with the digging.

The machine-gun nests were gone now, victims of Hellfire missiles, but the troops in trenches were harder to kill. Fortunately for the Cubans, the trenches were not straight, but zigged and zagged around trees and stones and natural obstacles.

The young commander was dead now, killed by a single cannon shell that tore his head off when he tried to look over the lip of a trench to find the SuperCobras. Most of his officers were also dead. One of the SuperCobras had been shot down by machine-gun fire. A Cuban trooper with an AK-47 killed the pilot of another with a lucky shot in the neck.

The first chopper managed to autorotate down, and the crew jumped from their machine into a empty trench. The copilot of the second machine flew it out of the battle and headed for the refueling and rearming site the marines had established in a sugarcane field between silos three and four.

The SuperCobras on site were almost out of ammo, and they too went to the refueling site, where they were fueled from bladders and rearmed with ammo brought in by Ospreys from *Kearsarge*. Then they rejoined the fray.

The noise of eight assault choppers hovering around the battlefield that centered on the barn did the trick. One by one, the Cubans threw down their weapons and climbed out of their trenches with their hands over their heads.

Several of the SuperCobras turned on their landing lights and hovered over the barn, turning this way and that so that their lights shown over the men living and dead that littered the ground.

Minutes later an Osprey landed just a hundred feet from the entrance to the barn. Toad Tarkington was the last man out. He was ten feet from the V-22 and running like hell when it lifted off and another settled onto the same spot. Marines with rifles at the ready came pouring out.

With his engines running and the canopy closed, Major Carlos Corrado taxied his MiG-29 toward the runway at Cienfuegos. Two men walked ahead of the fighter with brooms, sweeping shrapnel and rocks off the concrete so the fighter's tires would not be cut. They weren't worried about this stuff going in the intakes: on the ground the MiG-29's engines breathed through blow-down panels on top of the fuselage while the main intakes remained closed.

Inside the fighter Corrado was watching his electronic warning equipment. As he suspected, the Americans had a bunch of radars aloft tonight, everything from large search radars to fighter radars. He immediately recognized the radar signature of the F-14 Tomcat, which he had seen just a week or so ago out over the Caribbean.

Yep, they were up there, and as soon as his wheels came up, they would be trying to kill him.

Carlos Corrado taxied his MiG-29 onto the runway and shoved the twin throttles forward to the stop, then into afterburner. The MiG-29 rocketed forward. Safely airborne, Corrado raised the landing gear and came out of afterburner. Passing 400 knots, he lowered the nose and retarded the throttles, then swung into a turn that would point the sleek Russian fighter at Havana.

Inside the barn at silo one, Toad Tarkington took in the carnage at a glance. He was the first American through the door.

Cannon shells and shrapnel from Hellfire warheads had played hob with the wooden barn structure. Holes and splintered boards and timbers were everywhere—standing inside Toad could see the landing lights of the helicopters and hear Americans shouting.

Apparently several dozen men had taken refuge in the barn; their bloody bodies lay where the bullets or shrapnel or splinters from the timbers cut them down. The floor and walls were splattered with blood.

Toad found the wooden door, got it open, used his flashlight to examine the steel inner door. He set three C-4 charges around the combination lock and took cover.

The charges tore the lock out of the door and warped the thing so badly it wouldn't open. Toad struggled with it, only got it open because two marines came in to check out the interior and gave him a hand.

The stairway on the other side of the door was in total darkness. Not a glimmer of light.

With his flashlight in his left hand and his pistol in his right, Toad slowly worked his way down.

He saw lightbulbs in sockets over his head, but they were not on. Once he came to a switch. He flipped it on and off several times. No electrical power.

At the bottom of the stairs he came to a larger room. The beam of the flashlight caught an instrument panel, a control console. A bit of a face . . .

Toad brought the light back to the face.

A white face, eyes scrunched against the flashlight glare. An old man, skinny, with short white hair, frozen in the flashlight beam, holding his hands above his head.

The radar operator in the E-3 Sentry AWACS plane over Key West was the first to see the MiG-29 get airborne from Cienfuegos. He keyed the intercom and reported the sighting to the supervisor, who used the computer to verify the track, then reported it to Battlestar Control.

The AWACS crew reported the MiG as a bogey and assigned it a track number. They would be able to classify it as to type as soon as the pilot turned on his radar.

Unfortunately, Carlos Corrado failed to cooperate. He left his radar switch in the off position. He also stayed low, just a few hundred meters above the treetops.

There are few places more lonely than the cockpit of a single-piloted airplane at night when surrounded by the enemy. Corrado felt that loneliness now, felt as if he were the only person still alive on Spaceship Earth.

The red glow of the cockpit lights comforted him somewhat: this was really the only home he had ever had.

The lights of Havana were prominent tonight—he saw the glow at fifty miles even though he was barely a thousand feet above sea level. He climbed a little higher, looking, and saw a huge fire, quite brilliant.

Carlos Corrado turned toward the fire. Perhaps he would find some airborne targets. He turned on his gun switch and armed the infrared missiles.

The E-2 controller datalinked the bogey information to the F-14 crew patrolling over central Cuba at 30,000 feet. There should have been two F-14s, a section, but one plane had mechanical problems prior to launch, so there was only one fighter on this station.

The bogey appeared on the scope of the radar intercept officer, the RIO, in the rear seat of the Tomcat. He narrowed the scan of his radar and tried to acquire a lock on the target, which was merely a blip that faded in and out against the ground clutter.

"What the hell is it?" the pilot demanded, referring to the bogey.

"I don't know," was the reply, and therein was the problem. Without a positive identification, visual or electronic, of the bogey, the rules of engagement prohibited the American pilot from firing his weapons. There were simply too many American planes and helicopters flying around in the darkness over Cuba to allow people to blaze away at unknown targets.

The darkness below was alive with lights, the lights of cities and small towns, villages, vehicles, and here and there, antiaircraft artillery—flak— which was probing the darkness with random bursts. Fortunately the gunners could not use radar to acquire a target—the instant they turned a radar on, they drew a HARM missile from the EA-6Bs and F/A-18s that circled on their assigned stations, listening.

The F-14 pilot, whose name was Wallace P. "Stiff" Hardwick, got on the radio to Battlestar Control. "Battlestar, Showtime One Oh Nine, request permission to investigate this bogey."

"Wait."

Stiff expected that. Being a fighter pilot in this day and age wasn't like the good old days, when you went cruising for a fight. Not that he was there for the good old days, but Stiff had sure heard about them.

"That goddamn Cuban is gonna zap somebody while the people on the boat are scratching their ass," Stiff told his RIO, Boots Von-Rauenzahn.

"Yeah," said Boots, who never paid much attention to Stiff's grousing.

Carlos Corrado saw that a building was on fire, burning with extraordinary intensity. Never had he seen such a hot fire. He assumed that the building had been bombed by a cruise missile or American plane and began visually searching the sky nearby for some hint of another aircraft.

He flew right over the V-22 Osprey carrying Tommy Carmellini and Doll Hanna back to the ship and never saw it.

A lot of flak was rising from the outskirts of Havana, so Carlos turned east, away from it.

In the black velvet ahead he saw lights, and steered toward them. At 500 knots he closed quickly, and saw helicopters' landing lights! They were flying back and forth over a large barn!

They must be Americans—they sure as hell weren't Cuban. As far as he knew, he was the only Cuban in the air tonight.

Corrado flew past the area—now down to 400 knots—and did a 90-degree left turn, then a 270-degree right turn. Level, inbound, he retarded the throttles of the two big engines. Three hundred knots... he picked the landing lights on some kind of strange-looking twin rotor helicopter and pushed the nose over just a tad, bringing the strange chopper into the gunsight. Then he pulled the trigger on the stick.

The 30-mm cannon shells smashed into Rita Moravia's Osprey with devastating effect. She was in the midst of a transition from wing-borne to rotor-borne flight and had the engines pointed up at a seventy-degree angle. The rotors were carrying most of the weight of the twenty-ton ship, so when the cannon shells ripped into the right engine and it ceased developing power, the V-22 began sinking rapidly.

The good engine automatically went to emergency torque and transferred some of its power to the rotor of the bad engine through a driveshaft that connected the two rotor transmissions.

With shells thumping into the plane and warning lights flashing, Rita felt the right wing sag. Some of the shells must have damaged the right transmission!

The ground rushed at her, even as cannon shells continued to strike the plane.

She pulled the stick back and left, trying to make the right rotor take a bigger bite.

Then the machine struck the earth and the instrument panel smashed into her night vision goggles.

In the missile control room, Toad Tarkington held his flashlight on the old man as he produced a candle from his pocket and a kitchen match. He lit the match and applied it to the candle's wick.

One candle wasn't much, but it did light the room. Toad turned off the flashlight and stood there looking at the old man.

Muffled crashing sounds reached him, echoed down the stairwell, but no one came. Toad's headset was quiet too, probably since he was underground.

"Do you speak English?" Toad asked the white-haired man in front of him.

The old man shook his head.

"*Español?*"

"*Sí, señor.*"

"Well, I don't."

Toad walked over and checked the man, who had no visible weapons on him.

He had a handful of plastic ties in his pocket. These ties were issued to every marine for the sole purpose of securing prisoners' hands, and feet if necessary. Toad put a tie around the old man's hands. The man didn't resist; merely sat at the control console with his face a mask, showing no emotion.

"Cuban?" Toad asked.

"*Nyet.*"

"Russki?"

The white head bobbed once, then was still.

Toad used the flashlight to inspect the console, to examine the instruments. This stuff was old, he could see that. Everything was mechanical, no digital gauges or readouts, no computer displays . . . the console reminded Toad of a the dashboard of a 1950s automobile, with round gauges and bezels and . . .

Well, without power, all this was academic.

His job was to get that damned warhead out of the missile, then set demolition charges to destroy all this stuff, missile, control room, and all. He left the Russian at the console and opened the blast-proof door across the room from the stair where he had entered.

Another stairway led downward.

Toad went as quickly as he dared, still holding the flashlight in one hand and his pistol in the other.

He went through one more steel door . . . and there the missile stood, white and massive and surreal in the weak beam of the flashlight.

The aviation radio frequencies exploded when Rita's plane was shot down as everyone tried to talk at once.

Battlestar Control finally managed to get a word in over the babble, a call to Stiff Hardwick. "Go down for a look. Possible hostile may have shot down an Osprey."

Stiff didn't need any urging. He rolled the Tomcat onto its back, popped the speed brakes, and started down.

"Silo one," Boots said. "This bogey is flitting around down there like a goddamn bat or something, mixing it up with the SuperCobras and Ospreys. Let's not shoot down any of the good guys."

"No shit," said Stiff, who was sure he could handle any Cuban fighter pilot alive. This guy was meat on the table: he just didn't know it yet.

Carlos Corrado pulled out of his strafing run and soared up to three thousand feet. He extended out for eight or nine miles before he laid the fighter over in a hard turn.

He had seen helicopters down there, at least two. It was time to use the radar.

As he stabilized inbound he flipped the radar switch to "transmit." He pushed the button for moving targets and sure enough, within seconds the pulse-doppler radar in the nose of the MiG-29 had found three. The rest of the drill was simplicity itself—he selected an Aphid missile, locked it on a target, and fired. Working quickly, he selected a second missile, locked on a second target, and fired.

He had to keep the targets illuminated while the Aphids were in flight, so he continued inbound toward the silo.

One of the SuperCobras exploded when an Aphid drilled it dead center. The second missile tore the tail rotor off its target, which spun violently into the ground and caught fire.

Carlos Corrado flew across the barn, holding his heading, extending out before he turned to make another shooting pass.

Toad Tarkington found the circular steel ladder leading upward in the missile silo and began climbing.

When he reached the catwalk he walked around the missile, examining the skin. There was the little access port, six inches by six inches, with the dozen screws! That had to be it.

Toad Tarkington put the flashlight under his left armpit and got out a screwdriver.

He had three screws out when the flashlight slipped out of his armpit and fell. It bounced off the catwalk and went on down beside the missile, breaking when it hit the grate at the bottom.

The darkness in the silo was total.

Toad Tarkington cursed softly, and went back to taking out screws. He worked by feel. Someone would come along in a minute, he thought, bringing another flashlight. If someone didn"t, he would take the time to go find another.

The trick, he knew, would be to hold on to the screwdriver. He only had one, and if he dropped it, it would go down the grate.

He heard muffled noises from above, but he couldn't tell what they were. It didn't really matter, he decided. Getting this warhead out of this missile was priority one.

Carefully, working by feel, he removed the screws from the access panel one by one. When he had the last one out, he pried at the panel. It came off easily enough and he laid it on the catwalk near his feet.

So far so good. He carefully stowed the screwdriver in his tool bag and wiped the sweat from his face and hands.

Okay.

Toad reached up to find the latch that the ancient Russian engineer on television had said should be here. God knows where the CIA found that guy!

Yep. He found the latch.

He rotated it. Now the latch on the left. He was having his troubles getting that latch to turn when the lights came on in the silo.

From instant darkness to glaring light from twenty or more bulbs.

Toad Tarkington pulled his arm from the missile, clapped his hands over his eyes and squinted, waiting for his eyes to adjust.

He could hear a hum. Must be a fan or blower moving air.

No. The hum was in the missile, just a foot or two from his head. Something winding up. The pitch was rising rapidly.

A gyro?

What was going on?

Toad started down the ladder, moving as fast as he could go, intending to go to the control room to see what in hell was happening.

He heard a grinding noise, loud, low-pitched, and looked up. The cap on the silo was opening.

Holy . . .

He still had his tools. If he could get that access panel off and cut the guidance wires, the wires to control the warhead . . .

Toad Tarkington scrambled back up the ladder.

The little six-by-six access hole gaped at him. He ran his arm in, trying to reach the other latches that would allow the large panel to come off.

He got one open. The gyro had ceased to accelerate—it was running steadily now, a high-pitched steady whine.

Holy shit!

He was out of time: the fire from the missile's engines would fry him to a cinder.

He heard the igniters firing, popping like jet engine igniters.

The rocket motors lit with a mighty whoosh.

Toad grabbed for the access hole with both hands, held on desperately as the missile began to rise on a column of fire.

The noise was beyond deafening—it was the loudest thing Toad Tarkington had ever heard, a soul-numbing roar that made his flesh quiver and vibrated his teeth.

Rising . . . the missile was rising, dragging him off the catwalk.

He clung to the access hole with all his strength,

The missile came out of the silo, past the floor of the barn, accelerating, going up, up, up. . . .

The tip of the missile burst through the rotten, shattered roof and threw wood in every direction.

As it did Toad curled his feet up against the fuselage of the missile, released his hold on the access hole, and kicked off.

He flew through the darkness, bounced on the collapsing roof, felt the blast of furnace heat as the rocket motors singed him, then he was falling, falling. . . .

Stiff Hardwick couldn't believe his eyes. He had his F-14 Tomcat down at 4,000 feet, fifteen miles from silo one, and was impatiently waiting for Boots to sort out the villain from the other airborne targets in the area when he saw the ballistic missile rising into the night sky on a cone of white-hot fire.

"Jesus Christ!" he swore over the radio, "the bastards have launched one."

"Lock it up, Boots," Stiff screamed, still on the radio, although he thought he was on the intercom. "Lock it up and we'll shoot an AMRAAM." The acronym stood for advanced medium-range air-to-air missile.

Boots was trying. The problem was that the ballistic missile was essentially stationary in relation to the earth. It was accelerating upward, of course, but its velocity over the ground was close to zero just now. The designers of the F-14 weapons system did not envision that the crew would want to shoot missiles at stationary targets, so Boots was having his troubles.

Frustrated, he snarled at Stiff, "Go to heat, goddamnit. Shoot a 'winder at that exhaust."

"A 'winder ain't gonna dent that fucking thing," Stiff replied, his logic impeccable. He was on the ICS now. "We'll come up under it and shoot as it accelerates upward."

"Okay! Okay!"

And that is what he did. As the missile accelerated upward, Stiff Hardwick kept his nose down, punched the burners full on and accelerated in toward the launch site, then pulled up to put the climbing, accelerating ballistic missile in front of him.

Now Boots got a radar lock.

The symbology on the HUD was alive, showing the target, the boresight angle, the drift angle. . . .

Stiff Hardwick lifted his thumb to fire the first AMRAAM. As he did an infrared missile from Carlos Corrado's MiG-29 went up his right tailpipe and blew a stabilator off the F-14.

Jake Grafton heard all of it. "A missile is in the air! Just came out of silo one!" was the shout over the radio.

He picked up the red telephone, the direct satellite connection with the White House.

"Mr. President, I don't know what happened, but apparently the Cubans have launched one."

The president must have heard the shouts over the net the same as Jake did. His question was, "What is the target?"

Jake had the targets memorized. "It came out of silo one, sir. The target is Atlanta."

"Thank you, Admiral," the president said mechanically, and hung up.

When Toad Tarkington came to the night was quiet. He was lying on cool earth, the sky above was dark . . . and there was a marine standing over him with his mouth moving.

He was deaf. He had lost his hearing.

Toad sat up, fell over, forced himself into a sitting position again. He ached all over, every muscle and tendon screamed in protest. But he was alive.

He got to his feet, swaying. The marine helped steady him.

The barn was right there beside him.

He pulled his pistol, staggered for the entrance.

The interior was a shambles, the stench nearly unbearable from bodies fried and seared by the exhaust of the missile.

Toad pulled boards out of the way to get to the open door that led down to the control room.

The lights were still on. Using a palm on one wall to steady himself, he descended the stair.

The old man was still sitting at the console, still wearing the tie around his wrists.

He looked at Toad dispassionately.

"You bastard," Toad said. He said the words but he could barely hear them. "You foul, evil old man."

A young marine who had followed Toad down the stairs grabbed the whitehaired old man, shoved him toward the stairs. "Get going, you old fart! Upstairs, upstairs."

Tarkington sagged to his knees on the floor, then stretched out. He was so tired. . . .

Boots VonRauenzahn pulled the ejection handle, and both he and Stiff Hardwick were launched from Showtime One Oh Nine a fraction of a second apart.

Stiff got his wits about him as he hung in his parachute harness in the night sky. He could see the ballistic missile accelerating into the sky—it was now a bright spot of light amid the stars—and he could see the burning wreckage of his Tomcat as it fluttered toward the ground.

He couldn't see the MiG-29 that had shot him down. He could hear him though, a rumble that muffled the fading roar of the ballistic missile heading for space.

What he didn't know was that Carlos Corrado had decided that his fuel state didn't allow him to jab the Americans anymore this night. He was on his way back to Cienfuegos. With his radar off.

The SPY-1B radar aboard *Hue City* acquired the rising ballistic missile as it rose over the rim of the earth and transmitted the information by datalink to *Guilford Courthouse,* which picked up the missile on its own radar seconds later.

Hue City's tactical action officer (TAO) in the Combat Control Center reached out and pushed the squawk-box button for the bridge, notifying her captain. "Sir, we have a possible ATBM threat, bearing one hundred seventy-five degrees true." An ATBM was an antitactical ballistic missile threat.

The information from the SPY-1B radar was fed into the Aegis weapons system, which used the radar to control SM-2 missiles. The TAO waited for the computer to present the specifics of the target's trajectory.

Her orders were to shoot down any missiles launched from Cuba over the Florida Straits. To do that, she would use the latest version of the SM-2 missile, of which her ship carried eight. *Guilford Courthouse* also carried eight of these weapons, which had an extraordinary envelope. They could fly as far as 300 nautical miles and as high as 400,000 feet, about 66 nautical miles.

The ballistic missile that was flying now was still climbing and accelerating. The trick was to shoot it over the Florida Straits before it got out of the SM-2 envelope.

The captain was on the squawk box. "You may fire anytime," the old man said.

The TAO was Lieutenant (junior grade) Melinda Robinson. Her mother had wanted her to be a dancer and her father wanted her to take up law, his profession, but she chose the navy, confounding them both.

Just now she concentrated on the computer presentations on the large, 42-inch by 42-inch console in front of her.

"Two missiles," Robinson ordered. She was tempted to fire four, but the Cubans might launch more ballistic missiles, so she couldn't afford to run out of ammo.

"Fire one," she said.

The SM-2 Tactical Aegis LEAP (lightweight exoatmospheric projectile) missile roared from the vertical launcher in front of the ship's bridge in a blaze of fire.

Two seconds later a second missile roared after the first.

Guilford Courthouse also fired two missiles.

The solid fuel third-stage boosters of the SM-2 missiles lifted them through the bulk of the atmosphere, and finally separated at an altitude of 187,000 feet. The second stages ignited now, lifting the interceptor missiles higher and higher.

At 300,000 feet the second stage of the missile pitched over and ejected the nose cone of the missile, exposing the infrared sensor of the kineticenergy kill vehicle. The motor continued to burn for another sixteen seconds, carrying the kill vehicle higher and still faster. At 370,000 feet the kill vehicle was aligned by its GPS-aided inertial unit and was ejected from the missile.

Tracking the target now at 375,000 feet of altitude, the kill vehicle homed in on the ballistic missile's final stage at 6,000 miles per hour.

And hit it.

The second missile missed by a hundred feet, the third struck a piece of the target missile, and the fourth missed by seven feet.

"Admiral Grafton, *Hue City* reports the ballistic missile was destroyed over the Straits."

Jake picked up the telephone to the White House and waited for someone to answer.

"*Hue City,* an Aegis cruiser, reports the Cuban missile was destroyed over the Straits."

The president didn't say anything, but Jake could feel his relief. When he did speak, he sounded tired. "How many warheads are still in those missiles?"

"Only one left, sir. Number four. There are no Cubans there but the marines are having trouble getting the warhead out of the missile."

"Are you destroying the missiles when they are sanitized?"

"Yes, sir. A magnesium flare ignited near the nose cone. The heat melts it, then finally ignites the solid fuel and causes an explosion in the silo."

"You destroyed the warhead manufacturing facility?"

"Yes, sir."

"All that's left is the lab at the university?"

"That's correct."

"I want it destroyed, Admiral."

"There will be casualties, sir, American and Cuban. That thing is smack in the middle of downtown Havana."

"I understand that. Destroy it."

"We'll do it tomorrow night," Jake Grafton said.

Toad Tarkington found Rita putting a bandage on her copilot, Crash Wade, who had smashed his face into the instrument panel when their

Osprey crashed. Half the marines aboard had been injured, but by some miracle only two were killed. The Osprey was a total loss.

Toad put his hands on Rita's shoulders. She turned and he saw a large goose-egg bump on her forehead, one already turning purple. One of her eyes was also black and slightly swollen.

He knelt beside her. "How's your head?"

"I'm okay. Didn't even knock me out."

"And Crash?"

"The wound that's bleeding is pulpy—I think his skull is smashed. He doesn't seem to recognize me or anybody."

When she had Wade's wounds bandaged, she and Toad walked over to a tree and sat down. "Somebody said a MiG shot us down, Toad. Cannon holes all over the right engine nacelle. I couldn't save it."

She was so tired. When he leaned back against the tree she put her head down in his lap.

CHAPTER TWENTY-TWO

By dawn Jake Grafton had five biological warheads locked up aboard *United States*; five intermediate-range ballistic missiles had been melted and burned in their silos; and every uniformed American and flyable military aircraft was out of Cuba. It had been a tight squeeze.

Over half the SuperCobra helicopters lacked the fuel to return across the Florida Straits to Key West, nor was there room for them on the decks of U. S. ships off the Cuban coast. More fuel in flexible bladders was flown in from *Kearsarge*. The choppers were refueled, then launched for Key West. Four of the SuperCobras had been shot down, and one had suffered so much battle damage it was unsafe to fly and had to be destroyed.

Prowlers and Hornets armed with HARM missiles continued to patrol over central Cuba all night, ready to attack any radar that came on the air. Above them F-14s cruised back and forth, ready to engage any bogey brave enough to take to the sky.

Several Cuban Army units probed gently at the marines guarding the silo sites while they prepared to withdraw, but a few bursts of machine-gun fire and mortar shells from the marines were enough to discourage further attention. The marines eventually disengaged and pulled out un-molested.

When he landed his MiG-29 at Cienfuegos, Major Carlos Corrado found that he couldn't get fuel. Two cruise missiles had destroyed the fuel trucks and electrical pumping unit; all fueling would have to be done by hand, a slow, labor-intensive process. Disgusted, Corrado walked to the nearest bar in town, where he was a regular, and proceeded to get drunk, his usual evening routine. By dawn he was passed out in his bunk in the barracks, sleeping it off.

In Havana the next morning, Alejo Vargas summoned the senior officers of the Cuban Army, Navy, and Air Force to the presidential palace for a verbal hiding.

"Cowards, fools, traitors," he raged, so infuriated he quivered. "We had them in the palm of our hand, and all we had to do was make a *fist*. A red-handed apprehension of the American pirates would have brought the applause and respect of the Cuban people. A haul of American prisoners in uniform would have given us instant credibility. *This* was our chance."

"*Señor Presidente,* the troops would not obey. They refused to attack. When the troops refuse to obey direct orders, what would you have us do?"

"Shoot some generals," Vargas snapped. "Shoot some colonels. Scared men fight best."

"If we shot the generals and colonels the men would shoot us," General Alba explained, and he meant it. "The Americans are too well equipped, too well trained, too well armed. Their firepower is overwhelming. To fight them toe-to-toe would be suicidal, and the men know that."

Alba's logic was unassailable. To complain now that the Cuban Army, Navy, and Air Force did not do what he, Vargas, knew they could not do was illogical and self-defeating. No military force on the planet could whip the Americans in a stand-up fight, which was precisely why he had spent the last three years developing a biological-warfare capability.

Temper tantrums will get me no place, Vargas reminded himself, and willed himself back under control. He sat down at his desk, made a gesture to the others to seat themselves.

"Gentlemen, we must move forward. I have trust and confidence in you, and I hope you have the same in me. You are of course correct— we cannot overcome the Americans militarily. We must outwit them to prevail. With your help, it still can be done."

They sat looking at him expectantly.

"The laboratory where the biological agent for the warheads was created is in the science building of the University of Havana. Last night the Americans destroyed the warhead-manufacturing facility and our six operational ballistic missiles. All the American cruise missiles, the airplanes, the assault troops were employed to that end. Tonight the Americans will try to destroy the laboratory."

"Why did they not attack the lab last night?" Alba asked.

"You are the military man—you tell me. Perhaps they lacked sufficient assets, perhaps they did not have political support to create massive amounts of Cuban casualties or sustain significant American casualties— I do not know. The most likely explanation is that they were afraid of inadvertently releasing biological agents. Whatever, the lab is still intact and capable of producing polio viruses in sufficient quantity to supply a weapons program. The minds directing the American military effort will not ignore that laboratory."

"*Señor Presidente,* what would you have us do?"

Alejo Vargas smiled. He leaned forward in his chair and began explaining.

"Tell me what happened," Jake Grafton said to Toad Tarkington when Toad got back aboard the carrier. The sky was gray in the east by then, and Toad was filthy and bone tired.

A stretcher team from the ship's hospital met the Osprey on the flight deck and took Rita and Crash Wade below for examination.

Toad told his boss everything he thought he would want to know about the battle around silo one, about the missile rising, holding on to the tiny open access port, kicking off as the missile went through the barn roof, falling. . . .

He didn't tell Jake that he was so scared he thought he was going to die, and he left out how he felt when they told him Rita had been shot down just in front of the barn. He didn't mention how he felt when he realized she was alive, bruised up but alive. He didn't have to tell him, because Jake Grafton could read all that in his face.

The admiral listened, looking very tired and sad, and said nothing. Just nodded. Then patted him on the shoulder and sent him to take a shower and get a few hours' sleep.

The young CIA officer, Tommy Carmellini, sat in the dirty-shirt wardroom with a stony face, his jaw set. Chance was dead and he didn't want to talk about it.

He talked about the mission when Jake Grafton asked, however, told the admiral how it had gone, assured him that all the cultures in the building had been destroyed.

"The problem is that the bastards may have cultures stashed anyplace. Vargas may have a potful under his bed, just in case."

"Yes," Jake Grafton said, "I understand."

He did understand. To be absolutely certain of eradicating all the poliomyelitis virus in Cuba, he would need to burn the whole island to a cinder.

Jake went to his stateroom and tried to get a few hours' sleep himself.

Tired as he was, sleep wouldn't come. He tossed and turned as he thought about the battle just ended and the one still to come. What had he learned from last night's battle?

What could go wrong tonight?

After an hour of frustration, he took a long, hot shower. This time when he lay down he dozed off.

Two hours later he was wide awake. He put on a clean uniform and headed for his office.

Toad was already there huddled with Gil Pascal. "Rita's okay," he told Jake. "Crash Wade didn't make it. Amazing, isn't it? One dead, one just bruised."

"Can Rita fly tonight?" Jake asked.

Tarkington swallowed hard, nodded once.

"She's the best Osprey pilot we've got," Jake said. "She's got the flight if she wants it."

"She'd kill me if I asked you to leave her behind."

"She probably would, and you such a handsome young stud. What a loss to the world that would be."

"The Osprey that is bringing the survivor from *Hue City* will be here in twenty minutes. I'll bring him to your cabin."

"Hector Sedano's brother?"

"That's correct, sir. And the message said he wants to go back to Cuba."

Maximo Sedano parked his car on the pier so he wouldn't have to carry his gear very far. Scuba tanks, wet suit, flippers, weight belt, mask, he had the whole wardrobe.

He got all that stuff aboard the boat, checked the fuel, then cast off.

The gold was in Havana Harbor; he was sure of it. He had a chart that he had laid off in grids, and he had labeled each grid with a number that reflected a probability that he thought reasonable. The area off the main shipping piers didn't seem promising, nor did the busy areas by the fishing piers. The area off the private docks where Fidel had kept his boat seemed to Maximo to be the most likely, so that was where he would look first.

He took the boat to the center of the most promising area and anchored it.

It was inevitable that people would see him, so he had told everyone who asked that he was studying old shipwrecks in Havana Harbor. He knew enough about that subject to make it sound plausible—he could talk about the American battleship *Maine* and three treasure galleons that went on the rocks here in the harbor during a hurricane.

If he found it, he would not let on. If he found the gold, he would leave it where it was until he could come back for it with paid men and the proper equipment.

If.

Well, every man needs a dream, he reflected, and this was his. Better this than dying defending a ballistic-missile silo. Those fools.

The gold was near. He knew it. Sitting here on the boat he could feel its power.

God damn you, Fidel.

Juan Sedano, El Ocho, got out of the Osprey with a look of wonder on his face. The airplane, the aircraft carrier, the jets and noise and hundreds of foreigners, few of whom spoke his language—it was quite a lot for a young man who had never before been out of Cuba.

He got out of the Osprey wearing a set of navy dungarees, a white T-shirt, and a *Hue City* baseball cap, and carrying a pillowcase containing clothes, underwear, toilet items, and souvenirs given him by the men and women of *Hue City*, everything from photographs of the ship to CDs and *Playboy* magazines.

Toad Tarkington met Ocho on the flight deck and led the tall, broad-shouldered young man into the island and up the ladder to the flag bridge, where Jake Grafton and an interpreter, a lieutenant fighter pilot of Latin descent, were waiting. Jake took Ocho and the lieutenant into his at-sea cabin, where the three of them found chairs.

"When did you leave Cuba?" Jake Grafton asked Ocho after the introductions.

"Six or seven days ago," the lieutenant said, "he isn't sure. He lost track of the days at sea."

"Tell him that Fidel Castro is dead, that his brother Hector is in prison."

The Spanish-speaking junior officer did so.

Ocho's reaction was unexpected. Tears streamed down his face. "He asked me not to leave Cuba. He must have known that Fidel was dying, that something was happening. I left anyway."

He wiped at the tears, embarrassed. "I love my brother. He is my idol, a true man who believes in something larger than himself. I cry because I am ashamed of myself, of what I have done. He asked me not to go and I refused to listen."

"Tell me about Hector," Jake Grafton asked gently.

The admiral had expected to spend five minutes with the boy, but the five minutes became fifteen, then a half hour, then an hour. Ocho told of going to meetings with Hector, of the speeches he made, of his many friends, of antagonizing the regular priests and the bureaucrats while he spread the message of a coming new day to anyone who would listen, and many did.

Jake gave Ocho part of his attention while he thought about the lab in the science building in the University of Havana.

When Ocho finally began to run dry, Jake picked up the telephone and called Toad. "I'm in my at-sea cabin," he said. "Have the guys in the television studio play that tape we downloaded from the satellite this morning on the television in this stateroom. No place else."

"Yessir."

Toad called back in three minutes. "Channel two, Admiral."

Jake turned on the television.

In a few seconds Fidel Castro came on the screen. He was obviously a sick man. He was sitting behind a desk, wearing a green fatigue shirt.

"Citizens of Cuba, I speak to you today for the last time. I am fatally ill. . . ."

The young lieutenant translated.

"I wish to spend a few minutes telling you of my dream for Cuba, my dream of what our nation can become in the years ahead. It is imperative that we end our political isolation, that we join the family of nations as a full-fledged member. To make this transition a reality will require major changes on our part, and a new political vision. . . ."

Jake Grafton moved closer to the television set, adjusted his glasses, and studied the image of Fidel Castro. The man was perspiring heavily, obviously in pain, and every so often he would move slightly, as if seeking a more comfortable position.

"For years I have watched with admiration and respect," Fidel continued, "as Hector Sedano moved among our people, making friends, telling them of his vision for Cuba, preparing them for the changes and sacrifices that will be necessary in the days to come."

Fidel winced, paused, and took a sip of water from a glass setting nearby. Then he continued:

"We as a nation do not have to give up our revolutionary commitment to social justice to participate as full-fledged members of the world economy. We would be traitors to the heroes of the revolution and ourselves were we to do so. In the past few years the Church, in which so many Cubans believe, has come to understand that one cannot be a true Christian without an active commitment to social justice, the commitment that every loyal Cuban carries in his breast as his birthright. The Church has changed to join us. Now we also must change.

"The time has come for this government to renounce communism, to embrace private enterprise, to act as a referee to ensure that every Cuban has a decent job that pays a living wage and every enterprise pays its fair share of taxes . . ."

In less than a minute Fidel reached his peroration:

"Hector Sedano is the man I believe best able to lead our nation into this future."

The tape ended anticlimactically a few seconds later. A tired, haggard Fidel spoke to someone off-camera, said, "That's enough."

Jake Grafton reached out, turned off the television.

Ocho was stunned. "I thought Fidel was dead!"

"He is dead. He made this tape before he died."

"That was not a live performance?"

"No. A film, a videotape."

"And you have it!" Ocho's eyes were wide in amazement. "They must have played the videotape on television, and you copied it. But if it has been on television in Havana, why is Hector in prison?"

"The tape has never been on television," Jake said. "As far as I know, you are the very first Cuban to see it since it was made."

Ocho stared, trying to understand. Finally he asked, "What are you going to do with it?"

"I was wondering," Jake Grafton said, "if you would take it back to the lady who gave it to us. I believe she is your aunt by marriage, Mercedes Sedano?"

"Mercedes!" Ocho gaped. "She was Fidel's mistress. Why did she give you the tape?"

"You will have to ask her. Will you return the tape to her?"

"Of course. When do you want me to do this?"

"This evening, I think. By the way, are you hungry?"

"Oh, yes. I like the hamburger. *Muy bueno.*"

Jake and the lieutenant took Ocho to the flag wardroom for lunch. Ocho talked of baseball, of Cuba, of his brother Hector, and Hector's dreams for a free Cuba. He talked even with his mouth full, so the lieutenant who was translating didn't get much to eat. Jake let the young Cuban talk.

After lunch the admiral asked for Tommy Carmellini, so Toad Tarkington went looking for him. Carmellini was asleep. He smelled of liquor, which Toad ignored—after all, the man was a civilian.

When Toad got Carmellini into the admiral's office, he asked the chief petty officer to bring coffee, which Carmellini accepted gratefully.

"I've been thinking about your comment," Jake Grafton said.

"What comment?" Carmellini asked between sips of hot black coffee.

"About Vargas having jugs of cultures under his bed."

"Umm." Carmellini drank more coffee. When he saw that the admiral was expecting him to say more, he shrugged. "That was a flippant comment. I'm sorry."

Jake Grafton scratched his chin. "I thought it was . . . profound, in a way."

"How's that?"

"We can't burn the island down."

"That would be impractical," Carmellini agreed. "We'd have eleven million Cubans to house and feed afterwards."

"So where does that leave us?"

Tommy Carmellini searched the faces of the naval officers.

"There's a presidential directive against assassinating heads of state," the CIA man said cautiously.

"I have seen references to such a directive," Jake Grafton said, "though I haven't read the thing."

"Trust me. It exists."

"Friend, I believe you. That's sound public policy and I don't have anything like that in mind. Our objective is the lab and the cultures: that's more than enough to keep us busy. You've been there before and know the layout. Will you go back with us tonight?"

Tommy Carmellini nodded slowly. "I appreciate your asking, Admiral. I'd be delighted."

"We are planning a military assault. It is going to be a holy mess, I think. Vargas will probably ambush us on the way in or booby-trap the lab to blow up after we've fought our way in there. Maybe both."

"He's that kind of guy," Carmellini agreed.

"Hector Sedano's brother is aboard ship. He was picked up floating in the ocean north of Cuba two days ago after the boat he was on sank. Everyone else aboard drowned or was a victim of shark attack. This kid is either Hector's brother or a liar of Clintonian dimensions. They call him El Ocho. I want you to talk to him, feel him out. He impressed me as an extremely competent, capable young man. Talk to him, then come back and tell me what you think."

Toad Tarkington was in the Air Intelligence Center studying satellite images and radar images from an E-3 Sentry AWACS plane circling flying a race track pattern over the Florida Straits. The University of Havana science building was at the center of all the images.

"What's happening in Havana?" Jake asked.

"The streets are full of people," Toad said. "Especially around La Cabana Prison. Do you think they are there to break Hector out?"

"They're there because he is," Jake muttered, and used a magnifying glass to study the infrared images of the science building.

Toad pointed at the picture with the tip of a pen. "Tank," he said. "Vargas is going to be waiting with his guns loaded."

"Is he taking cultures out of the building? Do any of the specialists in Maryland have any opinions on that?"

"No one has seen any milk trucks. He'd be a fool to haul that stuff through Havana in a regular truck."

"Desperate men do foolish things," Jake Grafton said, and laid the magnifying glass back on the table.

As the sun was setting, Jake received a call from the White House. "I just watched that tape of Fidel," the president said over the encrypted circuit.

"It's impressive. We are going to deliver it to the woman who gave it to us, see if she can get it on television tonight."

"Maybe that will pan out," the president said. "The American Interest Section in Havana says that the crowd outside the prison is restless. Local police are nowhere in sight."

A wave of relief swept over Jake Grafton. "That's the best news I've heard today, sir."

"I'm really worried about those viruses."

"Sir, we'll do what we can."

"Just what are you going to do, Admiral?"

"Improvise as I go along. Do you really want to know?"

"I guess not," the president said heavily.

Alejo Vargas was in the office area across the hallway from the lab in the University of Havana science building when General Alba came in with old General Rafael Zerquera, the titular head of the Cuban armed forces, the chief of staff. The old man was at least eighty-five, probably a bit more, and he walked with a cane. With the two military men were several ministers, including Ferrara and the mayor of Havana. Behind them were six young officers, all wearing sidearms.

"*Señor Presidente*," General Zerquera began, and looked around the room for a chair. He found one and his aide helped him to it, though Vargas had not invited anyone to sit.

The general looked around slowly, taking everything in. Through the window one could see the air lock across the hallway that led to the sealed laboratory.

"I called your office, called the Ministry of Interior—they could not tell me where you were. The army knew, however."

Vargas said nothing.

"I saw a missile launched last night—everyone in central Cuba saw or heard it." The old man shook his head, remembering. "Weapons to destroy cities, kill millions—Fidel knew that if the Yanquis ever found out about the missiles, they would seek to destroy them. He was right. And he knew that if the missiles were ever used on the United States . . ."

Zerquera cocked his head, looked at Vargas. "So you launched at least one, and it never reached its target."

"What's done is done," Vargas snapped. "How do you know the missile did not reach its target?"

"Because we are still alive," Zerquera said. "If you think the Yanquis will not retaliate, you are a dangerous fool."

Vargas had to restrain himself. Zerquera had many friends; it would be impossible to stop tongues from wagging if he were shot here, in front of these junior officers.

"And then there is this lab," Zerquera continued blandly, gesturing at the window glass and the laboratory beyond. "Here you grow the poison to murder Cuba. If you use this on the Americans, they will retaliate. If it escapes, Cubans will die horribly."

Vargas took a deep breath before he answered. "We are moving the cultures."

"Moving them where?"

"To a place where they will be safe."

"Excuse me, *Señor Presidente*, for my failure to understand. What other place in Cuba has the sealed ventilation system and biological alarms and other safeguards that exist here?"

"There are none."

"So there is no place safer than this building."

"Tonight the Americans will probably attack this building in order to destroy the cultures. They burned several facilities last night that contained cultures, and they will probably burn this one. I am not a prophet, yet I make that prediction with a great degree of confidence."

"The president of the United States can destroy this building and everything it contains with a telephone call," General Zerquera said softly, "and there is nothing on earth we can do about it. In my opinion the viruses should be destroyed, if it can be safely done. An escape of the polio viruses from whatever containers they are in will kill vast numbers of our people unless the containers are housed in a specially prepared place, like this laboratory."

Vargas looked exasperated. "You exceed your authority, General, when you—"

Zerquera stopped him with a hand. "No, no, no! *You* exceed *your* authority when you endanger the Cuban people in order to gratify your ambition."

"Do not cross me, old man," Vargas snarled.

"I am not going to interfere in politics, Alejo. I never have. The Cuban people will decide who they want to lead them—neither you nor the exiles nor Fidel nor the president of the United States can dictate who the Cuban people will choose. For forty years they wanted Fidel, a loquacious eccentric with much personal charm and too little wisdom, in my opinion. Yet a new day has come."

Vargas gestured angrily. "These others have brought you here with lies about me."

General Rafael Zerquera got to his feet. He leaned on his cane, examined every face, and ended with his eyes on Vargas. "A nation matures much like a man does. Youth makes mistakes: with age and experience comes wisdom."

"You waste our time," Vargas said through his teeth.

"You will not remove the cultures from this building. The risk to the population is too great."

Vargas stepped forward to slap the old fool, but one of the aides stopped him with the barrel of a pistol pointed right at his face.

"Another step, *Señor Presidente,*" the young man said, "and you are dead."

Zerquera turned and headed for the door. He went through it, then took the elevator up to street level. The civilians followed him. Alba and the young officers stayed.

"You, Alba? You have betrayed me?"

"I obey my conscience," Alba said, and posted his men in front of the lab.

"Kill anyone who tries to remove anything from that room," the general told them.

As the last of the daylight faded, a helicopter from USS *United States* crossed the southern shore of the island of Cuba flying northwest. The helicopter stayed low, just above the treetops. In the cockpit both the pilot and copilot were wearing night-vision goggles. Behind them in the bay sat Tommy Carmellini and Ocho Sedano. A .50-caliber machine gun was mounted in the open door. The gunner wearing night-vision goggles sat on the jump seat, looking out.

Overhead EA-6B Prowlers and F/A-18 Hornets with their HARM missiles ready crossed the coast at the same time. These airplanes were there to attack any Cuban radars that came on the air tonight. So far, all was quiet. Above the Prowlers and Hornets, F-14 Tomcats patrolled back and forth.

One of the F-14 pilots was Stiff Hardwick. He and his RIO had ejected last night almost on top of silo one, so they had ridden home in an Osprey. The RIO, Boots VonRauenzahn, sustained a green-twig fracture to the left arm; he was sporting a cast tonight and couldn't fly. The junior RIO in the squadron, Sailor George, drew the short straw and was sitting behind Stiff tonight.

Stiff had had a hell of a bad day. First the shoot-down by a Cuban fighter pilot, then he endured a day of razzing from his peers, all of whom had a great laugh at his tale of woe, then tonight he had to fly with Sailor, a quiet woman who never had much to say around the testosterone-charged ready room.

On the way out to the plane this evening, Boots had put his good arm around the shoulders of his pal, Stiff. "Sailor will take good care of you. Don't fret the program, shipmate."

Stiff snarled something crude in reply and stomped off.

He was the sole victim of the entire Cuban Air Force—fighter pilots generally ignored helicopters, so the Osprey and choppers destroyed by the MiG pilot didn't register on Stiff's radar screen. He was never, ever going to be able to live down the ignominy of last night. His squadron mates would probably tattoo a ribald memorial of his disgrace on his ass some night when he was drunk or chisel it on his tombstone. His skipper had almost put somebody else in his place on the flight schedule tonight—Stiff begged shamelessly: "You gotta let me fly," he sobbed, "give me a chance to redeem myself."

"You aren't going to do anything stupid out there, are you?" the skipper asked, his voice tinged with suspicion.

"Oh, no, sir," Stiff assured the man.

So here he was, off to slay the dragon if he came out of his lair. And that goddamn Cuban fighter jock was probably still swilling free beer on the tale of the damned Yanqui who pulled up in front of him and lit his afterburners.

Actually Carlos Corrado hadn't thought much about his aerial victory. He awoke in the early afternoon with a blinding headache and treated himself to his usual hangover regimen—a cup of coffee, a cigar, and a puke.

He felt a little better this evening but thought he should forgo food. He would eat after he flew, he decided.

The powers that be didn't call the base today, of course, because the telephone system was hors de combat. Alas, a desk-flying colonel drove down from Havana.

"Please stay on the ground, Corrado. I would make that an order, but knowing you, you would disobey it. So I ask you, please do not fly tonight. Please do not allow yourself to be shot down. Please do not shame us."

Carlos Corrado told the colonel where he could go and what he could do to himself when he got there.

Tonight he sat on the concrete leaning up against a nose tire of his steed, which was parked between two gutted hangars. The troops had worked all day getting the MiG-29 fueled, serviced, and armed. It was ready. Now all Corrado needed to know was where the Americans were and what they were up to. Of course there was no one to tell him.

The walls of the hangars were still standing and magnified the sounds of the sky. As he chewed on his cigar butt, Corrado could hear jets running high. The growl was deep and faint.

The planes were American, certainly, and they had fangs. If he went heedlessly blasting into the sky, his life was going to come to an abrupt, violent end.

Where were they going?

Havana? He thought they would go there last night and they never got near the place.

Of course, the headquarters colonel knew nothing. At least, he had nothing to say. Except that Corrado was a fool. Only a fool would attack the American war machine head-on, he said.

Corrado got out a match and lit the butt. He puffed, coughed, chewed on the soggy mess.

Well, hell, we're all fools, really. Does any of this matter? And if so, to whom?

Rita Moravia settled the V-22 onto the flight deck of the *United States* and watched as Jake Grafton came trotting out from the island. Toad and a dozen marines carrying aircraft flares followed him. The marines had their rifles slung over their shoulders and wore their Kevlar helmets. Under the red lights shining down from the ship's island superstructure, the shadowy procession looked like something from a dream, a vision without substance.

She felt the substance as the men trooped up the ramp in the back of the plane and the vibrations reached her through the fuselage. Soon Jake Grafton was looking over her shoulder.

"Toad says you're okay. Now tell me the truth."

"I'm okay, Admiral." She turned and flashed him a grin. The bruise on her forehead was yellow and blue now.

"Whenever you're ready," Jake said, and strapped himself into the crew chief's seat.

CHAPTER TWENTY-THREE

It was a rare summer night, with a clean, clear sky, visibility exceeding twenty miles. A series of rain showers had swept the Florida Straits earlier in the evening, cleaning out the haze and crud.

Major Jack O'Brian sat in the cockpit of his F-117 looking at the cities below as he flew down the west coast of Florida, out to sea a little so as to avoid airplanes on the airway. O'Brian had one radio tuned to his squadron's tactical frequency, which he was merely monitoring in case the mission was scrubbed at the last minute, and on the other he listened to Miami Center. He wasn't talking to the air traffic controller either. His transponder was off. He was cruising at 36,500 feet, 500 feet above the flight level, so he should miss any airliner that he failed to see. Of course, an airliner going under him would not see him because his plane was midnight black and the exterior position lights were off.

The stealth fighter was also invisible to the controller at Miami Center, who had his radar configured to received coded replies from transponders. Even if the controller chose to look at actual radar returns, the skin paints, he would not have seen the F-117, which had been designed to be invisible to radars at long distances.

This feature also hid the stealth fighter from the American early-warning radars that were sweeping these skies looking for outlaw aircraft that might be aloft in the night, such as drug smugglers. And in just a few minutes it would hide it from Cuban radars probing the sky over the Florida Straits. If there were any.

Completely unseen, a black ghost flitting through the night, Jack O'Brian's F-117 passed Tampa Bay and continued south toward Key West. It was flying at Mach .72 to conserve fuel. The fighter had tanked over Tallahassee and would tank again in just a few minutes over two hours near Tampa. But first, a little jaunt to Havana.

Navigation was by global positioning system, GPS. The pilot had entered the coordinates of his destination into the computer before he even started the engines of his airplane, and now the computer and autopilot were taking him there. All he had to do was monitor the system, make sure everything functioned as it was designed to.

O'Brian sucked on his oxygen mask, reached under it to scratch his nose, readjusted his flight gloves, and generally fidgeted around in his seat. He was nervous—who wouldn't be?—but quite confident. After all, there was very little danger as long as the aircraft's systems continued to work properly. The craft truly was invisible at night. Of course it did have a small infrared signature and could be seen by an enemy searching the skies with infrared detectors, but there was no reason to suspect the Cubans were doing any such thing.

Barring a freak accident, like getting hit by a random unaimed artillery shell or having a midair with a civilian plane, the Cubans would never know the F-117 had even been around. Certainly they would never see it on radar or with the naked eye.

The Cubans might get wise when and if he dropped some bombs, but even so, there was nothing they could do about an invisible bomber.

The biggest risk, Jack O'Brian decided, was having a midair with one of the other three F-117s that were out here prowling around.

The second plane was running twenty miles back in trail, a thousand feet above this one, and the others an equal distance up and back, all with their own hard altitudes. Jack glanced again at his altimeter, just to be sure.

Key West came into view on schedule, a bit off to his left. The lights of the other Keys looked like a handful of pearls flung into the blackness of the night.

Then Key West lay behind and the lights of Havana appeared ahead. Jack O'Brian reduced power and set up a descent.

Angel One, the helicopter from *United States*, landed in the cane across the road from Doña Maria Sedano's house. Ocho got out of the chopper and walked across the road toward the house. Tommy Carmellini trailed along behind him.

Mercedes was standing on the porch as Ocho walked up. They launched themselves at each other, hugged fiercely. Mercedes didn't even glance at Carmellini, who was dressed in a civilian shirt and trousers but had a pistol strapped to his waist.

Mercedes kept her arm around Ocho, took him into the house where his mother was sitting in a chair.

Carmellini sat on the porch, watched the occasional car and truck go by. The vehicles slowed, their passengers gawking at the idling helo, but they didn't stop.

Soon Ocho came outside with Mercedes. She had the videotape in her hand. Ocho introduced Carmellini.

"If the videotape is to have maximum effect, it should be aired immediately," Carmellini told Mercedes, who held the tape tightly with both hands.

"We are going to get Hector out of prison," Ocho said, anxious to explain. "We could take you to Havana television and leave you, if you wish."

Mercedes nodded, so Ocho put his arm around her and led her to the helicopter. Doña Maria was visible in the door of her cottage; Ocho waved at her before he climbed into the helo.

Jake Grafton used a infrared viewing scope to examine the streets of Havana. He was sitting in the copilot's seat of the V-22 Osprey, which Rita had racked over in a right bank, orbiting the downtown. The city was well lit—not as well lit as an American city, but almost. The central core of the city was dark—the electrical power had yet to be restored.

The area around the University of Havana seemed deserted. No tanks, no armored personnel carriers, no barricades, apparently no troops. The streets looked empty.

Strange.

Or maybe not so strange. Maybe the lab was empty, the viruses moved to God knows where.

Everyone in Cuba seemed to be in the streets around La Cabana Prison; at least a hundred thousand people, Jake estimated. Bonfires burned in the streets near the prison, huge fires that appeared as bright spots of light on the infrared viewing scope.

He looked for the antiaircraft guns which he knew were there. He found them, but at this altitude he couldn't see people around them. "Go lower," he told Rita. "Two thousand feet."

Still circling to the right, she eased the power and let the Osprey descend.

Jake turned his attention to the prison, an island of darkness on the edge of the stricken city center. The main gate was an opening in a high masonry wall that surrounded the huge old stone fortress. The gate seemed to be closed, but at this altitude and angle, it was difficult to be sure. Immediately behind the gate sat a tank—Jake had seen enough of those planforms to be absolutely certain. Two more tanks sat in the courtyard . . . and some automobiles. Jake adjusted the magnification on the infrared viewer. Now he could see individuals, walking, standing in knots, talking through the fence—yes, the main gate was closed.

Two antiaircraft batteries sat beside the prison, old Soviet four-barreled ZPUs with optical sights. They were useless against fast movers but would be hell on helicopters.

The roof of the prison was flat, and apparently empty. No. Correct that. Snipers on the corners. Damn!

Jake checked the radio to ensure he was on the proper frequency, then keyed the mike. "Angel One, this is Battlestar One, where are you?"

"Angel One's on it's way to the television station to deliver a passenger."

"Let me know when you lift off from there."

"Roger that, Battlestar."

"Night Owl Four Two, call your posit."

Jack O'Brian in the F-117 replied, "Night Owl Four Two is overhead at ten."

"La Cabana Prison is our object of interest tonight, Four Two. I want single bombs, all to stay within the walls. Can you do that?"

"We can try, sir. You know the limitations on my equipment as well as I do."

"Your best efforts. Lots of friendlies outside the wall. First target is the antiaircraft battery inside the prison walls on the north side. Do you see it?"

"Wait." Seconds ticked by.

"Got it."

"The second target is the antiaircraft battery on the south side."

"Night Owl Four Four is on station at eleven thousand, Battlestar. Why don't we each run one of those targets? I'll take the north one."

The two F-117 pilots discussed it and Jake approved.

Jack O'Brian had several possible ways to drop the bombs he carried in the internal bomb bay. If he were bombing through a cloud deck or in rain or snow, he would release the unpowered weapon over the target and let it steer itself to the GPS bull's-eye through use of a GPS receiver, a computer, and a set of canards mounted on the nose of the weapon. Tonight, since the sky was reasonably clear, he would illumine the target with a laser beam while overflying it, and let the unpowered bomb fly itself to the laser-designated bull's-eye. If O'Brian could keep the laser beam directly on the spot he wished the bomb to hit, he should be able to achieve pinpoint, bomb-in-a-barrel accuracy.

Once again O'Brian carefully checked his electronic countermeasures panel, which was dark. The Cubans were off the air, which was comforting.

Now he adjusted the focus of the infrared camera in the nose. The display blossomed slowly, continued to change as he got closer and the grazing angle increased.

He could see the gun plainly owing to the camera's magnification. He sweetened the crosshairs just a touch as the airplane motored sedately toward the target, still cruising at ten thousand feet, and turned on the laser designator, which was slaved to the crosshairs.

Jack O'Brian checked his watch. "Night Owl Four Two is thirty seconds from drop."

"Four Four is a minute out."

"Don't turn on your laser until you see my thing pop."

"Roger."

Armament panel set for one bomb, laser mode selected, laser designator on, master armament switch on, steady on the run-in heading, autopilot engaged, crosshairs steady on the target—no drift—system into Attack. A tone sounded in his ears and was broadcast over the radio on the tactical frequency. O'Brian knew that several people were listening for that tone, including the pilot of the other F-117 Night Owl Four Four, Judy Kwiatkowski.

He watched for unexpected wind drift. Not much tonight—what little wind there was was well within the capability of the bomb to handle.

Counting down, the second hand on the clock on the instrument panel ticking . . . The release marker marched down and he felt the thump as the bomb bay doors snapped open. Immediately thereafter the bomb was released, the tone stopped, then the doors closed again.

With the bomb in the air, it was essential that the crosshairs on the laser designator stay precisely on the target because the bomb was guiding itself toward this spot of invisible light.

He took manual control of the crosshairs, kept them right on the artillery piece beside the old fortress.

The aspect angle of the target was changing, of course, as the airplane flew over it and beyond. Now it was behind the plane, the crosshairs right on the target.

Then, suddenly, the antiaircraft artillery piece disappeared in a flash as the five-hundred-pound bomb struck it dead center.

Thirty seconds later the gun on the south side of the building was hit by Judy Kwiatkowski's weapon.

"Very good, Night Owls," Battlestar said. "The next target is the tank nearest to the main gate. I think one bomb will discourage the tankers. Four Four, I want you to bomb the main gate. Tell me if you see it."

"Four Four has the target."

"How long until the weapons hit?"

"Give us ten minutes to go out and make another run."

"Ten minutes will do fine," Jake Grafton said, then turned to Rita.

"After the bombs hit the tanks and main gate, I want you to land on the roof. The guys in back will go out shooting and take care of the snipers. Let me go talk to Eckhardt and Toad." Both officers were riding in the back of the Osprey with the grunts.

Jake unstrapped and got out of the copilot's seat. In a moment Lieutenant Colonel Eckhardt climbed into the seat and used the infrared scope. "See the snipers?" the admiral asked. "I want you and your people to shoot them or capture them, whatever."

"Yes, sir." The colonel got out of the seat.

"Ten minutes, Rita. Start your clock."

"Aye, aye, sir," Rita said, and began figuring the best way to approach the prison.

A man from the control tower ran to find Carlos Corrado and tell him that American aircraft were over Havana. The people in the tower heard the news on short-wave radio from headquarters.

"Havana."

Corrado threw away his cigar butt and got into his flying gear.

Five minutes later he was taxiing. He didn't stop at the end of the runway to check the systems or controls, but added power and stroked the burners. The big fighter responded like a thoroughbred race horse and lifted off after a short run.

Of course he left his radar off.

Still, the crew of the U.S. Air Force E-3 Sentry over the Isle of Pines picked up a skin-paint return of the MiG almost immediately.

"Showtime One Oh Two, we got a bogey lifting off Cienfuegos, looks like he's on his way to Havana on the deck. Try to intercept. Over."

Stiff Hardwick had been airborne for an hour and ten minutes. The recovery aboard *United States* would begin in exactly thirty-five minutes. This bogey was on the deck using fuel at a prodigious rate, and when Stiff came swooping down from 30,000 feet his fuel consumption would also go through the roof. Fuel would be tight. Very tight. If he had to stroke the throttles to drop this turkey, he was going to need a tanker.

"One Oh Two will probably need a tanker."

"Roger that. Showtime One Oh Seven—" this was Stiff's wingman, who was orbiting a thousand feet above Stiff "—remain on station."

"One Oh Seven aye."

"Showtime One Oh Two is on the way," Stiff told the E-3 controller.

"That's the spirit," Sailor Karnow said from the rear cockpit.

"Shut up, babe. Just do your thing and keep the crap to yourself."

"You got it, dickwick. I'm behind you all the way."

The helicopter landed in the street in front of the television station and Mercedes stepped out. Ocho waved as it lifted off, leaving her standing there with her hair and skirt blowing wildly, clutching the videotape.

El Ocho, alive and well! It seemed like a miracle. Truly, she had thought he was dead, lost at sea.

"I have seen the tape," Ocho had shouted over the noise of the helicopter as they rode above the lights of Havana. "Fidel wanted Hector to lead Cuba. His opinion will sway many people."

Yes, she nodded, fighting back tears.

364 ★ STEPHEN COONTS

"Why did you give the tape to the Americans?"

"Vargas would have taken it from me," she replied.

Ocho accepted that because he knew it was true. That tape would destroy Alejo Vargas.

"Make them show it on television," Ocho had shouted. "We will get Hector out of prison." He grinned broadly, showing all his teeth. The future was arriving all at once.

She watched the helicopter disappear into the night sky, then turned and walked into the television station.

One of the most horrifying threats any soldier can face is being in the bull's eye of a modern guided weapon. The stealth fighters were out tonight, dropping their weapons with extraordinary precision. The bombs came in too fast for the human eye to follow, especially in the light conditions prevailing in Havana this night. For the Cuban troops surrounding the old prison, it was as if a giant invisible sharpshooter were somewhere in the clouds hurling bombs.

The two bombs on the antiaircraft guns frightened the soldiers and made the crowd nervous. Watching from the Osprey, Jake Grafton thought for a moment the crowd might stampede: with this many people jamming the streets that would be a human disaster. Still, he could not take the risk the guns or tanks would open fire on the inbound helicopter or the Osprey, both of which he wanted to land on the prison's roof.

Through the infrared viewer Jake could see the soldiers instinctively moving away from the tanks. He could see men getting out of the hatch, jumping to the ground, walking away.

On the street the crowd was also pushing back, crowding away from the old fortress.

Minutes passed and nothing happened. The packed rows of humanity on the street seemed to relax, to thin as the people instinctively sought their own space.

Jake heard the first bomb tone come on. An officer—Jake assumed he was an officer—climbed up on one of the tanks, waved his arms at his men.

The bomb tone ceased: the weapon was in the air.

Now the officer standing on the tank put his hands on his hips—Rita had the Osprey down to a thousand feet, only a mile from the building, set up to begin her transition to helicopter flight, so the activity in the prison courtyard was as clear to Jake as if he had been watching it on television.

"Angel One, this is Battlestar One. Come on in."

"Roger that, Battlestar."

The Cuban officer was still standing on the tank when it disappeared in a flash as the bomb hit it.

When the cloud of smoke and debris cleared, no one was moving within a hundred feet of the blasted tank, of which only tiny pieces remained. The bomb must have penetrated the armor in front of or behind the turret, Jake thought.

Now the second bomb tone ended. Cuban troops were running out of the prison complex through the main gate, which Jake belatedly realized was open. The men were dropping their weapons, throwing away their helmets and running as fast as their legs could carry them.

The five-hundred-pound bomb from Night Owl Four Four exploded in the gate and the running men disappeared in a flash.

"Put it on the roof," Jake Grafton told Rita Moravia.

"Okay, I got this guy," Sailor Karnow told Stiff Hardwick. "He's bogey one."

The symbol was right there in front of Stiff on the heads-up display.

"About thirty miles or so," Sailor said matter-of-factly. She would sound bored if they were giving her an Academy Award. That was another thing about her Stiff didn't like. Well, the truth was, he hated her guts, but he knew better than to say so in the new modern politically correct gender-neutral navy to which they both belonged. A few off-the-cuff remarks like that to the boys could torpedo a promising career.

"Lock the son of a bitch up," Stiff told his RIO.

"You can't shoot this dude," Sailor said, still bored as hell. "There are four stealth fighters flapping around down there, three Ospreys and a helicopter, or did you sleep through the brief? You can't shoot without the blessing of Battlestar Strike, which you ain't likely to get."

Twenty-five miles now. Stiff had the F-14 coming down like a lawyer on his way to hell, showing Mach 1.7 on the meter. He was fast crawling up this MiG's ass.

"Don't just sit there with your thumb up your heinie, honey. Get on the goddamn horn."

"Battlestar Strike," Sailor drawled on the radio. "This is Showtime One Oh Two. We got us a situation developing out here."

Rita didn't use her landing light until the last possible moment, snapping it on just in time to judge the final few seconds of her approach. As it was, only one of the demoralized snipers on the roof took a shot at the plane, a wild, unaimed shot that punched a hole in the fuselage near the port gear and spent itself against a structural member. Then the marines charging out of the back of the beast fired a shot over his head and the sniper threw down his rifle. The other snipers had already done so.

In seconds the chopper from *United States* came out of the darkness and set down alongside the V-22. Tommy Carmellini and Ocho Sedano came scrambling out.

All this was new to Ocho. With wide eyes he looked at the Osprey, at the marines, at the skyline of Havana, at the bonfires in the street and the tens of thousands of people.

Toad Tarkington appeared at Jake's elbow. "I think I know how to get off this roof," Toad said.

"Lead on," Jake told him.

"Uh, Showtime One Oh Two, negative on the permission to shoot. That's negatory, weapons red, over."

"Strike, goddamn it," Stiff Hardwick roared, "We're sitting right on the tail of a goddamn MiG on his way to Havana to kill some of our people. I got the son of a bitch boresighted."

"Showtime, there are too many friendlies over Havana. Weapons red, weapons red, over."

"How about I pop this guy with my gun? Request weapons free for a gunshot. Over."

"Wait."

Stiff was off the power, idling along at about 400 knots, five miles behind the bogey. Of course, the bogey didn't know he was there. The Cuban MiG-29s had very primitive electronic detection equipment, which consisted of a light and an auditory signal in the pilot's ear. These devices told Carlos Corrado he was being looked at by an American fighter radar but failed to tell him where or how close the thing was, the two pieces of information that he needed the most.

As he closed on Havana and listened to the tone and watched the light, which didn't even flicker, Carlos Corrado pondered on the irony of knowing American fighters were out there somewhere and not being able to do anything about it. If he turned on his radar, he would beacon to the Americans, who would then come at him like moths to a flame. His only chance was to keep the radar off.

If the Americans launched a weapon at him, he had a few flares he could punch off, of course, and some chaff. It was not much, but it might be enough. If it wasn't, well, he had had a good life.

Carlos began looking right and left as he crossed the suburbs of the city. Amid all the lights he spotted some fires, and the center of the city was dark, without power, but all in all, Havana looked pretty normal. Amazing, that!

"Battlestar Strike, this is Showtime. Still waiting on that permission. This MiG is posing right here in front of me, begging for it. Do I zap it or what?"

"We are still checking with the air force," Battlestar told Stiff, "trying to find out exactly where everyone is. Don't want any accidents out there, do we?"

Stiff keyed the intercom. "Assholes," he roared at Sailor Karnow. "They are all stupid fucking assholes."

"I hear that," said Sailor, sighing. "I've known it for years. I should have joined the WNBA."

Toad Tarkington led the procession along the dark corridor of La Cabana prison. Apparently the power had not yet been restored after the high-voltage towers fell. Everyone following Toad had a flashlight.

The corridors were alive with echoing sound, shouts, curses, doors clanging, screams, shots.

"Hurry," Grafton shouted, and ran toward the shouts.

As he suspected, the mob was in the building. As he and Toad rounded a corner, their flashlights fell on a solid wall of humanity dragging two uniformed officers. Carmellini shouted. The human wall halted.

"This is Ocho Sedano," Carmellini shouted, "Hector's brother. He is here to free Hector."

The man dragging a fat officer by the collar of his uniform demanded, "Who are you?" Obviously drunk, this man had the commandante's pistol in his hand, but he didn't raise it or point it. The flashlights were partially blinding him, but he could still see the front end of Toad's M-16.

"We are here at El Ocho's request." Carmellini proclaimed loudly. "He has asked for our help to free his brother Hector."

The mob moved forward, probably in response to a surging push from the people behind.

"Give us the officers," Jake said to Carmellini, "and we will bring Hector from his cell." Carmellini shouted the message in Spanish.

The members of the mob didn't like it, but they were facing six rifles in a narrow stone corridor. The people at the head of the mob released the officers and turned to shout at those behind them.

The marines grabbed the two officers and pushed them away along the corridor.

Carmellini talked earnestly to the officers. "They will lead us there," he told Jake. "Colonel Santana arrived an hour ago. He was with the commandante until just a few minutes ago."

"Hurry," Jake Grafton urged. "The mob is out of control." He had drawn the .357 Magnum he wore in a holster around his waist and now had it in his right hand.

"Showtime One Oh Two, Strike, the air force is having trouble confirming the location of all their machines."

"Strike, this guy is hanging it out, begging for it, trolling right over the damn city looking for some white hats to zap. Are you gonna cry at the funeral after he kills some of our people?"

This comment was of course grossly out of line: Stiff Hardwick was a mere lieutenant—an O-3—and the decisions in Strike were being made by an officer with the rank of commander—O-5—or even captain—O-6. He was going to be in big trouble when he got back to the ship, but he didn't care. The primary object of war was to kill the enemy, and by God, the son of a bitch was right there. He'd deal with the peckerheads later.

Another minute passed. They were over the heart of Havana now. The oily black slash of Havana Harbor was quite prominent, as were the dozens of fires that now surrounded the walls of the old La Cabana fortress.

"This guy is starting a turn," Sailor told Stiff, referring of course to the bogey.

Carlos Corrado should have been searching the night sky over Havana for the planes he knew were here, but he wasn't. He was only human. He was looking at the red warning light and listening to the buzz that told him that a hostile fighter's radar was illuminating his aircraft.

The light and tone had been on for five minutes now. The miracle was that Carlos Corrado was still alive. Five minutes in front of an aggressive American fighter pilot was about six lifetimes . . . and *still* the American hadn't pulled the trigger!

Carlos didn't know why, but he suspected the reason had something to do with the fact they were tooling over the rooftops of Havana.

Ocho Sedano and the Americans ran through the corridors of La Cabana Prison until they came to a massive steel gate. It was closed but unlocked; they used the commandante's keys to lock it behind them. Then they entered a cellblock full of men screaming to be freed. Hundreds of arms reached through the bars, trying to reach the Americans.

The guards led them to Hector, who was in a cell in a corridor off the main cellblock. "They have no key to the cell," Carmellini told Jake.

"Use C-4. Blow it," the admiral said.

Hector reached through the bars and got his hands on Ocho. They hugged while Jake Grafton held the flashlight and Tommy Carmellini set the explosive.

"Have you seen Santana?" Carmellini asked Hector.

"Yes. He was here."

"Where is he now?"

"He heard you coming and ran."

When the plastic explosive blew the lock apart on Hector's cell, Ocho jerked the door open and hugged him fiercely. "I apologize, Hector," he said. "Please forgive me."

Jake Grafton dragged them apart. "There is no time," he shouted, and pushed them toward the corridor.

The sounds of the mob tearing at the steel bars that barred the way into the cell block could be heard above the shouts of the men in the cells.

Toad led his party the other way. Another door, precious seconds wasted while the officers fumbled for a key, then they were through and going up a stairway. More stairs, then along a long, dark corridor lit only by flashlights.

As they rounded a turn someone ahead fired a shot at them. The bullet spanged off a wall, and miraculously failed to connect with human flesh.

Suddenly sure, Tommy Carmellini told Jake, "It's Santana. You go on. I'll get the bastard."

"We don't have time for personal vendettas," Jake Grafton snapped.

"I'm a civilian, Grafton. I can take care of myself. Go on!"

Jake led his party onward.

When they came out onto the roof the Osprey's position lights and flashing anticollision light revealed a crowd of at least three hundred people. They completely surrounded the Osprey and helo and the marines with rifles who held them off. The pilots must have shut down the engines due to the large number of people nearby. Lieutenant Colonel Eckhardt walked back and forth behind the marines, an imposing martial figure if ever there was one. Fortunately no one in the crowd seemed to be armed.

Jake and Toad forced their way through the crowd.

It was Ocho who stepped in front of the crowd and began to speak. "This is my brother Hector, the next president of Cuba."

The crowd cheered lustily.

"I am El Ocho. I wish to know if you love Cuba?"

"*Sí!*" they roared.

"Do you believe in Cuba?"

"*Sí!*"

"Will you fight for Cuba?"

"*Sí!*"

"Will you follow me and put Hector Sedano in the presidential palace?"

"*Sí! Sí! Sí!*" The crowd breathed the word over and over and swarmed around Ocho.

"Come," said Jake Grafton, and pulled Hector toward the Osprey.

CHAPTER TWENTY-FOUR

As Jake Grafton and the others climbed the stairs toward the roof of La Cabana Prison, Tommy Carmellini doused his flashlight and held it in his left hand. He stood in the darkness waiting for his eyes to adjust to the dim light.

He had a pistol that the marines aboard ship had given him, a 9-mm, that felt cold and comforting in his grip. He closed his eyes, listened to the cheers and shouts from the roof, waited until he heard the chopper and Osprey get airborne.

Finally the corridors of the old fortress grew quiet.

Santana was in here someplace.

Jake Grafton had his thing and he was hard at it. William Henry Chance had his thing, trying to control biological and chemical weapons in Third World countries, and he had died doing it. Tommy Carmellini's thing was cracking safes. Sure, he was doing it for the CIA now instead of stealing diamonds from rich matrons, but somehow that wasn't enough. There comes a time in a man's life when he begins to tally up the score. When Carmellini realized Grafton wasn't going to take the time to step on the cockroach Santana, he knew he had to.

He stepped forward now, walking the way Hector had indicated that Santana had gone.

Taking his time in the near-total darkness—there was just enough light to see the outline of the corridor—walking, listening, walking, listening again, Tommy Carmellini moved to the end of the corridor and stopped.

He could hear metal on metal, as if someone was trying to open a lock. The sound came from the corridor on the right.

Tommy Carmellini bent as low as he could get, eased his head around the corner.

Yes, the sound was clearer now.

Ever so slowly he edged around the corner, crossed the corridor to the other side, began moving forward into the blackness, toward the sound.

The noise stopped.

Carmellini froze. Closed his eyes to concentrate on the sound.

The pistol was heavy in his hand.

The sound began again.

Forward, ever so stealthily, moving like a glacier, just flowing slowly, silently, effortlessly. . . .

The man was just ahead. Working on a lock. Probably on one of those steel gates.

Again the sound stopped.

Carmellini froze, not trusting himself to breathe.

The other man was here, he could feel him. But where?

Time seemed to stop. Tommy Carmellini held his breath, stood crouched but frozen, knowing that the slightest sound would give away his position.

Santana was . . .

Suddenly Carmellini knew. He was right . . .

There! He pointed the pistol and pulled the trigger.

The muzzle flash strobed the darkness, and revealed Santana swinging the butt of his rifle, swinging it at Carmellini's head.

He tried to duck but the rifle struck his shoulder and sent him sprawling. He held on to the pistol, triggered two more shots, which came like giant thunderclaps, deafening him with their roar.

The flashlight was gone, lost when he fell. His left shoulder was on fire where the rifle butt struck him, his arm numb. He could hear Santana running, shuffling along, the sound fading.

He felt for the flashlight with his right hand, couldn't find it, paused and listened and searched some more. There! He picked it up without releasing the pistol. Now he put the pistol between his legs, tried to work the flashlight with his right hand. It was broken. He set it on the floor out of the way.

He listened, heard the faintest of sounds, then nothing.

Tommy Carmellini slowly got to his feet and began moving back the way he had come, after Santana.

"Showtime One Oh Two, Battlestar Strike. You are cleared to engage the bogey with a gun. Weapons free gun only, acknowledge."

"Weapons free gun only, aye," sung out Stiff Hardwick, and jammed his throttles forward to the mechanical stop. The engines wound up quickly; Stiff eased the throttles to the left, stroked the afterburners. The big fighter leaped forward and began closing the five-mile gap between the two planes.

Carlos Corrado glanced over his left shoulder, for the hundreth time, expecting to see nothing, but this time he saw the plume of flame that was Hardwick's burners. *The Yanqui must be right behind me.*

Enough!

He slammed the throttles to the hilt, dropped the left wing and pulled right up to six Gs. The MiG-29 then showed why it was one of the most maneuverable fighters in the world—it turned on a dime.

As it did, Carlos Corrado fought the G and flipped his radar switch to the transmit position.

Leveling up after a 180-degree turn, the radar scope came alive . . . and there was the American—close. Too close! Jesus Christ!

Without time to even consider the problem, Carlos Corrado punched off an Aphid missile, which roared off the rail in a blaze of fire straight for the F-14.

Sailor Karnow saw the bogey wind into a left turn, and called it to Stiff, who instinctively lowered his right wing to stay in the MiG's rear quadrant.

What Stiff wasn't prepared for was the unbelievable quickness with which the MiG-29 whipped around and pumped off a missile.

The sight of the fiery exhaust of the Aphid missile coming at him from eleven o'clock and the wailing of the ECM in his ears, telling him that he was being painted by a MiG-29 pulse-doppler radar, reached Stiff

Hardwick's brain at the very same instant. Before Stiff could react in any way, the missile shot over his canopy inches above his head. Fortunately for Stiff and Sailor and their progeny yet unborn, the Aphid had not flown far enough to arm, so the missile passed harmlessly.

"*Holy shit!*" Sailor shouted into her oxygen mask.

Stiff Hardwick hadn't spent the last four years flying fighters for nothing—his instincts were finely honed too. As the Aphid went over his head, he jerked the nose of his fighter toward the closing MiG, visible only as a bogey symbol on the HUD, and pulled the trigger on the stick. The 20-mm M-61 six-barreled cannon in the nose lit up like a searchlight as a river of fire streaked into the darkness.

Carlos Corrado saw the finger of God reaching for him and slammed his stick back, then sideways. The MiG's nose came up steeply and the right wing dropped in a violent whifferdill that carried it up and out of the way of the fiery stream of cannon shells.

Completing the roll, Carlos Corrado pushed the nose of his MiG downward, toward the city, and let the plane accelerate without afterburners, the light of which would beacon to the American. Or Americans, if there were more than one, which was probable.

Carlos pulled out just above the rooftops and thundered across the city. He had lost track of the enemy's location because he could not see him visually or with his radar. He desperately needed his GCI site just now to call the enemy's position, but of course the GCI people had been knocked off the air and were either dead or drunk.

Still, the contest appealed to his sporting instincts. He decided to try for one in-parameters missile shot before he called it a night and went looking for a bar.

His radar was still on, still looking at nothing.

Without further ado, Carlos pulled the stick back and let the MiG's nose climb. Up past the vertical, G on hard, the MiG used its fabulous turning rate to fly half of a very tight loop. Upside down with its nose on the horizon, Carlos slammed the stick sideways and rolled upright. The F-14 was out to his left, turning toward him. Corrado flipped his switches to select an infrared missile, turned toward the American until he got a tone in his headset, and squeezed it off.

Then he killed his radar and turned hard ninety degrees right to exit the fight.

"Oh, no," Stiff Hardwick swore as he saw the missile coming at him from ten o'clock.

He lit his afterburners and dropped the right wing slightly and willed the Tomcat to accelerate, trying to force the missile into an overshoot, while he punched off chaff and flares with a button on his right throttle.

The missile tried to make the turn but couldn't. Perhaps the IR seeker in the nose locked onto a flare. In any event, as it flew past the tail of the Tomcat its proximity fuse caused the warhead to detonate, spraying shrapnel into empty air.

The MiG-29 was gone. It had disappeared.

"You know, dickwick," Sailor Karnow told her pilot, "I think God is really trying to tell us something."

Carlos Corrado knew that he had had more than his share of luck this night. Although he was flying a tremendously maneuverable airplane, the electronic detection and countermeasures systems were generations behind the F-14 that had followed him around. Why the F-14 had not shot him down he couldn't guess, but he was wise enough to know that luck sorely tried is bound to turn.

He decided to put his MiG on the ground while it was still in one piece. Fortunately there was an airport nearby, Havana's José Martí International, right over there in the middle of that vast dark area. Since there was a war on, someone had turned off the runway lights.

Corrado pulled off the power, let the fighter slow to gear speed, then snapped the landing gear down. Flaps out, retrim, and swing out for an approach to where the runway ought to be. On final he turned on his landing light and searched the darkness below.

There! Concrete.

He squeaked the MiG on and got on the brakes.

He left the landing light on to taxi.

"Showtime One Oh Two, the MiG is landing at José Martí." That was the air force controller in the Sentry AWACS plane.

Stiff Hardwick was climbing through five thousand feet at full power when he heard that transmission. Fortunately he had committed a map of the Havana area to memory, so he knew precisely where José Martí International lay. He cut the power and lowered the nose.

"What in hell do you think you're doing, Stiff?" Sailor demanded.
"Shut up."

"We barely got enough fuel to make the tanker as it is, pea brain. You go swanning around down here for a few more minutes begging that Cuban to give you the shaft and we'll be swimming home."

"I'm gonna get that Cuban son of a bitch. Gonna strafe him on the ground. Gonna kill that bastard deader than last week's beer."

Sailor Karnow knew the pilot was serious. Here was a frustrated man if ever she had met one. As the plane dove for the black hole that was José Martí International, she tried to reason with Stiff:

"You can't shoot the guy on the ground at a civilian airport. There's no lights down there, you might kill a bunch of civilians!"

"There he is! I can see the fucking guy taxiing—he's still got his landing light on! *There he is!*"

Sailor Karnow was losing her patience. "*You pull that trigger, Jake Grafton will cut your balls off, you silly son of a bitch!*"

Stiff Hardwick knew the jig was up. Sailor was right—he hated women who were always right. He reached up and safetied the master arm switch. And kept the Tomcat coming down.

Edged the throttles forward as he dropped lower and lower, boresighting that barely moving plane down there with the single landing light shining forward. The needle on the airspeed indicator crept past Mach 1.

The radio altimeter deedled, he kept going lower....

"Don't fly into the ground, you idiot!" Sailor pleaded from the rear cockpit.

The fear in her voice probably saved both their lives. Stiff eased back on the stick just a smidgen, an almost microscopic amount, so the F-14 rose another ten feet above the ground as it roared over Carlos Corrado's taxiing MiG-29 like a giant supersonic missile. The American fighter passed a mere four feet over the MiG's tail; the shock wave shattered the MiG's canopy.

Then Stiff pulled the stick back in his lap and lit the burners and went rocketing upward like a bat out of hell.

"Better get on the horn and get us a tanker, baby, or you're gonna be my date in a life raft tonight."

Sailor had the last word. "Honest to God, dickwick, you oughta think about taking up another line of work."

Tommy Carmellini wondered if he had managed to put a bullet into Santana. That was a lot to hope for, but still . . . three shots, and the man no more than five, six feet away?

With luck.

A man needs luck as he goes through life. Life is timing, and timing is experience plus luck.

Carmellini wondered just how much experience sneaking along dark corridors Santana had had through the years. He hadn't impressed Carmellini as the sneaking type. One never knew, though.

He found himself moving slower and slower, listening with his eyes closed, concentrating. He could hear . . .

Breathing. Coming from somewhere ahead. Definitely breathing.

Jake Grafton had Rita circle out over the harbor while he talked to other airplanes he had inbound. After a few minutes, he told her to fly toward the university.

Looking through the infrared viewer, he could see that the streets around the university were deserted. Not a car or truck moving, none parked, no people.

Alejo Vargas was down there, all right.

Jake got out of the copilot's seat and went aft to talk to Hector Sedano, who was sitting beside Lieutenant Colonel Eckhardt. Jake pulled one of the Spanish-speaking marines along to translate.

"Do you know of the biological-warfare laboratory in the science building of the university?"

No, Hector didn't. Jake took a minute to explain.

"My government has sent me to destroy the polio viruses that are in that lab, and the equipment that was used to grow them. Do you have any objection to me doing that?"

Hector did not, as long as innocent lives were not lost unnecessarily.

Talking loudly over the aircraft's high internal noise, Jake continued while the young marine, a buck sergeant, translated: "I promise you, we will proceed with all due care. The stakes are very high, those viruses must be destroyed. If you will join me in this humanitarian effort representing the new Cuban government, I believe the job can be done with a minimum loss of life."

"Tell me of this laboratory," Hector Sedano demanded. "What you know of it, and how it came to be."

The feeling was coming back in Tommy Carmellini's left arm. It hurt like hell now, like someone had tried to carve on his shoulder with a dull knife.

Ignore the arm. Listen!

He froze. He hadn't realized it, but there were cells on both sides of the corridor, cells with open doors.

Santana must be in one of them. Which one?

. A sound like a sigh.

He heard it! From the left, maybe ten feet.

Frozen like a chunk of solid ice, Carmellini didn't move. He continued to breathe, but very shallowly, taking all the time in the world.

Minutes passed. How many he couldn't say.

He could hear the murmur of the mob somewhere below. No doubt they had turned all the prisoners loose.

The other man was being extremely quiet. Extraordinarily so.

Carmellini finally began moving, reluctantly, ever so slowly, like the shadow of the sun as it marches across a stone floor. And he made about the same amount of noise.

He was in the cell, feeling his way . . . when his left foot touched something that shouldn't be there.

Like a cat he reacted, the pistol booming faster than thought.

In the muzzle flash he saw that Santana lay stretched on his back on the floor, his eyes open to the ceiling.

The bastard was dead.

From the cockpit Jake Grafton could see the crowds below on the streets. Rita had the Osprey flying at 2,000 feet, and Jake could see the swarms of people with his naked eye, without using the infrared viewer, though he used it occasionally to check on the progress of the crowd.

Rita swung the Osprey over the university district, and he picked out the science building.

He watched the mass of humanity flow into the district, surge along toward the science building.

He used the viewer, steadied it carefully and cranked up the magnification. Yes, the knot of humanity at the front of the crowd, that had to be around Ocho. El Ocho, as the Cubans called him.

The boy was fearless. This afternoon when Jake explained to Ocho that there was a strong probability that the soldiers would refuse to fire on the civilians, might even disobey their officers if ordered to fire, Ocho merely nodded.

Perhaps the ordeal in the ocean had toughened Ocho, or perhaps he had always been impervious to fear. That emotion affected people in an extraordinary variety of ways, Jake knew.

Looking through the viewer it was difficult to be sure, but apparently soldiers were joining the crowd with Ocho as he walked along.

He wanted to let Hector accompany Ocho, but his better judgment told him no. A single sniper, one frightened soldier, and the last best hope of Cuba might be dead in the street. With the viruses still in that lab, that was a risk Jake Grafton was not yet prepared to take.

As he watched, he wished he were with Ocho. That walk must be sublime, he thought.

Ocho Sedano knew a great many people because he had spent years accompanying his brother to speeches, sitting in planning sessions, helped him dig holes to hide weapons.

Many more people, however, knew Ocho. Every Cuban between eight and eighty knew of the star pitcher who threw the sizzling fastballs and hit home runs when his turn came to bat. Many people recognized him, shouted to him as he walked along, then decided to shake his hand and join the throng behind him.

As the human river turned the corner onto the avenue that led to the university, a knot of soldiers left the shelter of a doorway and came toward Ocho. He didn't stop, kept striding along the center of the street.

"Halt!" the senior officer shouted. He was a major. "You are entering a military area! You can go no farther!"

Ocho didn't even slow his pace. The soldiers had to join the crowd to keep from being trampled.

"You! Stop these people! This is a secure area, by order of Alejo Vargas."

"We will not stop." Ocho laughed. "Do you think you can stop the sun from rising?"

The soldiers hurried along, trying to talk to Ocho, who refused to slow his pace.

"You are El Ocho?" one of the younger soldiers asked.

"The days of Vargas are over, my friend," Ocho explained. "Give away your gun and come along with us."

The sheer numbers and weight of the people pushing along frightened the major, who had a pistol in his hand. Even as his subordinates handed their weapons to the nearest people in civilian clothes, he placed himself in front of Ocho, who didn't stop walking.

"I order you to stop, Sedano!" he shouted, and pointed the pistol at Ocho's head.

"You would make me a martyr, would you?" Ocho asked the major, who was trying to match Ocho's stride. "Look around you, man. No one can stop them."

The major fired the pistol into the air. His face was drawn and pale, almost bloodless. "Stop or I shoot you down, as God is my witness."

"*Mi amigo*," said Ocho Sedano, "For days at sea I was ready to die; all the fear drained from me. There is none in my heart now. My death will not stop these people: nothing can stop the turning of the earth. Still, if you feel you must kill me, make your peace with God and pull the trigger."

Then he smiled.

El Ocho was a madman, the major realized. Or a saint. The major wiped at the perspiration on his forehead, and handed Ocho the pistol.

Ocho passed the weapon on. He put his arm around the major's shoulders. "Come," he said. "We will walk to the promised land together."

Like a wall of water rushing along a dry arroyo, the human river flowed along the avenue toward the university as airplanes droned through the darkness overhead.

In the foyer of the science building, Alejo Vargas heard the airplanes. He looked at the politicians and young soldiers who waited silently behind him, blocking the doors to the stairs and the elevator, and he looked at his aides, who were nervously looking out windows, trying not to fidget.

Where was Santana?

The man should be here: he was Alejo Vargas's one loyal friend on this earth.

Vargas paced back and forth, stood in the doorway and listened to the airplanes, wondered if the troops he had hidden in the surrounding buildings were loyal, would still fight. Over two thousand heavily armed men were waiting for the Americans. This time the Yanquis would not escape: this time there would be prisoners to parade before the cameras, vanquished foes to kneel at his feet as Cuba cheered. This time . . .

A car rocketed up to the front of the building and a man leaped out, a uniformed colonel with the Department of State Security. He ran up the stairs, came running through the door, saw Vargas and ran toward him.

"The television," he said breathlessly. "On the television, they are showing a tape of Fidel."

"Yes?" said Vargas, his brows knitting.

"Fidel made the tape before he died. He wants Hector Sedano to be the president after him."

"What?" Vargas didn't believe a word of it.

"They run the tape, which takes about six minutes, then run it again, over and over and over."

"That's impossible," Vargas said, turning toward the politicians, who had moved closer. "Fidel made no such tape before he died. He wanted to make a tape naming me as his successor, but his illness prevented it."

"They are showing a tape on television," the colonel insisted. "Fidel says the nation must change, and Hector Sedano is the man to lead that change."

"It's a trick!" Vargas roared. "The Yanqui CIA is playing a trick on us." Every face was openly skeptical.

"Fidel is dead! Don't you people understand that?"

A rising symphony of babbling voices and helicopter noises came through the open door.

"What is happening?" Vargas demanded, turning in that direction. "Where are the soldiers?"

He saw heads climbing the stairs, many heads, then a mob of people in civilian clothes and army uniforms poured through the doorway, forcing their way in. The room filled rapidly.

People in the doorway stood aside for two men who walked through together, one a tall, rangy young man and the other of medium height, wearing a one-piece faded prison jumpsuit.

They stopped in front of Vargas.

Hector's voice was plainly audible to every person in the room when he said, "Alejo Vargas, I arrest you in the name of the Cuban people for the murder of Raúl Castro."

Vargas's hand darted inside his jacket for a pistol, but before he could get it out a dozen hands reached for him, pulled him to the floor, and took the weapon from him.

CHAPTER TWENTY-FIVE

Maximo Sedano spent the night aboard his yacht in Havana Harbor. He heard the planes and the explosions of bombs falling around La Cabana Prison, but he didn't go ashore. He had worked until night fell hunting for the gold that he was sure lay on the floor of Havana Harbor.

He found a great deal of junk and trash, but no gold.

As the bombs were falling he drank some rum, idly studied the skyline, thought about gold.

Thirty-seven tons of gold. My God, what a man could do with a fortune like that! Cars, yachts, women, all the good things in life.

He was filthy from the muck and pollution of the harbor. The water tank on the boat was not large, so he sponged off as best he could and resolved to take a shower ashore at the first opportunity.

The next morning he began diving as soon as the sun came up. Boats came and went and Maximo worked steadily. He changed tanks once.

The work was maddening. The most probable location for the gold was the marina anchorage, where Fidel and Che must have spent the nights they were anchored. Here is where they must have dumped the gold overboard!

Yet it wasn't on the floor of the harbor. He thought mud and sediment might have covered the ingots, but even when he dug, he could find nothing.

He wasn't being systematic enough, he decided as he lay exhausted on the deck of his boat, his broken fingers aching like bad teeth.

He knew he couldn't go on today, so he took the dingy and motored ashore. He had his empty tanks along for the harbormaster to fill.

Tired, working one-handed, Maximo took several minutes to get the small boat tied up and the empty air tanks onto the dock. He picked them up and carried them toward the harbormaster's shack.

The man was sitting inside reading a newspaper.

"Can you fill these?" Maximo asked.

The harbormaster looked up to see who was asking, then brightened. "Señor Sedano, of course. I am so delighted to hear about your brother. Congratulations."

"What?"

The look of surprise on his face must have shocked the harbormaster, who held out the newspaper. "Surely you know," he said. "Your brother Hector is the new president of Cuba."

Maximo took the paper, sank down into the only empty chair, stared at the headlines.

"What a night!" said the harbormaster, beaming like the sun. "History in the making. Hector and El Ocho, what a team!"

"Amazing."

"And look! The newspaper published a letter from your sister-in-law, Mercedes. Forty years ago Fidel hid the peso gold under the floor of the presidential palace. It's still there, every ounce of it. *Sixty tons of gold* the nation owns, eh! Isn't that amazing?"

The gray U.S. Navy ammo ship anchored in the bay and put a launch into the water. The coxswain brought the small boat around to a gangway. In a few minutes the trill of a bosun's pipe could be heard, then a series of bells over the ship's loudspeaker.

A group of officers and sailors in white uniforms came down the gangway and climbed aboard the launch.

The town of Antilla, Cuba, lay baking in the sun. The waterfront was lined with fishing craft. The only ships at the pier were two small coasters, about a thousand tons each. The launch maneuvered against the pier and Rear Admiral Jake Grafton stepped ashore. Gil Pascal and Toad Tarkington followed him onto the pier.

"That's the warehouse over there," Toad said, and pointed.

Jake just nodded. He waited as a knot of Cubans came walking out on the pier toward him.

"Where's the translator?"

"Right here, sir," said an enlisted man, who stepped forward beside Jake. He too was togged out in his best white uniform.

After the usual diplomatic greetings, Jake, Captain Pascal, and the translator went with the Cubans toward the warehouse, leaving Toad alone on the pier.

Tarkington strolled along, looking here and there, his arms folded behind his back.

He was standing near the head of the pier when he heard a noise. He stepped to the edge, leaned over.

A man in a black diving suit covered with muck and slime was dragging his gear out from under the pier into the sun.

"I was wondering where you guys were," Toad said conversationally.

"Some days you're the pigeon, some days you're the statue," the navy SEAL said. "Three days we've been living under here like harbor rats, watching that warehouse. We searched it the first night, Commander— the warheads were in there. And they're still there; the Cubans haven't taken anything out."

"Where's your partner in crime?"

"Over on the other side of those coasters. He'll be along in a bit. Think we could get a ride out to the ship? I've been dreaming of a hot shower, a hot meal, and a clean bunk."

"I think that can be arranged." Toad reached down, helped lift the diving gear onto the pier.

When the SEAL was standing on the pier beside him, dripping onto the splintered boards, Toad said, "How'd you like your Cuban vacation?"

"I want better accommodations for my next visit."

As the president of the United States feared, the aftermath of the second Cuban missile crisis, as the press called it, was a political disaster in Washington, with howls of outrage from the press and demands from frightened senators and congressmen for investigations and the resignations of everyone in the executive branch.

The president watched General Tater Totten retire from a distance, didn't go to the small Pentagon ceremony, let the White House spinmeisters whisper that Totten was somehow partially responsible for the journey to the brink of the abyss. Sensing that he couldn't win a whisper war, Totten kept his mouth shut and departed with dignity.

Amid the impassioned breast-beating and public denunciations, the director of the CIA decided that he too had had enough of Washington. He had a final conversation with the president in the Oval Office after he submitted his resignation but before the White House announced his departure.

"Sorry to see you go," the president muttered politely, not meaning a word of it. The director nodded knowingly.

"Don't know if this congressional investigation can be derailed or not," the president said, not willing to look the director in the eye. "A lot of what happened will be classified forever, so I don't really see what they stand to gain by stirring through the ashes."

"They'll investigate anyway," the director predicted gloomily. "That's what I want to talk to you about. At one of those meetings during the crisis you asked for the name of our top man in Cuba, and I wrote it down for you. I don't know if you ever looked at that name, but it would be absolute disaster if that person's name were revealed to a congressional investigator."

"After you wrote it down, I looked at the name," the president said, speaking slowly. "Not at the meeting, but later. Didn't expect to recognize it, but then was amazed that the last name was the same as the priest who was thrown in prison."

"Mercedes Sedano was Castro's mistress and an intelligence treasure. She told us of drug deals, Vargas's blackmail files, Fidel's secret bank accounts. . . . When she wanted the tape made of Fidel naming Hector as his successor, there wasn't time to go through the usual drops and cutouts, so she went directly to the American Interest Section of the Swiss embassy. None of this must come out, Mr. President. If the Cubans find out she was whispering to us, Hector Sedano's government might fall. And she might lose her life."

"That sheet of paper no longer exists," the president said. "I suggest you destroy the files."

A few minutes later as the director was preparing to leave, the president said, "I have never understood spies. Why did that woman betray her country?"

The director blinked like an owl. "I don't know that she did," he replied, and walked out of the Oval Office for the last time.

On a Wednesday morning in November Tommy Carmellini parked his car in a large parking garage in downtown Denver and got his backpack from the trunk.

The weather was gorgeous, a sunny, mild day with air so clear the peaks of the Rockies looked close enough to touch. Autumn leaves lay packed in gutters and windrows waiting for tomorrow's wind to blow them around.

Carmellini walked two blocks to the Sixteenth Street mall. While he was waiting for a free shuttle bus he bought a copy of the *Denver Post* from a vending machine. Like so many of the young people, he was dressed in tennis shoes, faded jeans, and a threadbare pullover sweater. An unzipped windbreaker was tied around his waist. A backpack hung over one shoulder. The shuttle bus stopped at the end of every block to let people on and off. Hanging from a strap, Carmellini kept his backpack pressed against the rear window of the bus.

At the western end of the mall Carmellini let himself be swept along with the flow of people into the regional bus depot. He found a bus to Boulder, climbed aboard, and dropped the fare into the change box, then eased into a window seat five rows behind the driver. He kept his backpack on his lap.

The bus filled quickly. In minutes the driver closed the door and pulled out of the station.

Tommy Carmellini opened the newspaper and examined the front page. All U.S. sanctions against travel and commerce with Cuba were lifted, and the U.S. was opening an embassy in Havana. There was a photo of the president of the United States shaking hands with Hector Sedano at a news conference in Washington.

Tommy flipped through the paper. On page four he found a short item reporting a Florida grand jury indictment of El Gato, a Cuban exile living in Miami, charging him with selling unnamed equipment to the Cuban government in violation of the laws existing at the time. According to the newspaper, El Gato was the only person indicted.

Carmellini folded the paper and tucked it in the seat pocket in front of him.

Cuba was long ago and far away. Of course he still read the news and classified summaries, and heard people talking about Cuba and the people he met there. Microsoft and Intel were building big factories in

Havana, and Phillip Morris was buying one of the oldest cigar companies for beaucoup bucks. Rear Admiral Jake Grafton was now an assistant to some bigwig in the Pentagon, Commander Toad Tarkington went with him as an aide, and Toad's wife, the newly promoted Commander Rita Moravia, was the executive officer of a fighter squadron. Hector Sedano was doing an enviable job running Cuba, and some fighter pilot nobody ever heard of named Carlos Corrado had been promoted to general and put in charge of the Cuban Air Force.

Life goes on.

Most of the seats on the bus to Boulder were occupied. The sun coming through the windows and the motion of the bus were very pleasant, and many people dozed. The seat beside Carmellini was empty, so he relaxed his grip on the backpack and closed his eyes.

He was awake when the bus crossed Davidson Mesa into Boulder, roaring down the turnpike at seventy-five. He marveled at the upthrust granite slabs of the Flatirons which formed a spectacular backdrop behind the town.

As the bus cruised by the university on its way downtown, Tommy Carmellini walked to the door by the driver and waited. He got off at the next stop and stood looking at the red stone buildings of the university as the bus accelerated away in a cloud of diesel exhaust.

He had a map in his hip pocket, but he had studied it so much he didn't need to refer to it today. He strolled along, readily recognized the student union, and went from there.

The buildings were built all of a pattern, and with throngs of students coming and going, seemed to proclaim the glory of man's quest for knowledge in the bright November sunshine.

Carmellini glanced at his watch a time or two, then strolled along with his hands in his pockets. He found the building he wanted, opened the door, and went in. He took the stairs up to the top floor.

The hallway was lined with doors, lots of doors. He walked along, examining them. Each door bore the name of a faculty member, and most had a small card advertising the faculty member's office hours taped to the frosted glass.

He found the one he wanted, checked the hours. He was early, by ten minutes.

He knocked.

No answer.

Should he wait here in the hallway, or ... perhaps the library? The hallway was empty, but someone could come along at any moment.

Of course the professor might not come at all. Carmellini recalled his own college days: a student could spend weeks trying to waylay a tenured assistant professor in his office.

Well, if this didn't work he would try something else. Just what, he didn't know.

He decided on the library. He turned and started down the hall. He had taken three or four steps when the door opened behind him and a man in his sixties stuck his head out.

"Did you knock?"

"Yes."

"Got a watch? Can you read? Office hours don't start for ten minutes."

"Yes, but—"

"Oh, come on in."

Carmellini carefully closed the door behind him. The office was tiny, merely a cubbyhole with a desk and computer for the professor and one extra chair. Bookshelves filled with books lined both side walls. A shelf under the window behind the professor was piled willy-nilly with papers, manuscripts, files. The glass in the window didn't look as if it had been cleaned in years.

"If this is about your thesis, we're going to need more time than I have available today, so—"

"You're Professor Svenson, right?"

"That's right." The professor had seated himself behind his desk. He looked up into Carmellini's face and adjusted his glasses. His features twisted into a frown.

"Your face doesn't ... You're? ..."

"Your name is Olaf Svenson?"

"What do you want?"

Tommy Carmellini unzipped the backpack, pulled out the pistol with the silencer. He thumbed off the safety.

A look of terror crossed Svenson's face. "The government has no evidence," he said. "They decided not to prosecute. They—"

Tommy Carmellini shot Olaf Svenson in the center of the forehead from a distance of four feet. Svenson collapsed in his chair, his head tilted back.

Carmellini stepped around the desk, put the muzzle of the silencer against the side of the professor's head and pulled the trigger twice more. Two little pops.

He bent down, retrieved the spent cartridges that had been ejected from the pistol, pocketed them, then safetied the weapon and returned it to his backpack.

He had touched only the doorknob. He extracted a handkerchief from his pocket and wiped the interior knob carefully, then pulled the door open. He pushed the little button to lock the door, then stepped into the hallway and pulled it shut. One hard twist of the cotton handkerchief on the outside knob, then he was walking away down the hallway and no one could ever prove he had been there.

Surrounded by young adults strolling, laughing, and visiting with each other on the sun-dappled grass, Tommy Carmellini walked across the campus with his head down, the backpack over his shoulder, thinking of Cuba.

HONG
KONG

To John and Nancy Coonts

ACKNOWLEDGMENTS

Doing background research for a novel like this is always an adventure. Friend and neighbor Gilbert Pascal, engineer and physicist, read and offered valuable suggestions on draft chapters as the tale developed. Paul K. Chan read and commented upon the manuscript.

The plot of this tale was a collaboration between the author and his wife, Deborah, who delights in dreaming up literary tangles.

Revolutions and revolutionary wars are inevitable in class society, and without them it is impossible to accomplish any leap in social development and to overthrow the reactionary ruling classes and therefore impossible for the people to win political power. . . .

The seizure of power by armed force, the settlement of the issue by war, is the central task and the highest form of revolution. This Marxist-Leninist principle of revolution holds good universally, for China and for all other countries.

—Mao Tse Tung

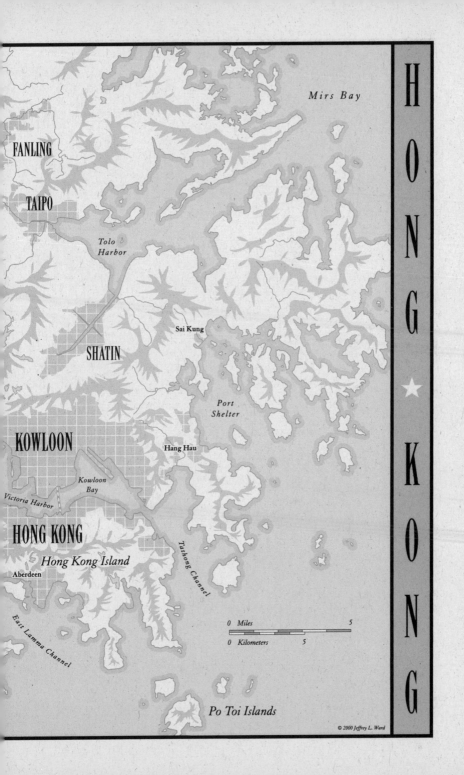

FANLING

TAIPO

Tolo Harbor

Sai Kung

SHATIN

Port Shelter

KOWLOON

Hang Hau

Kowloon Bay

Victoria Harbor

HONG KONG

Hong Kong Island

Aberdeen

East Lamma Channel

Tathong Channel

Mirs Bay

| 0 | Miles | | 5 |
| 0 | Kilometers | 5 | |

Po Toi Islands

© 2000 Jeffrey L. Ward

HONG ★ KONG

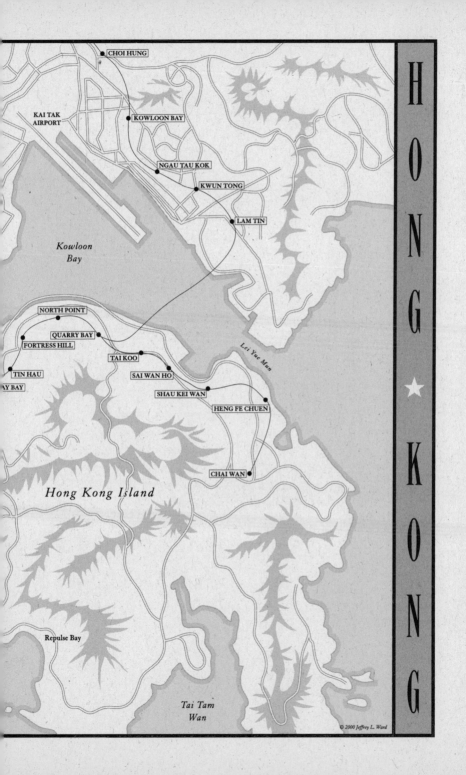

CHOI HUNG

KAI TAK
AIRPORT

KOWLOON BAY

NGAU TAU KOK

KWUN TONG

LAM TIN

Kowloon
Bay

NORTH POINT

QUARRY BAY

FORTRESS HILL

TAI KOO

TIN HAU

SAI WAN HO

AY BAY

SHAU KEI WAN

Lei Yue Mun

HENG FE CHUEN

Hong Kong Island

CHAI WAN

Repulse Bay

Tai Tam
Wan

© 2000 Jeffrey L. Ward

H O N G ★ K O N G

CHAPTER ONE

One tiny, red, liquid drop of blood was visible in the center of the small, neat hole in China Bob Chan's forehead an inch or so above his right eye. Chan's eyes were wide open. Tommy Carmellini thought his features registered a look of surprise.

Carmellini pulled off his right latex glove, bent down, and touched the cheek of the corpse—which was still warm.

Death must have been instantaneous, and not many minutes ago, Carmellini thought as he pulled the glove back onto his hand.

The diminutive corpse of China Bob Chan lay sprawled behind his Philippine mahogany desk in the library of his mansion on the south side of Hong Kong Island.

When Carmellini had eased the library door open a few seconds ago, he had seen the shod foot protruding from behind the desk. He scanned the room, then entered the library.

The side of the room opposite the door consisted of a series of large plate-glass windows accented with heavy burgundy drapes. Through the windows was a magnificent view of the harbor at Aberdeen. Beyond the harbor was the channel between Hong Kong Island and Lamma Island. A few lights could be seen on sparsely populated Lamma, and beyond that island, the total darkness of the South China Sea. Tonight the lights of the great city of Hong Kong, out of sight on the north side of the island's spine, illuminated a low deck of stratus clouds with a dull glow.

The band at the party on the floor below this one was playing an old American pop hit; the tune was recognizable even though the amplified lyrics were muffled by overstuffed furniture and shelves of books that reached from floor to ceiling.

Tommy Carmellini looked around, trying to find the spent cartridge. There, a gleam of brass near the leg of that chair. In the subdued light of the library he almost missed it.

He stepped over, bent down, looked.

7.65 millimeter.

That cartridge was designed for small, easy-to-conceal pocket pistols. Difficult to shoot accurately, they were serious weapons only at point-blank range.

Standing in front of the desk, he put his hands on his hips and carefully scanned the room. Somewhere in this room Harold Barnes hid a tape recorder eleven days ago when he installed the wiring for a satellite dish system.

Presumably Chan had ordered the system so that he could watch American television. Perhaps he was a fan of C-Span, which was broadcasting the congressional hearings concerning foreign—i.e., Chinese—donations to the American political parties in the last election; in the past ten days his name had certainly been mentioned numerous times in those hearings.

Alas, Barnes had left no record of where he hid the recorder. He had been shot in the head the night after he completed the installation.

Carmellini was certain Barnes would have used a recorder, not a remote transmitter, which would have been too easy to detect and find. One reason he was certain was that he had known Barnes, a quiet, careful, colorless technician who had gone through the CIA tradecraft course with Carmellini. Who would have suspected that Barnes would be the first of that class to die in the line of duty?

The mikes . . . Harold ostensibly spent four hours on the television satellite dish system, a system he should have been able to install in two. If he followed normal practice, he would have hardwired at least two tiny microphones, one for each track of the recorder.

The chandelier over the mahogany desk caught Tommy's eye. Ornate, with several dozen small bulbs, it would attract Harold Barnes like sugar attracts a fly.

Carmellini studied the chain that held the chandelier. There was a wire running down it . . . no, two wires—one black wire and the other smaller, carefully wound around the chain.

Barnes could have put a mike in the chandelier, another anywhere in the room—maybe the desk or over by the reading area—and hidden the recorder behind some books, perhaps on the top shelf. Surely there were tomes that didn't get removed from the shelves once a decade.

Carmellini stepped to the nearest bookcase, studied the spines of the books that filled the thing. Not a flake of dust.

A diligent maid would not be good.

So . . .

He pulled a chair over under the chandelier, then stood on it.

Aha! There it was, taped in the junction of the main arms of the chandelier. With the bulbs of the chandelier burning brightly, the tiny recorder would have been almost impossible to see from the floor.

Carmellini reached. In seconds he had the two reels out. Maybe three-quarters of the tape had been used, about six hours' worth.

Back on the floor, he was tempted to put the reels into his pocket, then thought better of it. He pulled up a trouser leg and carefully shoved them down into one sock.

He had a new tape in his other sock, but with China Bob dead, the recorder seemed superfluous. Should he cut the wires and remove the device?

How much time did he have?

If China Bob Chan killed Harold Barnes, why was the recorder still there? Was he waiting for someone to come for the tape?

Suddenly aware that time was fleeing, Tommy Carmellini pushed the chair back to its former position. He vigorously rubbed the uphol-stered seat of the chair to remove any marks his shoes had made.

As he straightened, he heard a noise. It seemed to come from the secretary's office. When he stepped in that direction the light in the smaller office came on.

Carmellini moved swiftly and flattened against the wall. The door to the secretary's office was to his right. He listened intently for foot-steps.

Carmellini desperately wanted to avoid being caught in this room with a dead man on the floor and a tape in his sock. True, he had diplomatic immunity as the assistant agricultural officer at the consulate, but the publicity and hullabaloo of an arrest and interrogation, not to mention expulsion from the country, would not be career-enhancing.

He heard the scrape of a chair being moved.

Coiled, ready to lash out if anyone came through the door, he approached it, staying back far enough that he remained away from the glare of the light.

Someone was sitting behind the secretary's desk, someone small. My God, it was a kid! A boy, perhaps ten or twelve.

Carmellini stepped back so he would be out of sight if the youngster glanced this way.

Now he heard a computer boot up.

There was one other exit from this room, at the far end. Carmellini didn't know if the door was locked, but it led to another suite of offices which opened into the hallway near the elevator.

He walked toward the door, moving quietly and decisively.

The knob refused to turn. Locked. There was a keyhole, but he could not see the brand name or type of lock.

He removed a leather packet from his pocket and unfolded it, revealing a carefully chosen selection of picks. He took one, inserted it in the lock.

As he bent down to work on the lock, he saw for the first time the heads of the bolts in the door. They had been painted the same dark color as the door to make them less noticeable.

Even if he got the lock open, the door was bolted shut.

He put the pick away and stowed the packet in an inside jacket pocket as he walked back toward the secretary's open door.

Standing at least six feet from the door, he moved so he could see inside.

The kid was at the computer, typing.

Now he sat back in the chair, waiting...

In seconds a naked woman appeared on the screen, a woman holding what appeared to be a giant penis in her hand. Now she—

Jesus, the kid is into porno!

Just what the woman was going to do with the penis, Tommy Carmellini never discovered, for at that instant the door from the hallway opened and a woman walked in. The boy took one look at the intruder and closed the screen, but not before the woman got a good look at it.

She cuffed him once, said something in Chinese.

The boy ran through the icons, closed the Internet connection as the woman spouted Chinese as quickly as her lips would move.

Carmellini stepped back against the wall and waited.

He heard the computer go off, heard the scrape of the chair and footsteps, then the door to the hallway close firmly.

He peered into the office.

Empty.

He opened the hallway door a crack, just enough to see the woman and boy disappear into the elevator at the end of the hallway.

He paused for a second, then went back into the library and scooted the chair under the chandelier. Installing the new tape in the recorder took about thirty seconds; then he found the on-off switch and turned off the recorder. He put the chair back where it belonged and rubbed the seat again.

At the door in the secretary's office, Carmellini checked to ensure no one was coming, then stepped into the hallway and pulled the door shut until it latched. Strains of Gershwin's "An American in Paris" were audible here.

As he walked toward the staircase that led to the rooms below where the party was being held, Carmellini stripped off his latex gloves and put them in his pocket.

Downstairs he found Kerry Kent sipping champagne and talking animatedly with a long-haired intellectual type who was gazing hopefully at her. Kerry was a tall English woman with a spectacular mass of reddish brown hair who spoke both Cantonese and Mandarin fluently. On most working days she labored as a translator at the Greater China Mutual Aid Society, an insurance firm, but in reality she was an officer in the British Secret Intelligence Service, the SIS. Tonight she was wearing an elegant dark blue dress that just brushed her ankles and a modest borrowed diamond necklace.

"Oh, there you are, darling," she said lightly, laying a hand on Tommy's arm. "I have been talking to this brilliant playwright—" She said his name. "His new play is opening next week in the West End. My sister told me quite a lot about it, actually. What a coincidence! When we get back to London we must see it."

Carmellini shook hands with the scribbler and gently led Kerry away. "Did anyone watch me come in?" he asked, just loud enough for her to hear over the hubbub of cocktail party chatter and music.

"I don't think anyone was paying much attention. What were you doing up there?"

"Watching porno on the Internet. Fascinating stuff! I'll tell you all about it later. Who is this sicko stalking you?"

He was referring to a Chinese man who was standing six feet away and openly staring at Kerry. When she moved, he moved.

"An admirer from the provinces, obviously, hopelessly smitten. All my life I've had this devastating effect on men. It's such a bore. I'm thinking of having chest reduction surgery to end these unwanted attentions."

That comment was intended as a joke, for Kerry had a slim, athletic figure.

Carmellini snarled at the staring man and guided Kent away by the elbow.

"Did you get it?" She meant the tape.

"It wasn't there. China Bob is stretched out behind his desk with a hole in his head."

"Dead?" A furrow appeared between her eyebrows.

"Very."

"You found the recorder?"

"In the chandelier. But the tape was missing."

Kerry Kent sipped champagne as she digested Carmellini's lie. Just why lying to her was a good idea he couldn't say, but his instinct told him not to trust anyone. Someone shot Harold Barnes, and another someone, perhaps the same one, put a bullet in China Bob Chan's head—and Carmellini had known Ms. Kent for precisely three days, not exactly a long-term relationship.

There were at least three ways to get from this floor of the mansion to the floor above: two staircases and an elevator. Carmellini had slipped up one set of stairs after he went to the men's room, which was out of sight of the ballroom, just down the hall toward the back stairs. Anyone in this room could have done precisely the same thing in the last few hours, and probably several of them had.

Perhaps the tape held the answer.

Carmellini scanned the crowd one more time, trying to fix the guests in his mind. The cream of Hong Kong society was here tonight.

"Tell me again," he said to Kerry Kent, "who these folks are."

She scanned the crowd, nodded toward a man in his sixties in the center of a small crowd. "That's Governor Sun Siu Ki, surrounded by his usual entourage—officials and bureaucrats and private industry suck-ups. The gentleman of distinction talking to him is Sir Robert MacDonald, the British consul general. The tall, blond Aussie semi-eavesdropping on those two is Rip Buckingham, managing editor of the *China Post*, the largest English-language daily in Hong Kong. Beside him is his wife, Sue Lin. Over in the far corner is the American consul general, Virgil Cole, talking to China Bob's sister, Amy Chan. Let's see, who else?"

"The fellow in the uniform with the highball, standing by the band."

"General Tang, commanding the division of People's Liberation Army troops stationed in Hong Kong. He's been in Hong Kong only a few weeks. The papers ran articles about him when he arrived."

"The man talking to him?"

"Albert Cheung. Educated at Oxford, the foremost attorney in Hong Kong. Smooth and silky and in the know, or so I've heard."

She continued, pointing out six industrialists, three shipping magnates, and two bank presidents. "These people are the scions of the merchant and shipping clans that grew filthy rich in Hong Kong," she said, and named names. "If ever a group mourned the departure of the British, there they are," she added. "Never saw so much of the upper crust chatting it up together."

Any person in the room could have gone upstairs and popped China Bob, Carmellini reflected. All of them had probably excused themselves and gone in search of the facilities once or twice during the evening. Or someone could have ridden the elevator from the basement or walked to the library from another area of the house. The field was wide open. Still, Tommy Carmellini took one more careful look at each of the people Kerry had pointed out, then said, "Perhaps we should leave now before the excitement begins."

"A marvelous suggestion. Let me say a few good-byes as we drift toward the door."

Five minutes later, as they stood waiting for the consulate's pool car to be brought around, Carmellini asked Kerry, "So what's on the agenda for the rest of the evening?"

"I don't know," she said lightly and turned toward him. He accepted the invitation and kissed her. She put her arms around him and kissed back.

"You are such a romantic," she said when her lips were free.

"And single, too."

"I haven't forgotten."

"I don't recall mentioning my marital status before."

"You didn't. Your reputation preceded you. Tommy Carmellini, un-married burglar, thief, second-story man . . ."

"And all-around good egg."

"James Bond without the dash and panache."

"Don't knock the recipe until you've tried it."

"You'll have to sell me."

"I'm willing to give it a go, as you Brits say."

"Tell me about the Internet pornography. Little details like that spice up action reports, make them interesting."

The consulate pool car pulled to a stop in front of them, and the valet got out. "I was saving that morsel for later," Carmellini said as he tipped the man and accepted the keys. "After all, the night is young."

CHAPTER TWO

The morning sun shone full on the balcony of the fifth-floor hotel room when Jake Grafton opened the sliding glass door. The bustle and roar from the streets below assailed him, but he grinned and seated himself at the small, round glass table. As he sipped at a cup of coffee he sampled the smells, sights, and sounds of Hong Kong.

His wife, Callie, stepped out on the balcony. She was dressed to the nines, wearing only a subtle hint of makeup, with her purse over her shoulder and her attaché case in her left hand.

As she bent to kiss Jake he got a faint whiff of scent. "You smell delicious this morning, Mrs. Grafton."

She paused at the door. A furrow appeared between her eyebrows. "What are you going to do today?" she asked.

"Loaf, read the morning paper, cash some traveler's checks, and meet you for lunch."

"When are you going to start on your assignment?"

"I'm working on it this very minute. I know it doesn't look like it, but the wheels are turning."

Today was the third day of the conference, an intense seven-day immersion in Western culture for Chinese college students. Callie was one of the faculty.

"I'm soaking up atmosphere," Jake added. "This trip was billed as my vacation, as you will recall."

Perhaps it was the rare sight of her husband in pajamas at eight on a weekday morning that bothered her. She smiled, nodded, and said good-bye.

As Jake worked on the coffee he surveyed the old police barracks immediately across the road from the hotel. The barracks was surrounded by a ten-foot-high brick wall, which hid it from people on the street. Three stories high, it was constructed of whitewashed brick or masonry in the shape of a T. The windows in the base of the T, which was parallel to Jake, revealed rooms with bunks, lockers, showers, laundry rooms, and a kitchen and dining hall, all set in from outside balconies that ran the length of each floor, much like an American motel. The top of the T was an administration building, apparently full of offices. Police cars filled the parking spaces around the building.

The lawn, however, was a military encampment, covered with troops, tents, fires, and cooking pots. Here at least five hundred People's Liberation Army, or PLA, troops were bivouacked, covering almost every square yard of greenery. Pencil-thin columns of smoke from the fires rose into the still morning air.

In colonial days the Royal Hong Kong police force must have been a nice life for single British men who wanted to do something exotic with their lives, or at least live their mundane lives in an exotic locale and make a very nice living in the process. Like most colonial police forces, the Royal Hong Kong force was famously corrupt, had been since the first Brit donned a uniform and strolled the streets.

Today Chinese policemen and soldiers scurried to and fro like so many ants. Jake wondered if there were any British policemen still wearing the Hong Kong uniform.

Jake Grafton drained his coffee cup and turned his attention to the English-language newspaper, the *China Post,* which had been slid under the door of the room early this morning.

The financial crisis in Japan was the lead article on the front page, which contained lengthy pronouncements from the Chinese government in Beijing. The article also contained a quote from the American consul general, Virgil Cole.

Jake read the name with interest and shook his head. He had flown with Cole on his last cruise during the Vietnam War, and the two of them had survived a shootdown. And he hadn't seen the man since. Oh, they corresponded routinely for years after Cole left the navy, but finally in one move or other the Graftons lost Cole's address, and the Christmas cards stopped. That was ten or so years ago.

Tiger Cole. After his broken back healed, he had gotten out of the navy and gone to grad school, then got into the high-tech business world in Silicon Valley. When he was named consul general to Hong Kong two years ago, *Fortune* magazine said he was worth more than a billion dollars. Of course, he was also a generous donor to political causes.

Maybe he should call Tiger, ask him out to dinner. Then again . . . He decided to wait another day. If Tiger didn't call, he would call him.

On the second page of the paper was a column devoted to a murder that apparently happened last night. The body was discovered just before press time. Jake recognized the victim's name—China Bob Chan— and read the article with a sinking feeling. As the key figure in a campaign finance scandal in Washington, China Bob had been getting a lot of press in the United States of late, most of it the kind of coverage that an honest man could do without. Chan's untimely demise due to lead poisoning was going to go over like a lead brick on Capitol Hill.

On the first page of the second section of the newspaper Jake was pleasantly surprised to find a photo of Callie with two of the other Americans on the seminar faculty, along with a three-paragraph write-up. Amazingly, the reporter even spelled Callie's name correctly. He carefully folded that page to keep.

All in all, Jake thought, the newspaper looked exactly like what it was, a news sheet published under the watchful eye of a totalitarian government intolerant of criticism or dissent. Not a word about why the PLA troops were choking the streets, standing at every street corner, every shop entrance, every public facility, nothing but the bare facts about China Bob's murder, not even an op-ed piece about the implications of his death vis-à-vis Chinese-U.S. relations.

Jake's attention was captured by several columns of foreign sports scores on the next-to-the-last page. Australian football received more column inches than the American professional teams did, Jake noted, grinning.

He tossed the paper down and stretched. Ahhhhh . . .

Someone was knocking on the door to the room.

"Just a minute!"

Jake checked his reflection in the mirror over the dresser—no need to scandalize the maid—then opened the door a crack.

A man in a business suit stood there, a westerner . . . Tommy Carmellini.

"Come in." Jake held the door open. "I'm not going very fast this morning, I'm afraid."

"Have you seen the morning paper?"

"China Bob?"

"Yes."

"I saw the story."

"It's true. Chan's as dead as a man can get."

"Let me take a shower, then we'll go downstairs for some breakfast."

"Okay." Tommy Carmellini sat down in the only chair and opened his attaché case.

When Jake came out of the bathroom fifteen minutes later, Carmellini was repacking his sweep gear in the attaché case. "No bugs," he told Jake.

"The phone?"

"Impossible to say. I have no idea how much impedance and resistance on the line are normal."

"Okay."

"How did you know the story was true?"

"Alas, I met China Bob last night a minute or two after he had joined the ranks of the recently departed. He was warm as toast and the hole in his head was brand-new. There was a spent 7.65-millimeter cartridge under a table a few feet away."

"Who shot him?"

"I didn't. That's all I know for sure."

"Do you have the tape on you?"

Carmellini sat and removed it from his sock. He passed it to Jake Grafton, who examined it cursorily and put it in a trouser pocket.

After they had ordered breakfast in the hotel restaurant, the two men talked in general terms about the city in which they found themselves. Jake told Carmellini that he and Callie had met in Hong Kong, in

1972. "Haven't been back since," Jake said, "which was a mistake, I guess. It's a great city, and we should have come every now and then to watch it evolve and grow."

Carmellini was only politely interested. "How come," he asked the admiral, "they sent me over here to help you out? You're not CIA."

"You sure about that?" Jake Grafton asked. Carmellini noticed that Grafton's gray eyes smiled before he did. His face was tan and lean, although the nose was a trifle large. The admiral had a jagged, faded old scar on one temple.

"Few things these days are exactly what they appear to be," Carmellini agreed. "As I recall, when I met you last year you were wearing a navy uniform and running a carrier battle group. Of course, the agency is going all out on cover stories these days."

Jake chuckled. "I was pushing paper in the Pentagon when they were looking for someone to send over here to snoop around. Apparently my connection to Cole from way back when got someone thinking, so . . . Anyway, when they asked me about it, I said okay, if my wife could come along. So here I am."

Carmellini frowned. "How did I get dragged into this mess? I had a pair of season tickets to see the Orioles and a delightful young woman to fill the other seat."

"I asked for you by name," Jake replied. "The new CIA director tried to dissuade me. Carmellini is a thief, he said, a crook, and last year when someone murdered Professor Olaf Svenson, Carmellini's whereabouts couldn't be accounted for. Seems that you were on vacation at the time, which is not a felony, but it made them do some digging; of course nothing turned up. No one could prove anything. Still, your record got another little smirch."

"He said that?"

"He did. Apparently your personnel file is interesting reading."

"You know how football players talk about adversity?" Tommy Carmellini remarked. "I've had some of that, too. And smirches. Lots of smirches."

"Uh-huh."

"So if you know I'm smirched, how come you asked for me?"

"My aide, Toad Tarkington, suggested you. For some reason you impressed him."

"I see."

Their breakfast came. After the waiter left, Jake said, "Tell me about last night. Everything you can remember."

Carmellini talked as he ate. "They have me working with this woman from SIS, a Brit named Kerry Kent. She's a knockout and speaks Chinese like a native. I've known her exactly three days and an evening."

"Uh-huh."

Carmellini explained about the party, about how Kent got two invitations and took him along as her date. Two hours into the evening, he explained, he saw his chance and sneaked upstairs.

"I was pretty spooked when I found China Bob all sprawled out. I got the tape out of the recorder and installed a new one, so anyone checking the machine would think the original tape didn't work. That was my thinking, which wasn't very bright on my part. I did have the presence of mind to turn the recorder off, so maybe anyone finding it will buy that hypothesis. Then again . . .

"By the time I got downstairs the thought occurred to me that I didn't know beans from apple butter. Anybody in Hong Kong could have killed China Bob, for any conceivable reason. Including, of course, my companion for the evening, Kerry Kent. She spent fifteen minutes in the ladies' just before I went upstairs, or so she said. Just to be on the safe side, when I got downstairs after retrieving the tape I told her it wasn't in the recorder."

Jake Grafton looked up from his coffee. "And . . ."

"And damn if she didn't frisk me when we were outside waiting for the valet to bring the car around. Gave me a smooch and a hug and rubbed her hands over my pockets."

"You sure she was looking for the tape?"

"She patted me down."

"Maybe she was trying to let you know she was romantically interested," Jake suggested with a raised eyebrow.

"I had hopes," Carmellini confessed. "She's a nice hunk of female, tuned up and ready to rumble. But she had me take her straight home. She didn't even invite me up for a good-night beer."

"I thought secret agents were always getting tossed in the sack."

"I thought so, too," Carmellini said warmly. "That's why I signed on with the agency. Reality has been a disappointment." Another lie, a little one. Carmellini joined the CIA to avoid prosecution for burglary and a handful of other felonies. However, he saw no reason to share the sordid details with his colleagues in the ordinary course of business, so to speak.

"Did she find the tape on you?"

"No. I had it in my sock."

"Did she have a pistol on her?"

"She didn't have a pistol in her sock, and believe me, there wasn't room for one in her bra."

"Her purse?"

"A little clutch thing—I gave it a squeeze. Wasn't there. Of course, whoever shot China Bob probably ditched the pistol immediately."

"So who are your suspects for the killing?"

"It could have been anybody in Hong Kong. Anybody at the party or anybody who came in off the street and went straight upstairs. Still, Kent or the consul general are high on my list. As I mentioned, she camped out in the ladies' just before I went upstairs. I saw Cole coming down the stairs five minutes before I went up."

Virgil Cole, the perfect warrior. Jake was the one who had hung the nickname "Tiger" on him, back in the fall of 1972 when Cole became his bombardier-navigator after Morgan McPherson was killed. This morning Grafton took a deep breath, remembering those days, remembering Cole as he had known him then. Those days seemed so long ago, and yet . . .

The Chinese employees of the Bank of the Orient had known the truth for days, and they had told their friends, who withdrew money from their accounts. As the news spread, the queues in the lobby had grown longer and longer.

This fine June morning a crowd of at least two thousand gathered on the sidewalks and in the manicured square in front of the bank, waiting for it to open. The bank was housed in a massive, soaring tower of stone and glass set in the heart of the Victoria business district, between the slope of Victoria Peak and the ferry piers. Its name in English and Chinese was of course splashed prominently across the front of the building in huge characters. In still larger characters lit day and night mounted on the side of the building at the twenty-story level so they would be visible from all over the island, from Kowloon, indeed, on a clear day from mainland China itself, was the name of the bank in Japanese, for the Bank of the Orient was a Japanese bank and proud of it.

After urgent consultations and many glances out the window at the crowd, which was growing by the minute, bank officials refused to open the doors. Instead, they called the Finance Ministry in Tokyo. While the president of the bank waited by the telephone for the assistant finance minister for overseas operations to return his urgent call, someone outside the bank threw a rock through a window.

One of the cashiers called the police. The police took a look at the crowd and called the governor, Sun Siu Ki. Sun didn't go look; he merely called General Tang Tso Ming, the new commander of the division of the People's Liberation Army that was stationed in Hong Kong.

A half hour later several hundred armed soldiers arrived. They spread themselves two deep across the street on each end of the crowd. They also surrounded a park across the street from the bank where many people were waiting. There really weren't enough soldiers to physically prevent the crowd from moving, so the soldiers did nothing but stand in position, waiting for orders. Then four tanks clanked up, ripping up asphalt, and stopped with their big guns pointed at the crowd.

General Tang arrived with the tanks. He looked over the crowd and the soldiers, had his officers adjust the placement of the troops, then went to the door of the bank and pounded on it with his fist. When it didn't open, he pulled his pistol and rapped on the door sharply with the butt.

Now the door opened.

General Tang and two of his colonels marched into the Bank of the Orient and demanded to see the president.

As they walked along the sidewalk toward the Star Ferry, Tommy Carmellini said, "Admiral, I'm really flying blind. The people at Langley sent me over here with orders to help you out, but they didn't tell me what this is all about."

"They sent me over here," Jake Grafton told the CIA officer, "because I knew Tiger Cole in Vietnam. Apparently I'm one of the few people in government who know him personally. Washington wants to know what in hell is going on in Hong Kong."

"What do they think is going on?"

They each bought first-class tickets on the ferry and went up on the top deck. As the ferry pulled out, Jake Grafton said, "China is coming to a crisis. The whole country is tinder ready to burn. One spark might set it off. The Communists want to stay in power by delivering economic prosperity, which can come only if the economic system changes. They are trapped in this giant oxymoron; they want economic change without social and political change. On the other hand, the United States wants a big piece of the China pie. So the American establishment has traded technology and capital for access to Chinese markets and low-cost labor. In other words, they have invested in the political status quo, which is the dictatorial Communist system."

Tommy Carmellini nodded his understanding.

Jake continued. "The Communist system distorts and corrupts everything. The only way a Chinese importer can get goods into the country is to obtain a government import license. These licenses are restricted to prevent private entrepreneurs from competing against state-owned enterprises. Enter China Bob Chan and a thousand like him. If you are an enterprising Chinese businessman, for a fee Chan will obtain for you an import license from a government official—in effect, he splits the bribe. This system ensures that the bureaucracy is corrupted from top to bottom. Every single person in government is on the take, party members, officials of every caliber and stripe, army generals, everybody. This system generates enormous profits that go into their pockets, and the industrialized West gets to sell high tech to China."

"Only the public loses," Carmellini murmured.

"Precisely. Anyway, to get specific, the Chinese government used China Bob Chan to make political contributions in America and grease the wheels to get American export licenses for restricted technology, some of it military. As a general rule, government licenses always create opportunities for graft of one sort or another, in China and America. In this case the PLA, the People's Liberation Army, wanted the American military technology. Unfortunately, China Bob pocketed about half the money the PLA paid him to do all this American greasing. The guy who dealt with China Bob on behalf of the army was General Tang, now the PLA commander here."

"Uh-huh."

"The story is that Tang was sent here to find and apprehend a political criminal, Wu Tai Kwong. Remember the man who stood in front of the tank in Tiananmen Square in 1989?"

"I thought he was dead."

"He may be. But dead or alive, he's public enemy number one; he gave the Commies the finger. These people are paranoid."

"That's an occupational hazard with absolute dictators," Tommy Carmellini said lightly.

"Anyway, that is what the army says it's doing here. In reality, Tang and the army are here to prevent a political uprising in Hong Kong. The CIA thinks China Bob Chan washed the money to finance the revolution."

"He was working both sides of the street?"

"The CIA thinks so. The politicians in Congress wanted someone to come over here and root around and give an independent assessment of how deep the consul general is in all this. The White House picked me, for lack of someone better."

"Virgil Cole?"

"That's right."

"Why you?"

"Well, basically, I got the impression that I'm supposed to worm my way into Cole's confidence and get him to say things to me that he wouldn't say to anyone else. That was the thinking in Washington, anyway. It stinks, but that's the sordid truth."

"Maybe it's all bullshit," Carmellini suggested. "Rumors go round and round. I'm an expert on rumors."

Grafton had his arms on the railing of the boat. "Cole is apparently having a relationship of some type with Amy Chan. Her father was a British soldier and her mother was a Chinese girl who came to Hong Kong when the Nationalist cause collapsed and Mao took over on the mainland. The mother got in just before the door slammed shut, took up prostitution to feed herself. She was supposedly really good-looking, became a high-class hooker, ended up falling for this Brit soldier and having Amy by him. Of course the soldier was a shit and went tooling off to Britain when his tour was up—seems he had a wife there, too.

"Anyway, Amy's mother saved her money and sent her daughter to America for an education. She had a degree from UCLA and was working at the American consulate processing visa applications when Cole arrived. They hit it off right from the start."

"Uh-huh."

"Her half brother was China Bob Chan. He used Cole as his poster boy to advertise his influence with the Americans. Amy had him over to the mansion every other night. China Bob paraded him in front of government toads, General Tang, everybody and anybody who came down here from Beijing. This has been going on about a year. Cole has been talking to congressional investigators, so he is aware of the intricacies of all this. Still, the Tiger Cole I remember from way back when wouldn't give a good goddamn what anybody thought about his love life."

"That's my impression of him, too," Carmellini mused. "I've seen his dossier and spent an hour or so with him, and I'd say you are pretty close to the mark."

"We're here to find out what Cole and China Bob have been up to," Jake said. "I want to listen to that tape you brought over. Callie will help me with the Chinese." He had the thing in *his* sock just now.

"I'll have to get a player out of the communications room at the consulate," Tommy Carmellini told Jake as they joined the throng waiting to get off the boat when it slid into its dock in the Central District. "It takes a special machine to play the thing."

"Let's get bugs in Cole's office in the consulate. Search his desk, see what you can learn. As soon as you can, open the safes and start going through the files. I want to see anything that implicates Tiger Cole in a conspiracy to overthrow the Chinese government. If there is not a shred of physical evidence, I want to know that, too."

"Jesus! Where'd you learn how to do investigations?"

"We don't have time for subtleties. I want to know what in hell is going on in Hong Kong, and I want to know *now*. If representatives of the American government are members of a conspiracy to overthrow the lawful government of China, that could be construed as an act of war."

As they walked out of the Star Ferry terminal, Tommy Carmellini nodded at the admiral and set off for the consulate on Garden Road.

The president of the Bank of the Orient was Saburo Genda. When General Tang and his officers were escorted into his office, he was on the telephone with Governor Sun, trying to explain the situation.

"We do not have money on hand to pay all the depositors waiting outside," Genda explained as patiently as he could.

He listened to a burst of Chinese, which he spoke reasonably well, then answered, "Of course the bank is solvent. Yes, we have reserves. Unfortunately, we just do not have sufficient cash in the vaults to pay all the people waiting outside. . . . Yes, we will open in a few hours. You have my assurances, sir."

He hung up the telephone and wiped his forehead.

Tang wanted to know why the bank wasn't open.

Genda ran through it all again.

"Get some money," General Tang said.

"We are trying, General, but since we don't have printing presses in the basement, we must obtain currency from other banks. We are in the process of doing that now."

Tang disliked being patronized, which he thought a slight on his dignity and his position, and he told Genda that in no uncertain terms.

He was just winding up when the telephone rang. Genda answered.

"Sir, the Finance Ministry in Tokyo is on the line."

Genda switched to Japanese and began talking into the telephone, leaving the general to stew. Tang felt out of place in this huge, opulent office decorated with tropical hardwoods and designer furniture, four stories high in a grand temple dedicated to the gods of money.

Tang Ming was a peasant's son, born during World War II, whose earliest memories were of his family fleeing before advancing Japanese troops.

He had spent his adult life in the army. From skin to backbone he was a soldier. A firm believer in the social goals of communism, he was, like a majority of his fellow countrymen, a cultural and racial xenophobe. Before his assignment to Hong Kong he had actually seen foreigners on only two occasions in his life, both official visits to Beijing. He had seen the foreigners at a distance, not talked with them.

Sitting in this huge office and watching an impeccably attired senior Japanese executive babble in a foreign tongue about matters he didn't understand made General Tang Ming restless and irritable.

Someone with a cellular telephone called the editor of the *China Post*, Hong Kong's leading English-language newspaper, and informed him about the restless crowd in front of the Bank of the Orient. The editor, Rip Buckingham, had heard rumors for the past two days about the possible collapse of the bank, so as he listened to the caller describe the crowd and the troops, his gut told him, *This is it.*

Rip called the newsroom and ordered four reporters and two photographers dispatched to the scene immediately. Then he extracted an eyewitness account from the caller while he jotted notes.

When he finally let the caller go, Rip automatically glanced out the window of his corner office at the giant Coca-Cola sign on top of the Bank of the Orient building, an imposing seventy-story skyscraper in Hong Kong's Central District. In a typical Hong Kong deal, the developer of the building played off competing consumer giants, one against the other, for the honor of having their logo prominently displayed on the masthead of the new bank building, the biggest one in the colony. Reportedly the local Coke bottler had paid a fee in excess of ten million dollars U.S. to the developer just for the privilege of putting a sign up there. That was in 1995, two years before the British turned over the colony to the Chinese Communists.

No one is building buildings like that in Hong Kong now, Rip thought bitterly.

Rip was an Australian who had enjoyed a wonderful, vagrant youth. He repaired slot machines in Las Vegas, worked as a motorman on San Francisco trolleys, sailed the Pacific and Indian oceans in the forecastles of rusty Liberian tramps, and bicycled across most of China, including the entire route of the ancient Silk Road, from Tyre on the eastern edge of the Mediterranean to Sian in central China. Finally, in his late twenties, Rip Buckingham came to rest in Hong Kong, where he got a haircut and traded his sandals for leather shoes. He even married a local girl.

Rip turned to the computer sitting on a stand beside his desk and began writing. He wanted to get the eyewitness account down while it was fresh and immediate. He was still working on it when his reporters began calling in on their cellular telephones. He folded the facts they had gleaned into the story he was writing and asked questions.

Unlike a reporter operating in a Western nation, Rip did not telephone the governor's officer or the police or the PLA to elicit comments or give those officials a chance to dispute the accounts his reporters were getting. He had done that years ago when he first took over the managing editor's position, and before long was told by some government functionary, "You can't print that." The police then came to the newspaper office to ensure that he didn't.

So far he had managed to avoid the wrath of the Communist officials who ruled Hong Kong. It hadn't been easy. He was, he often thought wryly, becoming a master at damning with faint praise. I'm the king of innuendo, he once grumped to his wife. Actually, as he well knew, he had escaped censorship only because his paper was published in English, a language that few government officials spoke with any fluency. All the Chinese-language newspapers had a squad of resident apparatchiks from the New China News Agency who had to approve everything.

As Rip worked on the story, a sense of impending doom came over him. There were several hundred banks in Hong Kong, most of them privately owned, yet China had no Federal Deposit Insurance Corporation. Chinese banks outside of Hong Kong were owned by the state and theoretically could not fail. Of course, if those state-owned banks were examined using Western accounting standards, all were insolvent.

The problem was the desperate financial straits of the Chinese government, which saw the privately owned banks in Hong Kong as a source of low-interest loans for noncompetitive state-owned industries that would collapse without cash infusions, industries that employed tens of millions of mainland workers.

The Japanese who owned the Bank of the Orient had refused to make those loans to the Chinese government. Now the bank was failing, and thousands of people were going to be flat-ass broke after a lifetime of work and saving.

What was the Chinese government doing to prevent that outcome, if anything?

As luck would have it, after he left the Star Ferry terminal Jake Grafton wandered along with the crowd, lost in thought. When he at last began paying attention to his surroundings he found himself in the square outside the Bank of the Orient, shoulder-to-shoulder with several thousand other people. The doors of the bank were apparently locked. From time to time people came out of the crowd to try the doors, which refused to open.

Armed soldiers in uniform were visible here and there, but they were well back, away from the crowd, and seemed to be making no attempt to disburse it or prevent people from approaching the door of the bank to rattle it, pound on it, or press their foreheads against the glass and look in.

Here and there knots of people argued loudly among themselves, waved passbooks, and stared openly and defiantly at the soldiers.

For a moment, Jake thought of wandering on, finding another bank to cash his traveler's checks. Surely they all weren't closed today.

Yet something made him linger. He found a few empty inches on a flower bed retainer wall and parked his bottom.

Meanwhile, in the executive suite of the bank, President Saburo Genda was getting bad news from the assistant finance minister in Tokyo.

"We will not loan the bank additional funds. I'm sorry, but the prime minister and the finance minister are agreed."

President Genda's forte was commercial loans to large companies. He had spent much of his adult life dealing with wealthy businessmen with a firm grasp of economic reality. He fought now to keep his temper with this obtuse government clerk.

"You don't understand," he said, his voice tightly under control. "We are experiencing a run on the bank. There is a crowd of several thousand depositors outside demanding their money. Without additional cash, the bank cannot pay them. Without more money, the bank will collapse."

"I am sorry, Mr. Genda," said the bureaucrat. "It is you who do not understand. The government has decided to let the bank fail. It would simply cost too much to save it."

"But—"

"The Bank of the Orient made far too many real estate loans in Hong Kong at astronomical evaluations. As you know, the market collapsed after the Communists took over. It may be twenty years before the market recovers. Indeed, it may never recover."

"Mr. Assistant Minister, your ministry has known about the bad loans for years. Your colleagues were working with us. We have the assets to pay our depositors, but the assets are in accounts in Japan and you have frozen them. Those funds belong to this bank! Make them available for us to pledge and we will borrow the cash we need locally."

"I am sorry, Mr. Genda. The government has decided to offset the bank's assets against the amounts the bank owes the government."

"You can't do this," Genda protested. "This isn't the way things are done. You are violating the banking regulations!"

"The decision has been made."

"Have you discussed the failure of the bank with the governor of Hong Kong or the Chinese government in Beijing?"

"We have. Since the bank is not Chinese, they did not choose to guarantee its debts."

Genda continued, almost pleading, trying to make the bureaucrat see reason. "This is a Japanese bank! Many of our senior people are former Finance Ministry officials. We have close ties with the government, extremely close ties."

"I am sorry, Mr. Genda," the civil servant said politely. "As I said, the decision has been made. We here in the Ministry expect you to take personal responsibility for the condition of your institution. Good-bye."

The assistant minister hung up, leaving Saburo Genda standing with the telephone in his hand, too stunned to hang it up, too stunned to speak to his subordinates standing around the room waiting for a report. He felt as if his head had just been separated from his body. In two minutes of conversation, the civil servant at the Finance Ministry had ruined him: He could never work in a bank again; his whole life had just been reduced to rubble.

"Open the bank," General Tang said in Chinese. "I order you to open the doors of the bank."

"The bank is ruined," Saburo Genda told the soldier, his lips barely able to form the words. "Tokyo refuses to guarantee our borrowings of cash to pay the depositors."

Tang Ming tried to understand. Foreigners! "But this is a bank. You have much money in the vault. Give it to the people who want it, and when you run out, tell them they will have to come back another day."

"Then the riot will occur in our lobby."

"You must have money!" Tang gestured to the crowd. "What have you done with all of their money?"

Genda had had it with this fool. "We loaned it out," he said through clenched teeth. "That is the function of banks, to accept deposits and make loans."

Tang Ming stretched to his full height. He looked at Genda behind his great, polished desk, a whipped dog, and his two colonels and Genda's secretary and the crowd beyond the window.

"Come," he murmured at the colonels and strode out.

The tangible anger of the crowd made Jake Grafton uneasy. He sensed it was high time for him to be on his way, time to be out of this group of angry Asians who were working themselves up for a riot.

Still he lingered. Curiosity kept him rooted.

Although he spoke not a word of Chinese, he didn't really need the language to read the emotions on people's faces. A few people were openly crying, weeping silently as they rocked back and forth in sitting positions. Others were on cellular phones, presumably sharing their misfortune with family and friends.

The number of wireless telephones in use by the crowd surprised Jake—China was definitely third or fourth world. There was money in Hong Kong, a lot of which had been invested in state-of-the-art technology. Still, most of the people in this square existed on a small fraction of the money that the average American family earned.

As Jake sat there with two thousand American dollars' worth of traveler's checks in his pocket that he could get cashed at any bank in town, the vast gulf between the comfortable, middle-class circumstances in which he had lived his life and the hand-to-mouth existence that so many hundreds of millions—billions—of people around the world accepted as their lot in life spread before him like the Grand Canyon.

He was no bleeding heart, but he cared about people. Always had.

He found people interesting, could imagine himself in their circumstances; this was one of the qualities that made him a leader, a good naval officer, and a decent human being.

General Tang Ming climbed into a small van with public address system speakers mounted on the roof. Sitting in the passenger seat of the van holding a microphone, the general explained the facts as he understood them: The bank had loaned all the money it had and had no more to pay to the people in the crowd. It would not open its doors.

Since waiting for an event that would not happen was futile, Tang ordered the crowd to disperse. The language he used was Mandarin Chinese, the dialect of northern China, of Beijing, and of most of the soldiers under his command. Unfortunately, it was not the language of the people in the crowd, most of whom spoke Cantonese or English.

As General Tang harangued the crowd in the street outside the Bank of the Orient over a loud, tinny PA system in a language few understood, the crowd became more boisterous. Some people began shouting, others produced stones and bits of concrete from construction sites that they threw toward the bank windows. Several men nearest the main entrance to the bank pounded on the door with their fists, shouting, "Open up and pay us!"

Others in the crowd, sensing approaching disaster, tried to leave the area by passing through the cordon of soldiers. Almost by reflex, the greatly outnumbered soldiers tried to hold the crowd back. They struck out with billy clubs and rifle butts. Inevitably the conflict panicked onlookers, many of whom gave in to their urge to flee all at the same time. Those in the center of the crowd began pushing those on the fringes toward the soldiers.

A shot was fired. Then several shots.

General Tang was still holding forth on the PA system from the passenger seat of the van when the first fully automatic burst was triggered into the crowd by a frightened soldier.

People screamed. More shots were fired into the crowd, random insanity, then the soldiers were either trampled or ran before the fear-soaked mob trying to escape.

A sergeant in one of the tanks on the edge of the park tried to aid the escape of his fellow soldiers, who ran past the tank in front of a wall of running civilians who were also desperate to escape. The sergeant opened fire at the civilians with a machine gun mounted on top of the main turret. The bullets cut down several dozen people before the gun jammed.

In three minutes the sidewalk and street in front of the bank contained only dead, dying, and wounded people, many of them trampled. More than a hundred people lay on the pavement and grass and in the flowerbeds, some obviously dead, some bleeding and in shock.

General Tang climbed out of the public address van and stood staring uncomprehendingly at the human wreckage. He hadn't recognized the muffled pops as shots since the public address system was so loud, and he was initially pleased when the people he could see from the van began to move. Alas, by then the situation was out of control. Surprised by the panic evident among the civilians he could see through the van's windshield, Tang stopped speaking and heard, for the first time, the shooting, the shouting, and the screaming.

Staring now at the people lying in the otherwise empty street, he became aware that several officers were beside him, shouting questions.

The thought that ran through the general's head was that the crowd should not have run. It was their fault, really. He certainly hadn't given orders for the soldiers to shoot.

"Pick them up," he said and gestured toward the dead and wounded. The officers beside him looked puzzled.

"Pick them up," General Tang repeated. "Take them to the hospital. Clear the street."

When the first shot was fired, a nervous Jake Grafton raked two old ladies from their perch on the retaining wall and shoved them onto the ground. Then he threw himself on top of them.

He didn't move until the shooting was completely over and most of the people on their feet had fled. Only then did he stand and look about him at the bodies, at people bleeding, at people like himself who had taken what cover they could find.

He helped the two old women to their feet. Neither was hurt. They looked about them with wide, fearful eyes. Without a word they walked away, away from the bank and the soldiers and the gunshot victims.

Jake Grafton lingered a moment, watching the soldiers check the people lying on the concrete. Then, with his hands in his pockets, he walked through the troops and along the street away from the square.

The soldier who fired the first shot was from a fishing village on the northern Chinese coast. Eighteen years old, he had been in the army for nearly two years. He had been in Hong Kong for two weeks and two days—he was counting the days so he could accurately report to his family when he next sat down with a scribe to dictate a letter. His name was Ng Choy, and now he was crying.

Sitting on the hard, clean, bloody pavement of the bank square, he couldn't stop the tears. The body of the man he had shot was lying beside him. In his panic Ng had triggered a burst of seven shots, all of which hit this middle-aged man in the chest. By some fluke, after the man was shot his heart continued beating for almost half a minute, pumping a prodigious quantity of blood out the bullet holes. The sticky mess was congealing now and turning dark.

Ng Choy didn't understand any of it. He didn't understand why he was here, what everyone had been shouting about, what the sergeant had wanted him to do, why this man had tried to wrestle him out of the way, and he didn't understand why he had shot him.

So he sat there, crying uncontrollably, while his fellow soldiers walked around him, carrying away the wounded and the dead.

Finally two soldiers picked up the corpse beside Ng, leaving him on the cold pavement with his rifle and the pool of sticky blood.

Rip Buckingham cradled the telephone automatically between his cheek and shoulder. "How many dead?" he asked the reporter on the line.

"Fifteen, the soldiers say. One woman died as they loaded her into the ambulance. At least forty more were injured by bullets. I estimate a dozen or two were trampled—it will be impossible to get an accurate count of the injured."

"Get to the bank officials. Find out why they wouldn't open the doors of the bank."

The story would be front-page news around the world, with a big, bold headline: 15 KILLED IN HONG KONG BY PLA TROOPS. The teaser under the main headline would read, *Crowd at Japanese Bank Fired Upon.*

Ten minutes later Rip was told, "I talked to a cashier. The officers of the bank are in a meeting and unavailable. The bank is insolvent. Tokyo refused to loan it any more money."

"*What?*"

"Yes. The Japanese are letting the bank fail. The word is Tokyo already poured twenty billion yen into it. Apparently that's the limit."

This story is growing by leaps and bounds, Rip thought.

He called a man he knew on a Japanese newspaper and asked for help. In twenty minutes the Tokyo newsman called back with confirmation from the Finance Ministry. The government of Japan had decided not to save the Bank of the Orient, a Japanese-owned bank headquartered in Hong Kong. After consultations with Finance Ministry officials, the Chinese authorities had elected not to intervene.

Rip looked at his watch. There was still time. He grabbed a notebook and his sports coat and headed for the door.

The army was cleaning up the mess in front of the Bank of the Orient, loading bodies in ambulances and the backs of army trucks. Rip stood watching for several minutes. There were few onlookers; the soldiers standing around didn't seem in the mood for gawkers. Yet because he wasn't Chinese, it was several minutes before the nearest soldier gestured for him to move on.

Rip went to the office tower entrance of the bank building and showed his press pass to the security guard. It took some talking and several hundred Hong Kong dollars, but eventually he managed to get into the executive suite on the fourth floor.

He explained to the receptionist that he wanted to talk to the president of the bank. He gave her his card: "Rip Buckingham, Managing Editor, *China Post*," with the *China Post* lettering in the company's trademarked style.

The receptionist told him to take a seat.

He looked at the art on the walls and at the magazines on the table. He really didn't expect to see any bank officer. He thought it would be helpful to see the street in front of the bank again, see it knowing it was an important place, so he could visualize the scene the reporters were describing to him. And he had the time before deadline. So he was surprised when the receptionist appeared in the doorway and said, "Mr. Genda has a few minutes. Come this way, please."

Saburo Genda had a corner office. Through the window Rip caught a glimpse of the last army truck leaving. Except for a few police guards, the square was empty.

Genda was slumped in a large stuffed chair beside the desk with his back to the square. He didn't look up as Rip entered, didn't pay any attention to him until the Australian was seated across from him. He had Rip's card in his hand. He glanced at it.

"So, Mr. Buckingham," Genda said in accented English, "ask your questions."

The Japanese executive looked, Rip thought, like he had slept in his clothes. He had the fashionably gray hair, the dark power suit and tie, the trim waistline . . . and he looked exhausted, worn out.

"What happened, Mr. Genda?"

"They killed the bank."

"They? Who is they?" Rip asked as he wrote down the previous reply in shorthand.

"The Finance Ministry. They seized our assets in Japan. They refused to let us draw on those assets for the cash we need to operate on a daily basis. The news leaked out, there was a run on the bank . . . We are out of business, insolvent. The bank has," Genda took a deep breath and exhaled, "collapsed." He raised his arms and let them fall to the arms of the chair. He looked at his hands as if he had never seen them before.

"You are saying the Finance Ministry chose to put you out of business?"

"Yes."

"Do you know why?"

"They said it was the bad real estate loans."

"But I thought they have known about those loans for years."

"They have."

"Then . . ."

"Someone in Japan made a decision, Mr. Buckingham. I don't know who or why. The decision was to make the bank fail."

"Make it fail? You mean allow it to fail."

"No, sir. When the Finance Ministry seized our Japanese assets, the

Ministry forced the bank to close its doors. There was no way it could stay open. They took a course of action that made the failure of the bank inevitable."

Rip made a careful note of Genda's exact words.

"Mr. Genda, I have heard that the Bank of the Orient refused the Chinese government's demands for low-interest loans. If the bank had made those loans, would it have failed today?"

Genda tried mightily to keep a straight face. He started to answer the question, then thought better of it. He lowered his head. He seemed to be focused inward, no longer aware of Rip's presence.

Rip tried one more question, then rose and left the office. He pulled the door shut behind him.

CHAPTER THREE

"Tell me again about Tiger Cole," Callie Grafton said to her husband. They were eating lunch on the balcony of their hotel room. Jake had related his adventure at the bank square this morning and the fact that Tommy Carmellini had dropped by for breakfast.

"I remember you and Tiger flew a plane from the carrier into Cubi Point during the final months of the Vietnam War," Callie said, "and I went to the Philippines to meet you. I remember meeting him at the airport when you showed me the plane before you left."

Jake nodded. He, too, remembered. "A few weeks after that we were shot down," he said.

"As I recall," Callie said, "he was tall, silent, intense."

"That was Tiger. He never had much to say, but when he did, people listened."

She had been a junior translator at the U.S. consulate in Hong Kong in those days. And now Tiger Cole was the consul general. Who would have guessed?

"Tiger broke his back in the ejection," Jake continued, recalling days he hadn't thought about in years. "After we were rescued he spent a long time in the hospital, then they sent him to Pensacola for rehabilitation. He finally said to hell with it and pulled the plug. I think he went back to college in California, got a master's in something or other, then got involved in the computer industry."

"I lost his address about ten years ago," Callie explained. "He sent us Christmas cards, then we moved or he moved or whatever."

Jake Grafton chuckled. "Sometimes life deals you an ace. Last month *Fortune* magazine said he was in on the ground floor of three big high-tech start-ups."

"And now he's the consul general," Callie said distractedly. "Why do you want me to translate this tape?"

Jake summarized his morning conversation with Carmellini while Callie finished her salad. "The tape may contain something worth knowing. China Bob was a rainmaker, a wheeler-dealer who played every angle he could find. Something on that tape might shed some light on what is happening in this town."

"You mean on what the Americans are doing to help make it happen?"

"If they are."

"This CIA officer, Carmellini? Do you trust him?"

"I met him last year in Cuba," Jake explained. "He was working with a CIA officer who was subsequently killed. The dead officer told me Carmellini was a safecracker before the CIA recruited him."

"That doesn't sound like anything I'd want on my résumé," Callie shot back.

"It may not take all kinds, but we sure as hell got all kinds."

"Are we going to do this tonight?"

"I don't know. Whenever Carmellini shows up with a tape player."

"I certainly don't want to sit around this hotel room all evening waiting for him."

"I didn't say we should."

"Why don't you call Tiger Cole, invite him to go to dinner with us?"

"You think he'd go?" Jake asked dubiously.

"For heaven's sake, of course he'd go! Unless he has another commitment, then he'd probably want to set something up for tomorrow. Call him. Tell him you're in town and want to have dinner. I always thought you saved his life after you two were shot down."

"That's true," Jake admitted. "But he's the consul general and pretty busy and—"

"You're a two-star admiral in Uncle Sam's navy, Jake Grafton. You can buy a drink anywhere on this planet."

Rip Buckingham was about ready to send the bank story to the makeup room when he received a telephone call from the governor's office.

"This is Governor Sun's assistant, Mr. Buckingham. Your newspaper is running story about tragedy in front of Bank of Orient? This morning?"

"Yes."

"Governor Sun Siu Ki has issued statement. Statement go in story."

The aide's English was almost impossible to follow, so Rip replied in Cantonese. "Read it to me," he said, trying to keep the dejection out of his voice.

"A crowd of justly outraged citizens gathered this morning at the Bank of the Orient to withdraw their money panicked when bank officials shamefully failed to open their doors," said the aide, reading slowly. "In the rioting that followed, several people were killed by the gallant soldiers of the People's Liberation Army while they were restoring order. The officials of the Bank of the Orient will be held responsible for this tragedy. . . ."

There were several paragraphs more, and as the governor's assistant dictated in Cantonese, Rip wrote it down in English, in his own private shorthand. He read it back to ensure he had it, then quickly typed out the statement on his computer. He put a note above the statement for the front-page editor, directing him to put the governor's statement in a box in the center of the page. However, he didn't change a word of his story, which gave the facts, without comment, as they had been gathered by his reporters.

When he had sent the story for the *China Post* on its electronic way, he called it up again and made some changes. His fingers flew over the keyboard, changing the slant of the story, trying to capture the despair of Saburo Genda and the hopelessness of the crowd waiting for money that rightfully belonged to them and would never be paid. He also tried to capture the callousness of the soldiers who used deadly weapons on defenseless people.

When he had finished this story, he E-mailed it and the governor's statement to the Buckingham newspapers worldwide. The *China Post* was owned by Buckingham Newspapers, Ltd., of which Rip's father, Richard, was chairman and CEO. Richard Buckingham started with one newspaper in Adelaide at the end of World War II, and as he liked to tell it, with hard work, grit, determination, perseverance, and a generous helping of OPM—other people's money—built a newsprint empire that covered the globe. Richard still held a bit under sixty percent of the stock, which was not publicly traded. A series of romantic misadventures had spread the rest of the shares far and wide; even Rip had a smidgen under five percent.

Thirty minutes after Rip E-mailed the story to Sydney, the telephone rang. It was his father.

"Sounds like Hong Kong is heating up," Richard growled.

"It is."

"When are you going to pack it in?"

"We've had this conversation before, Dad."

"We have. And we are going to keep having it. Sometimes in the middle of the night I wake up in a sweat, thinking of you rotting in some Communist prison because you went off your nut and told the truth in print about those sewer rats."

"All politicians are sewer rats, not just ours."

"I'm going to quote you on that."

"Go right ahead."

"So when?"

"I don't know that my wife or mother-in-law will ever leave, Dad. This is their place. These are their people."

"No, Rip. *You* are their people. You are the husband and son-in-law, and in China that counts for just about everything. You make the decision and they will go along with it. You *know* that."

"What about the *Post*?"

"I'll send someone else to run it. Maybe put it up for sale."

"Nobody is going to pay you serious money for a newspaper in Communist China, Dad. Not here, not now."

"We'll see. You never had a head for business, Rip. You are a damned good newspaperman, though, a rare talent. You come to Sydney, I'll give you any editorial job in the company except mine, which you'll get anyway in a few years."

"I'll think it over."

"The thought of you in one of those prisons, eating rats . . . Oh, well." Without waiting for a response, his father hung up.

The massacre in front of the Bank of the Orient was the hot topic of conversation among the American Culture conference attendees during the afternoon break. One of Callie Grafton's fellow faculty members told her about it as she watched the attendees whispering furiously and gesturing angrily. Three or four of them were trying to whisper into cell phones. Callie didn't tell her informant that Jake had been in the crowd in front of the bank and had given her an eyewitness account at lunch.

At least twenty people were killed, the faculty member said, a figure that stunned Callie. Jake hadn't mentioned that people were killed, only that there had been some shooting. Obviously he didn't want her to worry. "Ridiculous to worry, after the fact," he would say, and grin that grin he always grinned when the danger was past.

Through the years Jake had wound up in more than his share of dangerous situations. She had thought those days behind her when he was promoted to flag rank. An admiral might go down with his ship, it was true, in a really big war, but who was having really big wars these days? In today's world admirals sat in offices and pushed paper. And yet . . . somehow this morning Jake wound up in the middle of a shooting riot!

Perhaps we should go home, Callie mused, and then remembered with a jolt that Jake was here for a reason and couldn't leave.

She tried to forget riots and bodies and her husband's nose for trouble and concentrate on the conference.

Unfortunately, one of the attendees was a government official, a political officer sent to take notes of the questions and answers and jot down the names of any Chinese who might be "undermining the implementation of the laws," in the phrase the official used to explain his presence to the faculty.

This official was a bald, middle-aged party apparatchik, a generation removed from most of the attendees, who were students in their early to mid-twenties. The first day Callie Grafton found herself fixating on the man's facial expressions when any student stood to ask a question.

Angry at herself for feeling intimidated, she still had to carefully phrase her comments. While she could not be prosecuted for political deviancy, her participation in the conference could be terminated by this official on the spot. That sanction was used the very first day against a political science professor from Cornell. Callie was ready to pick up her notebook and follow him out the door, then decided a precipitous leave-taking would not be fair to the students, who came to hear her comments on American culture.

That first evening Callie remarked to Jake, "Maybe taking part in this conference was a mistake."

"Maybe," he agreed, "but neither of us thought so when the State Department came up with the invitation." State had procured a conference faculty invitation for Callie as a cover for the Graftons' presence in Hong Kong. "Don't be intimidated," Jake continued. "Answer the students' questions as best you can, and if the organizers give you the boot we'll see the sights for the rest of our stay. No big deal."

Today after the break, the questions concerned the American banking system. Hu Chiang had asked questions often during the last three days, and he was ready when the room fell silent.

"Mrs. Grafton," he asked in Chinese, the only language in use during the conference, "who decides to whom an American bank will lend its money?"

Hu was tall, more muscular than the average Chinese youth, Callie thought, which made him a fairly typical Hong Kong young adult, most of whom had enjoyed better nutrition while growing up than their mainland Chinese peers.

"The bank lending committee," Callie answered.

"The government gives the committee guidance?"

"No. Government sets the financial standards the banks must adhere to, but with only minor exceptions, the banks loan money to people and enterprises that are most capable of paying back the loan with interest, thereby earning profits for the owners of the bank."

This colloquy continued for several minutes as the party boss grew more and more uncomfortable. Finally, without even glancing at the listening official, Hu asked, "In your opinion, Mrs. Grafton, can capitalism exist in a society that lacks political freedom?"

The official sprang from his seat, turned to face Hu, and pointed his finger. "I can sit silently no longer. That question is a provocation, an insult to the state. You attempt to destroy that which you do not understand. We have the weapons to smash those who plot evil." He turned toward Callie. "Ignore the provocations of the criminal elements," he ordered peremptorily, closing the discussion. Then he sat heavily and used a cloth to wipe his face.

Callie was trembling. Although she could speak the language, she felt the strangeness of the culture acutely. She was also worried that she might somehow say something to jeopardize the conference or the people who had invited her.

"Mr. Hu merely asked my opinion," Callie said, trying to hold her voice steady. "I will answer the question."

The official's face reddened and his jowls quivered. "Go," he roared at her, half rising from his seat and pointing toward the door. "You insult China with your disrespectful attitude."

Callie gathered her purse and headed for the door. As she walked she addressed her questioner, Hu Chiang, who was still standing in the audience. "The answer to your question, Mr. Hu, is no. Political freedom and economic freedom are sides of the same coin; they cannot exist independently of each other."

"I got thrown out," she told Jake when she unlocked the hotel room door and found him on the balcony reading.

"I thought you would, sooner or later," he said and grinned broadly. "Still glad we came?"

She slumped on the side of the bed and held her head in her hands.

Jake put his arms around her. "Hey, I called the consulate. Tiger Cole wants us to come to dinner tomorrow night."

"I told you so," Callie Grafton said through her tears, then tried to smile.

Removing the tape player that would play the miniature tape he had taken from China Bob's library from the tech shop in the basement of the consulate presented Tommy Carmellini with several problems, the most intractable of which was that the device could not be in two places at once. Kerry Kent had access to the office. Carmellini thought that if she chose to look for the player while it was missing, she would realize that Carmellini had lied to her, that he didn't trust her. She might even conclude that she was a possible suspect in China Bob's murder.

The problem was that the tape player was a unique device that played a nonstandard small tape that held up to eight hours of recording, so Carmellini couldn't hope to buy one over the counter at a gadget shop.

Tommy Carmellini thought about all of this as he stood in the small shop staring at the one serviceable tape player. Or was there only one? The room was chock-full of electronic components and gizmos, perhaps he just didn't know what was there. He began searching under the workbench, then worked his way to the large steel filing cabinets that stood against the back wall.

Aha! On the top of the cabinet behind an obsolete commercial Sanyo reel-to-reel tape player was another small player that looked as if it could handle the tape from China Bob's. He got it down, blew the dust off it, sat it beside the first one. Yes. The same model, controls, etc. He plugged the thing in and found a tape in one of the drawers that looked like it would fit. When he had the tape properly installed on the reels, he pushed the Play button.

Nothing. The thing was broken.

Without a qualm, he put the working machine in his attaché case and left the broken one in its place. There were several headsets lying around, so he selected one and tossed it into the case, too.

He found Kerry writing a report in the office the CIA officers used. The senior man was there, Bubba Lee, schmoozing with two of the other permanent men, George Wang and Carson Eisenberg. All three were Chinese-Americans; Lee and Wang had two Chinese parents, Eisenberg had a Chinese mother. All could speak perfect Cantonese and pass for natives, which they often did. This morning they wanted to shoot the breeze about Harold Barnes, who had been in Hong Kong for only a couple of months before he was killed.

"I went to the police department this morning," Eisenberg told Tommy, "to see if they have developed any leads on Barnes. They were all atwitter over China Bob's murder last night. You and Kerry got out of there just in time. They kept everyone else until dawn, including Mr. Cole."

"Did they ever find the murder weapon?"

"Little automatic, nickel-plated?"

"Could have been."

"Found it in the secretary's office just outside the library, in the trash can."

"That makes sense," Kerry Kent said. "If I had just shot someone, I would want to get rid of the weapon as soon as possible."

Tommy Carmellini stared at her in amazement. She was either ditsy or had more brass than any broad he had ever run across.

Lee and the others spent a very pleasant half hour going over the Chan layout with Tommy, speculating about motives, generally rehashing everything, and reaching no conclusions.

Then, finally, the men returned to their offices, closed their doors, unlocked their private safes, and got on with the business of covert and overt espionage, leaving Carmellini to the gentle company of the British transplant, Kerry Kent.

"I wonder who has the tape," she said. "Barnes was always such a careful workman. One must assume the device worked and someone swiped the tape."

Carmellini shrugged.

"One has to assume," she continued, "that the tape is the key to the mystery."

"If you think I have it, you're barking at the wrong dog," he said.

She came over to the desk where he was sitting, squatted so her face was level with his. No more than twelve inches separated them. "You can trust me, you know."

"So you think I have it."

"I don't think you trust me."

"Whatever would give you that impression? I've known you three whole days . . . no, four now. Four delightful days of humdrum work and one evening of romance lite. You kissed me what? Twice? I trust you as much as you trust me."

"I never mix business and pleasure."

"So there's no hope for us? Wait until my mother hears the news; she had such high hopes. Now get up off the floor and go sit in a chair. A woman kneeling before me will give people the wrong impression and create a tragic precedent."

Kerry did as he asked.

"What I'd like to know," he said, "is how many people paraded through that library before and after me, looked over China Bob's corpse, then went back to the party and didn't say a word to anyone."

"This morning a request came in from the chairman of the congressional committee," she informed him. "Congress invited China Bob to Washington to testify."

"All expenses paid, no doubt."

"The poor man is probably better off dead," Kerry said firmly. "His position between the Chinese and the Americans was going to get scorching hot."

"Whoever shot him did him a real favor," Carmellini agreed. He picked up his attaché case and walked out of the office.

"I had just graduated from college when I first came to Hong Kong," Callie Grafton told her husband as they walked the streets of Kowloon, taking in the sights, sounds, and smells. "I felt like I had finally come to the center of the earth's civilization, the place where all the currents and tides came together.

"I remember my first ride on the Star Ferry as if it were yesterday. The white-and-green boat was *Morning Star*, very propitious, you must agree, for a girl making her way in the world for the very first time. All of the thirty-nine-ton double-ended diesel boats are named for stars, and between them made four hundred and twenty crossings a day between Kowloon and Central. Each crossing took about ten minutes, regardless of the weather or sea conditions. The boats began running at six-thirty in the morning and stopped at eleven-thirty at night. There were two classes of passengers—first class, which rode on the upper deck, and second, which rode on the main deck.

"Everyone who lived or worked or visited Hong Kong rode on these ferries. On days off I would ride the ferries a dozen times a day, looking at the people and listening to them talk, laugh, cry, giggle. . . . Chinese laborers and wealthy merchants and sons and daughters and wives and mistresses and teenage toughs, English civil servants and nannies, Australian adventurers, tourists from everywhere on earth, Europeans, Russians, American sailors, Malays, Filipino maids, Japanese businessmen, Hindus, Sikhs—everyone came to Hong Kong, to make money and a new life for themselves or just to see it, to learn the truth of it. All the roads of the earth lead to this place.

"I loved the city. It was British, colonial, civilized, grand and trivial, yet it wasn't. It was Chinese, but not quite. It was timeless, yet everyone was in a hurry and the city was being transformed before my eyes.

"From this city I could feel the power of China, the thousand million people, the ancient and the new, the way of the seeded earth. I came to think of China as a giant oak, deeply rooted and enduring through the centuries while the lives of men changed like the seasons.

"In this city I can still feel the pulse of the earth. I can stand in the crowded places and listen to the hundreds of voices, all babbling about the things that fill human lives. I can hear the generations talking of the things that never change, the dreams, ambitions, and concerns that make us human."

Jake Grafton squeezed his wife's hand, and they walked on.

Rip Buckingham's brother-in-law, Wu Tai Kwong, was a delivery driver for the Double Happy Fortune Cookie Company. Rip was happily married and living in Hong Kong when he learned that his wife's younger brother was involved in the anti-Communist movement in Beijing. The whole thing seemed innocent enough . . . until that same brother-in-law stood in front of the tank in Tiananmen Square in 1989 and had his photo plastered on every front page in the world. That incident made him a criminal. And a dedicated revolutionary.

Now, of course, he was a fugitive . . . and living in Rip's basement. Although he was a notorious political criminal and the object of the greatest manhunt in Chinese history, the government had no idea what Wu looked like now, where he was from, who his family was, or what name or names he might be using. Perhaps this was to be expected in a nation where public records were spotty at best, a nation where a significant portion of the population was illiterate and without identity papers of any kind, a nation with more than a hundred million migrants who roamed at will, looking for work.

Still, the Chinese authorities knew with an absolute certainty that sooner or later they would get their man. They had offered a large reward for Wu Tai Kwong. Human nature being what it is, they had merely to wait until someone betrayed him.

Wu Tai Kwong, being who he was, was not hiding. True, he wasn't broadcasting his whereabouts and he was using a false name and false identity papers, but he had no intention of stopping his political activities. He hated the Communists and intended to destroy them or be destroyed by them, whichever way fate spun out the story.

The tale could go either way, he realized. Someone who knew or suspected who he might be would tell someone, and so on, and the rumors would spread like ripples in a pond. Still, Wu had to talk to his friends, had to plan, to plot, to conspire against those he hated. He did so knowing that any day could be his very last, for he knew that once the Communists caught him they would execute him quickly, then broadcast the news of their triumph.

This afternoon he stopped his delivery van at various corners on Nathan Road and picked up the solitary people standing there waiting. He picked up four men and a woman in this manner, then found a quiet place to park near the old Kai Tak airport. These people knew him, knew his real name, knew the risks he took, and he trusted them with his life. Since they literally held his life in their hands, they also trusted him.

Today this "gang of six" discussed the current situation, the public anger at the failure of the Bank of the Orient, the predictable resentment against the PLA for shooting into an unsuspecting crowd.

"Is this the spark? Is now the hour?"

They debated the question hotly.

To overthrow the Communists, Wu Tai Kwong had argued for years, two things must come to pass. The great mass of people must be aroused against the government, and the army must refuse to fight the people.

"There are things still to be done," Hu Chiang argued. "We are almost ready, but not quite."

"The police know far too much," the woman replied. Alas, keeping the existence of a large subversive organization a total secret was impossible. People whispered, some tried to sell information to the authorities, others wanted to betray their colleagues and the movement for reasons that ran the gamut of human emotions. "There are too many leaks, too many people talking. We must wait no longer. Every day we wait the danger grows, yet we grow only marginally stronger."

"We are bribing the police," one man pointed out when his turn to talk came. "Every day the number of people who want money grows. It is inevitable that someone will take a bribe and turn us in . . . if they haven't called Beijing already. We must act now!"

Wu waved them into silence. "There is another factor. The Americans suspect that the American consul, Cole, has moved money into Hong Kong. They are trying to trace the money, find out where it went. China Bob Chan is dead, but the trail is not cold. If we wait too long, the Americans may decide to tell Beijing what they know . . . or suspect."

"So that is the decision?" Hu Chiang demanded.

"I will not make the decision," Wu told them. "We will vote. Now."

Only Hu Chiang voted to wait.

"Then it is decided," Wu told them. Even Hu looked relieved that the waiting was over, he thought.

"The longest journey begins with the first step. Let us begin."

As he started the van to drive away, Wu remarked, "We must win or die."

"Win or die," they murmured.

The house where the Buckinghams lived perched precariously on the side of the mountainous spine of Hong Kong Island, just below the Victoria Peak tram station. From it one had a magnificent view of the central business district, Kowloon, and the harbor.

The roof of the building was flat. Paved with tile and equipped with lawn chairs and sun umbrellas, it made a wonderful patio on almost any day clouds did not obscure the sun. At the head of the staircase was a small room with large windows that Lin Pe, Rip's mother-in-law, used as a greenhouse.

When he got home, Rip found his wife, Sue Lin Buckingham, on the roof sitting under an umbrella, reading. He removed a cold beer from the refrigerator in the greenhouse and sagged into a lawn chair beside her. As he summed up the events of the day, his wife put down her book and listened in silence.

Sue Lin was a rarity, a highly educated Chinese woman. She had never known her father, who died before she was born. Her mother made a small fortune in fortune cookies and insisted that her daughter get an education. Sue Lin spent her teenage years at a private school in California, then got bachelor's and master's degrees from the University of California at Berkeley.

Rip Buckingham, Australian bum and Chinese aficionado, fell for her the very first time he saw her. She had not been similarly smitten, but he persisted. Eventually he won her heart, a triumph that he still regarded as the great accomplishment of his life. She was, he thought, the most gracious lady he had ever met.

This evening she listened in silence to Rip's narrative of the Bank of the Orient debacle and his summary of Governor Sun's statement.

"The statement was really an order telling you how to write the story, wasn't it?"

"Yes, I suppose." Rip took a big swallow of beer, then stared glumly at his toes.

"The government may shut down the newspaper. You've been expecting it."

"I know. I just kept hoping it wouldn't happen." He swept his hand at the city before them. "This is our city, our place. We have done nothing wrong. The paper merely prints the news in a fair, unbiased manner. What's wrong with that?"

Sue Lin didn't reply. "Perhaps they won't shut you down."

Rip sipped some more beer. "It's time we thought about leaving."

"We can go anytime," his wife responded without enthusiasm. They both held Australian passports. "But I don't want to go without Mother. You know that. And Mother won't leave Hong Kong."

"She always said she wouldn't leave, sure, but this place is going to explode," Rip argued. It was hell trying to use logic on women who didn't want to hear it. "This isn't the city that it used to be. She *must* see that! And she had money in the Bank of the Orient. In the middle of listening to the reporters and writing the story, that thought ran through my head."

"Money or no money, she won't leave without my brother. Absolutely not."

"I guarantee you he won't leave alive. Not a chance in hell."

"He's all she has from her early life."

"Bull! She has both of you! I know there were three other children, but that was thirty-some years ago. They are adults with children of their own or they're dead."

"Rip, you don't understand."

"I *do* understand. And I think it's time your mother listened to reason. When this place explodes, your brother is going to be leading the revolution. The government is going to figure out who he is—who his mother is, who his sister is, who his brother-in-law is. While Wu is busy answering destiny's call, the Communists are going to put you, me, and your mother against the wall and shoot us dead. *We're running out of time!* If we don't leave we'll die here. We've *got* to get the hell out of China!"

"Don't be ugly."

"Why don't you listen to reason?"

Sue Lin held out her hand. He took it.

"Our world is coming apart," Rip told her. "Everything is cracking, breaking, shattering into thousands of pieces. I feel helpless, doomed. At any second the great quake will come and this little world where you and I have been so happy is going to cease to exist."

Tears ran down her cheeks. She turned her back on him and wiped them away.

They were sitting side by side, holding hands and looking at the city, when the cook called from the greenhouse and told them dinner was ready.

CHAPTER FOUR

Tommy Carmellini was waiting in their hotel room when the Graftons returned after dinner. He was sitting in the darkness well back from the window.

"Did the maid let you in?" Jake asked sharply.

"No, sir. I let myself in. I didn't want the staff to know I was here."

"Next time wait in the lobby."

"Right."

"Callie, this is Tommy Carmellini."

"Mrs. Grafton, you can call me Jack Carrigan. That's the name I travel under."

"So you have two names, Mr. Carmellini?"

"Sometimes more," he admitted, grinning.

"Most people are stuck with only one," Callie said, "the one their parents picked for them. It must be nice to have a name that you pick yourself and can toss when you tire of it."

"That *is* one of the advantages," Carmellini agreed cheerfully.

"I brought the tape player." He gestured toward the bed, where the device rested. "I don't speak Chinese. To me it just sounds like a bunch of birds twittering."

Jake flipped on the rest of the lights as Callie seated herself on the bed across from Carmellini. She eyed the tape player distastefully. "What's on the tape?" she asked.

Carmellini leaned forward and looked into her eyes. "A CIA officer was murdered just hours after he planted two bugs and a recorder in the library of a man named China Bob Chan. Two nights ago China Bob was shot and killed in that library by a party unknown. I got there before the body cooled and took the tape from the recorder. That tape is probably the best evidence of the identity of the person who killed Chan. In fact, it may be the only evidence we'll ever get. It also might shed some light on who killed the CIA officer."

"You told Jake that Tiger Cole, the consul general, might have killed Chan."

"Mrs. Grafton, anyone in Hong Kong could have gone into that library and shot China Bob."

Callie glanced at Jake, who said nothing.

"The recorder was voice-activated," Carmellini explained, "so that valuable space on the tape wouldn't be wasted recording the street noises that penetrated an empty room. When the sound level dropped below the electronic threshold, the tape would play on for a few seconds, then stop. Places on the tape where the recorder stopped were marked as audible clicks."

"We'll play it later," Jake Grafton said in a tone that settled the issue.

"Sure." Carmellini rose to go. "Nice to meet you, Mrs. Grafton." Callie merely nodded.

Buckingham Lin Su, or as she wrote it in the Western style, Sue Lin Buckingham, found her mother, Lin Pe, in her study consulting her fortune book. Lin Pe lived in her own three-room apartment in the Buckinghams' house. Just now she was smoking a cigarette which she had fixed in a short black plastic holder. The smoke rising from the cigarette made her squint behind the thick lenses of her glasses.

Sue Lin broke the news. The Bank of the Orient had collapsed, failing to open its doors today. Depositors trying to withdraw their money had been fired upon by soldiers.

Lin Pe took the news pretty well, Sue Lin thought, considering that her company kept all its accounts at the Japanese bank because it paid the highest interest rates in Hong Kong.

Lin Pe listened, nodded, and when Sue Lin left, got the accountant's latest summary from her desk and studied it.

The Double Happy Fortune Cookie Company, Ltd., was a profitable international concern because of one person—Lin Pe. Thirty years ago when she came to Hong Kong from a village north of Canton, she found a job in a factory that baked fortune cookies for export to America. Before she went to work there she had never even heard of a fortune cookie. The little fortunes printed on rice paper inside the cookies charmed her. She wrote some in Chinese and one day showed her creations to the owner, an alcoholic old Dutchman from Indonesia who also mixed the cookie batter and cleaned up the place at night, if he was sober enough. He translated a few, they went into the cookies, and Lin Pe had found a home.

When the Dutchman died five years later of cirrhosis of the liver, she bought the company from his heirs. It thrived, because Lin Pe was a very astute businesswoman and because the fortunes she put into her cookies were the best in the business.

About three dozen fortunes were in use at the cookie factory at any one time. Writing good fortunes was a difficult business. She was hard put to come up with three or four good new ones per month, which meant some of the old ones had to be used again. Lin Pe kept a book, her "book of fortunes," in which was recorded every fortune she had ever written and notations on what months it had been used. She changed the fortunes going into the cookies on a monthly basis.

Just now she put down the accountant's summary and consulted the fortune list she had constructed for use next month.

"Happiness will find you soon." She had used this fortune before and thought it one of her best. Other cookie people wrote "You will find happiness," but that was bland, without wit or snap. Lin Pe sent the happiness searching for you.

"Your true love is closer than you think." Love, Americans seem enamored with it. Many of the letters she received from restaurant owners in America pleaded with her to use more love fortunes in her cookies. Lin Pe had never been in love herself, so to write these fortunes she had to imagine what it might be like. This was becoming more and more difficult as the years passed.

"Beware . . . use great care in the days ahead." When she saw this fortune in her book, she inhaled sharply.

It was her fortune.

One cookie in three thousand contained that fortune. Yesterday she plucked a cookie off the conveyor belt as it was about to go into the packing machine, and that was the fortune inside.

She closed the book, unable to continue. She shivered involuntarily, then sat staring out the window.

Rip Buckingham disliked the Communists, and her son Wu hated them. Neither knew them like Lin Pe did, for she had lived through the Great Cultural Revolution. Occasionally she still awoke in the middle of the night with the stench of burning houses and flesh in her nostrils, listening for the shouts, the sobs, the screams. She had fled to Hong Kong to escape that madness; now the storm seemed to be gathering again out there in the darkness. She could feel its presence.

The money. Its loss was a disaster, of course, but perhaps the Japanese could be shamed into paying it back. The neat little men with their perfect haircuts and creased trousers must know the importance of keeping faith with their customers, even if the law didn't require it.

The cookie company could run a few days without writing checks. Lin Pe began considering whom she might borrow money from to meet the payroll. Rip and Sue Lin had plenty of money and would have loaned her all she wanted without giving it a thought, but Lin Pe was too proud even to consider that course of action. Amazingly, the possibility never crossed her mind. From her desk drawer she removed a private list of her fellow businesspeople and studied that.

Rip Buckingham's idea of the perfect way to spend an evening was to loaf in a lawn chair on his roof reading newspapers from all over the world as he sipped beer and listened to music. Occasionally he would pause to watch a ship slip through the harbor on its way to or from the open sea.

Hong Kong didn't have enough dock facilities, so many of the freighters had their cargo on- and off-loaded onto lighters, which were towed back and forth between their anchorages and the ships by tugboats. Flotillas of ferryboats were in constant motion crossing and recrossing the strait, fuel boats cruised for customers, tour and party boats dashed about, here and there someone sculled a sampan through the heaving ridges of waves and wakes.

Rip was not enjoying the view tonight.

He finished with a Beijing newspaper and threw it onto the pile with the Hong Kong dailies. He grabbed a Sydney paper and started flipping though it.

The problem was that he liked being a newspaperman. He liked going to the office, saying hello to everyone, reading the wire service stories, tapping away on his computer as the cursor danced along, then seeing it all in print. He liked holding the paper in his hand, liked the heft of it, liked the way that it felt cool to the touch. He liked the smell of newsprint and ink, liked the idea of trying to catch the world every day on a pound of paper. A newspaper was worth doing, and Rip Buckingham didn't want to do anything else.

And he wanted to keep doing it here. In Hong Kong.

He was still stewing, and trying to get into last Sunday's *Washington Post*, when his wife came through the greenhouse leading two men. Rip recognized them immediately—Sonny Wong and Yuri Daniel.

Wong Ma Chow, "Sonny," was a gangster, the leader of the last of the tongs. He made a huge fortune in Hong Kong real estate, then lost it in the collapse that followed the British departure. Since then he had returned to the service business. Whatever service you wanted, Sonny could provide . . . for a price.

Rip had seen Yuri Daniel, Sonny's associate, around town for four or five years. Rip had never before had any dealings with him, nor had he wanted to. Yuri was a Russian or Ukrainian or something like that, reportedly from one of those hopelessly poor, squalid villages in the middle of the vast Eastern European plain. Rumor had it that he left the mother country in a large hurry with a suitcase full of money taken at gunpoint from a Russian mobster. How much truth was in the rumor was impossible to say, but it was a nice rumor.

Yuri's expressionless face, with its cold, blank eyes and pallid features, certainly didn't inspire trust. Inspecting it at close range, Rip idly wondered why Sonny chose to be in the same room with Yuri Daniel.

"Hey, Sonny."

"Hey, mate. What do you hear on the Bank of the Orient thing?"

"At least fifteen dead."

"The lid is gonna blow off this place. People aren't going to take this lying down. Even I had money in that goddamn thing."

"Tea? Beer?"

"Beer would be great."

Sue Lin was still there, and now she nodded at Rip and went for the refrigerator.

"First time I've been up here," Sonny said, surveying the view from a chair beside Rip. "Hell of a view you got here, yessir. Hell of a view. You're right up here with the upper crust, looking down on the world."

Yuri sat on Sonny's other side, turned slightly away from the two of them. He hadn't yet said a word.

Sue Lin brought the beer, then left them. She paused at the door of the greenhouse and looked back, catching Rip's eye. She raked her windblown hair from her eyes, then went in, closing the door behind her.

". . . owned a building just below here some years back," Sonny was saying. He pointed. "That one right there, with the little garden on the roof. The value of that building went up to four times what I paid for it. I was collecting fabulous rents every month, then it all just . . . just melted away, like ice cream in the noonday sun."

"Yeah."

"One day, the whole thing . . ." He sighed.

Rip sipped a beer. Sue Lin had brought one for each of them. Yuri was looking at the ships in the harbor to the west.

"I always liked this view," Sonny said. "Always."

"Yeah."

"These are the last days of Hong Kong, Rip. It's coming to an end."

Rip didn't say anything to that. What was there to say?

"Got your message that you wanted me to drop by. So what can Wong and Associates do for the scion of the Buckingham clan?"

"China Bob Chan."

"Too bad, huh?"

"Got any ideas on who might have done it?"

"It wasn't me, Rip."

"Hey, Sonny. If I thought there was the slightest possibility, I would have respected your privacy. What I'm after is any background or insight you might be able to provide, not for attribution, of course. What was China Bob into?"

"You've been following the American thing . . . ?" Sonny began. "The PLA was giving him money to contribute to American political campaigns. Don't ask me why. The generals think the American politicos are as crooked as Chinese politicians. And they may be right—there was a guy in the American embassy in Beijing who was handing out visas to the United States to anyone who said he would go over there and contribute to the president's reelection campaign."

"Uh-huh."

"Chan was into the usual stuff here. And he was big into smuggling people, which I won't touch. It's too dirty for me, Rip, but not for China Bob."

"Where to?"

"Anywhere. Malaysia, Australia, America, anywhere people wanted to go, China Bob would do the deal. Course he didn't always deliver—it's a smelly business."

"Did he do passports?"

"S.A.R. passports, but no one wanted those," Wong said. Hong Kong became a Special Administrative Region of China in 1997 when the British turned over the colony. "I heard that for the right price—and the right price was very high—China Bob could produce genuine passports. That's not generally known around, I believe."

"Was he doing that a lot, do you think?"

"No country I know about is granting visas to people holding S.A.R. passports, so there isn't a lot of demand for those. The refugee problem has these other countries scared silly. The old British colonial passports are a dreg on the market—you can't get into America or Australia or Singapore or Indonesia or anyplace I know with one of those. Even Britain is worried about tens of thousands of Chinese refugees flooding in. No one is granting entry visas."

Rip sipped some more on his beer and waited.

"Guy like China Bob had a lot of deals going," Sonny said, thinking aloud. "The guy who sold China Bob blank American passports will deal with me, if you want. Faking an Australian visa on an American passport shouldn't be a problem."

"You and China Bob were sorta competitors, weren't you?"

Sonny bristled slightly at that remark. "Our businesses paralleled each other at times," he admitted. "There was room for both of us."

"You're talking a forged passport?"

"Genuine. The real thing, right out of the lock box at the consulate. The source is very reliable."

"Uh-huh."

"He's not honest, you understand, but he is reliable. That's a critical difference in business, one so few people appreciate."

"I think I see it," Rip told Sonny, who nodded as if he were pleased.

"I put the passport with Australian entry visa in your hands," Sonny explained. "You take your Chinese relative to the airport, put her on Qantas to Sydney. She breezes through immigration at both ends. Guaranteed."

"How much?"

"Twenty grand American. Cash. Half in advance, half on delivery of the documents."

Rip whistled. "Is that what China Bob was into?"

"He did a little of that. And he brought stuff in. He could get import permits for darn near anything; anything he couldn't get a permit for he could smuggle in. Money, import, smuggling—those were his main businesses, but he did some people, too. For fifty grand he could put your cousin on a freighter going to the United States. The Philippines were a real bargain, though, only about four thousand. Your cousin would be in a locked container with some other passengers. He'd have to take his own food and water with him, but he wouldn't get a sunburn. About eight days at sea, five hundred a day. Hell, Rip, it would cost more money than that to send him on a cruise ship."

"The passengers didn't always get there, though," Rip pointed out.

"Rip, I just couldn't say. Dumping the cargo at sea—something like that the people involved don't talk about. Oh, you hear whispers, but people like to whisper. Gives them something to do."

Rip waved away that possibility. He knew those kinds of things were happening, but he really didn't believe China Bob had gotten his hands that filthy for the paltry dollars involved.

Rip glanced at the Russian. On the other hand, Yuri looked like he would cheerfully cut your throat for cigarette money.

"Was Bob into Chinese politics, do you think?"

"Hey, Rip, I don't think the guy intentionally set out to die young."

"Well, he figured wrong somewhere, that's for sure."

"Everyone makes mistakes occasionally. Even China Bob."

"Think someone double-crossed him, one of his associates maybe?"

"I doubt if somebody shot him to get his wife. Wives being what they are, not too many people kill to get one. To get rid of one, yes." Wong snorted at his own wit. When the noises stopped, he said, "A double cross is likely. Though if I were a betting man, I would put my money on the PLA. Rumor had it Bob might go to America, embarrass a lot of important people." He shrugged.

"Thanks for coming by tonight, Sonny."

"Okay. Now tell me the real reason you called."

"I enjoy seeing your smiling face."

"I didn't shoot him, Rip. Bob and I did a lot of business together. His death leaves me scrambling, trying to salvage some things we had going. I'm not saying his death will be a net loss to me—I figure over time everything will balance out. You gotta be philosophical. These things happen."

"Uh-huh."

Sonny Wong gave up. "Great view you got here, Rip."

"Yeah."

"You ever want a passport for your mother-in-law, call me."

"I'll keep that in mind."

"Come on, Yuri. Let's go find some beds."

With her husband's help, Callie Grafton got the small tape reels properly installed on the player and pushed the play button. She was wearing the headset Carmellini had brought. Before her was a legal pad and pen on which she made notes and summarized the conversations as she listened. She made no attempt at a word-by-word translation. Occasionally she had to rewind the tape and listen to portions of conversations several times to make sure she had the meaning right.

Midnight came and went as she listened intently, occasionally jotting notes.

Finally she took a break, stopped the tape, and took off the headset. After she had helped herself to water, she muttered to her husband, who was out on the balcony watching the lights of the city; "What are you going to do with the tape after I finish with it?"

"I don't know. Depends on what's on it."

"I'm about halfway, I think. I don't understand everything I've heard, but Chan was apparently laundering money."

"For whom?"

"For the PLA. The money was going to America."

"Okay."

"The congressional investigators might be able to put voices and facts together to make something of all this."

"Perhaps."

She stood silently, stretching. Finally she lowered her arms and massaged his neck muscles. "Do you think Tiger killed him?"

"Hon, I don't know. I'm waiting for you to tell me what you think."

"What are you going to do if he did?"

"I don't know that either."

She went back inside and put on the headset.

It was three in the morning when Callie Grafton removed the headset and turned off the tape player. Jake was curled up on the bed, asleep.

She went out on the balcony and saw that rain had fallen during the night. Just now the air was almost a sea mist, which made the lights of the city glow wondrously.

She had listened to the ten minutes prior to the gunshot, which the tape captured, three times.

China Bob Chan had been a human, and presumably somewhere there was someone who cared for him, perhaps even loved him. Try as she might, Callie could work up no sympathy for the murdered man. He was gone and that was that.

She turned off the lights and lay down on the bed. She was so exhausted she wondered if she could relax enough to sleep. Then her eyes closed and she was out.

The sound of morning traffic coming through the open sliding-glass door woke Jake. Callie was asleep on the bed beside him.

Being as quiet as possible, he got up and put on running shorts, shirt, and shoes, made sure he had a key to the room, then slipped out and made sure the door locked behind him.

Down on the street the day was in full swing. People filled the sidewalk, all in a hurry, all rushing somewhere. Jake tried to stay out of their way until he got to Kowloon Park, with its semi-empty sidewalks. As he jogged through the park he passed morning exercise classes engaged in slow, stylized calisthenics that reminded him of ballet.

He ran the entire length of the park and out onto the sidewalks of

Austin Road, where he headed for the docks on the western side of the peninsula.

He had gone only a few dozen yards along Austin Road when he realized that he was being followed. Someone was jogging behind him, huffing loudly. And there was a car on the street, creeping along.

Jake Grafton glanced back over his shoulder, taking in the car and the man in casual pants who was running behind. He was a couple hundred feet back, and running was obviously not a sport with him. The guy was wearing the wrong shoes and carrying too much weight, for starters.

The thought of Callie asleep in a hotel room with the tape of China Bob's last hours on the bed beside her flashed through Jake's mind.

When he reached the street that ran beside the dock area, Canton Road, he turned left, south, to head back toward Tsim Sha Tsui on the southern tip of the peninsula. He kept his pace steady and tried not to look over his shoulder, though he did glance back once to make sure his tail had not collapsed on the sidewalk.

He veered left onto Kowloon Park Drive, just loping along.

Ahead was a ramp up to an overpass that went across the street and into the lobby of a major hotel. Looking neither right nor left, Jake took the ramp, made the turn at the top, and slowed just enough to go through the glass doors, which reflected the early morning glare.

His tail came thudding up the ramp, made the turn, charged for the door with his head down, inhaling deeply as he tried to get enough air to ease the pain in his chest. On the street below the car that had been keeping pace with the runner accelerated away.

Jake Grafton caught the tail by the throat as he came through the door and slammed him into a marble pillar, where the man collapsed, too stunned to move.

Glancing around to be sure no one was paying too much attention, Jake picked the man up by his pants and shirt and shoved him back out the door onto the ramp. There he slammed the man's head into the ramp railing, and the man passed out.

After he eased the heavy man to the concrete, Jake patted him down. He had a small automatic in a holster in his sock, so Jake relieved him of that and pushed it down inside his own athletic sock. A wallet . . . he didn't need that anymore, either. A few keys, matches, an open pack of Marlboros . . .

Grafton spent no more than ten seconds searching the man, then he straightened and went on into the hotel, leaving one middle-aged Western woman staring open-mouthed at him. No one else seemed interested.

Callie was still asleep when Jake let himself into the hotel room. The tape was still in the player.

Jake examined the pistol, a Chinese-made automatic, loaded. He put it in his luggage.

The wallet he had taken from the tail contained Hong Kong dollars and a variety of cards, all displaying Chinese characters.

He was toweling off after his shower when Callie awoke.

"Hey, beautiful woman, did you sleep okay?"

She sat up in bed, looked around at the bright room and the daylight streaming through the gauzy drapes.

"I don't know who killed that man, Jake."

"Couldn't tell from the tape?"

"Impossible to say. But China Bob was into everything. Everything! He smuggled people, money, dope . . . he was even bringing in computers and guns."

"Computers?"

"I couldn't make much sense of it."

"Was Cole on the tape?"

"I don't know. I don't know his voice."

"You'll meet him again tonight."

"I don't know that I want to."

"Hey, kiddo. We're the first team, okay? What say we have breakfast and see some sights?"

CHAPTER FIVE

The governor of Hong Kong, Sun Siu Ki, sat at his desk in City Hall puffing a cigarette as he listened to an interpreter translate Rip's story of the fatal riot in front of the Bank of the Orient from the *China Post*. A copy of the offending paper lay on the corner of the desk in front of him, out of his way. Spread out where he could read them were the front pages of three Chinese-language newspapers.

Sun couldn't believe his eyes or ears: Every editor in Hong Kong had apparently decided today was the day to tell the most outrageous lies about the government.

The copy of the leading Chinese-language paper had been hand-delivered to the governor's office by one of the newspaper's censors, who was horrified when he saw the paper rolling off the press. The lead headline and story on the Bank of the Orient failure was certainly not the one he had approved, and he wrote a note to the governor stating that fact.

The headline and story reported that Beijing had ordered the Bank of the Orient to close its doors since it had refused to lend money at superlow rates to customers designated by Beijing. The unspoken inference was that bribes in Beijing were the price of access to easy credit.

The censor had the presses stopped, but not before a truckload of the libelous papers had already left to be installed in vending machines in the northern area of Kowloon.

The other two papers carried slightly different versions of the same story. According to them the bank failure was the direct result of lending to unnamed politically connected entities who were unable to repay the loans, which had been made at ridiculously low rates. The morning editions of these papers had been distributed. The governor's aide bought these copies from vendors at the Star Ferry terminal on his way to work.

Everyone in Hong Kong was reading these lies.

The aide was in the next room, talking to the censors involved. Apparently both of them swore the stories were not the ones they approved for publication.

If the newspapers weren't enough, already this morning the governor had received a call from army headquarters: Several thousand people were sitting in the plaza outside the closed Bank of the Orient. They were peaceful enough, but they were there, a visible, tangible, unspoken challenge to the Communist government. As he listened to the interpreter, Sun Siu Ki was thinking about those people.

Behind his desk was a large window. Through that window, when he bothered to look, the governor could see a breathtaking assortment of huge glass-and-steel skyscrapers—one of which was the Bank of the Orient—designed by some of the world's premier architects. These buildings were the heart of one of the most vibrant, energetic cities on earth, a city as different from the old, decaying Chinese cities of the interior as one could possibly imagine. This difference had never impressed Sun Siu Ki.

A career bureaucrat, he was governor of Hong Kong because of his family's political connections in Beijing. He knew little about capitalism, banking, or the way Western manufacturing, shipping, and airline companies operated, and nothing at all about stock markets or the international monetary system. The wealth and dynamic energy of Hong Kong struck him as foreign . . . and dangerous.

A wise person once observed that Hong Kong was China the way it would be without the Communists. Nothing resembling that thought had ever crossed Sun Siu Ki's mind or caused him a moment's angst.

Baldly, he was in over his head. He didn't see it that way, however. Sun believed that he knew what he needed to know, which was how to surf the political riptides of the Communist upper echelons in Canton Province and Beijing.

The problem du jour was the defiance of the government's authority by the people in the streets . . . and the newspapers. As bad as the uncensored stories were in the Chinese press, the headline in the *China Post* was the most outrageous: 15 MASSACRED AT BANK OF ORIENT.

Sun Siu Ki had replaced a governor who didn't attack pernicious foreign ideas with sufficient vigor. If people saw that the Communists were too soft to defend themselves, they were doomed: They would be swept away, eradicated as thoroughly as the Manchus. Being human, the party cadres were doing their damnedest to prevent just such a disaster.

Many of the readers of the *China Post* were not Chinese. The newspaper's reactionary stories inflamed the foreign devils, and they wrote outrageous, incendiary letters to the editor, which that fool published. All this caused faraway officials of the foreign banks to fear the loss of their money. Foreigners thought only of money. The culpability of the *China Post* was plain as day to Sun Siu Ki.

He gestured the interpreter into silence and seized a sheet of fine, cream-colored paper with the crest of Hong Kong on the top. There were still many boxes of paper bearing this logo in the attic of Government House. Thrifty Sun saw no incongruity in using paper bearing the likeness of the British lion. He wrote out an order for the offending newspaper to cease publication and signed it with a flourish. After further thought, he wrote out an order for the arrest of the editor. A few weeks in jail would teach him to mind his tongue.

While he was at it, he wrote out arrest orders for all of the editors involved. The time had come, Sun told himself, to whip these people back into line and show them who was in charge.

With the newspaper editors dealt with, Sun began to ponder the best way to handle the protesters in front of the bank.

The CIA contingent was summoned to the consul general's office just minutes after they arrived at work.

"What's going on?" Tommy Carmellini asked Kerry Kent, because she was more fun to talk to than the three men. Prettier, too.

"Didn't you see the crowd in front of the Bank of the Orient when you came in this morning? The ferry from Kowloon was packed; the only topic of conversation was the demonstration they were on their way to join."

The consul general's office was large and sparsely furnished, apparently reflecting the taste of the current occupant. Virgil Cole was several inches over six feet, with wide shoulders and short blond hair that was suspiciously thin on top. Ice-cold blue eyes swept the people who trooped in and stood in front of his desk.

Carmellini had spent a few moments with the consul general when he checked in last week. Cole had said little, merely welcomed him to Hong Kong, shook hands, muttered a pleasantry or two, and sent him off. He had also attended a meeting that Cole had chaired.

Cole stood behind the desk now, looked into each face. "There's a crowd gathering in front of the Bank of the Orient this morning," he said without preliminaries. "Tang and the army will probably run them off before long."

No one disputed that assessment.

"I want to know what's going on in City Hall."

"We have some excellent sources there, sir," Bubba Lee began, but Cole waved him into silence.

"They are marvelously corrupt—I know that. The problem is our whisperers are too low on the totem pole. I want to know what Beijing is telling Governor Sun and General Tang and what those two are telling Beijing, and I want to know it now, in real time."

Lee took a deep breath and said, "The only way we can get that information, sir, is to tap the telephones."

"While you are at it, bug Sun's office. Do it today." Cole nodded curtly at Lee, then seated himself in the chair behind his desk and picked up the top document in his in-basket.

Apparently the spooks had been dismissed. Lee turned without a word and led his colleagues from the room.

Out in the hallway with the doorway closed, Lee faced them. "You heard him. He's the most garrulous man I ever met."

"A dangerous blabbermouth," Carson Eisenberg agreed.

"Nevertheless, he's given us our marching orders, so let's dive in. Carmellini, your star is rising."

As they walked toward the CIA office, Carmellini said, "Can anyone get us a couple of telephone company trucks and some uniforms?"

"Tommy, you are in a city where money doesn't just talk, it sings like Pavarotti. You can get anything in Hong Kong; the only question is the price."

"We need a floor plan of City Hall. Blueprints would be better."

"Blueprints, yes," said George Wang. "We bought them from a butler when the British were still in residence." He waggled his eyebrows at Kerry Kent, who stayed deadpan.

"Okay," said Tommy Carmellini, "this is how we're going to do it. . . ."

Rip Buckingham was in his office on the second floor of the newspaper, closeted with the newspaper's headline writer, when he heard a commotion on the stairs. By the time he got to the door the policemen were up the stairs and shouting fiercely at two reporters who were trying to keep them from coming in. One of the policemen, a sergeant, tired of a zealous reporter's interference and threatened to chop him in the side of the neck.

"Ng Yuan Lee, what are you doing?" Rip shouted in Cantonese, which froze the sergeant. He snarled at the reporter, who drew back.

"Rip Buckingham, I have a warrant."

"You're kidding, right?"

"No," the sergeant said, extracting a piece of paper from his pocket. "They have issued a warrant for your arrest, signed by the chief judge. The governor demanded it."

Rip Buckingham threw up his hands in resignation. He didn't, however, argue with the sergeant and his colleague, who were merely doing their jobs.

"I'm sorry, Rip," Marcus Hallaby, the headline writer, told him from the office door. "God, I'm sorry! I just didn't think the headline was that big a deal, and . . ." Marcus was crying. He was also half soused, precisely the same condition he had been in yesterday afternoon when he wrote the massacre headline, precisely the same condition he had been in for the last ten years. He covered his face with his hands and sagged against the wall.

"Hey, Marcus, it wasn't your fault," Rip said, trying to sound like he meant it. After all, he had been the one who always refused to fire Marcus when headlines irritated people he couldn't afford to irritate.

These little storms blew in several times a year. For a day or two there was lightning and thunder, then the sky would clear and Marcus would still be there, contrite, apologetic, slightly drunk.... The damn guy just couldn't handle life sober and Rip had never been able to condemn him for that.

"It was the story," he told Marcus. "And the governor..."

"We must shut down the newspaper, Buckingham," the sergeant said gently. "We have our orders. Everyone must leave the building. We will put a guard on the doors."

"Who gave these orders?"

"Governor Sun Siu Ki."

"May I see the paper, please?"

The order was in Chinese. Buckingham read it while the sergeant wiped his hatband and ran his hand through his hair. He ignored the curious staffers standing nearby and turned his back on Marcus, who was sobbing audibly. Rip folded the document and handed it back to the officer.

"Perhaps it will help if I tell all the staff in English what they must do." He said it easily, without even a hint of temper, and the sergeant agreed again. As a very young man touring China, Buckingham had learned the fine art of self-control.

Some of the staffers wanted to argue with the officers, but Buckingham wouldn't permit it. With sour looks, muttered oaths, and tears, the staffers—two-thirds of whom were Chinese—turned off the computers and office equipment and vacated the building. Buckingham remained the epitome of gracious affability, so he was given permission to have a private conversation with an assistant before the policemen took him away. Most of the staff milled helplessly on the sidewalk as the police car disappeared into traffic.

Jail held no terrors for Rip Buckingham. He had been incarcerated on several occasions in his footloose past when local policemen didn't know quite what to make of a six-foot-three Australian bicycling through forbidden areas, that is, areas in China off the beaten track, in which tourists were not permitted. He usually talked his way out of their clutches, but now and then he spent a few nights in the local can.

Fortunately his gastrointestinal tract was as impervious to bacteria as PVC pipe. Had his GI tract been more normal, one suspects he would not have strayed so far from tap water. He would probably be in Sydney now, married to one of the local sheilas, with one and a half blond kids, holding down some make-work position in his father's worldwide newspaper empire while the old man groomed him to follow in his footsteps, et cetera, et cetera.

As he rode through the streets of Hong Kong in the police car, wedged in the backseat between Sergeant Ng and his colleague, Rip Buckingham thought about the et ceteras. He also thought about his father, Richard Buckingham, and what he would say when he heard the news. Not the news his son had been arrested, but that the paper had been shut down.

Amazingly, for a man who owned fifty-two newspapers located in six countries, his father never really understood the romance of the printed word. Richard Buckingham saw newspapers as very profitable businesses with enviable cash flows. "Newspapers," he liked to say, "are machines for turning ink and paper into money."

Measured on Richard's criteria, the *China Post* had once been one of his best. B.C. Before the Communists.

Strange, Rip thought. He was thinking about the paper as if it would never publish again. Well, perhaps its day was over. For that matter, perhaps Hong Kong's day was over.

The Brits just turned over the keys and walked away. They went home to their unimpressive little island on the other side of the world and pretended Hong Kong never happened.

Maybe that was the wise thing to do.

Rip Buckingham shook his head, angry at himself. He was becoming demoralized. This was his city, his and Sue Lin's. She was born in Hong Kong, grew up here; he had adopted it.

Sue Lin loved Hong Kong.

Well, he thought defensively, he did, too. The city belonged to everyone who loved her. God knows, there were millions of people who did.

Despite his best efforts at keeping his spirits up, he was glum when the police car rolled through the gate of the city prison.

Damn Communists!

Sue Lin Buckingham told her mother that Rip was in jail, on a warrant demanded by Governor Sun Siu Ki. Policemen had arrested him, closed the newspaper. And this morning another riot was developing in front of the Bank of the Orient.

"Rip was foolish," Lin Pe told her daughter in Cantonese, the only language in which she was fluent. She spoke a little English, but only when she had to. She acquired most of her English from American movies which she watched on a VCR, running scenes over and over until she understood the dialogue.

The news about Rip annoyed her. He had no respect for authority! "He has been baiting the tiger with his news stories and editorials, and now the jaws have snapped shut. Only a fool spits in the eye of a tiger."

"The paper was losing circulation, Mother, and advertising." Sue Lin was tense, unhappy over the news of her husband's jailing, and her mother's simplistic reaction angered her. As if this lifelong capitalist didn't understand the dynamics of the marketplace! "The *Post* used to make money because it was *the* newspaper for Hong Kong bankers and businesspeople to read. Rip knew that he had to address the concerns of the people he wanted as readers or he would lose them. And when he lost them, he would lose the advertisers who wanted to reach them. It's that simple."

"Apparently Sun Siu Ki isn't concerned about Rip's advertisers," the mother snapped.

"Sun Siu Ki is an extraordinarily stupid bastard." Rip Buckingham's Chinese wife was no shrinking violet.

"That may be," her mother agreed evenly. These young people! "But he represents the government in Beijing, in precisely the same way that the old governor represented the queen in her palace in London. The difference, which dear Rip chooses to ignore, is that the English queen never laid eyes on a copy of the *China Post*. She didn't give a"—she snapped her fingers—"what Rip Buckingham said in his silly little newspaper in Hong Kong, on the other side of the planet. The people in Beijing don't share Queen Elizabeth's indifference. They apparently do read Rip's scribblings. They're a lot closer, their skin is a lot thinner, and Sun is their long right arm."

Sue Lin sank into a chair. "Oh, Mother, what are we going to do? Rip is in jail. No one knows how long they intend to keep him. They may even send him to a prison on the mainland."

Her mother's expression softened. "The first thing to do," she said, "is to call Albert Cheung, the lawyer. He knows everything. He will know what to do."

Lin Pe made the call. After talking to three people who pretended they never heard her name before in their lives, she got through to Albert Cheung, an illegal refugee from mainland China who was so smart that he won a scholarship to study law at Oxford. When he returned to Hong Kong, with a trace of a British accent and a fondness for tweeds, he managed to elbow his way to the top of the legal heap and into the inner sanctums even though he had no family in the colony. He had had a finger in every big deal in Hong Kong for the past twenty years. He was filthy rich and slowing down, yet he was too smart to pretend that he didn't remember Lin Pe.

"It has been years since I've heard from the chairman of the Double Happy Fortune Cookie Company, Limited," Albert Cheung said.

"You've been getting your dividends every quarter," Lin Pe told him. Albert took stock instead of a fee when she floated the initial public offering for her company on the Hong Kong exchange.

"Yes, indeed," he said. "I was wondering, have you ever thought of selling the company? Retiring to a life of leisure? Travel the world, see the Great Pyramids, the Acropolis—?"

"I've had some other things on my mind, Albert. Like getting my son-in-law out of jail."

"Rip Buckingham? See, I keep up. But I didn't know he was in jail. What has he done?"

"Sun Siu Ki closed the *Post* today and arrested him. Could you find out how long they intend to keep him?"

"So the tiger has him in his jaws?"

"Yes."

Cheung sighed. After a few seconds he said, "Many things are possible if you are willing to pay a fine. Would you—?"

"Within reason, Albert. I will not be robbed by anyone."

"I saw the headline in the morning *Post*: '15 Massacred at Bank of Orient.' And the PLA did the shooting. That headline was not wise, Lin Pe."

"I think Sun Siu Ki was just fed up."

"Perhaps the bank closing had—"

"Rip Buckingham's world is collapsing. He's been fighting back the only way he can."

"I'll see what I can do, Lin Pe. Give me your telephone number."

She did so, asked about his wife and children, then hung up.

"He'll see what he can do," Lin Pe told her daughter. "It will cost money."

"The newspaper will pay."

"The newspaper is finished," said Lin Pe. "It will never publish again."

"Richard Buckingham is a powerful man."

"Sun Siu Ki and the people in Beijing probably never heard of Richard Buckingham, and if they have heard, they don't care," Lin Pe said, which was, of course, true. To see beyond the boundaries of China had always been difficult. Even the queen of England, she reflected, knew more about the outside world than the oligarchy in Beijing.

"The next thing to do," Lin Pe said, "is to call your father-in-law. Someone from the newspaper has probably called him already, but you should do so now."

As her daughter walked from the room, Lin Pe added, "Don't forget, all calls out are monitored." She went back to writing fortunes.

Well, there it was. A way to get some money and get out before Wu Tai Kwong set China on fire. Sell the fortune cookie company to Albert Cheung!

The traders at the Hong Kong stock exchange had expected a wild ride in the aftermath of the collapse of the Bank of the Orient, but the ride was worse than anyone imagined it might be.

At the opening bell the traders were faced with massive sell orders, while the buy orders were minuscule. Prices went into freefall. Ten minutes went by before exchange officials finally learned that the computer system was at fault. Most—but not all—of the sell orders had an extra zero added just before the decimal, increasing the size of the orders by a factor of ten. On the other hand, some—not all—buy orders had their final digit dropped somewhere in cyberspace, shrinking them to a tenth of their original size.

The result was chaos. Since not every order was affected, the orders had to be checked by hand, which drastically limited the number of orders that could be processed. Unable to cope, officials closed the market.

Exchange officials quickly determined that they had a software problem, but finding the cure took most of the day. While they were working on it, one of the exchange officials was called to the telephone. The governor's aide was on the line demanding an explanation. For the first time, the exchange official mentioned the possibility of sabotage.

"Sabotage?" the governor's aide asked incredulously. "How could anyone do that?"

"Probably a computer virus of some type," he was told.

"Are you certain that is the case?"

"Of course not," the exchange official snapped.

Sun Siu Ki was on the telephone to Beijing when the phones went dead. He tried another line, couldn't even get a dial tone, so he motioned to an aide that there was a problem and handed the instrument to him.

Sun turned to General Tang, explained that Beijing wanted the bank demonstrators dispersed and, if possible, wanted to avoid a bloody incident that the press would publicize around the world, inflaming foreign public opinion. "Remove the press from the area," Sun advised, "before you remove the hooligans. That way the foreign press will be unable to use provocations as propaganda. Still, first and foremost, these hooligans must not be permitted to flout the authority of the state. That is paramount."

Tang understood his instructions and the priorities they contained. Both men firmly believed that the state could ill afford to give an inch to anyone challenging its authority or resolve. Perhaps they were right, because both men knew Chinese history and their countrymen.

In any event, they were determined men who believed that the party and the government could and should use every weapon in the arsenal, indeed, every resource of the state, to fight for the survival of the revolution. And if pushed, they were fully capable of doing just that.

The telephones had been off for ten minutes when Tang left the governor huddled with his aide, who tried to explain that the computers at the stock exchange had been sabotaged. As Tang rode out of the City Hall parking area in his chauffeur-driven car, two telephone repair vans passed him on their way in.

Three men wearing one-piece telephone company jumpers and billed caps climbed from the vans. Tommy Carmellini removed an armload of tools and equipment from the van he came in while Bubba Lee talked to the security guard in Chinese. Carson Eisenberg unloaded the equipment they needed from the other van. The men strapped on tool belts. When Lee motioned to them to follow, they picked up their equipment and trooped along in single file into City Hall.

Tommy Carmellini was worried. He was an obviously non-Chinese worker who didn't speak a word of the language. The other two spoke Chinese, of course, and they had assured Tommy that there would be no problem, but still . . .

When he walked into City Hall, Carmellini took the bull by the horns. The very first Chinese he saw, he brayed, as Australian as he could, "G'day, mate. Where's your switchbox?"

Carson Eisenberg repeated the question in Chinese, the official pointed and said a few words, and they were in!

The CIA officers went to work on the telephones. Since the system was an ancient government one, this involved picking up each handset and using a noisemaker that allowed a colleague in a manhole just up the street to identify the line and tap it. After each line was identified, there was much shouting in Chinese into the instruments for the benefit of the watching civil servants.

As the crew worked their way from office to office, Carmellini inspected the building and its security system. He did this as one of the uniformed guards stood beside him quietly observing his every move. Carmellini smiled at the guard, nodded, then ignored him.

The building looked modern enough. The hallways and rooms were spacious, with hardwood floors, but, like government offices the world over, looked crowded and cramped.

Carmellini was in the foyer of the governor's office examining the door locks and alarms when one of the staff began staring at him. Carmellini glanced at the man . . . and recognized him: It was the guy who had stared at Kerry Kent at China Bob Chan's party the other night!

The man's brows knitted; he knew he had seen Carmellini before but couldn't quite remember when or where. His puzzlement was obvious.

Carmellini headed for the hallway with his escort right behind.

The staffer followed.

Uh-oh!

He had seen a men's room a moment ago and he headed for it now, his entourage in tow. Inside he went into a stall and shut the door.

He listened as the staffer and the security escort chattered away, their remarks totally unintelligible.

Carmellini unzipped his overalls, shrugged them off his shoulders, and sat.

He sat listening for almost fifteen minutes, then flushed noisily and rearranged his clothing.

When he opened the stall door, the room was empty.

Carmellini was listening at the door of the men's room when he heard footsteps. He got away from the door just in time. It swung open, and the man, wearing a PLA officer's uniform, looked startled. Tommy nodded pleasantly and walked out.

The hallway was empty. He went down a flight of stairs, walked toward the service entrance, passed the table with the two security guards, and went out into the parking area. The other three men were still inside. Carmellini got behind the wheel of one of the vans and sat staring at the side of City Hall, waiting.

Everybody in Hong Kong seemed to be on their way to the Central District this morning. Public transportation facilities were packed, with long lines of people waiting to board subway trains, buses, taxis, and the Star Ferry at Tsim Sha Tsui. PLA soldiers at the Central District subway station, the MTR, tried to prevent people leaving the trains at that stop, but there were too many people and the soldiers were overwhelmed. Taxis and buses were directed not to discharge passengers when they stopped at the usual stops, so they stopped in the middle of city blocks and opened their doors. By ten in the morning at least ten thousand people were in the square in front of the Bank of the Orient and on the surrounding sidewalks.

That was the situation when General Tang arrived direct from the governor's office in City Hall. He became angry with his officers, whom he felt should have made greater efforts to prevent the crowd from gathering.

"Since we failed to prevent the crowd from gathering, now we must make it disperse," he instructed the staff, only to be told that the officers doubted they had enough soldiers present to make much of a show. Ordering the crowd to leave without sufficient soldiers to enforce the order would make the PLA appear ridiculous, an object of scorn.

"In accordance with your instructions, sir, we have used our men to prevent news media from congregating here."

"Why not prevent everyone from congregating?"

"We tried, sir, but we simply did not have enough men."

Tang lost his temper. "Why did you wait for me to tell you to get more men? This demonstration is a direct affront to the government. It is a crime against the state and will not be tolerated! Order the police to send all available men here. They should have been here already, preventing this crowd from gathering in an unlawful assembly."

"Sir, we have discussed this matter with the police, who say they have no spare men to send. All are engaged in law enforcement and traffic control duties elsewhere."

"Get more soldiers, as many as you need. Have them brought here by truck as soon as possible."

"Yes, sir."

Tang found a vantage point in a third-floor office of a nearby building. The civilians who worked for a shipping company were ejected and the soldiers moved in. From here Tang could see that the crowd below consisted of men, women, and children, all well behaved. People sat visiting with each other and, as the noon hour approached, ate snacks brought from home. Water and food vendors worked the crowd.

"Why have you allowed these vendors to congregate here?" Tang demanded of his staff. "Run them off."

The soldiers tried. The vendors promptly gave away everything on their carts and obeyed the soldiers, who laughed along with the crowd. Watching from above, Tang was coldly furious.

"Two hours, sir. We will have another two hundred men here within two hours."

"By truck?"

"Yes, sir. The trucks must go through the Cross-Harbor Tunnel, which is crowded at this hour."

Tang could contain his fury no longer. He stormed at the staff, berated them at the top of his lungs. When he had vented his ire, he retired to a private office and slammed the door.

Jake and Callie Grafton spent the morning cooped up with a flock of middle-aged British and American tourists riding a small tour bus around the coast of Hong Kong Island. They visited the mandatory jewelry factory—they looked but didn't buy—and rode a sampan to a fish restaurant in the harbor at Aberdeen.

A barefoot old woman in a loose cotton shirt and trousers, brown as a nut, with a lined, seamed face, sculled the tourists over. The restaurant was one of a half dozen in the harbor, all built on barges. Permanently anchored, covered with Victorian gingerbread painted in bright, gaudy primary colors, the restaurants somehow still managed to bear a faint resemblance to a pagoda.

These much-photographed temples of capitalism made Jake smile. Callie's mood, however, was somber; she hadn't smiled all morning.

After they had given the waiter their order—the waiter seemed to know an extraordinary amount of English, although Callie chatted with him in Chinese—Jake and Callie Grafton were left in semiprivacy with glasses of wine. They were seated in a booth by a window that looked across acres of fishing boats and the residential sampans of the boat people. Beyond the harbor were rooftops and high-rises, all the way up the mountain.

"You don't seem too happy about your glimpse into China Bob's affairs," Jake said tentatively.

"I'm sorry. I've got no right to be such a stick in the mud."

"Not your fault. The guy was a probably a shit."

"Sssh! People might be listening."

"I hope not."

"Let's just say he was a foul, evil man who made his living on the misfortunes of others."

"That would be fair."

"The tape was really hard to figure out," Callie explained, "and I don't think I've got it yet. I would say that at least half of the tape is made up of his side of telephone conversations. When he was silent too long, the tape stopped and one hears that infuriating beep, and the first few words of his next sentence are missing.

"Of course, he also had conversations with people in his office, and sometimes during those conversation he would take telephone calls.

"The tape is full of beeps, missing words, mumbled words, incomprehensible garble, and Chinese spoken too fast for me. Sometimes Chan and a visitor would both speak at the same time . . . sometimes they both shouted at the same time. Everyone around here smokes, have you noticed that?"

"Yes."

"They talk with cigarettes dangling from their mouth. . . ." She sighed. "The tape needs to be gone over by experts. All I got were snatches of conversation, words and phrases, sometimes a bit of give and take, usually just bits and pieces."

"And you don't know who killed Chan?"

"No. There is a beep—which means the tape was stopped—then a bit of a phrase, incomprehensible, and the shot. Nothing after that. The tape stops."

"Before that, what was on the tape?"

"Someone talking about an import permit for computers."

"Okay."

"And before that, an argument about money. It seems someone gave Chan money to give to people—I think in America—and he pocketed at least half of it, according to the man who shouted at him."

"You said Chan was into human smuggling?"

"That was the subject of several conversations, I think. Hard to be sure. I got the impression that it would be better for everyone if the cargo didn't survive the voyage."

"You aren't crying for China Bob?"

"I wouldn't mind throwing a shovelful of dirt in his face."

"Hmm." Jake took a sip of wine.

"Where's the tape now?" Callie asked. "Did you leave it in the room?"

"It's in my pocket."

"Oh. Okay."

"Along with a pistol I took off a guy who was following me this morning when I went jogging."

"You're kidding me."

"Nope. A little automatic. Loaded." Jake removed the man's wallet from another pocket and passed it to Callie. "See if you can figure out who this guy is."

She ignored the money, Hong Kong dollars equivalent to about forty dollars American, and examined each of the cards. "I don't know many Chinese characters," she said tentatively, "but none of this stuff looks like an official ID card. I would think that in Hong Kong everything is in English and Chinese."

She returned the documents to the wallet and passed it back. Jake took out the money and put it in his shirt pocket, so he could leave it on the table after lunch as a tip.

As they were eating lunch he realized that two people were watching him and Callie from the kitchen door and whispering together. One was a man who didn't look like he was kitchen help.

After a few minutes the man took a seat at an empty table by the door and devoted himself to studious contemplation of the menu.

"When we get back to the hotel," Jake said to his wife, "I want to see if I can get you a flight back to the states."

"I don't want to go back alone."

"And I don't want you in the middle of a civil war. I'm going to have a heart-to-heart talk with Cole, and then I think I'll go back, too. Sending me over here to root around was a bad idea from the get-go."

"You're worried about the man who followed you this morning, aren't you?"

"I'm getting worried about everything. We're in way over our heads."

As they rode the sampan back to the tour bus, he slipped the wallet into the water. When no one was looking, he did the same with the pistol.

Callie reached for Jake's hand. "Come on, Romeo, hold my hand. We're smack in the middle of an exotic city and I could use a little romance."

Lin Pe rode the tram down Victoria Peak. It was but a short walk from Rip and Sue Lin's house to the tramway, and the motorman always stopped on the way down when he saw her standing there. She stepped aboard and wedged herself in among a carful of plump, rosy-pink Germans. With barely a lurch the car continued its descent of the steep grade.

At the bottom she set off on foot, walking quickly, her small purse clutched tightly in her left hand.

Huge buildings rose on all sides, towering palaces of glass and steel. Around them traffic swirled on multilane streets that could be crossed only at over- or underpasses. Hiking the concrete canyons was strenuous, but Lin Pe could remember dawn-to-dark days in the rice paddies from her youth. Nothing could be as strenuous as those lean times, with too much work and not enough to eat.

The human sea thickened as she approached the bank square. Acres of people crowded the sidewalks and spilled into the streets. Most seemed content to stand right where they were since the bank square wasn't all that big. Still, Lin Pe pressed forward, worming her way through.

There were some soldiers about, but they were standing back, well out of the way. Lin Pe walked right by them and edged her way carefully into the middle of the square, where she finally found a tiny area of unoccupied concrete and sat.

The bank loomed before her like a dark, black cliff, blocking out the sun. When she looked straight up she could see a patch of blue sky.

She folded her hands in her lap and spoke to the woman beside her. They chatted politely for a moment—both had money in the closed bank—then fell silent, each lost in her own thoughts.

When Lin Pe had been very young there had been a man. He had worked hard and given her six children. One died in infancy; the three eldest she left behind with his parents after he died. The two youngest, Sue Lin and Wu, she carried away, one in each arm, when she decided she must go. Without her man, burdened with the children and his parents, both of whom were vigorous enough then but growing older, she would never be able to make it. She had too many children ever to attract another man. So she left.

She sat in the square thinking about the children she left behind, as she did for a few minutes every day. Finally her mind turned to fortunes. Thinking up fortunes had been the most important thing in her life for many years now, and she returned to it whenever the world pressed in.

"Go always toward the light" had been one of her favorites. The words seemed to mean more than they said, which was why the fortune appealed to her. She thought about it now, about what inner meaning might be hiding in the words.

By midafternoon Tang's officers believed they had enough soldiers to force the crowd to leave, so they sent a staff officer to man the loudspeaker mounted on a van.

Like a thick, viscous liquid, the thousands of people began slowly flowing outward from the bank square. The crowd was orderly and well behaved and obeyed the soldiers with alacrity.

Thirty minutes after the order was given, only a few hundred civilians were still in sight from Tang's third-story window.

He turned to his officers. "Wait for more soldiers, you said, so we waited. And when told to go, the people went like sheep. For hours they sat here illegally, in open and notorious defiance of the government. They have made fools of us again."

One of the senior colonels tried to argue that the reason the crowd dispersed in an orderly fashion was because there were so many troops in sight, but Tang was having none of it. The government had been defied; he could feel it.

"Another crowd may return tomorrow," Tang said, "so I want enough troops stationed on the streets to deny access to this square. And put four tanks in the square. We will advertise our strength."

One of the people who did not leave the square was Lin Pe. She was sitting against a curb with a flower bed behind her, and she was very small. The soldiers ignored her.

When she was almost the last civilian left in the square, Lin Pe slowly levered herself erect and turned her back on the bank.

Eighteen-year-old Ng Choy watched her leave. He didn't know her, of course. She was just a small, old woman, one of thousands he had seen in and around the square that day.

Ng Choy turned his attention back to the stain on the concrete where the man he had shot yesterday had fallen.

His rifle was heavy in his hands.

There were three of them, and they would probably have killed Tommy Carmellini if he hadn't been scanning the faces in the crowd. He was walking from the consulate toward the Star Ferry, trying to go with the ebb and flow of packed humanity. He was renting a room by the week in a cheap hotel in Kowloon until he found an apartment, and he was on his way there after work. Hordes of people jammed the sidewalks and spilled into the streets this afternoon, even more than usual for Hong Kong, a notoriously crowded city.

The eyes tipped him off. The man was fifteen feet or so away, standing by a power pole, when he saw Carmellini. His eyes locked on the American, who happened to glance straight at him. The man was several inches shorter than Carmellini and powerfully built. He left the spot where he had been standing on an interception course.

Instinctively, Carmellini turned and started the other way. And saw another set of brown eyes staring into his as a man closed in from the direction of a street vendor's cart.

Carmellini didn't hesitate. He leaped for this second man, so quickly that he took his assailant by surprise. Carmellini knocked the man down as he went over and through him and kept on going.

As he turned a corner he looked back, and that was when he realized there were three of them pushing and shoving people out of the way as they chased him.

Oooh boy!

Tommy Carmellini stepped off the jammed sidewalk and began running along the gutter, between the sidewalk and the traffic coming toward him. Behind him the three thugs did the same.

Of course he was unarmed.

Carmellini was carrying a thin attaché case that contained a Hong Kong guidebook, a Chinese-English phrasebook for tourists, and a Tom Clancy paperback. After he got through the first intersection he glanced behind him. His pursuers were successfully dodging traffic, still coming, so he tossed the case into the street and settled down to some serious running.

He loosened his tie and the top button of his shirt.

After three blocks the street became limited access and separated from the sidewalk. Carmellini stayed in the street.

The three thugs following had lost some ground.

As he went under an underpass a speeding truck grazed Carmellini and bounced him off the concrete abutment. He kept his feet but he lost a step or two. When he topped the underpass his pursuers were closer.

Oh, man! That damned tape. He didn't have it and he didn't know what was on it! Of course the guys behind him wouldn't believe *that*! No doubt they were out to get the tape and permanently shut his mouth.

A few more blocks and he was into the Wanchai District, today as tame and touristy as North Beach in San Francisco, but in its day home to some of the raunchiest whorehouses east of Port Said.

But how did they know about the tape?

As he ran he worked on that problem in a corner of his mind.

The crowd here was only a bit thinner than the throng in the Central District, but the night was young.

Running down the street in his suit and tie pursued by three thugs, looking futilely for a cop, Tommy Carmellini was a victim looking for a crime site. Twice he ran by knots of armed soldiers standing on street corners, and the soldiers made no move to stop him or the three men following.

Insane! Like something from a pee-your-pants anxiety nightmare.

He considered possible courses of action and rejected them one by one. Dashing through a nightclub, darting into a building, jumping on a moving truck . . .

When he saw the entrance to the MTR, the subway, he didn't hesitate. He charged down the stairs and hurtled the turnstile.

He went around two sharp turns . . . and there was his opportunity. About nine feet or so over his head was a scaffolding on the side of a wall, for repairing light fixtures or something.

Without even pausing, Carmellini launched himself. He caught the bottom pole—the scaffolding was of bamboo poles—and swung himself upward. He hooked a leg and was up, flat on the walkway, when the three men chasing him rounded the corner and shot underneath.

This wasn't the time or place for a breather.

Quick as a cat, Tommy Carmellini swung down and charged back up the stairs, fighting the stream of people coming down. Out on the street he slowed to a walk and joined the crowd flowing along Hennessey Road.

Kerry Kent. As he walked he remembered how she hugged him at the party as they waited for the car, subtly ran her hands over him. Could she be the rotten apple?

And if she wasn't, who was?

CHAPTER SIX

Jake and Callie Grafton had dinner in Tiger Cole's private apartment at the consulate. Jake wondered if he would have recognized the consul general if he had seen him on the street. Cole was several inches over six feet, with wide shoulders and thinning, sun-bleached hair. No doubt the hair was graying. . . . His eyes were as blue as ever and still seemed to look right through you, or perhaps it was only Jake's imagination, a trick of memory from years ago.

Small talk wasn't Cole's forte. He listened politely to Callie, who tried to fill the silence with the story of the conference fiasco, impressions of Hong Kong, and a running commentary on Jake's career through the years. She told him about Amy and about Jake's current assignment at the Pentagon, and wondered about Cole's life. His answers were short, almost cryptic, but he looked so interested in what she was saying that she kept talking. Finally, over the main course, she fell silent.

"You two are very lucky," Cole said, "to have found each other. You seem very happy together."

"We are," Jake Grafton said and grinned at his wife.

"I was married three times," Cole continued, speaking softly. "Had a girl by my first wife and a boy by my second. The boy died two years ago of a drug overdose. His heart just gave out. He'd been in and out of rehab facilities for years, could never kick the craving." Cole stirred his dinner around on the plate with his fork, then gave up and put the fork down. He sipped at the wine, which was from California.

"I wasn't a good father. I never understood the kid or the demons he fought. I thought he was stupid and I guess he figured that out."

"Jesus, Tiger!" Jake Grafton said, "That's a hell of a thing to say!"

Cole looked at Callie. "Now *that* is the Jake Grafton I remember. Was never afraid to say what was on his mind."

Grafton finished the last of his fish and put his silverware on his plate.

"I wondered about you," Cole continued. "Wondered if you were still the way I remembered, or if you had turned into a paper-pushing bureaucrat as you went up the ladder."

"I see you're still the silver-tongued smoothie who charmed your way through the fleet way way back when," Jake shot back.

"Yep, still an asshole." Cole flashed a rare grin. "My presence in the diplomatic game is a stirring testament to the power of political contributions. I knew you were wondering—that's the explanation in a nutshell."

"You owe Callie an apology for sitting there like a bump on a log letting her carry the conversation."

Cole bowed his head toward Callie. "He's right, as usual. I apologize."

She nodded.

"When I saw the newspaper article a couple years ago announcing your appointment, I had a chuckle," Jake said. "You're so perfectly suited for the diplomatic corps, why'd you take this appointment?"

"After the kid died I needed to get the hell out. I was wasting my life with people with too much money and not enough humanity. I didn't like them and I didn't like the man I had become. When this opportunity came I grabbed for it like a drowning man going after a rope."

"You certainly had some interesting experiences in Silicon Valley," Jake commented. "You helped design key networking software, you started a company that got one of the biggest contracts to make the Chinese telephone and air traffic control systems Y2K compliant.... Certainly sounds as if you had your plate full."

"You did some checking on me before you came to Hong Kong."

Jake Grafton chuckled. "I did. I made some inquiries when I got the chance to come to the conference here with Callie."

"The company did the bulk of the Y2K China stuff after I left."

"You were over here then, weren't you?"

"That's right. I had to put my shares in a blind trust."

"So just how advanced are the Chinese computer systems?"

Cole made a face. "They've bought some state-of-the-art stuff. Hong Kong is as wired as any American city. On the mainland it's a different story; only the most obvious public applications have been computerized. The reason their growth rate is so high is that they are leapfrogging tech levels. For example, the first telephone system some cities are getting is wireless."

Cole fell silent. It was obvious he didn't want to talk about computers or high tech, so Callie changed the subject. "Tell us about Hong Kong," she said.

A glimmer of a smile appeared on Cole's face, then quickly vanished. This was a subject that interested him. "The rich are getting richer and the poor are getting left farther behind. That happens throughout the industrial world, but in China there is no social mobility mechanism. If you are born a poor peasant you can never hope to be anything else. In an era of rapid change, that hopelessness becomes social dynamite. The reality is that the forces of social, economic, and political change are out of everyone's control, and the dynasty of Mao Tse Tung is numbered. Every day the tensions are ratcheted tighter, every day the pressure builds."

"These demonstrations in the Central District that the government is dispersing with troops—what is that all about?"

"A Japanese bank failed and the depositors lost their money. The Chinese government doesn't want to attempt to overhaul the banking system, which is state-owned and insolvent. The government has used the banks to fund bad loans to state-owned heavy industry. They can't fix the system, so they ignore the problem."

"Isn't that dangerous?"

Cole shrugged. "The state-owned industries and the banks are insolvent. To wipe out all the debts is to admit that socialism is a failure and fifty years of policy has been one massive error. To make that admission is to forfeit their mandate to rule."

"So there's no way out?"

"The crunch is inevitable."

"Since Callie got thrown off the platform at her conference and these demonstrations keep getting bigger and bigger, we thought we might go home early," Jake said, stretching the truth only a little. "I called the airlines this afternoon with no luck. There are no seats at any price. Everyone and their brother is trying to get out of Hong Kong."

"A lot of people are worried. They certainly ought to be."

"Someone said the troops are after a political criminal."

"The troops are hunting a man named Wu Tai Kwong, public enemy number one, which is a measure of how paranoid the government has become. The man who stood up to them in Tienanmen Square in 1989 has become a symbol of resistance and must be ruthlessly crushed."

"One brave man," Jake commented.

"Ah, yes. Courage. Courage, daring, the wisdom to wait for the moment, and the wit to know it when it arrives. That's Wu Tai Kwong."

"You speak as if you know him," Callie observed.

"In some ways, I think I do," Tiger Cole replied thoughtfully.

"So you think communism will collapse in China?"

"Communism is an anachronism, like monarchy. It's died just about everywhere else. It'll die here one of these days. The only question is when."

"What does Washington say about all of this?" Jake wondered.

Tiger Cole chuckled, a dry, humorless noise. "Wall Street doesn't like revolutions, and the market is the god Americans worship these days." He talked for several minutes of the politics driving Washington diplomacy.

Later, as they stood at the window staring up the unblinking commercial signs on the tops of the neighboring skyscrapers, Cole said, "The industrial West is operating on the same fallacy that brought the British to Hong Kong a century and a half ago. They think China is a vast market, and if they can just get access, they will get rich selling Western industrial products to people so poor they can barely feed themselves. 'It will work now,' the dreamers say, 'because the Chinese are going to become the world's premier low-cost labor market, earning real money manufacturing goods to be sold in the industrial West.'" Cole threw up his hands.

Callie asked, "Do China's Wu Tai Kwongs have a chance?"

"I think so," Tiger Cole said. "The little people have everything to gain and nothing to lose. The king has everything to lose and nothing to gain. There is only one way that contest can end."

"It's going to cost a lot of blood," murmured Jake Grafton.

"Lots of blood," Tiger agreed. "That too is inevitable. In China anything worth having must be purchased with blood."

Tommy Carmellini didn't go to his hotel in the evening; he went back to the consulate. He found the equipment he wanted on the shelves in the basement storage room, signed it out, then went upstairs to steal an attaché case. He found a leather one he liked in the CIA spaces under one of the desks. It was a bit feminine for his tastes, yet Kerry Kent would never miss it. Her desk was locked, of course, but the simple locks the furniture manufacturers put on the drawers could be opened with a paper clip. Carmellini settled down to read everything Kent had in her desk.

Letters from England—he gave those only a cursory glance. Lots of travel brochures, letters from girlfriends, two from men—lovers, apparently—a checkbook. He went through the checks, used her pocket calculator to verify that she was indeed living within her income, examined the backs and margins of the check register to see if by chance she had jotted down a personal identification number. Indeed, one four-digit number on the back of the register was probably just that. Tucked under the checks was a bank debit card.

Well, it was tempting. She had caused him a bad moment this evening. Either she sent the thugs or someone she reported to made the call, he felt certain.

Her desk took an hour. He checked his watch, then began on the desks of his CIA colleagues. All the classified documents were supposed to be locked in the fireproof filing cabinets or the safe. Tonight didn't seem like the evening to open those, but perhaps tomorrow night or the night after.

He was working on the boss's desk when he heard someone coming. He closed the drawers, went to his own desk, and selected a report from the in-basket. He had it open in front of him when one of the marines from the security detail stuck his head in.

"How's it going, sir?" the lance corporal asked.

"Just fine. Everything quiet?"

"As usual."

"Terrific."

"Gonna be much longer?"

"Couple hours, I think."

Twenty minutes per desk was sufficient for each of the three men. Other than personal items of little significance, Carmellini found nothing that aroused his curiosity.

Since he was doing desks tonight, he decided he might as well do Cole's. The consul general's office was locked, of course, but Carmellini had the door open in about eighty seconds.

A reasonable search of the bookcases, desk, and credenza would take a couple of hours. He checked his watch. The night was young.

Tommy Carmellini picked the locks on Cole's desk, opened the drawers, and began reading.

Tiger Cole had just said good-bye to the Graftons when his telephone rang. "Tiger?"

He recognized the voice. Sue Lin Buckingham. She didn't waste time on preliminaries. "I know Rip would want you to know, so I called. He's in jail. The authorities shut down the *Post* today and arrested him."

"Have you called a lawyer?"

"Lin Pe called Albert Cheung. I think Albert will get him out of jail tomorrow."

"Tell Rip to come see me."

"I'll tell him."

Cole hung up the phone and poured himself another glass of California Chardonnay.

He snorted, thinking about Jake Grafton and the innocent grin that had danced across his face when he admitted he had "made some inquiries." Yeah. Right. Grafton had probably read his dossier cover to cover.

So he already knew that Cole's company did all the Y2K testing and fixing on some of China's largest networks. . . .

Hoo boy. Talk about irony! He had thought the U.S. government would take months to figure out what happened in Hong Kong. It turned out some dim bulb in Washington who didn't have one original thought per decade decided to send Jake Grafton to look around.

Cole took another sip of white wine and contemplated the glass. He had spent most of his professional life around very bright people, some of them technical geniuses. Jake Grafton was a history major, bright enough but no genius, the kind of guy many techno-nerds held in not-so-secret contempt.

Grafton's strengths were common sense and a willingness to do what he thought was right regardless of the consequences. Cole remembered him from Vietnam with startling clarity: No matter what the danger or how frightened he was, Jake Grafton never lost his ability to think clearly and perform flawlessly, which was why he was the best combat pilot Cole ever met.

Yes, Cole thought, recalling the young man he had flown with all those years ago, Jake Grafton was a ferocious, formidable warrior of extraordinary capability, a precious friend and a deadly enemy.

Perhaps it was Cole's good fortune that fate had brought Grafton here. His talents might be desperately needed in the days ahead.

Cole checked his watch, then walked out of the apartment, locking the door behind him.

The sign on the door said, "Third Planet Communications." Cole used his key.

The office suite was on the third floor of a building directly across the street from the consulate. As luck would have it, Cole could look out his office window directly into the Third Planet suite.

With several hundred of the brightest minds in Hong Kong on its payroll, Third Planet was an acknowledged leader in cutting-edge wireless communications technology. In the eighteen months it had been in business it had become one of the leading wireless network designers and installers in Southeast Asia. Although Cole had put up the capital to start Third Planet, he didn't own any of the stock. In fact, the stock was tied up in so many shell corporations that the ownership would be almost impossible to establish. Cole was, however, listed on the company disclosure documents as an unpaid consultant, just in case any civil servant got too curious about his occasional presence on the premises.

Tonight Tiger Cole walked through the dark offices to a door that led to a windowless interior room. A man sitting in front of the door greeted him in Chinese and opened the door for him.

The lights were full on inside the heavily air-conditioned room, which was stuffed with computers, monitors, servers, routers—all the magic boxes of the high-tech age.

Five people were gathered around one of the terminals, Kerry Kent, Wu Tai Kwong, Hu Chiang, and two of Third Planet's brightest engineers, both women. Cole joined them.

"We're ready," Wu said and slapped Cole on the back.

Another warrior, Cole thought, shaking his head, a Chinese Jake Grafton.

"Is the generator in the basement on?" Cole asked. Through the years he had noticed that these kinds of petty technical details often escaped the geniuses who made the magic.

Yes, he was informed, the generator was indeed running.

"Let's do it," Cole said carelessly, trying not to let his tension show.

One of the female engineers began typing. In seconds a complex diagram appeared on the screen. Everyone watching knew what it was: the Hong Kong power grid. The engineer used a mouse to enlarge one section of the diagram, then did the same again.

Finally she sat looking at a variety of switches.

The other engineer pointed with a finger.

The mouse moved.

"Now we see if the people of China will be slaves or free men," Wu said.

Months of preparation had gone into this moment. If the revolutionaries could control China's electrical power grids, they had the key to the country. Hong Kong was the test case.

The engineer at the computer used one finger to click the mouse.

The lights in the room went off, then came back on as the emergency generator picked up the load in the office suite. The computers, protected from power surges and outages by batteries, didn't flicker.

Cole and the other witnesses rushed from the room, charged across the dark office to the windows that faced the street.

The lights of Hong Kong were *off!*

Tears ran down Cole's face. He was crying and laughing at the same time. He was trying to wipe his face when he realized Wu was pounding him on the back and Kerry Kent was kissing his cheeks.

When Cole got his eyes swabbed out, he looked across the street at the consulate. The emergency generator there had come on automatically, so the lights were back on.

Tiger Cole wondered how long it would be before it occurred to Jake Grafton to ask if Cole's California company had worked on the computers that controlled the Hong Kong power grid.

As they rode the ferry back to Kowloon, Jake asked Callie, "Did you recognize his voice?"

"Yes. He talked to Chan about computers. Chan was trying to cheat him."

"But you don't know if he killed Chan?"

"The identity of the killer is impossible to determine by listening to the tape."

"May I send it off to Washington?"

"Jake, do whatever you think is right."

"Well . . ."

"You didn't tell Tiger why you are here."

"I thought I'd call him tomorrow. Before we got down to business I wanted a social evening."

"I'm not going with you for that."

"I should see him alone," Jake agreed.

They had just gotten off the ferry on the Kowloon side and were walking toward their hotel when the lights went off. One second the city was there, then it wasn't. The effect was eerie, and a bit frightening.

Callie gripped Jake's arm tightly.

When the electricity went off all over the city of Hong Kong, it also failed at the new airport on Lantau Island. And in the air-traffic-control rooms at the base of the tower complex. Fortunately there were only a few airplanes under the control of the Hong Kong sector, and those were mostly freighters on night flights.

The air-traffic-control personnel worked quickly to get the emergency generators on so that the radars could be operated and the computers rebooted. The computers were protected by batteries that should have picked up the load but for some reason didn't. The emergency generators were on-line in three minutes and the radars sweeping the skies in three and a half.

The computers, however, were another matter. When the controllers finally got one of the computers on-line, the hard drive refused to accept new data via modem. Manually inputted data was changed in random ways—flight numbers were transposed, altitude data were incorrect, way points were dropped or added, and the data kept changing. It was almost as if the computer had had a lobotomy.

The second computer had the same problem as the first, and so did the third. The controllers worked the incoming flights manually, but without the computers they were in a severely degraded mode.

Inside the new, modern, state-of-the-art terminal, conditions were worse than they were in the tower. The restoration of power via emergency generators brought the lights back on, but the escalators wouldn't work, the automated baggage system was kaput, none of the flight display screens worked, the people-mover train refused to budge—its doors were frozen in place—and the jetways that allowed access to and from the planes could not be moved. Fortunately there were few passengers in the terminals and concourses, but those who were there were trapped until service personnel could get to them.

When power was finally restored from the main feeds, the computers still refused to work. The airline companies' reservations computers, fax machines, and Internet terminals seemed to be working fine, but the airport had ceased to function.

The technicians in the Hong Kong harbormaster's office were also having problems. The radars that kept track of the myriad of ships, barges, tugs, and boats of every kind and description in Victoria Harbor and the strait were working, but the computer that processed the information and presented it to the harbor controller was no longer able to identify or track targets. When the technicians tried the backup computer, they found it had a similar disease.

The people who had caused these problems sat and stood in front of the computer monitors at Third Planet Communications in a merry mood. Someone opened a bottle of Chinese wine, which they drank from paper cups.

The virus programs they had written and loaded on the affected computers seemed to be working perfectly. As Cole explained to Wu and Kent all those months ago, "Remember the chaos that was supposed to happen when Y2K rolled around, and didn't? We must make it happen now. Revolutions are about control, which is essence of power: We must take control away from the Communists. When the Communists lose their power they lose their leadership mandate. It's as simple as one, two, three."

Tonight Cole told Wu, "The revolution has begun."

He shook hands all around and headed for the door with a light step. Tomorrow would be a hell of·a day and he needed some sleep.

Tommy Carmellini hailed a taxi in front of the consulate. The driver took him back to his hotel via the Cross-Harbor Tunnel, creeping along through the blacked-out city with a solid stream of cars and trucks.

The rear door of the hotel was locked. To discourage thieves, no doubt, Carmellini thought as he opened it with a pick. The job took less than a minute. With the electricity off, of course there was no alarm when the door opened. There wouldn't have been an alarm even if the power had been on—the door wasn't wired, a fact Carmellini had ascertained fifteen minutes after he checked into the place.

He went up the back stairs and carefully unlocked his room. A old-fashioned metal key, thank God, because the card scanners in use at the new hotels would not be working, leaving all the patrons locked out of their rooms.

No one was in the room waiting for him.

Carmellini changed into black trousers, a long-sleeved dark shirt, and tennis shoes. The equipment from the consulate went into a knapsack, as did a roll of duct tape, a small flashlight, a glass cutter, a few small hand tools, and an extensive assortment of lock picks: everything necessary for a quiet night of burglary.

Kerry Kent lived in an apartment house on a side street off Nathan Road, a mile or so north of the Star Ferry landing at Tsim Sha Tsui. The building was about ten stories high, filled the block, and was ten or fifteen years old, Tommy Carmellini thought.

The street was unnaturally quiet. A few people were up and about at two in the morning, but without electrical power to drive the gadgets, the night was very still. Carmellini could hear traffic on Nathan Road and, from somewhere, the rumble of a train.

He checked the scrap of paper where he had written the apartment number.

Kent's pad should be on the seventh floor, he decided, and went into the building to examine the apartment layout. The elevators weren't working so he climbed the dark staircase. Okay, the first floor was the one above the ground floor, so she would be on the eighth floor.

He walked along the hall until he found the apartment that corresponded to hers, which was twenty-seven.

Back outside on the sidewalk he examined the windows and balconies, counted upward. Okay, Kent's was the balcony with the two orange flowerpots and the bicycle chained to the rail.

He stood on the sidewalk just a moment, adjusting his backpack, listening, looking. . . .

When he was sure no one was observing him, Tommy Carmellini leaped from the sidewalk and grasped the bottom of the wrought-iron slats in the railing on the first-floor balcony. He could tell by the feel that the iron was rusty. Would it hold his weight?

Using upper-body strength alone, he drew himself up to the edge of the balcony floor and looked. And listened.

When he was convinced it was safe, he pulled himself up hand over hand until he could hook a heel over the rail, which squealed slightly in protest.

In seconds he was balanced on the rail, still listening. . . .

He straightened, examined the underside of the floor of the balcony above him. He reached up for the rails, grasped them, and gradually gave them his weight, making sure the slats and railings were not too rusty or broken.

Up the side of the building he went, floor by floor, silently and quickly. Two minutes after he left the street, he was crouched on Kerry Kent's balcony examining the door, which was ajar. For ventilation, probably, since the night was warm and pleasant. As he listened for sounds from inside the apartment, he examined the windows of the apartments across the street, looking for anyone who might have watched him climb the side of the building.

Only when he felt certain that he was unobserved did he remove two tiny remote microphones, bugs, from his backpack, and a roll of duct tape. Using a knife, he trimmed two pieces of tape about two inches long from the roll and stuck them on the front of his shirt, where they were accessible. Then he returned the knife and tape roll to the backpack.

Due to the low probability that Kent routinely swept for bugs, these would transmit to a recorder as long as their batteries lasted, a time frame that depended on how many hours a day noise was generated in the apartment. They should last a couple of weeks if she didn't watch too much television or leave the radio on continuously. Months if electric power wasn't restored to the building.

The recorder had to be nearby, outside if possible, where Carmellini could get at it without too much effort. He planned to find a place to install it after he got the microphones in place.

Just to be on the safe side, he removed the backpack, which contained the burglary tools he wouldn't need since she left the sliding glass door ajar, and placed it on the floor out of his way.

Now he got to his feet, crouched to present as small a silhouette as possible to any casual observer, and inched the door open with his latex-clad fingertips. Applying steady pressure, he got the door moving and kept it moving, as slowly as possible.

When he had it open enough, about fourteen inches, Carmellini stood, turned sideways, and stepped in.

Moonlight was the only illumination. As his eyes adjusted to the gloom Carmellini could see that the apartment consisted of just one room and a bath. The kitchen area, a sink and stove, was located in the inside corner of the room to the right of the door. The area to the left of the door was the bathroom. The rest of the apartment, which was about the size of a standard American motel room, contained a Western-style bed, a few chairs, and a dresser. A television sat atop the dresser. Posters of famous paintings adorned the walls.

And in the bed, asleep apparently, were Kerry Kent . . . and a man. From this angle Carmellini could see only his hair—the man appeared to be Chinese. Kent's bare leg stuck out from under the sheet and light blanket that covered them.

Carmellini stood in the darkness listening. Heavy, deep, rhythmical breathing.

From where he was standing he examined the apartment, looking for a place for the bugs.

The head of the bed certainly looked inviting. It was some kind of wooden latticework; he could reach in and stick a bug on the back of the top of the headboard. It should be out of sight there and safe enough, unless someone moved the bed and examined the headboard.

The other one . . . perhaps under the bedside nightstand that held the telephone.

The decisions made, Tommy Carmellini stepped forward with bugs and tape ready.

Like a silent shadow he moved to the edge of the bed and bent down. He reached up under the nightstand and was affixing the first bug when Kerry Kent's deep breathing stopped.

She was facing away from him, thank God, but she might turn over. He froze.

Yes, she was turning toward him. He waited until she had completed her move and was breathing regularly again, then he felt to make sure the tiny transmitter's antenna was hanging down freely. It was. Now he slowly stood, staying perfectly balanced, moving at the speed of a glacier, making no noise at all.

To get the other bug behind the headboard meant that he had to reach across her, above her face, and put it in place without jiggling the headboard in any way, for the movement of the headboard would be transferred to the bed.

He didn't let his limbs come to a stop but stayed fluidly in motion, each move thought out and planned so that he stayed balanced on both feet.

He got the tape, with the bug in the center of it, in the proper position and pressed firmly so that it would stick to the wood. The antenna seemed to be hanging in place behind one of the lattices.

He had pulled his arm back and was ready to turn when her breathing changed abruptly and she awoke. One second she was asleep, the next she was awake. Just like that.

Carmellini stood frozen. He was about eighteen inches from her head. If she decided to get up to go to the bathroom, this was going to get very interesting.

Can a person feel the presence of another human being, one absolutely silent and motionless?

There are those who swear they can. Tommy Carmellini believed that some people could, and he stood now willing his heart to beat slowly lest she hear it.

For the first time he was also aware of the faint voices and traffic rumble that could be heard through the open balcony door, which had of course been almost closed before he arrived. Would she notice the noise? Or the coolness of the night air?

She turned in bed again, rubbed against the sleeping man.

Oh, great! She'll wake him!

She mumbled something in Chinese . . . and the man stirred.

He turned, put his arm around her.

Seconds passed, his breathing deepened.

Tommy Carmellini realized he was sweating. Perspiration was trickling down his nose, down his cheeks. He dared not move. . . .

If I don't relax, she's going to smell me!

The seconds dragged. She adjusted her position in the bed . . . and finally, little by little, her breathing slowed and grew deeper.

Carmellini began moving toward the open door. He didn't walk, he flowed, gently, steadily, smoothly. . . .

On the balcony he debated if he should close the door. If it made a noise now . . . no! The risk was too great.

After scanning the other balconies and the apartment buildings across the street to ensure he didn't have an audience, Carmellini went over the rail. He leaned back, checked the balcony below as best he could, then lowered himself onto the railing. Balancing carefully, he released his grip on the wrought-iron slats above and coiled himself to go down another floor.

In half a minute he was standing on the street. He was wiping his hands on his trousers when the electrical power was restored to the neighborhood, bringing the lights on. Televisions and radios that had been on when the power failed blared into life.

What is it his mother used to say? "You're going to get caught, Tommy, one of these days. Sneaking around like you do ain't Christian. People'll get mean when they catch you sneaking, one of these days."

One of these days, he thought. *But not today.*

He began looking for a place where he could hide the recorder.

As Tommy Carmellini walked south on Nathan Road toward his hotel, a van whipped to the curb and a man jumped out with a bundle of paper in his arms. He put the stack on top of a newspaper dispenser, cut the plastic tie that bound it together, then got back in the van, which rocketed off down the street.

Carmellini paused by the stack and took a sheet off the top. A flyer of some type. In Chinese, of course.

He folded it and put it in his pocket.

Wonder what that is all about?

CHAPTER SEVEN

Governor Sun Siu Ki didn't have newspapers to worry about this morning; he had shut down the politically incorrect rags and jailed the editors. No, the rag du jour was a flyer that had been distributed by the tens of thousands throughout the Special Administrative Region, the old colony, of Hong Kong.

The flyer, titled *The Truth,* was a single sheet of paper printed on both sides with Chinese characters. It contained a highly critical account of the Bank of the Orient debacle and shooting, blaming the entire incident on the Chinese government's attempted looting of the bank and on the overaggressiveness of the People's Liberation Army. The sheet called for mass demonstrations to demand that the authorities cease requiring bribes from banks, release the jailed newspaper editors, and allow the publication of uncensored news. The sheet was signed by a group calling itself the Scarlet Team.

"This is outrageous, inflammatory, antirevolutionary criminal propaganda," the governor told his assistant, who agreed completely with that assessment. "Have the police find the people who did this and arrest them." Sun hammered on the desk with his fist as he added, "I will not tolerate these criminal provocations! Find these people!"

"Yes, sir," said the aide.

The governor wadded up the offending flyer and threw it into the wastebasket beside his desk.

He took a deep breath, then tackled the next item on the morning's agenda. "Has electrical power been restored throughout the city?"

"Yes, sir. Apparently so. The engineers are still trying to determine why the load was lost in the first place. Unfortunately power fluctuations apparently caused extensive damage to the computer systems at Lantau Airport and Harbor Control."

"When will the systems be operational again?"

The aide didn't know the answer to that one. He would find out and report back, he said, which didn't please the governor.

Everything seemed to be going wrong all at once. As if to emphasize that fact, the secretary came in to announce that the ministry in Beijing was on the telephone.

The minister was worried. Questions were being asked at the highest levels. Did Sun need more help handling the situation in Hong Kong?

"No, certainly not," Sun replied. "Criminal elements are taking advantage of events that are out of anyone's control, but the government is firmly in charge."

Because Albert Cheung was somebody important, the warden of the prison had Rip Buckingham brought to his office. There was a room in the prison for lawyers and clients to meet, but it consisted of a long table with chicken wire down the middle and a guard at each end. There was no privacy.

Albert had known the Chinese warden a long time—he slipped him a handful of currency when they shook hands. After the guards brought Rip, the warden and guards left together, leaving Rip and Albert alone.

"I thought Lin Pe might call you," Rip said, sinking into a stuffed chair. "You'll have to excuse my odor. They're having trouble with the showers and soap."

"Lin Pe called me yesterday. Yesterday I went to see Governor Sun. We negotiated. I went back this morning and we negotiated some more. To make a long story short, he wants a hundred thousand Hong Kong." Actually Sun Siu Ki had wanted two hundred thousand, but Albert had beaten him down. This he didn't mention. He didn't like to discuss money with his clients, except when absolutely necessary. Discussing money offended his sense of dignity.

Rip grunted noncommittally. He was thinking how clean and comfortable Albert Cheung looked. Wearing an impeccable gray suit and conservative silk tie, he looked as if he had just stepped out of the Pall Mall Club in London. Rip was wearing filthy khaki chinos, a nondescript blue shirt, and penny loafers without socks. His clothes looked like he had worn them day and night for a month, although it had been only two days.

"Your wife wants you home," Albert said tentatively.

Rip Buckingham didn't want to talk about his wife. She had come to visit him yesterday and the prison staff had refused to let her in unless she paid a bribe. That, Rip knew, was pretty much standard procedure these days. Sue Lin refused to pay. Or so one of the guards told him last night. That certainly sounded like her, Rip reflected. She was tough, and Rip liked that a lot.

He picked up a pencil from the warden's desk and stroked it with his fingers as he asked, "What do I have to do to reopen the paper?"

"Sun and I did discuss that matter," Albert acknowledged.

"How much?"

"Well, it's not that simple. Apparently people in Beijing have been talking to the governor."

"Uh-huh."

"You'll need to sign a contract with Xinhua for editorial services. That will cost you so much a month." Xinhua, the New China News Agency, was the Communist government's propaganda organ.

"How much?" Rip asked idly.

"I don't know. It probably won't be nominal."

"We sometimes run Communist government press releases as news," Rip told the lawyer, "but only if they're newsworthy. My staff decides. You'd be amazed at the reams of trash bureaucrats generate. My readers aren't interested."

"You don't have to print anything you don't wish to print. However, the agency will assign an editor, who must approve anything that you do want to print."

"Censorship."

"Call it that if you like."

"For Christ's sake, Albert!"

"Rip, be reasonable. This isn't a comfortable little chunk of England anymore, with British judges and British law. *This is China!* You have to go along to get along."

Buckingham said a dirty word.

"Give me the authorization to pay Sun and I'll get you out of here. You think about the paper. We'll talk later."

Rip broke the pencil in half and tossed the pieces on the warden's desk. "I won't publish the paper under those conditions," he said. "I can tell you that right now. But it isn't my paper. It belongs to Buckingham News, Limited, which may soon be looking for a new managing editor."

"Buckingham News, that's your father, right?"

"Rich owns about sixty percent of it, I think. My sisters and I own small pieces, some of the stock is in executive compensation plans, and the rest is owned by some hot dollies Dad took a fancy to. He gave them stock certificates instead of diamonds."

"Does that work?" Albert asked curiously.

"Dad says it depends on how many shares you give them," Rip said, his face deadpan. He shrugged. "Buckingham News pays no dividends, there's no market for the stock, and Dad has absolute control. About all a shareholder can hope for is that the certificates will be worth real money someday. One might think of it as a sort of pension plan for the women."

"What does Mr. Buckingham do with the profits if he doesn't pay dividends?" asked the Hong Kong attorney. "I assume there are profits."

"He buys more newspapers, cable television networks. He got into satellite distribution of television signals years ago. He said that technology would ultimately have a greater impact on the human race than the invention of movable type. Certainly it's going to have a greater impact on the third world."

Rich may be a noxious old fossil, his son reflected, but he had vision. Rip told the lawyer, "As a matter of fact, I think Buckingham News owns the company with about fifty percent of the satellite dish business in Hong Kong."

"Very progressive," said Albert Cheung.

"In any event, the women seem happy and Dad appears to be doing all right."

"Wonderful, wonderful."

"Quite. But I don't know what Dad will do about the *Post*. The only principle to which he is irrevocably and totally committed is making money."

"Yes."

"A lot of money."

Albert Cheung looked interested. "I like money myself," he remarked blandly.

"Go pay the man and get me the hell out of here," Rip Buckingham told the lawyer. "The company in this place is fascinating but the food isn't anything to brag about."

"Mr. Cole, there's a Rear Admiral Grafton on line one."

"Thank you," Cole said to his secretary and picked up the phone. "Hello, Jake."

"I just called to thank you for last night. It was good seeing you again."

"And you."

"I was wondering if I could drop by today and have a chat about government business? Could you give me an hour or so?"

"Come at lunch and I'll buy."

"About twelve?"

"See you then."

When Sue Lin heard her brother, Wu, come in, she went downstairs to his room and knocked. He immediately opened the door. He was here to change clothes, which was about all he ever did at this house.

"We need to talk," she said softly in English, worried as always that the domestics would overhear.

Only two years older than Sue Lin, Wu had always awed her, ever since she could remember. Never had she met a man with his inner calm, a man whose strength radiated like heat from a fire. He was, she thought, the most masculine of men, a man so strong emotionally and spiritually that nothing on this earth could shake him.

Of course he attracted people, men and women, like a magnet attracts iron filings. In a reflective moment Rip had compared Wu to Christ. "If he was preaching a new religion he could convert the world," Rip said, and Sue Lin thought Rip was probably right.

As Wu looked at her his face softened. "Of course," he said, nodding gently. "May I continue to change, or would you like to go upstairs?"

"Go on," she said, motioning toward the closet, and told him about Rip being arrested and the newspaper closed.

"I have heard," Wu said. "I am sorry for Rip."

"Albert Cheung will get him out, but the paper . . . the governor will probably keep it closed."

She sat in the only chair in the small room. "The day has almost arrived, hasn't it?"

"Its coming was inevitable," Wu replied calmly. Sue Lin had never seen him excited—she didn't think anything could disturb his inner peace.

"Rip is worried. If the authorities finally learn that you are my brother, Lin Pe's son, Rip thinks they will take their frustrations out on us."

"Rip is probably correct," Wu said softly. He rarely raised his voice. "His understanding of the scope of the official mind seems quite complete.".

"He wants us to leave Hong Kong now."

"Sister of mine, I advise you to obey your husband."

"Mother will not leave."

"Her destiny is not yours."

"Wu, for God's sake, you must tell Mother to leave! She will listen to you! She ignores my pleas."

Wu sat on the bed and took his sister's hand. "Leaving China would cost Lin Pe her life. *This* is who she is. On the other hand, you have your husband, your life together, which you can live anyplace on the planet. Lin Pe does not have that."

"Are you saying that Rip and I should leave you two here?"

"This country, these people, they are my life also."

Sue Lin Buckingham jerked her hand from his grasp. "I think the new maid is suspicious of you. She watches you from the window, pretends she knows no English when it is obvious she understands some of it. She may be a police spy."

"What would you have me do?"

At that Sue Lin threw up her hands and left the room.

Albert Cheung drove Rip to the building that housed the newspaper. It was raining again, a steady drizzle. Albert wanted to take him home but Rip insisted on going to the office.

There were two policemen with shotguns standing under an over-hang outside the building.

Albert pulled his Mercedes into the alley that led to the parking area in back. "Thanks, Albert," Rip said and released his seat belt.

As Rip reached for the door handle, Albert put a hand on his arm and said, "Wait a minute, Rip. I want to give you some advice, if you'll listen."

"I'll listen. I won't pay for your advice, but I'll listen."

"It's time for you to go. Take your wife, go back to Australia. That is your place. That is where you belong."

Rip growled and reached for door handle.

"Listen to me," Albert said sharply. "The British are gone. For one hundred and fifty years this city was a part of Britain. It was as English as tea and toast. No more. Those days are *over*. And everyone has to adjust to the new reality."

"I've adjusted. I just don't like it."

"Like it or not, Hong Kong is now part of China, and China is an absolute dictatorship. The British ways—free speech, democracy, open, honest government, a tolerant, pluralist society, the rule of law, open debate about the public's business, fair play—all that is dying or dead. People here must jettison the old ways and adopt the new. They have no choice—*they have to do it!* I've been reading your paper: You rail against the incoming tide."

Rip tried to rebut Albert Cheung. "I have tried to fairly—"

" 'Fairly'? Don't be ridiculous. *Fair* is a British concept, not Chinese. There is nothing you can do."

"This is my home, too," Rip said savagely.

"Stop playing the fool. Get on a plane."

Rip sat for a moment listening to the slap of the windshield wipers. "Why don't you leave?" he asked the lawyer.

"I happen to be Chinese, you may have noticed. And there is money to be made here."

"There are six million people in Hong Kong without anyplace else to go."

"You're wasting your breath trying to save the world, Rip. You won't get a halo. You won't even get a thank-you."

"Don't charge me for this advice, Albert." Rip got out of the car, shut the door firmly behind him.

Albert Cheung sped away without another look at Rip.

Maybe the cops would have let him in the building, maybe not; Rip didn't try. He went around back and unlocked his motorcycle, an old Harley-Davidson he had imported from Australia.

Motorcycles were popular in Hong Kong—mainly Japanese bikes, fast and fuel-efficient—but not as ubiquitous as they were in Singapore or Bangkok. The British always discouraged motor vehicles for private use by making it expensive to register one or get a driver's license. The Communists continued that policy. Still, a lot of people today had the money or political connections, so there were more and more motorcycles. Those who couldn't afford to go first-class rode Chinese iron. With no demand for forty-year-old Harleys, thieves weren't interested, or so the theory went. Rip always locked his anyway.

He turned on the fuel cock, adjusted the choke, and started kicking. The engine caught on the third kick.

He was warming the engine when the woman who ran a small newsstand across the street came looking for him.

"Rip, why have the police closed the building?" Originally from Hunan Province, she had lived in Hong Kong at least twenty years. Rip had deduced that one time by questioning her closely about Hong Kong news stories she could remember.

"The governor has ordered the paper closed, Mrs. Guo," Rip told her. "He didn't like what he read."

"You did not go to jail? I heard they arrested you."

"I went to jail." He gave her a brief summary, then said good-bye. "My wife is waiting for me. She worries."

"Yes, yes. Go home to her." Mrs. Guo went back along the alley with her head down, as if she were walking against a storm. Hard times . . .

The Chinese are used to hard times, Rip reflected. They've never known anything else.

He put the motorcycle in motion.

The streets were still crowded. Traffic sprayed water on Rip, who had to concentrate to keep his motorcycle under control.

Rip had first seen Hong Kong as a teenager in the mid-eighties, when there were still vestigial traces of the nineteenth-century city, and large swatches remained unchanged from the days of World War II. Back then many people could talk for hours about the Japanese occupation from their personal experience. Not many of those old people were left, of course, and few people now asked about the old days. Nobody cared anymore.

That was the way of the world, Rip knew. Certainly the way of China. The past—good or bad—was soon forgotten. There was always today to be lived through and tomorrow to prepare for. Venerable ancestors were, of course, worthy and honorable and all that, but, alas, they were quite dead.

It was that Chinese focus on the now that intrigued Rip Buckingham. For the Chinese, he thought, all things were possible. Coolies and peasants from the rice paddies had built this modern city, were constantly transforming it, and in turn were transformed by it. It was an extraordinary metamorphosis.

Today not a single building remained from the nineteenth century. The commercial buildings were fifty-story-plus avant-garde statements in steel and glass. Mile after mile of high-rise apartment buildings housed more than six million people. The thought of living in one was a daunting prospect for Westerners, but the fact remains, six million people were decently housed.

As he rode the Harley through traffic and tried to ignore the drizzle and road spray, Rip Buckingham marveled again at the raw power of this great city. Chinese signs were freely intermingled with the logos of international corporations and brand names. Rip thought this mixture symbolic of Hong Kong, where East and West met, transforming both.

Hong Kong was a vast human stew, and by choice Rip was right in the middle of it.

He inched his way up the narrow, twisty roads that grooved the northern face of Victoria Peak, then guided the motorcycle into a driveway and triggered a radio-controlled garage-door opener in a house glued to the side of the peak. Buckingham News actually owned the place, which was a good thing since Rip could never have paid for it on his salary.

As he was getting off the machine inside the garage his wife came through the door.

"You're soaked," she said.

"Doesn't matter. I stunk from jail."

She kissed him.

He hit the button to close the outside door, then led her up the stairs to the living room. A large window looked out on the Central District and Kowloon across the strait. As Rip told his wife about jail and the governor, he automatically glanced outside. Kowloon was almost hidden in the rain and mist.

"I called your father."

"What did he say?"

"Just that you should call when you could. I asked him if I should hire Albert Cheung, and he said yes."

Rip stretched and nodded. "I need to take a shower, put on some dry clothes. I'll call him later."

"What are we going to do, Rip?"

"I don't know," he said, meaning it. "This place is our life. Sun Siu Ki just took it from us."

"They won't let you keep publishing the *Post*."

"I know."

"Things are changing."

"I know. *I know!* You told me. The police told me. Albert Cheung told me. I know, I know, and *goddamn,* I resent it."

"Mother won't leave without my brother."

Rip took his wife's hand. "I know that, too," he said gently and kissed her.

An hour later, after he had a long, hot shower and put on fresh clothes, Rip called his father's office in Sydney. Soon Rich's voice boomed through the instrument.

Rip told him about the cease publication order and the demands of Sun Siu Ki.

"Dad, I don't think we should run the paper under these conditions. It's censorship. Knuckling under to the Communists will cost Buckingham News its standing in the international community, and that ultimately will mean loss of ad revenue all over the globe."

"That paper is worth a hundred million," Richard Buckingham thundered into the telephone.

Rip had to hold the instrument away from his ear. The old man sounded like he was in the next room.

"Bloody Chinks! A hundred million!" Rich ripped off a couple oaths, but the volume was going down. "All the bloody lies they've told the last fifteen or twenty years, about how great it was going to be in Hong Kong when they took over . . . Makes me want to puke!"

"Yessir," Rip agreed.

"And the bloody Brits." Richard added them to his list. "Believing those lies . . ."

"Maybe it's time to pack it in," Rip said reluctantly, trying to get back to the business at hand. "Maybe in a few years the government here will see the benefits of a free press."

"They don't really have a choice," Richard rumbled. "The world has outgrown censorship. But you're right—we can't buck the bastards head-on. Pay off the *Post* employees. Send me the names and qualifications of everyone who wants to work for another Buckingham paper and is willing to move. We'll see what we can do." There was a second of dead sound, then he added, "Move at their own expense, of course."

"Yes, sir."

"I'd like to see you and Sue Lin. Come on home."

"In a few weeks. We have to wrap up some things here."

"Righto, mate."

"And Dad? Thanks."

"For what?"

"For seeing this my way."

"See you in a few weeks."

Richard Buckingham hung up the telephone and sat staring out the window at the artsy-fartsy roof of the Sydney Opera House. He called in Billy Kidd, who had been his number two since Richard was the publisher, editor, and sports writer of the *Wangeroo Gazette*.

"The Commies have shut down the *Post* in Hong Kong," he began. After Richard told Billy what he knew, he added, "I want a story about the shutdown and I want it on the front page of every paper I own. Call Rip at home and have him write it. Use a file photo of him."

"Righto."

"Top of the front page, Billy." Richard picked up a legal pad and pencil from his desk and handed it to Billy, who could take a hint. He began taking notes.

"Billy, someday those Commie bastards are going to regret screwing with me. Bad press is the only lever I have, and by God, I'm going to use it."

Richard Buckingham got out of his chair and paced the office. "Put the one-baby story on the telly chat shows again. More Falun Gong persecution stories. Bang the drum every day. And I mean every day, Billy. A new, different, bad slant each and every day."

"Whatever you want, Richard. But I don't think that—"

"And I want something about those hundred million migrants roaming around China that the Commies are cracking down on. I'm tired of reading about these lawless vagrants threatening the economic prosperity of the new China. The corrupt, venal Communist regime is threatening the economic prosperity of the new China. They are prosecuting the harmless kooks in the Falun Gong movement, jailing people whose only crime is to want a little bit of life's sweetness. Massive pollution, sweatshops, child labor—China's the last big sewer left on earth, and that's the way we'll write it from now on. Fax it to the managing editor of every paper."

Billy finished taking notes and asked sourly, "Anything else?" He had been with Richard Buckingham too long to cower.

"Communism is as dead as Lenin. The Buckingham newspapers and television networks are going to trumpet that news loud and clear. Find a politico to write it, somebody important or somebody who wants to be important."

"You—"

"And why does the free world tolerate the crimes against humanity that the Chinese government perpetrates on those who can't defend themselves? Maybe an article, 'Tiananmen Square Revisited.'"

Billy scribbled furiously. "You're the boss," he said.

"You're damn right I am," Richard roared. "Those bloody Chinks didn't like the coverage they got from the *China Post*—they're going to shit when they see the press they're getting from now on. When anybody anywhere says anything bad about Red China, I want to read it in the papers and hear about it on the telly news shows. From this day forward Buckingham News is the world's foremost voice urging the overthrow of the Communists in Beijing."

Rich punched the air and sat down. "You and I are going to do at least one good thing before we go, Billy-boy," he said conversationally.

Billy Kidd launched himself from Richard's office. Billy knew that when Richard was on a tear you didn't get many openings, so he bolted at the first one he saw.

An hour later Richard called Billy on the intercom. "Don't we own a big piece of a direct TV company in Hong Kong?"

"That's right. China Television, Limited. Very profitable."

"Sell it as fast as you can. Maybe a competitor will buy it. Get what you can and let's move on."

"Richard, I know you're angry, but China Television is worth serious money. Satellite television is here now; China is on its way to becoming the largest market on earth. Those little dishes are selling like Viagra."

Richard Buckingham's answer was matter-of-fact. "I'm going to piss on a lot of Commies, Billy. I don't want something of mine hanging out where they can cut it off, throw it in the dirt, and stomp on it. Get rid of China Television—we'll take the loss out of their hides."

Billy refused to quit. "No one will pay what it's worth," he insisted.

Richard was patient. "Billy, with the Communists in power, nothing in China is worth real money. That's the lesson the Americans and British and Japanese are going to learn the hard way."

A man was waiting on the street when Jake stepped out of the hotel. He was standing under an overhang to stay out of the rain. As Jake walked along the sidewalk with Callie's umbrella, the man got into a car that had been parked in the taxi space in front of the building.

Jake ignored the tail. He was acutely aware of the Chan tape in his pocket. For some reason he was relieved that he had ditched the wallet and pistol he had taken from the man who had followed him yesterday.

As he entered the ferry terminal, the car outside pulled to the curb, and two men got out of the rear seat.

Jake saw them board the *Star of the West* just before the gangplank came over. The second man aboard had a bandage on his head; this was the fellow whom Jake had relieved of wallet and pistol. He boarded on the lower deck. The other man came to the upper deck, where Jake was, but he stayed well away from the American.

Exiting the Central District ferry terminal, Jake hailed the only taxi he saw. He didn't bother checking to see what the men following him did.

When Jake entered Cole's office, Cole came around his desk and shook hands. "We have a choice," he said. "We can have lunch served here, go to the cafeteria, or slip down the street to a restaurant with wine and all the trimmings. What will it be?"

"Here, if that's okay with you?"

"Here it is. Have a seat and let me talk to the secretary."

In a few minutes Cole was back. He sat in one of the black leather guest chairs beside Jake.

"I guess I should have leveled with you last night," Jake said. "I'm here on official business. A lot of Washington bigwigs are getting nervous about the situation in Hong Kong. More to the point, they are getting nervous about China Bob Chan and your relationship to him. They managed to talk the White House into sending me over here to talk to you, see what I can find out, and report back."

A look of puzzlement crossed Cole's face. "Why you?"

"Someone found out that we flew together way back when, the politicians are embarrassed about China Bob, I was getting on a four-star's nerves at the Pentagon, someone with some stroke at the National Security Council thinks I can work miracles. It all happened at once, so here I am."

"Uh-huh."

"When this trip got suggested, I initially said no. Then Callie was asked to do the culture conference, sort of as a cover. . . ." He shrugged.

"Ask your questions."

"Are you or your friends having me followed around town?"

"You're being followed?"

"Two men followed me here this morning. Presumably they're outside somewhere, waiting for me to come out."

Cole looked genuinely surprised. "Jake, I have no idea."

"I guess it all boils down to this: Are you or are you not a member of a conspiracy to overthrow the government of China?"

Cole whistled. "Jesus! You flew all the way over here from Washington to ask me that question?"

Jake Grafton scratched his head. "Well, I think the folks in Washington expected me to be a bit more circumspect, but, essentially, yeah. If the answer to that question is no, the next question is, Have you ever given advice or anything of value to anyone whose goal is the overthrow of the government of China?"

Cole pinched his nose, looked at Grafton, and grinned. The grin started slowly and spread. Jake knew he didn't grin often.

Finally Cole broke into a laugh. He was still chuckling when the secretary came in with a tray. On the tray were two bowls of soup, several sandwiches, and a couple cans of Coke. Tiger Cole's face returned to its normal detached expression. As the man left the room the consul general muttered, "I always serve American drinks to guests. Today is Coke day. Tomorrow is Pepsi."

Cole tasted the soup. "You are a rare piece of work, Grafton. When they taught you to go straight for a target way back when, you learned the lesson well."

Jake tried the soup himself. It was something Chinese, a watery vegetable, okay but nothing to write home about. No crackers in sight. He popped the can of Coke and took a sip. At least the drink was cold.

Cole pointed his spoon at Jake, then decided to use the spoon on the soup. Once a chuckle escaped him.

They ate in silence. Finally Cole finished soup and sandwich and leaned back in his chair to sip on the soft drink.

"Do you know how ironic this is, that of all the people on this planet, you, Jake Grafton, are the one who comes flying out of my past to ask about my future."

"I haven't asked about the future," Jake shot back. "It's the present the weenies in Washington are worried about."

"Ah, yes. The present."

Cole walked around the desk and stood at the window looking out. He couldn't see much, merely a gloomy forest of skyscrapers with glass sides on a dreary, rainy day.

"This warm front is supposed to get out of here tonight," he said. "The next three or four days will be bright and sunny."

"Uh-huh." Grafton finished his Coke and set the empty can on the tray along with the dirty dishes.

Cole returned to the desk, sat in his regular chair, folded his arms on the desk, and looked Jake Grafton in the eye. "Some ground rules. We'll play this game my way or not at all."

Grafton adjusted his position in his chair. "What are the rules?"

"I'll answer your questions completely, frankly, truthfully, but you can't tell a living soul for one week."

Jake thought about that. "The problem," he said after a bit, "is that you are in the diplomatic service of the United States. If a private citizen wants to saddle up and ride off to a revolution, that's between him and whoever is running the universe this week. If a diplomat does it, that's a different case altogether."

"A point well taken," Cole said. "I gave this some thought while we ate. Let's do this: If you will agree to the conditions I stated, complete silence for a week, I'll write out a letter of resignation, leave the date blank, and give it to you. You fill in the date anytime you wish and see that the people in Washington get it—no sooner than a week from today."

Now it was Jake Grafton's turn to go to the window and look out. "Why don't you just tell me some lie to get me out of your hair?"

"Ooh boy, that's rich! Coming from you. When they asked you way back when whether or not you had ever bombed an unauthorized target, what did you say?"

"I said yes."

"Indeed you did. You were the rarest of rarities, a truly honest man. Sorry, but I don't have it in me to lie to Jake Grafton."

"Listen, Tiger. I can't stay silent for a week. Not if you tell me you're up to something you shouldn't be up to."

Cole cocked his head and looked at Jake with an odd expression. "What should I be up to?"

"Don't give me that!"

"Do you know what these Communists are? Do you know what they represent?"

Jake Grafton leaned across the desk toward Tiger Cole. "If the government of the United States told me to pull the trigger," he whispered hoarsely, "I'd be willing to personally send every Communist in the world straight to hell. But as long as I'm in the United States Navy I don't have the luxury of choosing that course of action without orders. Neither do you when you're representing the United States of America. Write out that resignation and date it today. I'll send it in for you."

Cole leaned back in his chair and rubbed his eyes.

After a bit he asked, "When are you going to send it in?"

Grafton threw up his hands. "I don't know!"

Cole spun around to the PC that sat on a stand near the desk, turned it on, put stationery in the printer tray, and started typing. Three minutes later a letter rolled off the printer. Cole read it through, signed it, then handed it to Grafton.

Jake took his time reading the letter, then folded it carefully. "Got an envelope?"

Cole got one from a drawer and handed it across the desk.

Jake put the letter in the envelope, then stowed it in an inside breast pocket of his sports coat.

"Any more questions?" Cole said.

"Want to tell me why?"

Cole leaned back in his chair and stretched. He looked out the window at the slabs of skyscraper glass while he collected his thoughts, then turned his attention back to Grafton.

"I should have died that December day in 1972 when I was lying in the jungle muck in Laos with a broken back. Would have died, too, if I had been flying with an average mortal man. But no! As fate would have it I was flying with Jake Grafton, the warrior incarnate. Jake Grafton wasn't leaving that jungle without me—it was both of us or neither of us. So he fought and we both lived. I can close my eyes and remember it like it was yesterday. That moment was the most important of my life."

Cole turned toward the window and the gloomy, rainy day. "And I remember the day I became a millionaire," he continued, speaking softly. "We did an initial public offering. I went from owing thirty-three thousand dollars in student loans and two thousand on an old Chevy to a net worth of twenty-three million bucks just like *that!*" He snapped his fingers, turned back toward Jake, and snapped them again.

"One day in September three years ago I became a billionaire. The tech stocks were going up like a rocket, the valuations were . . . but you know all that. You see, we designed software for complex data networks and wireless telephone systems and burglar alarms and car security systems and toys that talk . . . magic technoshit. Stuff. In a world full of stuff, we were the kings of the new magic stuff. The world beat a path to our door.

"So there I was, filthy rich, able to buy anything on the planet . . . and none of it meant pee-squat. My boy died of dope, and I got the hell out. That was where I was when I was asked to help overthrow the Communists."

Tiger Cole leaned forward in the chair. "I've been in Hong Kong two years and gave a hundred million or so to the revolution, and the value of my stock holdings has just kept climbing. I'm worth *two* billion dollars, Jake. *Two billion!* I've squandered my life on bad marriages to stupid women. Wasted it, and the system gave me *two . . . billion . . . dollars.*"

Cole spread his hands, as if that explained everything. Obviously he thought it did.

"Who asked you to help overthrow the Communists?" Jake Grafton said.

"Ahh . . ." A trace of a smile appeared on Cole's face. "You already know or you wouldn't have asked."

Jake Grafton stood, went to the door of the office, and pulled it open several inches. He looked back at Cole, still sitting behind the desk. "Some dreams are bigger than others," he said.

Cole nodded.

"The sandwich was okay. The soup's terrible."

Jake Grafton pulled the door completely open and walked out of the office.

CHAPTER EIGHT

Rip Buckingham was on a squash court batting balls against the wall when Tiger Cole arrived at the athletic club. "I heard the governor shut down the paper," Cole said after he closed the door to the court.

"Yep. I spent a couple of nights in the can."

"You've been begging for it for years."

"Already I feel cleaner, closer to God. I'm going to try to get arrested more often, work up to once or twice a month."

They played hard for twenty minutes, then returned to the dressing room. They were the only men in the shower. As the water ran, Rip told Cole, "The rain is supposed to stop tonight. Wu says tomorrow is our day."

"Okay."

"Kerry is counting on your help with the computers."

"I can't guarantee anything. We need another week to verify our methodology."

"We don't have a week."

"I didn't think he'd wait."

"Hard to believe the time has come."

Cole just nodded. He thought, life's transitions always come at the worst possible time.

"How about the governor? What is he saying to Beijing?" Rip knew that Cole had had the CIA bug City Hall.

"He doesn't have a clue," Cole said. "If the Chinese government knows what's going down, they haven't told him or Tang."

"I'd like to bring Sue Lin and her mom to the consulate," Rip muttered, barely loud enough for Cole to hear above the sound of running water.

"Rip, we've been all through that three or four times. Take them to the Australian consulate."

"If it goes bad the PLA will overrun the Australians. The Americans are the only people they don't have the balls to take on."

"Take the women to the airport tonight and put them on a plane to Sydney."

"The old woman won't go, can't go—doesn't have a passport—and the daughter won't go without the old woman."

"For Christ's sake! Have your father send a private jet; land them somewhere in the damned outback. There has to be at least one immigration official in Australia who can be bought."

"There are probably dozens, but the women don't *want* to leave."

"Rip, it's time to stop sweating the program. If we lose we'll all be dead. The women know that."

"Jesus, another philosopher!" Rip glowered at the older man.

Cole was right, of course. Still, Rip thought he would feel better if he had somehow managed to get Sue Lin and Lin Pe out of the line of fire. If that made him an unrepentant chauvinist, so be it.

"Had a talk with Sonny Wong a few nights ago," he told Cole. "The bastard says someone in your consulate is selling him genuine American passports."

"Think he was lying?"

"No."

Tiger Cole finished washing and went into the dressing area. When Rip joined him, he said in a low voice, "That explains a lot."

"A lot of what?"

"China Bob Chan knew far too much. He and Sonny did dozens of deals together through the years."

"So who's leaking?"

"Only two people have access to the passports. One of them has to be in on it, maybe both. One of them is a woman who sleeps with one of the CIA dudes."

"Didn't one of consulate staffers just in from the states get killed a week or so ago?"

"A CIA officer. Shot to death on the street after he planted bugs in China Bob's library."

They finished dressing in silence and left separately.

The bakery for the Double Happy Fortune Cookie Company was housed in a warehouse near the Chinese University in the New Territories. After the Dutchman died, Lin Pe moved the bakery here for a reason: Even though wages for cooks and laborers were low, wages for students were even lower. By paying students more than the going wage, Lin Pe managed to staff her business with some of the brightest, most talented workers in Hong Kong.

The cookie packaging and storage facilities for bulk bakery supplies were located on the first floor. The actual baking of the cookies and printing of Lin Pe's fortunes occurred on the second floor. In the company offices on the third floor where Lin Pe had kept the books by hand for many years, banks of computers manned by students studying computer and electrical engineering were operating around the clock. Behind the warehouse several delivery vans were parked, as well as a half dozen full-sized trucks that were used to transport overseas cookie shipments to the airport.

Wu Tai Kwong had taken the situation as he found it. The bakery employees were now one of the key cells of the revolutionary committee; threads ran from the bakery to dozens of cells in the university and in factories and offices all over town. From there, the threads ran all over China. Wu Tai Kwong well knew that a local uprising in Hong Kong was doomed; he was playing for much bigger stakes.

This afternoon he lingered on the loading dock with several of his key lieutenants smoking, watching the rain fall, and making last-minute plans.

The time for waiting was over. The spontaneous protests in front of the failed Bank of the Orient had deeply impressed Wu and his friends. The willingness of unarmed citizens to defy the PLA was, Wu thought, a direct measure of the depth of their antigovernment feelings. The Communists also understood that fact, which was the reason they reacted so violently to peaceful protests.

The conspiracy dynamic was also pressing mercilessly. As the organized circle of government enemies expanded, secrecy became nebulous. The enforcers who had ruthlessly punished security lapses when there were relatively few conspirators—and even executed government spies—became powerless as the group expanded exponentially. Whispers at the rank-and-file level became impossible to prevent. Absolute secrecy could be enforced only in a few key cells. Fortunately Virgil Cole, the American, had signed on a year ago and contributed vast sums of money, money that was used to bribe the regular and secret police and anyone else whose silence was deemed necessary.

The government in Beijing knew it had sworn blood enemies, of course, but Beijing was far away, with dozens of layers of corrupt officialdom between here and there. Still, even an absolutely corrupt government could bestir itself if the threat was perceived as grave enough.

Time, Wu told his friends, was running out. Now or never. Fight or submit. Fight or die.

Today his friends watched his facial features as he talked, listened intently to every word. Wu recruited them to his vision and held them enthralled with the power of his personality, nothing else. Energy radiated from him, life, *power* . . .

Some of the women who came within his personal orbit thought of him as a semireligious figure, a modern-day Buddha or Confucius. He wasn't: Wu Tai Kwong was a fierce, driven man of extraordinary personal courage who had ordered executions of traitors and occasionally pulled the trigger himself. He believed in himself and his convictions with a righteous fervor that ordinary people would label irrational. What the people who knew him well saw was a man with the wisdom, courage, determination, and titanic ego necessary to lead a nation as large as China into a new day.

Wu removed a cell phone from his pocket. "Do we go?" he asked them one last time.

Positive nods all around.

Wu dialed the number.

One ring, two.

"Hello." Cole's voice. How well Wu knew it.

"Go," he said and flipped the mouthpiece shut, severing the connection.

"The new day is almost here," Wu said now to his friends and laughed heartily. He would have laughed on Judgment Day. His laughter seemed to calm the taut nerves of those around him, some of whom forced themselves to smile.

Wu Tai Kwong took a last drag on his cigarette, tossed the butt into a rain puddle, got into the delivery van he normally used, and drove out of the Double Happy Fortune Cookie Company parking lot.

He joined the flow of traffic in the crowded street and crept along toward the first light. The windshield wipers fought a losing battle with the rain, which was coming down harder now than it had all day. Perhaps it was only his imagination.

Another van pulled out in front of him, inched its bumper out into the space between Wu and the vehicle ahead, and of course he had to let it in.

The driver got the van into the traffic stream ahead of Wu, and of course didn't make it through the first light.

Sitting behind the van, thinking of rain and soldiers and millions of angry people, Wu failed to take alarm when the back door of the van ahead opened and two men hopped out. They slammed the door closed, then one stepped to the passenger door of Wu's van and one to the driver's door. They jerked the doors open.

The man on Wu's side had a pistol in his hand, one that he seemed to produce from thin air. Wu looked left—the man climbing into the passenger seat also had a pistol, one pointed at Wu's midsection.

"Put the van in park," the man said standing beside him, "and move over. I'll drive."

Wu floored the accelerator. The van jumped forward, smashing into the back of the vehicle ahead. The man standing on the driver's side fell to the street while the man on the passenger's side who was half in and half out hung on to the door for dear life.

Wu slammed the vehicle into reverse and cranked the wheel over as he jammed the accelerator back down.

A bullet smashed the driver's window. Wu felt the thump of the wheel rolling over the fallen man just before the van impacted the vehicle behind. Wu kept the accelerator mashed down, the rear wheels squalled. . . .

The man on Wu's left was inside the vehicle now, swinging at his head with a pistol. Wu drove his right hand into the man's teeth, then slammed on the brake and tried to get the transmission in reverse.

The engine stalled.

In the silence that followed Wu could hear the gasping oaths of the man in the passenger seat. He was grinding on the starter when the man hit him a glancing blow in the head with the pistol.

Wu tried to elbow the man, punch him in the face, but he passed out when the man hit him in the head with the gun a second time.

Jake Grafton unlocked the door to his hotel room and couldn't believe his eyes. The room was trashed. The bed had been stripped, the mattress stuffing strewn everywhere, the furniture broken, the television smashed . . . every item of clothing he and Callie had brought to Hong Kong lay somewhere in the middle of that mess. Even the carpet had been peeled back around the walls.

"Callie?"

He walked into the room, checked to make sure she wasn't in the bathroom or closet or lying under the mess or behind the dresser.

"*Callie?*"

He knew what they had been searching for—the tape. They didn't find it because it was in his pocket.

Where was Callie? She could be downstairs, or shopping, or getting her hair done. . . .

"*Callie!*" He roared her name.

A woman peered through the open doorway from the hall. A Chinese woman, the maid. She asked something in Chinese.

"The lady who was here?" he replied. "Where did she go?"

The maid shook her head uncomprehendingly, stared in amazement at the sea of trash.

Jake Grafton brushed by her and hurried along the hallway. Unwilling to wait for an elevator, he charged down the stairs, trying to think.

He raced for the manager's office and blew by the secretary. The manager was a Brit. "Someone trashed my room"—he gave the man the number—"and my wife is missing! Call the police!"

The man stood gaping at Jake, so Jake repeated it, then went charging out of the office.

He had to find a phone.

Fumbling with the telephone book, barking at the operator, he finally got through to the American consulate. "Tommy Carmellini, please."

In less than a minute Carmellini was on the line.

"Grafton. This morning someone did a real messy search of my hotel room. My wife is missing."

Several seconds of silence followed as Carmellini digested the news. "The tape," he said. "Did they get it?"

"No. Who was it?"

"God knows."

"*I* want to know."

"Well, I sure as hell don't know what to tell you, Admiral. If they snatched your wife, you'll probably be hearing from them."

"Unless they have plans for making her talk."

Carmellini didn't respond.

"Is the consul general there this afternoon?" Grafton asked.

"I don't know."

"I'm coming over there. See you in about a half hour. Find me a weapon."

Jake Grafton slammed the telephone down and marched through the lobby to the street. He passed two uniformed police on their way into the building and didn't stop.

Tiger Cole was in his office. With Carmellini in tow, Jake stormed past the secretary and barged in. Cole was on the telephone. ". . . the trade agreements can be interpreted as—" One look at Grafton's face stopped the words.

"May I call you back, Mr. Secretary? A crisis has arisen here that I must deal with." He listened for a second or two, muttered something, then hung up.

"What in the world—?"

"Someone trashed my hotel room searching it and my wife is missing." Jake came around the desk and seized Cole's lapels. "If you know who has her or where she is, now is the moment to come clean."

"*Hey!*" Cole tried to pull Grafton's hands off.

The admiral held on fiercely and lowered his face toward Cole. "If anything happens to Callie I'll kill you," he snarled. "*Anything!* Do you understand me, Cole?"

The consul general became very still. "I understand, Jake."

Grafton released Cole and straightened.

"Who has her?"

"I don't know. Tell me about it."

Jake sat on the desk. He described the room. "When I left her to come here for lunch, she was fine. Going to go downstairs for lunch, but she said she would be waiting for me when I got back from the consulate. She wasn't, and the place had been violently trashed. Whoever did it was looking for this!" He pulled the tape from his pocket and showed it to Cole. "This is the tape from China Bob Chan's library, removed from the recorder within minutes after his death."

Cole's brow knitted. "How'd you get it?"

"Mr. Carmellini gave it to me. He was sent over here to help with my investigation. The death of Harold Barnes seemed a good place to start."

Jake turned to Carmellini. "Anything of interest on your searches or bugs?"

"No, sir. Not yet."

"What's he searching?" Tiger asked.

"Everything in this building," Grafton barked. "Safes, filing cabinets, desks, hard drives, databases, trash cans, everything. I want to know what the fuck is going on in Hong Kong and I want to know *now*!"

Cole took a deep breath. "Did you bug this office, Carmellini?"

"Yes, sir."

"Disable the bugs and leave us alone. Admiral Grafton asked a question and he deserves an unrecorded answer."

Carmellini took less than a minute to remove the hidden wireless microphones. One was stuck to the eraser of a pencil, one of a dozen pens and pencils protruding from a coffee cup on Cole's desk; another was pinned to the window curtain behind his chair.

When the door closed behind Carmellini, Cole said, "I don't know who kidnapped your wife."

"Did you know it was going to happen?"

"No. I'm amazed that it did."

"Let's take it by the numbers. What in hell are you mixed up in?"

"As you surmised at lunch, a group of revolutionaries is about to kick over the lantern. I'm one of them."

"Uh-huh."

Cole raised his hands questioningly.

"Did your group kill Harold Barnes, or have him killed?"

"To the best of my knowledge, no."

"Don't start that quibble shit with me, Cole! You are ten seconds away from a phone call to Washington. Did anyone in your group kill Harold Barnes? Tell me what you think."

"No."

"Who killed him?"

"I don't know. I thought at the time it might be someone in the CIA who was in bed with China Bob."

"Where did China Bob fit in all this?"

Cole took a deep breath and leaned back in his chair. "I wish I knew the correct answer to that. I was using him as a conduit to get untraceable money into Hong Kong to fund the revolution. About a hundred million American dollars went through his hands."

"Your money?"

"Yes."

"*Jesus,* Tiger! What in the hell are you doing, man?"

"Violently overthrowing the Communist government of China. I thought it was a great investment."

"Did the thought ever cross your mind that perhaps the best thing you could do for your fellow Americans was let the Chinese solve their own problems?"

"I'm not going to justify my actions to you or anybody else," Cole said coldly. "I've done what I believed was the right thing for my fellow man—all of them. You and the people in Washington can put that on my tombstone or stick it up your ass, I don't care which."

"Okay, okay." Jake held up his hands. "What else was Chan into?"

"He smuggled some computers into the country for me."

"Was he making campaign contributions to American politicians?"

"I believe so."

"Who supplied the money?"

"The PLA."

"What else was he up to?"

"Anything that would turn a dollar. Chan liked money and had a finger in every pie in town. That's probably what got him killed."

"Someone thought he knew too much about too many things?"

"I suspect that's the gospel truth."

"Did he know your money was going to fund a revolution?"

"I believe he thought I was in the drug business, but he may have guessed the truth at some point."

Jake Grafton held both hands to his head. "I can't believe this shit!"

Cole smacked the desk with the flat of his hand. "Don't give me any sanctimonious crap! I won't listen to it! Thirty years ago America's liberals refused to fight for freedom in Asia—now they're partners with the propaganda ministry of the Communist government as investors in China.com. Anything for a goddamn buck! Yeah, I'm funding a revolution. If the warm, well-fed, comfortable, educated establishment bastards in America lose some money or bleed a little, it'll break my slimy heart."

Jake Grafton took his time answering. "You can't give freedom to people, Tiger. It's something they have to earn for themselves. If they don't want freedom enough to fight for it, they won't value it."

"The Chinese are going to fight, all right," Cole shot back. "They're going to do their share of bleeding."

"Okay," Jake Grafton said.

When Cole calmed down, he asked, "Did Callie listen to the tape that Carmellini brought her?"

"Yes."

"All of it."

"She said she did."

"Who knew about the tape?"

"Carmellini, and whoever he told. He brought us a special player and earphones to listen to the thing. I presume he got them out of the closet here at the consulate."

Tiger Cole took a deep breath. "Let's make some assumptions, see where they take us. Let's assume that whoever grabbed Callie is interested in the contents of that tape."

Jake Grafton nodded.

"We know China Bob was taking money from the PLA to give to American politicians," Cole continued. "And we know he wasn't passing all of it along. The PLA has figured this out, too, but I fail to see why they would care what was on that tape. If a PLA officer killed China Bob, he wouldn't care if the American government knew it. The Chinese government doesn't care. Oh, Beijing might be embarrassed about the congressional revelations, but the government really doesn't *care*. Do you understand me?"

"I guess."

"For these people, Beijing is the center of the universe. What the Americans think or don't think is as important as the shape of the craters on the back side of the moon."

"Okay."

"The only reason the PLA would want the tape is because there's something on it that threatens them. If they knew about the revolutionaries, they wouldn't need the tape. Do you agree?"

"I'm listening."

"That leaves someone else Chan dealt with. Not me, because it's too late for you or anyone else to stop the train. The danger to the revolution is past."

"I accept that for now," Grafton said. "If the shit hits the fan tomorrow. If it doesn't . . ."

"The tape would be of value only to someone who doesn't know the timetable, someone who thinks that he can sell the information that's on it or use it for blackmail. He's assuming that the world he knows is still going to be there, otherwise the tape has no value."

Jake took the tape from his pocket and placed it on Cole's desk. "Do you have anybody who could translate this for me?"

"Yes. Kerry Kent."

"Is she in the building?"

"Yes." He pushed the button on the intercom and said his secretary's name. "Is Mr. Carmellini waiting out there?"

"Yes, sir."

"Please have him go to the CIA office and ask Ms. Kent to come see me."

When he released the intercom button, Cole told Grafton, "She's a British SIS agent on a foreign assignment. She works here."

"Do you want the Brits to hear this?"

"I don't think she'll pass it along to London."

"Think or know?"

"She's Wu Tai Kwong's girlfriend."

"I'm not going to sit here for six hours while she listens to the tape. Gimme your best guess. Who snatched Callie?"

"The first possibility that pops into my head is a local gangster named Sonny Wong. I have reason to believe that people in this building are feeding him information, maybe even selling him passports."

"Do you know who these people are?"

"Suspicion only."

"What else is Wong into?"

"His primary occupation is smuggling: refugees, dope, diamonds, guns, whatever will earn a buck."

"Where do I find this star of the social register?"

"You need to see a man named Rip Buckingham. He's a friend of mine. I'll give you his address. We won't call because the telephones might be tapped, but I'll write a note for you to take with you. Go over to his house."

"Does he know about the plan for revolution?"

"Yes."

"He's one of the inner circle?"

"Yes."

"What does he know?"

"As few of the specifics of my business as possible. Like all good conspirators, we compartmentalize all we can, just in case. Obviously he knows details that I don't. He's as familiar with the big picture as I am, of course."

Jake Grafton could sit still no longer. He walked to the window and back, rubbing his hands. "I need a weapon, a pistol. Got one you could loan me?"

Cole hiked a foot up on his lower desk drawer, pulled up a trouser leg, and pulled down his sock. He was wearing an ankle holster. "It's a five-shot Smith and Wesson thirty-eight with a two-inch barrel," he said as he unstrapped the holster. "The police will get real pissy if they catch you toting it around. About all it's good for is shooting yourself."

"Would you have done that if they arrested you?" Jake murmured.

"Hell no. I've got diplomatic immunity," Cole said.

"Is immunity bulletproof?"

"Nope. Which is why I carried the pistol."

Cole was writing down Rip Buckingham's address on a Post-it when the intercom buzzed. The secretary's voice came through the box. "Sir, Mr. Carmellini is back with Ms. Kent. And there is a call from a Mr. Wong. He says he has something that might be of interest to you."

Cole looked up and met the unblinking gray eyes of Jake Grafton.

"Send Carmellini and Kent in," he told the box, "and I'll take the call." When Carmellini and Kent were seated beside Jake Grafton, Cole pushed the speaker button on the telephone.

"Cole."

"Mr. Cole, my name is Sonny Wong. I don't think we have ever formally met, but you may have heard someone mention my name." Wong spoke decent English, but the accent was unmistakable.

"I have indeed heard your name."

"I have come into the possession of several items you may wish to redeem, Mr. Cole. One is an American lady named Grafton."

CHAPTER NINE

The color drained from Jake Grafton's face as Tiger Cole said, "I'm listening."

"You may remember our mutual friend, China Bob Chan? It seems that a tape recording was made in his library the evening he died."

Wong paused. Cole said nothing. Kerry Kent looked at Tommy Carmellini, who kept his gaze fixed on the telephone.

"Still there, Mr. Cole?"

"Yes."

"This lady has listened to the tape. I don't have the tape, mind you, just the woman. She heard you shoot China Bob, Mr. Cole."

"So?"

"You have diplomatic immunity in China, but the American State Department might take a dim view of murder. Conceivably, the American government could waive your immunity and turn you over to the Chinese for trial. A federal indictment in the United States is more probable. This woman could put you in prison for the rest of your life."

"I'm still listening."

"The other item I have is even more marketable. Amazingly, with the entire resources of the Chinese government devoted to the search for public enemy Wu Tai Kwong, I have managed to apprehend the criminal."

"Why are you telling me all this?"

"I think the authorities would be very interested in both of my prizes, Mr. Cole. As you know, they have offered a very tempting reward for Wu. I propose to sell both these people to you or to the Chinese government. Think it over."

"You son of a bitch! Who are you trying to bullshit? Sun will throw you in the same hole he's got waiting for Wu. If Wu won't talk, I will."

Sonny chuckled. "You underestimate the gratitude that will overflow Sun's hard little heart if I produce Wu Tai Kwong. Waving Wu's head in Beijing will make Sun's fortune—the bastard may wind up as our next premier."

"You're the biggest liar west of Little Rock."

"Everybody has a price."

"What's yours?"

"Fifty million American dollars."

"I think you're trying to hijack the revolution."

"Hijack it? I'm trying desperately to profit from it."

"Without Wu, there won't be a revolution."

"Crap," shot back Sonny Wong. "No one can stop it now. You'll lead it yourself. Or I will."

"I'd be a fool to pay."

"You'd be a fool not to. Your choice."

"Fifty million?"

"Yep. Transferred by you into a Swiss bank account. You have three days to make the transfer or I make a delivery to the People's Liberation Army."

Cole took a deep breath. "What account?"

"One of my colleagues will call you with the information, a Mr. Daniel. Should you decide to redeem one person and not the other, discuss that with Mr. Daniel."

"I'll want to talk with both parties right now to make sure they are alive and well cared for."

"Discuss the details with Mr. Daniel."

"If anything happens to them I—" Cole began but he was talking to a dead telephone.

He pushed the button to cut the connection.

They all sat staring at the telephone.

After a moment, Grafton said, "Callie said the tape is inconclusive.

She said anyone listening to it couldn't determine who fired the shot that killed Chan." He picked up the tape from the desk, fingered the reels, then laid it down again.

"It's money Wong's after," Cole muttered. "If he doesn't get money, he'll probably kill her."

"But he wants the tape," Jake objected. "Wants to know what's on it."

"Yeah. He and China Bob did a lot of business together. God only knows what the two of them talked about. He wants the tape, too."

"Wu Tai Kwong?"

"The political criminal."

"Why would you care about him?" Tommy Carmellini asked.

"Who do you think is leading the revolution?"

"I guess I hadn't put two and two together."

"Wu isn't his real name. As fate would have it, he's Rip Buckingham's brother-in-law. If we can overthrow the Communists and Wu lives long enough, he's going to be the first elected president of the new Republic of China."

"And Wong wants you to pay a ransom for him?"

"If I don't pay for Wu, Sonny Wong will indeed turn Wu over to the People's Liberation Army, which will pay Sonny the posted reward and execute Wu."

"Fifty million dollars is a lot of kale," Tommy Carmellini remarked, rubbing his chin.

"Callie and I have been pretty diligent savers and investors," Jake said, "and we have about one-fifth of one percent of that amount."

Cole waved a hand dismissively. "I'll pay it," he said.

"They may kill them anyway."

"We'll set up a trade. They produce Wu and Callie, I make the call authorizing a wire transfer of the money. When the money is in his bank, we leave."

Jake Grafton shook his head slowly. "He'll have to kill you and Wu after you make the call. Wong can't afford to let Wu live to send an army to hunt him down. Hell, he'll have to kill us all so nothing leaks out."

Cole's face wore a blank expression. His mind was obviously going at a mile a minute.

"How come this Wong knows so much about the revolution?"

"He's involved, obviously."

"Obviously. How is he involved? What's his role in all this?"

"Not now," Tiger Cole said, frowning. "I can't tell you now."

"*Goddamn you!*" Jake Grafton roared. "That asshole kidnapped my wife!"

"I'm sorry, Jake," Tiger Cole said.

The admiral struggled to get himself under control. He played with the pistol, checked it, then pulled up his trouser leg. When he spoke again it was in a normal tone. "If you had nothing to do with Callie's kidnapping, you have nothing to apologize for," he said as he strapped the ankle holster to his right leg. "If you did, I'll kill you, Cole. It's that goddamn simple."

"How did Sonny Wong capture Wu Tai Kwong?" Carmellini asked.

"Everyone in Hong Kong knows Wu is somewhere in the city," the consul general replied. "The revolutionary movement has more leaks than the *Titanic*."

"So why hasn't Wu been arrested before?"

"Because we've paid off the police." Cole shrugged. "Everyone in the Chinese government is corrupt, all of them. This is the third world!"

"Can we get help from the police to get Callie back? Wu?"

"Beijing has posted a huge reward for Wu. The cops are corrupt, but you are fooling yourself if you think no one will call the PLA to turn him in. They will!"

"Okay," said Jake Grafton. "Let's talk about Callie. Only a few people knew she was going to listen to that tape. Carmellini, you're one of them. Who'd you tell?"

"No one, Admiral."

"Somebody figured it out."

"Kerry Kent," Tommy said bitterly.

"You ass," she hissed and went for him with her fingernails.

Carmellini grabbed her wrists. He was far too strong for her. "Don't play the injured lover with me," he sneered with all the contempt of a man who had never been in love. "I've heard that song before. You're the number-one suspect on my list."

"I trust her," Cole said, in a tone that ended the argument.

Carmellini pushed Kent away. If looks could kill, he would have received a fatal wound just then.

"The postmortem can wait," Jake Grafton said. "We've got other fish to fry." He picked up the tape from Cole's desk and put it in his pocket.

The maid brought Rip the cell phone. He was sitting on his roof under a dripping umbrella. The air was now a fine sea mist; occasionally a whisper of breeze tossed a handful of droplets on his face, almost like a kiss.

The maid didn't look at him, merely handed him the phone and left.

Rip pushed the button and answered.

"Rip, this is Sonny Wong."

"Hey, Sonny."

"Got some bad news for you, Rip. Hate having to deliver it like this, but the world is pressing in, if you know what I mean."

"Like what?"

"Like I have your brother-in-law as an unwilling guest."

"My brother-in-law?"

"Yeah. Wu. Remember him? Drives for the Double Happy Fortune Cookie Company? Is wanted by the government for political crimes? The million Hong Kong dollars reward? That brother-in-law."

"Jesus, Sonny, I thought we were friends."

"We are, Rip, but this is business. Hong Kong is about to blow up in our faces, no thanks to your brother-in-law, who has done everything within his power to light the fuse. It's been a grand party, but it's over. A guy has to look out for number one. You and I are not friends ten million American dollars' worth. That's what it will cost you to see Wu in one piece again."

"I don't have that kind of money, Sonny. You know that."

"Ah, but your father does. Call him! Tell Richard Buckingham that if I don't get the money, your brother-in-law Wu Tai Kwong will be turned over to General Tang Tso of the PLA, who will probably shoot him before he writes the reward check. Or strangle him. For some reason, those guys still like to strangle people. So old-fashioned and messy. Uncivilized too, but probably very satisfying on some level. Almost orgasmic."

"You're a perfect bastard, Sonny."

"Not quite perfect but I'm working on it. If I were Richard Buckingham's heir, like a certain person I know, I wouldn't have to be. You know what I'm saying? It's an accident of birth, really, that I was born in a sewer, poor as a flea on a starving rat, and I've been digging and scratching every minute since then to get out of it."

"Let me talk to Wu."

"You're going to have to take my word on this, Rip. Wu is sleeping right now; I don't want to wake him."

"How do I know you've got him?"

"If you're really worried about that point, I'll have someone drop by with a finger. What the hell, he's got ten. He'll never miss a few."

"Okay, okay."

"You talk to Richard. I'll call you back in a few hours, give you the particulars on a Swiss bank account that I'm trying to fatten up. You can plan on transferring the money there."

With that Sonny hung up.

Rip went inside looking for Sue Lin. He found her in the kitchen. "Where's the maid?"

"The new one?"

Rip nodded.

"After she gave you the phone, she went downstairs, got her umbrella, and left. Didn't say a word to me. I happened to look out the window and saw her walking toward the tram."

"Wu's been kidnapped."

"*What?*"

"Sonny Wong has him. He wants ten million American dollars or he'll turn him over to the government and collect the reward."

She sat and put her face in her hands. Rip put his arms around her shoulders and found she was shaking.

"Hey." He knelt in front of her, opened her hands. Tears streamed along her cheeks. "Hey."

"I've seen this Sonny Wong," she whispered. "He is evil."

"Sue Lin, I've known him for years. Yeah, he's a crook, but he's always been straight with me. He's just wants money. Unfortunately we looked like an easy mark."

"He'll kill Wu."

"We'll pay the money. I'll bet he'll let him go."

"With the city full of people who worship Wu?" she protested, shaking her head. "Sonny Wong will kill him and take the first plane out before anyone finds out the truth."

The sound of a man groaning woke Callie Grafton. She opened her eyes and looked around. It took several seconds before she realized what she was looking at. She was in a small stateroom, perhaps on a ship, lying on a narrow bed, a lower bunk. Across the aisle, almost within reach, lay a man with his back to her. He was the one groaning.

Blood stained his shirt and the sheet on which he lay.

She extended her arm . . . and felt a sharp pain roar through her skull. Slowly she put her hands to her head and pressed. She had the mother of all headaches.

Her head throbbed with every heartbeat. Gradually the pain seemed to ease somewhat, and once again she extended her hand to the groaning man.

His back was warm.

Callie moved, painfully, until she could touch the man.

She swung her feet over the edge of the bunk and sat up, which almost split her head with pain. In a minute or so the pain lessened and she could see and function.

Ever so slowly, she stood, turned the man over, and examined him.

His left hand was bloody. She looked. His little finger was missing, leaving only an oozing, partially scabbed wound.

She tore at the sheet, finally got a strip off it, and wrapped the strip around the man's hand as a crude bandage.

He had stopped groaning. When she finished she realized his eyes were open and he was looking at her with intelligent brown eyes. He was Chinese, in his mid-thirties perhaps.

"You've lost a finger," she said in Chinese.

"They cut it off."

She sat back down on her own bunk, put her aching head in her hands. It was coming back: the knock on the hotel room door, the voice—she thought it was the maid or bellman. When she opened the door, several men rushed in. They grabbed her mouth to keep her from screaming and threw her on the bed and one of them produced a hypodermic.

That was all she remembered. That and the fear.

Now she was sitting in a stateroom . . . she could feel the boat rocking in the waves. It must be a small ship to rock like this. There was a round porthole with the glass painted over; a bit of light leaked through the scratches in the paint. That light was all that illuminated the tiny room.

When she turned her head she could see that the man on the bunk had rolled over. Now he was looking at her.

"Does your hand hurt?"

"Not too much," he said.

"Who are you?"

"You wouldn't know me."

"Do you have a name?"

"Wu."

"I'm Callie."

"Callie." He said it experimentally.

"Where are we?"

"I think we have been kidnapped. They knocked me out, so I don't know."

"Me, too."

She still had her watch, which was unexpected. Almost three o'clock. The men had burst into the hotel room about ten A.M.

She wondered if it were the same day.

She lay down and thought about her husband.

"Commander Tarkington?"

"That's right." Tommy Carmellini pressed the telephone to his ear to help himself concentrate. The voice that sounded in his ear from the other side of the Pacific was certainly clear enough.

"My name is Tommy Carmellini. We met last year in Cuba. Do you remember?"

"Yes." Tarkington sounded sleepy. The telephone call had awakened him.

"Admiral Grafton asked me to call you. He needs your help." Tarkington was Jake Grafton's aide.

"I got a pencil. Shoot." Now Toad was alert.

"His wife has been kidnapped," Carmellini said.

"Callie Grafton? *Gawd damn!*" The Toad-man whistled through his teeth.

Carmellini glanced around the office. Kerry Kent and the three CIA dudes were all staring at him, listening to his every word.

"We believe the man behind it is a Hong Kong citizen named Sonny Wong," Carmellini continued. "I don't know his real name. He is associated with a Russian national named Yuri Daniel. The admiral asked me to call you. He wants the CIA to run those two through the computers and see what they can come up with. Wong may have some bank accounts in Switzerland or some other bank haven. Look for passports, visas, travel records, wire transfers, anything."

"Okay." Toad's voice was crisp and businesslike.

"Have the National Security Agency set up a study of telecommunications traffic in the Hong Kong area. Obviously we are interested in the Graftons, Sonny Wong, Yuri Daniel, kidnapping, ransom, anything along those lines."

"I'll talk to them in a few hours. Tell the admiral I'll go through the agency director's office. Shouldn't be a problem. Anything else?"

"That will do it for now."

"Heard anything about Callie? Is she okay?"

"We don't know."

"Does this Wong dude want money or what?"

"Money."

"Wow!" said Toad Tarkington. "That Wong must have really bad karma—I can smell it from here. Jake Grafton is the last man on the planet I'd want blood-crazy mad at me. You tell the admiral I'm on my way to the office as soon as I get my pants on."

Jake Grafton sat at the conference table in Cole's office and tried to clear his thoughts. There was stationery in the trays under the computer printer, so he helped himself to a couple of sheets. He took a U.S. government black ballpoint from his shirt pocket and clicked the point in and out while he collected his thoughts.

The National Security Adviser had sent Jake to Hong Kong to find out what was going on; the man was entitled to know.

Jake wrote quickly in a clear, legible longhand detailing what he had learned. The consul general was involved in a conspiracy to overthrow the Chinese government and had resigned. Cole had been in the building when China Bob Chan was killed, may have talked to him, and may have been somehow involved in his death. The enclosed tape was made in Chan's library by the recorder planted by Harold Barnes and should be listened to by Chinese-language experts.

He wrote two pages total, then put the handwritten sheets and the audiotape in a large padded envelope, which he sealed. He wrote the National Security Adviser's name on it and handed it to Cole.

"I want you to send this to Washington in the next diplomatic pouch. The Chan tape is in there."

"Okay."

"I'm relying on your honor, Cole."

"I am well aware of that fact, Jacob Lee, and will try not to take offense at the fact you felt the need to point it out."

"I'm all out of apologies," Grafton replied coolly.

"I'll put the envelope in the pouch," Cole said. "The problem is the airlines—nothing is coming in or going out of Lantau since the air traffic control computers crapped out."

"Did you have anything to do with that?"

"I certainly hope so."

Jake scratched his head, trying to make up his mind. "I want the tape in the bag and on its way," Jake said finally, "so I won't be tempted to trade the damned thing to this Wong asshole for Callie."

"Okay."

"And the time has come for you to resign." Jake took Cole's letter of resignation from his pocket and tossed it on the desk. "Fax that thing to Washington."

"Now?"

"Right now."

Cole took a deep breath. "Okay," he said.

The intercom buzzed. "Mr. Cole. There's a small package here for you. The sergeant at the gate brought it up. He says you should see it."

"Is he still there?"

"Yes, sir."

"Have him bring it in."

The marine was square as a fire plug and togged out in a khaki shirt and blue trousers with a red stripe up each seam. He looked pale.

"Did you X-ray the package, Sergeant?" Cole asked.

"Yes, sir. There's no bomb. Looked like a bone."

"A bone?"

"Well, three little bones. Jesus, sir, it looks like a finger."

Cole cut the brown wrapping paper away from the box with a letter opener, then cut the tape that held the top on.

Jake Grafton was looking over Cole's shoulder when he opened the box. It was a finger, all right, freshly severed, if the still-soft blood was any indication.

"Thank you, Sergeant," Cole said softly and sent the marine on his way.

Jake Grafton stood still as a statue, staring at the finger.

"It isn't Callie's," he said.

"Probably Wu's," Cole muttered and used the intercom to ask the secretary to have Kerry Kent come up to the office.

While they were waiting Jake walked around the office looking at Cole's memorabilia. He was thinking of Callie, wondering how he was going to get her back, when he realized he was looking at an old photo of himself and Tiger Cole. The thing was in black and white, framed, sitting on an out-of-the-way shelf behind the conference table. He and Cole were standing in front of a bomb-laden A-6 in their flight gear, obviously on a flight deck. Neither man was grinning.

Those were simpler days.

Kerry Kent knocked, then came charging into the office. She looked into the box, and clapped her hand over her mouth.

"Those bastards," she said between clenched teeth. "Those fucking bastards."

Victoria Peak and the tops of the buildings were wreathed in fog when Jake Grafton walked out the front entrance of the American consulate. The rain had stopped, leaving the air tangibly wet, thick, warm, and heavy.

He walked slowly, taking his time, watching for people who might be paying attention to him.

He had to will himself to walk slowly, to analyze and think logically about the situation and what he could do to affect it.

The tension in everyone he met was visible—all the pedestrians were on edge, regardless of age, sex, race, or how they were dressed. Without smiles or nods, the people walked briskly with their heads down, avoiding eye contact, avoiding each other, hurrying toward the great unknown.

He stood in line and bought a ticket on the tram, then waited a minute or two with the crowd for the tram to descend the mountain. He let other people board the car in front of him, arranging it so he was one of the very last aboard, and told the motorman where he wanted off.

The car got underway almost noiselessly as the cable pulled it up the tracks. The only sound Jake could hear was the faintest rumble from the wheels, or perhaps he was only feeling the vibration of the steel wheels on the steel rails. The grade was about thirty percent, he estimated. A series of stairs ran alongside the cable car's track for those in the mood for a serious climb.

No one in the car spoke. All studiously avoided looking at each other as the car silently climbed the steep grade. The buildings slid past and the fog thickened.

The car stopped at a tiny platform about three-quarters of the way up the side of the mountain. Jake got off, then the car resumed its journey and disappeared into the fog.

He walked along the street, found the right house, rang the bell.

A man opened the door, a man in his late thirties, perhaps even forty.

"Rip Buckingham?"

"Come in, please."

When the door closed behind him, Jake said, "I suppose Wong called you."

"Yes. My wife is upstairs. Wu is her brother."

They sat at a table in the kitchen, with a window beside them that gave a view of some nearby housetops amid the gloom.

"Cole said they took your wife."

"Yes."

"Sonny won't be able to stay in Hong Kong after this."

"If he gets fifty million from Cole, he won't want to."

"He also wants ten million from me. From my dad, actually, Richard Buckingham."

"Buckingham News?"

"Yeah."

Jake considered the situation in silence as he sized up Rip Buckingham and tried to figure out how much steel was in him. Finally he said, "Wong won't be able to live comfortably anywhere if he releases Callie and Wu alive to testify against him. Switzerland isn't an extradition haven."

"After Wong gets his money, he'll kill everybody who might cause him trouble," Rip said heavily. "A man once told me that four hundred Chinese each paid Sonny fifty grand American to go to America. The ship sailed away and was never seen again."

"Twenty million dollars," Jake muttered after doing the math in his head.

"I don't know if the story is true," Rip continued, "but I know Sonny. He doesn't take unnecessary chances."

Tommy Carmellini had his equipment set up in the attic of the consulate. He had worked for three nights bugging and wiring selected offices, one of which was the CIA office. Another was the consul general's. Grafton wanted to know what was going on—Carmellini intended to find out.

Just now he settled into the folding chair he had stolen from the immigration office and donned a headset, which was plugged into the amplifier. The tape recorder was recording all the microphone inputs simultaneously for later study. Without interfering with the recording, he flipped through the channels, listening to various bugs in turn, sampling the audio.

The CIA office was his main concern. He listened to them chat, matched up voices with the faces in his memory. They were still squeezing the juice from the kidnapping. Well, an admiral's wife doesn't get snatched every day.

Kent also knew that Sonny Wong claimed he had Wu. She wasn't sharing that tidbit with the others, Carmellini noticed. In fact, she was sharing very little.

A remark of Bubba Lee's set the tone. "Man, calling Washington and telling NSA to get on the case—that Grafton *is* somebody."

"Yeah, but who?" That was Eisenberg.

"An admiral in the navy. Don't they sometimes get posted to the intel community?"

"Sometimes."

"Well, that sailor has some stroke, or thinks he has."

"Thinks he has, yeah."

"Do you buy it about Sonny Wong? Does a snatch sound like something he would do?"

"Never can tell, man. Things are getting twangy tight around this town. Riots, people shot in the streets, power off half the night . . ."

"Did you hear about the airport?" Was that Bubba Lee? "The computers out there rolled over and died. People trapped on the concourses, no water in the fountains or toilets, flights canceled. I heard someone went crazy and threw a chair though a plate-glass window."

"Whole goddamn town is falling apart."

"Hey, the whole goddamn *country* is falling apart, if you ask me."

There was more of it, thirty minutes or so. At some point Carmellini realized that there were only two men talking. Eisenberg had been silent a long time, as had Kerry Kent. Maybe they were no longer in the room.

Didn't Cole say Eisenberg knew the woman in the passport office?

Carmellini flipped to that microphone. A loud conversation in Chinese drowned out everything else in the room.

Disgusted, Tommy Carmellini turned the selector to listen to the mike in the consul general's office.

Yep, there was Kent.

"—might kill him. I've been saying for months that he should have an armed bodyguard around the clock. Does anyone pay any attention to the fears of a woman? What does *she* know? What could *she* possibly contribute to this—"

"He didn't want a bodyguard! You know that. Stop this goddamn whining."

"Whining? They may *kill* him!"

"Indeed. He's been a fugitive for a dozen years, with his life hanging by a thread. The revolution continues regardless. The world keeps turning, the tide is coming in . . . at last!"

"What are you doing to get him back alive?"

"I'm paying the damned ransom."

"What else?"

"What else do you think I should do?"

"I don't know!" she moaned. "I only know that I want him *alive*! I need him, China needs him—*everything* depends on him. *Everything!*"

"Tell me some more about Sonny Wong," Jake Grafton said to Rip Buckingham, "everything you can remember." They were still in Rip's kitchen, seated in front of the window. The rain had stopped and the fog was lifting, revealing the skyscrapers of the Central District.

"Sonny's the head of the last of the old-line Hong Kong criminal gangs, or tongs," Rip told the American. "He's sort of an anachronism, a fossil from the wilder days."

"Kidnapping isn't anything new," Jake said sourly.

"No," Rip admitted. "I thought Sonny was above poopy little capers like this, but apparently not."

"I want to know everything, who his associates are, what he does for money, where he lives, what he eats, his habits—vices, women, kids, everything."

"What's on your mind?"

"I want my wife back."

"That may be impossible."

Jake Grafton gripped the edge of the table and squeezed as hard as he could. All these years, ups and downs and ins and outs, good times and hard times, the tiny triumphs and disasters and little victories that fill our days . . . to have her life end here, now, snuffed out by a criminal psychopath who wants money?

When his muscles began quivering from the exertion, Jake Grafton released the table. He rubbed his hands together, thought about Callie, about their adopted daughter, Amy. "Let's hope not," he said to Rip, so softly that the Australian almost missed the response.

CHAPTER TEN

British consul general Sir Robert MacDonald spent a long afternoon with his staff writing a situation report for the Foreign Office. While so engaged he received a telephone call from the foreign minister in London, who was worried.

"The PM wants to know what in the world is going on out there," the foreign minister said after the usual pleasantries.

"The authorities are having some public relations difficulties," replied Sir Robert, never one to overlook the obvious. He had gone to school with the PM, who loathed him. Forced to accept Sir Robert into the government, the PM had sent him as far from London as he possibly could. "A few technical problems too, I'm afraid," the consul general continued. "Rather inconvenient when the power goes off at odd hours."

"The Buckingham newspapers published a provocative piece in to-day's U.K. and American editions," the foreign minister informed Her Majesty's Hong Kong representative. "I wonder if you've seen it?"

"Afraid not. The locals shut down the *China Post,* which was Buckingham's little rag hereabouts. Of course, they shut down all the newspapers—I'm sure my staff sent you that information in the morning report."

"Richard Buckingham signed this piece himself. He says that a revolution is about to sweep China, one that will overthrow the Communists."

"His son was the editor of the *China Post*," Sir Robert replied. Rip had been a thorn in MacDonald's side since the day the man arrived from London. "Governor Sun tossed him in jail," he said, unable to keep the satisfaction completely out of his voice. "He's out now, of course. Perhaps he had something to do with the article."

"I see," the FM said slowly.

"It's always a mistake to quarrel with a man who buys ink by the barrel," Sir Robert continued, repeating a comment his wife had made to him on several occasions when he took offense at *China Post* editorials. "Richard Buckingham can say anything he wants in his newspapers and there's jolly little the Chinks can do about it. But talk of revolution is rot, pure rot. The Communists are firmly in control. They have a division of troops in the colony."

Sir Robert still referred to Hong Kong as a colony, which it had ceased to be in 1997, even though his staff and the Foreign Office had repeatedly requested him not to.

"The Orient Bank fiasco was very poorly handled," the consul general told the foreign minister now. "I expressed our dismay at the senseless loss of life. Appalling. I told Sun that myself. Still, the Chinese brook no nonsense from dissenters." That was a serious understatement. The authorities were positively paranoid about dissenters, which caused them diplomatic problems throughout the Western world, including the U.K.

The FM was not so sure about the Communists' control of the political situation. "The world turns," he said. "I seem to recall that a few years ago everyone thought that the Communists in Russia had a firm grip—"

"China is not Russia," Sir Robert shot back, quite sure he was on solid ground. "The conditions are completely different."

"I'll convey your views to the PM," the foreign minister said wearily.

"Do that," Sir Robert said. "Good-bye."

He was amazed at the credulity of the people in London. Of course, they were eight thousand miles from the scene of the crime, but still . . . a revolution? Here? Because Richard Buckingham said so in his newspapers?

Governor Sun also had a busy afternoon. Between calls from Beijing demanding detailed facts he didn't have and issuing directives that made little sense, Sun huddled with key members of his staff, who were trying desperately to establish why the electrical power had failed last night throughout the S.A.R. and why so many of the computers that controlled critical government functions were on the blink.

"Could it be sabotage?" Sun demanded. Like so many of the bureaucrats in Beijing, he had a healthy respect for the unvoiced anger of the people. Baldly, he feared the people he ruled. Repeatedly throughout Chinese history rioting mobs had overthrown dynasties and warlords. Anger and frustration could transform peasants into fierce giants capable of slaying dragons, and Sun well knew it.

Like so many Chinese officials who had held office as the dynasties rose and fell through the millennia, Sun instinctively wanted to control the people he ruled, ensure they stayed in their place, obedient and quiet. For that to happen in this day and age living conditions in China had to improve, which inevitably caused expectations to rise faster than they could be met. It was a vicious cycle with a bad ending; Sun didn't want to be the man on the spot when the music stopped and whole thing exploded.

Then there were the reactionary capitalist forces that the Communists had struggled against since the first day of the Long March. Always the reactionaries were there, waiting for a misstep, a mistake. Waiting.

Sun's aides knew his fears, and they thought they knew the seething maelstrom that was Hong Kong. They soothed him now, told him that there was no evidence of sabotage, when in fact they had no knowledge of why the computers had failed. "A voltage spike, the engineers think," the aides told the governor, who wanted to believe.

"A voltage spike" was the message he gave to Beijing.

American consul general Virgil Cole was not telling his government the truth either. Unlike Governor Sun and Sir Robert MacDonald, who thought they were reporting the truth to their superiors, Cole was lying and knew it. He knew precisely why the power went out last night in Hong Kong and he knew why the airport and harbor computers had failed. He knew what had happened and he knew the plan for going forward.

Of this, he told the United States government precisely nothing.

The Chinese desk at the State Department wanted reports and updates and answers to specific questions, all of which Cole farmed out to his staff. He told the staff more or less what he wanted them to tell Washington, which was the truth as far as it went, but not the complete truth, not by a long shot.

Cole blamed the crisis on the Chinese government's demand for loans at nominal interest rates, loans the government had no intention of ever paying back. The nongovernment stockholders in Hong Kong banks were taking their money and clearing out, which was the root cause of the Bank of the Orient failure. The shootings of unarmed civilians were directly due to the incompetence of the officers of the People's Liberation Army and a government that was paranoid of any dissent whatsoever.

Subsequent problems—power and equipment failures—Cole cavalierly blamed on technical incompetence. When the CIA resident, Bubba Lee, told him of Sun's "voltage spike" explanation to Beijing, Cole tossed that into his latest report to Washington.

During his tenure in Hong Kong, Virgil Cole had repeatedly told the American government that the Chinese government was a corrupt tyranny, with a gross disregard for human rights. The ruling oligarchy was paranoid, cowardly, greedy, technically incompetent, and devoid of personal honor. Cole had said all this so many times the people in Washington laughed about it, yet in the past he had made sure he didn't make himself so obnoxious that the powers that be would fire him. Oh no.

He referred his staff now to some of his past missives on governmental incompetence. When they returned with drafts of the reports Washington demanded, Cole read them with interest, made a few corrections, signed the things, and sent them off.

Lying to the government was a bad business, of course, and he had fretted over it for a year. When you put garbage in, you got garbage out. His conscience used to trouble him more than it did now, although it still twinged him a little.

This evening his lies didn't even make the long list. He was thinking of Wu Tai Kwong, Callie Grafton, and all the things that had to be done. The letter of resignation was also on his mind. It had been faxed off hours ago, and he was now awaiting an explosion from Washington.

It was time to go. He didn't need the consulate anymore.

If the Chinese arrested him, they knew far too much and the revolution was doomed. But they didn't know. So there was a chance, a good chance, he believed.

Time was running out. Lives were at stake, millions of lives. Tens of millions. *Hundreds of millions!*

He looked out the window. The frontal clouds had dissipated; blue sky was visible up there between the towering glass skyscrapers. Across the way was the Third Planet office. With the sky the way it was, the windows there were opaque.

Although Cole didn't know it, inside those offices Kerry Kent and Wu Tai Kwong's top lieutenants were holding a council of war. There were seven of them, each in charge of a specialized group of fighters. They were Wu's friends . . . although perhaps disciples might be a better description.

They took the news of Wu's kidnapping badly. Three of them were for finding Sonny Wong and demanding Wu's immediate return as the price of Wong's life.

Kerry Kent tried to dissuade them. "Sonny Wong has thought of that move," she argued. "Virgil Cole will pay the ransom. If he doesn't, we'll get Wu back in pieces. Do you want Wu alive or Wong dead?"

"That's Wong's choice," Hu Chiang said tartly.

"No, it's ours," Kerry shot back. "We've a revolution to fight. I want Wu back more than anyone in this room, but first and foremost, we must continue the fight that is his life. And ours. That is our first priority."

Hu was not persuaded, but two of Wu's other friends took up Kerry's argument. "The hour is *now*," Wei Luk argued. "Wu Tai Kwong is a general in our army, it is true, but even generals are soldiers. Our cause is more important than any one person. We must not jeopardize it by taking sides in an internal squabble."

"Internal squabble?" Kent said incredulously. "Sonny Wong wants fifty million American dollars from Virgil Cole. That's ransom."

"Cole should have donated his money to the cause," Wei Luk replied stoutly. "If he had, he would not now need us to stop the revolution to save his pocketbook."

"His pocketbook? You fool! Wu Tai Kwong's life is at stake. Sonny Wong is threatening to murder him!"

"Perhaps he merely threatens. I think Cole is too worried about his money."

Hu Chiang managed to stop this fruitless argument. "Enough!" he shouted. "*Enough!* Kerry Kent said the revolution must be our first priority, and I agree. We cannot stop the revolution to search Hong Kong for one man. We must strike now. If we do not, for any reason, we endanger the lives of every member of the Scarlet Team. Let Cole pay the money. There will be time later to deal with Sonny Wong. There is nowhere on this earth he can go to escape us."

Wei Luk agreed with that, and so did the others.

Around sunset two men came to the door of the stateroom—it *was* a stateroom, Callie had decided, in a yacht or small ship. She and Wu had tossed and turned on their bunks all afternoon. Worried as she was, she still fell asleep for an hour or two, which she attributed to the drug they had injected her with. She still felt groggy, unable to focus properly.

One of them stood in the door and motioned to Callie. "Come with us," he said in Cantonese. She went. Pretending she didn't know Chinese would require some serious acting. She didn't feel up to the effort, so she didn't try.

One in front, one behind, they led her along a narrow passageway lined with doors. She got a glimpse out a porthole, saw that this deck was six or eight feet above the waterline and that the yacht was tied to a pier. It was some kind of yacht, she decided, an old one, though still maintained in excellent shape.

The man in front opened a door off the passageway, held it and motioned her through.

A man sat behind a small desk. He was not Chinese; European, perhaps, of medium height and weight, perhaps a hundred and fifty pounds. With a bony head and thin face and pinched nostrils.

"Sit," he said in English, and she took the only empty chair.

The two men who had brought her came into the small room—

which was no bigger than the stateroom where she had spent the day—and stood with their backs to the door.

"Mrs. Grafton," the man said and pushed a sheet of paper and ball-point pen an inch or two toward her. "We wish you to write a statement."

Russian. With that accent, he was a Russian.

She made no effort to pick up the pen.

The Russian waited a few seconds, then said, "Pick up the pen. You will write with it."

When Callie failed to obey he reached across the desk and slapped her, a stinging slap. He was remarkably quick with his hands.

Tears came to her eyes, which infuriated her. She sat there staring into his face through her tears.

"Perhaps I should explain. Pick up the pen or we will break your left arm."

She reached for the thing, got it in her right hand, put both hands back in her lap.

"Very good," the Russian said. "A first step. We make progress."

He leaned back in his chair and made a steeple with his fingers. "Before you begin writing, I will explain what we want. You listened to a tape that was recorded in the library of China Bob Chan the evening that he died. There were various conversations on the tape. Who were the people talking and what did they say?"

She looked at the pen in her right hand, so she didn't see the slap coming. God, the man was quick as a cat.

"Look at me, Mrs. Grafton. I am not nice. Nice is not a thing I have. I want something from you and I will hurt you to get it. I will cut your face, break your bones, break your head, cut out your eyes, watch men rape you . . . whatever it takes. I do not care if you live or die. Do you understand me?"

She nodded.

"Good. Very good!" the Russian said. He folded his hands on the table in front of him. "Did you listen to the tape?"

She decided not to talk. If you don't resist evil you become a part of it, she told herself. She saw the slap coming and went with it, but still the blow numbed her face. And another. And yet again.

She felt herself starting to go out, slipping away. Her eyes refused to focus.

Hands grabbed her roughly, held her in the chair. When she could focus again Wu was there, with a man on each side holding him. Wu's hands were bound by plastic ties and the ties were secured to his belt.

"Mrs. Grafton," the Russian said carefully. "Listen to me. I want to know what you know. If you do not talk, I will kill this man who spent the afternoon with you." That said, he drew a knife and inserted the point into Wu's arm. The color drained out of Wu's face, but he said nothing.

"He is very tough," the Russian said, grinning at Callie. "But he bleeds." He made a lengthwise cut in the man's arm about four inches long and wiped the knife on her blouse. "If you do not answer my questions I am going to cut him into little pieces and feed him to the fish."

He was as good as his word. He slowly inserted the knife into Wu's bicep, at least an inch deep, and slowly drew it down toward his elbow as the blood welled from the cut.

"I'll talk," Callie said, unable to watch.

"Where is the tape now?"

"My husband has it."

"Who brought you the tape?"

"Tommy Carmellini."

"Is Carmel—is he CIA?"

"Yes."

"Does your husband work for CIA?"

"Navy. He is in the navy."

"Why did Carmel bring him the tape?"

"Because I speak Chinese and Carmellini doesn't."

The Russian thought about that for a moment, then went on. "Did you hear China Bob Chan on the tape?"

"I think so."

"Virgil Cole?"

"Yes."

"Who else?"

"I don't know."

He lunged for her, his hand swinging, and she jerked back. One of the men behind her grabbed her hair.

The Russian slapped her, then said again, "Who else?"

"I didn't recognize the other voices."

The Russian glanced at the man behind her, and he released her hair.

She had cut her tongue on the inside of her mouth. The blood tasted coppery and felt slimy, and she had to swallow it.

"I am going to ask a question, Mrs. Grafton. I want the truthful answer. No lies, please. Lies will be very bad for you. Do you understand?"

"Yes." This time it came out a whisper. Blood was still streaming from Wu's wounds and dripping on the deck.

"Who killed China Bob Chan?"

"I don't know."

"Oh, Mrs. Grafton, I hoped I would not need to hurt you, and now you lie to me. Too bad, too bad."

The Russian came around the desk and reached for her. Callie spit blood in his face. When he blinked and drew back to avoid it, she slashed at his face with the ballpoint.

One of the men behind her jerked her half out of the chair, turned her, and hit her so hard she passed out.

When she came to she was in a cold, cold place, in absolute darkness. She felt around her . . . and felt something cold, like cold, dead flesh.

She was in a meat locker.

And she was freezing. Sore, not completely conscious, she curled up in a fetal position to try to conserve her body heat.

Rip Buckingham wanted to talk. He had been carrying this great burden in his breast for months and months and finally here was someone he could tell, someone who also had a huge stake in how the tale would end, someone with whom he could share his fears.

He started by telling Jake everything he knew about Sonny Wong, and then he couldn't stop. He told him about Lin Pe and Sue Lin and Wu Tai Kwong, about Wu's romance with the British SIS agent Kerry Kent, told him how Kerry approached Virgil Cole and asked for his help, how Cole agreed to help fund the revolution and teach key cell members the fundamentals of cyberwarfare.

"Soon," Rip said. "Very soon. The revolution will start and the world as we know it will come to an end."

Jake Grafton listened without saying a word. He knew some of it, surmised more, but Rip filled in the gaps and made the story whole.

"They are going to find out who Wu really is and come for Lin Pe and Sue Lin. They are going to drag them off to prison, strangle them. The Chinese think like that. If I can't shoot you I'll piss in your well and strangle your mother."

"And the women refused to leave," Jake suggested.

"How did you know?"

"If they had agreed you wouldn't still be here, would you?"

"I suppose not."

"How soon is soon?"

"Tonight maybe. Tomorrow. Tomorrow night. I don't know, but it's got to happen quickly."

"Does this Sonny Wong know the timetable?"

"Only if he has a spy at the very top levels of the Scarlet Team. Each cell has a name. The top one is the Scarlet Team."

"How do you start a revolution, anyway?"

"Wu never told me. He didn't want me to know too much."

"Well, let's you and me go see if we can find Mr. Wong."

Rip didn't think much of that idea. "He won't have Callie or Wu with him," he objected.

"I want to see him."

"Why?"

"I want to talk to the man," Jake explained. "Give him a reason not to harm Callie."

"Sonny isn't the kind of man who is easily convinced of anything," Rip explained. "Especially where money is involved. Talking won't do any good."

"That depends on what we say," Jake said patiently. "And how we say it. You'll see. I'm fairly good at delivering messages."

"I can't see how this will help," Rip protested, but Jake's mind was made up.

They rode the tram up the mountain—because the first cable car was going up—and got a taxi at the visitors' center on top. "Wong has a floating restaurant in Aberdeen," Rip told the admiral, who wondered if it was the same one that he and Callie had eaten at yesterday. He hoped not. The thought that Wong might have made a dollar off him rankled.

"Whenever I want to talk to the guy I leave a message there," Rip continued. "For all I know, Sonny sleeps there sometimes. One other thing I forgot to mention: He has an associate, not a partner, but a chief lieutenant. The man is Russian, Yuri Daniel. Avoid him if you can. Just being around him makes my skin crawl."

To Jake's relief, Wong's was not the restaurant where he and Callie had eaten. It was the next one down, gaudy as a painted whore, sporting enough lights to decorate the White House Christmas tree.

Jake and Rip lined up at the same little wharf and took a sampan across the choppy black water to the restaurant. The main dining area was almost empty.

"With air traffic screwed up and all the electrical problems, the tourists are staying in their hotels," Rip opined.

The maître d' let them have their pick of window seats, then left them.

"I'm not hungry," Jake said. "Let's go see if Wong is around. Where are the offices?"

"The second floor, or deck, I think." Rip pointed to a small black door near the kitchen entrance.

"Lead on."

The door was unlocked. Rip pushed it open. There was a man sitting inside. Rip spoke to him in Chinese, asked if Wong were around.

The man looked Rip over, asked his name, then went upstairs.

In about a minute a medium-sized Chinese man in his fifties came down the narrow stairs. He broke into a grin, which revealed crooked teeth. "Rip Buckingham, as I live and breathe," the man said in English. "This is a surprise. Who is your friend?"

"Jake Grafton."

"I'm Sonny Wong," the Chinese man said but didn't offer a hand. "Come upstairs. We'll talk there." He turned and led the way back up the narrow staircase. Rip and Jake followed. The man who had been sitting in the foyer also came along.

Wong's office was roomy enough, furnished with a practical desk and some overstuffed chairs, and decorated with the stuff curio stores sold to tourists, stuff that looked valuable but probably wasn't—carved elephants, ivory pagodas, here and there a hand-carved chess set.

Sonny Wong turned to face his guests. "So, Mr. Grafton, did you come to buy your wife back?"

"I came to explain why you should release her unharmed."

"Oh, no harm come to her if Virgil Cole pay the money I asked. If not . . ."

"Cole will pay," Jake said, looking around, then focusing on Sonny. "You got a nice life here in Hong Kong. Rip tells me you've got a lot of stuff, a restaurant, houses, apartments, boats, money, women. . . . Virgil Cole is going to pay you. If you send my wife back alive and in the pink, you can continue to live your good life here in Hong Kong. We'll chalk this little episode up as an adventure and go on down the road."

Sonny smiled. He looked at Rip. "Do you think Cole would pay more to get you and Mr. Grafton back alive?" He turned toward the telephone on his desk. "Why don't we ask him?"

Jake Grafton drew Cole's .38 snub nose from his right trouser pocket, turned, and shot the guard at the door square in the heart. The shot was like a thunderclap in that small space.

Wong turned, quick as a cat, but too late.

Jake Grafton rammed the barrel of the snub nose against his lips.

"If you even twitch, I'm going to blow your brains all over that desk." He stared into Wong's eyes, trying to see if the man would do something stupid. Then he felt his pockets.

Rip Buckingham was standing frozen, staring at the dead man by the door, his jaw slack.

Jake marched Wong backward around the desk, opened and closed drawers. Sure enough, in one he found a pistol, a small automatic. It felt heavy enough.

"Rip."

Buckingham turned toward him. Jake tossed him the automatic with his left hand.

"See if this is loaded."

"I don't know . . ."

"Pull the slide back, see if there is a shell in the chamber."

Rip bent over slightly, his long hair falling across his face. He used both hands on the pistol. "It's loaded," he reported.

"Find the safety, put it to the off position."

After several seconds, Rip said, "Okay."

"Fire a shot into that chair."

Rip extended the pistol to arm's length, aimed, and pulled the trigger. The shot wasn't as loud as the boom from the snub nose, but it was loud enough.

"You're armed," Jake told him. "Go search all the rooms on this deck. Make sure Callie and Wu aren't here. Shoot anyone who looks at you cross-eyed. No conversation, just shoot them. Go!"

To his credit, Rip Buckingham went.

Keeping the snubbie against Wong's teeth, Jake began searching his desk. The papers were written in Chinese, which was no help to Jake. He tossed the stuff all over as he scanned it, looking for . . . well, anything. Anything at all.

"You want to call the police?" Jake asked Wong.

Wong didn't reply.

"We can tell them about the kidnapping, have them call the American consul general, who will verify that the wife of an American flag officer was kidnapped by you and you personally demanded a ransom. American trade being what it is with China, I think the authorities might take a damn dim view of your activities, Mr. Wong."

Jake didn't call the police because Callie would probably be dead by the time the police got to her. He didn't say that, of course, but that was the nub of it.

He marched Wong back around the desk and made him sit in a chair while he searched the dead man. This man was also armed, another small automatic. Jake pocketed it.

He sat across from Wong, kept the .38 in close to his body, and pointed right at Wong's solar plexus.

"I misjudged you, Mr. Grafton."

"If I knew where she was, Wong, I'd kill you here and now and go get her."

"I believe you."

Jake sat silently, staring at the Chinese. For his part, Sonny Wong kept his mouth shut and didn't move.

The minutes crawled by. The telephone rang. Jake didn't answer it. After four rings the noise stopped.

Jake heard no shots, no shouts, no loud noises. Which was a good thing for Sonny Wong, because he would have been the first to die. Jake thought the man knew that, for he sat silently and still.

Eight minutes later, Rip returned. He had put the automatic in his pocket. "There were some living apartments," he told Jake, "some men who looked at me curiously, but your wife and Wu aren't here."

"Let's go," Jake said, rising from his chair. "Wong, you'll lead the parade. The thing you'll feel in your back is the barrel of this pistol. Honest to God, if there is any trouble from anyone, I'm going to empty this thing into your back. Now let's go."

Down the stairs they went. They went out into the dining room, then into the kitchen. Five people were there, four men and a woman, preparing dishes for the patrons. Jake stood so they couldn't see the pistol he had on Wong and had Rip get everyone out of the kitchen.

When all five had left, Jake told Rip, "Go out into the main dining room. Announce that there is a small fire in the kitchen and everyone should leave in an orderly way. Customers and employees, everyone. Don't let them panic. Just herd them off this barge."

"A fire?"

"A small fire."

Rip looked around the kitchen, looked at Sonny standing there with a blank face, looked at Jake. "What about the people upstairs?" he asked.

"Working for Sonny Wong, they take their chances. If they have time to get out, good for them. If they don't, too bad. Now do as I say."

"What about Wong?"

"He can leave with me or die here. His choice."

Rip Buckingham took a deep breath. "When you deliver a message, you really deliver, Grafton."

Jake walked Wong over to the stove, a large gas burner with blue flames from several of the jets. Nearby was a deep-fat fryer full of hot grease. Jake turned the flames under it up as far as they would go.

He traced out the gas lines, which were routed along the junction of the deck and bulkhead. Through a door, into a storage room. There it was, a tank of bottled gas or propane, Jake couldn't tell which.

Jake led Wong to the door to the dining area. He pushed it open a crack, watched Rip getting the small crowd off the floating restaurant onto sampans. Some of the employees kept looking toward the kitchen, but Rip insisted that Sonny himself wanted everyone to leave.

"Give me your shirt," Jake said to Wong.

The Chinese unbuttoned the short-sleeve shirt and handed it over. With the pistol right against Wong's neck, Jake marched him to the deep fat fryer and dipped the shirt in. When it had absorbed a fair amount of grease, he tossed it onto the stove. The grease flared up.

Taking a step sideways to get a good view, Jake thumbed back the hammer of the revolver and aimed at the gas line. He missed with the first shot, but his second was rewarded with a loud hissing of escaping gas.

Jake eared back the hammer one more time, put the pistol against Wong's lips.

"There is no place on this planet you can hide, Mr. Wong. If any harm comes to my wife, I'm declaring war on you."

Then Jake ran. Out the kitchen door, across the dining room as fast as he could scramble toward the sampan dock at the main entrance. He heard Sonny Wong running behind him.

The kitchen exploded with a dull boom.

Rip Buckingham was standing alone on the dock. There were no boats.

The fire came out the kitchen door; the dining room quickly filled with smoke.

Jake said, "Shall we?" to Rip, took a last look at Wong, then dove into the black water. Rip was right behind him.

CHAPTER ELEVEN

When the van brought Eaton Steinbaugh home after his radiation treatment, his wife, Babs, was waiting by the curb. He felt like hell. Babs helped him inside. He wanted to go to the study and lie down on the couch, and today she let him. Usually she insisted he go to the bedroom and get in bed, but not today.

"You got an E-mail," she told him.

"Did you print it out?" he whispered.

"Don't I always?"

She handed him the sheet of paper. The message was from Hong Kong, somebody in Hong Kong—he had never before seen that E-mail address. The body of the message was a series of letters, arranged as if they were a word. He counted the letters. Twelve of them.

The letters appeared to be a code. And they were, but the code wasn't in the message. The twelve letters *was* the message.

He handed the sheet of paper back to Babs.

"Want to tell me what that means?" she said sharply.

"Within four hours."

"Cole?"

"Yes."

"Really, Steinbaugh, I don't know about you. Sick as you are and you're messing in other people's business. All away around the world, in China, no less."

"Umpf."

"They could prosecute you."

"For what?"

"How would I know? Something, that's for sure."

"They already did that," her husband replied. "Years and years ago." When he was twenty he spent two years in a federal penitentiary for hacking into top-secret Pentagon computer files. Of course he was thrown out of the university and ended up never going back. That was over ten years ago.

"Prison didn't teach you a damned thing, obviously," she snapped, and walked out with her head down.

A husband dying of cancer was a heavy load, and he appreciated that. Not much left for Babs to smile about.

Virgil Cole!

It was really happening.

Cole promised him it would. "Have faith," he said. "The time will come."

"I might be dead by then," Eaton Steinbaugh told Cole. He hadn't been diagnosed with cancer then. Maybe it was a premonition.

"Hey, man, the Lord might call us all home before then. Just do your best to make it work when the hour comes."

"They might change the codes. They might change the system."

"If they do, they do. That's life. I don't want you to guarantee anything. Just do the best you can and we'll all live with it, however it turns out."

Babs was sure as hell wrong, he reflected wryly, about what he learned in prison. While doing his time he taught a computer course for the inmates. Every day he had hours alone on the machine, hours in which he was supposed to be preparing lesson plans. He spent most of those hours hacking into networks and databases all over the globe. What he didn't do was tamper with the data that were there, so no one came looking for him. Locked up with nothing to occupy his mind, the hacking kept him sane.

That was then. Today just getting into a network was tougher, and a lot of the security programs had alarms that would reveal the presence

of an unauthorized intruder. System designers finally were waking up
to the threat.

But Eaton Steinbaugh had also learned a few things through the
years. One was that getting in was a lot easier if you had access to the
software and constructed a back door that you could use anytime you
wanted.

He became a back door specialist. As soon as he was released from
prison he was heavily recruited by software companies. Through the
years he took jobs that interested him, and the demand for his skills
forced the companies to pay excellent wages. For his own amusement,
when he designed or worked on networks, he put in a trapdoor for his
own use.

He was working for Virgil Cole's company when Cole called him
in one day. Cole found one of the back doors, which was the first time
anyone ever managed that trick.

That Cole! He was one smart cookie, shrewd and tougher than cold-
rolled steel. Steinbaugh had never met a man like him.

Cole didn't fire him. Just told him to do a better job on the back
doors or take them out.

He was working for Microsoft when Cole telephoned him eighteen
months ago, wanted him to accept a job with Cole's company, which
Cole was no longer with, go to China to do some Y2K remediation.

Steinbaugh had always refused Y2K remediations, which he regarded as mind-numbing grunt work, but he did it because Cole asked.

On his way to Beijing he went through Hong Kong and dropped
in to see Virgil Cole at the consulate. Cole took him to the best restaurant in town, which was French of course, where they ate a five-star
gourmet dinner on white linen in a private alcove and sipped on a two-
thousand-dollar bottle of wine.

"You didn't have to do this for me, you know," Eaton Steinbaugh
told Virgil Cole.

"I needed an evening out, and you're a good excuse."

They were sipping cognac and sucking on Cuban cigars after dinner
when Steinbaugh remarked, "When you stop and reflect, life's contrasts
are pretty amazing, aren't they?"

"What do you mean?"

"Well, I grew up in blue-collar Oakland, Dad worked on road-
paving crews, we never had a whole lot. Then I wound up in prison,

which was a bummer. Since then I've been all over the world, married, had a kid, and here I am in Hong Kong having a five-star dinner with a billionaire, just like I was somebody. You know?"

Cole laughed. Later Steinbaugh realized that Cole had hoped for this reaction, indeed, had played for it.

"I spent a lifetime working to get here, too," he said. "The low point in my life was a night in Vietnam. I was a bombardier-navigator on A-6 Intruder aircraft. One night near the end of the war the gomers shot us down."

"I didn't know that," Steinbaugh said.

Cole continued: "I remember lying in the jungle with a broken back waiting for the North Vietnamese to find and kill me. I was absolutely certain I had come to the end of the road. And I was wrong." He lifted his glass in a silent toast to Steinbaugh, and drank. Steinbaugh did likewise.

When he had his glass back on the table, Cole said, "If the Chinese people can get rid of the Communists, who knows, perhaps in the fullness of time they too will have some of the same opportunities that have enriched our lives."

"Yeah," Steinbaugh agreed, for the comment seemed innocuous enough.

"I want your help to make it happen."

Steinbaugh wasn't sure how to answer that.

"I want you to install some of your back doors," Cole said, looking him straight in the eyes.

"Where?"

"On some systems in Beijing. You're going to be working on some systems in the Forbidden City, the Chinese Kremlin. I want you to install back doors so that when the time comes, you can get into those systems and control them, screw them up, or disable them."

"When will the time come?"

"When the revolution starts."

"Jesus Christ!" Steinbaugh's eyes got big in surprise. He had sort of suspected that Cole had something on his mind when he asked him to come to see him in Hong Kong on his way to Beijing, but in his wildest imaginings he hadn't envisioned anything like this. "A revolution! Me screwing with government computers to help a revolution—wouldn't that be an act of war or something?"

"I'm no lawyer," Cole said, "but I suspect you're right."

The consul general's cigar had gone out, so he fussed over it, scraped off the ash, and got the thing smoldering again. When he saw that Eaton Steinbaugh was still listening, he went into specifics, some of which were very technical.

Steinbaugh was even more amazed, then he wasn't. Cole didn't do anything by guess or by God. He had thought about this, about what he wanted.

"Cyberwarfare," Steinbaugh said.

"That's right. We must divert the government's attention, confuse them all to hell, make it as difficult as possible for them to figure out what the threat is. That's the first goal. Second, we want to make it difficult for the Communists to respond militarily to the real threat when they figure out what it is. Third, we must deprive them of control over the people, the economy, the course of events. If we can deprive them of the power to make things happen, we will win."

"We?"

"You and me."

"Oh, come on."

"The revolutionaries."

"You're one of them?"

"Yep."

"Goddamn," Steinbaugh said.

Of course he agreed to do it.

Eaton Steinbaugh had pretty well finished the Beijing assignment when he got sick and had to go home to California. He was just thirty-five years old, and the doctors said he had terminal cancer. He mailed Cole a note, told him he'd better hustle the future right along, make it happen soon. Cole knew what he meant.

Now, today, this message arrived.

Within four hours.

One more message to go.

Steinbaugh got up from the couch and turned on the computer. He had set up the E-mail system so it would notify him immediately of any incoming mail.

Babs heard the computer noises and came to the door.

"You're really going to do it, aren't you?"

"Yes."

"You're a damned fool, Eaton. As if you don't have troubles enough, a dying man about to face the Lord and answer for all you've done, bad and good. I don't know how many felonies you're going to commit now."

"Neither do I. This is sort of fun, huh?"

She shook her head and went back to the kitchen.

Well, Babs was Babs. She was a good woman, although she knew absolutely nothing about computers, which were his passion. Truthfully, she didn't know much about men, either, or at least Eaton Steinbaugh—didn't know why he did what he did, made the choices he made. She thought him a fool for hacking as a young man and for his back doors, which he had made the mistake of mentioning a few years ago when they were talking about how fascinating his work was. Practical and unimaginative as always, she thought him a complete flaming idiot for helping Cole. He knew that, and somehow it didn't matter. She had never had any romance in her soul. Still, he loved her and she loved him, each in their own way, and that was good enough for this life.

When Jake Grafton got back to the consulate with Rip Buckingham, Tiger Cole's office was in an uproar. Even though it was almost midnight the lights were on, the secretary and two hovering aides looked white as ghosts, and Cole was on the phone. Since it was midnight here, it was noon in Washington.

Cole was standing beside the desk holding the telephone to his ear, looking out the window.

Although Jake didn't realize it, Cole was looking straight at the windows of the office of Third Planet Communications. There was a man at the window looking this way, but with the lights behind him, Cole didn't recognize him. Cole hoped the man was Hu Chiang on a break—Third Planet was going to be a busy place a bit later tonight.

On the telephone an undersecretary of state was demanding to know what the hell Cole had been up to in Hong Kong. The fax of Grafton's letter to the National Security Adviser had apparently found its way to his desk, and the undersecretary was shouting.

"A gross breach of trust, Cole. Outrageous! I have called the Justice Department. The lawyers there are recommending that the FBI investigate you for a possible treason prosecution. Do you hear me? *Treason*!"

"I don't know what to say, Mr. Podgorski. I suppose this incident will be an embarrassment to the administration."

"An embarrassment? You suppose? It'll be a nightmare, Cole. How could you? You know the president is on a tightrope over China, and now *this*!"

"Darn. What was I thinking? A public discussion of the administration's willingness to deal with tyrants won't win you any friends, I fear."

"Public discussion? Is that a threat?"

"You don't think I'm going to plead guilty to some trumped-up political charge or refuse to talk to the press, do you?" Cole asked dryly. "Prosecutions are political acts. I promise you that you will be reading my repeated requests that the administration stand up for the human rights of China's enslaved citizens in *The New York Times*. This whole issue is going to get a full, complete, open airing. Perhaps my friends in Congress will decide to hold hearings."

"Asshole! You asshole! I'm sending the FBI to arrest you. They'll be on the next plane."

"I'll pack my toothbrush," Cole told Podgorski and hung up the telephone.

"Sounds like it hit the fan in Washington," Jake Grafton said.

"They are agitated. My resignation was sudden, unexpected. After mature reflection, I suspect they will claim executive privilege covers my resignation and the reasons for it. They may even refuse to acknowledge I was an appointee of the administration."

Cole grinned. He did it so rarely that the effect was startling, as if a powerful light had been turned on. And as suddenly as it appeared, it was gone.

"Why are you dripping on my carpet?" Cole asked. His gaze went to Buckingham. "Both of you?"

"Little fracas at Sonny Wong's restaurant in Aberdeen," Jake said.

Rip added, "Grafton started a fire. We had to swim for it."

"Did you kill him?" Tiger Cole asked, referring to Sonny.

"No." Jake sighed. "I was sorely tempted. I almost wish I had.

Wanted to put the fear in the bastard. Maybe he'll send her back. Even if he doesn't, maybe he'll keep his hands off her."

The secretary looked at the admiral like he was insane. Both the aides were trying to keep control of their faces, with little success.

Rip Buckingham was beside himself. He shooed the secretary and aides from the room. When they were gone, he whispered hoarsely at Cole, "This man's crazy. He shot a man dead in Wong's office. Pulled a gun from his pocket and shot him right in the bloody ticker. Didn't say a bloody word, just . . . bang."

Cole shook his head. "That sure sounds like Jake Grafton."

Jake pulled the pistol from his pocket, opened the cylinder, and picked out the empties. "Need some more shells. Some gun oil too, if you have any. Salt water isn't good for these things."

Buckingham sank into a chair and put his head in his hands.

"I called my attorneys in California," Cole said. "They need a day to sell some stock, raise some cash. They will be ready to wire-transfer the money to that Swiss account the day after tomorrow."

"The day after tomorrow," Grafton echoed. "When Wong calls, why don't you tell him that he has to take them to a neutral place? I'll meet him there. When I see them safe and sound, I'll call you and you can wire the money. That way killing us won't solve his problem."

"It'll be a start."

"To be safe," Jake explained, "he has to kill Wu and you and everyone in the revolutionary movement who might oppose him or seek revenge. If all of you are in one place, after he gets the money he can just blow up the building and solve his problem."

"Okay. But how are you going to get Wu and Callie out of harm's way after he gets his money?"

"I don't know yet. I'll have to think about it."

"I don't think it can be done," Tiger Cole said softly.

"Sonny can't afford to be known as the man who killed Wu," Rip said. "Sure, a lot of people know that he kidnapped Wu. But if he kills him . . ."

Cole opened a desk drawer, extracted a small box, and walked to the chair where Buckingham sat. "This is your brother-in-law's finger," he told Rip. "Sonny Wong had it delivered this afternoon."

Buckingham looked in the box and turned pale.

"We need Wu alive. China needs him."

"Don't patronize me," Rip said crossly. "I'm a big boy."

"How about doing another story for your dad? The last one was very good—got 'em in an uproar in Europe and Washington."

"Okay," Rip said, brushing the hair back out of his eyes. He handed the box back to Cole.

"You can use a computer in the office across the street. More on the coming revolution, about the goings-on in Hong Kong. E-mail it to Richard for tomorrow's papers. We want to make damn sure the world knows who the guys are in the white hats."

Rip took a deep breath, his eyes still on the box.

"What do I say about Wu?"

"Don't mention him by name. 'Unnamed patriots' is the phrase. Nothing about Sonny Wong."

After Rip left, Cole used the intercom to ask the secretary to get Jake some clean clothes from his apartment. Then he asked the admiral, "Want a drink? I got some bourbon."

"Yeah."

"What did you tell Wong?"

"Not to harm Callie."

"I'm sorry, Jake. Sorry you and Callie got mixed up in this."

"Yeah."

Jake was buttoning one of Cole's shirts when there was a knock on the door. Tommy Carmellini stuck his head in.

"I thought I'd find you here, Admiral. You left a note on my desk asking for a report?"

"I did. Come in."

Carmellini dropped into an overstuffed chair and watched Jake put on his wet shoes over dry socks. "You want it here, where Mr. Cole can hear?"

"Yep. What have you found out?"

The CIA officer removed a small notebook from an inside jacket pocket and flipped it open. "The clerk selling the passports to Sonny Wong is a woman named Elizabeth Yeager." He spelled the last name. "She delivers the passports to her bedroom buddy, Carson Eisenberg, a CIA guy who is on Wong's payroll. She's been making false computer entries and writing up files to cover the thefts, so all the numbers will match when the department is audited."

"How did you find out this information?"

"I opened the safes down there, checked the logbooks, then went into the secured cabinets."

"Jesus!" Cole said. "And I thought this place was reasonably secure."

"Not even close," Carmellini shot back.

"Do you have Eisenberg's contact?" Jake asked.

"Name, phone number, and address. And I got his banking information, where he's been depositing the cash he got from Wong."

"What else?"

"Kerry Kent has been talking to some people in her apartment in Chinese. Don't know what it means without a translator, and don't know which translator around here I can trust. I sent the tape off to Washington."

"Uh-huh."

"The consul general uses English in his office, fortunately. He had a conversation earlier today with Kerry Kent about a plane that was supposed to arrive at seven this evening at Lantau Island. She was worried that with the airport closed, the plane couldn't land. Cole didn't think that would be a problem."

Carmellini looked at Cole. "Was it a problem, sir?"

"You're still taping conversations in this office?"

"Yes, sir. After you and the admiral had your little talk, I wired you up again."

"Goddamn you, Carmellini! I told you—"

"Can't fire me," Carmellini said smugly and grinned. "I work for him." He jerked his thumb at Grafton.

"Don't be a prick."

"It's genetic. Folks often remark upon that fact. You'd think I worked for the IRS or—"

"Can it," Jake Grafton snapped. "Anything else?"

"Yeah. Cole's been lying to you."

Grafton's eyes narrowed. He glanced at Cole, then concentrated on Carmellini. "Explain."

Carmellini extracted a sheaf of folded paper from another pocket. "The National Security Agency has been doing some intercepts on certain E-mail addresses, and they passed along some dillies that Cole had been sending and receiving."

Cole sat down behind his desk. He didn't look too upset.

"Seems that Mr. Cole has been E-mailing people in the states about something called York units. They are supposed to be on that plane."

"York?"

"York units. Don't know what those are, but it is obvious to me from reading this correspondence that Mr. Cole is not a traitor, that certain people in the United States government are cooperating with him and providing him with technical and logistical support. Six York units, tech manuals, computers, WB cell phones, the list goes on and on."

"I know what York units are," Jake muttered and glanced again at Cole. As usual the consul general's face revealed nothing of its owner's thoughts.

"Anything else?" Jake said to Carmellini.

"That about covers the waterfront, I think."

Jake looked at Cole. "What do you want to do about Eisenberg and the Yeager woman?"

"Can't prosecute them with illegally obtained evidence."

"They don't know how we got the evidence," Carmellini pointed out.

"Have the personnel officer call them in and fire them," Cole said to Carmellini. "Then give them a choice: They can go home and be prosecuted for theft and espionage, or they can stay in Hong Kong. If they want to stay, run them out of the consulate. Tell them if they ever show up in the states again they *will* be prosecuted."

"Yes, sir."

Jake frowned at Carmellini. "We're going to need some weapons that have a little more oomphf than this thirty-eight. Send the head marine up here and let me talk to him."

Carmellini nodded and headed for the door.

"Take the bugs with you," Jake added.

There were three of them, tiny things, cleverly hidden. Carmellini pocketed them, then left the room and closed the door behind him.

"Want to tell me about it?" Jake said.

"The administration wants the Communist era in China to end, and they are willing to help the rebels make it happen. But they don't want anyone to know they helped."

"You're the fall guy?"

"I suppose. They had to have someone to blame and I volunteered.

I thought you had figured that out. Life in California was getting to be a burden that I couldn't carry, and . . ." Cole shrugged.

Jake just nodded. He finished off his whiskey in one gulp and set the glass on the table by the couch.

"I guess the left hand and the right hand are still strangers in Washington," Cole added.

"Yeah," Jake Grafton replied. "They never tell all of it."

"Do you know these people who kidnapped us?" Callie Grafton asked Wu Tai Kwong between chattering teeth. He had used a piece of sheet to wash her wounds after she was brought back to the stateroom around midnight. He thought she had had a mild concussion, but she was shivering uncontrollably from her hours in the meat locker.

"I know them," he replied. He had ripped a sheet into strips and wrapped them around the cuts in his arm. The bleeding seemed to have stopped.

"They wanted to know what was on the tape. The CIA had a bug hidden in China Bob Chan's library and taped the conversations there the night he died. I listened to the tape."

"Sonny Wong is worried about what you heard."

"You think?"

"He might be on the tape."

"So who is Sonny Wong?"

"A gangster. Maybe the last big one in Hong Kong. There are many little gangsters, people who want to be big, but Sonny *is* big. Makes lots of money."

Callie wrapped herself tighter in the blankets. She couldn't stop shivering. Her face hurt like hell and she was bruised and ached all over, but the deep cold she felt was worse.

"Is this about money?" she asked. "Is that why we were kidnapped?"

"I think so." Wu sat down on his bunk. His hand and arm were hurting. He rested his elbow on his knee with the hand elevated. "Cole has so much. The temptation was too much for Sonny."

Callie waited for Wu to say more. She saw a broad-shouldered, medium-sized Chinese man of about thirty years, not handsome, not ugly, the kind of man who could melt into any crowd bigger than three. Or could he?

There *was* something . . .

"Sonny Wong is the security chief," Wu said. "Every revolution needs someone to enforce secrecy or the whole thing will collapse of its own weight. That is his job."

Callie began to see it. "So if someone talked to the police . . ."

"Sonny heard of it. He had people in every cell who reported to him. He plugged the leaks."

"He killed people who talked?"

Wu lowered his head. "Sometimes," he admitted. "Sometimes people saw the error of their ways and agreed to talk no more."

"He's a thug."

"An enforcer. It takes more than dreamers with stars in their eyes to make a revolution."

"He's the dirty end of the stick."

The metaphor threw Wu. Callie didn't feel like explaining.

"You trusted him that much?" Callie pressed.

"No one else wanted the job. No one wanted blood on his hands."

"How did you know this loyal murderer wouldn't betray you?"

"I didn't know. Anyone could have betrayed me, any hour of any day."

"Who is your thug in Beijing, Shanghai, et cetera?" Callie asked.

"Sonny has friends throughout most of China. Really, there was no one else who could do the job."

Callie was unwilling to leave the subject. "So you must have known that someday Wong might turn on you, take over the entire organization, put himself at the head? There is plenty of precedent, I believe. Saddam Hussein and Joe Stalin leap immediately to mind."

"That was a possibility," Wu Tai Kwong reluctantly admitted.

"So what did you plan to prevent that move from succeeding?"

"I planned to kill him before he killed me."

"Looks like you may have miscalculated," Callie snapped.

Thoroughly disgusted, she carried the blankets into the tiny bathroom and shut the door. The door had no lock.

CHAPTER TWELVE

Virgil Cole's daughter, Elaine, was an associate professor of mathematics at Stanford University. She was attending a women's political caucus in Washington, D.C., when she received a coded E-mail from her father. Like the message received by Eaton Steinbaugh, the E-mail consisted of a nonsense word, a dozen random letters, from an address in Hong Kong.

She received the message at noon when she checked her E-mail on her laptop in her hotel room. She got off-line, left the computer running, and gazed about her distractedly, the political meeting forgotten.

She opened the drapes on the window. Georgetown was visible but none of monumental Washington, which was out of sight to the right.

She had a small notebook in her computer case. She got it out now, opened it, and examined the notes she had written there. The handwriting was neat, almost compulsively so. She had made the notes the last time she was in Hong Kong visiting her father, over spring break.

Being Virgil Cole's daughter had always been a mixed blessing. He was quiet and unassuming, brilliant and rich. Somehow her mother's second husband never measured up. He was very nice, and yet... When she was young she had thought her mother was crazy for not staying with her father, but as an adult, she could see how difficult

Cole was, especially for her mother, who was neither brilliant nor quiet and unassuming.

Perhaps it had all worked out for the best.

Except for her half brother, of course, who had never come to grips with the fire in his father's soul.

A Chinese revolution. Yes, that was Virgil Cole. A great impossible crusade to which he could give all of his brains and energy and determination would attract him like a candle attracts a moth.

She had never seen him so full of life as he was in April during her visit.

A crusade! A holy war!

She had seen the fire in his eyes, so of course she said yes when he asked her to help. He didn't come right out and baldly ask. He explained what was needed, how the worm programs were already in place and at the right time needed to be triggered from a location outside of Hong Kong, triggered in such a way that the identity of the person doing it could never be established . . . beyond a reasonable doubt.

He explained the worms, how they were designed, and she carefully wrote down the instructions she needed to make them dance.

She played with her computer keyboard, checked the E-mail again.

So the revolution was *now*.

And she was going to help.

And she might never see her father again.

She was mulling that hard fact when the execute message came. She turned off the computer and stored it carefully in its carrying case. She left the case on the bed and took only the notebook with her.

She caught a taxi in front of the hotel and told the driver she wanted to go to the main public library.

Sure enough, the library had a bank of computers that allowed Internet access. The librarian at the desk near the computers was a plump, middle-aged woman. "The fee is a dollar," the lady told Elaine, who dug in her purse for a bill. "Such a terrible irony—the computers are here for people who can't afford their own, but the users must help defray the cost."

"I understand."

"Everything costs, these days," the librarian said. "We're fighting the battle with the library board to get the fee eliminated, but so far they won't yield."

"Yes."

"Our only rule is no pornography. If people keep calling up pornographic sites, I'm afraid the computers will have to be removed."

"Do you check to see what people are viewing on the Net?" Elaine asked, pretending to be horrified at this privacy intrusion.

"Oh, no," the librarian assured her. "But people do walk behind the cubicles, and they talk, you know!"

"Indeed they do. I'm here today to do some research for my thesis."

"Let me know if you need any help," the librarian said and turned to help the next person, a pimpled teen with unkempt long hair who looked as if he might be very interested in porno.coms. As Elaine walked away, the library lady began briefing this intent young man on the evils of cybersex.

With the notebook of passwords and computer codes on the table beside her, it took Elaine less than fifteen minutes to get through the security layers into the main computer of the central bank clearinghouse in Hong Kong. Once there, she began searching for the code that her father assured her would be there.

Virgil Cole answered the ringing cell phone on his office desk with his usual "Hello." He listened a moment, then broke the connection.

"The York units are in," he told Jake Grafton, who was stretched out on Cole's couch thinking about his wife. "Want to see them?"

"I thought Sergeant York was a paper program."

"It's hardware now."

"You got six?"

"That's right."

"Steal 'em?"

"No."

"Buy 'em?"

"Not quite. Let's say the American government retains legal title and I have custody."

"Let's go look." Jake reached for his shoes. "I was wondering how you red-hot revolutionaries were going to avoid being massacred by the division of troops the PLA has stationed in Hong Kong. This is it, huh?"

There was not much traffic on the streets at this hour, but Jake

Grafton paused in the entrance way of the consulate. Half hidden in the shadows, he restrained Cole with a touch on the arm while he scanned the street in both directions.

Only when he was sure there was no one waiting did he mutter at Cole and step through the entrance.

Cole led the way across the street and along the sidewalk for fifty yards. They went down the first alley they came to, then down a ramp to a loading dock under the skyscraper. A tractor-trailer rig was flush against the loading dock.

Cole climbed the stairs, nodded at two men sitting on the dock, and knocked on the door. A man carrying an assault rifle opened the door. Cole and Grafton went in.

The Sergeant York units were two-legged robots about six and a half feet tall. The legs had three knees—back, front, back—with three-pronged feet. They had articulated arms and, where human hands would be, three flexible grasping appendages, almost like jointed claws, which ended in sharp points. Two were hinged to close inward and one outward, almost like an opposed thumb.

Mounted on the right side of the torso on a flexible mount was a four-barreled Gatling gun that fired standard 5.56 millimeter rounds from a flexible belt feed. Capacity was two hundred rounds.

And the York units had heads mounted on flexible stalks that could turn right or left, be raised or lowered. Two Yorks were standing on the concrete floor back-to-back, turning their heads and looking about with an ominous curiosity.

"The best part," Cole said with more enthusiasm than Grafton thought he had in him, "is the tail. What do you think of the tail?" The prehensile tail was only about eighteen inches long, thick where it came out of the body and tapering quickly.

"It's cool." Jake could think of no other reply.

"The engineers wanted three legs, and the army absolutely refused to buy the thing if it had more than two—they were worried about their image. The tail was my compromise. It helps with stability, balance, agility, shock absorption. . . . With the tail the York is quicker and faster, and can leap higher. And it gives us room for more batteries, which are heavy."

"What were those soldiers thinking?"

"Yeah."

Three Chinese men were watching Kerry Kent walk a York out of the semitrailer. She used a small computer unit, much like a laptop. There were no wires. Like Grafton the Chinese men watched the Sergeant York robots and whispered to each other.

Jake Grafton felt mesmerized by the spectral stare of the robots that were outside the trailer. Their heads never stopped moving. They had no mouth or nose, but in the eye-socket position—the widest part of the head—were two cameras. The one on the right side had a lens turret on the face. As Jake inspected the nearest one, the turret rotated another lens in front of the left camera, if it was a camera.

"What the hell are these things looking at?" he asked Cole.

"Us, the room we're in, everything. They are learning their surroundings."

"Smart machines?"

"These things use a combination of digital and analog technology in their central processors so they can learn their surroundings without having to carry around computers the size of grand pianos. It's a neural network, modeled on the human brain. That breakthrough in computer design was one of the advances that took robot technology to another level."

"I see," Jake said as the third robot walked to a spot beside the other two and came to a stop. It tilted its head a minute amount, almost quizzically, as it scrutinized the two men.

"One of the fascinating things about neural networks," Cole continued, "is that the network needs rest periods or the error rate increases. Nap times."

"What is that thing looking for?" Jake asked, indicating the curious York.

"Just checking for weapons. When they're in a combat mode, they fire on unidentified persons carrying weapons."

"They can't shoot at everyone with a weapon. How do the Yorks separate the good guys from the bad guys?"

"It's a complex program, based on physical characteristics—such as size, clothing, sex, possession of a weapon—and aggressive behavior. Some behavioral scientists worked with our programmers to write it."

"Sex?"

"Most soldiers are men. That's a fact."

"I see."

"My main contributions to the Sergeant York project were some breakthroughs in ultrawide bandwidth radio technology. They communicate with their controller and with each other via UWB, which as you probably know has some unusual characteristics, unlike UHF or VHF.

"So these things talk to each other?"

"They are a true network—what one knows, they all know. Information is exchanged via UWB on a continuous basis, which means that these six are soon working from a very detailed three-dimensional database. Each unit also contains a UWB radar, so it can see through walls and solid objects. Very short-range, of course. The radars are off-the-shelf units, stuff being used to inspect bridge abutments for cracks and look for lost kids in storm sewers."

"What about the stalk on top of the head?"

"There is a flexible lens there for looking around corners. The sensor on the right side of the head works with visible light, the left with infrared. At night the sensitivity on the right sensor automatically increases so it can handle starlight."

The fourth York walked out of the truck and took a position beside the others but facing off at a ninety-degree angle.

"These units are prototypes," Cole explained, "not the refined designs the U.S. army will get as production units. These lack sensors in the rear quadrant, so they usually want to face in different directions so they will get the three-hundred-and-sixty-degree panorama."

"They 'want'?"

"Sergeant York has artificial intelligence. The operator can position the units, monitor their performance, override automatic features, approve target selection and the like, but these things can be turned loose on full automatic mode—then they fight like an army. They *are* an army. We developed them to fight and win on the conventional battlefield, the tactical nuke battlefield, and urban battlefields like Mogadishu. The Somali experience was the catalyst for their development."

Jake whistled, and two of the York units turned their heads to look at him.

"I guess I forgot to mention audio. They have excellent hearing in a much wider frequency spectrum than the human ear can handle."

"How much battle damage can they sustain?"

"A lot. They are constructed of titanium, the internal works are shielded with Kevlar, and Kevlar forms the outer skin. Still, mobility is their main defense."

"Two legs and a tail . . . how mobile are they?" the admiral asked.

Cole pointed to the Kevlar-coated areas on the nearest York's leg, the shapes of which were just visible under the skin. "The major muscles are hydraulic pistons; the minor ones are electromechanical servos—which means gears, motors, and magnets. A couple of ring-laser gyros provide the balance information for the computer, which knows the machine's position in relation to the earth and where the extremities are; it uses the pistons and servos to keep the thing balanced. York is extremely agile, amazingly so considering it weighs four hundred and nine pounds without ammunition."

"Power?"

"Alas, batteries. But these are top-of-the-line batteries and can be recharged quickly or just replaced in the field, a slip-out/slip-in deal. In addition, since the outer layer of each unit's Kevlar skin is photoelectric, outdoors on a sunny day the batteries will stay pretty much charged up as long as excessive exertion is not required of the unit."

Jake Grafton shook his head, slightly awed. "How much does one of these damned things cost?"

"Twice the price of a main battle tank, and worth every penny. They can use every portable weapon in the NATO inventory. Hell, they can even drive a hummer or a tank if you take out the seat and make room for the tail."

"Uh-huh."

All six were out of the semitrailer now. They arranged themselves in a circle, each facing outward. They made a small whining sound when they moved, a sound that would probably be inaudible with a typical urban ambient noise level.

"Preproduction prototypes," Cole said when Jake mentioned the noise. "The production units won't make those noises."

Kerry Kent came over, her wireless computer in her hand. "Let me introduce you to Alvin, Bob, Charlie, Dog, Easy, and Fred."

She was referring to the small letter on the back of each unit's head and on both shoulders. The nicknames were slight twists on the military phonetic alphabet system.

"The New York Net," Jake Grafton said. He wasn't trying to be funny because he wasn't in the mood: The thought merely whizzed through his cranium and popped out about as fast. Kent and Cole looked at him oddly without smiling.

She showed Jake the computer presentation. "Each unit can be controlled by its own computer, or one computer can control as many as ten units. When I'm in network mode, I can see what each unit is seeing or look at the composite picture." She moved an icon with a finger and tapped it. Jake leaned forward. The picture did have a remarkable depth of field, although it was presented on a flat screen.

She tapped the screen again. "As you can see, I can designate targets, tell specific units to engage it, or let the computer pick a unit. I can assign each unit a task, tell it to go to a certain position, assign targets, basically run the fight with this computer. Or I can go to an automatic mode and let the system identify targets in a predetermined order of priority and engage them."

"What if your computer fails or someone shoots you?"

"The system defaults to full automatic mode, which happens to be the preferred mode of operations anyway."

Jake shook his head. "The bad guys are going to figure out what they are up against pretty quickly. Maybe rifle bullets will bounce off these guys, but grenades, rockets, mortars, artillery?"

"Mobility is the key to the York's survival," Kerry rejoined. She tapped the screen.

Charlie York stirred. It tilted its head back to give itself a better view of the overhead, which was about twelve feet up. It crouched, swung its arms, and leaped with arms extended.

It caught the edge of an exposed steel beam and hung there, its tail moving to counteract the swaying of its body. Everyone in the room exhaled at once.

Jake stood there for several seconds with his mouth agape before he remembered to close it. The dozen Chinese men in the room were equally mesmerized. After a moment they cheered.

"The units can leap about six feet high from a standing position," Kerry Kent explained. "On the run they can clear a ten-foot fence. They normally stand six feet six inches high; at full leg extension they are eight feet tall."

"Very athletic," Cole said, nodding his head. He didn't grin at Jake, but almost.

"How long are you going to let Charlie hang from the overhead?" the admiral asked Kent.

Her finger moved, and Charlie dropped to the floor. The unit seemed to catch itself perfectly, balancing with its hands, arms, and tail. Now Charlie looked at Jake, tilted its head a few inches.

In spite of himself, Jake Grafton smiled. "Wow," he said.

A half dozen men began checking the Yorks, inspecting every visible inch. They had been trained at Cole's company in California as part of a highly classified program. One man began plugging extension cords into the back of each unit to recharge the batteries. The other men busied themselves carrying crates of ammunition out of the back of the semitrailer and stacking them against a wall.

"So tomorrow is the day?" Jake muttered to his former bombardier-navigator.

"Yep," said Tiger Cole.

"Another big demonstration in the Central District?"

"Yep. The army will be there. We'll strap them on with the Yorks."

"Jesus Christ! A lot of civilians are going to get caught in the cross fire."

Cole nodded once, curtly.

"Do it at night, Tiger. Maximize the advantage that high tech gives you. These Yorks probably see in the dark as well as they do in the daytime."

"This isn't my show." Tiger's voice was bitter. "I argued all that and lost. Revolution is a political act, I was told, the first objective of which is to radicalize the population and turn them against the government. Daytime was the choice."

"Explain to me the difference between your set of high-minded bloodletters and the high-minded bloodletters you are trying to over-throw."

"That's unfair and you know it. You know who and what the Communists are."

Grafton let it drop. This wasn't the time or place to argue politics, he decided. After a bit he asked, "Why only six of these things? Why not a dozen?"

"It will be a couple years before the first production models come off the assembly line," Cole told him. "We got all there are."

"I hope they're enough."

"By God, so do I," Tiger Cole said fervently.

"Here's a sandwich and some water, Don Quixote," Babs Steinbaugh said. She scrutinized the computer monitor. The E-mail program was still there, waiting.

Eaton Steinbaugh sipped on the water. The sandwich looked like tuna salad. Babs read his mind: "You have to eat."

He took the duty bite, then laid the sandwich down. Yep, tuna salad!

"China is so far away," she mused. "What can you do from here?" Here was their snug little home in Sunnyvale.

"Everything. The Net is everywhere." His answer was an over-simplification, of course. Steinbaugh didn't speak a word of Chinese, yet he knew enough symbols to work with their computers. He wasn't about to get into a discussion of the fine points with Babs, however, not if he could help it.

"This Cole . . . is he paying you anything?"

"No."

"Did you even ask for money?"

"We never discussed it, all right? He didn't mention it and neither did I."

"Seems like if you're going to do the crime, you oughta get enough out of it to pay the lawyers. For Christ's sake, the man's filthy rich."

"Next time."

She grunted and stalked away.

Babs just didn't appreciate his keen wit. Next time, indeed!

As he waited he thought about the trapdoors—sometimes he referred to them as back doors, because he had installed them—which were secret passages into inner sanctums where he wasn't supposed to go. While in Beijing he had worked on the main government computer networks in the Forbidden City. The powers that be didn't want to let him touch the computers, but Cole's company had the contract and the Chinese didn't know how to find the problems and solve them, so they were between a rock and a hard place. After much bureaucratic posturing and grandstanding, they let him put his hands on their stuff.

The network security system was essentially nonexistent. That was deplorable, certainly, but understandable in a country where few people had access to computers. Constructing and installing a back door was child's play once he figured out the Chinese symbols and Pinyin commands. A Pinyin dictionary helped enormously.

Installing back doors in other key government computer systems was not terribly difficult either, for these computers all were linked to the mainframes in the Forbidden City.

Like all top-down systems, the Communist bureaucracy with its uniform security guidelines and procedures was extremely vulnerable to cybersabotage. The best ways to screw with each computer system tended to be similar from system to system, but what worked best with railroad timetables and schedules usually didn't work at all for financial systems. Putting it all together was a sublime challenge, the culmination of his lifelong interest in logical problems. Eaton Steinbaugh enjoyed himself immensely and was bitterly disappointed when the reality of his cancer symptoms could no longer be ignored.

His illness did create another problem, however, one that he took keen interest in solving. The whole point of triggering the inserted code programs from outside Hong Kong was to prevent compromising the computer facility there—Third Planet Communications. But the person doing the triggering was going to leave a trail through the Internet, a trail that government investigators could later follow back to the guilty party.

Unless the guilty party disguised his tracks, made the trail impossible to follow. One way to do that was to use a generic computer, one dedicated to public use, so the identity of the user could never be established beyond a reasonable doubt. Due to his illness, Steinbaugh thought he might be unable to leave his home. He spent a delightful week working up a way to cover his trail through cyberspace and thought he had the problem solved. He wrote a program that randomly changed the ID codes buried throughout his computer's innards—called "cookies"—every time the codes were queried by another computer. He liked the program so much that when the China adventure was over he intended to post it on the Internet for the use of anyone seeking to screw with the commercial Web sites that were constructing profiles of visitors to sell to advertisers and each other, a practice that formed the slimy foundation of E-commerce. Of course, if he wasn't as clever as he thought he was, the FBI was going to be knocking on his door one of these days.

Not that it mattered. In or out of jail, Eaton Steinbaugh only had a few months to live, at the most.

Today, when the computer on his desk began signaling that he had an incoming E-mail, he began pecking at the keys in feverish anticipation.

Yes, there it was. From Virgil Cole. A series of numerals. He counted them.

Eleven.

That was right. Eleven random numbers. The guys at NSA would undoubtedly rack their brains for days trying to crack the code that wasn't there.

As soon as possible.

That was the message.

Start as soon as possible.

Too excited to sit, Steinbaugh got up, stretched, stared at the screen. Start with a bang, he decided.

He sat back down and began.

In less than a minute he was at the door of the main government computer in Beijing looking for his back door.

He typed. Pushed the Enter button.

Nothing.

Don't tell me those bastards have changed the access codes.

Not to worry. He had anticipated that possibility.

There! He found it.

He typed some more, inputting a code that no one else on earth knew.

And voilà!

In, in, in!

Ha ha ha ha ha!

Eaton Steinbaugh consulted his notebook, the one in which he had painstakingly written everything, just in case. A copy of the book was in his lawyer's hands, with instructions to send it to Cole when Steinbaugh died.

He found the menu he wanted, typed some more.

In three minutes he was face-to-face with a critical operational menu, one that gave him a variety of choices. He stared at the Pinyin, consulted his notebook, carefully scrolled the page . . . yes. Here it was.

He moved the mouse. Positioned the cursor over the icon just so. Clicked once.

Sure enough, the system now gave him access to yet another system, with another menu.

This menu had five choices: safe, arm, fire, self-destruct, exit.

He positioned the icon over the one he wanted, then clicked the button on the mouse.

Just like that. That was all it took.

Sue Lin Buckingham was waiting for Rip when he got home. He had written another story for the Buckingham newspapers predicting imminent revolution in Hong Kong and sent it to Sydney via E-mail. It would be published under his father's byline, of course, as the first one was.

"Your father sent an E-mail," Sue Lin said. "He will wire the money to Switzerland tomorrow."

Rip just nodded. All the members of the Scarlet Team had been in the Third Planet office except Wu and Sonny Wong. Amazingly, the team was going on with the plan despite the fact that one of their members had kidnapped the leader.

Wu had put it together, pushed the entire population of Hong Kong—and China, for the revolutionary movement was nationwide— toward this day with the force of his personality and leadership ability. Now he was a prisoner, held for ransom to enrich Sonny Wong, and nothing could be done!

Rip Buckingham stared at his wife's drawn features. "I don't know what to say," he told her. "I saw Wong earlier this evening at his restaurant. He has Wu, all right. Perhaps Wong will release your brother, perhaps he will kill him. Regardless, we march on."

"Can't the senior leadership force Wong to release Wu?"

"There isn't time for that distraction, they say." Rip's upper lip curled. "Some of them seem to think Sonny will share the money with them."

"You think?"

"I don't know what to think."

Rip threw himself in a chair. "I once saw an avalanche in the Andes," he mused. "It started slowly enough, but once it began to move no power on earth could stop it. The moving snow carried everything with it—trees, rocks, dirt, more snow. It got bigger and bigger and moved faster and faster. . . ."

He looked at his wife. "Perhaps they are right. Perhaps going forward is our only choice."

She poured him a glass of wine.

"Have you told your mother?" he asked.

"Not yet."

The military base in the arid lands of western China was not a garden spot. Too far from the ocean to receive much moisture, its weather was dominated by the Asian continental high. In the summer the area was too hot, in the winter far too cold, and too dry all the time. High peaks with year-round caps of snow were visible to the north and southwest. And always there was the wind, blowing constantly in a vast, clear, clean, open, empty sky.

The high desert was as physically different from the humid coastal lands of China as one could possibly imagine. Still, for the Chinese, the reality of the place was determined by a far different factor, one that had nothing to do with terrain or weather: The high desert was very sparsely populated.

For people who spent their lives in densely populated urban or rural environments, surrounded by relatives and cousins and lifelong friends, life in the empty desert was cultural shock of the worst sort. The isolation marked each and every one of the soldiers. Some it broke, some it made stronger, all it changed.

The primitive living conditions at the base didn't help. True, China had developed the high-tech industries that created the nuclear weapons and intercontinental ballistic missiles that were the reason the base existed, but the troop barracks were uninsulated and the men used latrines. The water was not purified, so minerals stained the teeth of the men who had been here for years.

Lieutenant Chen Fah Kwei hated the place. Tonight he was the duty officer in the underground bunker that housed the missile launch controls. There were six missiles in this complex, new ones outfitted with the latest fiber-optic ring-laser gyros and high-speed guidance systems.

Truly it was an honor to be the soldier in charge of this arsenal of national power, but Lieutenant Chen wished his transfer to Shanghai would come through soon. He had honor enough to last a lifetime, and he wanted to live someplace with eligible women, laughter, music, books, films. . . .

Tonight he thought longingly about these things while he inspected his teeth. He was using his knife blade for a mirror. As he studied the reflection of his open mouth in the highly polished blade, he decided that, indeed, the minerals were turning his teeth yellow. He tried to consume the minimum amount of water, swallowed it as quickly as he could, but still the minerals were ruining his teeth.

Glumly, he glanced at the monitors of the main computer, which displayed the status of the six missiles in their silos. Bored, sleepy, and homesick, he was playing with his knife when he felt the first thump, a physical concussion that actually rocked his chair.

At first he thought it was an earthquake, but nothing else happened.

He glanced at the monitor.

Missile One. The status had gone red. Silo temperature was off the scale, hot. Now the fire light began flashing.

Stunned, he stared at the monitor for several seconds while he tried to comprehend the information displayed there.

A fire! There was a fire in Silo One.

He flipped a switch on the panel before him, and instantly a black-and-white television picture of the inside of the silo appeared on a monitor mounted high in the corner of the control room.

He stared at the picture. He couldn't see anything. The missile wasn't there. All he could see was . . . was . . .

Flames.

Flames!

He pushed the red alarm button on his console. He could hear the distant klaxon, which was ringing here, in the barracks, and in the fire station. Men to fight the fire, that was what he needed.

He looked back at the television . . . and the set was blank. The fire had burned up the camera or the leads.

The computer monitor . . . Still getting readouts, but they were cycling. The temperature was going through thirteen hundred degrees Fahrenheit. Missile fuel and liquid oxygen must be feeding the fire. At those temperatures the concrete of the silo would burn, the cap would rupture, and nuclear material from the warhead might be ejected into the atmosphere, to be spread far and wide by the wind.

Lieutenant Chen Fah Kwei pushed another alarm button on his panel. The wail of the siren warning of a possible nuclear accident joined the blare of the klaxon.

What had happened?

The missile must have ruptured, spilling fuel all over the interior of the silo, where it caught fire.

That must be—

Even as those thoughts raced through Chen's mind, he felt another thump in the seat of his pants.

The monitor. *Silo Two!*

His fingers danced across the controls, bringing up the camera.

A sea of fire.

Sabotage?

The telephone rang. Chen snagged it.

The colonel. "Report," he demanded.

"Sir, the missiles are blowing up in the silos. Two have gone."

Even as he spoke the third missile exploded.

"Impossible," the colonel told him.

"The silos are on fire!" Chen screamed. "I can see the fire on the television monitors. The temperatures are unbelievable. The concrete will burn."

"Activate the automatic firefighting system."

"Which silos?"

"All of them," the colonel roared.

Chen did as he was told. The firefighting system would spray tons of water into the silos as fast as the huge pumps could supply it.

The system was on and pumping as the missiles in Silos Four, Five, and Six exploded in order.

The control room was crammed with people shouting into telephones and talking to each other at the top of their lungs when Chen realized that one explanation of the tragedy was that the self-destruct circuits in the missiles had been triggered.

Of course, he had not triggered anything. The safety caps on the self-destruct switches were still safety-wired down. To destroy a missile in flight, the appropriate cap had to be forcibly lifted and the switch thrown before a self-destruct order was sent to the computer.

But what if the computer received or generated a self-destruct order without the button being pushed? Was that possible? It seemed to have happened six times!

Perhaps, Lieutenant Chen thought, *the thing I should have done after the first explosion was turn off the main computer.*

CHAPTER THIRTEEN

Ma Chao was a fighter pilot in the air force of the People's Liberation Army. Based at Hong Kong's new international airport at Chek Lap Kok on Lantau Island, across the runway from the main passenger terminal, his squadron was equipped with Shengyang J-11 fighters, a Chinese license-built version of the Russian-designed Sukhoi Su-27 Flanker, one of the world's premier fighters.

Major Ma's squadron came to Hong Kong in 1997 upon the departure of the British. For Ma Chao and his fellow pilots, the move to Hong Kong had been cultural shock of the first magnitude. They had been stationed at a typical base several hundred miles up the coast, across the strait from Taiwan. Ma Chao had grown up in Beijing and attended the military academy, where he was selected for flight training.

His first operational posting was to the squadron where he still served, almost twenty years later. When he first reported the squadron was equipped with the Chinese-made version of the Russian MiG-19, called the F-6.

The F-6 was the perfect plane for the Chinese air force. It was a simple, robust, swept-wing day fighter, easy to maintain and operate, adequately armed with three 30-millimeter cannon and two air-to-air heat-seeking missiles. Although the fuel capacity was relatively limited, as it was in all 1950s-era Soviet designs, the plane's single engine was powerful enough to give it supersonic speed.

Ma had loved the plane, which was a delight to fly. Unfortunately he didn't get to fly it often. The fuel and maintenance budget allowed each pilot to fly no more than two or three times a month, and then only in excellent weather. Fearful that the undertrained pilots might crash if they tried to fly aggressively, the generals insisted that the planes be flown as near to the center of their performance envelopes as possible. These doctrine limitations were universal throughout the air force.

Although the Chinese licensed the Su-27 design from the Russians for manufacture in order to upgrade the capabilites of their air force, the set-in-stone training limitations did not change. Ma and his fellow fighter pilots were strictly forbidden to perform aerobatic maneuvers or stress the airplanes in any way that might increase the risk of losing the plane. Consequently, their fortnightly training flights consisted of a straightforward climb to altitude, followed by a straight and level intercept under the control of a ground-based radar operator—a ground-controlled intercept, or GCI—then a return to base.

Ma Chao had spent his adult life with this system, never questioning it. The revelation occurred in Hong Kong a month after he arrived. One evening a woman he had come to know showed him a videotape of an Su-27 aerobatic performance at a Paris air show years before. Ma was astounded by the airplane's capabilities, which had been there all the time, waiting for the pilot with the courage to utilize them.

It seemed that all the assumptions upon which Ma Chao's life was based were equally suspect. Ma Chao soon discovered that Hong Kong, with its high-tech, high-rise, high-rent hustle and bustle and diversity, was as close to paradise as he would ever get. Every trip away from the squadron spaces was sensory overload, a cultural adventure that Ma and his friends found extraordinarily fascinating.

When he was finally approached by members of Wu Tai Kwong's Scarlet Team, he was an easy recruit. From the cockpit of an Su-27 he could see the future. Wu Tai Kwong was absolutely right: The great city of Hong Kong that Ma Chao flew over every two weeks was the future of the Chinese people; the rice paddies and poverty of the mainland were the past.

This June night Ma Chao was in the barracks preparing for bed when his cell phone rang. The cell phone was one of the wonders of the new age—Ma hadn't even known such things existed until he came to Hong Kong. This one was very special and could not be purchased commercially. This phone handled normal cellular telephonic communications well enough, but it also received covert wide bandwidth messages that were broadcast over commercial television signals. Since the WB signals degraded normal television reception slightly, this technology was never going to be approved for commercial use.

Tonight the message was a single line of traditional Chinese poetry. Ma Chao knew precisely what the code meant: Tomorrow!

Sonny Wong also knew what the message meant when he heard it. The senior leadership of the Scarlet Team had decided that the cause was more important than Wu Tai Kwong.

Sonny was certain that would be the decision, but it was nice to see events work out as he had predicted they would.

The government had provided the opening; the Scarlet Team would lead the revolution of the Chinese people. Sonny Wong would collect fifty million dollars from Virgil Cole and ten million from Rip Buckingham, a nice comfortable fortune that he would keep in Switzerland. This pile would be his safety net, his rainy day money, to be used if the Communists proved too tough to crack.

Once he had the money, he would eliminate Wu, Virgil Cole, and Hu Chiang. With these three out of the way, he would be in position to take over the Scarlet Team.

Yes, indeed, thought Sonny Wong, if he played his cards correctly, he could conceivably wind up as the next ruler of China. Emperor Wong. President Wong. Premier Wong. Whatever.

Or he could sell the Scarlet Team to the Communists and retire rich, rich, rich...live on the French Riviera, play baccarat at Monte Carlo....

The loss of the restaurant this evening was an irritant, but only that.

He had dealt with brashness and disrespect before—and those fools were long gone. Jake Grafton was as good as dead: Sonny had already given the order.

Many of the students at the University of Hong Kong were not asleep this night. They were huddled together in apartments and bars all over the city. When the WB cell phones rang and they heard the coded message, a cheer went up.

Then they dispersed, went home to try to sleep a few hours and prepare for the day to come.

One of the people with a WB cell phone—made in California and smuggled in by China Bob Chan for Third Planet Communications—was Lieutenant Hubert Hawksley of the Hong Kong police. Hawksley had come to Hong Kong as a soldier in the British army way back when and liked it so much he wangled a police job when his army enlistment was up.

Other British policemen left when Hong Kong was turned over to the Communists, but Hawksley stayed. Through the years he had enjoyed a fine income, very little of which came to him in his pay envelope. He found the oriental way of life congenial and thought he understood the Chinese. Try as he might, he could not imagine that the Communists would be less corrupt than the colonial British. That opinion proved to be prophetic.

One of Hubert Hawksley's many professional acquaintances was Sonny Wong. Sonny had paid Hawksley quite a pile of money over the years. The thing about Sonny was that he was regular. Every month as regular as the post the money arrived. Cash.

One day a year or so ago Sonny had approached Hawksley at the floating restaurant, one of Hawksley's hangouts. He had joined the policeman at the bar, torn up Hawksley's tab, and ordered a beer himself.

"Are you hearing any rumors these days?" Sonny wanted to know when he finally got around to business.

"About what?"

"Sedition. Treason. Antirevolutionary goings-on."

"All the time," the policeman said genially. "The regime is vigilant. The secret police are on the job."

"They pass intelligence to you?"

"Of course. We keep them informed, they keep us informed."

"I was wondering if you might make me a copy of any information you receive along those lines. My friends and I would be willing to pay."

"How much?" Hawksley asked sharply.

"Five thousand Hong Kong a month."

"My risk is large," Hawksley replied.

"Six, then."

"Seven."

Sonny paused to think that over. "Of course," he said, "our long-standing arrangements would be unaffected."

"Of course."

"In addition to knowing what the state security people tell you, we would like to . . . shall we say . . . edit . . . any reports along these lines that the force passes to state security."

"Ahhh . . ."

Hawksley ordered another glass of stout while he thought about whom he would have to bribe to make that happen. He explained the organizational reality to Wong, then tried to estimate what the responsible people would need in the way of money to help Wong out.

"They mustn't know my name, of course," Sonny muttered. "Some of them might take my money and whisper my name. That would be bad."

"Not cricket," Hawksley agreed.

They settled on a figure of twenty thousand Hong Kong, which had to be adjusted up a couple of thousand when one of the captains on the force proved to be greedier than Hawksley had estimated.

Since then Hawksley had learned a great deal about the Scarlet Team, and he had passed much of what he learned right back to Sonny. Various people had tried to betray Wu Tai Kwong, of course, and they had disappeared from Hong Kong, never to be seen again. A few people thought they could become police informants, one or two wanted to explain about sabotage plans.

At one point Hawksley knew so much he began to fear for his life. He wrote down what he knew, made a copy, then gave the copy to Sonny with a remark or two about the original.

Sonny had merely smiled, raised the money to twenty-five thousand a month.

Still, Hubert Hawksley begin to think seriously about early retirement and a return to England. He mentioned these plans to Sonny one day, and Sonny tried to dissuade him.

"I know too much," Hawksley told the gangster.

"Not at all. Anyone in your position is going to learn a great deal, and you are a reliable man. The next man might not be. Stay awhile, see this through. Earn all the money you can. Leave Hong Kong a wealthy man."

He stayed, of course.

And now, in the wee hours of the morning, the WB cell phone given to him by a woman trying to avoid prosecution for theft squawked into life, waking Hawksley from a sound sleep. He knew the significance of the message. Afterward he lay awake in the darkness thinking about what was to come.

Today, he decided, was going to be an excellent day to call in sick.

All over China the special cell phones rang, stimulated by a WB signal piggybacking on the signals of every television station in the country, and all over China the owners of the cell phones listened with mixed emotions.

For some, the message was a signal for a mission that had to be accomplished on an agreed timetable. For others, the signal meant to wait a little while longer. For all, it was a message heralding the coming of a new day.

The single-sheet flyers were piled willy-nilly on street corners, in subway, store, and office building entrances, and in the entrances to the endless blocks of government-owned apartment buildings. The headline on the front page trumpeted: BANK RECORDS WIPED OUT IN MASSIVE COMPUTER FAILURE.

The story began:

A massive computer failure last night at the Hong Kong bank clearinghouse wiped out the computerized records of member banks, which are all the banks in Hong Kong. Sources say that the computerized account records of the borrowers and depositors of the affected banks have been destroyed and will have to be reconstructed from backup tapes where they exist, and by hand from written records, which all banks maintain, before the banks can again open for business. The task will take weeks.

It is common knowledge that various high government officials have demanded and received personal loans at ridiculously low interest rates from Hong Kong banks, which were the only banks affected by the clearinghouse computer failure.

The story continued, citing no sources but implying that the government had willfully destroyed the bank records to hide official corruption.

Very little of the story was true, a fact Rip Buckingham had pointed out to Wu weeks ago when he was asked to write it. "The government," Wu said, "has told so many lies that people are ready to believe the worst. The goal is to put government officials on the defensive. The story in the flyer must create doubt in people's minds."

The story did more than that, though. It called for a general strike and a mass demonstration in the Central District today to protest the malfeasance of the government.

Lin Pe was up at first light. She had been rising at that hour ever since she could remember and saw no reason to change at this stage of her life. She used the early morning hours to work on her fortunes or the books of the Double Happy Fortune Cookie Company, occasionally to correspond with friends. Every few weeks she had to sign all the company checks that her accountant had prepared, payroll and suppliers and utilities and the like. The checks were there on the table, but since the bank collapsed, it was ridiculous to sign them.

This morning she got out the fortune book and sat reading while she waited for a good idea to arrive. When inspiration was hard to find, as it often was, she would wait patiently. If she didn't think about too many other things a good idea would show up eventually.

She had a lot on her mind these days: Wu, the frozen accounts at the Bank of the Orient, her daughter Sue Lin, Rip, whether she should sell the cookie company to Albert Cheung....

Sue Lin knocked, then came into the room carrying a flyer.

"Mother," she said, "all the banks will be closed."

Lin Pe read the story, then laid the flyer aside and sat looking out the window at the great city. "I can't meet my payroll," she said softly.

"Oh, no one will expect to be paid," Sue Lin said dismissively. "Too much is happening." She sat down facing her mother and told her about Wu's kidnapping.

Old Lin Pe listened to everything her daughter had to say and asked no questions. When Sue Lin ran out of steam she sat silently looking at her mother, who rubbed her hands together, then smoothed her hair.

"Wong will kill him after he gets the money," Lin Pe said finally.

"Maybe not," Sue Lin said, unwilling to cross that bridge. She felt so helpless. "What can we do?"

Her mother sat staring at the wall, saying nothing.

As Jake Grafton walked the streets to the ferry landing in the hour after dawn, he had to thread his way around the citizens of Hong Kong, who were engrossed in the flyers that littered the streets and sidewalks.

Jake had tried to get some sleep on the couch in Tiger Cole's office, but he had tossed and turned, unable to stop thinking about his wife. He had dropped off for a few minutes, only to have a nightmare about her, which woke him and left him unable to get back to sleep.

At one point Tommy Carmellini came in, wanting to tell him what he had heard on his listening devices. About the only thing worth reporting, according to Carmellini, was a call Kerry Kent got earlier in the evening. "She said yes, paused, yes again, paused, no, then an-other yes and hung up."

"So?"

"I don't know who called her, but it wasn't a social friend."

"Doesn't sound like it," Grafton agreed.

As the sun rose he had stood at Cole's window watching the traffic on the street below and the people on the sidewalk reading the flyers.

Cole wasn't there. He had gone out at some point. No doubt he is off leading the charge, Jake thought gloomily.

He couldn't shake the thought that this mess was Cole's fault.

If the bastard had minded his own business, stayed in California getting rich making magic technoshit for robots and the like, Callie would be safe and sound, not in danger of being murdered by a goddamn Asian gangster.

That thought made him angry. There would be plenty of time later for recriminations, but now was the time to figure out how to rescue Callie.

That's the mission, Jake, and it's high time you put the brain in high gear and got cracking.

He decided that he should go back to the hotel. If by chance Callie had been released, perhaps she would go there. The chances were small, but still . . .

"Goddamn it!" He had said the words aloud, then stood there grinding his teeth.

He needed a bath, a shave, and a change of clothes.

If Sonny Wong has any sense, someone will be waiting to ambush me as I walk out the front door of the consulate.

With that thought in mind, Grafton went out the back of the compound in a truck that had just delivered a load of fresh vegetables. When the truck stopped for a light two blocks down the street, Grafton raised the rear door and jumped down, then lowered the door and slapped it twice.

Now, walking through the streets, he was struck by the number of youngsters and the elderly out and about on a weekday morning. They weren't the dressed-for-success business types who filled the Central District office towers during weekdays. These folks wore jeans and cotton pants and T-shirts. They carried backpacks and sacks of food.

The damn fools are going to the big demonstration!

Governor Sun Siu Ki read the news of the clearinghouse computer disaster in the flyer labeled *The Truth* as he dressed for the day. An aide had brought him one of the sheets.

"Is this true?" he demanded, waving the offending paper at the aide.

"Yes, sir. The director of the clearinghouse called us with the news at three this morning. The entire clearinghouse staff is working now to determine the extent of the damage."

Sun was not the swiftest civil servant in Hong Kong, but he wasn't stupid. "How did the writers of this flyer get the news so quickly, get it printed and onto the streets?"

"Sir, we do not know. These flyers were thrown out of trucks all over the S.A.R. as early as five A.M."

"This computer failure the story speaks of, could it have been sabotage?"

"We do not know."

"Find out," Sun snapped. "Immediately," he added and shooed the aide out.

The story was libel, of course. Well, probably libel.

Sure, there were grotesquely greedy men in government—there had been misfits and rogues in every government in every age since the world began. And of course some of these misfits might have twisted arms in the Hong Kong banking community. But to suppose that these people, if they did owe money to the local banks, would destroy the banks so they wouldn't have to pay it back? The whole thing was preposterous, pure poppycock.

And even if the story were true, this rag should never have printed it. The sole purpose of such a story was to lower the people's respect for the government and the men who made it function.

Mao would never have tolerated such disrespectful diatribes from anyone, Sun told himself primly, and certainly he should not.

Regardless of what the bureaucrats in Beijing thought, the time had come to take off the gloves with these people. Show them the government's steel backbone and this type of libelous misbehavior will stop.

Sun was capable of applying the pressure, of crushing enemies of the state. He didn't have many skills, but at least he had that one. He picked up the telephone on his desk and told his secretary to call General Tang.

Tang came to City Hall by car to confer with Sun. The two of them ate a hurried breakfast of rice and fish at Sun's desk while they waited for a call to Beijing to be returned. An aide came in and told them that the subway trains refused to operate this morning. "It is the doors," the aide said. "The administrator of the system says the doors will not open on the trains."

"Can't they be opened manually?"

"Yes, but then they cannot be closed. The chief engineer blames the fluctuations in the power grid."

When the minister in Beijing called, he was obviously distraught. "First Hong Kong, now the nation is under attack. We do not even know who the enemy is, and he is wounding us seriously."

Sun didn't have a clue what the minister was talking about. He made noises anyway.

The minister explained: "Several hours ago our ballistic missiles exploded in their silos, starting horrible fires that threaten to contaminate large areas. Last night the Hong Kong and Shanghai banking systems collapsed, the stock exchanges cannot open, the railroad dispatch computer refuses to come on-line, refineries all over the country have had to shut down to prevent dangerous conditions progressing to explosions and fires . . . and every air traffic control and GCI radar in the country is mysteriously broken. The nation is wide open to an aerial invasion, and we won't know it is coming until enemy troops arrive at the gates." His voice rose an octave here.

The minister paused to get himself under control. "Obviously the nation is under cyberattack. The telephone network has been used to sabotage critical computers. The premier has decreed that the telephone system be shut off on the hour, in ten minutes, until such time as the critical systems can be brought back on-line, our enemies identified and rendered harmless, and future attacks of this sort guarded against."

Sun couldn't believe his ears. He pushed the mute button on the speaker phone and asked General Tang, "What is a cyberattack?"

"Computers," Tang replied.

The minister was still going on, about how Sun should notify Beijing immediately of any change in the situation in Hong Kong, and then he hung up, leaving Sun staring at the little telephone speaker on his desk, quite unable to grasp the import of what he had just heard.

"They are turning off the telephone system?" he asked General Tang. "So he said."

"The Taiwanese," Sun said bitterly. "I have argued for years that China must bring those rascals to heel. Events will prove me right."

"I suspect the Japanese," General Tang shot back. "They are our natural enemies."

They finished eating in silence, each man deep in his own thoughts.

When they pushed the plates back, they discussed the situation. They were on dangerous ground and they knew it. The nation under cyberattack from unknown enemies, the power of the government being tested here in Hong Kong . . .

The right course of action was unclear. Still, they were the men who would have to answer to Beijing for inaction as well as action.

When he had heard Tang out, Sun issued his orders. "Today many unhappy people will congregate in the Central District. They will once again attempt to embarrass the government." The British legacy was still causing problems, Sun thought sourly. "That challenge to the government's mandate to rule is, in my judgment, our most important problem. Put your troops in the downtown and refuse to let the demonstrators in."

"The subway problems will keep people from coming into the Central District," Tang remarked. He assumed that most of the city's citizens would want to demonstrate against the government, an assumption that Sun didn't challenge.

"The time has come to be firm," Sun declared. "We must show the people the steel of our resolve. Show them the might of the state they hold in such contempt."

Lest there be a misunderstanding, Sun added darkly, "I abhor the useless effusion of blood, but if we do not hold our ground now, that failure will cost more blood."

"We will give the order to disperse, then enforce it."

"We must tell the people," Sun told the general. "Go from here to the television studio. Stand in front of the camera and tell the people to stay home. Tell them the nation is under attack, but we shall prevail because we have the resolve of a tiger."

"Only one television station is still operating," the senior aide informed them. "The others have had power outages or equipment failures."

"All?" Sun demanded.

"Yes, sir. During the night they went off the air, one by one."

"Sabotage," said Tang. "Could this be related to the nuclear weapons disaster?"

"Impossible," the governor opined. "Here in Hong Kong we are dealing with criminal hooligans."

Had the brain trust in City Hall asked about the situation with the radio stations, they would have been more alarmed. Of Hong Kong's dozens of stations, only one was still on the air. The morning DJ at this station atop Victoria Peak was a Hong Kong personality named Jimmy Lee, easily the most popular man on the south China coast.

Lee was funny, irreverent, crazy, with it, and cool, a combination that delighted the young people and brought smiles to the faces of everyone else. Listening to Jimmy Lee was always a breath of fresh air.

Jimmy Lee wasn't himself this morning, though. The man was constitutionally unable to keep a secret—it wasn't in him. Everything he knew eventually slipped out, usually when he least wanted it to. Normally this trait didn't do him any harm since his off-kilter personality was his stock-in-trade. For the past two weeks, though, Jimmy Lee had been the possessor of a huge secret, one that had grown heavier with each passing day.

He had joked so much about Wu Tai Kwong, the phantom political criminal, that Wu had concluded Lee could be an ally. So one morning one of Wu's lieutenants was waiting when Lee finished his morning show.

At first Lee didn't believe the man knew Wu Tai Kwong, as he said he did, but the man's serious demeanor and his anti-Communist sentiments assuaged his doubts. The man returned to the station for private conversations week after week for months. Lee finally realized that the man wasn't a government agent and that he indeed knew Wu Tai Kwong.

Eventually the man enlisted Lee to become a spokesman of the revolution. Two weeks ago he was told about the upcoming battle of Hong Kong, presented with a cell phone, and told about the message that he would receive on the designated day.

Jimmy Lee had not told a soul this fantastic secret, which was a remarkable testament to the supreme effort he was making to control himself. He had thought deeply about it for two weeks, brooded upon it, had nightmares about it. The reality was that the revolutionaries wanted him to commit treason . . . when the telephone rang.

Treason! If the revolution failed, Jimmy Lee's life would be forfeit. The government would hunt him down and execute him publicly.

This morning Lee was almost incoherent on the air. He played songs but babbled nonsense when he had to speak. He had never been able to resist food, was almost a hundred pounds overweight, yet this morning he was unable to eat. Sweating profusely, nauseated, able to talk only in monosyllables, he was questioned by his producer . . . and he told everything.

The producer refused to believe Lee. He was unaware that this was the last radio station on the air in Hong Kong. He knew nothing about the disasters in the stock market, the airport, the subways . . . none of that had been published by the government, which like all Communist governments was loathe to admit or discuss problems.

Lee talked on. He produced the cell phone. He told about meeting a friend of Wu Tai Kwong's, told about how the army would be confronted today, about the explanations he was to make over the radio . . . and then he produced the cassette.

The producer put the cassette into a player and listened to a minute or two of it while Jimmy Lee hyperventilated.

The male voice on the cassette was as calm and confident as a human can be, calling for people to rally behind the freedom fighters, obey the revolutionary leaders, and kill PLA soldiers who refused to surrender.

The producer turned off the cassette player and sat chewing his fingernails while he considered what he should do. The first thing, he decided, was to let the New China News Agency censor listen to this tape. The man worked for the government, knew how things worked. He would know what to do about the tape.

Lin Pe was not thinking of resolve, although she had as much as the governor and then some. She was thinking of the strange ways human lives are twisted by chance, or fate, call it what you will.

She dressed in her newest clothes, brushed her hair, made herself look as nice as she could. In her purse she put her notebook—so she could write down any fortunes that crossed her mind in the course of the day—two rice cakes, and a bottle of water. She ensured the house key was already in the purse, then went to find her daughter, who was giving the maids their daily instructions. The television was on—General Tang was telling people to stay home.

When Sue Lin finished with the maids, she told her mother, "Rip wanted us both to stay home today. He said the streets will be dangerous, there may be shooting." Her mother would respect Rip's opinion, Sue Lin knew, more than she would her daughter's, for her mother had not lost her lifetime habit of deference to men.

"I think the rebellion will begin today," the old lady said calmly. "Today is the beginning of the end for the Communists."

"Richard Buckingham is paying the money today, Mother. Wu Tai Kwong will probably be home this evening."

Lin Pe merely nodded. Then she went out the door and along the street toward the tram, which would take her down the mountain to the Central District.

The matter was quite simple, really. Her son thought this struggle was worth his life. That being the case, it was worth hers, too.

CHAPTER FOURTEEN

At the Victoria ferry landing, people were streaming off the overloaded ferries from Kowloon and patronizing a small army of food vendors, who were selling fish and shark and rice cakes as fast as they could fry it. Not many children, considering. Here and there Jake Grafton saw people reading sheets of *The Truth,* sometimes three and four people huddled together looking at the same piece of paper. The people looked somber, grim, though perhaps it was just his imagination.

Not many people were interested in going to Kowloon, so there was no line. Jake went right aboard the ferry *Star of the East.*

As the boat approached Kowloon he could see the sea of humanity waiting to board the ferries to Victoria. With the subways out of service, this crowd was to be expected. The terminal was packed, with a large group of people outside on the street, waiting to get inside.

As soon as the boat tied up, Jake was off and walking at a brisk pace. Outside the terminal the crowd swallowed him. He thought about getting something to eat in McDonald's, which was about fifty yards away, but it too was packed full, with people waiting to get into the place.

For the first time since he had arrived in Hong Kong the sheer mass of China threatened to overwhelm him. People everywhere, densely packed, all talking, breathing, shouting, pushing . . .

He made his way along Nathan Road and turned into the street that led by his hotel. Fewer people here, thank God.

The manager was in the lobby trying to calm a crowd of tourists from Germany. The common language was a heavily accented pidgin English.

So sorry, the manager explained, but the airlines had canceled all flights; daily bus tours of Hong Kong were canceled; trains to Canton, Shanghai, and Beijing were not running; telephone calls to Europe were not going through; credit cards could not be accepted for payment of bills; money-changing services at front desk temporarily suspended. So sorry. All problems temporary. Not to worry, all fixed soon. So sorry.

Behind Jake he heard an elderly British male voice say with more than a trace of satisfaction, "Bloody place is falling apart. *Knew* it would! Wasn't like this in the old days, I can tell you."

In the corner an American college student was trying to comfort his girlfriend. In the snippet he heard, Jake gathered that the girl was worried that her parents would be worried.

Jake waited until the manager made his escape from the unhappy Germans, then waylaid him. He told him his name, reminded him of the trashed room, wanted to know where his luggage was.

The manager signaled for a bellhop, then spoke to the uniformed man in Chinese.

Jake was escorted to the elevator and taken to the top floor of the building. They had laid out his and Callie's luggage in a three-room suite, the best in the house, probably. The sitting room and bedroom both had balconies.

The crowd was so dense it intimidated Lin Pe, and she had lived in dense Chinese cities much of her life. There was an intensity, an anticipation, that seemed to energize the people.

She fought against the flow of people and managed to get aboard a ferry to Kowloon, as it turned out the last one, because the authorities demanded that the Star line stop carrying demonstrators to Victoria and forced the crews off the boats.

In Kowloon Lin Pe began walking. On Nathan Road she caught a bus and rode it north for several miles, then transferred to a bus going to Kam Shan, near Tolo Harbor. She got off the bus at Shatin and walked a quarter of a mile through town. Shatin was huge, with more than a half million people living there now. Lin Pe remembered when it was just a small town, not many years ago.

She stopped at a small corner grocery where she knew the proprietor. After the usual polite greetings, she found a seat on an empty orange crate under a sign advertising scribe services. The letter writer would not be here for hours, but people with little to do often passed the time by sitting here, so no one would say anything.

From her perch on the orange crate she could see the entrance to the main PLA base in the New Territories. Nothing much seemed to be happening on the base, which was good.

From her bag Lin Pe extracted her WB telephone. She turned it on, then called in and reported that she was in position. Then she turned the phone off to save the battery.

Jake Grafton took a shower, shaved, and put on clean clothes that fit; Cole's were too large. He strapped the Smith & Wesson to his right ankle and put on the shoulder holster containing the Model 1911 Colt .45 automatic he had requisitioned from the marines at the consulate. Over this he donned a clean sports jacket. He put a hand grenade in each pocket. Just another happy tourist ready for a day of fun and games in good ol' Hong Kong.

He checked with the hotel operator to see if he had any messages. Yes, a voice mail. He listened as the senior military adviser on the National Security staff told him that his mission was canceled, he could come home anytime.

He tried to return the call and got as far as the hotel operator. All lines overseas were out of service. So sorry.

So Tiger Cole and the Scarlet Team had isolated the place.

He turned on the television. Only one channel was still on the air—the others were showing test patterns or blank screens.

Oooh boy!

Jake Grafton went out on the bedroom balcony, which also overlooked the police station. Not many troops on the lawn. He could hear a helicopter circling overhead, though he couldn't see it.

There was a division of troops in Hong Kong, Tiger said, China's best ... with tanks, artillery, and twelve thousand combat-ready soldiers.

Jake's attention was drawn to the street in front of the hotel, eight stories below him. A convoy of trucks had pulled up alongside the hill and wall of the police station, and people were streaming from every truck.

In thirty seconds the street was a sea of people. A van-type truck was sitting at the main gate, the driver talking to the guard.

On the street the people were removing ladders from the trucks. My God! They were armed. Assault rifles, it looked like.

The ladders went against the wall, people swarmed up them.

As they reached the top of the wall, they got off the ladders, walked along the wall. There must be interior ladders or stairs, Jake thought.

The driver was out of the truck at the gate, holding a pistol on the guard. People ran by the truck into the compound.

Jake had a grandstand seat. In less than a minute, several hundred armed civilians were running through the compound.

Shots! He could hear shots! Some of the soldiers were shooting! And being shot at!

The reports rose into a ragged fusillade, then slowed to sporadic popping.

A dozen or so soldiers wearing green uniforms lay where they had fallen.

Now a convoy of trucks came streaming through the main gate.

In two minutes all the shooting stopped, even the occasional shot from inside the administration building. Several of the trucks were backed up to a loading dock, and a small human chain began passing weapons out of the building. As fast as one truck was loaded, it pulled out and another took its place.

Jake Grafton looked at his watch. The time was 8:33 A.M.

Welcome to the revolution!

He had to get to Victoria while he still could. Cole had said the Scarlet Team intended to confront the People's Liberation Army with Sergeant Yorks. That would be the acid test. Either the Yorks could stand up to trained troops or the revolution would be over before lunch.

But all those people heading for the Central District—Grafton wondered if he had what it takes to sacrifice innocent people for the greater good. He thought of Callie and concluded that he didn't.

The New China News Agency censor assigned to Jimmy Lee's radio station listened to the Wu Tai Kwong cassette tape with a growing sense of horror. Jimmy Lee was sitting on a nearby stool near collapse—the producer had taken his place at the microphone. The tape sounded authentic. Any doubts the censor had were wiped away by the conviction in that taped voice . . . and the call for people to kill PLA soldiers who refused to surrender their arms.

The censor called his superior officer on the telephone, but no one answered. Too early. His superior wouldn't come to work for another hour yet, and with the subway out, maybe not then. The man lived way up north in the New Territories.

The censor swallowed hard and telephoned City Hall.

He ended up with an aide to Governor Sun and began telling him of the tape and the upcoming battle in the streets.

Callie Grafton awoke stiff and sore from her beating the previous evening. Places on her face were blue and yellow, and one side of her face was severely swollen. Sometime during the night she stopped shivering . . . thankfully, but her ordeal had drained her.

Still, she was in better shape than she thought she would be. When those thugs were pounding on her she thought she might die.

She had awakened on and off during the night, waited fearfully for the men to return, to drag her off for another interrogation or session in the meat locker, but it didn't happen.

Perhaps this morning.

She tried to recall everything she could remember about the Vietnam prisoners of war she had met or read about. The men she had known were ordinary men who had endured torture, starvation, and beatings for years and somehow survived. One looked at them expecting them to be different somehow—and no doubt they were on the inside—but the difference didn't show in the facade they presented to the world. They looked ordinary in every respect.

Perhaps the lesson was that they were ordinary yet had somehow found extraordinary courage. Or maybe that courage is in all of us and we just don't know it. Or need it.

I am as tough as those guys, she told herself, thinking of the POWs. She wanted to believe that even though she didn't.

"He wants me to implicate Cole in murder," she told Wu Tai Kwong. He nodded.

"What does he want from you?"

"A confession that he can give to the Communists, one that he can use to justify a fat reward for my capture."

"He will turn you over to the government?"

"I'll be dead by then. He'll give them my corpse and demand a huge reward. The confession will be the . . . how do you say it? The sauce upon the cake?"

"Icing on the cake."

"Knowing Sonny," Wu continued, "he has demanded money from everyone, Cole, the government, everyone. He keeps me alive so he can prove that I am alive, should that become necessary. Then he will kill me and sell my corpse."

"Do you really believe that?"

"He cannot set me free. I have many friends. I will find him and kill him, no matter where on earth he goes to hide. He knows that. He will kill me."

"Are you frightened?"

"Of what? Death?"

"Dying."

"Yes."

"But not of death?"

"I have achieved my dream. The revolution has begun. The regime is crumbling and the revolution will speed its collapse. Sonny Wong can do nothing to stop it. The government can fight, delaying the day of its doom, but it cannot prevent the inevitable."

A terrible smile spread across the face of Wu Tai Kwong. "I have won," he whispered. "I have undermined the levee—the sea *will* come in."

Despite the fact that she was no longer cold, Callie Grafton shivered. "When the regime collapses, what will happen then?" she asked.

"The people will execute the Communists. That is inevitable. And fitting. That is the fate of all dynasties when they fall. The Communists will go like the others."

Jake Grafton went out the main door of the hotel and turned right, headed for Nathan Road and the ferry landing. Two men who had been lounging against the wall followed him.

He glanced back just before he turned the corner—they were keeping their distance.

Rounding the corner, another man stepped away from the wall with a pistol in his hand. It must have been in his pocket.

Jake didn't think, he merely reacted. He dove for the pistol, seizing it and wrenching it away from the man.

No doubt Grafton's sudden appearance had startled the man, who must have thought that the sight of the weapon would freeze Grafton, make him stand still in the hope of not being shot. In any event, the American's move was so unexpected that it succeeded.

Jake Grafton's adrenaline was flowing nicely. With his assailant's pistol in his left hand, he hit him with all his might in the throat and dropped the man to the sidewalk, gagging.

Now he ran, fighting the crowd, toward the waterfront.

Soldiers were spread across the pier in front of the ferry landing.

They've stopped the ferries!

Jake veered right, toward the small basin beside the huge shopping mall for cruise ship passengers. In this basin small boats normally took on and discharged passengers for harbor tours.

There were a handful of tour boats tied to the pier, all of them sporting little blue-and-white awnings to keep off the sun and rain. Jake ran along the pier until he saw a man working on one. The engine was running, although the boat was still securely moored.

By now Jake had the pistol in his pocket that he had taken off the man in the street. He was going to have a nice collection of these things if he lived long enough.

He looked behind him. The people who had been following were apparently lost in the crowd, which filled most of the street.

He pulled out his wallet, took out a handful of bills, replaced the wallet in his hip pocket. He jumped down into the boat and waved the bills at the boatman, who was in his early thirties, with long hair that hung across his face.

The boatman said something in Chinese. Jake gestured toward Victoria. "Over there," he said and offered the money again.

The boatman ignored the money. He pointed back toward the soldiers and shook his head.

Okay.

Jake looked at the boat's controls as the boatman showered him with Chinese. The throttle was there, a wheel, a stick shift for a forward-reverse transmission . . . the boat was idling.

"Out. Get out!" Jake pulled the pistol just far enough from his pocket for the boatman to see it, then pointed toward the pier.

Frightened, the boatman went. As he did, Jake Grafton jammed the money he had offered into the man's shirt pocket. Must be my genial expression, Jake thought as he ran forward to untie the rope on the pier bollard.

With it free, he made his way aft as quickly as he could.

Where are the men who were following me? Did they lose me in the crowd?

That must be it. They're probably searching frantically this minute.

With the bow and stern lines loose, Jake scrambled back to the tiny cockpit and spun the wheel while he jammed the throttle forward. The boat surged ahead, caroming off the boat moored in front of it.

He didn't waste time but headed for the entrance to the basin.

There, on the pier! The men who followed him from the hotel! They stood watching. Now one of them removed a cell phone from his pocket and made a call.

There was a nice breeze and a decent sea running in the strait, so the little tour boat began pitching the moment it cleared the mouth of the basin.

Some soldiers around the ferry terminal were shouting and gesturing at him, so Jake turned his boat to the northeast, away from Hong Kong Island. *Those guys are itching to shoot someone,* he thought and decided to get well out of rifle range before he turned south to cross the strait.

In the helicopter circling over the police station, Hu Chiang also looked at his watch. The assault on the police barracks had gone like clockwork, for which he was supremely grateful. Wu Tai Kwong was supposed to be in the left seat of this chopper running the show; the others had insisted that Hu Chiang take Wu's place.

As he watched the trucks loading small arms at the police barracks, Hu Chiang wondered just where Wu was . . . and Sonny Wong. No one had seen Sonny in days.

He had almost refused to take Wu's place as the tactical leader. Generalissimo Hu Chiang—the thing was ridiculous. If the choice had been his he would have declined. Yet he remembered what Wu had said, so long ago when the revolution was just a dream: "The cause must be bigger than we are, worth more than we are, or we are wasting our lives pursuing it."

"We cannot make a utopia, fix all that is wrong with human society," he had told Wu.

"True, but we can build a civilization better than the one we have. To build for future generations is our duty, our obligation as thinking creatures."

Duty. That was Wu's take on life. He was doing his duty.

So Hu Chiang was in the chopper this morning, half queasy, trying to keep his wits about him as the faithful stormed the police barracks on the southern tip of the Kowloon peninsula.

From this seat a few hundred feet up he could see much of Hong Kong harbor, which was dotted with dozens of moored ships from all over the earth and squadrons of lighters and fishing boats. He could see the airport at Lantau, the Kowloon docks and warehouses, the endless high-rises full of people with hopes and dreams of a better life, the office towers of Victoria's Central District, and the spine of Hong Kong Island beyond.

The most interesting portion of the view was to the north, toward mainland China, hidden this morning in the June haze. Hong Kong was but a first step, then the revolution must go north, with or without Wu Tai Kwong or Hu Chiang. . . .

The radio sputtered again. The leader of the barracks assault was checking in. "Mission completed," he said, so proud he almost couldn't get the words out.

"Roger," Hu Chiang replied and directed the chopper pilot to circle over the entrance to the highway tunnel under the strait.

The army had it blocked off this morning, of course. Forty or so troops were visible, a truck, and . . . a tank!

Yep. There it sat, right in front of the harbor tunnel entrance, squat and massive and ominous.

Hu Chiang picked up the mike and began talking.

Another helicopter, this one belonging to the PLA, was circling over Victoria's Central District and the southern tip of Kowloon. General Tang was in the passenger seat. He had had the chopper pick him up at City Hall and was now looking the situation over.

He had certainly not expected the crowds that he saw coming toward Victoria's Central District from the west and east. Connaught Road was crammed with people, as were Harcourt Road and Queensway, an endless stream of people coming from the Western District, Wanchai, and Happy Valley, all headed toward Central.

He had his troops deployed in the heart of the Central District and around City Hall, with his headquarters in the square in front of the Bank of the Orient.

The troops there seemed to be properly positioned, but the size of the crowds stunned Tang. This massive outpouring of people in defiance of the government he had not expected. It was almost as if . . . as if the people *expected* to swallow the troops.

For the first time, General Tang wondered if Sun Siu Ki or the party leaders in Beijing understood what was happening in Hong Kong.

A cry for help from the Kowloon police barracks snapped General Tang back to unpleasant reality. He motioned to the pilot of the helicopter, who swung out over the strait and flew toward the southern tip of Kowloon.

The pilot pointed out another chopper to General Tang, who had trouble seeing it at first.

"A television station helicopter," the pilot said over the intercom. "I have seen it many times before. They must be taking pictures for the television."

That, of course, was the last thing that General Tang wanted. Television pictures of this mass outpouring of antigovernment sentiment would shake the regime to its foundations. The people in Beijing had no idea, none at all!

Tang waved angrily at the television helicopter. The pilot looked directly at him, then looked away.

"Can you talk to that pilot?" Tang demanded.

"Yes." The army pilot changed the channels on the radio and called the helicopter.

Hu Chiang didn't hear the army pilot's call because he was talking on a different frequency to the squad leader in charge of the trucks carrying the weapons from the police barracks. These trucks had to get through the tunnel to Victoria, so the tank and army troops were going to have to be neutralized. Hu's pilot heard the call, though, and told Hu about it on the intercom.

"Trouble," the television station pilot said. "If we ignore him too long, he will have everyone in the world shooting at us."

"Let's do it to him first," Hu said and pointed west toward the harbor as he spoke into the microphone on his headset. The pilot took the TV chopper in the indicated direction.

Tang forgot about the civilian helicopter when he got a glimpse of the police barracks and the uniformed bodies still sprawled upon the lawn, which had been used as a campground. Tang knew corpses when he saw them, and those men looked real dead.

He saw the trucks, which must be loading the weapons Tang knew were stored in the barracks.

He directed his pilot eastward.

The streets of Kowloon were packed with cars. With the tunnel to Victoria closed, there was no place for the Hong Kong Island traffic to go, so a massive traffic jam was the result. Traffic in the city was always bad, yet today it was impossible. People had abandoned the cars in gridlocked intersections. The weapons thieves were fools to assault the police barracks with the streets impassable.

They certainly weren't going to make a fast getaway in all this traffic. His order to close the tunnel, he thought with a bit of pride, may have proved their undoing.

He again spoke to the pilot, who took him east a half mile until the machine was over the entrance to the harbor tunnel.

The troops were where they were supposed to be, the tank was there. . . . They just needed to be told that there were armed criminals in the vicinity . . . to be ready!

He consulted the printed frequency list his staff had given him this morning, then dialed the radio to the proper channel. He keyed the mike and began speaking. When he did so he naturally looked down at the people he was talking to, the soldiers surrounding the tank.

He was three words into his message when the tank exploded.

The explosion was not a massive fireball: but a cloud of smoke that jetted from the side of the thing, then seemed to envelop it.

As if it were hit by a wire-guided antitank weapon, General Tang thought, then realized that was exactly what had happened.

Out of the corner of his eye he saw a streak of fire in the air, not large. Before he could react a loud, metallic bang shook the chopper, followed by a severe vibration, then a slew to the right.

"We've been hit," the pilot shouted over the intercom. He wrestled with the cyclic and collective, trying to gain control, even as the helicopter spun faster and faster to the right and began falling.

Michael Gao was a thirty-six-year-old security analyst with a finance degree from Harvard. He worked for one of the large American mutual funds that regularly invested in the Hong Kong market . . . when he was working. Just now he was engaged in high treason against the government of a sovereign nation. Dress it up any way you like, he thought wryly, shooting down an army helicopter with a Strella missile is going to be difficult to explain away in court. Ditto popping a tank.

He had wrestled with these issues a thousand times in the past year and always came back to the fact that he personally wanted the Communists out of power in China. He believed it would be better for everyone, including himself, if some form of democratic government were installed in Beijing. And he believed the conversion worth a major national convulsion. That being the case, it logically followed that he should personally commit himself to making it happen. So he had.

No going back now, he told himself as the helo competed the last few revolutions of its out-of-control spiral and smashed onto the top of a gravel dike around the tunnel entrance.

The chopper didn't explode or burn. After the dust from the impact settled, just a wisp of smoke rose from the crumpled wreckage. No one emerged from the cockpit—no doubt the crew was dead or dying.

No one rushed to their aid.

Michael Gao realized with a start that he was hearing the popping of small arms. He looked down from the top of the building where he stood and watched his friends snipe at the troops around the smoking hulk of the tank.

With a gut-wrenching certainty, Michael Gao knew that if there had been any men in the tank, they too were now dead. The armor-piercing sabot he had fired raised the temperature of the metals it penetrated so high that the materials forming the tank's interior would spontaneously ignite and cook the crew, if by some miracle they survived the initial concussion and thermal shock.

The soldiers near the tunnel entrance were lying in the street or trying to find cover. Bursts of automatic rifle fire created sparks where the bullets ricocheted off concrete and little puffs where they impacted. This was ridiculous! The rebels didn't have time for this.

Gao leaned over the edge of the roof, shouted to the man who was on the roof of the lower building across the street, the one facing the tunnel entrance. "Use the loudspeaker!"

The man picked up the microphone. "PLA soldiers! Lay down your arms. You are surrounded. We will kill you all unless you lay down your arms and surrender."

One by one, the demoralized soldiers threw their assault rifles on the street and raised their arms in the air.

When the general's helicopter went down, Hu Chiang told his pilot to circle back over the tunnel entrance. He arrived in time to see the last of the soldiers guarding the tunnel throw down their arms.

The problem was the cars and trucks that filled the streets from curb to curb . . . and the tank that smoldered in the tunnel entrance. In their planning sessions the rebels had anticipated both problems. They had two solutions, both painted yellow and made by Caterpillar. They were on flatbed trucks parked in the rubble of a building being demolished. Now they came clanking onto the street with their blades down.

Vehicles that couldn't move were bulldozed out of the way. Trucks were pushed up onto sidewalks, cars were stacked one atop the other.

All this was accomplished in a bedlam of people running, screaming, protesting, begging the armed rebels not to ruin their cars ... all to no avail. The bulldozers pushed and shoved and made a way, and soon the first truck carrying weapons taken from the police barracks armory was waiting near the tunnel entrance. The truck was covered with armed rebels hanging on every available protuberance.

One of the bulldozers backed up to the tank, and a cable was hooked to the thing. Then the dozer began pulling, dragging the tank out of the way.

When it was clear, the other bulldozer raised its blade and led the trucks into the tunnel.

Governor Sun's secretary thought the New China News Agency weenie on the telephone was some kind of flake. This story of Jimmy Lee falling apart, worried about committing treason ... Jimmy Lee? The top one percent of the top one percent of cool?

He put the radio censor on hold and told his colleague at the next desk, "Another nut case. This one wants to talk to the governor."

"The governor will refuse."

"I know."

"He will be angry you asked."

"What should I do? Perhaps the man is telling the truth."

The man at the next desk surrendered. "Tell the governor. Let him make the decision."

At Lantau Airport Ma Chao and his fellow fighter pilots were directed to don their flight gear and wait in the ready room, which they did. Apparently during the wee hours of the night Beijing had ordered a full alert.

Unfortunately, no amplifying orders had been received over the military radio communications net. The telephone system was down, silencing the faxes and computers. An old Bruce Lee movie was playing on the television.

The ready room was abuzz with speculation. Everyone seemed to have an opinion—the more outlandish, the louder the proud possessor proclaimed it. They argued, wondered, gestured, and guessed. The

Americans and Taiwanese were invading. The Japanese had declared war. There had been a coup in Beijing.

Ma Chao and his friends sat silently, taking it in, saying little. They thought they knew what was happening, but without explanations or verification from headquarters, they couldn't be certain. Nor was there a need for immediate action.

Patience was needed, and Ma Chao had plenty. Like all the pilots, he was wearing a sidearm. He had the flap unbuttoned so he could get it out and into action quickly.

As he listened to the fantastic scenarios that were being paraded before the group as quickly as they were concocted, he thought about the commanding officer and his department heads, all Communists, all loyal to the regime, as far as Ma Chao knew.

When the crunch came Ma Chao and his three fellow conspirators were going to have to take charge, and that probably meant they would have to shoot some of the senior men. Ma Chao sat in the ready room wondering if he could do it.

He had assured Wu Tai Kwong that he could. "I am a soldier," he said. "I have the personal courage to do what must be done."

"You could shoot men you have served with for many years?"

"I do not know," he finally replied, truthfully.

"Ah, my friend, on men like you the revolution will succeed or fail. You must use your best judgment, but you must not surrender. You must face unpleasant reality and do what the situation requires of you."

He had nodded, knowing the truth of Wu's words.

Wu always told the truth. All of it, never just a piece, and he never sugarcoated it. You got bald reality from him.

"Chinese pilots are poorly trained," Wu told him and explained how Western air forces trained their pilots. "You Chinese pilots fly straight and level, relying on the ground controller to find the enemy and steer you to him. What if the ground controller is off the air, or the enemy refuses to fly straight and level, waiting for you to assassinate him? What then? Could you improvise?"

Ma Chao did not answer. He thought about the question but refused to state a mere opinion.

"When the revolution begins," Wu said, "you will have to weigh the situation and make the best decision you can, then go forward confidently, aggressively, believing in yourself. There will be no one to give you orders. You must decide for yourself what needs to be done, then do it. What we require of you is the courage to believe in yourself."

Ma Chow thought about that courage now as he sat in the ready room waiting for the earth to turn.

Governor Sun's secretary found that his boss was tied up with an engineer who was trying to explain the difficulty with the subway doors. "The problem is in the computer," the engineer explained.

"The computer opens and closes train doors?"

"Yes," the engineer said, pleased that Sun was with him so far. "Something has gone wrong with the software. We must find the problem before we can fix it."

"I thought you said the problem was power fluctuations?"

"Power fluxes caused the problem with the software."

The secretary went back to the New China News Agency man he had on hold. "The governor is busy. Why don't you tell me the message? I'll write it down and give it to him when he has a moment."

"This is very important," the censor said. "The message is too important and too long to be written down."

The secretary rolled his eyes. "I'll have the governor call you. How is that?"

"I will await his call." The censor dictated the telephone number at the radio station, then hung up.

The secretary threw the call-back slip into the governor's in-basket.

The soldiers on duty at the Victoria end of the Cross-Harbor Tunnel heard echoes through the tunnel of the small battle in Kowloon. They also saw General Tang's helicopter crash and assumed, correctly, that it had been shot down.

They waited in nervous dread for what might come next. There were only a dozen of them, a small squad, manning a police barricade in front of the tunnel entrance. They were young, the oldest a mere twenty-four, from rural villages far to the north. They had joined the army to escape the drudgery of the rice fields. Only four of them could read the most basic of the Chinese ideographs.

They were armed with old Kalashnikov assault rifles and one machine gun. When they heard the clanking of the bulldozer coming through the tunnel, they assumed it was the tank that they knew had been positioned at the Kowloon end.

Relieved, they relaxed and the sergeant in charge walked down the tunnel to meet the tank coming the other way. He went about fifty yards and waited.

When he realized he was looking at a bulldozer, and behind it trucks, the sergeant knew something was happening that no one had told him about. He turned and scampered back up the tunnel, shouting to his men.

Unsure of what to do, the men waited for direction.

The uncertainty ended as the bulldozer emerged from the tunnel. Two men atop the dozer opened fire on the soldiers standing about.

The other soldiers might have killed these two men and some of the men following the dozer on foot if they had been given a chance, but they weren't. A machine gun atop a nearby building swept the tunnel entranceway with a long burst, sending the bullets back and forth, knocking the standing soldiers down like bowling pins.

The three-second burst was enough. Men emerging from the tunnel shot the survivors as the bulldozer rolled over two bodies. The trucks turned into the crowded streets and stopped. Men inside the truck beds began passing out assault rifles and ammunition to the crowd of young men and women who had been lounging there.

At the biggest television station in Hong Kong the atmosphere was strictly business as usual when Wei Luk and three other rebels walked in. There were no guards in the lobby, armed or unarmed, and no guards in the reception area; just two potted palms and large photos of the station's news stars. One of the stars was a man named Peter Po, who, like Wei Luk and his friends, had bet his life that communism could be successfully overthrown.

Wei Luk glanced at the smiling picture of Peter Po and then stepped over to the receptionist, a beautifully made-up young woman with an expensive coiffure and long, painted nails. She gave Wei and his friends a dazzlingly professional smile.

Their pistols were in their pockets, so they looked presentable enough. Wei Luk smiled, told the girl that he had an appointment with Peter Po.

"And these other gentlemen?"

"Them too."

She picked up the phone, pushed a button, waited a bit, then asked his name. He gave it.

"At the end of the hallway take a right," she told him after she had talked to Mr. Po, "then it's the third door on the left."

The girl pointed toward a green steel door with a small window. She unlocked it with a hidden button as Wei Luk pushed.

Po welcomed them into his office. He was wearing the television uniform, a suit and tie.

"I thought there was a guard," Wei Luk said.

Peter Po nodded. "I told him today would be a good day to stay home sick, and he agreed."

"Okay."

Peter Po looked at his watch. "When do you think?"

"I don't know. When the truck delivers weapons and more men, then and only then."

Fortunately Governor Sun had not yet realized that the rebellion had begun, so no one at City Hall had sent police or troops to secure the one operating television station or shut it down. A rebel broadcast would cause them to cure this error as quickly as possible, however. Until an armed force could be resisted, the rebels thought it wise to hold their tongue.

Yet the rebels were now inside and the police and army were out. Peter Po had a script and knew how to run the equipment in the building so that the rebel leadership could talk to the people of Hong Kong.

Wei Luk's orders were to ensure that the police and soldiers stayed out of the building, to the last man. "Fight until there are no bricks left stuck together," Wu Tai Kwong had told him.

"Take your places," Wei told his men now. He directed one of the men to go back to the lobby and sit with the receptionist.

"Let no one else through the door. Call when the truck arrives."

———

The crowd in the Central District of Victoria chanted antigovernment slogans, sang snatches of songs, surged along the streets carrying everyone with them, a giant human river.

The crowd came to a stop against the ring of PLA troops that surrounded the Bank of the Orient square. There were five hundred soldiers in the streets around the plaza, all armed with assault rifles and wearing riot-control shields and face masks. The trucks that had delivered them there were parked on the streets inside the military perimeter.

At the four corners of the plaza the officer in charge, Tang's number two, Brigadier General Moon Hok, had ordered machine guns placed in nests built of sandbags. In the center of the plaza he had placed two tanks. Between them sat a command car bristling with radio aerials.

General Moon was in the command car when he learned that General Tang might have crashed. While the PLA was attempting to verify why their helicopter had ceased all transmissions, Moon got out of the vehicle and stood looking at the sea of soldiers in the square and the huge buildings that surrounded it.

From a military point of view, the position was not a good one. The buildings were man-made high points that would afford an enemy excellent positions from which to shoot down into the square, creating a killing zone.

He called a colonel over, told him to assign squads to search each of the buildings adjoining the square. The colonel walked away to make it happen.

As Moon Hok listened to the noise of the boisterous crowd echoing through the urban canyons and the radio noise emanating from the command car, he decided to use his troops to push the crowd back one block in all directions, thereby putting the buildings that faced the square within his perimeter. Tang had told him to bring no more than five hundred men this morning because the square wouldn't physically hold any more; now he was contemplating holding nine blocks with the same five hundred men. They would be thin, very thin.

What if the crowd rioted, got completely out of control?

Could Tang be dead?

The noise of the crowd made the hair on the back of Moon Hok's neck rise.

He got on the radio and called for another five hundred men to join him. It would be hours before they arrived from Kowloon, but better late than never.

When Virgil Cole designed the Sergeant York units, he realized that the volume of data flowing from the sensors would require that each unit be individually monitored. Since a network was only as good as the data its sensors fed into it, he didn't trust a computer to make life-or-death decisions. The U.S. Army planners didn't want people completely removed from the loop, either. Consequently, part of the York system was a mobile command and control trailer where the people who monitored each unit sat at individual stations. Here a mainframe computer checked the sensor data and suggested possible courses of action to the human operators.

The trailer had also been on the C-5 Galaxy that delivered the York units and was now parked in an alley three blocks from the Bank of the Orient. Despite the fact that power cables led to it from mobile power units parked nearby, the trailer was gaily painted with surprisingly good graphic art. A sign on the side proclaimed the trailer to be a mobile museum exhibiting the latest in computer technology, sponsored by a well-known philanthropic organization dedicated to the education of the world's children.

Cole had huddled with the Scarlet Team members this morning, telling them what he knew of other team efforts throughout China. He repeated the litany of woes that the minister in Beijing had recited to Governor Sun, ticking them off on his fingers. "The government is inundated with troubles this morning," he said in summation. "The population is getting out of control in most of the major Chinese cities. Beijing is beginning to suspect that revolution is in the wind. When the people see how fragile the government's control is, the rebellion will spread."

"Wu Tai Kwong has done his work well," someone commented.

"We must do ours equally well," Cole shot back and went to check the sensor data feeds from each York unit. Six monitors were arranged in a row, all six labeled from left to right: Alvin, Bob, Charlie ...

Kerry Kent stood beside him, comparing her handheld tactical controller with the main monitor.

Satisfied, she stood back, took a deep breath.

"Worried?" Cole asked.

"Only about Wu," she replied. "This will go fine. You'll see. You built good stuff."

Cole waved the compliment away. "I won't authorize a transfer of money to Wong's account until Jake Grafton sees Wu and Callie Grafton in the flesh and calls me—they leave together when the Swiss have got the loot."

"Does Wong know that?"

"I told him when he called earlier. The bastard threatened to hack off more fingers, but we have no choice. We must be tough, insist on fair dealing, or the son of a bitch will take the money and kill them, sure as shootin'."

Kerry Kent took a deep breath. "When?"

"Tomorrow night is the earliest I could set up the wire transfer. We have to do it while the Swiss bank is open; they don't stay late for anybody."

The two-way radio had been busy all morning. Now the man monitoring it signaled to Cole. "The convoy has cleared the harbor tunnel."

"Cleared the tunnel, aye," Cole acknowledged.

He keyed the intercom mike on his headset. "The convoy has cleared the harbor tunnel. All units check in."

The operator at each monitor sang out, "Alvin ready," "Bob ready," and so on, in order.

Kerry Kent took control. "We are ready, Mr. Cole."

Since Kerry Kent was going to be fighting a revolution this morning and her boyfriend was a guest of Sonny Wong's, this should be a good time to search Kent's apartment, Tommy Carmellini thought. He used the stairs for this visit—the elevator was out of service—and picked the lock to get in.

He checked the small bathroom and closet to ensure that he was the only person there, then strolled slowly through the place taking inventory.

He had no idea what he was looking for. Kerry Kent, SIS double agent, revolutionary, anti-Communist warrior . . . maybe she had Mao's little red book under her pillow. He picked up the pillow and looked.

Well, no book, but a businesslike little automatic. He picked it up, checked the caliber. .380. She didn't use this on China Bob Chan.

The bed was as good a place as any to start. He put the pistol on the dresser, began stripping sheets. He examined the mattress inch by inch to see if it had a compartment for documents or the like. Apparently not. Nothing under the mattress, in the box springs, in the frame of the bed.

He piled the mess in the center of the bed and worked around it. Kerry's dresser was next.

The sea breeze and swells running in the strait this morning distracted Jake Grafton for a moment and made him smile. The salty wind cooled the perspiration on his forehead and filled his nostrils with the pungent scent of the Pearl River, flowing from deep in China. The pitching, bucking little tour boat was a handful and forced him to think about how he was going to bring the boat into the pier on Hong Kong Island.

Just which pier he should use was a problem. Who were the men on the sidewalk? Who hired them? Whom did the man call on the cell phone? They were undoubtedly watching him now, waiting to see where he landed.

He wanted to go back to the consulate, avoid the disaster that was about to happen in the Central District. When the shooting started the crowd might stampede, killing hundreds of people, perhaps thousands. Cole, you damned fool, getting smack in the middle of someone else's war!

The engine of the tour boat hummed sweetly. That was a lucky break. Thinking about possible observers, Jake took the boat in close to the shore and turned east. He motored along for five minutes before he found what he wanted, a low pier with empty cleats. Someone used this boat to make a living; Jake Grafton didn't want to deprive him of it.

He brought the boat in smartly toward the pier. Although he didn't own a boat, he had watched sailors handle small boats for years. With the prop engaged and the engine idling, he leaped onto the pier with a rope in his hand and dropped it over a cleat. Back onto the bucking boat as it kissed the tire hanging at the waterline, reverse the prop, let the bowline spring the boat in ... When he had the boat tied up fore and aft, he killed the engine.

The rock-solid pier felt good under his feet. He walked off the pier thinking about the thugs in Kowloon, wondering if they had been working for Sonny Wong.

CHAPTER FIFTEEN

Sergeant Loo Ping was told to search the Bank of the Orient tower, which stood on the north side of the square. He picked four men and went to the front door, which was locked. With his face against the glass, shielding his eyes with both hands, he could see that the bank lobby was empty.

He fired his rifle into the door lock. After three shots he pushed experimentally on the door. It gave, but a piece of the deadbolt still held it. He had two of the men put their shoulders against the door and push. The glass cracked, the broken lock gave way, and the door opened.

Sergeant Loo led his men inside. Of course the major hadn't told him what to look for. "Search the building," was all the major said, as if the object of the search was self-evident.

"People," Loo Ping told his squad now. "Look for people. If we find anyone, we will take him outside to the command vehicle for interrogation."

The soldiers moved off. One went to the basement, the others went to the elevators and pushed the button. Nothing.

Loo Ping led them to the staircase and they started up.

"What if we find money?" the youngest soldier asked, which amused the others.

"You think they leave money lying around?"

"This is a bank, isn't it? Perhaps there is money. They must keep it somewhere."

Loo Ping was a rice farmer's son himself and had never had a bank account. Of course there was money in a bank, even a failed one. Perhaps the major really wanted the soldiers to search for money.

"Money would be locked away in safes," one of the soldiers remarked now, which made sense to Loo Ping. The bankers certainly wouldn't leave money lying around.

The second floor was a huge open room, carpeted, full of desks, with a computer on each of them. The lights were off, so the only illumination came through the windows on the sides of the grand room. The soldiers stood at the door, marveling. Imagine what the room must be like when the lights were on and people were seated at every desk, counting money!

This morning there were no people, so after a bit the soldiers let the door close—amazing how the door silently closed by itself—and climbed another flight of stairs.

The third floor was like the second, a vast office full of desks and computers and wonderful white machines that did God knows what, and . . .

Something was standing in the center of the room, near the window overlooking the square.

It looked like a big man.

Loo led the way, the other three behind. All had their rifles in their hands so that anyone could see they were men with authority who must be obeyed.

The man at the window was huge! He turned to watch the soldiers walk between the rows of desks toward him. He had dark skin and was completely naked.

Loo Ping's steps slowed.

It wasn't a man.

No.

A machine? Nearly seven feet tall, the neck consisted of three flexible stalks. The head was narrow at the chin and top, widest at the eyes, with a stalk or flexible tube coming out the top. The legs reminded Loo Ping of the hind legs of a dog; he thought the feet looked like those of a chicken, with three prominent toes. And that tail! Something from a movie?

No!

A *robot!* That is what it must be!

One of the men whispered to Loo, tugged at his sleeve. "It has a weapon," the man said.

"Hey!" Loo Ping called, still walking forward, but slower.

He halted ten feet from the thing and looked it over. The letter C was visible high on its shoulders. Its hands were claws, and they held a launch tube for a wire-guided antitank missile. Another launch tube lay on the floor.

Now Loo realized the head was lowered a few degrees, so the eyes—they were really some kind of lenses—were looking right at him. One of them had a circular lens turret in front of it, and now the turret rotated, stopped with a click, then rotated again.

Nervous, Loo took a few steps sideways.

The head followed.

For the first time Loo Ping noticed that a multibarreled weapon of some kind was mounted on the right side of the robot's torso. Now the barrels began spinning, emitting a high-pitched whine, barely audible in this quiet room.

Loo Ping tightened the grip on his rifle, glanced at his three troops. They were still there, although they looked like they were going to run.

"Hey!" Loo Ping said again, facing the robot and moving the barrel of his rifle a little, so it pointed more at the robot. He searched for the safety with his right thumb.

"The gun is pointed right at you," the closest soldier whispered to Loo Ping. He was right. The spinning barrels of the weapon were pointed at Loo Ping's chest. He took another step to the right. The barrels followed.

"Ooooo . . ." he began, but he never completed the sound.

The robot's weapon fired, and Loo Ping felt the impact of the bullet as it hit him dead center in the heart. His blood pressure dropped to zero, and he was dead seconds after he hit the floor.

The robot swung its weapon and fired one bullet at the nearest soldier, then the next, and the next. Four individual aimed shots in less than a second.

The four empty cartridges ejected from the minigun's breech rattled like hail against the window glass, then fell to the carpeted office floor while the barrels of the minigun freewheeled to a stop.

The soldier Loo Ping had sent to search the basement walked through the door just as the minigun fired. As the reports echoed through the room, he dove back through the door and scrambled down the staircase.

"Someone is escaping," Kerry Kent said. She was watching the monitor intently, listening to Charlie York's audio in her headset.

"Let him go," Cole said. "He's no threat." He wiped his mouth with the back of his hand. Four uneducated kids dead in a heartbeat. His mouth was watering badly, like he was going to puke.

Charlie York turned back to the window. The turret on his right camera clicked to another lens, bringing the video of the plaza below into focus on Kent's monitor.

She checked with the other units. All okay, all ready.

Jimmy Lee, the King of Cool, was still babbling incoherently about Wu Tai Kwong and treason and not wanting to be executed. Lee's producer and the government censor stood wringing their hands.

Governor Sun hadn't called and in truth the producer doubted if he would. Still, Jimmy Lee was a celebrity of sorts, so he might.

The censor tried to place a call to Beijing but the operator said the lines were down. "This is a government emergency," the censor shouted, then wished he hadn't. The possibility that Jimmy Lee had gone off his nut and was babbling nonsense crossed his mind for the first time. He wondered just how hard he should press to get though to someone important.

He didn't have to worry. The operator told him that government business or not, the telephone lines out of Hong Kong were still out of order.

"Call army headquarters," the producer suggested.

"Why don't we just broadcast the news?" the censor replied. "Everyone will hear. What better way is there to warn the authorities of the plot?"

"What if Jimmy is crazy? Huh? Have you considered that? Maybe he's on drugs. The fool has used them before, remember?"

"All the telephone lines out of Hong Kong are down," the censor retorted. "The banks are closed, the subway isn't running, the airport is closed. . . . Jimmy says the rebels are attacking the computers. There is going to be an attack on the troops in the Bank of the Orient square. That sounds like truth to me."

"Okay, okay," the producer said. He eyed Jimmy, tried to decide if he was up to talking coherently. No.

He went into the studio and sat on the stool in front of Jimmy's mike. As he waited for the current song to end, he thought about what he was going to say. Tell it straight, he decided. Don't try to jazz it up like Jimmy would. Just act like a man with all his marbles.

Don't panic, people, but this is a rumor that may have some truth to it. Authorities, take action. You heard it first, folks, right here on the Jimmy Lee show.

The song came to an end. The producer flipped the switch to make his microphone hot and began speaking.

The people in the mobile museum trailer parked three blocks from the Bank of the Orient had a radio tuned to the Jimmy Lee show and a television showing the only station left on the air. Popular music had been coming from the radio and a Chinese soap opera from the television.

Someone called Kerry Kent's attention to the voice that came over the radio. A male voice, talking about the revolution that was just beginning, a revolution to overthrow the People's Republic. Troops were going to be attacked this morning in the Central District by armed rebels, who were trying to cause a major riot, a riot that was supposed to engulf City Hall and lead to the arrest of the authorities there.

"That isn't Jimmy Lee's voice," the man told Kerry ominously.

She looked at her watch. This wasn't supposed to be happening now.

"Have the people who are to guard the radio and television stations reached there yet?" These people could not be armed until the weapons came through the Cross-Harbor Tunnel.

"They are on their way. They haven't called in."

"What is going on at the radio station?"

No one could answer that.

Virgil Cole was watching now. Kerry Kent called Hu Chiang, who was still circling over the Central District in a helicopter. The feed from the chopper's television camera was displayed on a monitor in the trailer.

"You're over the bank square?" Kerry asked.

"Yes. I'm ready when you are."

Kerry turned to Cole. "The television and radio station guards are not yet in position, but a premature announcement is coming over the radio."

"Anything on television?"

"No."

"Are we ready?"

"We are waiting for the television and radio guards. When the hammer falls, we have to deny the government use of the media and keep it for ourselves."

"Is the army listening to Jimmy Lee?"

Kerry Kent stared at the monitors, which showed her what each of the Sergeant York units was seeing. Then she checked the computer-generated composite. "If they are, they haven't taken alarm yet," she said.

"Call the people on the way to the TV and radio stations. Get an estimated time of arrival. All they have to do is get there before the PLA does."

Kerry Kent nodded at one of the computer technicians, who picked up a WB phone and began dialing.

"Two hours," the radio operator told Moon Hok. That was how long the colonel at the barracks in the New Territories estimated it would take for the troops Moon requested to be loaded on trucks and transported to the Bank of the Orient square. Neither the barracks colonel nor Moon Hok yet knew that the Cross-Harbor Tunnel no longer belonged to the army, nor were they factoring in the gridlock conditions that prevailed in the streets of southern Kowloon. Still, Moon Hok knew the estimate was optimistic.

From where he stood he could hear the crowd chanting an antigovernment slogan, something about no more stealing.

Once again, Moon Hok thought bitterly, Tang and the governor had placed the army in an impossible situation. The crowd was definitely hostile and growing with each passing minute. In the streets leading to the square the people were packed to standing-room-only density.

Should they be allowed to remain where they were, or should he push them back and expand his perimeter?

While he was mulling his options, the radio traffic continued about the helicopter in which General Tang had been riding. It had crashed, according to an army officer who said he had witnessed the disaster from a vehicle a half-mile away. The helicopter had fallen near the Kowloon entrance to the Cross-Harbor Tunnel. Another officer chimed in, claiming he saw the missile that downed the chopper.

"It was shot down," he said on the radio net.

Shot down!

If the hostile population was now shooting at PLA helicopters, the entire situation had changed. This bank square was militarily indefensible. Perhaps he should load the troops in the trucks and get them out of here. Of course, that move would have political repercussions.

He decided to dump the whole mess in the governor's lap. He directed the radio operator to get Governor Sun on the radio.

But time had run out. Some of the civilians in the crowd outside the military perimeter were listening to the only radio station in Hong Kong that was on the air. These people were being entertained by Jimmy Lee's producer, who was describing the horrible, treasonous uprising that was about to take place in the Bank of the Orient square.

At first the people who were listening laughed. Then they stood looking at each other, wondering if this diatribe were true.

To a crowd that was already rowdy, the radio voice seemed to be describing the perfect way to vent their anger at the myriad of frustrations and injustices that were their lot in life.

The shouts became loud, angry, and the people began pushing forward toward the soldiers in the square.

Virgil Cole saw the crowd surge on the monitors. He pushed a button on his control panel so that the audio from the York units was in his headset. Now he could hear the angry chants.

"If the soldiers feel threatened, they'll fire tear gas or bullets, and the crowd will panic," he said to Kent, who was mesmerized by the unfolding spectacle. "Let's do it now."

The soldier who had witnessed Loo Ping's death at the hands of Charlie York stood now in front of General Moon, pointing at the Bank of the Orient building. He explained about the robot.

"A monster ten feet tall shot my sergeant and the other three men in my squad. Up there, on the third floor."

The general listened to this drivel, then walked away. The junior officers could handle the man. Monsters!

The man kept pointing at the third floor.

When he heard glass breaking, Moon Hok involuntarily glanced in the direction the soldier was pointing. He saw glass showering down . . . from a third-floor window.

Moon was about to tell one of the staff officers to have the soldier lead him to the monster in the bank when the nearest tank exploded. The explosion burned the general and tossed him through the air. He landed in a heap on the pavement, too stunned to move.

The York robot called Charlie dropped the empty launch tube for the wire-guided antitank missile and picked up another. While it was bringing the weapon into firing position, the second tank exploded. Dog York, in the building on the south side of the square, had fired that round.

Charlie aimed this missile at the command vehicle, then squeezed the trigger.

The missile pulverized the van, showering the men lying on the pavement with sheet metal and radio parts.

Having fired both the antitank missiles Charlie York had carried into the Bank of the Orient, Kerry Kent decided to have Dog York fire a rocket-propelled grenade at the machine gun nest on the far right side of the square. The York control screen was a Windows-based system—point and click—so in seconds she had a rocket screaming across the square. It struck the ammo feed on the side of the tripod-mounted heavy machine gun and destroyed it.

Seconds later Dog destroyed another machine gun on the far side of the square.

The tanks and two machine guns were out of action. Thirty seconds had passed, and every PLA soldier in the square was flat on his face or huddled behind a concrete planter wall.

The sounds of the explosions echoed through the urban canyons and were heard by more than a hundred thousand people standing and sitting in the streets. The energy level in the crowd soared as people craned their necks, trying to see in the direction of the square.

When the truck screeched to a halt outside the Victoria Peak television station, Wei Luk was standing in the doorway. With a huge sigh of relief, he watched a dozen university students with assault rifles pile out of the back of the truck and pass down a machine gun. They set up the machine gun where it had an excellent field of fire along the main street leading to the station, then took up positions around the building.

Wei Luk went back inside. The receptionist stared at him in wide-eyed amazement when he pulled a pistol from his pocket and directed her to unlock the door. Dazed, she pushed the button.

Wei Luk and his colleagues walked down the hallway toward the main studio, where they saw Peter Po and gave him the high sign.

Less than two minutes later the station had the feed from the camera in Hu Chiang's helicopter on the air. Peter Po began a voice-over, explaining to the television audience that the first battle of the revolution had begun.

In the museum trailer three blocks from the Bank of the Orient square, a cheer went up when the television began playing the aerial feed.

Virgil Cole turned to the shortwave radio that sat on a bench behind him. In less than a minute he began receiving reports from revolutionaries in television stations all across China that had picked up the Hong Kong signal from the satellite and were rebroadcasting it the length and breadth of the nation. With the program on the air, the revolutionaries would then abandon the stations, forcing all the personnel out and locking the doors of the buildings. When the authorities reacted, as they eventually would, they would have to break into the buildings to stop the broadcasts. And there would be no one there to arrest.

By then the damage would be done. The news would be out, the credibility of the government severely damaged.

Virgil Cole leaned back in his chair with a sigh of relief. *Finally,* he thought, *we have crossed the threshold. There can be no turning back.*

Alvin and Bob York were in a locked room in the basement of the building that stood on the west side of the square. The door was locked to discourage any soldiers who might be ordered to search the building. Now Alvin broke the lock with a twist of the door handle. Both units climbed the stairs toward the street level. The staircase was narrow with a low ceiling, with barely enough room for the robots when they tucked in their appendages and curled their backs.

Kerry Kent checked the video feed as the two units climbed the stairs to ensure all was well, then used the mouse to activate Easy and Fred.

Behind her Virgil Cole helped himself to another cup of coffee. He had spent five years of his life overseeing the design of the York units and had a huge financial stake in the company that manufactured them, so he should have been nervous about the Yorks' first operational trial. He wasn't. He had used up all his juice fretting the success of the nationwide television broadcast, which he thought more critical than the performance of the York units to the eventual success of the revolution.

He sipped the coffee and glanced at the monitors and wondered if he should have absolutely refused Wu Tai Kwong's demand to confront the PLA in front of an audience. He had confidence in the York units, but crowd psychology was a huge unknown—a stampede could kill thousands.

As he watched he remembered Wu's words: "Revolutions are made by people—the Yorks are just things. The people of China must see that others are willing to fight. We can give them something to fight for, but they must find the courage in their own hearts."

As the four York units that had been in hiding came running from the buildings, Charlie and Dog leaped through the broken glass of their respective third-floor windows. They used their hands and feet to cushion the shock of their landing on the concrete street, then they began running toward the center of the square.

Now all six Yorks were transmitting video and audio to the central computer in the museum trailer; in seconds the computer had transformed the six data streams into a three-dimensional picture of the square, the trucks, the decorative planters, trees, light poles, smoldering hulks of tanks . . . and the armed men who were rising from the pavement with their weapons in hand, staring wild-eyed at the huge, running robots, which attacked the crews of the two remaining machine guns.

Inevitably a few of the soldiers snapped their rifles to their shoulders to shoot, and instantly the system directed a York to engage. An onboard CPU slewed the minigun onto the target and triggered a round. Just one round per target, because unlike humans, the Yorks didn't miss.

The ring-laser gyros inside each York fed data to a separate maneuvering computer that kept it upright and balanced, the onboard sensors gathered data that was processed internally by the weapons-control computer and passed to the mainframe via UWB, and threats were identified and engaged in the order set by the controller before the battle began. In addition, the weapons-control computer passed information to the maneuvering computer so that it could move the unit to minimize the danger posed by low-priority threats, or threats the York had not yet had time to engage.

The computers and sensors operated seamlessly. Each unit engaged targets that threatened it and ran, leaped, swerved, and bounded to throw off the aim of opponents it had yet to engage.

The result was mass confusion. Officers shouted and pointed, gesturing wildly at the Yorks, which were leaping from truck to truck, running across the square, leaping up on the sides of the buildings and executing turns in midair while their miniguns hammered out aimed shots.

Soldiers who raised their rifles to aim at the sprinting Yorks were shot down, those who did nothing were not harmed.

One soldier threw down his rifle and stood erect in the center of the square with his hands in the air. One of the junior officers drew a pistol and pointed it at the erect soldier. He was immediately shot by two Yorks.

Other soldiers threw down their rifles, first a few, then many.

The firing slowed to an occasional shot, then stopped altogether.

The running Yorks slowed to a walk, then came to rest. Each one stood with its head turning, its sensors scanning, and the barrels of its minigun spinning, ready to fire. They were ominous, fearsome.

A cheer went up from the watching civilians, who ran into the square.

Burned and groggy from the concussion of the tank that had exploded nearby, General Moon Hok managed to get to his feet. He stood swaying, looking uncomprehendingly at his soldiers with their hands up. Then he took his first good look at the closest York, Alvin, whose sensors were scrutinizing him in return. The minigun followed his every move, but the shot didn't come.

The helicopter carrying Hu Chiang settled into the center of the bank square and Hu stepped out. The cameraman, his camera still going, piled out the back and focused his camera on Hu, who looked around, then walked over to General Moon Hok and demanded that he surrender his command to the revolutionary forces of China.

The civilians were running into the square now, many of them armed with weapons liberated from the Kowloon police barracks. They were taking weapons from soldiers and passing them to unarmed civilians. A few of the newly armed revolutionaries aimed their weapons skyward and pulled the trigger, just to see if they would shoot.

The Yorks nearly shot these people. Cole suspected what was coming and warned Kerry Kent, who safetied the Yorks' firing circuits just in time.

Moon Hok was in no mood to do or say anything to the people who had killed his soldiers and humiliated him, and Hu Chiang wisely decided that Moon's silence was good enough. He ordered one of the armed revolutionaries who had appeared nearby to jail Moon and his officers.

All this made excellent television. It got even better: From his hip pocket Hu removed a written speech that he and Wu Kai Kwong had drafted for Wu to give at this moment. Since Wu wasn't here, Hu read the speech to the unseen audience behind the camera as the cheering crowd gathered around him.

"We hereby proclaim the goals of the revolution: China shall become a free and democratic nation with a written constitution guaranteeing the rule of law, with leaders regularly elected by popular vote, a nation free of graft and corruption, a nation that protects its citizens from criminals, a nation where everyone shall have an equal opportunity to earn a living, a nation with free speech and freedom of religion, a nation that can take its place as a proud member of the world's family of nations. . . ."

The last half of the battle in the square was broadcast all over Hong Kong and mainland China. In Canton and Shanghai, in Beijing and Hunan Province and in villages all over the nation, people who happened to be near a television saw the Yorks standing in the center of the bank square surrounded by PLA troops with their hands in the air. Then the cheering crowd flowed into the square as if a dam had burst.

In Hong Kong City Hall someone called Governor Sun to the television. He was not in time to see the Yorks in action, but he watched as Hu Chiang landed in the square in the television station's helicopter and walked over to General Moon. He saw Hu accept General Moon's sidearm and he saw the first of the deliriously happy civilians stream into the square, hugging Hu Chiang and the surrendered soldiers and each other and gazing in awe at the York units.

"Radio Beijing," Governor Sun ordered peremptorily. "A revolution is underway in Hong Kong and we need more troops immediately to stabilize the situation."

The aide went off to do as he was told, leaving Governor Sun rooted to the spot, still staring at the television.

Nothing happened instantly in China, Sun well knew. It would take days for the government to reinforce the division of troops that were already here. Perhaps several weeks.

For the first time, Sun admitted to himself that he had misjudged the situation here.

His next epiphany followed immediately: The rebels would probably execute him if they could catch him. Chinese revolutions had never been bloodless affairs. This one wouldn't be either.

Jimmy Lee's producer stopped talking into the radio microphone when he realized that someone was standing beside him with a pistol, a pistol that was pointed at his head. He stopped talking in midword.

The pistol jerked, ordering him out of the chair.

A young woman of eighteen or nineteen years, an inch over four feet tall, took his place and began speaking into the microphone. "The Chinese revolution," she announced simply, "has begun. The island of Hong Kong has been liberated from Communist control."

Lin Pe watched the celebration in the Bank of the Orient square on the small television the Shatin grocer kept above his soft drink cooler. She watched as the cameraman inspected a York unit at close range—the thing towered a foot over everyone there and its head never stopped scanning—and the smoking hulk of a tank.

Hu Chiang appeared on television, behind him the crowd milled around, every now and then someone fired a shot into the air . . . the scene was festive, gay. No one even bothered to guard the unarmed PLA soldiers, who wandered through the crowd aimlessly, without direction.

Wu should have been here to see this, Lin Pe thought. He worked for a dozen years to make this happen, this *first step*!

The long journey had finally begun. She didn't know whether she should be happy or sad. She went back outside and sat down on the orange crate where she could see the gate of the army base and thought about everything.

She would tell Wu of this. In this life or the next.

———

In City Hall the governor and his staff were mesmerized by the televised spectacle, by the aerial shots of the crowd surging into the plaza, and by the simple, infectious joy that was apparent on every face.

They huddled around the television, which alternated between shots from the square taken with a handheld camera and aerial shots from the helicopter, which had taken off again. Through it all Peter Po gave the voice-over, as calm and collected as though revolutions were a weekly occurrence.

Hu Chiang's speech broke the spell in City Hall. Never known for an even temper, Sun exploded as he listened. He cursed Tang and Moon and the other PLA officers as incompetent, defeatist traitors. A call was put forth to the navy base. Sun demanded that all the gunboats steam up the strait and use their guns on the rebels celebrating in the Bank of the Orient square. The commander had caught the tail end of the televised debacle, and he agreed. Without much enthusiasm, Sun noted darkly.

Next he called the Su-27 squadron at Lantau. He got the squadron commander on the phone and demanded that armed sorties be flown against the rebels in the square.

"Drop bombs, strafe, shoot rockets . . . *kill the rebels! Stop the rot right here, before it spreads.*"

The colonel made him repeat the order to ensure he understood. "We will use a cannon to kill mosquitoes, eh?"

"Will you obey or must I call Beijing and have you court-martialed?"

"Bombs in the square will do a lot of damage, Governor. I just want to ensure you understand that. Afterward will be too late to complain."

"Kill the rebels."

"Bombs don't care whom they kill, Governor. Rebels, bankers, children, women, tourists, soldiers, policemen, whomever. That is what I am trying to explain."

"Obey my order!"

Next he called the chief of the metropolitan police and demanded he muster his officers and engage the rebels in armed combat. The police chief wasn't enthusiastic. Unlike the navy and air force commanders, he knew his men would be face-to-face with the robots he had seen on television.

"What are those things, Governor? What are their capabilities?"

"I do not know. Bullets will stop them, however."

"The army didn't seem to have much luck with bullets. What makes you think the police will do any better?"

"I have given the order," Sun said icily.

"So you have. But I tell you now, my men are police, not soldiers. They are trained in traffic control, not armed combat. I make no promises."

"Lead them yourself, coward!"

"If I am killed, whom will you blame for our defeat?"

Before Sun could give that disrespectful question the answer it deserved, he discovered that the chief of police had hung up.

Sun slammed down the phone. His chief aide was right there by the desk.

"Governor, you must report this matter to Beijing, but first, you must think of getting off this island."

"What are you saying?"

"Sir, the rebels will come for you, walk in the front door. The three or four policemen on duty out front cannot hold off armed rioters. You must not be here. You must not let them make a spectacle of you."

"You're right," Sun said, with more than a little gratitude in his voice. He telephoned the army base in the New Territories, asked for a helicopter to pick up him and his key aides on the roof of City Hall as soon as possible.

On the way to the roof, he stopped in the radio room. The operator called Beijing on the scrambled voice net.

Sun tried to quickly summarize the events of the morning. He told Beijing of his orders to the army and navy. "We need military reinforcements now," he pleaded with the minister.

The minister made no promises. "You must resist with the forces you have at your disposal," the minister said. "The rocket forces have had a horrible disaster, the trains cannot run until the computer systems get sorted out, the nation's electrical grid is experiencing spot failures, the telephone system is sporadic at best. We cannot get troops to you for some days."

"Air support? Could we have two more squadrons of MiGs or Sukhois?"

"The maintenance personnel, spare parts, and weapons all must be moved by road," the minister in Beijing informed Sun. "The move will take several weeks. I will give the order, but until they arrive, you must hold out with what you have."

Hold out with what we have.

Perhaps that is possible, Sun thought as he made his way up the stairs to the roof of City Hall. *If we can hurt the rebels in the square, then keep the remnants of the rebel forces on this island, prevent them from crossing the strait, perhaps it can be done.*

The chief of police was too old a dog to go running after every stick. He sat behind his desk at police headquarters watching the rebels celebrate on television.

After he read the flyer this morning, he ordered his policemen to stay away from the heart of the Central District. Apparently they had obeyed him, because he didn't see a single police officer on any of the camera's sweeps of the crowd.

A cop learns many things about the people he serves: who drinks to excess, who has a drug-addicted son or a pregnant teenage daughter, who takes bribes, who doesn't . . . who is fucking whom. In a society in which everything is for sale, everything has a price. A cop quickly learns to survive or he is eaten by the sharks.

The chief was busy surviving right now.

He tried to ignore politics when he could. Sonny Wong told him a year ago that rebellion was brewing in Hong Kong. Of course Sonny wanted to profit from that fact—that was a given. The rebels wanted change, Governor Sun and the Communists wanted to keep the status quo. One would win, one would lose.

Whoever won would need the police. And the police would need a chief.

This chief had no intention of ending up like China Bob Chan, with a fresh hole in his head and everyone in town breathing sighs of relief. Sure, China Bob made lots of money, got rich, had the big house and hot women and all the trimmings . . . and now he was sleeping in a hole in the ground because he knew too much about too many things.

Actually Sun wasn't a bad sort. The chief wondered now if he should have told the governor to get out of Hong Kong; the rebels would kill him if they caught him. Surely the man is bright enough to figure that out for himself.

The chief reached for the telephone, then thought better of it. He owed the governor nothing.

Michael Gao was on the roof of the building near the entrance to the Cross-Harbor Tunnel when he spotted the PLA helo running low, at treetop level, headed for City Hall on Hong Kong Island. He had a Strella launcher at his feet, so he lifted it, squeezed the trigger to the first notch to try for a heat lock-on.

And got one. He squeezed the trigger and the missile roared out of the launcher.

Away it went in a plume of fire. Straight across the street into the top story of the next building over.

He had another launcher, but he waited. Perhaps he would get a better shot. If he could get onto the sea wall ...

The chopper settled onto the roof of City Hall. Sun and three aides came running out. When they were aboard, the chopper rose into the air just enough to clear the railing on top of the building, then tilted into the wind.

The pilot turned to fly out over the strait, then he turned east.

Michael Gao ran with the missile launcher in his arms. People scurried to clear a path. He came to the sidewalk on the sea wall and hurriedly threw the launcher to his shoulder. The helo was speeding east over the strait, at least two miles away and low, no more than fifty feet above the water.

The missile's guidance unit refused to lock on to the helo's exhaust. The distance was just too great, the angle too large.

Gao lowered the launcher and watched the helo fly away.

Tommy Carmellini systematically examined every item in Kerry Kent's apartment, disassembled the lamps and clocks, took the television from its shell, examined the works. Did the same with the clock radio. Tapped along the floorboards, scrutinized the light fixtures, used a knife to slice the stuffing from the easy chair near the window, picked through every single item in her dresser . . .

Tommy Carmellini knew how to search an apartment and he searched this one. He found absolutely nothing that shouldn't be there.

Two hours later, discouraged and tired, he dropped his trousers and lowered himself onto Kent's commode. Before he did so, however, he lifted the lid on the back and examined the workings. Looked precisely like a commode should. Then he felt behind the tank to ensure that nothing was taped to the back.

As he sat answering nature's call, he picked up a magazine that Kent had arranged on a nearby stand. Flipped through the pages, looking to see if anything had been inserted. No.

A newspaper. He picked it up, shook it. Nothing fell out. He was about to put it back on the stand when he paused, looked again. *The Financial Times*, a week-old edition. Kent had it folded to the stock listings.

Idly Carmellini ran his eye down the listings. Column one, two . . .

Huh! There was a tiny spot of ink under the Vodafone listing, as if she rested the tip of her pen there for a moment.

He held the page up, scrutinized it carefully. Here was another spot, and another. Six in all.

Stocks. Investments. A portfolio. Well, even civil servants had portfolios these days. Hell, he had a little money in the market himself.

But he couldn't recall seeing anything about her portfolio in the apartment. Not a monthly statement, a letter from her broker, nothing.

Odd.

There should be something, shouldn't there?

CHAPTER SIXTEEN

Major Ma Chao and his three coconspirators were standing in the back of the ready room when the commanding officer and his department heads came in. Someone called the people in the room to attention.

"We have orders," the CO announced. "Governor Sun has directed us to bomb the rebels in the Bank of the Orient square in the Central District, and headquarters in Beijing has confirmed. We will launch four airplanes with four two-hundred-and-fifty-kilogram bombs each. Fortunately, the weather is excellent. We will coordinate the attack with a shelling by two naval vessels, putting maximum pressure on the rebels."

In the silence that followed this announcement the television audio could be heard throughout the room. The pilots had watched Hu Chiang make his speech, had seen the York units and the happy, joyous crowd that filled the square. They had listened to Peter Po explain the significance of the revolution, why the overthrow of the Communists was of the gravest national importance.

Now this.

There was certainly much to think about, including the fact that no pilot in the squadron had ever dropped bombs from a J-11. Although the plane was a license-built copy of one of the world's premier fighters, it had no all-weather attack capability; visual dive-bombing was the only option. Unfortunately the Beijing brass thought the risks of dive-bombing training too high, so it had been forbidden.

Major Ma turned sideways so his right side was partially hidden and drew his sidearm, a semiautomatic. He held it low, beside his leg.

"Sir," Ma asked, "did you verify the governor's identity? Agents provocateurs may be giving false orders."

This comment was grossly insubordinate and the commanding officer treated it as such. "*I* am completely satisfied that the governor issued these orders and that headquarters concurred," he said, daring anyone to contradict his statement. "The time has come to separate the patriots from the traitors," he added ominously. "I intend to follow orders, to bomb the rebels as directed by the government. Who will fly with me?"

The senior officers raised their hands, but not a single junior.

"You traitors are under arrest," the commanding officer snarled. "Now clear the room."

Ma Chao raised his pistol, pointed it at the CO. "It is you who are under arrest, Colonel. Drop your sidearm."

The CO was a true fighter pilot. He grinned broadly, then said, "We thought something like this might happen, Ma Chao, but we never suspected you. Some of these other little dicks, yes, but you surprise me. Too bad." He raised his voice. "Come in, Sergeant, come in," he called and gestured through the open door to people waiting in the hallway.

Three senior noncommissioned officers walked in. They were carrying assault rifles in the ready position.

The CO gestured toward the rear of the room. "Major Ma and those junior officers. Lock them up until we can interrogate them and find how far the rot has spread."

The NCOs pointed their rifles at Ma.

This was *it*! Now or never. Use your best judgment, Wu had said.

Ma steadied the front sight of his automatic and pulled the trigger. The bullet knocked the CO down.

"Anyone else?" Ma said, looking around.

The senior NCO grinned at Ma, then pointed his rifle at the department heads. "Your pistols, please. You are under arrest."

The lieutenant beside Ma couldn't contain himself. "I thought the sergeant was going to shoot you!"

Ma Chao thought the sergeant was on his side. He said he was last week, yet every week the earth turns seven times. Ma breathed a sigh of relief and walked toward the front of the room to see how badly the CO was hurt and to take charge.

When the trucks filled with troops left the PLA base, Lin Pe telephoned a number she had memorized. She recognized the voice that answered, a nice young girl who attended Hong Kong University. "Seven trucks have left the base."

Five minutes later Lin Pe called again. "Ten trucks filled with troops. They drove away through Shatin."

"Very good. Thank you for the report. We would like you to go back to Nathan Road and walk along it. Report any strong points that you see under construction."

Lin Pe said good-bye to the grocer, who had let her use his restroom, and walked through Shatin toward the bus stop. Her bag was heavy and she was tired, so she made slow progress.

Her son, Wu, had told her of the dangers of spying on the PLA. "They will shoot you if they catch you talking about them on the cell phone. They may arrest you because they are worried. They will be frightened, fearful men, and very dangerous."

"I understand," she replied.

"They may beat you to death trying to make you talk. They may kill you regardless of what you say."

"I understand," she had repeated.

"You do not have to do this," Wu told her.

"Someone has to."

"Ah . . ." he said, and dropped the subject.

Where in the world could Kerry Kent hide the information about her stock portfolio? Tommy Carmellini stood in the middle of Kent's kitchen thinking about that problem. He could have sworn he had searched everything there was to search, peered in every cubbyhole and cranny, pried loose every baseboard, looked in all the vents. . . .

The pots and pans were piled carefully against one wall. He had even peeled up the paper she had used to line her shelves.

Her attaché case wasn't here. Must be at the consulate.

The notebook . . . a spiral notebook had lain on her bedroom table. He had flipped through it, but . . .

He found it again, sat down in the middle of the bathroom floor in the only open space and went through it carefully. Halfway through the notebook, there it was. A page of multiplication problems, seven in all, and a column where she added the seven answers together. She hid it in plain sight.

He compared the numbers in the problems to the stock listings in *The Financial Times*. Okay, this stock closed at 74½, and here was the problem, 74.5 × 5400. Answer, 402,300.

He checked every problem. The correlation with the six stocks highlighted with a tiny spot of ink was perfect. One stock he couldn't find; only six were marked.

The total . . . £1,632,430.

A pound was worth what, about a buck fifty?

Wheee! She wasn't filthy rich, but Kerry Kent was certainly a modestly well-off secret agent, which was, as any self-respecting gentleman would tell you, the very best kind.

Almost two and a half million dollars.

On a civil servant's salary.

Perhaps her grandparents were loaded and left her a bundle. Perhaps she had a rich first husband. Then again, perhaps she was the world's finest stock picker and had done more than all right with her lunch money.

Or perhaps, Tommy Carmellini thought as he pocketed the worksheet and financial page, just perhaps, Kerry Kent was crooked.

Elizabeth Yeager's apartment was a walk-up in a small village setting on the south side of the island. As the taxi driver settled in to wait, Jake Grafton made his way past the craft shops that catered to the tourist trade, only some of which were open today, to the stairs of Yeager's building. Ivy and creeping vines covered the walls.

There were four mailboxes. Yeager's was Apartment Three. He pushed the button.

"Yes." An American woman's voice, tired and angry.

"Elizabeth Yeager, I have a message for you."

"What?"

"For you personally."

"Come on up." She buzzed the lock open.

The former consular employee opened her door just a crack. Jake Grafton slammed the door with his shoulder, and it flew open, nearly bowling her over. There was another woman sitting by the couch, a dumpy, middle-aged woman with graying hair.

"Who are you? What do you want?"

Yeager's eyes were red from crying.

"You're Yeager?"

"Yes."

"Some questions for you." He looked at the other woman. "If you wouldn't mind."

Yeager nodded at the woman, who glared at Jake as she swept past.

"It's a crime to break into people's apartments," Yeager said as she perched on the edge of a chair. "Don't forget, my neighbor, Mrs. O'Reilly, can identify you."

"That was the woman who was just here?"

"That's right."

"Ms. Yeager, I wouldn't be talking about crimes if I were you. Stealing passports, forgery, treason, kidnapping . . . If you ever go back to the states you may wind up spending the rest of your life in a cell."

"You're Grafton, aren't you?"

Jake nodded.

"I've nothing to say, so get out."

"Or what? You'll call the police?"

She merely glared at him.

"Perhaps you'll call Sonny Wong and he'll send someone over to run me off. There's the phone—call anyone you like."

He sat in the chair facing her.

"Bastard."

"Where's my wife?"

"I don't know." Yeager hitched her bottom back in the chair and looked obstinately away.

Jake Grafton tried to hold his temper, which was getting more and more difficult. If Yeager only knew. "My wife has been kidnapped," he explained patiently. "Her life is at stake. I think you know a great deal about Sonny Wong, where he can be found, where he stays, where his men operate from. I want to know all that. I'm not going to tell anyone what you tell me. I won't report it to the United States government. It'll be strictly between us, absolutely confidential."

She turned to face him again. "You're an officer in the United States navy. You can't touch me. *I know my rights!* I have nothing to say!"

He pulled the Colt .45 from under his sports jacket, pointed it at her head, and thumbed off the safety. As she blanched, he turned the muzzle a few inches and pulled the trigger. The report was like an explosion, overpowering in that enclosed space. The bullet smacked into the wall behind her.

He leaped for her, grabbed a handful of hair, put the muzzle against her nose.

"Your rights don't mean shit! Where is my wife, goddamn it?"

She swallowed hard. "I don't know." That came out a squeak.

"We're having a revolution in Hong Kong, Ms. Yeager. The police have crawled into holes and the army has its hands full. No one cares about you. I can break every bone in your miserable body. I can shoot you full of holes and leave you here to bleed to death and nobody on this green earth will give a good goddamn. Now I'm going to ask you one more time, and if you give the wrong answer, we're going to find out how many bullets it takes to kill you. *Where is my wife?*"

Elizabeth Yeager's eyes got big as half-dollars and the color drained from her face. She tried to speak; the words came out a croak. Then she passed out cold. At first Jake thought she was faking it, but she went limp as linguine.

"Shit!" said Jake Grafton, more than a little disgusted with himself. Scaring a woman half to death.

"Shit," he said again, and released his hold on Yeager. She slid off the chair onto the floor like a bundle of old rags.

He kicked the coffee table. It skittered away.

He had his chance last night. He should have stuck that revolver up Wong's nose and told him he was going to blow his fucking head off if he didn't produce Callie in a quarter of an hour.

Yeah.

He slammed the door to the apartment on his way out.

He had the taxi take him back to the consulate so he could watch the revolution on television. Since Cole had submitted his resignation and was technically no longer an employee of the United States government, Grafton probably shouldn't be in his office. In any event, no one had suggested he leave. He turned on the television and settled behind Cole's desk.

The thought that he should be doing something to find Callie gnawed at him. Just what that something was he didn't know.

When the time came, Sonny would produce Wu and Callie to collect his money, but once he got it, he had to kill them all. Wu, Callie, Jake, Cole, everyone who had firsthand knowledge of the kidnapping. If he didn't he was a dead man.

Sonny Wong would have enough shooters in the area to ensure no one escaped. You could bet your life on that.

Jake's thoughts wandered. Callie had a brother in Chicago, married with two kids in college. Her mother was in an independent living facility near her brother, and her father was dead.

Her father had spent his career on the faculty at the University of Chicago. Professor McKenzie. What a piece of work he was! It wasn't that the old man believed in Marxism, with its dubious theories of social change and mind-numbing economic twaddle—the feature he liked was the dictatorship of the elite. The professor was an intellectual snob. The great failing of the common man, in McKenzie's opinion, was that he was common.

Jake wondered just what the prof would have thought of the collapse of communism all over the world.

He snapped off the television and sat down behind the consul general's desk in the padded leather executive chair that usually held Tiger Cole's skinny rump. There was a yellow legal pad on the desk, so he helped himself to a pen and began writing a report to the National Security staff on the situation in Hong Kong. Fortunately the consulate had radio communications with the State Department, so the staff could encrypt the report and put it on the air as soon as Jake finished it.

He was scrawling away when the secretary stuck his head in. "Ahh . . . Admiral." He frowned, perhaps offended that Jake was using Cole's office.

"Yes," Jake replied, and kept going on the sentence he was writing.

"There's a telephone call, sir. Mr. Carmellini."

Jake picked up the instrument. "Grafton."

"Carmellini, Admiral. I'm over here at Kerry Kent's apartment checking her cupboard. It seems she has a sizable stock portfolio somewhere."

Jake stopped writing. He had the telephone in a death grip. "Tell me about it."

Carmellini did. He gave Jake the names of the companies he thought she owned shares in, the number of shares, and the values. He also gave Jake the information on the seventh stock, though he didn't know the name of the company.

"Anything else?" Jake asked.

"That's about it, unless you are interested in the brands of her clothes."

"Should I be?"

"Well, they strike me as expensive duds, better than I am used to seeing on government employees, but she's British and a hell of a lot richer than me. . . ."

"Better come on back to the consulate."

"Is the ferry still running? I know the subway is dead and the tunnel is closed."

"Hire or steal a boat," Jake said, and hung up.

He pushed the intercom button to summon the secretary. When he appeared, Jake told him, "I want to call the Pentagon on the satellite phone."

"Those circuits are all in use by the staff, sir, for official business. They are giving the National Security Council and State real-time feeds on the situation here."

"Terrific. I want to use a line."

"Who are you, sir? Really? I mean, I know you are an admiral on active duty in the navy, but using the consul general's office and—"

"I don't have time for this," Jake snapped. "Get me a line, and now. After you do that you call the Secretary of State's office and complain to them."

The secretary was offended. "I'll have the call put through. You can use the phone on the desk. Wait until it rings."

Okay: China Bob Chan was smuggling money and high-tech war equipment into Hong Kong. And he was a conduit for Communist money being given or donated to American politicians in the hopes of getting favorable export licenses. Sonny Wong was a professional criminal with ties to criminal gangs all over China. Cole was an American agent supplying money and highly classified weapons systems to the rebels.

And Kerry Kent? A British SIS agent, either covertly assigned or playing hooky. Cole's weapons system operator, WSO, wizzo in U.S. Air Force terminology. Screwing the head rebel. With money in the bank . . .

Cole didn't trust China Bob, so a CIA agent bugged his office and was killed before he could retrieve the tape. Then somebody shot China Bob Chan, and the whole tangled skein became a mare's nest.

Callie listened to the tape and heard . . . nothing.

She heard hours of conversation, much of it one-sided because Chan was on the phone, and probably all of it relevant if one knew more about Chan's business . . . but not otherwise. For Callie it was just noise.

Then she was kidnapped.

Money?

Wong threatened Cole. Callie could convict him with her testimony, he said.

How would he know? He didn't hear the tape.

What if he were assuming the tape contained something it didn't? Ahhh . . . !

The phone rang.

Jake picked it up and found himself talking to the Pentagon war room duty officer. He identified himself and asked for Commander Tarkington.

Twenty seconds later Toad was on the line.

"Are you sleeping there?"

"Up in the office. I was down here loafing, hoping you'd call."

"Got a job for you."

"Yes, sir. Fire away."

Jake gave Toad all the information he had on Kent's stock portfolio. "This is a straw we are trying to build with," he told Toad. "See what the NSA computer sleuths can come up with. The account probably won't be under her name. I would think it's probably with a London brokerage or the Hong Kong office of a London brokerage. This woman may have had access to stolen American passports from this consulate. If she has contacts in the Hong Kong underworld, she may have passports from anywhere, genuine or faked." Jake gave Toad a physical description of Kent.

When Toad had finished writing down the description, he told his boss, "I've been talking to the CIA. They say SIS is well aware of Kent's status with the rebels, though they refuse to admit anything. Officially the Brits say they never even heard of her."

"Forget that. Find the money. Find where it came from. An inheritance, divorce settlement, whatever."

"Heard anything from Callie?"

"No."

"I asked for permission to come over there to help you, but the President nixed it. Said he doesn't want any military personnel going in-country for any reason."

"I figured he'd say that."

"I've talked to the chairman." The chairman of the Joint Chiefs, Toad meant. "We shouldn't have a problem getting cooperation. When I find out anything, I'll call you."

"I'll be sitting right here," Jake Grafton said.

At that moment Callie Grafton was telling Wu Tai Kwong, "We need an escape plan." She had inspected every inch of the small stateroom where they were being held, as well as the tiny bathroom. She had looked at the door hinges, the window, the air vent, the beds, and didn't have a glimmer of an idea.

"Yes," Wu agreed after a moment's reflection, "a plan would be good."

"Do you have any ideas?"

"No." Wu raised his hands, then lowered them. The sheet strips around his arm were blood-soaked, but the bleeding seemed to have stopped.

She found the situation infuriating. She balled up her fists and shook them. "I don't understand you. You say they will kill you, yet you don't seem to be worried. You aren't figuring out how to get out of here. You're just sitting there."

"What else is there to do?"

She made an exasperated noise. She had been married so long she judged all men by her husband. Jake Grafton wouldn't be sitting calmly, waiting for the inevitable. Not Jake. He would be scheming and planning until he drew his very last breath.

She missed him terribly.

"Figure a way to get us out of here," Callie told her fellow prisoner. "There must be a way. We're on a ship, a small one I think, docked I believe, maybe anchored. When they come for me again—or you—we'll both jump them. Fight, claw, do whatever we have to. Get out. Get free. Stay alive. Let's find something we can use as a weapon. Anything."

Wu waited a while before he spoke. He had that habit, she noticed, and she didn't much care for it. He said, "You would like my mother, I think. She is much like you. She struggles with life, seeks to conquer it."

"And you don't?"

"We all do to some degree. My mother more than me. You are more like her, I think."

"You are supposed to be a revolutionary. By definition, revolution is struggle."

"Quite so. I struggle to change the world as man has made it. But life? When the rain comes, it does not matter whether you welcome it or hate it—the rain falls upon your head regardless."

"Everyone dies, too," Callie said acidly. "I don't know about you, but I'm not ready. I have a lot of good years left in me. I'm not going to be robbed of life by some hoodlum, not if I can do anything to prevent it."

"That's the rub," Wu said softly. "Preventing it."

The Luda-class destroyer, Number 109, came steaming west through Victoria Strait between the island of Hong Kong and the Kowloon peninsula. She had been ordered by the commanding officer of the naval base to sortie immediately and shell the rebels in the Bank of the Orient square, pursuant to the orders of Governor Sun.

Lieutenant Tan was the officer of the deck when the order was received, and he protested. The commanding officer was not aboard, the ship was not ready for sea. His protests fell on deaf ears. "Sail with the men you have aboard and shell the rebels as ordered," the base commander said.

Of course, the base commander was having his own troubles. A riot had broken out in the enlisted mess hall, probably instigated by the rebels. The officers who attempted to turn off the base television system had been met with sticks and garbage pail lids. The rioting sailors were making threats against the officers' lives.

Actually two destroyers had sailed, but Number 105 had gone dead in the water with an engine room casualty before it cleared the base breakwater. Sabotage, Lieutenant Tan suspected, but he didn't say so with the quartermaster and helmsmen within earshot. These two were surly, doing their duty with the minimum acceptable professional courtesy. No doubt they sympathized with their rioting mates and perhaps with the rebels in the bank square.

Number 109 steamed on alone.

Lieutenant Tan began thinking about the professional problem he faced. The gun to use for surface bombardment was the twin 130-millimeter dual-purpose mount on the bow. There was a similar mount on the stern, but it was out of service for some critical parts.

The bow gun would do very well. Unfortunately in this ship the Sun Visor fire control radar that was designed for this gun was never mounted, so the gun had to be aimed visually. The gun had an effective range of eight or nine miles; that was no problem. In fact, the ship was within maximum gun range now.

The problem, Lieutenant Tan told himself as he stared at the chart of Hong Kong on the navigator's table, was going to be putting the shells into the square. He was going to have to lob them in with the gun elevated to a high angle. Maximum elevation angle was eighty-two degrees.

If he missed the square and started scattering 130-millimeter, 33.5-kilogram high-explosive shells around the downtown, there would be hell to pay later. Regardless of what they said now, the governor and base commander would want pieces of his hide then.

Of course the designated gunnery officer was not aboard. Lieutenant Tan was the only officer qualified to lay the gun, and he also had to con the ship.

He was so nervous his hands shook. He laid the chart on the table so it wouldn't rattle and consulted the range and elevation charts for the gun. Shooting at a hidden urban target was going to be a challenge, perhaps an impossible one.

He put the binoculars to his eyes and studied the buildings in the Central District. The ship was about five miles from the downtown, he estimated. Needless to say, the buildings did not appear on his chart of the area's waters. If he could remember which buildings were which . . .

He asked the helmsman for the speed.

"Eight knots, sir."

He was studying the chart, measuring, when he heard the lookout.

"Bogey on the starboard bow."

What?

"Jet airplane, sir, looks like he's lining us up for a low pass."

Lieutenant Tan looked.

A fighter, two of them. They were completing the turn to pass the length of the ship, bow to stern. Dropping down, one trailing the other, not going too quickly, maybe three hundred knots . . .

Suddenly he knew. "*Air attack!*" he screamed. "Open fire!"

Flashes on the wing root of the lead fighter . . . the water in front of the ship erupted. Quick as thought, the shells began pounding the ship, cutting, smashing.

The glass in the bridge windows shattered, the helmsman went down, shrapnel and metal flew everywhere.

The attack ended in a thunderous roar as the jet pulled out right over the ship, and the next fighter began shooting.

Screaming . . . someone was screaming amid the hammering of the cannon shells . . .

Fire! Smoke and flame.

When the shooting stopped, Lieutenant Tan tried to stand. The ship was turning to port, out of the channel. The helmsman was lying on the deck, his head gone. Tan spun the helm to center the rudder, bring the ship back under control.

"Arm the see-whiz," he shouted, meaning the CIWS, the close-in weapons system that the Chinese navy had purchased from the Americans.

Behind him he heard the talker repeat the order. The talker was huddled on the floor, bleeding badly from a wound that Tan couldn't see.

Tan looked aft. Something was burning, putting out smoke. He rang for full speed on the engine telegraph, a bell that was answered. The ship seemed to accelerate noticeably as the gas turbine engines responded.

The jets were on a downwind leg, high out to the right over Kowloon.

"Forward turret, fire at will at the enemy planes," Tan ordered. "CIWS on automatic fire."

This time as the planes dove, the ship was going faster, perhaps twelve knots. The forward turret opened fire unexpectedly. Of course the gun crew was shooting visually, using an artillery piece to shoot at a fly, but the noise and concussion helped steady Tan. He huddled down behind the helm station as the fighter's cannon shells slammed into the base of the mast and bridge area.

The noise had become beyond human endurance—the twin 130-millimeter mount was hammering off a shell every two seconds. There was a pause as the first jet roared overhead, then the gun began again. Despite that racket Tan clearly heard the chain-saw roar of the 20-millimeter Gatling gun of the Phalanx close-in weapons system when it lit off, spitting out fifty tungsten bullets per second.

Then, suddenly, the guns fell silent. Only the roar of a jet engine changing pitch, then nothing. Tan rushed to the side of the bridge in time to see a man ejecting from a stricken fighter. Then the fighter rolled inverted and dove into the choppy water of the strait.

Pulling out, climbing away after his second strafing run, Major Ma Chao also saw his wingman eject and the plane go into the water.

The destroyer was on fire, smoking badly from the area behind the bridge.

The crew would probably forget about the mission to shell the square as they fought to save the ship.

That was enough.

Ma Chao's commanding officer had a bullet hole in a lung, and one of the squadron's planes had been shot down—status of the pilot unknown.

And so we begin.

"A good beginning." Rip Buckingham used those words as the title for the story he wrote for the Buckingham newspapers. He told the story as completely as he could, leaving out the Sergeant York robots, concluding with the surrender of General Moon Hok in the bank square. When the story was finished he printed it out, then went to his den. He had an antique cabinet in one corner, one that he hinted to the maid contained liquor, which was why he kept it locked.

Inside the cabinet was a shortwave radio, an unlicensed ham set, the existence of which was unknown to the Chinese authorities.

Rip plugged the radio into a wall socket and connected the antenna lead. He used the wire that held up the awning on the roof patio for an antenna. Rip checked the time and ensured that the radio was tuned to the proper frequency.

He plugged in a hand microphone, then pushed the key and transmitted. "Hey, Joe? You there?"

"I'm here."

"Got a story for you."

"Wait until I get a pen and paper."

The man who monitored the radio would take down the story in shorthand, transcribe it, and send it via E-mail to Rip's father, Richard. Tomorrow it would be in the Buckingham newspapers worldwide.

"I'm ready."

"Okay," Rip said, and began reading aloud.

The televised celebration in the bank square was still going on hours after General Moon's surrender. Jake Grafton wondered why the giant block party had gone on so long because he knew that Cole and the rebels must prepare for the next battle, the real Battle of Hong Kong. What he didn't realize was that the rebels had lost control of the crowd. It was now a mob.

Beyond the range of the television cameras, the mob began seeping away down the side streets, flowing toward City Hall, which was on the waterfront.

The four policemen in front of City Hall stood their ground when the rioters first appeared by the dozens. By the time the crowd numbered several hundred, they were nervous. Not a single soldier was in sight.

As the crowd swelled into the thousands and began packing the streets, the four policemen walked away. They merely took off their hats and gloves and walked off into the crowd.

The jets diving on destroyer 109 and the thunder of the guns galvanized the crowd, which had a ringside seat. When the pilot of one of the jets ejected the crowd fell silent, but when the destroyer, smoking badly and in obvious distress, turned and limped away to the east, the crowd cheered wildly.

As fishing boats along the shore rushed to rescue the pilot in the water, the television helicopter circled low over City Hall, transmitting the scene to the station on Victoria Peak, which broadcast it. Television stations in at least a dozen southern Chinese cities were still retransmitting the broadcast. Pictures of the mob around City Hall and the wounded destroyer retreating after an aerial attack, accompanied by Peter Po's professional voice-over, stunned audiences that had been allowed to hear nothing of the civil troubles in Hong Kong.

An hour and a half into the pirate show the mob stormed City Hall. No one led it, no one advocated it, it just happened.

Governor Sun was not there, of course, but three prominent Communists were. One was a Beijing appointee to the Court of Appeals, the other two were officials in the government of the Hong Kong Special Administrative Region. All three were dragged out of City Hall and beaten to death in the street as the camera filmed it from a hundred feet overhead.

Hu Chiang, Cole, Kerry Kent, and the rebel leaders were holding a council of war in the trailer in the alley when they were called to witness the storming of City Hall on television.

No one had much to say when they realized the crowd was beating the Communist officials to death.

"I hope the world gets a good look," Cole said to no one in particular.

"What do you mean?" Kent asked.

"That mob has just driven a stake through the argument that the Chinese are happier and better off under communism. We've heard the last of that crap."

The defeat of Moon Hok meant that the PLA had to temporarily abandon all hope of reinforcing its forces on Hong Kong Island. PLA radio traffic revealed that they were well aware that the Cross-Harbor Tunnel was in rebel hands.

The New Territories garrison was frantically appealing to Beijing for help. The government had plenty of problems of its own, most of which had been created by Cole's cybertroops. Still, given enough time the Communists would move additional troops from mainland China to Hong Kong. Eventually overwhelming military power would be brought to bear on the rebellious population of the former British colony. Obviously the rebels could not allow time to become their enemy's ally.

"We are in a life-or-death struggle," Hu Chiang told the rebel leaders when they gathered again around the map of Hong Kong mounted on the wall of the trailer. "We must never lose sight of that fact even for a moment, or all is lost.

"As we speak the PLA is constructing fortified positions and strong points beyond our perimeter at the tunnel exit. Our watchers report that tanks are being arranged as a defense in depth.

"Despite this, we still expect the PLA to assault the tunnel entrance to see how strongly it is held. If the resistance is weak, we anticipate they will press until we crack. On the other hand, should resistance be stronger than anticipated, we believe they will drop back and wait for us to shatter ourselves on their strong points."

Hu Chiang paused here, surveyed the faces of his audience. "The government in Beijing is pressing the local commanders for immediate action. The Communists see the revolt in Hong Kong as a political disaster that must be crushed before it spreads. Nor can we afford to wait. The government has an overwhelming military advantage and given enough time to marshal its forces, would crush us. We must convince the Communists that the real crisis is political, induce them to rush into action and fail to properly employ their military advantage.

"The fighter squadron at Lantau will keep the Chinese air force and navy off us for a few hours. While we enjoy air superiority, we will attack. Tonight, as planned."

No one objected.

"Let us proceed," Hu Chiang continued. "The York units will be moved through the tunnel and take up hidden positions outside our perimeter." He indicated those on the map that hung behind him on the wall. "We have weapons for almost a thousand soldiers now, counting those captured today. We have a dozen heavy machine guns and several trucks full of tear gas canisters, if we need it.

"We are organizing our supporters into military units and using these units to reinforce our tunnel perimeter in Kowloon. When we are ready to push our entire force through the tunnel, we will open our assault by attacking the strong points with the York units. Are there any questions?"

Cole broke the silence. "The PLA might attack before we are ready."

"They could. If a fireball like Wu Tai Kwong were leading them, they would. Fortunately, the division commander is dead and the deputy commander is our prisoner. I listened to their radio traffic, and I did not sense a burning desire to fight. They are being ordered to fight. Beijing is making dire threats."

"How would you characterize the morale of the common soldier?"

Hu Chiang paused a moment before he spoke. "We have interrogated some of the soldiers captured this afternoon. They are not Communists. They want the same things every Chinese person wants—a job, money to feed and raise a family, a better life. Make no mistake, many will fight fiercely, and others will refuse to fight or defect. We hope the Sergeant York units sapped some of their fighting ardor. They are confused. Too much has happened too quickly."

Cole grinned, and so did the others. "Let's keep them confused, shall we?"

For Jake Grafton the tension was nearly unbearable, the waiting hell. Soon the sun would go down behind Victoria Peak and all of the Central District would be in shadow.

He paced like a caged lion and paid partial attention to the television while he worried about Callie. Was she still alive? Would Sonny Wong release her tomorrow when Cole paid off? Was hunting her tonight the right thing to do?

When Tommy Carmellini knocked on the consul general's office door, Jake waved at him to come in. He sat on the couch.

"Did you swim the strait or what?"

"I persuaded a ferry captain to bring a whole boatload of folks over, kids wanting to enlist, mostly."

"Did you bribe him?"

"A little bit. I think he would have done it for nothing, but I wanted him to have some drinking money."

"Have you been through her desk and files downstairs?"

"A cursory look, yes."

"Go look again. I want to know everything there is to know about that woman."

Fifteen minutes later the telephone rang, and Jake jumped for it. Almost two hours had passed since he spoke to his aide, Toad Tarkington, in America over the satellite circuits.

"Grafton." He spit out the word.

"You were right, Admiral," Toad said with triumph in his voice. "There is an account belonging to an American woman, same age and physical description as Kent, at the Hong Kong office of a London brokerage. Turns out the American woman has been dead for six months, but her passport has never been turned in."

"How'd she die?"

"Traffic accident in Hong Kong."

"Her name?"

"Patricia Corso Parma." Toad spelled it, gave Jake the social security number, date of birth, and passport number. "She may be dead, but she opened the account four months ago and has been depositing money in hundred-thousand-American-dollar chunks."

"The way I figure this," Jake said, "Kerry Kent is somehow tied in with Sonny Wong. He's the guy who kidnapped Callie and Wu Tai Kwong, the rebel leader. I'm going to sweat her, see if she knows where Wong might be holding Callie. If she doesn't know, she might know somebody who does."

"Okay, boss," Toad said.

Jake looked up and realized that Tommy Carmellini was standing near the desk, looking out the window. He must have just reentered the room.

"If anything happens to me," Jake said into the telephone, "I want you to make damned sure Wong and Kent don't have fun spending any of this money. Have the CIA screw with their bank records. Okay?"

"You got it, boss," the Toad-man replied. "But you be careful, will ya?"

"Yeah."

"When you see Callie, tell her that she's been in my thoughts, mine and Rita's."

"Yeah."

"Take care," was Toad's good-bye.

When Jake replaced the telephone on its cradle, Carmellini tossed a passport on the desk in front of Jake. American, with the blue cover. He opened it. Patricia Corso Parma. Staring at him from the page, however, was an excellent picture of Kerry Kent.

"Where did you find this?"

"Taped inside the air return ducting in Kent's cube, downstairs. I found a screwdriver in her desk and went looking for something to unscrew."

CHAPTER SEVENTEEN

"We need to talk," Jake said to Tiger Cole. He and Carmellini had just gotten through two circles of armed guards around the museum exhibit trailer and had been allowed to enter. Cole was watching the video from the York units, which were being positioned in preselected hiding places in Kowloon. Kent was at the main control panel. Beside her sat a Chinese student from Hong Kong University whom Cole thought brilliant.

"Give me two more minutes," Cole said.

"Where are you putting those things?"

Cole kept his eyes on the computer monitors. "In shops and basements, just getting them out of sight."

"This will be the acid test, huh?"

"They were designed for night fighting in urban areas. The official designation is AVSPU, for Assault Vehicle, Self-Propelled, Urban. The army put them in a class with hummers and armored personnel carriers."

When the last York was in place, Cole turned to Jake. "What can I do you for?"

"A short talk with you and Ms. Kent. Got a private place?"

"There's a tiny office at the end of this trailer."

"That'll do."

Cole spoke to Kent, and she got up from the control panel and followed Cole and Jake. Carmellini hung back, then followed her.

She glanced around at him, didn't say anything. She was wearing tennis shoes, jeans, and a pullover today; Carmellini had never seen her in anything but a dress or skirt. Her abundant hair was pulled back in a ponytail, making her look like the girl next door.

The office was small, with just a desk and two chairs. Jake snagged one and motioned Kent into the other. Cole stood. Carmellini waited until the door closed on the three of them, then went looking for Kent's purse.

Jake laid the passport on the small desk. "Explain this," he said to Kerry Kent.

She didn't reach for it. Jake passed it to Cole, who opened it, flipped through it, then tossed it back on the desk.

She nipped on her lower lip, but not a trace of emotion showed on her face.

After about ten seconds, she reached for the passport. She spent at least half a minute examining it, then laid it back on the desk.

"I never saw it before," she said.

"Wrong answer," Jake Grafton said sourly. "I know a lot and can guess at a lot more. Believe me, your future depends on how clean you come, right now."

"I'm a British citizen. I work for the SIS. I don't have to tell you anything."

"Another wrong answer," Jake said.

They were interrupted by a knock on the door. Cole opened it and Carmellini passed in a shoulder purse. Cole made room for him.

With another glance at Kent, Jake opened the purse, looked in. "Aha." From its depths he removed a Derringer, a small two-barrel single-action .22 caliber. "Would you look at this."

He opened the action. Loaded. Snapped it shut and passed it to Cole. "Want to talk now?"

"Why?" she said. "You don't know anything."

"You should have gotten rid of the gun. Do the British still hang people?"

"It was given to me."

"By whom?"

"Wu Tai Kwong."

"Wrong answer again. How about Sonny Wong?"

She leaned back in her chair and looked in every face. "You don't have proof of anything," she said. "Carmellini must have planted that gun in my purse."

Jake stood. "Tommy, stay here with Ms. Kent. Don't let her touch anything, call anyone, speak to anyone. We'll be back."

He walked through the door and Cole followed him.

"What was it about the pistol?" Cole asked as they walked to the York control console.

"Wasn't that CIA agent, Harold Barnes, shot with a twenty-two?"

A look of surprise crossed Cole's face. "I can't recall."

"I can," Jake Grafton said. He paused behind the York master control panel. "I read the report. Twenty-two slug at point-blank range above the right ear. The Hong Kong police turned the bullet over to the FBI."

"Kent?" He sounded skeptical.

"Perhaps. I'm guessing, but it fits. Now tell me, what would happen if someone changed some of the lines of the code that the Yorks use to separate the good guys from the bad guys?"

Cole pursed his lips thoughtfully. He went over to the keyboard and began typing. He spent two minutes studying lines of software code. "Looks okay," he muttered and came back to the control menu.

"But if one of the Yorks started shooting our guys, I would see it. I'm right here."

"That problem could be easily solved with a bullet."

"We've got to trust people," Cole responded. "There's no other way to do it."

"Wake up, Tiger. Kerry Kent and Sonny Wong aren't on the same sheet of music that you and Wu have been singing from. A wise man surrounds himself with people he trusts and checks on 'em constantly."

"You're right, of course."

"Where's your television helicopter?" Jake asked. "You and I need to take a ride."

"It's back at the TV station. The PLA would gladly pot it over Kowloon tonight."

"Call the station and have the pilot fly it down here. You and I need to borrow it."

"Want to tell me what's going on?"

"Not yet. Like she said, we need some proof. Call the station and get us a chopper."

The helicopter, a Bell 206 JetRanger, landed in the street. The pilot was a small man in his mid-twenties. As the chopper was making its approach, Jake turned to Tiger Cole and said, "We better take assault rifles, just in case."

"Okay." He borrowed rifles from two of the men guarding the trailer.

The pilot flew the helicopter between the office towers of Victoria, then dropped to fifteen feet above the waters of the strait. They flew over the trucks and armed rebels who were guarding the tunnel and kept going. Cole pointed to a building, and the pilot slowed to a hover over the street in front of it. He let the chopper descend straight down, cushioning it at the bottom, until the skids kissed. Cole got out and led the way.

They were in front of a laundry. Not many civilians around, although heads peered out windows all along the block. With Cole leading, the two men went through the laundry, out the back, and down an alley. Forty feet or so down the alley, they knocked on a back door. It opened a crack.

Cole said something in Chinese, and the door opened.

A York unit, Alvin, stood near the front of the building, which was a shoe shop. A curtain hung between it and the shop door. It stood facing the curtain, a belt-fed machine gun in its hands and an electric cord hanging from its back. "We're charging the battery," Cole explained, gesturing at the cord.

"Yeah. Are there any access panels on this thing?"

"Yes. Three, actually. One in his abdomen under the UWB radar, one in his back above the electrical socket, and one in the back of his head."

"Open 'em up. Let's take a look."

Cole didn't hesitate. From a trouser pocket he produced a small cloth bundle. He unrolled it, revealing four tools. One looked to Jake like a plain Phillips screwdriver. Cole used it to open the panels.

From his shirt pocket he produced a penlight. "This is a regular flashlight or a red-light laser. I use it to check the sensors. Use the white light." He showed Jake the control.

Jake peered into the back of Alvin's head. It was full of wires, contacts, and component connections. "Take a look," Jake told Cole and held the penlight for him.

"What are we looking for?"

"Anything that isn't supposed to be there."

"Looks okay to me."

"Next panel."

Of course, they found what they were looking for in the last panel, the one on the abdomen. Cole almost missed it. A tiny bare wire, no more than an inch long, protruded from the top of a solid black plug-in component.

Cole used his fingers to remove the connection, then began tugging on the bare wire. It turned out to be six inches long, a small antenna, and was connected to a small radio receiver, a AAA battery, and a blasting cap buried in about three ounces of malleable plastique explosive.

"A bomb."

"If it went off, what would it do?"

"Destroy the main power supply. The York will just stop, wherever it is. Think Kent did this?"

"She had access and motive."

"How did you know it was here?"

"Someone paid Kent a lot of money in the last four months," Jake replied. "A million and a half pounds. I'm betting it was Sonny Wong. He then kidnapped Wu and Callie and demanded fifty million American from you and ten from Rip, Wu's brother-in-law. He's your security chief, and he's dirty."

Cole used a pocketknife to cut the wires leading to the head of the blasting cap, which protruded from the plastique.

Jake continued. "Either Sonny Wong is going to kill you, Wu Tai Kwong, and the folks loyal to Wu, then take over the rebellion and lead it himself, or he sold the rebellion to the Communists. They pay him, he wipes out the rebel leadership—at a profit, which he pockets— and disables the Yorks. The PLA defeats the rebel army and hangs a couple hundred traitors as an example to everyone. Voilà! everything is once again copacetic in Communist heaven."

"We've kept a tight rein on everything."

"You're planning a goddamn revolution involving hundreds—for all

I know thousands, maybe tens of thousands—of people all over China and you think the Communist leadership didn't get wind of it? Maybe in Oz, baby, but not in the real world. Hell, man, the folks in Silicon Valley are selling high-tech secrets to anyone with money. You know that! Cash is king! Sonny Wong may be a patriot, but he can be bought. Kent's a chippie; you could buy her for pocket change."

"Okay, okay." Cole shook his head. "Yeah. Okay."

"You better visit all these Yorks and see what Ms. Kent was up to in her spare time. I'll take the chopper back to the barn and have a little chat with our lady friend from SIS."

"Okay," Cole said. "Send the chopper back for me. I'll meet him where it is."

"Give me the bomb." Jake held out his hand. Cole handed it to him. "When you get back, Carmellini and I are going to need some weapons. What have you guys got in inventory?"

"A little bit of everything for the Yorks."

"I need two silenced submachine guns, a couple of silenced pistols, and two fighting knives."

"You going to get Kent to tell you where Callie is?"

"Uh-huh."

"Don't do anything you'll regret."

"I intend to get my wife back alive," Jake Grafton said. "Whatever happens to anybody who gets in the way is their tough luck."

Tommy Carmellini and Kerry Kent were still seated in the small office at the end of the museum exhibit trailer. "Any problem?" Jake asked.

"She offered me some money."

Kent was staring at a spot on the wall, her face a mask.

"Anybody talk to her, she talk to anybody?"

"No, sir."

Carmellini got out of the chair and Jake sat. "I don't have a lot of time," he said to Kent. "I'm not going to fool around. I want the truth and I want it now."

She didn't say a word.

"You understand that you're never going to see a dollar of that money. It's history. Forget about it. The SIS will confiscate the account. What we're talking about now is your life."

Jake Grafton leaned forward and stared across the desk into Kerry Kent's eyes. In spite of herself, she found she couldn't look away. "Tell me where my wife is. If I get her back safe and sound, you live. If I don't, you die. It's that simple."

She said nothing.

"Carmellini," Jake said. "Get me a roll of duct tape."

The CIA officer went through the door.

Almost too quickly for the eye to follow, Kent lashed out at Jake Grafton's throat with the cutting edge of her hand. Jake took the blow on his forehead and went for her with both hands. He got his left hand around her neck, his thumb on her windpipe, and squeezed for all he was worth while he used his right to pop her hard in the nose.

Cartilage shattered and blood spattered everywhere.

The fight went out of her. Grafton released his grip.

She sat dazed, bleeding freely, then her eyes focused again.

She held her shirttail to her nose, exposing her bra. Jake didn't take his eyes off her. Amazingly, he felt better.

"Asshole," she hissed. "Hitting a woman."

Carmellini opened the door, then paused. Jake stood up and took the tape.

"We'll tape her to this chair. Put her in it."

That didn't take much wrestling. Jake began wrapping tape around her. "Put her hands behind her."

"What about her nose?"

"Never heard of anyone dying of nosebleed. If she croaks we'll put her in the medical textbooks."

Kent screamed. Jake punched her again, medium hard, and she stopped.

"One more time," he told her. "I enjoyed that."

He used almost the whole roll of tape on her. "Now," he said, removing the bomb that had been in Alvin York from his pocket. "Here's how we're going to do this. You are going to tell me where my wife is, and Mr. Carmellini and I will go get her. If we return with Mrs. Grafton, we'll come in here and disarm this bomb. If we don't return . . . well, I guess you'll die when Sonny pushes the button to pop the Sergeant Yorks."

Carefully, with her watching, he twisted the wires that ran to the blasting cap back together. "There."

"You're an American naval officer," she whispered. "You can't do this to me."

"Everyone keeps telling me that. Actually, I was thinking of taping this bomb to your head. What do you think, Tommy?"

"Asshole," she hissed. The blood covered her mouth and shirt. She was a hell of a mess.

"Get the WB phone out of her bag."

Carmellini did as he was told.

"I doubt if she memorized the phone number. Look for something with phone numbers written on it, a little pad, her checkbook, anything."

Kent's eyes widened.

"You were supposed to blow the Yorks with the cell phone, weren't you?"

She lost control of her face.

Jake continued. "We'll just tape the bomb to your head. If anything happens to Callie, I'll call you. How's that?"

Her eyes narrowed. She wiped the blood on her mouth off onto her shoulder.

"She doesn't think you'll really kill her," Carmellini said.

"I won't have to," Jake told him. "All I have to do is tell these people how she betrayed Wu and them. If Wu dies, she won't live another ten minutes. They'll kill her with their bare hands."

Her head was down now. Blood still flowed from her nose.

"He's holding them on a yacht, the *China Rose*." Her voice was a husky whisper. "It's at the Kowloon docks."

Jake Grafton lifted her head. He looked straight into her eyes. "You'd better pray we find them alive and get back here. Without me you're dead. Understand?"

They put tape over her mouth and punched a small hole in it so she could breathe. Then they left her, locking the door behind them.

"Sorry about that," Jake said to Tommy Carmellini as he used a rag to wipe blood from his hands. "When you left the room she turned wildcat, so I punched her in the nose."

"Glad it was you and not me. I knew Harold Barnes. He didn't deserve what he got."

"Cole is going to give me some weapons. I don't know what is on that ship. Maybe two people, maybe fifty. You want to come along?"

"Yeah."

"Ain't in your job description. When you're dead the story is all over; the movie ends right there. If you've got a woman somewhere and big plans, I understand."

Carmellini shrugged. "Going places people don't want me to go is what I do."

Jake tossed the bloody rag in a corner. "I'm going to kill anybody who gets in my way," he said. "No questions asked, no hesitation."

Carmellini glanced at the closed office door. "And Kerry Kent gets off with a busted nose."

"Oh, I doubt it," Jake said, sighing. He gestured to the people conferring in front of the map and checking the computer monitors. "She betrayed these people. If they don't kill her, Wu Tai Kwong will."

When the helo brought Tiger Cole back from Kowloon, he had five more small bombs with him. "Okay," he told Jake Grafton, "you've convinced me. She sold us out. There was a radio-controlled bomb in every one of the Yorks."

"Only one?"

"God, I hope so. I inspected them as carefully as I could. We could take them out of service for a week or so and disassemble each of them into a pile of parts and check every goddamn nut, bolt, and screw, but . . ."

"She says Callie and Wu are being held in a yacht tied up at the Kowloon docks."

"She being cooperative now?"

"That's probably not an accurate statement."

Cole snarled, "By God, I have a few things I'd like to ask her."

"Hey, she isn't going to tell you anything you don't already know. She did it for the money."

Virgil Cole shook his head, rubbed his eyes. "I just don't understand people like that. Maybe I've had too much money for too long. . . ."

"You were never that poor, believe me," Jake said. He handed Cole the sixth bomb.

"You said you wanted weapons?"

"And the use of your helicopter. I want to find this yacht before the light fades."

"Wong has a yacht?"

"Kent says he does. *China Rose*."

Cole's eyes lit up. "I've seen it! An older ship, steel, about two hundred and fifty, maybe three hundred feet long, with a little bridge and a massive salon aft. White with red trim." He looked at his watch. "The sun sets in about ten minutes. Go find that thing while I round up some weapons and clothes."

"Black."

"Today's your lucky day. Black is our uniform. I've got a truckful of black shirts and trousers. I'm trying to convince my friends that night is the time to fight."

Jake settled into the copilot's seat of the Bell and the pilot immediately lifted it into a hover. When he was above the power lines, the pilot eased the nose over and let the machine fly between the buildings toward the harbor.

They stayed low, the skids almost in the dark water, as they worked their way northwest up the Kowloon docks. Scanning the ships with binoculars, Jake fought down the sense of panic that welled up within him as the sun dipped below the horizon. Time was running out.

Coasters, tankers, container ships, tramps, fiber-optic cable layers . . . ships of every kind and description. They were Russian, Chinese, Japanese, Greek, American, and flag-of-convenience ships from all over the globe. Grafton hunted through them as the light faded slowly, inexorably.

Lin Pe worked her way along the nearly deserted streets of Kowloon. She was very tired and her feet dragged.

Unable to go farther, she sat on the sidewalk against a building, her bag clutched in her hand.

She had never seen the streets this empty. Those people who were out walked purposefully, determined, with quick glances up and down the street.

There were soldiers, of course. PLA trucks drove along the streets with soldiers sitting on the fenders, rifles in hand. At street corners soldiers directed traffic, waving civilian cars off the streets to make way for trucks.

And tanks.

Three tanks rumbled by Lin Pe, huge beasts with long, clumsy barrels protruding from their turrets. Their treads chewed up the pavement.

She got up and followed them, walking as quickly as she could. The tanks were faster than she was, but they didn't disappear from sight.

The three of them came to a halt at the intersection of Nathan and Waterloo roads. The intersection was about a mile north of the southern tip of the peninsula. One tank went through the intersection, then turned in the street. Gingerly the drivers maneuvered. One tank came to rest in the intersection, its nose and the cannon pointed south. One tank was parked on each side of the intersection, slightly back. The tankers on each flank pushed the barrels of their cannons through the glass windows of the corner buildings so they could also command the street and remain half hidden by the buildings. Two trucks stopped to discharge soldiers, who took up positions behind the tanks and the parked cars that lined the side streets.

Owners of parked cars came pouring from adjacent buildings. They scrambled to move their vehicles, some of which were already blocked in by the tanks. Shouting and pleading with the soldiers did no good. One officer pointed his rifle at several civilians and ordered them to leave. In seconds the last car that could be moved was gone, and the sidewalks were empty.

Lin Pe walked another block and found a store whose owner had yet to lock the door. He protested as she entered, but she insisted, talking loudly, refusing to leave. When the owner went back in the store to summon his wife, Lin Pe took out her WB cell phone and dialed the number she had memorized. It took her but thirty seconds to report the location of the tanks.

"Climb," Jake said to the helicopter pilot. He was desperate. There was little light left, and the *China Rose* was eluding him.

"If we climb the PLA may knock us out of the sky."

"Climb," Jake repeated, his voice hard and urgent.

The pilot hoisted the collective and the helo bounced upward; Jake fought against the downward G-force to hold the binoculars steady.

The pilot leveled at a thousand feet above the water. "Fly the whole waterfront again," Jake Grafton ordered, "especially the area by the amusement park."

But *China Rose* wasn't there. The haystack contained no needle.

Just when he was ready to admit defeat, he saw it.

"*There!*" He pointed. "Closer. Go closer."

The pilot turned the Bell and closed the distance.

Yes. There was just enough light to see the red trim, the small bridge, and the windows of the salon. A small boat hung on davits behind the stack. The yacht's name . . . he couldn't make it out. It must be *China Rose!*

The yacht—actually a small ship—was moored to a pier, the last of three large yachts on the north side. Three more were moored against the south side of the pier, which was at least two hundred yards long.

At the head of the pier stood a wire fence with a closed gate. On the quay itself were pallets of boxes, some Dumpsters, stacks of fifty-five-gallon drums, forklifts, trucks, some people walking. . . . Ocean-going general cargo ships were berthed at piers to the north and south.

"Over the quay." Grafton pointed out the direction he wanted to the pilot. He had to see how he was going to get onto the quay from the street.

In the last of the light he got his landmarks.

It was completely dark when he tapped the pilot on the shoulder and jerked a thumb toward Victoria. The helo turned and dropped the nose and accelerated out over the harbor. The pilot didn't turn on the exterior lights until he was approaching the shoreline of Hong Kong Island.

"Where did you see *China Rose?*" Jake Grafton asked Tiger Cole as they hunted through the clothes littering the floor of the truck for a pair of pants that might fit him.

"At a pier in Kowloon. Across from the yacht of a friend of mine, the *Barbary Coast.*"

"For Christ's sake, why didn't you say so two hours ago? I damned near didn't find it before the light faded."

"It just slipped my mind, until you asked. I saw it but paid little attention."

"Well, it's still there, on the end of a pier. If we had the time we could get a delivery truck, fake up some invoices, drive through the gate at the head of the pier and motor right up to Wong's gangway. No time, though. We gotta go as fast as we can get there."

"Why don't you land on my friend's yacht? Nikko Schoenauer. He's right across the pier. Has a helo pad on top of the salon."

"This guy German?"

"American as a hot dog."

"It must be nice having all these filthy rich friends."

"Nikko Schoenauer flew A-4s in Vietnam. He told me that he decided to get into a business that would always be popular, didn't pollute or use up scarce resources, with a product that people paid for with discretionary income, something nice to have but not necessary. His yacht's a whorehouse. He fills it with Japanese businessmen and sails off for weeklong parties and writes a fat check to a bank on the first of every month."

Jake glanced at Cole, who looked absolutely serious. "Whores 'n' More, eh? Tiger, you never cease to surprise me."

Jake pulled the shoulder holster containing the Colt on over the black shirt. Tommy Carmellini was waiting outside the truck with two silenced submachine guns and five magazines of ammo for each. He also produced a couple of marine fighting knives, one for each of them, and two sets of night-vision goggles. "First-class stuff," Jake said to Cole after he gave them a quick brief on the goggles.

Jake and Tommy put on the goggles, turned on the power. Idly Jake asked Tiger, "So you were visiting Schoenauer last week?"

"Yeah. The girls are kinda cute."

"I thought you were dating China Bob's sister?"

"Naw! China Bob was a snob. He wanted his sister married off to a decent husband. I was just another dude he was doing business with."

"Schoenauer's got a floating whorehouse, huh?" Carmellini asked. He had been standing outside the truck listening to Grafton and Cole.

"California girls mostly," Cole said. "They come and go. Refugees from suburbia and bad marriages. When they've gotten their batteries recharged, off they go back across the pond."

"Live in a yacht at the side of the road and be a friend of man."

"Something like that."

"We'll land on his boat and troop across the pier," Jake said, "if you don't think we'll be interrupting anything."

"I'm sure he won't mind," Tiger rejoined. "He can't get underway until he gets another load of clients, which won't happen until the airport reopens. Tell him I sent you."

Jake Grafton looked at his watch. "You ready?" he asked Tommy Carmellini.

"Yes, sir. Let's do it."

They stowed the weapons, ammo, and night-vision goggles in a drawstring bag, which they slung over their shoulders.

"When does the war start?" Jake asked Cole.

"In about two hours," Tiger replied, "unless the PLA kicks off the ball sooner."

"We'll be back by then," Jake muttered.

"Or dead," Carmellini added.

"You still got a handle on the electrical grid?"

"Yep."

"How about killing all power to that pier, or that area, in twenty minutes?"

"Sure. Hang tough, shipmate." Cole shook both their hands, then went back into the museum exhibit trailer.

"You scared?" Carmellini asked Jake as they walked to the helicopter, which was sitting in the street with the engine off.

"Hell, yes, I'm scared," Jake shot back. "That's a fool question. Why'd you ask it?"

"I wanted to make sure I wasn't the only one."

The helo pilot made sure both men were strapped in, then he pushed the starter, and the Bell's engine wound up with a whine.

Jake lied to Carmellini; he wasn't scared. He had been too busy worrying about Callie to be scared.

"Rip, Mother isn't here."

Rip Buckingham looked up from his PC. He was doing an in-depth piece on the revolution for the Buckingham Sunday editions.

"The maid said she left this morning and hasn't come back," Sue Lin said.

"Maybe she's at the cookie company."

"I called there. No one answers."

"Well . . ."

"Rip! She could be killed out there. If the government finds out she is Wu's mother, they'll throw her in prison. She'd die there. *Rip!*"

"For God's sake, Sue Lin, she's a grown woman, this is her town. She can take care of herself."

"But she can't!" Sue Lin sagged into a sitting position and began weeping. First her brother, now her mother. She was trying to be brave, but she just couldn't.

Rip cradled her head in his hands. "Sue Lin, your mother wanted to help. She wanted to be a part of what was happening."

"Why didn't you tell me? Why didn't you say no?"

"What right did I have to tell her no? She's Chinese—this is her country. These are her people."

"I'm your *wife*." She struck his hands away.

"Indeed. And it's time you realized that the future of China is more important than we are."

"What do you mean by that?"

"I mean it's time you realized that your happiness is not the most important thing in your mother's or brother's life."

"Is it the most important thing in your life, Rip? Answer me that."

"Don't ask me a foolish question, woman. You may not like the answer."

She rose from the floor and walked to the window. With her back to Rip she said, "You had no right to let her go without telling me."

"You would have said no. She wanted to go. What would you have me do?"

"If you love me, you will find my mother and bring her home."

He turned off the computer and stood. "You don't understand what love is. You think it is possessive, and it isn't. Sometimes you have to let go of the things you love the most."

He took a few steps toward her, then changed his mind. "I will try to find Lin Pe and help her do the job she volunteered to do. When it's over, if we're alive I'll bring her here."

Sue Lin didn't turn around.

He walked from the room and headed for the stairs.

———

This, Governor Sun Siu Ki thought, was without a doubt the worst afternoon of his life. His friends in Beijing had shouted, sworn, second-guessed, cajoled, and threatened him. He had been accused of being a dupe, a fool, a liar, and an incompetent imbecile. He tried to explain that the afternoon debacle was the fault of General Tang, now dead, and General Moon Hok, now a prisoner, but to no avail. The truth was that if those two soldiers had obeyed his orders to vigorously enforce the law and lay the wood to the outlaws, these riots would not have gotten out of control. They were afraid to use the military power the nation gave them. They were cowards.

Then the television showed the mob beating government officials to death. If that wasn't bad enough, the ministry in Beijing said that treasonous criminal spectacle had been seen by a large percentage of the urban population of China. It had even run on a television station in Beijing, the outraged minister told him, as if the failure of the media officials was Sun's fault.

So when his aide passed him a note saying Sonny Wong was on the phone, Sun Siu Ki was in a savage mood.

"Carrion-eater. Double-crosser. Traitor." He used all three of these phrases on Sonny when he picked up the telephone.

"Whoa, Governor. I know you're having a bad day, but there is a way out. I've told you that. I couldn't single-handedly stop these criminal combinations, but I can save the day."

"For money?"

"Of course, for money. I have a large organization that I support at my own expense, and we have done what the government could not—we have penetrated the rebel organization. Pay me the money and I will give you their heads."

"Beijing has not authorized the payment," Sun protested.

"I find their attitude beyond understanding. They are faced with a genuine rebellion that is getting worldwide press and inciting treason throughout China. The rebels are waging cyberwar against the nation. Government officals are being beaten to death by mobs, a spectacle played on every television on the planet"—this was only a small exaggeration—"and the government dithers over whether or not to pay me one hundred million American dollars to put a stop to all this. What are you people thinking?"

"Beijing has faith in the PLA," Sun explained. "Beijing is a long way from Hong Kong; from there they see the backs of ten million soldiers. Ten million soldiers are ten million soldiers. These traitors are causing huge problems, of course, but no ragtag mob is going to crush the PLA."

"You saw the robots on television today. Those robots are not a ragtag mob."

"Beijing was not impressed. You cannot extort money from them with movie props."

"Sun, you are as stupid as a snail. Wait until tonight. Tonight the robots will be in action. Tonight is the Battle of Hong Kong. When the PLA is losing, think of me. You know the telephone number." And Sonny hung up.

CHAPTER EIGHTEEN

Callie Grafton awoke with a start. She had been dozing, lost in despair, and suddenly she *knew*. The knowledge brought her wide awake. She sat up in her bunk.

"He's coming for me," she said to Wu, who was also awake. She said it first in English, then had to translate.

"Who is?" Wu asked.

"My husband. He is coming. I know it."

Wu didn't believe her, of course, but he had grown to like this strange American woman and her delicious accent.

"Us. He's coming for us." The faux pas of excluding Wu occurred to her now, and automatically she spoke again, correcting her error.

"How do you know he is coming?"

"I just know." She searched for words. "I can feel it. I can feel his presence, the fact that he is thinking of me, the fact that he is coming."

"Soon?"

"I do not know."

"Tell me of your husband," Wu said, to humor her.

Callie looked at him sharply. "You don't believe me and I don't expect you to, because I wouldn't if I were you. But Jake is coming. Perhaps I know it because I know the man."

She wrapped her arms around her legs. "All this time I have been worried because I didn't have an escape plan. Ha! I've got Jake Grafton."

"The knight in shining armor," Wu said.

"Laugh if you like. He'll come."

She was still sitting like that when they heard someone outside the door, then a key in the lock. Two men entered with weapons drawn.

"Come with us, Wu. Time to do some more work on your confession."

They handcuffed his hands behind him and took him away.

Two minutes later the key turned again.

The Russian, Yuri Daniel, stood in the open doorway looking at her. "You too, Mrs. Grafton. Your statement is ready to sign."

"I gave no statement."

"That wasn't a problem. I wrote it for you. Come."

Since he knew where he was going this time, the helicopter pilot kept the Bell JetRanger low, just above the water. He weaved around several junks and a fishing boat, then flew parallel to the coast for several miles. When he was on the extended centerline of the pier that held the *China Rose* and *Barbary Coast*, he turned for it.

"Wind's out of the north, a bit east," the pilot told Jake. "I'll land into the wind on the helo pad on the *Coast*."

"Yeah."

"Guns in or out?" Carmellini wanted to know.

"In the bags, I think. Don't want to scare 'em to death. But be ready, just in case."

The pilot kept the chopper so low that he actually had to climb to land on the *Barbary Coast*. A night landing on a tiny platform on a small ship, even one tied to a pier, was certainly not routine. The pilot's expertise was obvious.

As the helicopter settled onto its skids, Jake was looking across the pier at the *China Rose*. A few lights were on: on the bridge, over the gangway, and in a few of the portholes. The main salon aft was dark.

Safely on deck, the helicopter pilot shut down his engine. Jake and Carmellini got out, bags in hand.

Just in time to meet a man coming out the hatch from the bridge. He was about Jake's age, tan and graying.

"My name is Jake Grafton. Virgil Cole said you wouldn't mind if we landed on your boat."

When he heard Cole's name, the man extended his hand. "Name's Schoenauer. How long you going to be with us, Mr. Grafton?"

"Not long, I hope. Let's get off this weather deck and I'll explain."

Nikko Schoenauer led them to the bridge. He poured them coffee while Jake talked. Carmellini went straight to the pierside corner of the bridge and stood looking at *China Rose* through binoculars.

"Sonny Wong is rather a nefarious character, but this is the first time I've heard he indulged in kidnapping."

"I heard him ask for the ransom, so there is no doubt he's in it."

"I believe you, Mr. Grafton."

"It's Admiral Grafton," Carmellini said without turning around. "I'm just the civilian help."

Jake reached into his bag for the silenced submachine gun. "We're going over to get my wife back, if she's there. If it goes well, we'll return and ride the chopper off the pier. If it doesn't, friend Wong may pay you a visit."

"Hmm," Schoenauer said, looking at the submachine gun.

"If you have any weapons aboard, you might want to dig them out."

"Well, we do keep some old AKs, just in case we run into pirates. Pay off customs with a few bucks and they let us by. They know me, of course."

"Say, would you have any Vaseline and shoe polish around? Black shoe polish."

"I buy Vaseline by the quart. Shoe polish is another thing entirely— these days everyone wears tennis shoes—but I'll check."

While Schoenauer was gone the lights went out on *Barbary Coast, China Rose*, and the pier. In fact, the lights went off all along the waterfront.

Jake and Tommy got out their night-vision goggles and studied the *Rose*. "They had an electric eye rigged at the top of the gangway. Probably have a pressure pad too, so an alarm rings somewhere when you step on it. They're off until someone starts a generator."

"How many guys do you think?"

"I saw two before the lights went out. One was on the bridge. One walked along the main deck."

"I'd bet my pension there're more than two."

"Probably closer to twenty."

"Can we get aboard without using the gangway?"

"How about that stern mooring rope? It's in shadow. That'll be about it from the pier."

"Okay."

"I got this creepy feeling," Carmellini said, "that those sons of bitches know we're coming."

"Maybe. Just shoot first and it won't matter."

Schoenauer returned with two women. Jake couldn't tell much about them in the dark, but they were definitely Americans. He also had Vaseline and shoe polish. Jake smeared Vaseline over his face, neck, and hands, then applied the black shoe polish.

"Jake Grafton," one woman said as he smeared away. "It's a pleasure to meet you. Virgil told me about you. He said you were his very best friend on this earth."

Jake didn't know quite how to respond to that. "I'm sure he was just being polite."

"Oh, he didn't mean that he was your best friend, but that you were his, if that makes sense. He said you saved his life once."

"Long ago," Jake muttered, more than a little embarrassed.

"He said that Jake Grafton was the one man on this earth he would trust always to do the right thing, regardless of the stakes or the consequences."

Cole said all that? The crazy bastard!

"Hurry up," Jake urged Carmellini, who was also smearing himself with shoe polish. "They'll start an engine or generator to get power while we're standing here socializing."

As they were leaving, Carmellini asked Schoenauer, "You got an address or something where I can write to you?"

"Got a Web site," Schoenauer replied and told him the name.

"When I get some time off . . ."

They paused under a sheltered overhang on the main deck and used the night-vision goggles to check out *China Rose*. The small ship was dark, without a single light. Not even a battle lantern on the bridge. And no one was visible.

Due to the widespread power outage, only a glow of light from the sky enlivened the darkness.

"What if your wife isn't aboard?" Carmellini asked.

"We'll cross that bridge when we come to it," Jake said, trying not to panic. The CIA officer had hit squarely on the problem.

If she wasn't there, they would probably kill her unless he got to her quickly. And how would he ever find her in this city?

"So what do you want to do?" Carmellini asked.

"What I'd like to do is march straight across the pier and up the gangway and shoot anyone we meet, just go right on through them."

"Well, hell, why not?"

"Because we don't know where they are holding Callie or Wu, and Sonny Wong just might have someone guarding them with orders to kill them at the first sign of a commotion."

"Double ditto for Wu," Carmellini remarked. "Okay, what's your second option?"

"Walk down the gangway, turn right, go aft to their stern line, and up it. I'll climb it while you watch, then I'll watch while you climb. How's that?"

"I'll go first up the rope," Carmellini said. "I don't know what they told you about me, but sneaking around is my thing. I'm a burglar by trade."

"How in the world did you get in the CIA?"

"It was the CIA or prison. I'll tell you all about it sometime over a beer."

"Let's go," Jake said, and led the way down the gangway.

They walked along the pier, in no apparent haste, their weapons in bags over their shoulders. This was the most difficult part so far, Jake thought, as he willed his feet not to run.

When they reached the stern line bollard, Jake squatted behind it and donned the night-vision goggles. He saw no one on the *Rose*. Two people were visible on the bridge of the ship moored nose-to-stern of the *Rose*, but they didn't seem to be looking this way.

"Go," he whispered to Tommy Carmellini. The CIA officer already had the straps of his weapons bag over his shoulders, so he immediately crouched under the line, which was Manila hemp about three inches in diameter, and launched himself up it hand over hand. He kept his heels hooked over it behind him. In seconds he reached the rat guard, a platelike metal dish that surrounded the line and was supposed to constitute an insurmountable obstacle for rats trying to go up the line from the pier. Hanging on the line with one hand, Carmellini used the other to explore the catch that held the guard on the line, then release it. He dropped the guard in the water and continued up the line to the rail, grabbed it with both hands, swung a heel up, and clambered over.

Jake was taking his goggles off when the *China Rose*'s lights came on. The pier was still dark, as were the other ships. Someone had started an emergency generator, probably in the *Rose*'s engine room.

With the goggles back in the bag and the bag looped over his shoulders, Jake Grafton took a deep breath, then grabbed the line and swung out. As he suspected, the physical effort required was very high. Heart thudding, breathing like a racehorse, he was stymied by the rail and probably wouldn't have gotten over it if Carmellini hadn't grabbed him with hands like steel bands and literally lifted him over the rail onto the deck of the *Rose*. It was then Jake realized that Carmellini's buff physique was indeed rock-solid muscle; the thought had just not occurred to him before.

"You take the port side, work your way forward to the bridge," Jake whispered as they huddled out of sight under the rail. "I'll find a way down. Meet me below."

Carmellini's head bobbed.

Jake removed the submachine gun from his bag, made sure it was cocked and ready, then took the safety off. He pulled another magazine from the bag and held it against the forearm of the gun with his left hand. Carmellini already had his weapon in his hands. Now he went forward along the port side of the ship.

The little ship seemed deathly quiet. Almost too much so. Jake listened intently and heard the faint sounds of television. At least it sounded like television—a male voice, racing along in the up-and-down lilt of Chinese, allowing no breaks for conversation. He slipped up to the salon entrance and put his ear against the bulkhead.

A slight vibration—perhaps the generator?

He went forward along the starboard rail, walking as quietly as he could.

The first hatch he came to was a ladder down. He could hear television coming up the ladderway.

He looked down as much as he could without sticking his head down the hole. There didn't seem to be a passageway, so the ladder probably dropped right into a lounge of some kind. And that was where the people were.

Well, he could drop a grenade down the hole—he still had a couple the marines had given him—then go charging down after it went off, but everyone aboard would hear the explosion.

There had to be another way.

He walked on forward, looking for another ladder.

A lit cigarette arced out of the open bridge window toward the pier below. Tommy Carmellini saw it go and knew instantly what it was. The butt hit the concrete pier in a shower of tiny sparks.

He couldn't see the man who had tossed it. No, wait! He was walking in front of the open door at the top of the ladder. Now he was gone, back toward the helm in the center of the bridge.

Carmellini moved forward, almost a dark shadow.

He took a deep breath and exhaled slowly, silently.

You had to admit, this was living! Others could have the eight-hour days and houses in the suburbs; Carmellini liked living on the edge. He was certainly in his element now, although if he weren't very careful he could end up a corpse. That didn't worry him much. In fact, it added to the danger, so it added to the thrill.

He was thinking about the thrill when he got to the bridge ladder. He examined it for alarms, then experimentally put his weight on the lower step. Now the next.

The door at the top of the ladder was open, which Carmellini decided was a lucky break.

Or a trap.

He had had that feeling earlier, that they knew someone was coming. Was that just nerves?

Whatever, there was the open door, the dark bridge, and the man waiting up there.

He thought about sticking his head around the corner, then rejected that. If the man was expecting him, he would be in no position to shoot. He thought about jumping through the door, hoping he was faster on the draw. That option didn't seem so great, either. If the man was waiting for him he was dead meat.

Ah, I've watched too many movies, read too many thrillers. These guys are smugglers, thugs.

He decided to go in the third way, the tried-and-true Tommy Carmellini special way. He would sneak in, glacially slow, his weapon at the ready. And shoot the smuggler dude when he got a shot.

Up the last step, ever so carefully, weight balanced, weapon in left hand, so the barrel went around the edge at the same instant the eye passed it. . . .

There he was, by the navigator's table on the far side, bent over something. . . .

Slow as melting ice, Tommy Carmellini stepped onto the bridge, the gun leveled, his finger on the trigger. Carefully, purposefully, he scanned his eyes to ensure there was no one else on the bridge.

Just the one man.

Shoot him now or move closer?

Less chance to break a window with the bullets if I get closer.

Step . . . step . . .

Close enough. Sorry, pal!

He pulled the trigger. The gun coughed a short burst. Three shots in the lower back, to ensure he didn't punch one through the bridge window, breaking glass.

The man half turned and fell. Carmellini stepped forward to shoot him again in the head to finish it.

Something smashed him across the arms, ripping the gun from his grasp. His arms were numb! He couldn't feel his hands.

Another blow, this time across the back. The bag containing the night-vision goggles and spare ammo helped cushion the blow, but still he fell forward, sprawling on the deck. There was a room off the bridge, the captain's cabin. This guy must have been there!

"That twit!" a man's voice said conversationally. "I told him you'd be along sooner or later, and the fool wouldn't listen." The lights snapped on.

That voice . . .

"I heard about you, Carmellini. Harold Barnes told me."

Carson Eisenberg.

Another mighty blow across the shoulders. A pipe or a baseball bat. Eisenberg smashed Tommy across the ribs, over the head, almost broke his arm when he raised it to protect himself.

Carson Eisenberg was going to kill him. He was going to beat him to death with the pipe.

"You . . . cost . . . me . . . my . . . life . . . fucker!" Eisenberg accented every word with a blow.

Tommy Carmellini fell to the floor, reached for the gun, but his hands were too numb to hold it.

Whack! *"Bastard!"*

Desperate, Carmellini lashed out with a foot. And caught Eisenberg on a knee.

The ex–CIA officer lost his balance, and the pipe made a metallic ring as it struck something.

The knife! Carmellini realized he had it on his belt! Could he hold it with his numb hands?

He forced his right hand to curl around the handle. He got it out of the scabbard. And lost it.

Eisenberg was trying to scramble up from the deck. Carmellini kicked him again, this time with more force behind it. And again. Now Carmellini levered himself erect and aimed a kick at the man's chin.

He caught Eisenberg with his head coming forward and bobbing down as he prepared to shift his weight aft, over his legs. Eisenberg's head snapped back from the force of the kick. He went over backward and lay still.

Sobbing, Carmellini sank to his knees. His hands . . . he kneaded one with the other, felt along the forearms where the pipe had struck him. It was a miracle bones weren't broken. His shoulders, ribs, on fire . . . Eisenberg had given him a hell of a beating.

Can't stay here. . . . Gotta get the gun, get the knife, move on. To stay here is to die. Can't stay, can't stay, can't stay. . . .

He got the gun in both hands, checked it over as well as he could, then picked up the knife.

His forearms felt like they were broken, but they weren't.

Carson Eisenberg lay absolutely still, the back of his head touching his spine, his eyes open wide.

Carmellini wiped his eyes on his sleeve, smearing shoe polish, Vaseline, and blood, and staggered to the bridge door.

There was a light switch on the bulkhead, and he snapped it off. He waited until his eyes adjusted to the gloom before he stuck his head around the bulkhead and looked at the deck below.

Empty.

Where was Grafton?

The blood flowing from Kerry Kent's smashed nose gradually slowed to a drip. Her shirt and jeans were covered with it. She was thinking of all the things she would like to do to Jake Grafton when the door opened and one of the Chinese York controllers stuck his head in. He looked the situation over, then stepped into the room and pulled the door shut behind him.

She tried to talk, but all she got past the tape were grunts.

The man squatted in front of her and ripped the tape from her mouth. She almost screamed.

"Wow," the man said, staring at her nose and the blood.

"Cut me loose, goddamn it. Hurry."

As the controller slashed with a penknife at the tape that held her to the chair, she demanded, "Where in hell have you been? Why did you leave me sitting here bleeding?"

"Cole just stepped out to the porta-potty. He's been in front of the monitors continuously."

"Do you have a gun?"

"In my pocket."

"Hurry. Before he decides to ask more questions."

The controller jerked the tape away in great wads. Everywhere it touched her skin it tore the tiny hairs out. She bit her lip until it bled.

"What did you tell them?" the controller asked.

"Nothing. I told them nothing. They knew a lot without a word from me."

When the last of the tape came clear, she stood. There was not a rag in the room, nothing made of cloth. She pulled off her shirt and used it to wipe the worst of the blood from her face, then threw it on the floor.

"Give me the gun." She held out a bloodstained hand.

The controller passed it over. It was a 9-millimeter automatic, a fairly small one.

Kent checked the chamber to ensure it had a cartridge in it, then let the slide close. She pointed it up and thumbed off the safety.

"We're leaving," she said and jerked open the door.

Cole had just reentered the trailer and was standing ten feet away in front of the master York console when, out of the corner of his eye, he saw the office door fly open and Kerry Kent come boiling out. When he saw she had a pistol he dove behind the only desk in the place, so Kent's shot at him missed.

She knew that everyone in the place was armed. A shootout in here could end only one way, and Kerry Kent had no intention of dying for anybody's cause except her own. She ran. As she charged past the York control equipment she snapped off a shot into the main monitor and saw glass shatter, then she was flying out the door as fast as her legs would take her, the controller right behind.

One of the guards with an assault rifle tried to block her exit. She shot him in the chest and ran into the crowd before anyone else could get off a shot.

The main ladder to the belowdeck spaces in *China Rose* was in a thwartship passageway abeam the gangway. It was more of a staircase than a ladder. Jake Grafton eased himself down to the deck and looked as far as he could along the passageway. There were lights on down there and he could hear that television coming up the stairwell. It seemed to him probable that this passageway ran aft to the lounge where the television was located. Stateroom doors opened off both sides.

On the other side of the thwartship passageway was a closed hatch with a porthole in it. That probably was a ladder that led belowdeck to the crew's quarters and engine room spaces.

Okay.

He stood, grasped the long handle that rotated the dogs of the forward hatch, and put pressure on it.

The dogs rotated and the hatch came loose, ready to open.

As carefully and quietly as he could, he opened it, took it to its full one hundred and eighty degrees of travel, and hooked it over the latch that held it open. Yes, there was a regular ladder down.

He listened.

Voices.

And he was going to have to go down this damn ladder feet first!

He grasped the submachine gun with sweaty hands.

Maybe he should do the other side first.

Come on, decide, goddamn it! Callie is on this boat and her life—and yours—is on the line.

Forward. Then aft.

He stepped in, put his right foot on the first rung of the ladder.

The good news was that he had climbed ships' ladders all his adult life.

With his heart in his mouth, he went down as quickly as he could, swinging the gun barrel as he dropped below the overhead.

A short passageway with two doors off it, one port, one starboard, then another ladder down, and a door leading forward. He went to the open hatch and looked. Lights. Voices. The engine room spaces.

But first these compartments. Callie just might be in one of them.

The port door opened as he twisted the knob. A small stateroom, empty. The door to a tiny head stood open and he could see in. Also empty.

He tried the starboard door.

Locked.

He put the silencer right against the doorknob and pulled the trigger once. A ripping sound as the bullet smashed through the innards of the door lock.

He twisted the knob savagely, and it opened.

Another empty compartment. But wait!

The bunks were made up in this one.

He went back to the port compartment. Two messy bunks, wadded-up blankets . . . blood!

Had they held Callie here?

The door leading forward, this had to lead to the owner's stateroom. *Please God, let Sonny Wong be there right this very second.*

Grafton put his ear to the door and heard nothing.

Now he turned the doorknob.

Locked.

He used the gun on the lock. Instead of one shot, he accidentally triggered three.

This was the master stateroom, all right, complete with four portholes—two on each side of the ship—a king-sized bed, and Jacuzzi, but the stateroom and adjoining bathroom were empty.

Goddamn these sons of bitches.

He sensed that time was running out.

Hurrying, he descended the waiting ladder into the engine room.

Two men were fifteen feet aft, and they turned their heads as he came down the ladder. He hosed half a magazine at them, dropping them both.

Turning, going forward, hustling along, through a door into the accessories compartment.

Empty!

Aft again, running, checking for people . . .

There were another two men working on something on a workbench between the large diesel engines in the extreme after end of the ship. They saw him running toward them between the fuel tanks. One dove sideways to cover and the other pulled a pistol.

Jake managed to drop the gunman before he pulled the trigger.

A burst of Chinese came from the alcove where the other man had taken shelter.

Grafton didn't hesitate. He couldn't leave people alive behind him, or he and Callie and Wu and Carmellini would not leave this ship alive. He squirted a burst into the alcove as he ran by, then stopped and fired again, emptying the magazine in the gun.

Changing the magazine, he stalked forward, back through the engine room, past the bodies of the first two men he had killed. Even though he didn't want to, he looked to ensure they were dead. His stomach churned as if he were going to vomit.

Up the ladder he went, gun at the ready.

Jake Grafton saw the shadowy figure in the thwartship passageway as he climbed the ladder and almost shot him. At the last second he realized he was looking at Carmellini, who was swaying as if he were drunk.

"What happened?"

"Ran into an old colleague. He damn near killed me."

Blood was running down Carmellini's blackened face from a cut on his scalp.

"I've been forward and into the engineering spaces," Jake whispered. "Callie has got to be aft, down this staircase."

Carmellini wiped at the blood flowing from his scalp, then used a bloody hand against a bulkhead to steady himself. "Let's go," he muttered.

They descended the staircase together. The passageway at the bottom led aft to a swinging door, two actually, hinged on each side, with windows in each. There were doors—probably to staterooms or storage compartments—on each side of the passageway.

Motioning for Carmellini to hold his position, Jake walked the length of the passageway and peered through the window. He was looking into the dining facility. Four men sat there over bowls of Chinese food, smoking and watching a television mounted high in one corner. Beside Jake was a door to a refrigerated compartment. On the aft end of the dining hall was the door to the galley.

She had to be in one of these rooms off this passageway. Jake turned, went to the first stateroom door, and put his ear to it.

Nothing.

Voices at the next one, speaking in Chinese, it sounded like.

The next one nothing.

Carmellini motioned to him. He was checking the starboard doors. He was pointing to one. He came to Jake, whispered right in his ear. "English, a woman's voice."

"Chinese in this one," Jake said and pointed.

He went to the door Carmellini pointed out, and Carmellini took the door with the Chinese speaker. They looked at each other, then both turned the knobs at the same time and opened the doors.

The first thing Jake saw was Callie, facing him across a table. A man sat facing her with his back to the door. Otherwise the room was empty.

He couldn't shoot the man in the back because he might hit Callie.

The look on her face galvanized Yuri Daniel into action. He rose, spinning, reaching for a pistol in his belt, all at the same time. And found himself staring into Jake Grafton's face.

The Russian got the pistol clear of his belt when a burst from the submachine gun caught him under his chin and knocked him backward. Another burst, this time full in the chest, caused Yuri Daniel to collapse across the table.

"Oh, Jake, *thank God!* They have Wu in the—"

He had her then, jerking her through the door into the passageway, in time to see Tommy Carmellini empty a magazine through the open doorway of his compartment.

Carmellini charged through the doorway. Jake pushed Callie forward toward the staircase and ran aft, toward the dining hall, the gun leveled at his waist.

A glance through the door—three of the men were still watching television, though one was looking toward Jake. Perhaps he heard something.

Jake dug in his pocket, pulled out a grenade. He pulled the pin and let the lever fly off. He pushed the swinging door open a couple of inches and tossed the grenade.

The explosion made the doors swing on their hinges.

Then Jake stepped in and emptied the magazine at the men sprawled amid the tables.

As he changed magazines, the cook came running from the kitchen, shooting with a pistol.

The first shot thudded into the bulkhead as Jake was going down, the second hit a chair while he struggled to get the Colt .45 out of his shoulder holster.

Before the cook could fire a third shot, Tommy Carmellini killed him with a burst of submachine gun fire.

"Let's go, Admiral," he roared from the doorway. "We got 'em. Let's get outta here."

Jake finished changing magazines, then scrambled up. "Go, go, go!" he yelled.

Tommy Carmellini led the way with Callie and Wu right behind. Jake Grafton followed.

Jake called to Tommy, "Get them aboard the other ship and warm up the chopper. I'll be right along."

He ran up the nearest ladder to the topmost deck, above the salon, and went to the lifeboat, which had a canvas cover protecting it. Jake used his knife on the cover.

Sure enough, in the bottom of the boat was a can of gasoline that might contain two or three gallons. He shook it. Full, or nearly so.

Jake went to the hatch that led down to the engine room and emptied the gasoline can into the compartment.

From the foot of the ladder leading topside, he tossed a grenade, then scrambled upward.

He was nearly up when a jet of hot gases tore at him, almost causing him to lose his grip, as the explosion shook the ship.

Trying not to breathe the flames that singed his feet and hands, Jake scrambled for the gangway.

He was across the pier and up the gangway on the *Barbary Coast* when another explosion tore through the *China Rose* and flames jetted from her hatches.

"Are you all right?" Jake demanded of Callie.

"Yes, yes! Are you all right?"

Before he could answer the adrenaline aftershock hit him like a hammer and he vomited. He leaned against the passageway bulkhead aboard *Barbary Coast* and whispered, "Sorry about that," to Nikko Schoenauer, who was standing guard with an AK-47.

"Hey, forget it," said Nikko, who had overdosed on adrenaline a few times himself.

"Oh, Jake, I love you." Callie hugged him as tightly as she could while staying away from the shoe polish. She drew back. "You look like the wrath of God."

He took a good look at Callie under the *Barbary Coast*'s lights, which were brilliantly lit by the ship's emergency generator. "They really pounded on you," he said bitterly.

"It's over. Get me to a hot bath."

Wu and Schoenauer had a short conversation in Chinese. "Why not take a bath here?" Schoenauer asked the Graftons. "The helicopter can take these two—" he jerked a thumb at Wu and Carmellini—"to the Central District and come back for you in an hour." He turned to Carmellini and examined the cut on his head. "You need to have that stitched up."

Jake nodded his agreement.

Wu paused and rested a hand on Jake's shoulder. "Your wife save my life, maybe," he said in heavily-accented English. "She very strong woman."

He smiled at Callie and nodded once, then turned to follow Tommy Carmellini.

When Callie was up to her neck in bathwater, Jake told her, "For a while there I thought I might never see you again. When I saw the blood smears in that stateroom, I thought I was too late."

"I knew you'd come, Jacob Lee. I've never been so happy in my life as I was when that door flew open and I realized that terrible blackface apparition standing there was you."

While the Graftons cleaned up in *Barbary Coast*'s owner's stateroom, *China Rose* burned at the pier. No one came to fight the fire, although the crews of nearby ships gathered on deck to watch her burn.

Flames gradually spread throughout the ship. Finally the aftermost line securing her to the pier burned through, and wave action and the tide swung the stern well away from the pier.

When she sank an hour later in a welter of steam there wasn't a whole lot left. The black water of the harbor extinguished the last of the flames.

CHAPTER NINETEEN

The Cross-Harbor Tunnel was jammed when Rip Buckingham picked his way through it. People by the hundreds lounged against the wall and sat in the traffic lanes. Most were armed with weapons taken from the police barracks armory or soldiers who had surrendered in the afternoon, but there weren't enough weapons to go around.

Appointed officers were busy trying to organize the crowd into military units. To facilitate this process members of each unit were issued distinctive badges that attached to their clothes with Velcro. The plastic badges were in a variety of solid colors and simple shapes, such as circles, squares, triangles, and the like. The rebel organizers, Rip noted, stood in front of their groups and emphasized that everyone in the group must wear the group's badge, although they never told the volunteers why.

Rip knew. The badges allowed the York units to quickly recognize the wearer as a good guy, thereby freeing up York processing capability for other things.

The enemy would eventually catch on, of course, but by then the recognition patterns would have been routinely changed.

The tension in the air was palpable; it was impossible not to feel it. As Rip walked and listened to the excited conversations, which were echoed and magnified into an infinite chorus by the walls of the tunnel, the power of the moment almost overwhelmed him.

There was nothing these people could not do. They would pound at the rocks and shoals of the tyrant's forces like an angry sea and sweep them away, winning in the end, as inevitably as the spinning of the earth.

He reached the mouth of the tunnel and walked into the black night. The rebels had killed all electrical power in Kowloon. Looking north one could see the occasional glow of lantern light in a window, but that was all. The Kowloon skyline had completely disappeared. Members of the Scarlet Team were here at the mouth of the tunnel, working by flashlight with items on a long table.

Rip walked over for a closer look. Michael Gao was preparing a tiny radio-controlled airplane, a "bat," for flight. He held it in his hand, a black toylike thing with a wingspan of eight inches. With a two-bladed prop driven by a minuscule electric motor, the four-ounce bat could fly at about thirty miles per hour for several hours.

Gao nodded at a colleague in front of a control panel, who pushed a button, starting the bat's engine.

The controller waggled a stick; the ailerons, elevators, and rudder of the plane wriggled in sync. As Gao held the bat at arm's length, both men studied a monitor on the control panel.

Inside the bat was a miniature infrared television camera that continuously broadcast its signal. This signal gave the controller a real-time look at what lay beneath the bat. The signal was also processed by the York network, increasing the situation awareness of the York units.

When all was ready, Gao tossed the bat upward into the air at a thirty-degree angle. In seconds it disappeared into the darkness, and he reached for another one of the dozen that sat on the table.

"How close is the enemy?" Rip asked.

"They have a few scouts within a couple hundred yards," Gao told him, "but their combat units are about a mile back. They are building fortified positions in depth across the peninsula. We are trying to learn what is behind the leading edge of their forces. Are they or are they not going to attack us?"

"What do you think?"

"I don't know. The bats should tell us soon, then the brain trust will make some decisions."

"Okay."

"Have you heard? Wu Tai Kwong is back!"

Rip Buckingham hadn't heard. Relief flooded through him. His legs felt weak. He grinned and slapped Gao on the back.

"Did Sonny Wong release him?"

"No. He was rescued. I don't know much more than that. He landed in a helicopter moments ago."

"My mother-in-law is out there," Rip said, gesturing beyond the perimeter. "I am going to go find her."

"The PLA is out there, too. Do you want a weapon?"

"Have they started shooting civilians yet?"

"I don't know."

"I'll take my chances."

"Good luck," Michael Gao said, and held out his hand.

Rip Buckingham shook it, then walked away into the darkness.

"Losing the main monitor is no big deal," one of the controllers told Virgil Cole. "We'll just use another monitor for the primary display. I can't understand why she wasted a bullet on it."

Cole took a deep breath and exhaled carefully. He consciously tried to think like Jake Grafton. "She just wanted us to keep our heads down while she got the hell out of here, that's all."

"She might have caused real trouble if she'd taken the time to empty a clip into the CPU."

"And someone would have shot her," Cole muttered. "She ain't sacrificing any goddamn skin for the cause. Sonny Wong doesn't have enough money to buy that epidermis."

Wu Tai Kwong stood in the corner surrounded by his lieutenants, the Scarlet Team. He listened as they all tried to talk at once, smiled and said a few words now and then, then finally sent them back to their posts. Then he came over to Virgil Cole. A few minutes sufficed to tell the American of his adventures. The cuts on his arm had been stitched and bandaged, and he had been given an antibiotic for the infection. The stump of his finger seemed to be healing properly.

"We couldn't stop the revolution to turn Hong Kong upside down trying to find you," Cole explained.

Wu waved it away. "You did precisely the right thing, the same thing I would have done in your place."

"Your return saved me fifty million dollars."

"And I know you need the money," Wu said with a grin.

"Is Callie Grafton okay?"

"She is bruised but intact. Her spirit is unbroken. She is a warrior's wife. They wanted her to sign statements implicating you in many crimes, and she refused."

Cole didn't understand. "Why did she refuse?"

"She thought she was protecting you, doing the honorable thing. She would not have signed to save her life." Wu Tai Kwong's head bobbed as he thought of Callie. "With a thousand like her I could conquer the world."

"Jake Grafton and Carmellini?"

"Bloody but still on their feet."

Cole passed a hand across his forehead, then moved on. He gestured toward the monitors. "We are intercepting PLA radio traffic. Beijing has approved the use of heavy artillery. Governor Sun wanted a barrage laid on the tunnel entrance. We think the PLA is now positioning the guns at the army base preparatory to a barrage. We have launched bats to see where the guns are and estimate when they might open fire, but the question is: Should we keep our forces in the Cross-Harbor Tunnel while the barrage is underway or move them out now?"

The two men studied the computer presentations of enemy positions and the locations of the York units, then referred to the map on the wall. They were joined by a half dozen of the key lieutenants, who listened silently to the discussion.

"The PLA will probably attack after the barrage," Wu said after he had looked at everything. "Let's get the people out of the tunnel and position them in front of the PLA strong points. If we can do it without the PLA learning of the movement, they will think we are in the tunnel entrance rubble when they attack."

The orders went out immediately on the WB cell phones, and the volunteers in the tunnel began walking forward, into Kowloon.

Wu continued to study the map. "The winner of this battle," he said, "will be the side that controls the subway tunnel."

Cole looked at Wu with raised eyebrows. "That's very perceptive. I couldn't agree more. Your colleagues have been arguing with me about it."

"What do they say?"

"That the tunnel is too narrow and dark to get many people through, that the PLA won't bother with it."

"It will be difficult, certainly, but it is key. Most of the PLA officers are good soldiers—they will think of the subway. That is why I want them on our side."

Cole nodded vigorously. "We put a York in the tunnel at the Central Station. It's got four or five dozen men with it, which was about all that can follow efficiently. I was afraid to give them rocket-propelled grenades or antitank weapons for fear they might hit the York."

"You have done well, Cole," Wu said and bowed a millimeter. "I will go through the subway tunnel behind the York. I will have a WB cell phone, so keep me advised."

The artillery barrage, when it came an hour later, fell like Thor's hammer on the area around the entrance to the Cross-Harbor Tunnel, which was east of the Tsim Sha Tsui East reclamation project, a district of luxury hotels, restaurants, entertainment, and shopping complexes designed to profit from the tourist trade.

Nearby buildings absorbed direct hits from major-caliber shells, which began reducing them to rubble. Shells tore at concrete streets and abutments and gouged huge chunks from the levee. What the shells didn't do, however, was kill anyone. The rebels were no longer there.

Everyone in Kowloon heard the guns and felt the earth tremble from the impact of the shells. Windows rattled and broke, crockery fell from shelves, dust sifted from every nook and cranny.

Lin Pe was sitting in the entrance to an alleyway on Waterloo Road, a block west of the three-tank strong point at the Nathan Road intersection. Parked cars lined the side streets, including the one Lin Pe was on.

Ten minutes into the barrage a long column of troops marched south on Nathan Road and came to a halt behind the tank that sat in the intersection. The soldiers were eight abreast, all wearing steel helmets and carrying assault rifles and magazine containers.

The men stood nervously in line, peering about them in the darkness at the storefronts, looking up at the blank windows looking down on them, looking at each other and the tanks and the officers, who huddled together for a moment as they gestured and pointed at the buildings around them. The officers broke up their meeting in about a minute and began pulling squads of troops out of line and pointing to various buildings. The troops trailed off under NCOs. Then at least a hundred men peeled off and trooped down the steps into the Yau Ma Tei subway station, which was dark, without power.

Lin Pe removed her WB cell phone from her bag. When it synched up, she dialed the number she had memorized.

Whispering, she told the person who answered of the troops, where they were and what they were doing, how many she estimated there were. "They are going into the buildings, up on the rooftops, and down into the subway," she told the woman on the other end of the line.

Then she hung up.

An officer was staring at her.

She palmed the cell phone, pretended not to notice him.

He was wearing a pistol. Continuing to stare at her, he began toying with the holster flap as artillery shells rumbled overhead and the earth shook from their impact.

The man couldn't hold his feet still. All that dancing brought him a few steps closer, and he continued to toy with the holster. Now he pulled the pistol, took his eyes off her long enough to check it over.

When he looked again at Lin Pe, the officer still had the pistol in his hand. He seemed to be trying to make up his mind about something.

Would he search her? Shoot her?

She stood, turned to the nearest garbage can, took off the lid, and began rummaging through it as the artillery continued to pound.

Several minutes later she half turned so she could see him. His pistol was in his holster and he had his back to her as he talked to another officer.

Lin Pe bent over the next garbage can.

As the barrage hammered the entrance to the Cross-Harbor Tunnel, Bob York led Wu Tai Kwong and fifty other men through the subway tunnel under the strait. They had entered at the Central District Station; now they walked as quickly as they could given the unevenness of the rails and ties and the fact that the only light came from flashlights.

The third rail was not hot, which was a blessing since people occasionally stumbled against it. Wu had almost refused to let them use the flashlight, but with the York leading the way, no PLA soldier was going to surprise this little band.

The impact of the artillery shells could be felt rather than heard, a series of thuds that made the rails vibrate.

"What will we do if the electric power comes back on?" one soldier asked Wu.

"We have it turned off. It will not come on."

"But if it does, a train might come through here."

"You must trust me," Wu told the nervous man, "as I trust you. We hold our lives in each other's hands."

Ironically, no one mentioned what Wu knew to be the worst aspect of the small, narrow tunnel: Any bullets fired in here would ricochet viciously. With its concrete sides and dearth of hiding places, this tunnel was a horrible place to fight.

Moving along, carrying two machine guns and a half dozen antitank rocket launchers, the rebels made good time. Still, Wu breathed easier when he felt the floor of the tunnel tilt upward and they began the climb to Kowloon.

They passed the southernmost subway station on Kowloon, Tsim Sha Tsui, and kept going. The next station was Jordan Road, and there they would stop. Beyond that was the station at the intersection of Nathan and Waterloo roads, Yau Ma Tei. Wu thought that PLA troops were somewhere between those two stations.

Twenty minutes after the barrage began, it was over. The rubble around the tunnel entrance was covered by a dense cloud of dirt and concrete particles, and there had been one casualty: a woman near the Tsim Sha Tsui East shopping development who went outside to watch and was hit by a sliver of flying metal. None of the other spectators was even scratched.

Breaking the silence following the barrage was the sound of running feet pounding the pavement. Four thousand troops of the People's Liberation Army charged through the streets toward the tunnel as fast as they could run.

The Alvin York robot stood behind the curtain in the shoe shop where it had been placed. In its hands it held a water-cooled machine gun. Belt after belt of ammo was draped over its shoulders. All of its sensors were in operation at the moment, but only three were feeding data to the network: the UWB radar in its chest and the infrared sensor in its face, both of which looked through the curtain that obscured him and the glass of the shop window, and the audio sensor. The main York processing unit used data from all the Yorks to update the tactical situation. In addition, the net was receiving data from the ten reconnaissance bats that were still circling unseen over Kowloon and feeding real-time infrared video into the system.

All this information was displayed in two- and three-dimensional form on the master control monitors. Cole and the York technicians watched intently and waited. The waiting was growing more difficult by the second. Cole wanted to hit the troops after the leading edge of the assault was well past in the hope that the Yorks could disrupt the rear, which would panic the people in the lead.

"They are coming down Nathan and the Wylie-Chatham roads," one technician said. "No doubt they will push down Austin, aiming for the tunnel."

"We've got the Yorks positioned well enough," Cole said. "They can't win the battle for us, though they will help. We're going to have to win it for ourselves." He turned to the man at another panel and said, "Call the field commanders and tell them where the enemy is."

Finally he touched the York operator on the shoulder. "Okay," he said. "Do it."

The operator slid the mouse over the Alvin York icon and clicked once.

Alvin reached out its left hand and tore the curtain down that hid it from people in the street. Only when the curtain was completely out of the way did it put its left hand back on the machine gun. Then it pulled the trigger, sweeping the gun back and forth, hosing bullets at the soldiers in the street, shattering window glass and knocking them down.

Alvin moved forward, right through the remains of the window to the street.

When it hit the sidewalk it turned north, away from the southern tip of the peninsula, and broke into a run. Alvin ran like a halfback. In seconds the York's erratic, shifting pace was up to twenty miles per hour, a terrific dash against the bulk of the running soldiers, who were still flowing down the street toward it.

The York fired the machine gun as it ran, a shot for each target, its titanium claw working the gun so quickly that many of the soldiers thought the York was firing a continuous burst. In addition, the 5.56-millimeter weapon in the chest turret was engaging targets, different targets, in aimed single-shot rapid fire.

Several times the robot shot at soldiers that were too close to fall by the time it got to them, so it ran over them, hitting them like a speeding truck, causing their bodies to bounce away.

Here and there soldiers managed to fire shots at Alvin. A bounding York running erratically at twenty miles per hour along a totally dark street packed with humanity was an extremely difficult target, so most of the shots missed. The few full-metal-jacket bullets that hit the York spanged away after striking titanium or Kevlar.

Fred York's nearest major threat was a machine gun nest in the third floor of a building on the corner of Nathan and Jordan roads. It left the apartment where it had been stationed and climbed the stairs to the roof of the building. In addition to the built-in weapon, Fred carried two antitank rocket launchers.

Children and householders stuck their heads out of their apartments to silently watch the robot pass, its machinery softly whining and the minigun barrel on the chest mount spinning ominously. Instinctively the civilians knew to say nothing, to make no noise, and to refrain from touching, but they could not resist the opportunity to see a York up close and personal.

Fred kept its legs flexed, so by bending its head it could get through the doors. When it straightened its head, the stalk on top dragged along the ceiling.

Once on the dark roof the robot moved quickly. It crossed the roof in three strides, saw that the next roof was only one story lower, and jumped.

An alley barred the way to the next building, which was two stories taller than the one the York unit was on. Without breaking stride Fred leaped the alley and went through a window of the taller building. Shards of glass cascaded to the street below.

Without electricity or the glow of city lights outside, the office building the York had leaped into was stygian. This mattered not a whit to the York, which went through the nearest door and made its way along the hall, looking for the stairs.

Down the stairs, whining ever so gently, the hulking machine moved along the hallway toward the office suite that held the machine gun nest.

It found the people and the gun with its UWB radar. There were four men behind an office wall. One man was leaning out the window, looking at the street below, and the others were loading the gun. Fred detected the metallic sounds of the ammo belt being inserted in the gun and the chamber being charged.

"How thick is that wall?" Cole asked the operator who was monitoring Fred's progress. Cole was standing behind him, looking over his shoulder.

"A few inches, I think. Typical commercial construction."

"Have him shoot through it. If that doesn't work, have him punch a hole in it and shoot through the hole."

The robot's minigun moved to slave itself to the aiming point, then fired. The soldier leaning out the window fell forward until he was lying across the sill.

Three more shots followed in less than a second. The other men around the machine gun fell to the floor.

"We're going to need that gun," Cole said. "Have Fred bring it along."

"It won't be able to maneuver very well carrying the launchers, the machine gun, and some ammo belts," the operator objected.

"If it needs to move quickly, it can drop anything that hinders it."

Dog and Easy York fought their way along the tops of the buildings toward the tank strongpoint at the Nathan-Waterloo roads intersection, one on each side of Nathan Road. On top of the buildings the fighting machines were at peak efficiency—there were no civilian spectators and no friendly soldiers, so everyone they saw they shot.

Running, leaping from roof to roof, scrambling up or down, shooting at—and hitting—every target that the sensors detected, the Yorks covered six blocks quickly.

Each York carried an antitank rocket, so when they were in range they stepped to the edge of the buildings and brought the launch tubes to firing position. The Yorks fired their rockets simultaneously.

Flames jetted from the open hatches of the tanks as the rockets penetrated the relatively thin upper deck armor and exploded inside.

The one tank that survived was half buried inside a corner store, with its gun punched through the store and pointing down Nathan Road. When the other two tanks were hit, the commander of this tank screamed at his driver, "Go, go, go!"

The driver popped the clutch and the tank leaped forward, collapsing the corner of the building that sheltered it. It accelerated across the sidewalk and bulled through a line of parked cars.

The tank crossed Nathan at an angle and rode up on the cars parked on the left side of the road, crushing them, as the driver struggled to turn the tank to the right to keep it in the road. The turn kept his left tread on top of the parked cars, which were squashed and ejected backward as the tread fought for purchase. PLA soldiers hiding in shop doorways and behind cars ran for their lives.

Into this bedlam the Yorks began tossing grenades. One of the grenades ignited fuel trickling from a crushed gasoline tank, and soon the car was burning in the street and casting an eerie glow on the storefronts and the wreckage.

Dog York was throwing its last grenade when it was hit in the back by two bursts of rifle bullets. It spun and found two PLA soldiers running toward it, shooting. They probably intended to push or throw it over the edge of the building, but they had no chance. With bullets bouncing off its torso, the robot leaped and grabbed each by the neck with its powerful titanium claws, killing them instantly. Then it tossed the bodies off the roof.

Easy and Dog descended the stairs in their respective buildings, hunting for PLA soldiers. There was a machine gun nest in a third-floor apartment of Easy's building. It tore its way through walls, killed the soldiers, and picked up the gun. With ammo belts draped over its shoulders, the York unit went into the hallway and descended the stairs.

Someone dropped a grenade down the staircase. The thing exploded a few feet from Easy, showering it with shrapnel, but it kept going.

Out in the street it attacked the soldiers there with the machine gun and the few rounds remaining in the minigun. The tank was long gone, careening south on Nathan Road, leaving a trail of crushed and damaged vehicles in its wake.

Dog came out of a building on the other side and began working in tandem with Easy, killing every enemy soldier they detected.

One soldier huddled behind a car heard a running York coming at him and threw down his rifle. He stood with his hands in the air.

The Yorks ignored him.

Seeing this, more and more soldiers threw down their weapons and stood, almost two hundred of them.

The shooting stopped. The two Yorks came to a halt in the center of the intersection back-to-back, one holding a machine gun, their heads turning back and forth, the barrels of their miniguns spinning silently.

In the control room, Virgil Cole looked the situation over, then ordered the operator to stop the spinning miniguns to save battery power.

The runaway tank tore south on Nathan Road, forcing the PLA soldiers in the street to scurry for cover or get run over. The panicked tank commander kept the hatch open so he could look up at the buildings, spot enemies with antitank weapons.

Alvin York, running north up the street, saw the tank coming and got between two parked vehicles, out of the way. As the tank passed, Alvin chased it.

The York was capable of a sustained pace of twenty miles per hour and even higher speeds in short, battery-draining bursts. Alvin used that speed now to catch the tank.

The tanker must have sensed the York coming, for he turned and looked back just as Alvin leaped onto the back of the machine and aimed the minigun at the tanker's head. One shot in the head killed the man.

Alvin pulled the body from the hatch and threw it backward into the street.

Then the robot climbed up on the turret and descended into the tank.

The driver pulled a pistol and emptied it at Alvin. Bullets ricocheting inside the steel compartment killed the gunner, who slumped in his seat.

The out-of-control tank smashed over a line of cars, crossed a sidewalk, and buried itself inside a shop selling electronic gadgets. With the treads still spinning, the tank tore out the building's supports, causing it to collapse.

Inside the tank Alvin York reached for the screaming driver and tore his head from his body.

"*Jesus H. Christ!*" Virgil Cole exclaimed as he witnessed the gruesome scene on the computer monitor, two miles away. "Couldn't you just have the York shoot the guy?"

"He's on full automatic, sir," the controller responded. "The program is designed to allow him to conserve as much ammunition as possible."

"Sweet Jesus," Cole said, then turned away so he wouldn't have to look.

The Bob York robot saw the PLA soldiers advancing south in the subway tunnel toward the Jordan Road station and opened fire. It was standing in total darkness, partially hidden behind a pillar between the two train tracks. Wu had his men on the platforms on each side where they could not be hit by ricocheting bullets.

When the York opened fire, Wu shoved the muzzle of the machine gun he was manning around the edge of the platform and triggered a long burst. On the other platform another rebel did the same. The muzzle flashes lit the scene in a ghastly flickering light.

Wu waggled the barrel of the weapon, hosing the bullets into the tunnel. Up tunnel he glimpsed showers of sparks where the bullets bounced off concrete.

In that dark, closed space the din of the hammering machine guns and the strobing muzzle flashes were almost psychedelic.

Wu stopped firing when he saw Bob York leave its hiding place and begin advancing. He would like to know what the York was seeing, but the only way to find out would be by calling the command center— and the wide-band cell phones did not work in this tunnel. Wu knew because he had already tried it.

The York fired several more individual shots, then ceased. With his eyes closed, waiting for them to adjust to the darkness, Wu listened to the York until he could hear it no more. As the seconds passed he thought he could hear someone sobbing.

Well, there was no way around it. He was going to have to put his men on the track and advance.

"Let's go," he whispered and lowered himself over the edge of the platform. Two other rebels passed down the machine gun.

He had advanced fewer than fifty yards before he stumbled over the first body. He stumbled over six more bodies before he came to his first live man, who was moaning softly, begging not to be shot. Wu flipped on his flashlight. In the beam he found a PLA soldier on his knees with his hands in the air. The man's eyes were shut and he had blood flowing from a gash on his forehead.

One of the men with Wu Tai Kwong picked up the soldier's weapon and told him to follow along behind the rebels.

On the streets above the subway tunnel the PLA had ceased to be a fighting force. The soldiers were no longer under military control; they were either running for their lives, trying to find a place to hide, or surrendering.

After conferring with Virgil Cole on the WB cell phone, Michael Gao ordered the rebel assault force to advance northward up the avenues.

The firing was sporadic and dying down. Soon each rebel was carrying an armful of rifles and being trailed by a half dozen PLA soldiers.

Gao met Wu Tai Kwong at the street entrance to the Yau Ma Tei subway station near the Nathan-Waterloo intersection. They conferred briefly, decided to hold the prisoners in the center of the intersection with a few guards while the main force advanced with the Yorks up Waterloo Road toward the army base. Wu called Cole on the cell phone and told him what they wanted to do.

While the leaders conferred, people began coming out of the apartment buildings on the side streets and avenues. They were in a festive mood and proved hard to handle.

When Wu finally got his men moving toward the army base, the civilians followed. Indeed, they mixed freely with his troops, as if everyone were out for an evening stroll.

Another force of two hundred rebels, accompanied by Charlie York, advanced northeastward toward the entrance to the naval base. The rebels advanced cautiously. The command center had informed them that the naval base personnel had dug a trench near the gate to the base and were in it with machine guns, grenade launchers, and antitank rockets.

After consultation, the rebels decided to appear in front of the position and threaten it while Charlie York worked its way over the buildings to a flanking position. When it was in position, it could pin the enemy with a machine gun while the rebels made an assault.

Charlie York had no trouble getting into position. The building contained enemy soldiers, but fighting in a dark building was the forte of the Yorks. Using infrared sensors and UWB radar, the Charlie robot quickly found the enemy and exterminated them.

Standing in a fourth-floor window looking the length of the trench, Charlie opened fire with the machine gun that it held cradled in its arms. Each round was aimed, each round found a target.

The people in the trench saw only the muzzle flashes on the side of the building. With people dying all around him, one man pointed an antitank rocket launcher at the muzzle flashes and squeezed it off.

The rocket hit Charlie in the right arm. The impact ripped the arm from its socket and knocked the robot off its feet. Shrapnel from the shaped charge in the warhead damaged the minigun, rendering it useless.

"Damn!" said an exasperated Virgil Cole. "That's what happens when we sacrifice mobility, put a York in a fixed position and let people whale away at him. *Damnation!* We're going to lose a bunch of our guys carrying this trench if we don't get with the program, people! Don't let a York stand there like a statue until someone blows it into a thousand pieces! Now have Charlie jump down into the trench and get on with it."

Charlie leaped. . . . forty feet into soft earth. It fell when it landed, its left hand ending up six inches under the ground.

The robot scrambled to its feet and charged the nearest live man with a weapon. Fortunately it didn't have far to go, because without the right arm to assist in balancing it lurched badly.

The melee that followed was short and vicious. Using only its left claws, Charlie York tore at living human flesh. One man had an arm ripped off at the shoulder and began screaming, a high-pitched wail that lasted until Charlie hit him in the head, fatally fracturing his skull.

The darkness, the screaming, the maniacal superhuman thing that killed by hitting, ripping, or tearing—the nerve of many of the sailors broke. They dropped their weapons and ran, either back onto the naval base or over the lip of the trench toward the rebels.

In less than a minute it was over.

The man leading the assault group didn't learn that for another thirty seconds, when his WB cell phone rang. "You can advance now," the controller said.

Governor Sun Siu Ki listened to the radioed reports from the units in the field and watched the headquarters staff mark the positions on a table map of Hong Kong. The senior officer was Colonel Soong, a practical, down-to-earth military professional who had spent forty years in the army. He had tried to advise Sun of the reality of the military situation earlier in the evening but the governor refused to listen, replied with bombast and party slogans and quotes from Chairman Mao about being one with the people.

As the Yorks cut a swath through his combat forces and demoralized the rest, Soong suggested that Sun confer with Beijing, which he did via the radiotelephone.

The fall of the naval base was the turning point for Colonel Soong. It was then that he realized that he could not defeat the rebels with the forces he had at his disposal. He made this statement to Sun, who turned deadly pale.

After one more hurried conversation with Beijing, Sun got out his cell phone and made a local call.

"Sonny Wong."

"Governor Sun here, Wong." He took the time to exchange the usual pleasantries, perhaps as a way of composing himself.

With that over, he said, "I am calling to inform you that Beijing has decided to accept your offer. They are wiring one hundred million American dollars to your account in Switzerland."

"Rather late in the game, don't you think, Sun?"

"Governments are not like businesses—some things take time."

"I understand." Sonny let the silence build, then said, "I should wait until the money is in my account before I act, but since the hour is so late, I'll trust the government's good faith and move ahead expeditiously."

"Good! Good!" Sun said, genuinely grateful. "The government has committed to pay; it will honor its commitment, as it does all its obligations."

"Of course," said Sonny, a bit underwhelmed. "I'll let you get back to your pressing duties while I get on with mine."

When he severed the connection, for some reason Sun Siu Ki felt better.

Sonny Wong tossed the cell phone on his desk and broke into a roaring belly laugh.

Kerry Kent was sitting across from Wong. Her broken nose had been set, filled with packing, and taped into position. If she could have frowned, she would have.

"What's so funny?"

"We've *won!* That idiot Sun has talked Beijing into paying me a hundred million American."

"I told you Cole took the bombs out of the Yorks," Kent said. "We can't sabotage them. There is nothing we can do even to slow the rebels."

Sonny grinned pleasantly. "I know that and you know that," he said, "but the ministers in Beijing don't. By the time they figure out that we have done nothing to earn the money it will be too late. The money will be in my bank and they will be unable to reverse the transaction."

Sonny Wong laughed awhile, then poured himself a drink of good single-malt Scotch whiskey and lit a cigarette.

Damn, he felt good.

Too bad about Yuri. Too bad about the restaurant and the yacht. Grafton and Cole had screwed everything up and cost him some serious money. Before he left Hong Kong tomorrow he should probably settle that score.

But tonight, a drink. A laugh. One hundred million from the Communists in Beijing and ten million from their archenemy, Rip Buckingham's old man down under.

A good score, any way you looked at it.

Ha ha ha!

"Here's to revolution, wherever and whenever," Sonny Wong said and lifted his glass.

Rip Buckingham accompanied the rebels following the Yorks north on Nathan Road. He stopped to watch technicians service the Yorks, replace batteries, replenish ammo, oil and lubricate them. He looked over the herd of prisoners sitting in the center of the street—they didn't seem unhappy—then he went looking for Lin Pe.

He found his mother-in-law just where the controller said she was, in the entrance to the alley a block west of the Nathan-Waterloo intersection. The street was filled with a happy, joyous crowd, everyone talking at once. The glare of numerous small fires that the celebrants had built in the center of the streets lit the scene.

Rip sat down beside her. The old woman looked exhausted.

"We have won," he told her. "The PLA soldiers are surrendering by the hundreds, by the thousands."

"They really did not want to fight," Lin Pe said. "I could see that in their faces. Their officers made them fight."

They sat together watching the rebels stream up Nathan Road and turn east, heading for the army base. From where they sat they could see one of the still-smoking tank hulks. When the breeze gave them a whiff, the smoke smelled of burning diesel fuel and rubber, a nauseating combination.

"Why are you here?" Lin Pe demanded. "Why are you not writing this story for the world? That is your job."

"Sue Lin was worried. She wanted me to come. Since I love you both, I could not refuse."

After a moment to collect his thoughts, Rip said, "Wu was rescued earlier this evening. He is leading the rebels now. He was just here a little while ago, organizing the rebel forces. He led them up Waterloo Road toward the army base."

Lin Pe nodded. She had heard the news that Wu was alive and with the rebels earlier this evening from the girl taking cell phone calls. She didn't say that to Rip, though; she was so tired. And content.

In the midst of this raucous, happy crowd she could feel the common thread of humanity that ran down the long centuries of Chinese history from the unknowable past, through the present, into the unknowable future. Dynasties, wars, famines, babies born, and old people buried—these living people surrounding her now, filling the streets, were the sum of all that had ever been, and in their spirits and bodies they carried the future, all that would ever be.

She rested her head on her knees. With her eyes closed she could see her parents' faces as they were when she was very young, could remember the wonder she felt when she saw the sun rise on a misty morning, with the earth pungent and fresh after a night's rain. She remembered her husband, his face, the way he touched her, the feeling she had that their children were life the way it should be—these memories washed over her now, swept her along.

Lin Pe got out her notebook and wrote, "You are mankind."

She stared at the words, trying to decide if she had captured the nub of it.

Beside the first sentence she wrote, "You are the past and the future."

She gave it one last try: "Do not despair—life is happening as it should."

Sun Siu Ki's mood was just the opposite of Lin Pe's. His world was crashing in on him. The rebels owned Hong Kong Island. They had the only television and radio stations still operating in the S.A.R. and were filling the airways with their capitalist, imperialist filth. Rebels were in control at the airfield on Lantau and at the naval base. With six robots and an armed mob, they defeated the trained troops Colonel Soong had put in the field. In fact, the only real estate the government still controlled in the Hong Kong S.A.R. was the army base.

All this, Sun reflected, was a local disaster, like a fire or an earthquake. It was just his bad fortune to be here when it happened. Certainly his friends in Beijing would understand.

The only ray of sunshine in this miasma of doom was the certain knowledge that the huge Chinese army, armed with weapons featuring the latest technology—some of it purchased from the Russians and the rest stolen from the Americans—would in the fullness of time crush these rebels like a tidal wave coming ashore, overwhelming all in its path.

Six robots? Untrained civilians with captured rifles and limited ammunition? Amateur officers? They didn't stand a chance.

The sky to the east was pink with the coming dawn when Colonel Soong faced the brooding governor.

"The base is surrounded," the colonel said. "The rebels have completely encircled the perimeter of the base."

Sun got out of his chair and made his way to the map table. Grease marks on the map told the story.

"I have been begging Beijing to launch an air strike," Sun said. "Perhaps our comrades will deliver us."

The colonel didn't reply. He was fed up with wishful thinking.

"Will they attack?" Sun asked, referring to the rebels.

"Unless we surrender."

"Surrender?"

"They have not yet demanded our surrender, but we must consider it. They may attack without asking, or they ask and attack if we refuse."

"Why not use your artillery? You know where they are—hammer them into the earth."

"While we are hammering they will attack. There are too many people out there, Governor, for us to stop them."

Sun was incredulous. "What? A few thousand armed civilians against your trained soldiers?"

"We have about three thousand fighting men left on the base, counting every able-bodied man. My officers estimate there are more than two hundred thousand people outside the fence just now. Even if we set about slaughtering them with machine guns and artillery, they can push the fence down and overwhelm us before we kill them all."

Sun didn't believe it and said so. Soong took him to an observation tower to see for himself.

With the sun peeping over the earth's rim, Sun forced his tired legs to climb the stairs. From three stories up on the open-air platform near the parade ground—a structure normally used to train paratroops and review military parades—one could see the main gate and the road beyond and several hundred yards of the base fence.

The situation was as the colonel had presented it. Sun found himself staring at a sea of humanity. The people weren't under cover—they were standing and sitting almost shoulder-to-shoulder. People! In every direction, as far as he could see.

A soft moan of despair escaped the governor. He closed his eyes, swayed as he hung on to the railing.

He took time to compose himself, then said, "It would be a political and propaganda disaster if the rebels were to capture me. We mustn't take that risk. Order a helicopter warmed up."

"Governor, I don't think you understand. The rebels have the base completely surrounded. Yesterday they fired missiles at the helicopter you were in. If you try to leave, Governor, they will shoot you down."

A breathless messenger from the command center brought a ray of hope. "Bombers are inbound, sir. They have radioed for instructions. What targets do you wish them to attack?"

"The rebels around the army base?" The pilot of the leading Sian H-6 bomber asked this question of his radio operator.

"Yes, sir. That is the order. Here is the chart." The radio operator passed it forward to the copilot, who held it so the pilot could see.

The Sian H-6 was a twin-engine subsonic medium bomber, an un-licensed Chinese version of the Russian Tupolev Tu-16 Badger. First flown in 1952, the Badger was used only as a target drone or engine test bed in Russia these days. However, in China the H-6 was still a front-line aircraft in the air force of the PLA. This morning four of them were on their way to Hong Kong.

"The rebels are just outside the base perimeter," the radio operator said.

As the implications of the target assignment sank in, the pilot and copilot looked at each other without enthusiasm. To ensure the bombs fell on the rebels and not inside the base, they would have to bomb from a very low altitude. Since the navigation-bombing radar was useless at low levels, the bombardier at his station in the glass nose would merely release the bombs as the plane flew over the enemy. As long as the rebels lacked antiaircraft missiles or radar-directed artillery, the bombers should be able to strike their target. If the weather was good enough.

"What did you tell the base commander?" the pilot asked the radio operator.

"That we would try for the assigned target, sir."

"Tell the other airplanes to follow us in single file. We shall make a pass to locate the target, then bomb on the second pass."

"Yes, sir."

"We should be bombing on the first pass," the copilot objected on the ICS.

"I want to see what's there."

"We have been ordered to bomb—a first pass without bombing will merely wake up the rebels."

"When you are the pilot in command you can do it your way. Today we do it my way."

After he squashed the copilot, the pilot reminded his gunners to keep a sharp lookout. Alas, the Sian H-6 lacked a radar-warning receiver. The plane contained a single forward-firing 23-millimeter cannon and three twin 23-millimeter mounts: a remote on the top of the fuselage, one on the belly, and a manned mount in the tail. Only the tail turret was aimed by a fire-control radar.

The bombers were three miles high when they flew across the city of Hong Kong and turned eastward, out to sea, still descending. No low clouds this morning, the pilot noted, visibility five or six miles. He and the bombardier stared down into the haze as the planes flew over the city.

"I see the base," said the bombardier on the intercom.

"They should have sent fighters to escort us," the copilot said nervously as he searched the wide, empty sky.

"They did!" the tail gunner sang out. "At four o'clock, high."

The pilot looked in the indicated direction with a sense of foreboding. The briefing officer had specifically said there would be no escorting fighters. Rumor had it that the fighter pilots were politically unreliable. A civil war, the pilot told himself, was mankind's worst fear realized.

"Shengyang J-11s. Two of them." The tail gunner again.

"Uh-oh," said the copilot, who had also been told that the J-11 squadron at Hong Kong had joined the rebels. "What do we do now?"

"Those fighters may be hostile," the pilot told the tail gunner. "If they shoot a missile or line us up for a gunshot, be ready."

"Aye," said the gunner, his voice rising in pitch. Like everyone in the bomber, he knew he had little chance of hitting an incoming missile with his gun. In fact, he had never been allowed to fire his gun with real ammunition.

Ensuring he was out of 23-millimeter range, Major Ma Chow turned to get behind the four bombers, which were strung out in trail. His wingman stayed in a loose cruise formation several hundred feet behind Ma and slightly above the plane of Ma's turn.

Ma Chow was well aware of the fact that the bombers were defenseless against the two fighters, each of which was armed with four air-to-air missiles and one hundred and forty-nine 30-millimeter cannon shells. The fact that each plane was flown by a crew of his fellow countrymen also weighed heavily on him.

"What do we do?" his wingman asked over the radio.

"Let's try the radio," Ma Chow replied.

"Think they know we're back here?"

"If they don't, we'll tell them." The radios in Chinese warplanes could transmit and receive on only four frequencies, so it was a simple matter to try each of them.

Making a long, slow, descending turn in smooth air, the bombers dropped to a thousand feet above the water before they began their run westward toward the army base. Once in level flight the four bombers descended still farther, until they were only four hundred feet above the water.

Ma Chow locked up the trailing bomber with his radar and readied a missile.

"Bomber lead over Kowloon, this is fighter lead, over." The pilot and copilot of the H-6 heard the call in their headphones.

"What do we do?" the copilot asked, panic evident in his voice. "If we talk to them the authorities will call it treason."

"Bomber lead, this is fighter lead. If any of the bombers open your bomb bay doors, we will shoot you down. Please acknowledge."

The bomber pilot didn't know what to say, so he said nothing. He led the bombers around an island, then they straightened on course for the army base.

They crossed the waterline at about two hundred fifty knots, four hundred feet high.

There was no flak, of course, and no missiles. The planes flew in and out of splotchy sunshine over an immense, sprawling city. Ma Chow and the bomber pilots each wondered what the other would do as the tension ratcheted tighter and tighter.

"Target one mile," the bombardier of the lead bomber sang out on the ICS. He readied the bombsight so that he could designate his aim point as he passed over it; the sight would track that location mechanically and give him steering back to it.

Crossing rooftops, racing along a few hundred feet up with the rising sun behind them and the buildings casting long shadows ahead, the string of planes thundered toward the army base. Automatically the pilot retarded the throttles slightly, causing the speed to bleed off still more.

Then they saw the people. A horde of people, an endless sea of humanity extending for miles completely surrounded the base.

"Those must be the rebels," the bombardier said disgustedly as the lead plane swept overhead. "They aren't even armed."

"A few of them are," the copilot offered.

The pilot, also looking, said nothing. He had never seen so many people in one place at one time in his life.

When they were past the base the pilot trimmed the nose a bit higher and pushed the power levers forward. With the two engines developing ninety-five percent r.p.m., he stabilized in a cruise climb. Passing three thousand feet, he said to the copilot, "I think it's time we went home."

"They will shoot us for disobeying orders," the copilot objected.

"I saw no rebels, merely civilians."

"Those *were* the rebels," the copilot said obstinately. He was something of a fool, the pilot thought.

"You would bomb them, would you?"

"I have a wife and son at Quangzou," the copilot replied, naming the town near the airbase they left before dawn.

"Life is full of shitty choices," the pilot shot back. "Are you suicidal? If we open the bomb bay doors those fighters will swat us out of the sky."

Before the copilot could think of an answer to that verity, the tail gunner sang out on the ICS, "Number two has dropped his landing gear! He's turning out of formation. And there goes number four! They must be going to land at Lantau."

There it is! the pilot told himself. *Make up your mind.*

He retarded the throttles; with the nose in a climb attitude, the speed bled off sharply. Now he reached for the gear handle and moved it to the down position. As the hydraulics hummed and the gear extended, the pilot said to the copilot, "Better hope it's a short war."

Three of the bombers dropped their landing gear and turned for the airfield at Lantau. Only one continued to climb away to the northeast. Ma Chow's wingman went with the landing bombers while Ma Chow followed the one climbing out. As it passed twenty thousand feet he broke away.

He did a large 360-degree turn while he watched the lone H-6 disappear into the haze. When it was completely gone, he checked his compass, then dropped the fighter's nose.

Down he went toward the city below, accelerating rapidly. In seconds the plane was supersonic. He kept the nose down, let it accelerate.

Passing five thousand feet, Ma Chow engaged his afterburners. The airspeed slid past Mach two.

The tail of the fighter was hidden by a moisture disk condensing in the supersonic shock wave as Ma Chow flew across the PLA base below a thousand feet. Then he lifted his fighter's nose and rode his afterburner plumes straight up into the gauzy June morning.

Wu Tai Kwong and the members of the Scarlet Team were standing outside the closed main gate in plain sight of the PLA troops behind the gate and perimeter fence and in the observation tower when the shock wave of the racing fighter hit them like an explosion. When the crowd realized what it was, they cheered lustily.

Every person in the crowd looked up to watch the fighter disappear into the haze over their heads.

Wu listened to the fading roar of the engines and glanced at the hands of his watch, which were creeping toward seven o'clock.

At two minutes before the appointed hour, Wu nodded at Virgil Cole, who had a portable York control unit hanging from a strap around his neck. He used the unit to walk Alvin York forward and stop it next to Wu, who examined the robot with interest. This was the first time he had seen a York up close in the daylight.

When the Scarlet Team had looked it over, they stood aside, giving the soldiers on the other side of the fence their first good look. Cole walked the York to the closed metal gate, stopping it just a few feet short.

As the seconds ticked away, the crowd gradually fell silent. All that could be heard was the buzzing of the television helicopter overhead. Looking around, Cole tried to guess how many people were there. A quarter million, he thought, more or less. Most were unarmed, of course, but that was not the point. In human affairs numbers matter.

At precisely seven o'clock, Wu Tai Kwong nodded at Cole and he clicked on an icon.

Alvin York stepped forward, seized the gate, and tore it from its hinges. The robot threw the gate off to one side, then walked through the opening with its head scanning and minigun barrel spinning. Behind it walked the Scarlet Team, and behind them, all the people in the world.

The waiting soldiers threw down their rifles and stood aside. Alvin York and the Scarlet Team walked on by.

The Scarlet Team was not around when the crowd found Governor Sun hiding in a storage closet in a barracks. They dragged him outside and stripped him naked.

By the time Wu and Cole fought their way through the packed humanity, it was too late for Sun. The crowd used their fingernails to rip the flesh from his bones, then they pulled his limbs from their sockets and wrenched them from his body. He screamed some, then succumbed. Even if Wu could have reached Sun's person, it is doubtful that anyone could have stopped the mob.

The blood riot was captured by the television camera a few hundred feet overhead. Fortunately the human wave that swarmed over the base was fairly well-behaved and Wu's armed men were able to prevent wholesale looting of the military stores.

By noon the crowd had thinned considerably, and by midafternoon Wu's lieutenants began herding civilians off the base so they could see what was left.

Wu and Cole departed soon after Sun's death. They had much to accomplish and very little time.

CHAPTER TWENTY

Jake and Callie Grafton went to bed in the consul general's suite in the U.S. consulate while the rebels were fighting the PLA in Kowloon. After the television chopper brought them back to the consulate from the *Barbary Coast*, Jake merely nodded at the marines at the gate, who snapped him smart salutes, and walked through. He informed the consulate duty officer that he was expecting a call from Washington, which was an untruth of a low order of magnitude.

The duty officer was juggling telephones as he tried to coordinate the efforts of the staff, which was trying desperately to keep Washington informed of the progress of the battle in Kowloon as they learned of it. The duty officer muttered "Yessir" at Jake, who wandered off with Callie in hand. When the duty officer was out of sight, Jake made a beeline for Cole's bedroom.

They were under the covers with glasses of champagne on the nightstand ten minutes after they locked the door.

"I have a serious question to ask and I want a serious answer," Callie said.

Jake sipped champagne and wriggled his toes under the silk sheets. *Silk sheets!* God, how these billionaires lived! "Sure," he said, to humor her.

"Okay, here goes: If you were asked, would you accept an appointment as an officer in the Free Chinese Navy?"

"Have you been mulling that for the last two days?"

"I just wondered. What's your answer?"

"Hell, no. They might not make me an admiral. I'm not going to join anybody's navy unless they make me an admiral."

"What if they offer to make you an admiral?"

"I'd have to think about it."

"Really?"

"No. I'm pulling your leg. Turn out the lights and let's snuggle."

"I'm too sore to make love," she said.

"And I'm too tired. Turn out the lights, lover, and let's pretend until we collapse."

She reached and got the lights. "Do you mean it? If Wu Tai Kwong asks, you'll say no?"

"He won't ask, but if he does, I'll say what an honor it is to be asked, blah blah blah, but unfortunately blah blah blah."

"You're absolutely sure?"

"You and I are hitting the road the first chance we get. We are going back to the land of Coke and hot dogs as fast as we can get there."

"Level with me, Jake."

"You're really serious, aren't you?"

"Yes."

He thought about how he should say it. "If you hadn't been kidnapped, I wouldn't have had to kill those guys tonight. I'm not blaming you; I just don't want to have to fight this fight. This is a Chinese civil war—it's *their* problem. I'm willing to fight for my country and my family, and that's it. Sure, those guys tonight got what they had coming, but I'm not God, don't want His job. If we go home we're out of it. Do you understand?"

"Yes." She *did* understand, and she felt relieved.

"I was damned worried about you, Callie. Staring at the spectre of life without you was not pleasant. Maybe it's post-traumatic shock—I don't want you out of my sight, not for the foreseeable future."

"I was pretty worried, too," she whispered. "I kept thinking there was something I should be doing to get out, and I finally calmed down when I realized you'd come for me if you could. Jake Grafton was my ticket out."

"You're one tough broad, Callie Grafton."

"It's crazy to tell you this: I *knew* you'd come. I could feel your presence." She was going to say more, but he lowered his mouth on hers and the thought got lost somewhere.

It turned out he wasn't too tired and she wasn't too sore.

Afterward, as they lay back-to-back, she remarked, "That's the first time I ever took a bath in a whorehouse," but her husband didn't respond. He was already asleep.

An hour later the telephone rang. After he grappled with the thing, Jake managed to get it up to his ear.

"Grafton."

"That call you were expecting from the states is on line two, sir. Before you answer it . . . we just received a flash message appointing you the American chargé d'affaires in Hong Kong. Orders are coming via satellite now—tomorrow afternoon the American and British navies are bringing a half dozen ships to evacuate non-Chinese citizens who wish to leave."

Jake took a few seconds to digest all that, then said, "Who is on line two?"

"The Secretary of State, sir."

"Thanks." Jake sat up in bed, turned on the light, then pushed the button for line two.

He gave Callie the news while he dressed.

"Oh, Jake, I wanted to go home, too."

"It'll be a few weeks, at least, the Secretary said. The main thing is to get out the non-Chinese people who want to leave."

"Will that be many people?"

"Who knows?" he said as he strapped on the ankle holster. "The real question is what the Communists will do. I assume the rebels will leave Hong Kong soon. Maybe the Communists will try to retake the city. Maybe they'll sail their navy down here and assault the place. I don't know and neither does anyone in Washington. On the other hand, if the Chinese try something big the recon satellites will pick it up and Washington will give us a warning—a few hours, anyway—for whatever that's worth." He reached for the shoulder holster, decided he didn't want to wear the heavy Colt, then changed his mind and put it on.

"Some of the Americans won't leave," Callie said. "And you know that a lot of the British and Australians will refuse to go. This is their home."

"They stay at their own risk. They're betting Wu Tai Kwong and Tiger Cole can protect them. In my opinion, that isn't a very good bet."

He bent over and kissed her. "Get some sleep. If I'm going to be responsible for the way the consulate staff performs, I'd better find out what they're up to."

"I'm not leaving this city without you," she told him as he started out the door.

Jake grinned at her. "I didn't figure you would."

Callie didn't think she could get back to sleep, but she was so exhausted she soon drifted off.

The sun was up and Jake Grafton was drinking coffee at Tiger Cole's desk in the consul general's office when the rebels walked into the army base. He was on the satellite telephone to the State Department when the television showed Governor Sun Siu Ki being torn to pieces by the mob.

The power was on throughout the city, so everyone in Hong Kong who wasn't in the streets got to watch the rebels' final victory.

When the conversation with Washington was over, Jake Grafton went to the window and pulled back the drapes so that the morning sun shone full in the office. He was standing at the window looking out when he heard a voice at the door. Tommy Carmellini, sporting a bandage on his head.

"Just the man I wanted to see. Come in and drink a cup of coffee."

"I hear you're now the head hoo-ha around here."

"Yep. You're still working for me."

"I dunno, Admiral, if I'm up to it. Another night like the last one and I'll be a hospital case."

"Thanks, Tommy, for everything. You saved my wife's life when you figured out that Kent was up to her eyeballs in this mess."

Carmellini was still there when Callie came in.

"Did you get some sleep?" she asked her husband.

"No."

He kissed her and held her awhile before he told her that the rebels had won in Hong Kong. The city was theirs. "At least for a little while," he added under his breath.

The three of them were eating breakfast when the secretary buzzed and announced Cole.

He breezed in, dirty and tired and elated.

"We've won the first campaign," he told them.

"Congratulations."

"And congratulations to you," he said to Jake. "The secretary said you are now the chargé d'affaires."

"I'm moving right up the ladder. Who knows how high I'll go? How about some breakfast?"

"I'm starved. Order me some while I tell you all about it."

Jake picked up the telephone and dialed the kitchen. When he hung up, he waited for Cole to finish his summation of the night's adventures, then told him, "A federal grand jury in Washington has issued a warrant for your arrest. Washington announced it an hour ago. You are officially a fugitive."

Cole shrugged. "I volunteered. I'll live with it."

"So where do you guys go from here?"

"Shenzhen, which is a special economic zone right across the border. It's actually sort of a suburb of Hong Kong. We'll cross the bridge this evening and try to take the town. If all goes well, we'll head for Canton in a day or so."

"How are you going to get there?"

"The old-fashioned way—we're walking. We'll move the York units and our heavy weapons and ammo by truck, but the people will have to hoof it. We've got ten thousand men and women under arms, about half of them former soldiers who volunteered. With the trains out of commission, walking is our only viable option."

"Can you win?" Callie asked. "Can you really topple the Communists?"

"If we can convince the people that the Communists have lost the mandate of heaven, the right to rule, then, Yes. Mao Tse Tung always said political power grows from the barrel of a gun, and he couldn't have been more wrong. Every dictator who ever lived believed that fallacy. The truth is that power comes from the consent of the governed. So far the public reaction to the rebellion, at least in Hong Kong, has been better than anyone hoped. Wu always argued that the people were ready—events seem to be proving him correct."

"You've bet your life that he was correct," suggested Tommy Carmellini.

"Life is meant to be lived," Cole replied and helped himself to a cup of coffee.

He grinned—a rarity for Tiger Cole—then offered a coffee toast, "To life and good friends, wherever they are."

They were finishing their breakfast at the conference table by the window, enjoying the morning sun and their last hour together, when the secretary burst through the door. "Admiral, I'm sorry, but—"

He was knocked out of the way by Charlie York. The one-armed robot limped into the room and took up a position near the window, facing the three people around the breakfast table. A few wires hung from the robot's shoulder where its arm had been attached, and the minigun turret was visibly damaged. The skin was spattered with a dark substance, probably a mixture of blood and mud.

Behind the robot came Sonny Wong and Kerry Kent. Kent's nose was taped in position on her face. A portable York control unit hung from a strap around her neck.

Sonny Wong had a pistol in his hand, a nasty-looking automatic. He pointed it at Cole, then at Grafton, as he said, "Sorry to interrupt your breakfast, my friends, but we owed you a social call."

"The marines let them in, sir," the secretary squeaked, "because they thought they were with Mr. Cole."

Sonny pointed the pistol at the secretary. "If anybody comes through that door I'm going to shoot these people and turn loose the York. Tell that to the marines. Now get out!"

The man went, pulling the door closed behind him.

Kerry Kent sat in the consul general's desk chair and put the control unit on the desk. Jake saw that she was stirring the cursor around while Wong talked.

"We have both won, Mr. Cole: You have conquered Hong Kong and I have relieved the Chinese government of a great deal of money."

Sonny parked his rump on the edge of the desk, one leg dangling, the pistol negligently pointed in their direction.

"What do you want?"

"I owe this man here"—he gestured with the pistol at Grafton—"some serious pain. He killed more than a dozen of my associates and destroyed several major assets of mine, a floating restaurant and a large yacht. Capital assets worth twelve million American dollars burned or went to the bottom, Admiral, thanks to you. You are a real pain in the ass."

"You should have left my wife alone," Jake said calmly.

"Nothing personal, but I was trying for a lever to pry some money from Mr. Cole, who has more than is good for any man. He couldn't spend it in five lifetimes. I merely wished to help him with that chore."

"I should have killed you when I had the chance," Jake said, still speaking in a conversational tone.

Sonny Wong grinned. The truth was he felt damned good. "Too late now, Grafton. Too late, too late."

"Where did you get the York?" Cole asked Sonny.

"It was being repaired. Miss Kent had to shoot several of the technicians when they proved uncooperative, but the York seemed glad to see her."

Cole finished the last bite of his breakfast and put the knife and fork on the plate. Carmellini moved his feet back under his chair.

He truly is evil, Callie thought, staring at Sonny. She had never seen him in the flesh; he wasn't anything like she had imagined. Short, pudgy, a round, youthful-looking face—he didn't look like anyone's idea of a career criminal. He was, though.

"I'm ready," Kerry Kent announced triumphantly. She smiled at Carmellini. It wasn't a nice smile. "After Charlie does the admiral, he's going to do you, Carmellini, you sneaky bastard."

The coffeepot, creamer, and sugar bowl sat on a highly polished silver tray. Jake reached for the edge of the tray with his left hand, pulled it a little closer so he could reach the coffeepot better. The York unit was about fifteen feet away, staring at him.

Jake poured himself a cup of coffee and set the pot on the table, away from the tray. He then looked again at Wong, who was saying, "Tell you what, Cole. I will give you a chance to save yourself and your friends. Use the satellite telephone. Call your banker in California. Tell him to wire the fifty million to my Swiss account. There's been enough violence in Hong Kong. Pay me the money and get on with your quest."

"I don't have that kind of cash available at a moment's notice," Cole remarked evenly.

"Perhaps your banker can be persuaded to find some lying around somewhere. Miss Kent has programed the York. I am out of patience and time. We have played the game and you have lost. Step over here and pick up the phone."

Callie was staring at her husband. *He's going to kill that man,* she thought, *and regret it for the rest of his life.*

"We just want to go home," Callie said, causing Wong to look at her.

Jake reached for his coffee cup with his left hand and knocked the cup over. As he started to rise to avoid the coffee splashing across the table, he drew the Colt .45 from its shoulder holster with his right hand. He thumbed off the safety as he swung the barrel and shot at Sonny Wong.

Sonny was looking the wrong way when Jake drew and he wasn't ready, so he was a second behind, which was just enough. His shot missed Jake's head by three inches and smacked into the wall behind him.

Jake Grafton didn't miss. His shot hit Sonny in the middle of the chest. His second hit him high in the throat, snapping his head back, and his third went through Sonny's heart.

When the first bullet hit Sonny, Kerry Kent screamed and lifted the York control unit up in front of her face.

She was still screaming when Jake Grafton put his fourth shot through the control unit and hit her in the forehead, tearing off the top of her head and spraying a blood mist.

The York unit lurched forward as Kent's corpse toppled to the floor.

Jake tilted the edge of the silver tray with his left hand. The creamer and sugar bowl fell over. Jake turned the tray to catch the sun, then shined the brilliant reflection into the sensors of Charlie York. The robot froze, blinded.

Jake concentrated on keeping the reflected sunbeam in the lenses of the York's visual and infrared sensors.

"Oh, Jake," Callie murmured.

"Now what?" Jake said to Cole as he slowly holstered the pistol.

"Jesus, man, you shouldn't have shot a hole in the damned control unit."

Cole scrambled for it, picked it up, and turned it over in his hands, inspecting it.

"Oh, boy!" said Tommy Carmellini, who had dashed around the table and was checking Wong's pulse. "I don't think Mr. Wong expected that."

"Ruined the bastard's day," Jake muttered.

"Is he dead?" Callie asked.

"Pretty much," Carmellini replied, and went to take a squint at Kent. A glance was enough.

"Ruined," Cole said disgustedly, and tossed the control unit on the desk.

"Well, don't just stand there, Dr. Frankenstein," Jake said, his voice tightly controlled. "Turn the son of a bitch off."

"That's just it, Jake. Without the control unit, I can't."

"Isn't there an on-off switch or something?"

"Ah, no. The thinking was that the enemy could flip a switch as well as we could. The control unit is the only way to communicate with a York."

"Go get another one."

"Okay, but I don't think it'll do any good. Kent probably slaved the York to this unit so no one else could give it extraneous commands."

The sun was moving. In a couple of minutes Jake was going to lose it. As the beam wavered on Charlie York's face, he steadied the tray with both hands.

"Start thinking!" he said to Cole. "Gimme a plan!"

"Maybe you'd better get the hell out of here!"

"What if the damn thing then kills you people?"

"Kent said—"

"She lied to everyone—her whole life was a lie." He stared at Charlie York, trying to think. "What are the York's shortcomings, its vulnerabilities?"

"We just started the testing process when we had to stop. We ran out of time."

"No shit!" Jake took a deep breath, then exhaled. "Okay, everyone out of the room. All you people clear out, now! Go down the hall and get in one of the offices and close the door."

One by one they went around behind him and out. Callie was last. "Jake . . ."

"Go on, Callie. I want to know you're safe."

"Jake!"

"Go! Let me think for a minute."

There it stood, a big, massive mechanical monster with one arm and a damaged minigun, blinded by the sun.

It *was* going to kill him.

Perhaps he should just sit still, refuse to be a threat.

But Kent said she had told the York to kill *him*! As the York was looking at his face, she probably designated him as a target, bypassing the threat recognition program. Or was she merely using a figure of speech? Or just flat lying?

He was about to find out. In a few seconds the sunbeam would be gone and . . .

Holding the tray as steady as he could with his left hand, he drew the Colt .45 again. The distance to the York was about ten or twelve feet. God, the thing was intimidating!

With his elbow on the table, he aimed at the York's visual light sensor behind the lens turret. Got the sights lined up, held them as still as humanly possible, and squeezed the trigger.

The gun bucked in his hand.

The York's head snapped back from the impact of the heavy .45 slug, but the sensor lens appeared intact. So did the lens in the turret.

Bulletproof glass! Of course!

He had two more rounds left, so he aimed at the left sensor, the infrared one.

The York jerked again from the impact of the bullet, yet when its head came erect the lens still appeared to be okay.

The last shell.

Another hit. Again to no apparent effect.

He gently laid the empty Colt on the table, trying not to disturb the beam of light reflected from the tray.

On the table was a squeeze bottle of ketchup. Jake picked it up with his right hand. Still pretty full.

Now!

He flipped the tray at the York and ran for the door.

The York was right behind him.

As he went through the outer office, he grabbed a chair and hurled it at the York's feet.

Like a champion hurdler, Charlie York launched itself up and over. And lost its balance on landing and fell in a crash.

Inertia caused the unit to do a somersault.

And it rolled forward onto its feet and kept coming!

Jake dashed along the hallway as fast as he could go. He risked a glance over his shoulder. The York was twenty feet back, lurching along, touching the wall occasionally with its left hand to steady itself.

Callie opened a door, pushing a chair on rollers. "In here," she urged Jake as she sent the chair flying along the corridor toward the York, who again attempted to hurdle it. This time the chair caught one foot while it was in the air, and the York landed in a thunderous crash on its head and good shoulder.

Jake slammed the door closed. Carmellini, Cole, and Callie were there along with five or six consulate personnel. "I told you people to get outta here," Jake protested.

"In line, quick," Cole said. "It'll look through the wall."

A half dozen of the quickest thinkers got into a tight knot, then they separated.

The door shook from the impact of Charlie York's fist.

"Where's the nearest swimming pool?" Jake demanded of Cole.

"The hotel, three doors down the street."

"Meet me there," he shouted as the York's left fist smashed through the door. "Bring extension cords."

He jerked open the door to the adjacent room and dashed through it just as the York ripped the door to the room he had left completely off its hinges.

The robot charged into the room, then examined the features of each person there. Clearly it was unsure which of the humans was the designated target.

Grafton was not there. With its UWB radar the York had seen one person leave, so after no more than a four-second delay, it turned and charged after Grafton, lurching as it went, slightly off balance.

As he left the adjacent office Jake had locked the door behind him. He ran down the corridor as the York smashed at the wall, punching holes in the dry wall with its fist, ramming it, making dust come out in clouds.

Jake was going for the stairs when he reconsidered. He pushed the button for the elevator and stood there waiting while the York tore at the wall behind him. A leg came through, the head, now the arm.

He could hear an elevator coming, a high-pitched whine. There were two elevators, so he looked at the floor numbers over the doors. The elevator on the left was a floor away . . . stopping on this floor . . . the doors opened as the York crashed completely through the wall into the corridor.

Jake wormed his way between the opening doors and jabbed the down button as the York came tearing down the hall, each leg driving hard.

The elevator door took its own sweet time closing.

If it gets its claws in the door, the door won't close!

The elevator closed in the York's face, with the hand reaching. . . .

The York slammed its fist into the exterior door, making the whole elevator shake.

Jake's eyes went to the floor indicator. The elevator had been going up, so the up arrow was there. Before his eyes the arrow flipped to a down indication, and the elevator doors began opening.

Jake pulled out the emergency stop button. An alarm rang somewhere.

The door opened about two inches and stopped.

The York got its two claws into the opening and began tugging.

The door creaked.

If Charlie York had had two hands, the door would probably have failed. With only one hand, the robot could get insufficient leverage.

The ringing alarm bell only added to Jake's adrenaline level.

The York was right there in front of him, its head only inches away.

He pointed the plastic bottle of ketchup at the York's face and squeezed with all his strength. The ketchup squirted out, covering the York's sensor lenses.

When its vision clouded, the York withdrew its claws from the crack in the elevator door and brought its hand in front of its face. Fluid squirted from an opening in its wrist onto the sensor lenses. The doors remained frozen open about two inches, so Jake could still see the York.

With the alarm ringing steadily, Jake opened the emergency escape door on top of the elevator car and grabbed it with both hands. He swung his feet, wriggled wildly, and got one shoulder through.

The York tore at the door again. It got its hand through and used the middle joint of its arm for leverage.

It's learning, he thought. *The damn thing is learning!*

Jake got both shoulders through the opening, now his chest, then he was sitting on the side of the hole. The York had the doors open a foot now.

He swung his feet up just as the York lunged for him.

His sports coat was torn and inhibiting his movements. He jerked it off. He was about to throw it away when the stalk on the top of the York's head came up through the hole.

He tossed the coat over the stalk, forcing the York to lower itself down and use its hand to pull the coat away.

Meanwhile Jake was climbing the ladder in the elevator shaft.

He pushed the emergency exit button by the door two floors above. The door slowly opened. Jake dashed through the door, paused and looked back, just in time to see the stalk on top of the York's head disappear into the exit hole.

The York is coming!

The York will undoubtedly use the stairs, the door to which was twenty feet away.

Jake pushed the button for the elevator. He went over to the stair door, opened it a crack, and listened.

The damn elevator alarm was still going off, masking the sound of the climbing York.

Jake heard the other elevator arrive and the door open.

He turned . . .

And found himself staring at the York, which was charging him as fast as its legs would churn.

He tore open the stair door and dashed downward, taking the stairs three at a time. Charlie York was right behind.

Goddamn Cole! This fucking machine is too smart by half.

Even crippled, the agility of the York was awe-inspiring.

Jake vaulted a rail to gain a little distance, then did it again.

He slammed open the door at the bottom of the stairwell and charged through, right past two marines with assault rifles.

They turned and knelt.

As the York blasted through the door the marines opened fire in full-automatic mode.

The impact of the bullets staggered the York and gave Jake another second of lead, but that was all.

Fortunately the York didn't attack the marines. It ignored them and ran by, limping slightly, using its hand on whatever was handy to help stay balanced.

Jake ran through the metal detector at the main entrance, blasted through a group of American tourists waiting to talk to consulate personnel about leaving Hong Kong, and on out the front door.

The York was four seconds behind him.

"Jesus!" one tourist exclaimed to a marine guard. "What in hell was that?"

"A York unit," the sergeant replied.

"Who was it chasing?" the tourist's wife asked.

"That is our new chargé d'affaires."

"Oh, Lord," the woman moaned. "Why in the world did we ever leave Moline?"

There wasn't much traffic, so Jake sprinted across the street without breaking stride and ran into the next building, a huge office tower. The entire first floor consisted of a variety of shops, the interior walls of which were floor-to-ceiling glass. The effect was stunning.

Jake Grafton glanced over his shoulder, checking that the York wasn't too close, then dashed into a shop that had an exterior exit.

Sure enough, the York attempted to cut the corner and smashed into the glass, which literally exploded from the impact.

Shards of glass flew everywhere as screaming shop girls dove for cover. The York stumbled, went to its knees. Jake hit the bar for the outside door, triggering an alarm, and blasted on through.

In the center of the reception area of the next building was a large pool filled with giant Japanese goldfish. Water trickled in from a slime-covered waterfall. The whole thing was ringed with a variety of stunning tropical flowers.

Jake leaped to a small rock in the center of the pool, then leaped on across to the other side.

Charlie York tried to make the same leap . . . and fell into the pool.

With legs and arm churning, it rose, slime dripping from the barrels of its minigun, and splashed wildly after Grafton, who gained three or four seconds on the York.

The next building was the hotel. The doorman shouted at Jake as he ran toward him, but the uniformed man cleared out of the way when he saw the York coming, still decorated with green pond slime.

People in the hotel lobby ran for cover, screaming, shouting, getting behind whatever was handy as Jake ran by, looking for a sign or symbol that might indicate the pool's location.

He slowed as he went by the front desk. "Where's the pool?" he roared at the little squad of clerks in their bright red blazers.

One of them pointed toward the rear of the hotel.

Jake ran that way.

He saw a short stairs, then a double door. Aha! A sign.

Two turns, one more door, and he found himself on the edge of a large swimming pool. He went around one side, slowed to a walk. His chest was heaving. Fortunately there was no one in the pool.

The York blasted through the door, slamming it open.

It saw Jake, started for him, then slowed, its head turning back and forth, scanning.

It came to a halt two yards past the shallow end, on the side opposite Grafton.

"Smart," Jake muttered. "The damned thing is too smart."

Obviously the York appreciated the dilemma. Regardless of which way it chose to approach Grafton, he could escape by going in the other direction. He could even escape by jumping in the water.

Unless the York could swim.

Naw! Four hundred–plus pounds of titanium and hydraulic fluid, Kevlar and computer chips?

The York began moving forward, toward the deep end of the pool. It removed a pole the maintenance personnel used to vacuum the bottom of the pole from its hook on the wall.

The pole was far too short to reach. Apparently the York realized that fact, for it cocked its arm to throw the pole like a javelin. The butt end of the pole hit the wall behind the York.

Charlie York moved toward the shallow end, where there was more room to throw the thing.

Jake retreated toward the deep end. He suspected the York could heave that light pole with excellent velocity, and he wanted all the distance he could get.

He was right. The pole came like a Zulu spear and nearly got him.

When it realized the pole had missed, the York bent down and began breaking off tile with its claws. Then it backhanded the pieces the length of the pool at Jake.

He misjudged the first one, which almost got him on the arm.

The odds were with the York. It had him trapped.

How long would it keep this up? How much of a charge was on its battery?

Enough, apparently.

Jake dodged piece after piece of tile.

Then the door flew open and Tommy Carmellini and Tiger Cole came blasting through. They had power cords in their arms.

Callie was right behind them.

The two men stopped dead, sized up the situation, then began looking around for a place to plug in the cords.

The York half turned, watched them, waiting—probably—for threatening behavior, which didn't seem to be coming.

As it turned its head to check Jake's location, Callie charged the thing. She hit it in the side with her shoulder, her legs driving as if she were an all-pro tackle taking out a nose guard. She heard Jake's shout, then the force of her charge carried her and the York into the pool, where they hit with a mighty splash.

Foam welled up, obscuring the water.

Jake ran around the pool toward them. If the York got hold of her . . .

He hit the water in a running dive.

He was stroking toward them when he saw Callie's head break water.

The York had used its hand to get itself erect, its feet on the bottom.

As it stood it saw Jake swimming toward it.

And went for him.

"Get out of the damn pool," Cole shouted.

Grafton managed to turn, to stroke toward the deep end. Over his shoulder he caught a glimpse of Callie climbing from the water.

The York followed Jake, walking on the bottom.

It went deeper and deeper, reaching for the man, who couldn't see how far behind the York was.

Terror flooded him. He was so tired.

"Get out of the damn pool!" It was Cole, shouting again.

Jake got to the end, reached up for the edge with both hands, and heaved himself up, out of the water.

The York was only ten feet behind. Its stalk was the only part that protruded above the water.

As Grafton got his feet out of the water, Cole threw one end of a plugged-in extension cord into the pool.

The York kept coming. There was just too much water and too little current.

It reached the end of the pool, turned, and started for the ladder in the corner.

"The damned thing is going to climb outta there," Jake shouted. "Get that cord out of the water and bring me a female end."

Carmellini ran down the side, meeting Jake halfway. The hundred-foot cord was plugged into a socket near the door to the room and appeared to be long enough.

Jake ran back toward the York, which was slowly and laboriously trying to climb the ladder with one hand.

It slipped and fell back in.

Jake slowed, walked the rest of the way.

The York grasped the top of the ladder railing with its only hand and climbed the first two steps. Now it needed to release its hold on the top of the railing while it balanced itself and get a new hold farther back so it could complete its climb. This was where it fell the last time.

This time it slid its hand along the railing. . . .

The damn thing had an uncanny ability to learn.

It was going to get up the ladder, onto the concrete . . .

Jake leaned in from the right side, the side with the missing arm, and jabbed the female end of the extension cord into the receptacle on its back.

The York froze, half in, half out of the water.

It had gone into its rest cycle.

Callie ran toward him. Jake turned and caught her as she threw herself into his arms.

CHAPTER TWENTY-ONE

"You guys have a way to go to perfect those York units," Jake Grafton told Virgil Cole as they drove through Kowloon on their way to the railroad station at Lo Wu, a mile or so from the border. The army was gathering there.

"If they were any better you wouldn't be here."

"I grant you that, but still . . ."

"Write a letter to my company, a guy named Harvey Keim. Tell him what you observed, what you think. He'll be pleased that you took the time to help."

Callie was sitting in the middle of the limo's backseat, between her husband and Cole.

"Is that all you two have to talk about? Those damn robots?"

"Well—" Cole said, coloring slightly. "I'm sorry it wasn't much of a vacation for you folks."

"I didn't mean that," Callie stated emphatically. "You guys haven't seen each other in twenty-eight years." She made a gesture of exasperation.

"It's been an exciting visit," Cole agreed.

Callie opened her mouth to speak, then closed it when she felt Jake squeeze her hand.

As they rode they watched the people walking beside the road. Many carried army weapons on their shoulders and a makeshift pack on their back. There were so many of them. . . .

"Looks to me like you have more than ten thousand troops," Jake commented.

"I was thinking the same thing."

"Be honest. How would you rate the chances of overthrowing the Communists?"

Tiger Cole thought a moment. "Fair. I think a majority of the Chinese people are ready for a change, and a revolution is the only way they're going to get it. Rebellion has busted out all over. There's fighting in every major city, units of the armed forces are refusing to fight the rebels, people are thinking seriously about what comes next. If the Chinese want change badly enough, they can accomplish anything. We'll just have to live the tale and hope it turns out well."

The driver pulled the limo to a stop as near to the station as he could. The passengers got out and stretched their legs.

The aroma of shark cooking in a deep-fat fryer wafted across them. A street vendor had set up business nearby.

The driver opened the trunk and passed out a sleeping bag and a small backpack. Jake had given Cole the Colt in the shoulder holster, which he was wearing. Now Jake helped Cole put on the backpack.

"This is ridiculous, you know," Jake said to Cole. "You're on the *Fortune* magazine list of five hundred richest Americans, and you boil your earthly possessions down to a pistol, a backpack, and a sleeping bag?"

"In the age of hypocrisy a man has to travel light."

"I've heard there is such a thing as underpacking," Callie remarked, "though I've never gone there myself."

"After a couple hundred miles I'll be down to a toothbrush and one extra pair of socks," Cole replied. "I'll give the backpack to some lucky soul who wants to make it into a hat."

Another car drove up. Rip Buckingham and Wu Tai Kwong got out, along with two women, one old and one in her thirties.

The younger woman had been crying. Rip took her in his arms and held her tightly as he swayed ever so slightly back and forth. He didn't seem to care who was watching.

"I wish you would stay," she whispered.

"I'm a newspaperman, Sue Lin. This is the story of a lifetime. I have to go."

"I know," she whispered.

Wu hugged the old woman, bent down and whispered something to her, then picked up his backpack and walked away. He looked back once, paused, then continued on into the crowd, which swallowed him.

Rip lingered. "I want you and Lin Pe to go to Australia," he said to his wife. "I mean it. No ifs, ands, or buts. I don't want to walk all over China worrying about you."

"We'll worry about you."

"That'll be enough worry for the whole family. Lin Pe, will you and Sue Lin do as I ask?"

Both women nodded.

He put them back in the car finally, murmured something to the driver. The car pulled into a gap in the passing traffic and crept away.

Rip came over to where Cole and the Graftons were standing. "Hello, Admiral. I owe you a debt of gratitude for rescuing my brother-in-law."

Jake just nodded and shook the outstretched hand. "Good luck, Mr. Buckingham. Don't be too harsh in your stories on the archcriminal Virgil Cole."

"I'll try to be objective and fair."

"I'll hold you to that," Cole said, serious as always. Buckingham winked at Grafton, shook Callie's hand, then shouldered his packs and walked away.

"How long will you stay in Hong Kong?" Cole asked Jake.

"A couple of weeks, according to the weenie at State. He's probably lying so I won't squawk too much. You know how it is—I'll leave when they tell me to go back to the states, and not before."

"I love Hong Kong," Cole said, quite unnecessarily. He stood looking around, breathing in the sights and smells and sounds. "It's a unique, magical place. Nowhere else quite like it."

Callie Grafton found herself nodding in agreement. She too found Hong Kong fascinating. "When you get back to America," she told Cole, "come see us. If you're broke, call and we'll wire you the price of a bus ticket."

That remark brought a shadow of a grin to Cole's features. "I'll remember the invitation," he said, offering his hand. Callie shook it, then Jake.

"There is one thing I still don't know," Jake said as Cole picked up his bags. "Who shot China Bob Chan?"

"Ooh," Cole said, grunting a little as he hefted his pack. "I did, of course. He knew too much."

"Why didn't the CIA tape pick up a conversation?"

"I knew the office was bugged, so I stopped in the secretary's office, and Chan stopped because I did. We discussed our business right there. He decided he wanted to show me a letter he had received, so he opened the door and walked across to his desk, me tagging along behind.

"You see, he knew everything and he wanted money, a lot of it. Even if I paid him off, I thought it probable that he'd tattle to the authorities with specifics they could check. So as I followed him to the desk I drew the pistol from my pocket and shot him in the head when he turned around. Bob didn't even see it coming. Not a bad way to check out, if you gotta go, and he did. Then I ditched the pistol in a trashcan and went downstairs and got on with the mixing and mingling."

"So you knew there was nothing on the tape that would implicate you?"

"I was pretty sure there wasn't, but the truth was that I didn't care. Still don't. I wouldn't pay ten cents for a videotape of me doing the shooting, if one existed. Sonny Wong never understood that simple fact, which tells you how bright he really was. You can tell State I shot Chan if you want to—now that the revolution has begun, it just doesn't matter."

"Doesn't sound like you're planning on returning to the states any time soon."

"I'm not." Cole sucked in a bushel of air and let it out. "Life's an adventure. I've been a high-tech exec long enough, been a diplomat, been rich, been to all the black-tie parties I can stand. Now I'm going in this direction, going wherever the road leads."

"Keep the faith, shipmate."

"Yeah, Jake Grafton. I'll do that. For you and me and all of those guys who fought the good fight in their time."

They shook hands, then Tiger Cole walked out of Jake Grafton's life.

Jake turned to Callie. "I hate to say this, but I'm up to my ears in work at the consulate. Want to have the kitchen make us a pizza and help me tackle the paperwork?"

"Yes," she said and put her arm around his waist as they walked back to the car.

AUTHOR'S NOTE

Alas, there is no "correct" way to render the Chinese language into English. Prior to the Communist takeover of China, the widely used Wade-Giles system of transliteration gave us Hong Kong, Peking, Mao Tse Tung, Chiang Kai Shek, etc. The Communist bureaucracy spawned a new system, Pinyin, to transliterate Mandarin, which the bureaucrats decreed would be *putonghua*, or "common speech," i.e., the "official" language of China. (Mandarin is the language of northern China; the language of southern China is Cantonese.)

Unlike Wade-Giles, Pinyin often fails to present phonetic clues to English speakers, or, amazingly, the speakers of any language that uses the Roman alphabet. For example, *qi* in Pinyin is pronounced *chee*. We anglicize or transliterate Paris, Rome, and Moscow, and the French, Italians, and Russians seem unruffled. Why must Hong Kong become Xianggang?

For reasons we can only speculate about, in the last two decades American and British newspaper editors have embraced Pinyin with remarkable fervor, which leads to nonsense such as "The President ate Peking duck in Beijing."

In his excellent book, *The Making of Hong Kong Society* (Oxford: Clarendon Press, 1991), Dr. W. K. Chan points out that there are at least fifty-four different ways of presenting any Cantonese name in

English. Faced with this plethora of choices, the author has spelled the names in this book in a way that seemed to him easiest for an English speaker to pronounce. Any complaints should be addressed to the Pinyin troglodyte in Peking, or Beijing, or wherever.